ATLANTIS

A TALE OF THE EARTH

ROGER J. DIDIO

Cover art:
  "The Visitor" by Scott Moore
  "Atlantean Pyramids" by Bob Chernow
Cover design by Bob Chernow

FIRST EDITION

Library of Congress Catalog Card Number: 99-90617

ISBN 0-9672760-0-4

This book is dedicated to the women in my life—Cynthia, Anne Riess, Granny, Aunt Mary, Mother Earth—to my Circle, to Wisdom, and to the Divine Feminine in each of us.

CONTENTS

ALPHA

CAUSE

EFFECT

OMEGA

ALPHA

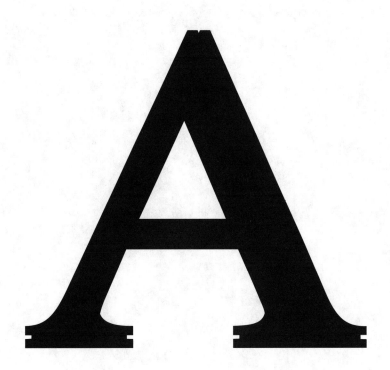

PROLOG 1

But one of the soldiers with a Spear pierced his side, and forthwith there came out blood and water.

—*John 19: 34*

At the beginning of the Dreamtime, in Primordial Chaos, I was in the Spirit, and I saw. Within the swirling mists of light and color, behold the Dreamer of the Dream in purest form.

Not awake, but not aware he sleeps. Dreaming a strange and fearful Dream, in which he sees himself as alien unto himself. Seeing illusions all about, yet fully convinced of their reality.

*****

Before the beginning of Time, a child is born—titanic son of the Thunderer and his Queen. Hideous, grotesque, deformed—not a fitting child for such noble and mighty ones as these. Repelled by his deformity, they cast him out of Heaven, forcing him to live deep within the Earth.

*****

Far beneath the Fire Mountain, the Blacksmith labors at his forge, stoking the fires that burn fiercely within the Heart of the Great Mother. Forging the universe from the raw materials—the dross of matter—in the primordial furnace of the Earth.

On a ledge above his head crouches Salamander—the Beast of Fire—who dwells with him inside the volcano. From its piercing eyes, red light blazes, filling the chamber with lightning.

Fire, smoke, and heat—incredible, omnipresent, all-encompassing heat—these are the elements of the Blacksmith's world. The thunderous hiss of steam as it rises from the boiling, bubbling pools of lava, the roar of the furnace, the striking and crushing hammer as it smites the anvil—these are the never-ending sounds that fill his ears.

The cavern surrounds him on all sides, its slick, moist walls blackened with soot. Naked save for a leather apron, glistening with perspiration, he pauses to mop his brow, resting one bare foot on the anvil, hefting the hammer, gift of his father—God of Vengeance and Justice.

Powerful muscles rippling, the raw, primal man leans backward, craning his mighty neck to watch the molten living rock as it rises through a hole above his head. Shooting upward with enormous force and pressure, welling up and collecting in the caldera, it finally spews forth in a geyser of leaping liquid fire.

Smiling with appreciation for the Mother, the artist and artisan returns to his labor. Hammer and anvil are the tools of his trade. Hammer and anvil—the Duality—active and passive, positive and negative, the male and female formative processes of Nature.

Smelting the ore, he pours the molten liquid. Forming the metal, tempering the steel, molding it in the artificer's fire. Laboring outside the bounds of Time, for as long as it takes until the work is completed.

"It is finished!" he exclaims at last. His fierce expression softens, and he looks at his masterpiece with pride and satisfaction. "The Spear—whoever shall possess it with an understanding of the powers that it serves, that same one shall hold the destiny of the world in his hands, for good or evil."

In response, a mighty Voice from the heavens cries out to the master craftsman. "The Spear cannot exist by itself. As with all things, there must be two. As you have created the Spear, so also shall you create the Sword."

The Blacksmith obeys, doing as the Voice had commanded. At last, from out of the steaming, swirling mist, he exclaims again, "They are finished—the Spear and the Sword, the *Talisman of Power* and the *Hard Lightning!*"

Now the heavenly Voice speaks a second time, summoning the messenger. "O Winged One, come forth. I charge you with the delivery of these gifts. Take them to the surface, to the world of humankind, and place them at the beginning of the Grail Path. For it is by these weapons that the human ones shall learn to walk along the Path and learn the way to enlightenment and the Consciousness of Freedom.

"Each shall oppose the other. The Spear shall bring death and destruction, suffering and change. The Sword shall be the counterbalance, bringing peace and harmony, cooperation and serenity. Long shall they last, passing from hand to hand, from age to age, from form to form. One against the other, holding the *Tension of the Opposites*.

"Indestructible, all-powerful, beautiful. In the world, but not of the world. Until the final day when they will be laid aside in favor of a better way."

"I obey," replies the Winged One. A flash of color, a rush of feathers, and the shimmering messenger is gone.

The gifts are brought to the surface, to be given to that strange new creature who walks upright and erect, hairless and bold, fragile and fierce. Beloved child of the Creator and the Great Mother.

PROLOG 2

*So the King and Merlin departed,
and Arthur said, "I have no sword."
"No force," said Merlin.
"Hereby is a Sword that shall be yours."*
—from Sir Thomas Mallory's, *"Le Morte d'Arthur"*

On the bosom of the Great Mother, the *Mystical Pair* stand ready to receive—the Two, the Twins, the Opposites. One light, the other dark; one following the straight path, one following a darker, more tortuous path. No matter—the goal is the same, the destination is the same.

FOR THEY SHALL WALK THROUGH THE AGES
ALONG THE GRAIL PATH,
AT THE END OF WHICH
LIES THE LAPSIS EXCELLIS—
THE PRECIOUS STONE, THE HOLY GRAIL.

GRADUALLY DEVELOPING
THE INNER LIFE OF THE SOUL,
STEP BY STEP,
DEGREE BY DEGREE.

ROMANCING THE GRAIL,
BEGINNING IN DULLNESS AKIN TO SLEEP,
WALKING THROUGH DOUBT AND FEAR,
ARRIVING AT A SINGLE POINT IN TIME—
AT THE MOMENT OF SPIRITUAL AWAKENING,

WHEN THE THIRD EYE OPENS
TO A MARVELOUS AND GLORIOUS VISION.

BEHOLD!
THE HIDDEN SECRETS OF THE UNIVERSE ARE REVEALED,
AND THE MEANING OF HUMAN DESTINY.

From out of the swirling mists they appear—the Spear and the Sword. The Twins reach out. The gifts are given; the gifts are received. The Twins part, going their separate ways for now, each to meet again, many times, many times, many times...

CAUSE

EARTH, AIR, METAL, FIRE, WATER

CHAPTER 1

I have woken from the sleep of ages
and I am not sure
if I am really seeing, or dreaming
or simply astonished
walking toward sunrise
to have stumbled into the garden
where the stone was rolled
from the tomb of longing.

—David Whyte, *"Easter Morning in Wales"*

It is the In-Between Time! Night has not quite passed, and the new day has not yet been born, as I come to sit on the sacred rock at the edge of the sea to watch the sunrise. A single point of light glows in the eastern sky—that wanderer known to all as the Morning Star.

The morning music is sweet upon my ears—the rhythmic splashing and crashing of the waves, the cries of the gulls, the deep, full-throated song of the osprey. And beneath it all, the sound of my own heart beating in time with the steady pulse of life at the edge of the sea.

I listen to the crying of the gulls as they feast on clams and mussels and seaweed. Far overhead, soaring majestically on the wind, an osprey searches for a fish to bring back to her nest. Brown pelicans float gently on the waves, now and then dipping their heads beneath the surface to swallow a fish. And the sandpipers dart back and forth between the ebb and flow of the waves in their ceaseless efforts to grab a morsel of food without getting their feet wet. The beach is alive, pulsing with life, and I alone am present to witness it. There is not another soul to join me on this glorious morning—not like before, when the birth of a new day would be celebrated by the whole community.

No, those days are gone, as are the Lighthouse and the Dragon Path and the mound on the hillside and the great city itself. Gone, too, are the beautiful men and women and children who lived there, with their long auburn hair and their dark, smooth skin and their deep, wide smiles—who drew their life from this great, watery world. All gone—with the crashing of the waves and the shifting of the sands and the ebb and flow of the tides and the ever-changing ways of the world.

The sky is ablaze with color in motion—a wheel of color turning before me from deep blue to pink and orange and gold, like an artist's palette run riot. The water has an almost silky look and texture, sparkling and shimmering like the crystal-blue iris of a planet-sized eye reflecting an image of Heaven back up to itself for its own admiration. The ever-present thunderheads far out to sea take on a luminescent glow, silhouetted against a backdrop of blues and pinks and oranges and golds, and outlined in a border of color so vivid that it can only be experienced, not described.

As I gaze to the east, the sky glows redder and redder, as if a giant furnace were being stoked just out of sight below the horizon. My heart beats a bit faster in anticipation. Even though I've seen the sun rise every day of my life and I'm now so very old, the excitement never fades.

I try to guess the exact moment of its coming, but try as I might, I never can. So I focus all of my senses at the point that glows reddest, draw in my breath, and simply wait.

A sound fills my ears, first just a whisper, then building to a mighty roar. Is it the wind and the waves, or is it coming from somewhere inside myself? And do I hear a Voice in that sound? I can never tell, and I've stopped trying to answer such foolish questions. Better to give myself fully to the experience and enjoy the mystery—what I can never explain but can always experience—the mystery of the birth of a new day.

The creatures with whom I am sharing the beach sense too that the moment is at hand. All is silent now, an instant of timelessness, hushed and still. A snatch of a poem from the *Book of Life* flickers across my memory...

> ALL LIVING HEARTS ARE TRANQUIL
> WITH A STIR OF DEEP ANTICIPATION,
> FOR THE TIME OF EVERLASTING THINGS
> IS NOW AT HAND.

I hold my breath and draw myself fully erect. And suddenly, a brilliant green flash bursts up out of the water, followed instantly by the glowing pink crescent of the newborn sun.

How huge it is, how beautiful! How swiftly now it climbs out of the water! The birds resume their feeding, the surf continues to flow in and out, the pulse of the Mother continues to beat, and life continues undisturbed.

And as the sun rises—a full circle now, suspended just above the horizon—I gaze steadily eastward into its brilliant red-orange face, as Time begins to spiral inward upon itself, and I am transported into that fiery center, where all of the trappings of society and the thin veneer of civilization slip away, the years and memories spin backward, past recorded history, past the destruction and the great flooding, past the Time of Tribulation, and I remember Atlantis!

*****

Atlantis! My former home, the land of my ancestors and yours, that magical, mystical kingdom at the edge of the sea where the first humans—the first ones like yourselves—lived for so long in peace, harmony, and tranquility. At the height of their civilization, they had mastered the world—wealth beyond measure, knowledge beyond measure, beauty beyond measure, power beyond measure. Yet neither their vast stores of gold nor their glorious civilization could save the Atlanteans from their own hubristic egos. They lost control, forgetting the ancient Truths, succumbing to the temptations of rampant technology and the pleasures of the material world.

Thus it was that the *Time of Tribulation* began, and their entire civilization collapsed in a cataclysm that was as swift as it was terrible. In just a single day and a night, it was all gone, vanishing beneath the cold and gloomy depths of the Ocean of Atlas, leaving not a trace behind.

But that is the end of the story, not the beginning. I want to tell you the good things first, the wonderful things about Atlantis. How they created the most magnificent civilization ever to grace the face of the Great Mother Earth, a vast and mighty empire that endured for thousands of years and touched every corner of the globe—from its highest mountains to its deepest caverns, from the ocean depths to the vastness of outer space.

Atlantis! Where we knew dragons and wizards and conversed with the animals and the elementals and all manner of spirits. Where we moved enormous blocks of stone to build pyramids and monuments and scientific instruments and temples. Where we attuned our lives to the rhythms and cycles of the seasons. Where we flew effortlessly and almost instantaneously along the Straight Paths through the sky and under the sea and deep inside the Earth and even into outer space. And where we harnessed the power of lightning and the forces of Nature.

Would you like to hear the story of Atlantis, the true story of what really happened? I would like to tell it to you. In fact, I must tell it to you, at this time of impending disaster coupled with tremendous opportunity—as a warning and a gift for your world, to inspire not fear, but hope. I approach the telling of this tale with mixed feelings. First, there is great joy in the telling, coupled with a sense of relief at being able to speak my truth at last. I've waited a long time to tell this story, but you were not ready to receive it until only a moment ago.

But I have been preparing its telling for, oh, I don't know how long, and now that the moment has arrived, it has brought other emotions—like sorrow as I relive the memories of that doomed civilization, and pathos as I experience once again all of those feelings that the Atlanteans felt—the fear, panic, frustration, and helplessness of those who chose to follow the truth but were ultimately powerless as the natural course of events swept over them. And most of all, I remember the astonishment of those in power that a disaster of such magnitude could be happening to them—for they were, after all, Atlanteans, the proud, the mighty, the invincible!

Finally, I'm feeling fear—fear of what might be if you do not listen to my tale and hearken to the lesson of the Atlanteans, who had developed a highly advanced civilization that was technologically not so very different from your industrialized world of today. So many similarities between a civilization that existed so long ago and your civilization—between antediluvian Atlantis and modern Twentieth Century society. So many similarities, yet so many differences...

For you see, that world—Atlantis—for all of its high science and technology, was a global society breaking apart and "sinking" beneath the waves of fear, egocentrism, and outer-directed thinking into the darkness of the *Spell of Matter*.

And what was this spell? Quite simply, a falling from awareness of the interconnectedness of all things in their mad, unnatural dash for power, status, and wealth. And an arrogance that what they were doing was perfectly natural, their divine right as the superior beings on the planet and, indeed, in the whole universe. Such hubris does not go unpunished!

Could you have heard my tale even a few short years ago, you descendents of the Ancients, you whose entire culture is based on the upside-down, fearful, illusionary world first spawned so long ago in Atlantis? I think not, for you would not have listened, and even if you had, you would not have understood, for you were too caught up in the spell of building cities and establishing kingdoms and enslaving your brothers and sisters and lining your coffers with gold.

But all of that is changing now. You are beginning to awaken, beginning to return to an understanding of a more natural state of existence—one based on harmony and cooperation rather than competition, plenty and abundance rather than scarcity, love rather than fear. Your world, with its focus on science and technology, for so long a fragmented society, is starting to come back together out of separateness and rise into the light of Spirit, breaking the "spell" and becoming a global village once again.

Yes, I know all about this. I know, for I was there. I witnessed it all, and I have been charged with telling the tale, waiting only until the time was right. And now the time is right! So come with me on a journey back into the dimmest recesses of your own minds. You remember, don't you? You hold the memory of the Ancients in your hearts.

*****

Once upon a planet, when the world was fresh and new, a great civilization lay spread out across the globe. It is gone now, leaving no trace of its former glory, and it was glorious! This is that civilization's story. This is the tale of Atlantis.

What marvels I have to show you! Step up and out with me now. We are not limited by physical laws. Space and distance cannot impede our progress. Time cannot force us to wait for its slow passing. Gravity cannot hold us down. Soar with me far out into the ether, for this is a magical and inviting world with ample room to fly.

From far out in space, behold! A beautiful blue-white world lies suspended in inky blackness, floating gently in a velvet sea of peace. From this distance, there are no borders, no divisions, only perfect unity and oneness. From this distance, it appears that all is in harmony, all is well.

Moving closer, we begin to discern geographical shapes and patterns—continents, mountains, oceans, islands. This is the body of the Great Mother, the Earth. So much activity! So much creativity! So much life! Great cycles turn and turn—the seasons of the year, the passing of the zodiac, the passage of the Moon around the Earth, the Earth around the Sun.

> To everything there is a season.
> And a time to every purpose under Heaven.

An unnamed philosopher penned those words in Atlantis, and we have remembered them in our most sacred writings ever since.

Above the Earth, the air itself is alive—the breath of the Great Mother. At sea level, her blood courses with life. On the land, her flesh glistens and sparkles.

See the ebbing and flowing tides, ocean currents, air currents, bubbling volcanoes, and geological upheavals. Land, air, and water in constant motion, producing giant storms—tornadoes, hurricanes, cyclones, typhoons, blizzards, waterspouts—and gentle rains that nourish the land and sustain all life.

Wind—transient and elusive, shifting soil and sand, eroding the red rock. Hear the Voice in the whirlwind carrying messages from the intangible, insubstantial realm of Spirit!

Water—liquid light, carving out deep canyons in the soft, porous limestone, grinding jagged granite peaks into smooth, rounded hills, reshaping coastlines. See the deluge come, the purifying waters washing away the old order, sanctifying the new one!

Fire—generative power of the sun, racing across prairies and through forests, consuming all in its path. Smell the scorched black earth, purified, purged, and made ready for the new!

Wind, water, fire—these are but a few of the tools of the Artist-Mother, assisting her in her transition from one state to another, carving and sculpting the face of the planet into new shapes. While at the same time, in stark contrast to these fierce bursts of creativity, the Mother reveals her softer nature, painting glorious rainbows, sunrises, and sunsets, offering the gifts of light and color to all who would take the time to notice.

The continents themselves, we see, are in constant motion, huge land masses floating on a sea of molten rock, sometimes resting gently, other times crashing into each other with enormous force and pressure. Earthquakes, volcanoes—we watch in awe as the land splits open, releasing gigantic, pressurized fountains of steam, water, mud, and lava.

We gasp in astonishment as the Great Mother transforms herself before our very eyes. Behold a never-ending cycle of creativity in constant motion, constant change. Behold the Round of Existence!

Entering the atmosphere, we soar over oceans and land masses, looking down on a vast and sunny landscape. As we draw closer, we begin to discern great areas of civilization—the vast Atlantean network that lies spread across the entire surface of the planet.

At the bottom of the world, far to the east, we find all that remains of Lemuria, oldest of the provinces. Once a tranquil, isolated land, it is now being torn asunder by the violence of war. For the Lemurians are different, somehow, not so much in appearance, but certainly in attitude. Being different in Atlantis was once not only tolerated, but encouraged. Now, however, during the Time of Tribulation, it is a death sentence, and those in power are intent on punishing the Lemurians and subjugating them to the will of the State. Day after day, month after month, year after year, the Atlanteans rain down fire and death from the sky. Day after day, month after month, year after year, the Lemurians resist and stand fast.

South of the equator, in the middle of the Sea of Peace, lies Mu. Already beginning to feel the effects of the final breaking up of the land, the province of Mu nevertheless is still fair and great. Here, mental pursuits are highly valued, and Moo, their wise, kind, and beautiful queen, is highly favored, bringing the great gifts of education and healing to all of her people. It is rumored that the people of Mu are actually becoming invisible, gradually evolving out of their bodies, so intent are they on mastering the secrets of the human mind and heart.

North of the equator, nestled in the fertile crescent of the life-giving River Nile, Al Khemia glows like a cool emerald amidst the burning desert sands. You know their monuments today—the pyramids, the Sphinx—although you no longer recollect their purpose. You think they were preoccupied with thoughts of the afterlife and immortality, but it was so much more than that. For it was here, in this province most familiar to you, that the arts of science, astronomy, mathematics, and architecture were honed to perfection. Artistry in stone—form following function—they developed a technology that enabled them to shape and manipulate ponderous blocks of stone, thus effecting the construction of gateways to other worlds and portals to other dimensions.

At last, Turtle Island, the largest of the provinces, located in the West in a most favorable position, blessed by harmonious planetary and cosmological influences. A land of such diversity—from black, rugged seaside cliffs to emerald forests, from countless acres of pristine prairie to snowcapped mountains, from gently rolling golden hills to soft white sandy beaches.

Such diverse people, too, the natives of Turtle Island. Perhaps the most spiritually evolved of the Atlanteans and the most connected to the Earth—they know and love the Great Mother and understand her ways far more deeply than any other Atlanteans. And the Mother loves them too, blessing them in countless ways—with gentle climate, abundant good health, and prosperity.

Ten provinces in all, thousands of communities, each a unique point of light, each connected to the others by a system of aligned tracks that are sometimes discernible along the surface of the Earth, other times visible only as shadows or light paths. So extensive were they, so deeply etched were these sacred Straight Paths into the Atlantean landscape, that they are visible even today, if one knows where to look and what to look for. The *straight and narrow paths, the old straight tracks*, they are spoken of even now by those who remember, however dimly, these earliest and most extensive of the markings that your early brothers and sisters have scored on the face of the Earth.

The communities were also connected to each other by a marvelous and highly sophisticated communications system—amino acid and crystalline structures that pulsed with life! In your world, you would call this computer technology, but you would not even be close to describing what, in truth, this highly spiritualized information network really was. You have no frame of reference, you see, for describing a living system that was so far advanced over your lifeless circuitry that you perceive it not as science, but as magic!

And of course, the provinces also were connected to each other by time-honored traditions and a common heritage and Source. Together they honored the ways of the ancient masters, or simply "the Ancients," as the founders of Atlantis were lovingly and respectfully called.

Still circling the globe, still traversing the blue-white planet from a distance of but a few miles, now we see other areas, too—areas of devastation and emptiness, destruction and solitude. You wonder what could have happened. How could a world so beautiful, so ordered, so highly advanced also contain such empty and desolate places?

Some of this destruction was caused by massive geological shifts, because the Great Mother is constantly active and ever-changing. But other destruction was human-made, caused by lengthy wars and the power of thermonuclear weaponry that eventually sank and destroyed the highly advanced Atlantean civilization.

Do you recognize these dead places? You should, for the power that was unleashed in the final conflagration was of such magnitude that they remain barren and relatively lifeless even today, so many thousands of years later. Of course you know them by name— the Sahara, the Gobi, the Outback.

Let us slow down now and move closer still, hovering above our final destination. The island of Atlantis, seat of the empire, center of the world, or simply, home. Rising up out of the Ocean of Atlas like a precious and sparkling emerald, opposite the mouth of what today is known as the Mediterranean Sea, Atlantis is home to a wide variety of plants and animals, including many that are extinct in your world. Home, too, to other creatures— the Atlantean race.

From this altitude, we can see sprawling metropolitan areas—centers of commerce, education, and the arts—interspersed among rolling farmland, forests, and plains. Moving sidewalks, elevators, and electromagnetic sleds carry residents and visitors from place to place. Those desiring to travel faster and farther take "the Way," a global transportation system that harnessed the subtle energy forces of the Earth's electromagnetic field, moving at incredible speeds over the ground, under the sea, and through the atmosphere and beyond. And most glorious of all, a mighty Temple in the center of a mighty city, surrounded by a Great Pyramid, a royal Palace, elegant mansions, and lush gardens.

For eons, this was Paradise. The basic needs for food, clothing, and shelter were taken care of, or rather, they had been until the Sons of Belial rose to power. Money as you know it today was nonexistent in Atlantis. Luxuries were exchanged via a sophisticated barter system based on love, cooperation, and trust.

Listen as they converse with each other? Are the words familiar to you? Can you remember speaking them yourselves? It is the Language of Light—the *Solara Maru*—the root language for your sacred tongues of Sanskrit and Hebrew.

From our vantage point a few miles above the surface, we see a populous and mighty Nation-State, overflowing with abundance and wisdom and knowledge. Overflowing, too, with violence and greed and corruption and vice. Here it was where early humankind, your ancestors, dwelt for ages in peace and happiness until the coming of the Sons of Belial.

Alighting now, we step into the antediluvian world, which you can barely remember, save for fanciful legends of the Garden of Eden, the Elysian Fields, Mount Olympus, and other paradises. This was the home of those whom your collective universal memory depicts as the gods and goddesses of antiquity—in reality the kings, queens, priests, priestesses, poets, scientists, and artists of Atlantis.

The actions and adventures you attribute to them in your myths have become larger than life as you've retold the stories over the millennia. You see your ancestors as separate from yourselves—mightier, nobler, greater in every way. In truth, however, those who came before you were not omnipotent gods and goddesses, but mortals like yourselves, with all of the attendant human passions, aspirations, nobilities, and frailties that you experience today.

Your recollection of them is confused because your collective memory suffered such a great shock after the final cataclysm. As you know, some escaped in ships and on rafts. Washing ashore in the provinces, those few survivors—exhausted and tattered and barely coherent—carried with them tidings of the appalling catastrophe, which have survived even into your own time in various flood and deluge legends. The time has come for you to acknowledge the truth—that which you have tried to mythologize, those whom you have tried to deify, are but your confused attempts to recall the real history of your own heritage.

We stand at the gateway to Atlantis. Let us step out onto Atlantean soil, traverse Atlantean ways, speak the Atlantean tongue, share the Atlantean experience. There is nothing to fear. Stand by my side as I guide you. Narrow your focus and perspective, attune your senses to a particular time and place, to particular events, to particular people. Become willing to entertain new ideas, new possibilities.

Welcome to the antediluvian world. Welcome to Atlantis. Welcome home!

*****

In this most marvelous and fabled world, there lived two very wonderful people—a man named Adima and a woman named Cybele. As individuals—male and female—they had risen up out of the Duality and joined together for a great and noble purpose. This is their story.

The man—Adima—was a being of many skills and talents—a lover and a warrior. His first loves were his family and his art. He was a husband and father, musician and storyteller, visionary and seer—an eloquent speaker and a Truthsayer. He talked and played with spirits, and they talked and played with him. He was, as his name indicated, *a Seeker of Wisdom.*

As a warrior, he was strong and athletic, a bold doer of deeds, well versed in the martial arts, skilled with sword and lance and bow and fists and feet. He was a member of the Atlantean Council of Elders, a position of political power and prestige, where he protected and served not only Atlantis, but his family and community as well. And as a man, he had his faults, ofttimes thinking too much—"too much in his head," as his wife was fond of saying. Sometimes fear paralyzed him. Sometimes he was reluctant and even unwilling to do his part. His greatest battle was always within his own mind.

The woman—Cybele—never having lost touch with the Great Mother, was a woman of many skills and talents—an artist and a creator. She had an open heart and manifested the attributes of unconditional love, innate harmony, compassion, and the healing presence. She had a close understanding of and relationship with Spirit, and talked and played with her Inner Beloved. She was, as her name indicated, *the invisible light that is married to the fire that turns the wheel of Creation.*

At home, she was wife and mother. In the Temple of Poseidon, she was counselor, healer, and teacher, serving her Atlantean community and family as priestess, a position of spiritual power and prestige. She was wise, a keeper of knowledge who gathered the truth, spoke it from her heart, and nurtured all who came to her.

And like the man, the woman, too, had her faults, ofttimes choosing to run away and disconnect from the world when life pressed in and overwhelmed her. Instead of being quiet, she often got busy in the outer world, and when circumstances did not go as she wanted or expected them to, she had a tendency to flee instead of turning inward for the answers.

For a time, this man and this woman lived separate lives, both having their own experiences and doing their own learning, according to the Plan. When they reached maturity, however, they came together at the appointed time and were married, also according to the Plan. Their union was wonderful, and from their joining, the twins were conceived and brought forth—a boy named Alta and a girl named Charis.

It is from the time when the twins were twelve years old that this narrative begins, just before dawn on the first day of the most important celebration of the Atlantean calendar. The family, along with others of the Children of the Law of One, had spent the holiday eve outdoors in the pine forest at the easternmost edge of the great island.

To the adults, it was the occasion of the Winter Solstice, which marked the beginning of the new year and the return of the sun and new life energy. To the children, however, it was simply the Dragon Festival—a time of singing, dancing, parades, storytelling, and magic.

I, too, was there, although my presence probably went unnoticed by most of the people. They had a tendency not to notice me, or to ignore me if they did notice, which was partly my fault because I rarely made an effort to announce my presence, especially in a great crowd. I much preferred to wander quietly and unobtrusively among the throngs, watching, observing, paying attention to the smallest of details as I stepped inside their very thoughts and shared their experiences. Without the distraction of conversation, I could attend to recording the particulars of each important event in the history of Atlantis.

I remember that morning so well, the Festival of the Dragon in the Year of the Child. It was a time of beginnings and endings—it was the beginning of the supremacy of the Sons of Belial; it was the beginning of the great breaking up of the land; it was the beginning of the Time of Tribulation; it was the beginning of the end of Atlantis.

CHAPTER 2

...to apprehend the mysterious and divine laws of life, and by means of the profoundest inner concentration, to give expression to these laws in their own persons.

—the *I Ching*

In the cool darkness just before dawn, the child stirred in her sleep. "Wake up, Charis," whispered her mother. "It's almost first light."

The little girl opened her eyes. It was still dark. A cool breeze brought a chill to her bare skin, and she nestled deeper into the warmth of her mother's arms. A feeling of peace and safety enveloped her as she lay listening to the sounds of the forest—birds singing, crickets chirping, and soft, excited whispers as many people gathered together.

The others are already awake, she thought, sensing them moving in the semidarkness, although their bare feet made almost no sound on the soft, pine needle-covered ground. She thought about her father and brother. They'd be awake by now, too, probably making preparations at the beach. That was okay, though. She didn't need to be there for that. She was comfortable just like this, lying beside her mother, feeling the older woman's heart beating in harmony with the rhythm of the surf crashing on the great cliffs to the east.

Charis smelled the morning air and inhaled deeply, tasting the salt spray on her lips. Even in the darkness, she could feel her mother smiling as she stroked her hair and coaxed her into full wakefulness. "Come on, sleepyhead. You don't want to miss the Dragon, do you?"

That did it! She was up with a bound. Already the first streaks of pink and gray light shone on the eastern horizon. As she dressed, she could feel the excitement and the sense of anticipation. This was her favorite day of the year. This was the day the Dragon came!

"You look pretty today, Mother," Charis said as she adjusted her robe. It was similar to the one her mother was wearing, the traditional crimson priestess gown, shimmering and glistening as it caught the early morning light.

"Thank you, Charis," smiled Cybele. "You look pretty, too."

It was amazing how much they resembled each other. Both had long, auburn hair and the dark red complexion typical of most Atlanteans. Even at twelve, the girl showed all the signs of growing up to look just like the slender, graceful woman who was her mother. But there was one notable exception; Cybele's features were more sharply defined and her expression rather serious. On the other hand, Charis' features were softer. She was more playful and shared her father's penchant for adventure.

In the distance, someone began drumming. "There's the drum," said Cybele. "Time to get started." Holding hands, mother and daughter began walking toward the sound.

"Isn't the forest lovely?" Cybele looked at her daughter. "Take a deep breath and smell the morning. Feel the spirit of the place."

It was a glorious morning, a perfect day for the festival. As usual, it had rained for most of the night, but that did not matter. Indeed, rain was always welcome, for Atlantis was a watery world. There was water everywhere; Atlanteans depended on it for their livelihood and their very existence. They were one with the water. And rain on festival day meant that good favor was to be theirs throughout the coming year. Now the air was sweet with the smell of pine needles and campfires and the crisp, salt air. Together they inhaled deeply. "It smells like pine and campfires," giggled the child. "And it feels like magic, doesn't it?"

"These woods have always been magical," Cybele reminisced as they walked. "When I was a little girl, younger than you, I came here to play and explore." She pointed down a narrow path that branched off deeper into the forest. "It was near here that Sophia first taught me the secrets of the herbs and how to use them for healing."

Indeed, it was a sacred, magical place—an old-growth forest of towering pines that stretched from the edge of the sea all the way inland to the mountains. And as vast as the forest was, so were its myriad life forms and mysteries. Yes, the forest contained so many wonderful things for those who were attuned to its secrets and knew where to look.

"Who is Sophia, Mother? You always talk about her, but I've never met her."

"She is my teacher. One day soon, your father and I will take you and Alta to meet her. She will be your teacher, too." That day won't be far off, Cybele thought as she looked at her daughter. Her little girl was growing up so quickly. She noticed her dark good looks, lithe body, and budding femininity. The child was getting taller and stronger every day. What will she grow up to be? mused Cybele. Will she be a priestess, as I am? Will she want to learn about the healing ways? What will the future hold for my children if the Sons of Belial have their way?

Her reverie was interrupted as they stepped out onto the main thoroughfare, a well-trodden path leading straight from the beach to the center of the marketplace. *The Good Red Road*, as it was commonly referred to, was busy that morning. Those of the Children of the Law of One who had not spent the night in the forest were coming in now from the city. There was quite a crowd—some travelling singly, others in groups, some rushing on ahead, others lagging behind.

Several people waved to them. "Namasté," said a woman, greeting Cybele with the traditional salutation of honor and respect. "We're looking forward to hearing your invocation this morning." The woman smiled at Charis. "Good morning to you, too, child. Are you ready to catch a glimpse of the Dragon this year?"

Charis nodded her head enthusiastically. Each year, she tried to spot the ever-elusive Dragon, but was never quite able to do so. The fabulous creature was only visible for the briefest of instants just before the sun rose out of the sea. It flashed a brilliant green, then vanished from sight as it sped toward the land to do its work. You had to look very carefully, or you'd miss it. Her brother claimed that he had seen the Dragon last year, but she really doubted it. He just liked the attention it got him from the rest of the children when he told the story. Well, maybe this year she would see it, too.

As they drew closer to the beach, they could hear the steady beat of the drum more clearly. The light, too, was changing from the deep filtered green among the trees, growing pinker and brighter with each step they took. People began to quicken their pace.

"Come this way, Charis."

The child followed her mother as she left the path and walked through the trees toward the booming sound of the surf and the drum. They were heading for a particular place—a sacred site with which they were long familiar. Rounding a corner, they stepped out of the forest onto a rocky ledge. And even though they had been there many times before, even though they knew exactly what to expect, they were still awed by the unspoiled beauty of the place—awed by the sights, sounds, and feelings of that sacred, natural cathedral at the place where the land met the sea.

Spread out before them lay an incredible panorama. To the east, directly in front of them, great black volcanic cliffs sloped sharply downward to meet the deep blue waters of the Ocean of Atlas. Huge waves crashed into the jumbled mass of rocks, tossing up glistening fountains of white spray and filling the air with a sound not unlike thunder. Birds of all kinds circled overhead or perched on the rocks, singing their morning songs and dropping clams and mussels from the heights to crack the shells and feast on the tender meat.

The light glowed pink, the sounds of drums, birds, and surf filled their ears, the wind caressed their bare skin and fluttered their gowns, and time seemed to stop. Cybele let her eyes roam over the horizon, drinking in the beauty and grandeur of the moment.

To the north, a Lighthouse stood silhouetted against the skyline. It was an immense structure of unknown antiquity. Since before anyone could remember, the Lighthouse had stood on its solitary perch atop the rocks, guiding seafarers safely into the harbor. Shipwrecks in Atlantis were unheard of, thanks to the Lighthouse Keeper and his light.

"I don't like that place," said Charis, following her mother's gaze.

"For goodness sake, why not? What's not to like about a lighthouse."

"It's haunted, that's what's not to like," Charis explained patiently. "There's a hobgoblin who lives there, and it leads travellers down the forgotten paths and gets them lost in the bogs and desert places. Anyway, that's what all of my friends say, and I'm not taking any chances by going there and finding out."

Cybele cast an amused glance at her daughter. "Well, I'm sure if you were to know the truth about the place, you'd be amazed at your gullibility," she chuckled. "But if I were you, I wouldn't worry about haunted lighthouses and hobgoblins today. Why not concentrate on all of the wonderful things around you. In fact, look up there."

Charis clapped her hands delightedly as an osprey soared overhead.

"It's a great sign to see Hawk on such a morning," said Cybele. "She's bringing a message for everyone. Pay attention and see if you can hear what she has to say."

So Charis ran off to follow beneath the great bird as it soared majestically on the breeze. Cybele watched for a few moments, then turned her gaze eastward. The ocean lay before her as far as her eye could see. She thought about Turtle Island and the other Atlantean provinces that lay beyond the horizon. How immense was the Atlantean kingdom, whose diverse parts were spread across the globe. Although she could not see them, she knew they were part of Atlantis nevertheless, and that they would be celebrating, too, on this first day of the new year. Like those hidden parts of ourselves, she mused. We can't see them, but still they are within us. Atlantis is a vast empire; we are vast beings.

She looked at the Children of the Law of One gathering on the cliffs. They were people of all shapes and sizes and colors. Some wore ceremonial garb, others the traditional dress of Atlantis—those flowing silk robes whose multicolored patterns and airy design were favored by men and women alike. Others were mostly naked. As she turned her gaze southward along the coast, she saw the figures of a man and a boy walking toward her.

"Here come Father and Alta," Charis announced, rushing up all out of breath from climbing on the rocks as she had followed the bird.

Cybele watched as her husband and son approached. How handsome they are! she thought. And how alike! Each had the same auburn hair and ruddy complexion. But while Adima had a rough, masculine quality and could be darkly brooding at times, not so with Alta. Like his sister, he was lithe and agile and full of fun, always ready to explore and run and go on a new adventure. There was no doubt that he and Charis were twins.

"C'mon, Charis," Alta exclaimed, grabbing his sister by the arm. "Let's go see the Dragon Path."

"Come right back," Adima called after them, enjoying the children's excitement as much as they were. Turning to his wife, he pointed to a number of musicians. "We've got excellent music this year. In addition to the drummers, we've added cymbals, gongs, strings, and horns. There's even a chorus to help with the singing. I'm looking forward to hearing the music they've prepared to accompany your poetry."

Cybele smiled and put her arm around her husband's waist. Together they enjoyed a quiet moment while the twins ran off on their exploration.

The Dragon Path to which Alta had referred was located a short distance down the beach. Carved from the solid rock, this channel ran from the water's edge straight inland for several hundred yards to a massive earthwork mound higher up on the cliff. "Tell me again about the Dragon, please!" Charis tugged at her brother's sleeve, her face aglow with excitement as they stood in the channel.

Eyes sparkling in the morning light, Alta pointed eastward to the ever-reddening horizon. "Look out there," he exclaimed, just as enthused as his sister as he told what he knew of the forthcoming visitation. "When the sun rises on festival day, the Dragon rises too." The boy stomped around, arms flailing wildly as he pantomimed a sea serpent rising up out of the waves. His sister giggled with delight.

"It travels on the sun's rays straight across the water to this very spot," he continued, pretending to fly as he assumed a dragon would fly, "then it follows this path straight up the cliff and into the tunnel." He pointed uphill toward the Dragon Mound. Quartz face gleaming white in the sun and topped by the round, grassy hillside, it reminded Charis of an Atlantean flying machine. A small black hole gaped like an omniscient eye in the center of the eastern wall.

The children scrambled up the rocky path. "It's so dark. What's in there?" Charis asked, trying to be brave as she peered intently into the opening.

"It's dark now," said her brother, "but it won't be for long. Father showed me earlier. This stone passageway leads to a large stone room deep inside the mound. There are other rooms, too, but I didn't have time to look into all of them. Anyway, along the back wall of the main room, there are lots of wonderful stone carvings."

"What do they look like?" Charis was fully entranced by the vivid description her brother was painting.

"They look like spirals, kind of like the ones Mother has on her jewelry and that are hanging up in the Temple of Poseidon. Father said they're in honor of the Great Mother."

"I get it!" Charis exclaimed, taking up the story. "Mother told me about this. On Winter Solstice day, which is today, exactly at sunrise, the sun shines into the passageway and lights up the symbols on the back wall. And that's when the Dragon brings the life energy to pass through the land and the people."

"Exactly," Alta nodded. "And then..." He was interrupted by the crashing of a gong.

"We'd better get back," said Charis, looking at the sky. "It's almost time."

Indeed, it was getting much lighter now. The children scrambled down over the rocks and joined their parents at a high point on the headland. And just in time. As if at a prearranged signal, the drumming ceased, and all were silent. The Children of the Law of One sat, knelt, or stood in various postures of expectation and meditation. Stepping forward, Cybele stood before the crowd, raising her voice in prayer.

"Great Mother, you who are the source and nurturer of all life on Earth, we honor you on this Solstice morning. Amid the spirits of our ancestors, we come together today in this great moment of renewal.

"Great Mother, yours are the sacred energies of Nature united with the creative forces of Father Spirit. Through your sacred marriage, the Earth is revitalized with light and power emanating from the Heavens. Through your sacred marriage, the fertility current passes through and reanimates the land and the people with the life force.

"Great Mother, as the sun once again begins its slow passage toward summer, we celebrate your gift—the gift of rebirth. And we thank you for a new growing season and a new beginning, whereby you ensure the continuation of life and abundance for us and all the Earth."

Cybele stopped speaking, and all eyes turned toward the horizon, which grew redder and redder. There was no sound save the wind and the surf. All was ready. It was time.

The Dragon arrived with spectacular swiftness—first a brilliant flash of green, then the pink arc of the sun rising out of the sea. Spellbound, they watched the light travel across the water, touch the beach, rise up along the Dragon Path, and fill the passageway in the mound. Instantly, a trumpeter sounded a single note—softly at first—a pure, clear tone, rising in pitch and volume simultaneously with the flow of the light toward the land. It was immediately answered by another and another, their perfect harmonies piercing the silence and swelling to a joyous fanfare.

One after another, more instruments joined in—bells, whistles, strings, cymbals, drums—producing a great, harmonious sound. The people raised their voices in song. Singing gave way to dancing, and all were joyful with the promise of a wonderful new year. The celebration lasted for quite a while. By the time the last notes had faded on the wind, the sun was an hour old.

In the ensuing silence, Cybele drew her family into a little circle. They sat cross-legged on the rocks, holding hands in the customary way—palms lightly touching, left hand up in a gesture of receiving, right hand down in a gesture of giving. They took a moment to center themselves and attune to the new energies of this sacred festival day, then they headed home for the ritual breaking of the fast.

CHAPTER 3

The most beautiful and deepest experience a person can have is the sense of the mysterious. It is the underlying principle of religion, as well as of all serious endeavor in art and science. He who never had this experience seems to me if not dead then at least blind.

—Albert Einstein

At one level, I speak to you of Atlantis...its science and history and culture. But in a larger sense, I also speak to you of mysticism and spirituality and their place in your lives. Some might argue that mysticism and spirituality serve no purpose in the modern world, that they are outdated and outmoded, leftover remnants from the time of witch doctor-priests and their unsavory cohorts. The Children of the Law of One, however, believed that the two were inseparable, that science and mysticism came together in synthesis, and this was reflected both in their daily habits and routines and in all of their endeavors in the arts and sciences.

Were they mystics as you understand the term today? They appreciated the experience of life, but they looked beyond the experience to its higher purpose. Cybele spoke of it often in her teachings in the Temple of Poseidon, reading from the *Book of Life*:

> BEHIND ANYTHING THAT WE EXPERIENCE THERE IS SOMETHING THAT WE CANNOT QUITE COMPREHEND AND HOLD WITH OUR MINDS, SOMETHING BEAUTIFUL AND SUBLIME, SOMETHING THAT COMES TO US ONLY INDIRECTLY.

In this sense the Children of the Law of One were mystics. They came into the world with an innate sense of wonder, which they never lost. Indeed, they developed and honed this sense, tempering it with humility at their lack of understanding of the great secrets and the massive forces of which they knew so little.

They delighted in opening their minds and humbly trying to follow the advice in the *Book of Life*:

> REACH OUT, TAKE HOLD, AND GRASP A SENSE
> OF THE LOFTY STRUCTURE OF ALL THERE IS.

Mystery and magic were delicious, to be tasted and savored and enjoyed for their own sake. *"After all,"* they asked, *"what is the worth of consciousness if it cannot possibly encompass the mystery of the ineffable?"* To have thought otherwise would have limited them, limited their creativity. They could not have accomplished all that they did if they had restricted themselves and kept within the confines of the secular and the mundane.

This philosophy was central to what Adima and Cybele taught their children. "To deny spirituality and mysticism is to deny an essential part of yourselves," Adima stressed. Cybele added, "It is to miss the complete picture. So let your minds soar and imagine all possibilities. All that's necessary is an open mind."

So Adima and Cybele were taught, so they taught their children, and so I offer you these teachings as I unfold the tale of Atlantis. For there is much more to this story than a morning festival at the beach, more than the love between a man and a woman and their children. There is romance and passion and magic and intrigue. There is hatred and greed and corruption and murder. There is human achievement unparalleled in the history of the world. There is destruction unparalleled in the history of the world. There is danger. And there is opportunity!

*****

"I saw an osprey at the beach this morning, Father," Charis said gaily as the family walked home through the woods.

"Osprey, the Fish Hawk. A powerful sign." Adima smiled at his daughter, proud of her and the maturity she had been demonstrating lately. Both she and Alta were quickly leaving the ways of childhood behind. "What did the beautiful sea bird say to you?"

Charis knew better than to respond quickly. The obvious answer would have been, "Nothing. Birds can't talk!" But she knew her father well enough to know that he was trying to get her to think about something. Both Adima and Cybele often used examples from nature to teach lessons to the children. So Charis thought about it. Birds can't talk, so what could it tell me without talking? she mused. What other ways could it let me know something or send me a message? She walked in silence for several moments. Finally she said, "I can't be sure, but maybe Osprey was telling me something about the festival and why it's important."

"Very good. And why do you think this message was delivered by Osprey?" Adima asked, his voice gentle and resonant.

"That's the part I'm not sure of." Charis was puzzled. "If I want to know something, I can just ask you or Mother, can't I? Why should I have to try to figure out what an animal is telling me?"

"Of course you can ask us, and we'll be glad to answer if we can," Adima nodded. "But sometimes Mother and I might not be there when you have a question, or we might not know the answer. It is important that you and Alta understand that there are times when humans don't have all the answers. At those times, you need to look elsewhere.

"One of the places where we can look is in Nature, with the animals. Each animal has a special medicine, a special teaching or healing gift that it offers us. Hawk is a messenger. We can learn from Hawk by observing its behavior—how it lives in its community, how it protects its nest and its young."

Charis was beginning to understand her father's teaching. "I get it! Osprey was at the festival too, just like we were. Maybe it's a mother getting ready to make a nest and have babies, and it wants to get some of the Dragon Current for itself."

"So the message is...?" prompted Adima.

"The message is that it's time to get ready for spring and summer." Charis was quite proud of herself.

"Quite possibly," Cybele took up the teaching as they turned onto the trail leading to their home. "Osprey is connected with Nature. It knows that the days will start to get longer and the new growing season is at hand."

"And it flies," Alta chimed in. "It soars effortlessly through the air, over land and water. It can go anywhere it wants. It's free." The boy extended his arms and threw back his head in imitation of a soaring bird, spinning around in ever-widening circles. The others watched in amusement as he spun faster and faster. Suddenly, not paying attention to where he was going, he stumbled over a root and sprawled headlong into the bushes.

"Ouch!" he grunted as he tried to extricate himself from the clutches of the branches. He was pretty well caught. The thorns grew such that the only way out lay in going deeper into the thicket. "From bird to mole," he cried as he disappeared from sight, crawling through the tangle of undergrowth. A moment later, he called, "Father, come and take a look at what I've found."

"It looks like our bird needs landing practice." Adima laughed as he walked around to where Alta was calling from the other side of the thicket. "Let's go pull the thorns out of him."

Still laughing, he came to where Alta was standing, looking at something on the ground. "What do you make of this, Father?" The boy pointed to his discovery.

Adima looked down, a deep frown darkening his handsome face. There were the remains of a recently abandoned campsite. A cooking fire was still smoldering, and bits of food and trash were strewn about. In the soft earth were several deep footprints, the unmistakable signs that people had been there for quite a while. He was troubled by the location of the campsite—so out of the way, so obviously hidden—and the footprints themselves. These campers were not barefooted or wearing sandals, as was customary among the Children of the Law of One. No, whoever made these footprints wore hard-soled footwear. There was something different about this, something sinister. He could sense it. Someone had wanted to hide.

It was a good hiding place. The thick bushes offered concealment from prying eyes and passersby. They also provided an unobstructed view of the beach. With good viewing lenses, an observer could stay concealed and still know exactly what was going on, then get out of the way without ever being seen. It was only by chance that Alta had happened to stumble and then crawl to the exact spot where the spies had been hiding.

Adima spoke to Cybele as she and Charis joined them. "Looks like somebody's been watching us but didn't want to take part in the festival. Perhaps they're shy." Stooping to take a closer look at the ground, he noticed the distinctive pentagram markings in the dirt. He recognized the geometric shape immediately, and then he knew. The mark was the insignia of the Sons of Belial. It appeared everywhere—on their clothes, their icons, even their bodies. To see the mark here could only mean one thing—the Sons of Belial had been observing the morning ritual.

Fear rose in Adima's throat. Men had been watching them, men who did not want to be seen, men who did not approve of the festival and who did not like the Children of the Law of One or their ways. These men considered themselves different from the Children of the Law of One and harbored ill will toward them. They were, if not outright enemies, at least potential troublemakers.

He felt he had to do something, but what? Confrontation meant retaliation, they'd proven that in the past. Yet they had to be confronted somehow. When he thought of these men and what they might do, he felt the old familiar sensations, the warm, tight waves of anxiety as they spread through his stomach. He thought about his family. What would happen to his loved ones if they were accosted when he was not there to protect them? He looked at Cybele, who nodded knowingly. Not wanting to frighten the children, she said, "Looks like someone's either been hunting or was shy about coming to the ritual. There are people like that. Too bad! They would have been welcome. Let's clean up this campsite and go home. I don't know about the rest of you, but I'm hungry!"

For the rest of the walk, Adima remained quiet, doing his best to silence his thoughts and remain calm. Now he understood for himself the message carried within the shrill cry of Osprey. "Beware!" Or at least, "Be aware, attend!"

He glanced upward as a passing cloud suddenly obscured the sun. A dark shadow and a challenge! The man shivered as a chill flowed along his spine. Visibly shaken, he allowed the full import of the warning to course through him.

Attend to the omens from the Spirit world, attend to the signals from the Earth, and attend to the signs from the people of Atlantis itself. Attend, see the larger view, and be responsible. For an event of great import is coming!

CHAPTER 4

The Prime is the root of all things and exists before Heaven and Earth. From this source, the universe comes into being. Undifferentiated, the Ether forms a unity. Divided, it makes Yin (Heaven) and Yang (Earth). Quartered, it yields the four seasons. Forming into a sequence, it produces the five elements (wood, fire, metal, water, and earth). The four seasons and the five elements move regularly in endless cycles.

—the *Tao Te Ching*

From the Lighthouse Keeper's Journal

Morning of the Dragon Festival
Month of the Winter Solstice
Year of the Child

Far above the world, day after day, year after year, I look down on Atlantis, admiring its beauty by day, shining my light by night, that all may see in the darkness. From on high, so near the Great Creator, everything looks peaceful and calm, ordered and serene. Would that it were so!

On this first day of the new year—the Festival of the Dragon—I am reminded of a beautiful Atlantean song that describes the creation of the universe. The melody will one day be forgotten, and over the eons, the song will come to take many forms, but its essential truth will remain unchanged.

In the beginning,
Long ago, yet even now,
Is the Eternal One,
Without form, beyond definition.
From the eternal Oneness
Came the first division,
When the Great Idoil,
The Hand of God,
Came forth
To birth the great stone.
Thus spake the Eternal One:
"Burst asunder, Idoil
And let the visible be born from you."
And bursting asunder,
A great stone came forth,
Bearing all Creation.
From the eternal Oneness
Came the first division,
The appearance of the opposites—
Duality.

The Idea became manifest,
The Word became flesh,
And the universe sprang into being
When the Eternal One,
The Root of All Things,
Divided into two.
And it was good.

Now these "two" are called by many names—Yin and Yang, Heaven and Earth, Female and Male, Mother and Father, Matter and Spirit. Everything in the world, and in the human body in particular, has this dual nature, this yin and yang aspect.

YIN, THE FEMALE PRINCIPLE
—SOFT, DARK, COLD, AND WET.
YANG, THE MALE PRINCIPLE
—HARD, BRIGHT, HOT, AND DRY.

The two principles exist together and cannot be separated. There is no yin without yang, just as there is no night without day. The Atlantean people, together with all life, are carried along in the unceasing flow of the whirling stream of yin and yang.

In a healthy community, just as in a healthy person, yin and yang are in a state of constant flux. They are also in a state of balance, like a Great Pendulum hanging suspended at the midpoint, holding the Tension of the Opposites.

So it has been in Atlantis for countless thousands of years, the yang of daily life complemented by the yin of sleep at night, each state balancing the other, with both necessary for wellness. The results have been twofold—a healthy society that fosters mental, physical, and spiritual growth for all of its people; and healthy people who maintain balance and harmony and apply it to their lives in proportion to their needs.

For a time, dis-ease was almost unheard of in Atlantis because its people knew and applied the Three Principles of Wholeness, as written in the *Book of Life*:

WELLNESS INCLUDES ALL OF THOSE PHYSICAL AND METAPHYSICAL ASPECTS OF BEING WHICH ARE INTERCONNECTED AND INSEPARABLE.
ALL DIS-EASE CAN BE TRACED TO SOME FORM OF DIS-HARMONY.
WELLNESS PREVAILS IN ONE'S ATTUNEMENT TO NATURE, TO HARMONY.

Such are the Children of the Law of One and the path they travel. Atlantis has risen to technological, physical, and spiritual heights because its people are connected and attuned to the power of love, working in harmony with all of the planetary and cosmic processes. Their successes, as demonstrated by their great wealth, prosperity, and worldwide empire, are the direct result of taking direction from within, from Spirit, and applying the lessons in the outer, everyday world.

Now, though, all of that is changing, and a dark time—a Time of Tribulation—has descended upon Atlantis. Others have arisen in our midst who follow a different path, a convoluted, shadowy path grounded in fear, drama, and competitiveness. Seeking outside themselves for direction, they have let their egos and their fear dictate and motivate their behavior.

And so the Great Pendulum has begun to move out of stasis and swing too far to one side, and the Atlantean civilization is beginning to disintegrate. None of this has happened overnight, of course. It has taken centuries to build Atlantis, just as it is taking centuries to destroy it. The final catalyst came when the Sons of Belial rose to power. The cult had been trying for years to gain control of Atlantis. Finally, twenty-five years prior to today's Dragon Festival, they succeeded, and the results have been devastating.

The first thing they did was to discard the old ways that no longer serve them, replacing them with alternative philosophies more suited to their goals of absolute power and worldwide domination. Now they have adopted recent but untested scientific breakthroughs that are in direct opposition to the traditional ways of thinking and perceiving the world. These new patterns of thought are giving rise to a modern technological civilization that is at odds with the ancient ways.

They indulge to excess, upsetting the yin-yang balance of the body of the Great Mother, and signs and symptoms of this imbalance have begun to appear both in the fabric of Atlantean society and in the Earth herself. At first these changes were minor, subtle, and often unseen, but now they are plainly visible for all who take the time to notice.

Things are out of control! The Sons of Belial are guiding their development to exaggerated and dangerous extremes. They have taken charge and control distribution of everything, from knowledge to food to livelihood to healing.

From my observation point high up in the Lighthouse, I gaze down upon my beloved world, and I weep. Something terrible is happening to our society. It has become corrupt from within, and the same thing is happening deep within the Great Mother Earth, a dark cancer festering, oozing, and growing—silent and deadly.

The universal wave of inspiration is gone from Atlantis. The land is becoming more and more fallow; even the sea is refusing to yield of her bounty. Both our society and the Earth herself are on the brink of eruption, and few on either side even have an inkling of what is about to befall them!

*****

Simultaneously with the Dragon Festival, another landmark event was taking place in Atlantis. In contrast to the openness of the Dragon Festival, however, this one was taking place in secret, in the deep, dark vaults below the Great Pyramid. And while the purpose of the Dragon Festival was to bring life and renewal, the purpose of this other event was to bring death and destruction.

In the alchemist's laboratory, the Adepts of the secret society gathered. Silent figures glided into the room from dark anterior chambers, their faces shrouded by heavy hoods that almost completely concealed their features. Not a word was spoken as they took their places in a circle around the perimeter of the room. All was silent, and the air was charged with tense anticipation.

The subterranean chamber was lit by a strange, pale luminescence that came from several dimly glowing crystals. They seemed almost to be alive, pulsing silently and eerily.

Their dim light revealed various scientific and magical apparatus scattered haphazardly around the room, equipment of mysterious, sinister origin and purpose. A grisly jumble of instruments, manuscripts, skulls, animal specimens, and assorted mystical objects lay interspersed among lab benches. These, in turn, contained mortar-and pestles, flasks, beakers, and retorts aboil with foul and noxious concoctions and distillations, from which wafted the acrid odor of smoke and pungent chemicals.

Off to one side, a low fire was burning in a furnace, heat being the fundamental requirement for every alchemical process. Conspicuously absent, though, was an altar—an appurtenance that most alchemists deemed essential to the spiritual aspects of their pursuit.

And everywhere there were the crystals—crystals of all shapes and sizes and colors, some connected to others by copper tubes and wires, others standing alone on great slabs of marble. For Atlantis was a crystal-based society. The crystal was their main tool for generating power and for healing. Not natural crystals, but manufactured ones, created through artificially forced growth, yet as pure as the natural product—cut, polished, totally symmetrical, and absolutely flawless.

A few stood almost twenty-five feet in height and ten feet in diameter, clear and shining and faceted with twelve sides sloping upward to a single point. The others were smaller, approximately four to five feet in height, in every color imaginable. Those colors gave the crystals their specific properties and vibrations—energy that could be utilized for various purposes, both good and evil.

Shakala stood in the center of the Circle of Adepts. Tonight was the first time that the master alchemist had allowed so many of them to come into his laboratory, and he was in a state of great excitement. Actually, anxiety is a better word, he thought as he swallowed dryly and looked around. His fear was almost palpable. The room was too dimly lit for the light to penetrate into the corners or up to the ceiling, but the alchemist knew that it rose to a great height. And he could sense all of the unseen eyes upon him, staring out at him expectantly from their places in the shadows. In the center of the stone floor he had etched an inverted pentagram, that magical symbol so common to Atlantean ritual science and the Sons of Belial. In its pure and upright form, the icon represented the human body, the upper triangle being the Divinely-inspired head. In its present inverted orientation, however, the figure symbolized the darker, shadowy side of the magical alchemical processes being invoked in the crucible of the alchemist's laboratory.

Above this diagram, Shakala had constructed a copper wire grid two feet wide and six feet long—large enough for an adult to lie upon. The squares that composed the grid were exactly one-and-one-quarter inches on each side. The grid was similar to the ones used in the Temple of Poseidon for the treatment of ailments affecting the physical body, with two important differences. Suspended through the midst of this cagelike structure was a gigantic black crystal. Although it was highly polished, the crystal reflected no light as it swayed ever so gently on its pendulum. From the four corners of the grid, metal rods rose up and out of sight into the gloom.

Shakala was excited about this night, excited about this device that he had built. That was why Belial and the others had invited themselves to his laboratory. They wanted to witness a very special event—the testing of his new device.

He had protested that it was too soon to test, that he was dealing with the transfer of electromagnetic energy as conducted through the crystals. In order for the energy to traverse the grid properly, the crystals had to be perfect. If a flaw existed anywhere, the flow would be interrupted, and a massive explosion would result. Shakala had asked for more time to experiment, but the Master would have no part of it.

"The time has got to be now," Belial had insisted in a voice as cold and hard as the granite that encased the room in which they stood. "We cannot wait any longer."

The alchemist shuddered as he thought of the events to come. How his friend and co-worker would be placed on the grid and how the energies would surround him and literally transport him, body and soul, to the Dark Place, a place where no light ever reached. Would he be able to control the vast forces? Would he be able to keep his friend safe? Would the device even work, or would it fizzle out in a shower of sparks and a puff of ozone?

"Please let them reconsider," Shakala whispered silently. But there was to be no turning back this night. The device was right in front of him, and all were gathered to watch him turn it on. A sudden wave of intense panic swept over him as he looked around the room. There is no escape, he thought. I'll never be able to break away from the Sons of Belial, and if I try, I'll suffer the same fate as those who have tried in the past.

Quickly he put such thoughts out of his mind as he busied himself with last-minute preparations. These were his friends, he reminded himself. There was no need for him to escape. He was home, right where he belonged. He remembered with pride Belial's response when he had gone to the Master and told him about the experiments and their potential results. "Well done, Shakala," Belial had praised him. "Continue your work, and let me know when all is ready. If you are successful, you will be well rewarded. Of course, if you fail... But I know you won't fail me."

Shakala's thoughts were interrupted by a powerful voice from the shadows. "Let us begin.

"We have convened this meeting of the Sons of Belial because there is a cancer in Atlantis that needs to be dealt with and removed. You who are loyal to the cause will understand the necessity of keeping our thoughts pure and not contaminating them with other vibrations that distract us from our true and single purpose. I am speaking, of course, of the Children of the Law of One. Their ways are not our ways. Their goals are not our goals. They are weak, we are strong. They envision a better world, we want to dominate this world."

The Voice from the darkness was deep and penetrating, vibrating with the energy of pure evil. Separate and apart it seemed to be, as though coming not from a man, but from a disembodied wraith from the netherworld. The men who comprised the Circle of Adepts, inured as they were to the dark effects of black magic, shuddered in spite of themselves, knowing that the voice of the Beast was speaking through the Master.

"Today begins their most sacred time of year," the voice continued, growing stronger and louder as the Beast worked itself into a frenzy of rage at the target of its hatred—the Children of the Law of One. "They are planning many events to mark this time and celebrate. So we have chosen this day to demonstrate our power to them. Even as we speak, some of us are in their midst, observing them, learning their ways, uncovering their strengths and their weaknesses. We will use this information to prey upon those weaknesses while avoiding their strengths. The result will be a demonstration of power such as has never before been seen in Atlantis, a demonstration of power that will leave no doubt as to who is in control.

"The day is coming when the Children of the Law of One will cower in fear whenever the name of Belial is spoken. They will bow in our presence, they will worship us, and they will be completely subservient to us." Screaming in demonic rage, the unseen power behind the leader of the Sons of Belial roared forth its hatred of the Children of the Law of One until, finally, it grew silent, its fierce anger spent. No one moved or dared to speak, their silence born of fear of the Man-Beast in the shadows. At last the Beast spoke again, quieter now, gentler, fully confident and self-assured.

"Today marks the beginning of their year. It is also the beginning of our rise to supremacy in Atlantis. All has been prepared. To those of you who have labored so long and hard, we say, 'Well done.' This morning you will see the fruits of your labor as we activate the device for the first time. In the days to come, you will watch people scream in panic, not knowing what is befalling them as the ground beneath their feet shakes and the wind roars in their ears." The chilling laughter with which the Beast punctuated this last remark sent shivers of fear through even the most hardened of the Adepts. The Beast went on.

"Before there is any damage, however, we shall stop the device. For we do not wish to destroy. We simply desire to instill wonder and fear. They will wonder what has happened and why, and they will fear the time when it will happen next."

Again that demonic laugh from beyond the realms of mortal man. "And it *will* happen again," the voice assured them. "Already we have plans for employing similar devices on Turtle Island and in the other provinces. We are thoroughly prepared, and we have planned well. All is in readiness for the Dark Time to begin—our time, the time of the Sons of Belial."

There was an almost imperceptible pause, as though the Beast were rearranging itself, moving out of the body of the man it had temporarily borrowed and through which it had revealed its sinister plan. Then the voice of Belial returned.

"But that lies before us. Right now, we need to deal with the immediate situation. Our device needs to be tested. We need to ensure that it works properly. To ensure success, one of our number has volunteered to step onto the grid and be subjected to the rays. He takes a great risk, and we honor him for that. The danger is great, but so are the rewards. Bring the hero in."

From one of the dark tunnels, several men entered the room, escorting a draped figure. It was Lus, a learned Adept and long-standing member of the Inner Circle.

For the first time, the giant figure of Belial stepped out of the shadows and moved to the center of the room. He was a mightily-muscled man, his immense height and massive girth accentuated by the sinister black robe that covered him from head to toe. Removing his hood, the Master let his gaze travel slowly around the assemblage. His pale face shone ashen white; his coal-black eyes exuded absolute authority; his whole demeanor radiated absolute power as he came face to face with Lus.

"Lus, my faithful servant, you are volunteering to test the device. You have remained loyal to the Sons of Belial and have worked long and hard to ensure success. For such valor there can be only reward.

"You will be bathed in the rays of the black crystal and transported body and soul to the Dark Place. Once there, you will record your experiences, so that you may teach us about this place of no light. After a proper amount of time, we shall bring you back, and you will tell us what you have learned."

Belial drew back into the shadows as Lus stepped into the cage. There was no struggle; he seemed calm and collected. Neither was there fear or cowardice. His was the face of absolute confidence, the face of a brave warrior about to set out upon a glorious adventure.

"Let the experiment begin."

As though it were a single living being, the Circle withdrew well beyond the safety markings on the floor. The alchemist made a few adjustments to certain rods and connections, then fastened a wire from the large rod in the ceiling to a corresponding rod on the grid. Stepping back, he made a great show of intoning a sacred chant and invoking the etheric forces, sending a clear message that he, Shakala, knew deep secrets and controlled powerful forces.

It began almost imperceptibly, barely noticeable in the silence...a low vibration welling up from the center of the room. Within seconds, the throbbing increased in intensity, and the copper rod began to glow blue-white as a current of energy ran down from above. When the current reached the tip of the rod, a single spark arced across the intervening space to the wire grid. The Adepts watched spellbound as the lifelike energy danced across the grid, enveloping Lus in an electric cocoon. The man was still visible within the current, but his form had taken on a vaporous, transparent quality. Suddenly, the energy level intensified, and the vibration rose to a high-pitched whine. An acrid-smelling smoke began filling the room, which was growing warmer by the second.

"It isn't supposed to behave like this!" Shakala cried, holding his hands over his ears in a vain attempt to ease the pain of that awful sound. "Something has gone terribly wrong. We've got to get him out of there!" He rushed forward, but the thick smoke, flying sparks, and enormous heat made access to the grid impossible. The alchemist was helpless.

From within the energy field, Lus uttered a long, piercing scream of agony, a desperate wail of utter despair, so full of pain and terror as to be coming from the very depths of hell itself. And then he was gone. He just disappeared, vanished into nothingness.

After a time, how long Shakala never really knew, the glow faded. A few remaining sparks still flickered across the metallic circuits, the vibration still echoed throughout the chamber, but Lus had vanished utterly. Through the smoke, everyone rushed to the grid, but it was unrecognizable as the device it had been when they had started. The metal rods were bent and broken, and the wires had been melted into a tangled, lumpy mass. The floor was deeply gouged and scorched by the enormous heat. And shattered bits and shards of what had been the black crystal lay everywhere.

The Adepts were dumbfounded. At first, no one moved or spoke. Then Belial turned to Shakala.

"Take whomever you need and rebuild this device as quickly as you can. You are to use all your skills, all your resources, all your energy. Lus is gone. That is unfortunate. However, we must rebuild the device, correct our mistakes, and try again. Perhaps we can rescue Lus, perhaps not. But the important thing is to perfect the device and try again. Remember our goal. We cannot fail. We will try again in twelve hours. Do not fail me, Shakala." With that, Belial turned and walked out of the room, leaving the alchemist and the Adepts in the midst of their disaster and loss.

CHAPTER 5

There is an appointed time for everything,
And a time for every affair under the Heavens.

—Ecclesiastes, 3:1

The Dome was nestled on a granite ledge at the end of an inland lagoon that branched off the *River of the Rising Sun*, one of the four great rivers that flowed north, south, east, and west to the sea from their common source at the center of the island. When they were first coupled, Adima and Cybele had found this spot together. Like all Children of the Law of One, they understood the importance of living in a harmonious environment. So the newlyweds had gone on a quest to find a suitable site, a place that was both natural and spiritual. First, each one prepared separately, spending a day and a night in prayer and meditation with their respective mentors. Then they had come together to begin their search. Walking hand in hand, each told the other what they were looking for.

"I asked the Goddess of Wisdom," Cybele had said. "She showed me a place where the vital force flows through and connects all things, maintaining balance between us and Nature and bringing harmony, health, and prosperity to our lives and our surroundings."

Adima, too, had sought the advice of Spirit. "I was sitting on the headland meditating," he replied, "and I had a vision in which I saw a field—roughly rectangular and undulating—lying at a bend in the river where it turned east to travel the last mile straight to the sea."

"The life force would be strong in such a place," Cybele agreed. "Let us hope we can find it."

It did not take long. They followed a trail through a particularly pleasant section of the forest. It wound through the woods for a while, then meandered through a wide meadow full of wildflowers, where the birds were feeding and singing and nesting. All the while, the couple headed east.

"We're getting closer. I can feel it!" Cybele exclaimed as they walked up a low hill. At the crest, they knew they had indeed found their perfect site. Before them was a magnificent view of the river below and the sea some miles distant. The top of the hill ran level for several yards, then descended onto a natural, rocky plain leading to the water's edge. A strong wind blew, and the waters of the lagoon sparkled deep blue in the morning sunshine. The site was perfectly suited to reflect the natural earth energy as it traveled along the straight section of the river leading to that point.

"The wind and the water come together with great force here," said Cybele, attuning herself with the energy of the place. "The Dragon Current is strong in this spot."

"Living here will bring us balance," said Adima, feeling what he could not see, expressing what he could not explain, knowing in his heart that they would dwell in this wonderful place that had just been given to them.

So, on the land to which they had been guided by Spirit, they had built their home. What Nature had not provided, they added in the form of vegetation, walls, and artwork. "Let's be imaginative," Cybele had suggested after studying the site for some time and feeling the good energy of the place. "We must create and maintain a connection between ourselves and the land and Spirit. It will be like a miniature version of the city. We'll build the dome in the center—our own temple—and everything will radiate out from there—spacious gardens, fountains, benches, and statues."

Her excitement was contagious. "We'll call it *Elysia*," her husband had named the site, "which means *manifest beauty and harmony within*." In the days that followed, they had set to work, instinctively following the principles of geomancy as written in the *Book of Life*:

> PLACE EVERY PLANT, TREE, AND STONE IN ACCORDANCE WITH THE LAWS OF MATHEMATICS AND MUSIC AS THEY ARE EXPRESSED IN THE GEOMETRY OF THE EARTH'S SURFACE.

In their youth and enthusiasm, they felt they were doing something new, something different, something no one had done before. Yet in reality, they were practicing an ancient Atlantean art. Atlantis was not beautiful and harmonious by accident; its people had made it that way. It was planned. For thousands of years, Atlantean astronomers had studied the sky, the planets, and the stars, while Atlantean geomancers were studying the Great Mother herself. The astronomers discovered great cosmic forces and energy currents emanating from the five planets—Jupiter, Mars, Venus, Mercury, and Saturn. The geomancers discovered similar patterns running above and through the Earth itself. They called them "the lines of the Dragon Current."

In conjunction with these discoveries, Atlantean mathematicians were studying numbers and measurements, particularly how numbers were structured and what they symbolized. By observing Nature, they realized that every natural event followed certain cycles and patterns. "What numerical patterns correspond to those in Nature?" wondered their greatest thinkers. Once they determined those patterns, they asked the next logical question. "How can we set them up as models in the conduct of human affairs?"

Thus was the foundation laid for the marvelous Atlantean Code of Science, which was far more mystical and spiritual than technological. It was founded on three great principles, which they recorded in the *Book of Life*:

> THERE EXIST ENERGY STREAMS ACROSS THE EARTH
> AND THROUGHOUT THE UNIVERSE.
> THESE ENERGIES ARE RESPONSIBLE FOR
> THE RENEWAL OF ALL LIFE ON THE PLANET.
> ALL NATURAL PRINCIPLES ARE PART OF A SINGLE PRINCIPLE
> THAT UNIFIES ALL OF THE INDIVIDUAL ARTS AND SCIENCES.

As the centuries wore on and the scholars and thinkers learned more and more, a great spiritual teaching grew out of their discoveries. They came to believe that the Great Creator first laid down a pattern of number, from which all else proceeded. "NUMBER," they wrote in the *Book of Life*, "CAN THUS BE REGARDED AS THE FIRST ARCHETYPE, OR PARADIGM, OF NATURE."

For this reason, they expressed their discoveries mathematically. They came to value those studies that were particularly numerical—arithmetic, music, astronomy, and geometry. They were especially interested in stereometry, the study of geometric solids and the structure of the universe. "All of these are naturally interrelated," the Ancients said. "They all follow the same rules because of their numerical nature, because of their closeness to the essence of things, because of their closeness to the Great Creator."

To manifest these spiritual principles in the physical world, Atlantean geomancers, mathematicians, and architects constructed a vast web of astronomical and geometrical lines across the face of the Earth. Along these lines, they built great geometrical figures in relation to the positions of the heavenly bodies. The most important task was locating the correct place to build, the place with the best combination of spiritual forces. Using magical rites, Divine omens, dreams, and visions, Atlantean geomancers selected their sacred sites.

Once the site was selected, they built elaborate and precise figures—circles, ellipses, and other geometrical shapes. Thus was Atlantis created.

"Superstition!" cried the Sons of Belial whenever anyone told the ancient tales or talked about applying such spiritual scientific principles to new construction. Nevertheless, the Children of the Law of One continued to implement this ancient art even into modern times. And so, following the age-old practices, Adima and Cybele had done their work well, re-creating in miniature the Earth's harmony, "bringing Heaven down to Earth," as Cybele expressed it.

In the center of this harmonious garden, they placed the dome itself, a graceful, beehive-shaped structure anchored into the living rock and rising above the top of the foliage. It was designed to provide them with shelter from the elements, for the ever-changing Atlantean weather brought dampness, rain, fog, and mist as often as it brought warmth and sunshine. Numerous openings allowed energy to flow in and out of the structure. The entire eastern wall was glass, offering a magnificent view down the river to the Ocean of Atlas. Everything was open and airy, designed to catch the sunlight and the ocean breezes, which carried different fragrances at different times of the year—orange and lemon in spring, frangipani in summer, jasmine in fall, eucalyptus in winter—all intermingled with the cool, ever-present aroma of cypress, cedar, and pine. The result was a recreation of the Ideal as described in the *Book of Life*:

> A BRIDGING OF OPPOSITES TO MAKE A HARMONIOUS WHOLE,
> HARMONY BEING THE WAND OF THE MIDDLE PATH.

*****

"That was fun," said Alta as they came into the dome from their excursion at the beach. "It was good to see all those people and be among friends celebrating and having a good time."

"Oh, look, there are the dolphins!" Charis pointed at two dorsal fins circling in the water of the lagoon. "Let's go see if they have a message for us."

"Can we eat outside, please? Alta called out as he rushed to join his sister, who was already at the water's edge.

"Yes, we'll eat outside. You two go ahead and we'll be right along." Cybele began preparing the ritual meal while the children went to welcome their visitors. The traditional breaking of the fast always took place outdoors, weather permitting.

In fact, the family spent more time outside than in. A flagstone terrace wrapped itself around the eastern side of the dome and spread to the edge of the lagoon. As a young man, Adima had cut and laid each stone himself—shaping them, positioning them, and mortaring them into place. As he worked, Cybele toiled beside him, sculpting and molding the clay for the walls and paths, preparing the soil to receive the seeds and seedlings, placing the pipes and gutters that would carry fresh rainwater to the gardens, fountains, and pools.

Theirs was an arduous task, but also a labor of love, and they had the almost inexhaustible energy and enthusiasm of youth to sustain them long after their muscles began to wail in protest. When at last they were finished, the newlyweds had stepped back and proudly surveyed their work. Even today, it was still their pride and joy.

Beneath clusters of tall trees, soft grasses served as cushions upon which they might relax, meditate, and pray. At the water's edge, alabaster benches offered a place to sit and enjoy unobstructed views of the lagoon and the Ocean of Atlas. Around the perimeter, neatly trimmed shrubs and berry bushes gave home and food to nesting birds. While flowing throughout the garden, gentle streams, pools, and bubbling, spraying fountains sang cheerily by day, rippled soothingly by night.

Yes, Elysia was a mystical, magical place. When the sun was shining, the garden was alive with butterflies and songbirds, and the air was filled with color and sound. When the rains came, fog rolled in from the east, shrouding terrace and trees in a gray, misty vapor, imparting a mysterious, magical aura to the place. It was at such times that Adima and Cybele loved their home the most, for there on the terrace, in the hushed and muted silence, peering into the gloomy, swirling fog, they felt closest to the Creator and the Great Mother.

It was not unusual for dolphins and birds to come by to talk and play. They were part of the family. At certain times of the year, even the great sea turtles came by to see what was going on. The dome was a natural sanctuary, and the animals seemed to sense that it was safe for them to rest there awhile—that they were loved and welcomed.

Which was good, because lately it seemed that the animals were not welcomed anywhere else in Atlantis. Much of their native habitat was being destroyed. The once vast salt marshes that made up the borderlands between the main island and the Ocean of Atlas were dwindling, and those that were left were becoming increasingly polluted by toxins and noise.

As the Sons of Belial expanded trade and manufacturing, it was at the expense of Nature and the animals, not in cooperation with them. More and more, Adima was treating sick animals or animals who came to Elysia to die. "But these dolphins look healthy enough," he remarked as he watched the sleek, playful mammals and listened to them squeal and whistle in their unique language.

"What are they saying, Father?" asked Charis. "What's the message?"

"Now hold on a minute, child," Adima laughed, pleased that his lessons were being taken to heart. "You don't have to look for a message every time you see an animal. Yes, they often have something to teach us, but sometimes they just come by for fun, not because they're trying to tell us anything. Sometimes the message is simply, 'Hi, how are you?'"

"I think we should invite them to share our repast," suggested Cybele, carrying a large tray of fruit, bread, berries, and juice out to the table. "Think they'd like fish?" She handed a plate of mackerel to Alta, who immediately began feeding the tasty morsels to the dolphins.

As always, the ritual meal was sacred and wonderful. First, Cybele made the customary prayers and ceremonial offerings of corn and tobacco. Then came the partaking of nourishment, the family enjoying the bounty provided by the Great Mother through her union with the Dragon Current. All over Atlantis, the scene was the same. Families and friends gathered together, spirituality and sacredness intermingled with joy and laughter. Talk naturally centered around the festival and the events that lay before them. The children were all excited about the upcoming events.

"So what have you two got planned for the rest of the day?" asked Adima, a twinkle in his eye as he watched his children enjoying themselves. Their excitement was contagious—he and Cybele could not help being as enthused as the twins.

Alta spoke up between mouthfuls. "First there's the Dragon Parade," he bubbled. "Then, we're going to be actors in the Dragon Play."

"You're going to be telling the Dragon Story, aren't you?" Charis wanted to know, eagerly tugging at her father's sleeve. She certainly hoped so. It was her favorite part of the festival. Every year, just after sunset, Adima dressed in the traditional costume of the Bard, played his drum, and told the *Myth of the Dragon*. The children looked forward to this; in fact, everyone did. It was one of the highlights of the festival.

"Don't forget the Sacred Wedding," Cybele reminded them. "This day isn't all fun and games, you know. There are some important spiritual practices to which we must also attend. The sun rose this morning on a new year. We want to make sure that the rest of the year is as prosperous as it promises to be today."

It is important to remind the children of their spiritual responsibilities, Cybele thought as she watched them enjoying themselves. So many of the young people were falling away from the old ways, getting caught in the outer world and the materialism that was so rampant around them. Many were starting to forget why they really held the festival and performed the rituals.

A question from Alta reminded her that this was true. "Mother," the boy asked, "why do we worship the sun?"

Cybele knew what had prompted the asking. There was a growing faction among the Children of the Law of One that was becoming increasingly fanatical, if that was the right word. While many were falling away from the ancient ways completely, others were going in the opposite direction, becoming obsessed with spiritual dogma and forming cults to worship inanimate objects and nonexistent deities, in many cases believing more in the words of the myths than the spirit behind them.

She explained patiently, repeating herself many times for emphasis and clarity. "The Children of the Law of One do not worship the sun. We respect the sun because we depend on it as a source of light and heat and power. But we do not worship the sun. The Great Creator sang the sun into being, along with you and me and all created things. Therefore, worship and awe are reserved for the Creator of the sun, not for the sun itself. Do you understand?"

Alta was not convinced. "But my friend says that the Sun God should be worshipped and honored."

Cybele paused for a moment before replying. When she did answer, she spoke not as the twins' mother, but addressed them in her other voice—that of spiritual teacher. "Of course," the priestess shook her head sadly, "there are those who mistake the sun for the sun's Creator. Even among the Children of the Law of One, there is imbalance." Almost as much as there is among the Sons of Belial, she thought to herself.

*****

With the meal finished, the children, anxious to be on their way, could wait no longer. Amid squeals of delight, they hugged their parents good-bye and hurried off into the city, making plans to meet in the Marketplace at midday for the Dragon Parade. Taking advantage of a few moments alone, Adima and Cybele discussed the footprints they had seen at the beach and what they might mean.

"It's the Sons of Belial," Adima declared as he cleared away the remains of the meal. "I know it." His wife looked at him, her intuition sensing the anxiety in his voice even as he himself felt the old, familiar waves of fear churning in his solar plexus. "You can't be around them for as long as I have been and not know when they're up to something. I'm really very worried. This is as dangerous a time as there has ever been in Atlantis. Perhaps our very existence is at stake."

This was by no means an idle or dramatic exaggeration; Adima knew what he was talking about. Despite his relatively young age, he held an important position on the Council of Elders, the main governing body of Atlantis. Thus he was privy to many of the inner workings of the Atlantean government. And that government was embroiled in turmoil.

Until recently, Atlantis had been a society based on cooperation, sharing, and love. Now, though, greed had taken over. To gain power and keep it, the Sons of Belial had begun by targeting the workers, taxing and burdening and otherwise mistreating the land's producers. As they grew in power and influence, they expanded their attack to science and the arts, instituting strict policies that suppressed any knowledge that did not conform to official State policy—a policy that was really about getting power, keeping it, and having absolute rule over the masses.

Under the guise of protecting the children and maintaining high moral standards, they had destroyed many of the documents relating to Atlantis' spiritual science, even banning the age-old practices of geomancy and astronomy. Most frightening of all, they had established an elite caste of spiritual leaders whose main purpose, it seemed, was to aid and abet the State-sponsored suppression. Led by Lilith, High Priestess and favorite consort of Belial, theirs was a sinister, covert mission—to jealously protect the "secrets" and keep them out of the hands of the "uninitiated," all for the public safety, of course.

Despite his fear of the consequences, Adima had spoken out publicly in an address to the Council of Elders, decrying such practices and warning of dire consequences. The results had been less than satisfactory. Adima had become a virtual outcast, shunned by all but a small minority of the Elders. These few expressed their dissatisfaction with State policy through a public censure of the Sons of Belial. Such an inflammatory action served only to deepen the already-wide rift between himself and Belial. Adima vividly recalled the dark, terrible expression of rage on the giant's face as a scribe had read the harsh words of censure:

"As a result of this rejection of the mysteries and of traditional scholarship, Atlantean philosopher-students are losing the ability to fully appreciate the system of names, numbers, and symbols they have inherited from the Ancients."

Yet after all, they were only words, since the Council minority had little power to enforce their will when the votes were called. So the Sons of Belial continued their ways, and no one seemed willing or able to stop them.

"Why do they do this?" Cybele took her husband's hand and walked with him out onto the terrace, where they sat on a stone bench at the water's edge, talking, feeding the birds, and watching the dolphins cavort in the wake of the pleasure craft sailing by on their way into the city.

"It's quite simple, really," Adima explained. "Their motives are very easy to understand if you just put yourself in their place. From their point of view, the Sons of Belial have always been the 'have nots,' or at least, the poorer cousins, struggling for acceptance and recognition and status. It has taken them a long time to achieve success. They're not going to let it go easily."

Cybele snorted in disgust, not prepared to accept what she considered to be a trivial explanation. "The problem is, they don't know how to handle success," she replied. "They might be quite advanced politically and economically, but they've got a long way to go spiritually. It's like giving children a great fortune and watching them squander it all in a day on things they don't need or even know how to use. They've got the wealth and the power but are hardly mature enough to use them wisely."

Adima nodded in agreement. "They believe in the Scarcity Principle—that if they give something away, they lose it; it's gone, and they can't get it back. And they're not about to give away the power for which they've struggled so long. Consequently, they hoard. They also believe in managing and controlling everything. They certainly don't see the Great Mother as a living organism. They see an inanimate ball of rock whose enormous resources are to be exploited and used to their advantage. All of which leads to the amassing of more material wealth than they could ever possibly use."

He paused for a moment so as not to speak over the noise of a small flotilla of gaily painted boats cruising up the river. Apparently, the celebration in the city was already well under way. Waving to the revelers, Adima turned back to his wife and continued. "So they take over the smoothly-running natural processes, and the inevitable result is going to be global destruction. Aren't the provinces reporting blights, droughts, and severe changes in the weather patterns around the globe? Haven't we already had two major earthquakes and tidal waves right here at home?"

They sat in silence for a few moments, each lost in thought. Cybele tossed some crumbs to a seagull that had landed at her feet. The bird pecked at them hungrily. "Isn't there a way to reason with them?" she finally asked. "Isn't there a way to compromise? They're not stupid men. They must understand the ramifications of what they're doing."

Adima shook his head. "Their vision is too shortsighted," he replied sadly. "We can't agree on anything. Council sessions are an armed camp. It's as much a war as if we had turned weapons on each other." In his mind, he could almost hear the shouts and accusations, could almost see the finger-pointing and other physical gestures bordering on violence. And above it all rose the mocking laughter of Belial—arrogant, supremely self-assured, and in absolute control.

"They think of today's festival as just another opportunity to subvert the Children of the Law of One. They know we don't pose a danger to them, that we won't retaliate. Most of us, myself included, fear them. Some of us may even hate them. But the Children of the Law of One are nonviolent. We won't take any direct hurtful action against the Sons of Belial no matter what they do or say. On the other hand, they would fight without provocation—even maim and kill—to get what they want."

Cybele rose and paced back and forth along the deck. "And what is it that they *do* want?" she asked in frustration. "I really need to understand this. What motivates them? How do they think and behave? The only way we're going to be able to heal our world is to understand them and not be afraid of them."

Adima sighed as he leaned on the railing and looked into the sparkling blue waters of the lagoon. "They want power, pure and simple." His voice was harsh and loud. "They want to rule Atlantis completely. They want to get control of the wealth and the military and the Temple and the priestesses, and thereby control the lives of the Atlantean people."

"Why?" Still Cybele could not understand.

"Because it's profitable!" came the stinging reply. "And they don't want to stop with our island. They want to rule Atlantean provinces around the world. Even now, they're abusing the working classes to the point where their status is one of virtual slavery."

Again the fear welled up inside him, stronger now, even more palpable. Should I tell her the rest of it? he debated silently, pausing to feel the cold, icy ball in the center of his own source of power. Do I inflict my fear on her, or do I try to protect her at all costs? Of course he already knew the answer. Where the man was confused and full of doubt, the woman was intuitive and wise. What the one could not comprehend alone, perhaps the two together would be able to understand. He had no choice but to reveal to her the secret he had been carrying in his heart for so long.

Gently Adima reached out and took his wife's hand, looking deeply into her lovely dark eyes. "I must tell you something else," he said softly, "not to frighten you, but so that you will know the whole truth." He sighed deeply. "This is the time predicted by the prophets," he began, quoting from memory an ancient, almost forgotten prophecy:

> DURING THE TIME OF TRIBULATION,
> ATLANTEAN SOCIETY, LIKE THE LAND ITSELF,
> WILL CRUMBLE AND BEGIN TO BREAK APART.
> AND THE FATHERS WILL FALL ASLEEP!

There! He had revealed the whole truth at last.

As the whispered words drifted out across the lagoon, Cybele drew in her breath and squeezed her husband's hand tightly. From childhood she had heard of this prophecy, spoken in whispers among the crones in the Temple, of a Dark Time that would come upon Atlantis. It had frightened her then, and she had not spoken of it in years. Now it had come to light once again. There was no need to converse in words. After so many years of living together, each knew the other's thoughts and feelings almost as well as they knew their own. Yet she had no idea that Adima had known of this, and she thought of how it must have frightened him to have carried the secret alone for so long.

They sat in silence for several minutes, each contemplating how the prophecy might manifest in their world. There was much to the prediction that Cybele could not remember, and she made a mental note to ask Sophia about it the next time they met. There were tears in her eyes as she thought of the pain and anguish that was being inflicted so needlessly. Didn't these men have any understanding of abundance? Finally she broke the silence. "Why are the Elders letting them get away with it?" she wanted to know.

Still holding her hand, Adima took another deep breath. "Right now, the Sons of Belial's influence is subtle," he replied gently. "They're doing everything in the name of progress, ostensibly for the betterment of Atlantis and for the good of all. They argue a strong case. They're eloquent men, and they appeal to people's fear.

"It's very subtle, and it's very powerful. The picture you and I have painted here this morning would never be accepted by the populace. Most people don't even think anything is wrong.

"At least," he corrected himself, " they don't think anything is wrong with having the Sons of Belial in power. Yes, they're aware that Atlantis has lots of problems, but they're coming to accept the Sons of Belial's explanations as to the cause of those problems and to hope that they will know how to resolve them in the future."

Adima stopped speaking and gazed down the river, while Cybele closed her eyes and sat still for several more moments. She knew her husband was not given to exaggeration. He was a wise and discerning man, and she trusted his political assessment of the situation, knowing it to be both intuitive and accurate. She could hear the anxiety in his voice, and she sensed his frustration and unease. Feeling his gaze on her, she opened her eyes and looked at the man she loved. "Where and how do you fit into all of this?" she asked, trying to focus on feelings instead of facts for the moment.

"Fortunately, I still have a lot of respect and influence with the King and the most senior Elders," Adima answered, "so the Sons of Belial haven't tried to oust me yet. But that time is coming, I can feel it. I don't know when or how they'll make their move, but it will come inevitably." He stared off into space for several moments, fingering a long, dull scar on his cheek. It was nothing more that a thin white line running diagonally through the darker flesh, a pale reminder of what had once been a terrible, frightful wound. He did not even look at his wife, and when he continued to speak, the fear in his voice was palpable. "And somehow they'll try to oust you, too. We're too powerful together. They'll have to break us up and destroy our sphere of influence. I'm trying to keep a low profile and not antagonize anyone unnecessarily, but I'm afraid, because we're going to be powerless to stop this."

"I'm afraid, too," said Cybele, taking his hand. Her priestess self was speaking once again. "But let me remind you of something. We have a great inner strength and many allies, both here and in Spirit. You know that we have grown stronger by facing our fears and knowing both sides of ourselves, the Light and the Dark. We know that the darkness cannot do us any harm if it is brought to the light. We may have to walk in the shadow for a while, but we carry our Inner Light with us. That light can never be extinguished, despite the Sons of Belial's plans to the contrary."

Adima shook his head. "I just wish I knew how this was all going to play out," he interjected, slapping his open palm against the unyielding white stone in frustration, as if it held an answer that would help them if only he could get it to respond.

Cybele continued, choosing for the moment to not acknowledge his fear. "I don't know how it will turn out for you and me," she went on. "We might come through this unscathed, or we might get bruised and scarred a bit. That does not matter. The point is that we are willing to do what we are called upon to do, in spite of our fear. But this I do know—the Great Mother is more powerful than any of us can imagine. She will never let herself be destroyed!"

Adima knew his wife's words were true. She was a wise counselor and healer, and he knew better than to question her spiritual insights. "So what do we do?" he whispered.

Cybele's reply was brilliant in its simplicity. "We focus our attention on love and healing instead of getting caught up in the fear cycle along with the Sons of Belial. To them, the world is an object over which to exercise dominion. It is theirs to do with as they please. To the Children of the Law of One, the Earth is a living creature, our Mother, as alive as we are, with every part connected to every other part. Remember that our ways do work. In fact, the principles behind our spirituality and science are far better adapted to the interests of the living Earth than are those of the Sons of Belial."

Shouts of laughter from a passing sailboat interrupted their conversation. "Well," sighed Adima, waving to the boaters, "you're right. Thank you for reminding me and for helping me to stay focused. We'll need to keep reminding each other of our real goals and purpose as we go through this. For now, though," he jumped up and took his wife by both hands, twirling her around and into his arms, "let's leave the outcome to Spirit and put aside our fears. Otherwise, we're going to be late for the celebration."

"And we surely don't want to miss that," Cybele exclaimed, ruffling her husband's hair and kissing him lightly on the cheek. "For this is a day of joy!"

CHAPTER 6

Sit down before fact like a little child, and be prepared to give up every preconceived notion, follow humbly wherever and to whatever abyss Nature leads, or you shall learn nothing.

—T.H. Huxley

From Young Shakala's Journal
Evening
Third Day of the Month of the Rook
Year of the Magus

Today I was introduced to the mysterious and magical world of the alchemist. Teacher was so enthusiastic, so thrilled with the potential and power he held in his hands. And so mysterious, too, so intriguing as he stared out at us from behind his lectern, dressed in his dark robes and pointed hat, his bulging pouch and glowing wand lying on the table before him.

"Throughout the world," he began, "in our mythology, folklore, monuments, and customs, there can be found traces of the ancient and esoteric Atlantean science—a science whose ideals and methods are based on ritual magic and alchemy."

A flash of flame and smoke, a quick whiff of brimstone, and I am instantly caught up in the spell. "Ritual magic and alchemy!" What potent implications they hold for me as I begin my studies in the university. What possibilities they pose. What doors they might open and mysteries reveal!

As an alchemist, my primary goal is to bring about the fertile union of the two elements in Nature referred to as sulphur and mercury. Sulphur represents the solar or cosmic energies; mercury represents the Earth Spirit. By using the Earth herself as the retort for this great chemical infusion, I shall be able to produce what is referred to in our great and mysterious *Book of Mysteries* as...

THE ANIMATED MERCURIUS—THAT MOST MAGICAL AND MYSTICAL OF SUBSTANCES FROM WHICH LIFE IS BORN AND SUSTAINED.

Apart from the symbolism, though, the practical application of all of this is the production of energy—life-giving, vitalizing, powerful energy—enough energy to power the great island and all of the provinces around the world!

Teacher explained that the alchemists believe the works of the Great Mother to be innately flawless; however, the natural world can be even further enhanced by human efforts. It is further written in the *Book of Mysteries*...

JUST AS ALL METALS ASPIRE TO BECOME GOLD,
SO THE EARTH'S DESTINY IS TO BECOME
THE PERFECT REFLECTION OF THE HEAVENLY PARADISE.

I have decided. There is no turning back now. My course is set!

*****

Shakala knew this once and even believed it to be true. But somewhere along the way, he had lost sight of this lofty and spiritual objective. He had always wanted to be an alchemist, but he never quite made it. He had garnered enough knowledge, but he had never gotten the opportunity to use it, and that had produced in him a deep and gnawing resentment, a bitterness that was literally eating away at his body.

Deep in thought, he pondered the events he had witnessed just a few hours before. He had wanted to be at the festival, but he hadn't dared after what he'd witnessed. He kept thinking of Lus. Where was his friend? What was he experiencing? To be utterly alone in absolute darkness for all eternity! Shakala's finite mind could not comprehend things in such absolute terms.

How long was forever? How dark was the absence of light? How alone was "completely alone?" What was going through Lus's mind? Was he screaming? Was he aware of himself, or did he lie dreaming in some altered state of consciousness? Was he feeling trapped, afraid? Was he conscious, or even sane? "Better to be insane or unconscious," Shakala shuddered. He had to stop thinking about it, he told himself, or he would lose his own mind right there on the spot!

"How did I ever get myself into such a predicament?" he asked aloud, but of course he knew the answer. He remembered the first time he'd heard about such a device. It was not a reality then, just a story that frightened him very, very much.

As a boy, his grandfather had told him of a time when certain of the Elders had conducted secret experiments in Atlantis. Such experiments, it was rumored, had resulted in the creation of incredible, grotesque monsters. To destroy the monsters and to punish the experimenters, the device had been built. "And that's where all boys and girls will go if they're bad," his grandfather had warned him ominously. "So you'd better behave." The stories had done their work well, because the young Shakala had been a very well-behaved little boy.

He also had held the image of the device and the Dark Place in his mind for all those years. They haunted both his waking thoughts and his dreams. As a result, he grew into a young man who found it difficult, if not impossible, to make friends and develop lasting, meaningful relationships. To him, life became a series of disappointments. Feeling helpless and hopeless, he blamed others for all of his problems.

Grandfather may have had the best of intentions, but his stories had deeply frightened the child. Even after the old man had explained that these stories were not true, just legends told around the fire to scare young children into that delicious sense of terror that they simultaneously love and hate, the boy was not convinced. He had been deeply wounded, his sense of trust had been destroyed, and he was never able to recover.

"I'll be good," little Shakala had vowed each night before drifting into a restless, uneasy sleep. "I'll never do anything to get myself in a situation like that. Please, gods, don't ever let anything like that ever happen to me, please, please, please." Such were his prayers to the nameless, ogre-tyrant gods he'd worshipped and feared over the years, hoping to appease them and avoid their wrath against his miserable, pitiful self.

As he grew older, however, the lure of earthly wealth and power overcame the fear of spiritual punishment and retribution. His grandfather's stories receded, buried deeply in his subconscious as the young student was caught up in the new scientific thinking—ideas that were leading him to create devices that would bring enormous wealth and power to whomever possessed their secrets. And he was one of those possessors, because he had the skills and knew how to construct the devices and control the energies.

Before long, the budding scientist began to think of such a device in a different way, not as an instrument of torture to punish bad children, but as a tool to be used for the good of all society. So he had begun his research into all of the ancient and secret lore of the Atlantean mysteries. The results had been positive and encouraging. He had come to realize that such a device was indeed theoretically possible, and actually quite simple to build.

He had tried to explain his theories to whomever would listen. Some smiled indulgently, others scoffed outright. Even those who were willing to listen couldn't quite grasp what he was saying. What seemed quite simple to Shakala was apparently far beyond others' limited ability to comprehend. "No matter, though. They don't need to understand just now. They'll understand just fine after I build it and it works," he said to himself.

He had never been respected or needed, only tolerated. Ever since his grandfather had died, he'd been convinced that he was in the way. He had few friends, so he withdrew into a world of books and learning, reading whatever he could get his hands on, devouring one volume after another. It didn't matter what he read—legends, spiritual tomes, research journals, or scientific treatises. His mind was like a sponge, soaking up vast amounts of data from the almost infinite storehouse of Atlantean knowledge.

When the time came, he was apprenticed to the scientific masters in Al Khemia. There he learned how to assimilate and apply all of the myriad facts he'd gathered over the years. He learned geomancy and astronomy, mathematics and stereometry, music and architecture—all of the great sciences of Atlantis. The masters were impressed with his talent and aptitude. He learned quickly, and he showed great promise, but he was never given the opportunity for which he had been yearning—to be invited to learn the deeper scientific secrets. He had asked on numerous occasions, but the answer had always been "No." So he had been forced to watch others, less skilled and less talented than he, rise up through the initiatory ranks while he was left behind and ignored. "Someday," he thought, "I'll get my chance. Someday, I'll show them." But that "someday" never came. Until the visitor had appeared.

One evening as he was working late, a stranger entered the lab. Shakala had seen this older man before, but they'd never spoken. He knew the rumors, though, of how the older man had had the potential for greatness but was something of a loner, almost an outcast among the other students. He'd done something, it was whispered, but no one knew what, or if they did, they weren't telling. As a result of that mysterious, perverse deed, he had been expelled from the Science Academy.

On that fateful evening, the man approached, speaking frankly and boldly. He told Shakala how he admired his work, how he'd been watching him for a long time, how others were watching, too. He spoke at length of how unfair it was that Shakala had been passed over so many times, considering what great talent the young alchemist had. "Now," the stranger concluded, "you do not have to wait any more. My friends are very interested in you, and they want you to join them. They recognize your talents. They want you to help them. They, in turn, will reward you by taking care of you, initiating you into the mysteries, and giving you all the wealth, power, and recognition you deserve. What say you?"

Shakala was sold. They were offering him everything he had ever wanted to replace the lack he perceived everywhere in his life. They were offering wealth, power, fame—none of which he would get if he stayed where he was—everything he needed to make his life complete.

So Shakala had accepted. That was how he came to join the Sons of Belial and work for them as they developed their scientific engines. He'd quickly risen to a high place among the Adepts, having made one breakthrough after another in the development of crystal technologies and energies. The experimental device was his pride and joy, the crowning achievement of his work. But the first test had been a dismal failure. Did that mean that the hypothesis itself was a failure? He hoped not, but it could well be so. Only time would tell, time and more experimentation.

Rebuilding the device had been easy. They had the materials and the tools, and his assistants had completed a new one in just a few hours. They would be testing it again just after dark. Figuring out what had gone wrong, however, was quite another task. Shakala had no idea what had gone wrong. He surmised that there had been a flaw in the giant black crystal, that somewhere within the cut and polished stone, a tiny imperfection had caused a distortion of the energy current, resulting in an explosion. Since the crystal itself had been shattered into a million pieces, there was no way to find the flaw and prove his theory. He could only guess. And if he guessed wrong, if there was some other defect in his design, then this second experiment was going to fail, too. And how would he explain that to Belial?

Belial was not someone who accepted failure from his subordinates. The Master would not tolerate another mistake or any more delays. Already there had been too many postponements because Shakala was being cautious, wanting to make sure that he understood all of the ramifications of the experiment before turning on the device. But Belial had other agendas—political agendas that could not wait for Shakala's more careful approach. The Master had a deadline for when he needed the device to be ready, and he was bound and determined to have it working by then, regardless of the cost.

Well, this time the cost had been Lus's life. What would the cost be next time—not just the cost to the Sons of Belial, but the cost to Shakala himself? The alchemist did not allow himself to think of what the cost might be to Atlantis. The experiment had generated an amazing amount of heat and energy, concentrated into a small space. The goal was to capture and control that heat and energy and focus its power outward in whatever direction the operator intended. In short, it could be an amazing force, used for good or evil, depending on the motives of the operator. It was Belial's intention to use the device as a weapon.

"But if something went wrong at this low frequency," mused Shakala, "what might go wrong if and when we turn up the power?" The alchemist shuddered to think about it. He had seen the burn marks on the floor, how deeply they were cut into the solid granite. That took an enormous amount of heat and energy. "What will happen the next time?" he wondered. "What will happen if the power gets unleashed, gets out somehow into the atmosphere or into the ground? How will we shut it off?" They'd tried in the first experiment, but to no avail. Fortunately, the energy had dissipated before anything more serious had happened. But what if it could not be contained the next time? What if the device did not get shut off in time? There was the very real risk of environmental damage, perhaps major environmental damage!

Atlantis, Shakala knew, sat on a major geological fault, one that had made its presence felt several times in the long history of the island continent. He shuddered to think what might happen if that fault were to become active now, when there was so much life on the island, when they were on the verge of creating a new society. His thoughts were interrupted by a knock on the door. "We're ready for you, sir."

"I'm on my way," the alchemist sighed and walked with his assistant back toward the lab.

*****

Deep below the surface of the Earth, below the caves and tunnels, below the bottom of the sea, deep in the mantle, far out of sight of the land dwellers, other, even more potent forces were at work. Magma oozed, a fault line slipped. Heat—like in the Alchemist's oven and the Blacksmith's furnace, so necessary for transformation—was building. And as the heat increased, water turned to steam, rock turned to lava, and huge pressures began to build. Titanic forces were gathering, forces far beyond the comprehension of the Sons of Belial and their puny and arrogant efforts to control them.

As the Atlanteans walked the surface of their world, deep in her fiery Heart, the Great Mother was preparing, making ready to rid herself of the parasites that were infecting her. Taking the first steps in her own self defense, taking the first steps in healing the great wounds that were being inflicted upon her, taking the first steps in protecting herself and all of the myriad innocent life forms who nurtured themselves at her life-giving bosom. How could they not know her thoughts? How could they not hear her sighs? How could they not feel her grief and pain? How could they not taste her salt tears?

Others knew, others heard, others felt, others tasted. And along with the Great Mother, they wept.

CHAPTER 7

There were giants on the Earth in those days, and also afterward ... These were the mighty men who were of old, the men of renown.

—*Genesis 6:4*

"Let's take the horses," suggested Cybele. "The Good Red Road will be crowded, and this is a holy day. We haven't ridden in such a long while. It will be fun to travel on horseback." This was no idle suggestion, but rather one having great spiritual significance. She had been looking forward to this, her favorite holiday, for weeks, hoping the weather would be fair and warm. Now, on such a gorgeous day, she was as eager to ride as the twins had been to see the Dragon.

For horses had been revered in Atlantis since its earliest days, Horse being their first domesticated animal. That had been such a great leap forward that it was likened to the discovery of fire. Where once they had been slow, plodding, and earthbound, in that singular moment when the Atlanteans first climbed on Horse's back, they became free and swift as the wind. Not long after, they invented wheeled vehicles, and over the ensuing years they built great racecourses for the development of speed in horses. Even the ceremonial war chariot of Poseidon, the first king and legendary God of the Sea, was drawn by a team of twelve great horses—six black, six white; six male, six female.

Now, although Atlantean technology had risen to vast heights and they moved along the Straight Paths over land and sea in self-powered, lighter-than-air vehicles, the Children of the Law of One still revered the sacred animals and the old ways. So Adima and Cybele saddled up and ventured forth into the countryside, laughing and talking and singing the sacred, joyful songs. As they rode, Adima smiled, remembering the first time Horse had welcomed him upon its mighty back, when he was but a little boy. He had been fascinated by the great beast, and when his father had lifted him up, the child imagined himself being lifted up and out of his ordinary life into a world of great promise and adventure. Sitting astride the stallion, he had felt for the first time a sense of his own personal power. He still felt it today, stronger than ever.

"Yeeeee!" the man whistled shrilly, urging his mount into full gallop and waving at Cybele to follow suit. The animal needed no further persuasion, for it had been bred to run. Man and beast fairly flew through the meadow, the miles passing swiftly beneath Horse's flying hooves. At last, coming to the top of a rise, as if on signal, the great animal stopped and reared up on its hind legs, whinnying its joy and exuberance for all to hear.

There was much to be joyful about, and Horse was inviting them to pause and appreciate the beauty that surrounded them on all sides. It was an invitation that could not be refused. And so, reaching out and taking each other's hands, husband and wife gazed with love upon their wondrous world.

The view was breathtaking. From where they stood on the hill, the entire Atlantean countryside lay spread out before them. To the west, virgin forests stretched for miles and miles, their cool, deep greens flowing in waves over the land. Rising gradually at first, then ever more sharply, the ancient trees provided animals and humans alike with a welcome respite from the tropical heat. Glittering waterfalls flowed like silver ribbons through the verdure. Soft, wide meadows of wildflowers punctuated the slopes with brilliant dots of blues, reds, oranges, pinks, and yellows. Then suddenly, over a mile in the air, in a shocking burst of pink and black, the naked volcanic rock thrust itself upward—stupendous granite sentinels rising ever more sharply to the dazzling, snowcapped summit. These were the Mountains of the Moon, source of the four rivers, the backbone of the great island continent.

To the north, the Great Plain flowed like a golden inland sea for mile after fertile mile, gradually ascending far on the horizon to the elevated purple table lands where the royal family dwelt in unimaginable splendor. Bisecting the center, like a gigantic, pearl-white serpent, the River of the Rising Sun crawled its way peacefully across the land. Born in the eternal snowfields atop mysterious Mount Kylene, the fresh glacial water provided abundant nutrients for the acres and acres of rich, black farmland before finally commingling with the warm brine of the Ocean of Atlas far to the east. It was an overwhelming open space—the whole of which was covered with temples, palaces, tombs, pyramids, and pillars, each one a work of art in its own right, each one adorned with jewels, mosaics, etchings, and sacred inscriptions. Viewed from this height, the geometrical arrangement of the buildings, monuments, obelisks, and the interconnecting lines that joined them was evident. This was the embodiment of Spiritual Engineering—that sacred form of science whereby the pattern on the Earth conformed to a corresponding pattern in the Heavens.

AS ABOVE, SO BELOW.

Atlantean geomancers were quite fond of quoting the *Book of Life*.

The lovers squeezed each other's hand tightly, too overcome to speak, enraptured by the beauty of their homeland. Everywhere was evident the highest quality of beauty and order, embodying metaphysical principles in which scientific and poetic truth were united in harmony. For the Atlantean geomancers had a deep understanding of the hidden nature of the countryside. Further, they knew that all aspects of life and growth, both large and small, conformed to certain basic patterns.

A hill here, a district there, each connected by a system of straight paths, each with its unique center and balance, each with its hidden nature, each named for its counterpart in the sky—the Sun, the Moon, a star; or, rather, with the spiritual principle which that heavenly body represented. The full purpose of this terrestrial geometry was both clear and important to the Atlanteans, and they wrote about it in the *Book of Life*:

OUR LIVES ARE ENRICHED BY MEANS OF A FORCE ACTIVATED THROUGH
THE CORRECT GEOGRAPHICAL RELATIONSHIP OF THE SACRED CENTERS.

Adima, Cybele, and the twins were attuned to these principles. The Children of the Law of One were attuned to these principles. Thus, the placement of the centers, the accuracy of the lines, and the way in which they chose the sacred spots in the landscape were of utmost importance, because the flow of the Dragon Current followed the course of their man-made alignments.

It was a most elaborate landscape—both spiritual and practical—and quite capable of supporting a dense population. And here, at the southeastern tip of the continent, round and white and gleaming in the sunshine, the first kings had built a city of magnificence to match the glory that so rich a land would soon achieve.

Adima smiled and shook his head, trying to conceive of the monumental effort it had taken to produce such grandeur. For this city, itself named Atlantis, was a work of art whose construction was of incalculable expense and magnificence. In shape it consisted of concentric rings of land and waterways, spreading out across three belts of water and two of land. Interspersed throughout each ring, there were springs, both hot and cold, some for the use of the royalty, others for the citizens, still others for beasts of burden. The outer rings held a racecourse and private homes. The inner harbors were dotted with all kinds of seagoing craft, from sailing boats to cargo ships to vessels of war.

Spanning the canals was the Avenue of the Gods, a broad, paved thoroughfare leading from the Gates of White Pearl—which opened onto the Great Plain—inward and upward to a central hub. There, on a high hill ringed by three canals, where Poseidon and Cleito—founders of Atlantis—had conceived Atlas and his twin brother, Gadir, the Atlanteans had erected their most magnificent structures.

Cybele shared her husband's sense of wonder, her priestess-mind fully aware of the Divine inspiration and assistance that had made such achievement possible. Like the great Nation-State itself, the architecture was on a monumental scale. Many of the structures were made of enormous blocks of stone, cut and hewn to geometric perfection and placed seamlessly together, the joints scarcely perceptible, no wider than the thickness of a strand of hair.

It was masonry to a degree of artistic perfection the likes of which the world has not seen since. Yet there was no heaviness. Pyramids, geodesic domes, tetrahedrons, and other shapes dominated the skyline in a light and airy architecture that was part of the environment, the sacred geometry blending harmoniously with the living flora and fauna. And there, in the very heart of it all, covering a square eighteen hundred feet on each side, the Ancients had raised a great temple to Poseidon, whom they loved. The spiritual power center of Atlantis, the original structure was begun in antiquity by Atlas, eldest son of the founders and first high king. Over the centuries, each succeeding king had added to its adornment until the Temple had become, according to the *Book of Life*:

...AN ABODE AMAZING TO BEHOLD FOR THE
MAGNITUDE AND BEAUTY OF ITS WORKMANSHIP.

From the vast eastern courtyard, in the center of which rose a gigantic statue of the Sea God riding a golden chariot through the waves in the company of dolphins, wide boulevards and rose-trellised paths led to the structures that made up the royal residence. And such a Palace it was, with its three thousand rooms, half above ground, half below— a grand maze of courts, chambers, colonnades, statues, and pyramids.

The sight of so many buildings gathered together in a single space—inlaid as they were with mosaics and jewels, silver and gold and that most precious and sacred of all metals, orichalcum—was more than the first-time visitor could comprehend. Courts, halls, gateways, pillars, obelisks, monolithic figures, and sculptures were massed in such profusion that it was scarcely possible to take it all in. For a time, Adima and Cybele could do naught but gaze upon the loveliness of the Atlantean Heart Center, feeling powerful waves of love reaching out to them and to all visitors that day.

"Come, you are welcome," the city seemed to beckon. *"Step within, for you are home."*

"It's alive," Cybele spoke at last, breaking the reverie by voicing her feelings. "The city itself is alive!"

Adima nodded in agreement. It was true. He sensed the lifeblood coursing through its veins, heard the rhythmic beating of its mighty heart, felt its sweet breath kiss his cheek in welcome. Even though he and Cybele saw it each day, the city and countryside seemed to take on a special glow during the holidays. The commonplace, the mundane, was relegated to the background, while that which was mystical, magical, and sacred came to the forefront for all to behold.

Behind them, glistening white in the sunshine, lay Elysia and the mound by the sea where the Dragon had first appeared that morning. From there, the Good Red Road ran for thousands of miles around the perimeter of the island, a sacred artery along which countless pilgrims trod on their sojourns from city to city, shrine to shrine, center to center. On the eastern headlands stood the huge and mysterious Lighthouse, solitary and aloof at the edge of the Ocean of Atlas. Like the legendary winged Guardian, Hermes, who was born and had his sanctuary in a cave on the sacred summit of Mount

Kylene, the Hermit of the Light dwelt alone, ever vigilant, watching and observing from his vantage point high above the world, protecting the ships from dashing themselves on the jagged rocks, his light illuminating the channel and providing safe passage into the harbor.

It was said that they were brothers, and that the hermit was as old and as wise and as powerful a magician as the Winged One himself. But no one really knew for sure, so seldom did the ancient one leave the tower to walk amongst his countrymen. Still, the rumors persisted, as did the tales of hauntings, visions, and other eerie encounters said to occur in the vicinity of the Lighthouse.

Outside the city walls, Lake Moeris sparkled in the sunlight. Built by the Ancients, it was an engineering marvel, a vast, artificial container over four hundred and fifty miles in circumference and three hundred and fifty feet deep—a complex system of subterranean channels, floodgates, locks, and dams. Yet it was so much more than that—for, in truth, Lake Moeris was a spiritual reservoir, an enormous chalice containing the sacred substance by which the Great Plain was kept fertile and irrigated—the life-giving waters of the River of the Rising Sun.

And well within the city, just beyond the Temple and Palace, stood the marvel of the race—the Great Pyramid. Power source, accumulator and transformer of cosmic energies, connector of Heaven and Earth, its four visible sides rose steeply upward from an immense bedrock base to a tiny, almost invisible crystal point high above the world. Built to last for all time, this veritable mountain of stone, this wonder of wonders, monumentalized the entire code of Atlantean scientific knowledge.

"What's going on over there?" Cybele pointed toward the magnificent structure, around which appeared to be a bustle of activity.

Adima followed her pointing finger with his eyes. "There shouldn't be anything going on; this is a holiday. I would imagine that the Sons of Belial are working instead of celebrating. They won't take part in the festivities, of course. Work is far too important for such trivial nonsense as a Dragon Festival. Well, whatever it is they're doing, I'm sure we'll hear about it before long."

The business at the Pyramid was quickly forgotten as they rode down the hill, across the Great Plain, and through the Gates of White Pearl. The city was alive with color and music and all manner of artistic adornment.

The Atlanteans were a romantic and spiritual people who looked past the surface appearance of things to the deeper meaning and experience. They were great poets and artists, yet their subject matter was often beyond the scope of words. So, where there was no literal expression of sufficient scope to comprehend the principles to which they were referring, they used symbolic language and art. These were expressed in their music, literature, painting, drawing, sculpture, and architecture. And in the "languages" of these art forms, the images were not fixed in rigid interpretations but had manifold meanings.

Cybele remembered how excited the twins had been to discover the esoteric meaning behind the symbols. "Rings and circles represent continuity, marriage, land, and water," she had taught them as soon as they were old enough to understand such abstraction. "A circle with an inscribed cross symbolizes peace and also serves as an icon map of the city."

"What are those?" Charis had wanted to know, pointing to a cluster of spirals and arrangements of interlocking dots and circles.

"Such symbols represent infinity and the sacred paths and circles of the landscape," Cybele explained. "They also serve as guides for those who travel such paths. Can you tell me what the wheel represents?" She pointed to an ornately carved wheel inscribed on a flaming solar disc.

"It looks like the sun," Alta ran his fingers over the shining surface. The metal and stone were cool to the touch.

"You're right," his mother congratulated him. "The wheel depicts attributes of the sun and solar power, with its hub as the sun itself and the spokes as its rays. Of course, you already know that each of the heavenly bodies is expressed by a particular color. Can you remember them?"

Charis piped up first. "The Moon is silver," she proclaimed, "Jupiter is yellow, and Mars red." She paused, letting her brother get in on the fun.

"And Venus is blue, Mercury white, and Saturn black," Alta had finished proudly.

That teaching had happened many years ago, at their first Dragon Festival, but the twins never forgot. Neither did Cybele. Now she smiled as her eye was drawn to a huge painting of a Dragon passing through a winged circle. "The twin symbols of alchemical fusion," she translated the meaning instantly. The Dragon was a concrete expression of the Divine powers of life-giving. The Blue Dragon represented the yang, or positive, side of the magnetic force known as the Dragon Current; the White Tiger was the yin, or negative, side.

As they rode toward the Marketplace, horses' hooves clicking rhythmically on the cobbled pavement, Adima and Cybele savored the sensory stimuli flowing over them from all directions. The city was crowded with visitors from many, if not all, of the provinces, from nearby Turtle Island to far-off Lemuria, with whom a fragile and uneasy truce had been declared. Conversations were in many dialects, loud, animated, and friendly, interspersed with gestures and touching and hugging and much laughter. The weather was warm, so most of the people were dressed in airy, flowing garb. The material shimmered and glistened, not just lightweight but light itself—sparkling and iridescent, stylish, functional, and beautiful.

Minstrels strummed their lyres and sang their gay and festive songs. Puppets danced on strings, much to the delight of children and adults alike. Street vendors hawked their wares, from food to balloons to trinkets. Cool ocean breezes carried the pleasant smells of incense and flowers and roasting chestnuts and cedar. The city was showing itself off today, and proud to do so.

"Mother! Father!" Alta and Charis where right where they said they'd be, merrily engaged in a game of Paper-Wood-Fire-Metal-Earth with some friends. Both parents smiled, remembering their youth and how much they had enjoyed this delightful pastime, which was based on several scientific principles.

As every child knew, certain influences went well together; others could not lie happily in conjunction. This was demonstrated by the relationships between the five material principles. Wood fed fire but ate up earth. Fire produced earth but consumed metal. Earth produced metal but soaked up water. Metal produced water but destroyed wood. Water produced wood but destroyed fire. There were really no winners or losers in such child's play, and certainly no rules, just a lot of joy and laughter as the children took turns being one element or another and tumbling on top of each other.

"There are Suonare and Suristes and Hu!" cried Cybele, pointing to a group of friends sitting on a blanket in the shade of the Marketplace's ancient sycamores.

"I see you're ready for the parade," Adima said warmly as he handed the horses over to a groom who stood ready to attend to them. The horses would be as pampered as the humans this day. Their friends made room for them on the soft grass.

"The parade should be starting very soon," Suonare said. "We got here early to get a good viewing spot. I want to see the King. Of course, you two don't get excited about such things. You see the royal family all the time."

"Believe me, it's not as glamorous as you make it out to be," laughed Cybele. "They're human, like we are. They just have a lot more people around them and a lot more things to do and attend to. Like today, for instance. The King will be in the parade and put his hand to the plow to symbolize the importance of agriculture, but then he'll be so busy receiving ambassadors and dignitaries from the provinces that he won't have any time for himself to enjoy the holiday."

"Actually, I'm just as glad when I don't have to visit the Palace," Adima joined in. "It's too busy, too hectic and frenetic. Lots of noise and commotion. You can't hear yourself think. I much prefer the quiet of the Temple gardens or the forest or my own terrace on the lagoon. By the way, Hu, what's going on over at the Pyramid? We saw a lot of commotion over there as we were riding in."

The older man shook his head disgustedly. "Some kind of science experiment," he snorted. "They're testing some new device for Belial's weather control project. I don't know why they have to do it today. But they say they're on a tight schedule and can't wait. They've been working tirelessly for months now, and conditions are supposedly just right today for whatever it is they need to do."

Their conversation was interrupted by music and revelry. The children stopped their game and came running over. Everyone stood up. First, there was a blast of trumpets as the Dragon-clearers ran through the streets, symbolically opening the way and announcing the imminent arrival of the Dragon. Minstrels danced in the streets, singing a mock warning to all whose homes happened to be situated on the Dragon Path, reminding them that they must, on festival day, leave all portals open, for it was unwise to obstruct the Dragon Parade.

> *Attend, ye who dwell upon the Dragon Path,*
> *For on this day the Dragon passes through the land,*
> *And all who stand in its way*
> *Might be struck dead or taken off,*
> *Never to return!*

Instantly, doors and windows were flung open, for the Atlanteans were not just passive observers, but active participants in the ritual. It was all done in a spirit of fun and laughter, of course. Everyone knew that the Dragon wasn't going to strike people dead or whisk them away, but they did respect the tremendous natural forces that ran through the land.

Such forces were held at bay by other Atlantean contrivances—the Logan stones that dotted roads and fields—huge, magical boulders so precariously balanced that they could be set rocking at a touch. Such mysterious stones and other isolated piles of rock were traditionally associated with the invocation of fertility. These great megaliths, set up on the high moors and coastal cliffs, played an important part in the generation of the terrestrial current and its transmission down the alignments of pillars and stones.

And so the parade wended its way through the city, led by minstrels with painted faces and dressed in motley, the characteristic dress of jesters and fools, strewing rose petals and singing to the crowd as they danced past. It was a carefree, colorful party that marched through the streets, reaching out to young and old alike, taking them by the hand and inviting them to join in the parade.

Alta and Charis leapt up as the papier-mâché Dragon came into view, taking their places beside the mythic creature as it passed by on its seasonal journey to reanimate the Spirit of the Community.

"Tend to the Dragon as it passes over the sacred centers," the minstrels reminded the crowd, referring to the belief that the Dragon traveled along certain invisible lines of terrestrial magnetism, pausing at each sacred site, *"and join in the singing of the Dragon Songs."*

This was a most important tradition, for each part of the community was responsible for looking after its particular stretch of the Dragon Path. At each neighborhood center, the people sang a local episode in the history of the creation of Atlantis. The Marketplace was no exception.

The parade paused as the minstrels gathered the children in a circle, strummed their lyres, and played their pipes. Everyone joined in the singing.

> *Imagine!*
>
> *From mountain peak to mountain peak,*
> *Far as the eye can reach,*
> *The fairy chain stretches*
> *Across the whole wide world.*
>
> *Descending from the high places,*
> *Over ridges, banks and knolls,*
> *Over mounds and earthworks,*
> *Through groves of trees.*
>
> *Through the valleys far below,*
> *Great standing stones to mark the way,*
> *Out across the fertile Plain,*
> *Entering in through the gleaming gates.*
>
> *Lo! See it now!*
> *From afar the Dragon comes*
> *Along the Straight Paths.*
>
> *Flashing fire—*
> *A beacon in the High Places*
> *Tops a rise,*
> *Crosses a ridge,*
> *Drawing closer, ever closer.*
>
> *Follow the beam, friends, one and all,*
> *Along the fiery Dragon Path.*
> *The Dragon fire blessing all,*
> *Sparkling as it passes.*
>
> *To which we cry,*
> *Just keep straight on!*
> *Just keep straight on!*

Thus the parade continued on its way, forming with each successive ritual what the Atlanteans called a *line of songs* woven between the geometric centers of their landscape.

"That was fun!" the twins bubbled as the Dragon passed out of sight. And they knew the best part of the parade was yet to come. As one, the people rose, jostling for position, pressing forward eagerly, hushed, expectant, lining each side of the Avenue of the Gods. The pavement itself seemed aware and ready, waiting for those most sacred and magical of travelers to grace its cobbled stones. Gadir—King of Atlantis—was coming!

Again the trumpets burst forth in a mighty fanfare. Now not Dragon-clearers came into view, but warriors in full dress regalia, stepping in time to the rhythm of twelve beating drums. How straight and true they marched, in perfect formation, looking neither right nor left. Feathered plumes dancing in the breeze, ceremonial shields and lances sparkling in the sunlight, they were an ancient army—the Elite Guard, escorts of the King.

Alta and Charis felt the excitement in the air, their own hearts beating in harmony with the great drums as the royal warriors passed by.

"Here he comes!" Suonare cried, pointing to a chariot just coming into view at the far end of the street. It was a magnificent golden vehicle, encrusted with jewels and inlaid with ebony and ivory—an exact replica, on a smaller scale, of the great war chariot in which Poseidon rode as he towered over the Temple courtyard—and drawn by two of the most noble and mystical creatures ever to grace the planet.

"The Centaurs! The Centaurs!" The twins shouted in unison with every other child in the Marketplace. Parents lifted smaller children up. Youngsters sat on fathers' shoulders. No one wanted to miss the opportunity to see the mighty creatures and partake of some of their magic. For these were, indeed, the Centaurs—purest of the mixtures that the Atlantean genetics experiments had produced, the only known mutants still alive. The others were all extinct—those creatures whose images continue to live on in the sense memory of the human race—unicorns, winged horses, nymphs, and satyrs.

So many of the mixtures had involved horses. The Atlanteans had wanted to be like Horse, and Horse had wanted to be like them. So they had tried to combine the best of both species. The results had, for a time, been successful, or so they thought, producing unicorns and winged steeds and the halflings. But then something had gone terribly wrong. One by one, the mythic creatures began to die, and no amount of genetic engineering or genetic healing was able to save them. Now they were all gone, save only these two. They were, in truth, the last of their kind, for further genetic experiments had been forbidden; too many dangerous aberrations had resulted.

Now here they were, drawing the King in his ceremonial war chariot—not as beasts of burden, but as honored cohabitors of the kingdom, gold and silver and splendid jewels encrusting their trappings and flashing brightly in the sunlight as they passed. Mystical and magical, the Centaurs were highly honored as dispensers of knowledge and harmony.

In the chariot's wake, a team of thoroughbred horses drew a golden plow. In just a little while, Gadir would use that most sacred tool of agriculture to ceremonially till the soil after it had been fertilized by the Dragon. He was heading there now, to a specially prepared area on the western side of the Temple. There, in the shadow of the Great Pyramid, he would take his place beside Belial and Lilith and preside over the Alchemical Wedding.

"Where is the King's consort, Father?" Charis quietly whispered in Adima's ear. He looked at her. How did she know the King had a consort? Indeed, how did she even know what consorts were?

"She and the King are no longer together," he whispered back softly, stifling his surprise. "She has returned to Mu." Alas, it was too bad, he thought as he watched the procession pass. Apparently Gadir and Moo had felt as though they shared nothing in common.

The courtiers, Elders, and priestesses, however, all felt differently. They liked the Queen of Mu. They all hoped she'd be the one. But she was not, just another in a long series of failed romantic trysts, and another disappointment for the Court.

Adima looked at the King riding alone in his chariot. "A king without a queen is unbalanced," he muttered under his breath. "Every kingdom needs both in order to be whole. Atlantis is no exception."

So Gadir rode past, smiling and waving and all by himself—no Queen at his side, a King without balance, without his feminine complement. A living exemplar of a nation out of balance.

*****

"It's time for me to be on my way to the Temple," Cybele declared as the royal retinue passed out of sight. "It wouldn't be right to keep the King and the High Priestess waiting or for me to show up late for the Wedding ceremony." She kissed her husband and the children and walked off.

"We'll follow right along," Adima called after her, waving good-bye, "and meet you afterwards."

"Wedding ceremony!" snorted Hu, as they started in the direction of the Temple. "The High Priestess doesn't care a whit for the sanctity of the Wedding ceremony. The only part of the Wedding ceremony that the High Priestess cares about is how good she looks in her robes in front of the crowd. Now in my day..."

"Never mind about 'in your day,'" chided his wife. "How dare you criticize her that way! Do you want to be struck dumb? Besides, it won't do any good to go reminiscing about how good things were way back when, nor will it do to go complaining about the High Priestess. Give her the benefit of the doubt. She means well. She's been High Priestess for a long time and really has the people's best interests at heart. Yes, she's a little bit vain, but we all have our faults. She really cares about the festival and the people and the prosperity of Atlantis."

Her husband was not convinced. "As far as I'm concerned, the only prosperity she cares about is her own," Hu retorted as they approached the outer precincts of the Temple.

"Shhhh, lower your voice," cautioned his wife. "You're in the Temple courtyard. Have some respect! Besides, it doesn't matter anyway, because she's just a figurehead. The real benefit of the Wedding comes from the fusion, not from anything the High Priestess does."

Adima frowned as he listened to their conversation. It was so typical of conversations among the Children of the Law of One these days. Someone complaining that the old ways were not being honored anymore, or that a leader's spirituality was not what it appeared to be. Others, fearing that they'd be struck down for daring to criticize or profane such sacred people, defended the "keepers of the faith" as being beyond reproach.

He thought about the forthcoming ritual, the third of the day's festivities. This was the crowning glory, really, because while the other events were of a symbolic and spiritual nature, the Alchemical Wedding was very, very physical. Preparations had been underway for weeks in anticipation of the event. "The King is coming, the King is coming," cried the heralds day after day in the Marketplace. Indeed, any visit by the King was such a rare event that it was treated with special attention and consideration.

More figurehead than ruling monarch, it was not often that King Gadir actually came into the city, preferring the seclusion of his private estates on the northwestern edge of the Great Plain, in the foothills of the Mountains of the Moon. He was a hard man, more absent than present, more calculating politician than benevolent leader, more tyrant than steward—taxing, squeezing, and choking the very lifeblood out of the people. Or rather, he allowed the Sons of Belial to do so, all in the name of progress and maintaining a strong and vigorous kingdom.

Not that Gadir was inherently evil. He was, rather, weak and selfish, self-indulgent and seldom present, attending to the needs of his people only when he thought about it, only when affairs of State did not get in the way of his personal affairs.

Adima thought of one of his favorite adages from the *Book of Life*:

> THE STATE OF THE KINGDOM IS A DIRECT
> REFLECTION OF THE STATE OF MIND OF THE KING.

This was certainly true in Atlantis—Atlantis was divided within itself just as the King's loyalty and time were divided between his personal interests and his royal duties to his subjects. Thus, the King's persistent absence from the lives of his subjects was perceived by many as tacit approval of the methods of the Sons of Belial.

Others, however—Adima included—perceived Gadir as a King who had sold out his people, forgotten his obligations and duties, and lost sight of his sacred function. Perhaps Gadir had never even understood any of this to begin with. However it had come about, the King of Atlantis now reigned over a divided Kingdom.

Still, the legends of the great Atlantean kings of the past lived on in the hearts of the people—kings who took great delight in their subjects, kings who blessed them, nurtured them, and offered them the benefits of their wisdom and vision. Such titanic men, who had over the ages become almost demigods—Poseidon, Atlas, and the rest—had no illusions about their kingly roles and duties. They assumed both the rights *and* the responsibilities of kingship, not because their own talents and graces had raised them to preeminence, but because they knew they had been Divinely appointed to assume and carry out a sacred trust. In those most ordered and balanced and perfect kingdoms of the past, such benevolent kings took from their subjects only that which was necessary for the survival of the kingdom. And, like his subjects, each king lived according to the customs and responsibilities of his rank.

Such legends had a powerful hold over the Atlantean people. They wanted to believe that Gadir was a good king. They wanted to believe that he had not abdicated his sacred trust. They wanted to believe that he was the embodiment of Atlas in physical form, ruling with the twelve kingly attributes of love, wisdom, temperance, patience, benignity, prudence, benevolence, kindness, tolerance, mercy, humility, and justice. Thus it was that the people had scurried about in a great hustle and bustle, making all manner of preparations, according to the ancient traditions. Now, the kingdom had assembled, and all was in readiness on the western side of the Temple.

Throughout the vast complex, select royal warriors and guards lined the pathways and stood at attention, while overhead, looking down on his beloved subjects from high above, the titanic statue of Poseidon—ever-present reminder of the glory that was Atlantis—smiled on his people, blessing his subjects and his kingdom. The entire ritual was designed to reflect the cosmic order, and the King, who represented the solar principle, the Sun, was the central figure. Gadir sat enthroned on the western side of the Temple overlooking the Great Plain, while beside him Belial, the lesser priestesses, and visiting dignitaries from the provinces took up their positions. On each side of the Temple itself, a regiment of the Elite Guard stood at attention, royal warriors facing each of the cardinal points of the Atlantean realm. On the lawn, spreading out from the Temple to the Great Pyramid, stood court officials and military and religious functionaries, all placed according to their roles of office. Interspersed throughout them all, the people themselves stood, the whole human assembly forming a magic pattern that symbolized the Divine authority by which Atlantis was governed.

And as the humans had formed themselves, so they had designed the landscape to conform to the same principles. Extending in a straight line due west from the Temple, various standing stones and other sacred objects were decorated with flowers, spirals, symbols of fertility, and the undulating Serpent—symbol of the current of life energy—forming a colorful map of the Dragon's route across the landscape. Of course, it was not the paintings or symbols themselves that produced the release of Life Essence, but the rock on which they were drawn. It was the energy from these rocks that created rain and fertilized plants and animals. The paintings and ritual songs served to stimulate its flow and benefit the creatures with which the current of a particular spot was associated.

From where he stood, Adima could see far out across the Great Plain of Atlantis, all the way to the snowcapped Mountains of the Moon rising thirty miles to the west. The vast fields were lying dormant now, waiting for the start of the new growing season. He marveled at the science, technology, and human effort that had produced the vast network of circles and standing stones spread out across the Great Plain.

Marked by the geomancers, the stone circles were located according to the nature of the celestial body they represented and the strength of the natural magnetic current that flowed through the site. Every stone circle had an affinity with a certain part of the human body, thereby forming giant figures that stretched right across the face of the landscape. Interspersed among the stone circles was a series of upright stones that were strategically placed so as to take advantage of the natural magnetic current that flowed through the area. In the exact center of the Plain, a great lightning rod rose in the form of a specially placed and carved marble obelisk.

When construction was completed, the Ancients recorded an important reminder in the *Book of Life* so that all would understand the meaning and purpose behind so monumental an effort:

> THE ENTIRE VAST CONTRIVANCE IS ESSENTIAL TO THE GREAT WORK OF ATLANTEAN ALCHEMY, WHICH FORMS THE CLIMAX OF ALL OUR RITUAL— THE INTRODUCTION OF SOLAR AND ATMOSPHERIC ENERGY INTO THE TERRESTRIAL LIFE CURRENT.
>
> STONE PILLARS ARE THE CONDUIT, RECEIVING THE LIGHTNING AND, THROUGH THEIR LIVING QUARTZ OR METALLIC CONTENT, UNITING HEAVEN AND EARTH IN THE SAME WAY AS DOES A LIVING TREE.

What was about to occur was the *Alchemical Wedding*, the marriage between Mother Earth and Father Spirit, consummated through the Sacred Lightning. This most solemn and sacred of ceremonies was presided over by Lilith, High Priestess of the Temple of Poseidon, with whom Adima and Cybele had long acquaintance.

The weather was cooperating nicely. Great clouds had been building in the west all afternoon. Now they were moving east and almost in position over the Temple. This was a natural phenomenon—clouds came in from the ocean in the morning, picked up moisture over the mountains and plains at midday, then returned to the sea in the late afternoon, dropping their water in the form of rain and thunderstorms. Such was the Atlantean hydrologic cycle, on which they depended to water their crops, give drink to the residents of the city, and keep their world green and alive.

Adima glanced skyward as lightning flickered in the distance and thunder rumbled far off in the west, then turned his gaze toward the Temple veranda. Cybele and the other priestesses were there, awaiting the arrival of Lilith. He looked at his wife as she sat behind the dais. Deep emotion flooded over him as he admired the woman whom he loved. How passionate she was, how kind and gentle! Yet there was so much more. For the soft, regal persona of priestess was balanced by a strong infusion of warrior energy.

Even after all their years together, his heart still pounded a bit faster whenever he saw her. It was not infatuation, he knew, for with each passing day, his love for her grew ever stronger, ever deeper. "She is so beautiful," Adima thought. "I love her so, and I'm so proud of her." He wondered what Cybele would think of the conversation he had just heard. What was she thinking as she sat beside the King of Atlantis, waiting for the ritual to begin?

Actually, if he could have read her mind, he would have seen that Cybele's thoughts were, in fact, quite similar to those which Hu had voiced. The ceremony was no longer what it once was. It was originally intended for everyone to be involved. The prayers and rituals were in the vernacular of the people, and all had participated. This very day, however, something had changed radically. Only moments ago, out of earshot of the crowd, Lilith had issued a stunning edict to the priestesses, banning all but herself from playing an active role in the ceremony.

Cybele did not appreciate such overt and hostile abuse of power. In fact, she was quite upset, although she remained outwardly poised and unemotional as she sat beside the King. Her mind, however, was filled with memories of rituals past, coupled with anxiety about the future. She thought about her childhood and what the old women had told her when she had been initiated, that once these now-secret rituals and invocations had been common property. Everyone had taken part—because they were supposed to!

At the time of the founding of Atlantis, the Ancients had appointed the first high priestess and her priestesses as the Keepers of Knowledge, charging them with the sacred task of preserving the memory of Atlantean world-order through the ages. These women understood their sacred role as it was described in the *Book of Life*:

> ATLANTEAN TRADITION COINCIDES WITH THE FIRST MOMENT OF HUMAN
> ENLIGHTENMENT AND IS BASED ON CONSTANTLY RENEWED REVELATION.

Atlantean priestesses maintained the philosophic schools that codified this learning and understanding into the full body of Atlantean learning and lore. Their work helped illuminate the work of future generations such as the Pythagoreans, the Platonists, the medieval transcendental magicians, the Hebrew cabalists, and the Christian Gnostics.

They developed a method for gaining certain "INCOMMUNICABLE KNOWLEDGE," as they described the process in the *Book of Mysteries*:

> THROUGH A HIGHLY MYSTICAL COURSE OF STUDY, WE PREPARE OURSELVES
> AND OUR STUDENTS FOR INDUCED MOMENTS OF HEIGHTENED PERCEPTION.
> AT THESE TIMES, ASPECTS OF THE HIDDEN UNIVERSE STAND OUT CLEAR
> AND ORDERLY TO THE INNER MIND.

As they gained further insight into past and future events, the priestesses came to understand numerical relationships and proportion, and how these elements achieved balanced expression through the arts of geometry, music, and poetry. In short, they became the keepers of the sacred history of Atlantis, a history that was open and available to all.

Now, though, spiritual practices in Atlantis were being controlled by the High Priestess and her favorites, and as far as Cybele was concerned, their motive was to gain personal power. The secrets of spiritual invocation, once common property, had become exclusive to those appointed by the Sons of Belial to procure the seasonal renewal of fertility and interpret Divine Will through the heavenly portents. Thus Lilith, established in a position of authority, began to extend her influence and activities and to make demands on the population for sacrificial offerings.

Cybele shivered as a deep rumble reverberated over the land. Great thunderheads loomed black on the horizon, and with each passing moment, the light grew dimmer and dimmer. It was only late afternoon, but the huge masses of clouds were effectively blocking the sunlight, combining with the lightning and thunder to produce a most surreal effect—darkness in the middle of the day!

Within this preternatural twilight, Lilith stepped from the inner precincts of the Temple and came forward to greet the crowd. Respectfully, everyone grew silent as she began to speak:

"O Atlanteans, we know that the creative gods traverse the country along the Straight Paths. At certain seasons of the year, these paths become animated by a vital force that fertilizes the Earth and gives new life to plants and animals. To ensure the seasonal return of this force, we perform certain rites."

These *rites* to which the High Priestess was referring were formed around knowledge recorded in the *Book of Life*:

> EVERY FOOD, PLANT, AND ANIMAL HAS A CENTER WHEREBY THE
> PERFORMANCE OF THE PROPER RITUALS WILL RELEASE THE LIFE ESSENCE OF
> THAT PARTICULAR PLANT OR ANIMAL AND THEREBY BRING ABOUT ITS
> INCREASE.

Again thunder boomed across the heavens, and the light grew dimmer and dimmer. "I'm afraid of the thunder," Alta confessed, pressing closer to the man beside him. He could barely make out his father's features in the gloom.

"Don't worry, son," Adima squeezed the boy's hand. "All is safe. The alchemists and geomancers have done their work well. The great rod serves to draw the lightning to itself and down into the Earth, so there is no danger to us. We know how to control these forces." I hope! he thought to himself.

There had never been a mishap, but one never knew. True, lightning strikes were a natural occurrence in the fields, but there was always a danger. And he wasn't too thrilled about being that close to the lightning, either, having been struck by a rogue bolt when he was but a youth. An intuitive sense, however, told him that he *would* encounter the lightning once again, and quite soon now.

The High Priestess continued, her disembodied voice echoing in the growing gloom. "In order that plants should grow, it is necessary to fuse the electrical current of the atmosphere with the streams of terrestrial energy. So now we invoke the atmospheric forces and ask them to enter the flow of the Earth current."

With that, Lilith turned to the west and called forth the Sacred Lightning. When it came, it was an awesome and eerie spectacle, hearkening back to a time when the Earth was young and being shaped by huge and cataclysmic forces of Nature.

Over and over again, a staccato of searing, jagged bolts arced from Heaven down to Earth, drawn by those silent stone sentinels far out on the Great Plain. Each fiery flash illuminated the darkened landscape for the briefest fraction of a moment. In that flickering, transient light, faces and obelisks appeared and disappeared, thunder cracked and boomed, and the ground trembled under the awesome forces of the Great Mother.

When the Dragon arrived, it did so with astonishing fierceness and beauty, dancing across the sky and seeking its most sacred target—the gigantic marble obelisk rising up to the heavens from the center of the Great Plain. Moving at incredible speed, a terrific bolt of lightning arced out of those boiling black clouds, striking the obelisk and traveling straight down the stone and into the Earth. As it passed, the Dragon's breath warmed the living rock, filling it with the Life Essence until the pillar glowed a fiery red.

Time and again the Dragon struck, flashing from one stone megalith to the next, all across the Great Plain. It was a sight that would be forever burned into the memories of the Children of the Law of One and the Sons of Belial alike—great flashes of lightning diving straight down from a jet black sky, striking the standing stones, then dancing from one to the next as the Plain was bathed in the energy of the Dragon Current. The people watched, spellbound, awed by forces beyond their ability to control or comprehend. There was no rain, just the massive lightning energy as the Dragon and the Fire God danced from stone to stone to stone.

Although the memory would linger forever, the Mother's spectacle itself lasted just a few moments, and when it was over, the smell of ozone drifted across the Plain on the wind.

The Alchemical Wedding had been consummated. The Earth was fertile once again. The Dragon had come and gone, and now the light returned in all of its glory. The huge clouds parted, revealing the mossy green tips of the Mountains of the Moon, and behind them, a great flaming orange ball sinking slowly into the west. Behind the clouds, emanating from the center of the sun itself, the great healing rays spread out and down upon the land. The people of Atlantis cheered and applauded and embraced each other in their exuberance, for this was a message of great import—Divine assurance that those golden rays would, indeed, bring to life all that the land produced.

Very quietly, the King arose and walked out onto the lawn, where a perfect square of rich volcanic earth had been prepared for the ceremonial tilling. Putting his hand on the golden plow, he addressed the crowd.

"My people..." He paused for effect, scanning the vast throng, looking directly into their eyes. "What we have just witnessed is the act of union between Earth and Heaven. It is indeed necessary for the continuation of life; for if there is no lightning, the Great Mother becomes barren.

"We know that lightning has a beneficial effect on the nitrates of the soil, through which they can be absorbed by plants, thus ensuring the seasonal return of fertility." Gadir's voice deepened, resonating with kingly authority as, just for a moment, he believed once again.

"As the sun's rays purify a running stream of water, so we pray that the fertility of the subterranean streams be sustained by the introduction of the atmospheric influences of the Dragon Current. Now I take the plow and till the soil. Let the growing season begin! Let prosperity reign!"

A thunderous cheer rose from the crowd. Amid smiles and laughter, the King walked out among the people, taking hold of their hands and chatting with his subjects.

A blessing, Adima thought in amazement. The King is blessing us! Maybe things are going to turn out better than I thought. Maybe he does care.

Gadir came to Adima, who took the royal hand gratefully. "I am so delighted to see you, Highn..." he began, but the King had already let go and moved on, even as Adima's words trailed off into empty space in the wake of the royal monarch's passing.

The King's hand had been clammy and cold, his grip weak. But Adima was excited nevertheless, as were all of the vast assemblage. They had touched the King! Or rather, the King had touched them! "Kings have a healing touch," his mother had told him when he was a boy. Would the people be changed now, somehow healed and blessed by the touch of this great man? Adima wondered, and he hoped it would be so.

As the King moved through the crowd, Adima watched him closely. He looks just like a regular man, he realized, just like me...a bit older, a bit different shape and size. But he did not observe the differences, just the sameness. After a while, the King ascended the Temple steps and turned to address the great throng one last time. Now not just Adima's, but all eyes were upon him, all ears attuned to hear his words and receive his blessing.

Gadir did not speak long. At first, his banter was light and pleasant. He joked and laughed and got the people to do so, too. But gradually, his message grew darker, more serious, more demanding—grim and to the point, surprisingly dire and somber for such an auspicious occasion. Perhaps the people had not expected good tidings and loving oratory, but neither were they prepared for the King's furious call for additional labor and sacrifice in order to ensure victory in the war with Lemuria.

"I know you work hard," Gadir boomed, his jaw taught, his eyes intense. "I know you toil in my service seven days a week, from early morn until late at night, sometimes all night. I know how tired you are, how you miss your families and friends, how taxing this is. All I can say is 'thank you.' And my greatest fear is that you will stop."

His tone grew harsher and louder. With clenched fists and dire threats, the King exhorted the people to step up their efforts, increase production of the Atlantean war machine, and sacrifice, sacrifice, sacrifice. "For the glory of Atlantis!" he cried. "To ensure peace and prosperity and freedom!"

And, in fact, most of the Atlanteans believed him. Most nodded their heads in agreement, shouting their assent, applauding long and loud with each new exhortation.

"You cannot stop. You cannot rest. No family priorities, no other commitments. Only your service to me, to achieve success. For the glory of Atlantis is all that matters, regardless of the cost. If we win the war with Lemuria, we will be free. It will have been worth it. There is no satisfaction in losing, and that is what will happen if I ease up on my demands on you. We shall lose, and I shall have failed. I cannot let that happen. I *will* not let that happen."

Gadir lowered his voice, eyes burning as he pronounced sentence upon his people. "So there is no rest for you, not even one day in seven. No rest. No blessing. I will drive you and drive you and drive you. As I drive myself. I demand this of myself, so it is my right to demand it of you. I have sacrificed family and friends and personal goals. So I have the right to demand that you do likewise."

He paused again, his expression a strange combination of fierceness and helplessness as he bestowed his final gift. "I am the King. Do as I do. I am the King. You exist to serve me and ensure that victory is mine. I am the King. I must succeed at all costs. Even at the expense of you and your very existence. This is my blessing to you."

In the hush that followed, he shot his subjects a baleful look, then cast a sidelong glance at Belial, as though seeking the giant's approval. When it was not forthcoming, Gadir turned and left the dais, disappearing within the Temple precincts. Almost as one, the people stood and cheered, for they felt that the King had acknowledged them and their work, recognized their contributions "to the Cause," even justified and blessed "the Cause" itself. Their labor was holy because the King had declared it so.

What other choice did they have? For to have admitted the truth would have been to admit that their world, was indeed broken, and that Gadir was in fact an Ogre Tyrant. But Adima knew better, and he did admit the truth, if only to himself for the moment. Belial must have put him up to this, he realized. The King would never have had the audacity or insensitivity to give such a fiery oration on his own, not on such a day of joy. No, there had to be an ulterior motive, and when he saw the smug expression and satisfied smile upon that pale white face, Adima knew that he had hit upon the real source of the diatribe.

For several moments, he sat in glum silence, having seen not the beloved King blessing his equally beloved kingdom, but the Ogre Tyrant—raging and threatening, taxing and demanding, placing even greater demands on an already overburdened, overtaxed, and decaying kingdom—squeezing, dark, selfish, vicious, and greedy.

When Cybele came to join him, he smiled wanly. "You go on ahead," he gently patted her arm. "I'll be along soon enough. There's something I must attend to right now."

The priestess understood. She could read her husband's feelings almost better than he could read them himself. She knew he was deeply troubled by what he had just witnessed, and that he needed to be alone for a while. So they made plans to meet later for supper.

Thus, as the people made their merry way to the Dragon Play, Adima sought the solitude of the Garden of the Heart. There was much to think about, much to sort through. He needed a quiet sanctuary where his mind could distinguish between reality and illusion. He needed to write.

As he made his way through the crowd, friends and acquaintances accosted him, asking his opinion of the speech, his thoughts on the war, his feelings about one thing or another. Although he responded politely, Adima chafed at the delay. It seemed as though he would never reach his destination.

Actually, however, it did not take as long as he thought. In only a few moments he had arrived at the gardens. Now here he was, safely nestled in comfortable surroundings. There were the reflecting pool and the fountain. There was the main trail winding through the trees. And there, beneath a stately elm, was a place to rest. For all of this he was grateful, truly grateful.

Heaving a sigh of relief, Adima dropped his pouch on the grass and walked over to the Fountain of Ablutions. It was customary for all who entered the garden to cleanse themselves of any impurities they might be carrying, so as not to despoil the sanctity of such a holy space. He washed his hands and face in the cool cascade, drank his fill of fresh water, then returned to the elm tree. Alone now with his thoughts, he sprawled on the soft grass. Great, leafy branches shaded him, the mighty trunk supported his back, the Earth upheld him.

Eyes closed, he breathed deeply three times to silence the chatter in his brain. At last he was ready. The Silence had come, and with it, the Truth—to fill his mind and dwell within him and change him.

In the stillness, the Warrior-Poet opened his mind's eye to a vision of the Kingdom of Atlantis. There it was, shining clear and bright before him. Ever so quietly, a Voice whispered in his heart, instructing him to take a long, hard, honest look at his world. Reaching into his bag, he took out his pen and his journal. Opening to a clean, fresh page, he recorded the date and the time. Closing his eyes once more, he paused to listen to the Voice of Truth, letting the Muse speak through him. Then he began to write.

*****

From Adima's Journal...
Afternoon
First Day of the Dragon Festival
Month of the Winter Solstice
Year of the Child

The Warrior's Renunciation

When a Warrior serves under an Ogre Tyrant, is he still a warrior, or has his status been reduced to nothing more than a serf? Today I sat in the presence of the king. I am glad I did, for now I know the truth.

It has been written, "The State of the Kingdom is a direct reflection of the state of mind of the King." How true! I know that now. Today I saw an insane king, an Ogre Tyrant, squeezing the jugular of the kingdom, crushing the heart of the kingdom, sucking the lifeblood of the kingdom. And I see the kingdom dying as a result.

The people might think that they are blessed, but they are not. They are cursed. They are without hope, forlorn. Without friend or ally, because the king has become the Ogre Tyrant. He has sold out his people, forgotten his obligations and duties, lost sight of his sacred function. Perhaps he never even understood any of this to begin with.

There is no sacredness in the kingdom anymore. Spirituality has fled, leaving in its wake a pestilence. And with the fleeing of Spirit, so flee I.

This Warrior no longer feels allegiance to the king. For my eyes have seen truly. My heart has felt truly. The king has abdicated his sacred trust. The relationship between the king and myself, once a Holy Relationship based on mutual respect and trust, has degenerated, through the king's own wishes, into a relationship based on the subordination of one man's will to that of another!

For when I swore allegiance to the king, I became not his servant or slave, but rather his voluntary companion, one who would take pride in defending both king and kingdom and fighting his wars. In return, I expected the Good King to take affectionate care of me and all of the warriors and reward us for our valor. The Good King is who I vowed to serve—the Good King, "Protector of Warriors," "Dispenser of Treasures," "Ring-Giver."

But that king is gone, leaving no protection, dispensing no treasures, giving no ring. For who is protected now in the kingdom? Dead and broken bodies lie everywhere. Where is the treasure? In the place of the Good King now stands the Ogre Tyrant, who has failed to honor the sacred trust because of his ill temper, avarice, and weak will, thus alienating this great Warrior. For it is not merely a physical security and treasure that I seek from my relationship with the Good King. The significance is more spiritual than material—a kind of visible proof that in this relationship we are realizing ourselves to our fullest potential, that we are congenially and successfully united with one another.

But that can no longer be. The Good King is dead, and this Warrior needs to pick up his shield and sword and lance, mount his horse, and ride on. No need to honor the bargain. It has already been broken—not by me, but by the Ogre Tyrant. No need to give my life in service to the Ogre Tyrant. No sacred trust or responsibility to honor any more. All contracts are revoked, rescinded, and disavowed.

O King, I release you and myself from all vows, arrangements, and agreements between us, and we are free to go our separate ways. These are the consequences of your actions, O King. You are free to accept them and learn from them, or deny them, as you see fit. As I am free to go my way in peace and serve in another kingdom, or even establish a kingdom of my own.

There is no enmity between us, no hostility, no regrets, no remorse. I shake the dust from my feet, take up my family and my possessions, mount my horse, and move on, leaving you in peace. And although you may not bless me, I bless myself, and I bless you, and wish you well.

CHAPTER 8

Spiraling into the center, the center of the shield.
I am the weaver, I am the woven one.
I am the dreamer, I am the dream.

—Author Unknown

Far out in the Ocean of Atlas, far removed from the activities of the Dragon Festival, Dolphin swam freely, attuned to the rhythm of the moon and the tides, in direct communion with the Great Mother. As Keeper of the Sacred Breath of Life, Dolphin sensed what the Mother sensed, experienced what she experienced, felt what she felt. Indeed, it had always been thus, ever since Dolphin had been taught to breathe in that new and wonderful way, using its breath to induce altered states of consciousness and align itself with other dimensions of life.

For so long, Dolphin had lived in the peace of the Mother's gentle cycles and rhythms, matching its tiny heartbeat to her great heartbeat, partaking of her bounty and her nurturing. Now all of that had changed. The Mother was sick!

What was the Gray One to do? "Spirit will know," realized Dolphin in that way of intuitive knowing shared by all creatures attuned to the Mother's love. "I shall ask Spirit for the solution."

And so, using the power of the breath, Dolphin moved into the Dreamtime, a mystical state of consciousness described in the *Book of Mysteries* as...

> THAT ENDLESS AGE THAT PRECEDED ATLANTIS AND WHICH STILL CONTINUES TO FLOW IN A DIMENSION NORMALLY BEYOND HUMAN PERCEPTION.

What Dolphin experienced was frightening indeed. All of the gods were in a panic. "What is happening to the Mother?" asked Dolphin in the First Language, the language spoken by all who knew and loved the Great Mother. "How do we help her? Is she dying?"

"It would appear so," replied the gods, "and we are helpless. We must ask her what is wrong and why she is so sick." And so they did, calling out to the Earth, asking her to reveal her feelings and explain why she was so troubled.

Up spoke the Great Mother, reminding the gods that she had done her part in abiding by the agreement between herself and their King regarding the possession of her Daughter.

"When my Child is with me," the Mother said, "I cause all things to flourish, and the Earth has Spring and Summer. During her stay in the Underworld, however, I am sad, and so the Earth lies fallow. But Life does not die, because my Daughter always returns at the appointed time, and the cycle repeats itself. I have prepared the Earth beautifully and have done my part and kept the bargain. So have you, O gods. The Earth is abundant. I have set a bountiful table and dressed myself gloriously. I have prepared a great feast and invited all to come and partake of my abundance in the beauty of my natural settings."

The Great Mother paused and heaved a deep sigh. When she continued speaking, there were tears in her eyes.

"But some of my children—selfish and ignorant of my ways, greedy and wanton— have evil intentions. They are destroying my body and squandering my gifts—even raping, gouging, depleting, and polluting my flesh and blood, with no regard to my feelings or to the effect on themselves and on me.

"They are not even aware that I am alive and hurting, sick and dying. They are even less aware that as they are doing this to me, they are doing it to themselves."

The Mother turned her misty eyes to the Gray One. "Dolphin, this is the message you must carry back to the world of the humans," she instructed. "You are the link. Seek out the wise and kind Hermit of the Light, for he remains connected to me, and give him my message. I will not let myself be destroyed. I will protect myself and do whatever it takes to restore my health and rid myself of the mad revelers who are destroying me. Yet I know that there is much that is good and kind and noble about my children. Lest they perish completely, I shall give them time to prepare. The Wise One will know what to do."

And so, the Messenger of the Dreamtime returned to the Ocean of Atlas, swimming back and forth before the Lighthouse, crying out in a loud voice, bidding the hermit to hearken to the call. Dolphin did not have long to wait.

From the tower on high, where he dwelt apart from worldly distractions, Enoch, Keeper of the Light, observed the rhythms and cycles of Nature, reading them, predicting and preparing for Dolphin's return. For a long time, the hermit had been awaiting a message from the Divine. Now Dolphin had crossed back over the threshold from the Dreamtime, bringing word from the Great Mother, and hopefully a solution that the Children of the Law of One might use to preserve the noblest and best parts of the Atlantean culture. "At least, I hope there is a solution," the old man muttered as he listened to the Gray One's call.

Gathering his robes about him, the hermit hastened out to the shoreline, carefully picking his way among the jumble of huge granite boulders that guarded the coast of Atlantis like grim, silent sentinels. Towering waves crashed and roared, making a sound like thunder as they slammed into the cliffs and tossed showers of white foam and spray high into the air.

The sky had faded from orange to violet, and the ever-present wind blew in strong gusts. The rocks were slick and black and dangerous indeed, but the old man knew the way well. Had there been anyone to notice, he would have looked strange indeed, standing on that jutting promontory overlooking a tiny, sheltered cove, silhouetted against a backdrop of billowing black clouds and the purple sky. But there was no one there. No one to witness the strange interaction between these two children of the Great Mother. No one to witness the incredible changes in the space-time continuum as the extraordinary interchange took place—when man and Dolphin joined in a moment of silent communion in the Non-Time.

"Come Dolphin," Enoch cried, his dark robe fluttering in the wind and his long white hair and beard streaming out behind him. "Speak the words of the Great Mother. Tell me what she would have me do."

Instantly, the wind and the waves grew calm, a hush fell over the beach, and a gentle current of warm air caressed the old man's skin. He stood absolutely still, waiting and watching, waiting and watching, gazing at his ghostly reflection in the dark waters of the cove. There it was, below the waves! Movement—a silvery-white streak rising up from the cold, slate-blue depths. From deep down it shot upward, a living arrow speeding straight and true, until...

In a burst of foam and spray, Dolphin broke the surface of the water, cleared its spout, and lifted its gray-white body upright in greeting. The hermit opened his arms and cried with delight, welcoming the Messenger of the Dreamtime, grateful that he had been chosen to receive the Mother's message. Then the Gray One spoke, and the hermit answered. Together the Keeper of the Sacred Breath of Life and the Keeper of the Light communicated, speaking in the primordial tongue, the sound-language of the Great Mother.

The sun had set by the time they were finished. In the darkness, the wind and the waves returned to their ceaseless movement. Dolphin returned to the sea, and the hermit returned to his aerie, his path through the rocks illuminated from on high by the brilliant beam of the light.

*****

As the sun slipped behind the Mountains of the Moon and dusk approached, the fires were lit and the evening meal was prepared and served at long tables spread out on the Temple lawn. A magnificent banquet it was, with all manner of the bounty of Atlantis— food from the sea, fruit from the great orchards, vegetables from the fertile volcanic soil, wine from the vineyards, pure water from the four great rivers. It was a feast of abundance, of thanksgiving for their great prosperity. After supper, Adima relaxed with his family and friends. He felt better now that he'd had a chance to write in his journal and unburden himself from the effects of his encounter with the King. He was ready to tell the Dragon Story. But first, a transformation had to take place!

Excusing himself, he made his way to a dark, secluded corner of the great lawn, out of sight of the revelers. Unslinging his pouch, he opened it and withdrew a few articles of clothing. He held up a flowing robe, remembering the first time he had heard the Dragon Story from his own father and how excited he had gotten trying to catch a glimpse of the elusive creature when it came. Of course, now that he was grown, Adima understood the scientific reasons underlying what happened, and he understood the mystical, spiritual principles as well. Slipping the robe over his head, he remembered those teachings from his university days. What was it the old geomancer had said?

"We Atlanteans acknowledge a mysterious Principle—a force, really—that animates the lines between our stone pillars, earthworks, and mountaintops. We further know that our lives are enriched when this force is activated through the correct geographical relationship of sacred centers. That is why we perform the Alchemical Wedding in the guise of ritual.

"This creative force traverses the country along paths that we acknowledge and use. Because these paths are animated by a vital force that fertilizes the Earth and gives new life to plants and animals, Atlantean geomancers and architects would as soon build a water mill in the Dry Place as situate a sacred site on a spot where the sacred influences are absent."

Adima smiled as he stooped to lace his sandals. The voluminous robe covered him almost completely. Not much of the man remained visible. The metamorphosis was almost complete. The worldly man would soon be transformed into the magical Bard.

"But the geomancer's dry science doesn't make for good storytelling," he whispered to himself as he donned the headdress and mask and stepped out onto the lawn. "Everyone would much rather listen to a romantic story about Dragons."

The weather had cleared, and it was a beautiful, balmy night. A soft, translucent mist spread across the horizon, and through the milky haze, a canopy of stars twinkled like cool diamonds far overhead. On the vast lawn, a huge bonfire burned brightly, and in its orange glow, a masked, magical figure glided silently through the crowd, drumming his drum and beckoning to the children to follow.

The mysterious being was dressed in a flowing saffron robe that covered its body from neck to toes in a shimmering cascade of ruby-red iridescence. In the glow of the firelight, a panoply of holographic images peered out from the rippling folds of the lustrous fabric—faces and figures—human, animal, and angelic—ever changing, ever flowing from form to form.

Surmounting its head like a crown, a corona of multicolored feathers shone like an angel's halo—white feathers from Eagle, Swan, Owl, and Hawk, interspersed with the colorful plumage of Turkey, Parrot, and Macaw. From beneath the plumed headdress, a carved, painted face—part human, part animal, part spirit—peered out at the crowd.

It was Esopa, traditional Bard of the Atlanteans, who gazed upon the world through the all-seeing eyes of Owl, who listened to the world through the sharp ears of the shaman, who spoke to the world through the wise lips of the Goddess of Wisdom. Seating himself comfortably on a large, smooth rock, Esopa took up his drum and started tapping out a rhythmic beat. It was the call to gather.

"He's going to tell the story," an excited youngster squealed, clapping her hands together in glee. Children and adults alike gathered around, sprawling on the grass, settling in, getting comfortable at the feet of the Bard. From her place in the crowd, Cybele looked at her husband as he sat ready to tell the story. He had grown older and wiser since the days of their joining, but in her eyes he was still the same innocent young man with whom she had fallen in love. Watching the faces of all who gathered round him, she could not help but share the joy and happy anticipation they felt in his presence. Adima had a way of making people feel welcome, comfortable, and most of all, valued. She knew why—it was the love that radiated from the goodness of his heart.

Esopa the Bard looked at the people around him—his children, his wife, his friends, even strangers. Tonight they were all one family. He smiled, closed his eyes, tapped softly on his drum, and began to speak in a gentle, rhythmic cadence.

> Come with me now on the breath of the wind,
> To a magical, mystical place.
> Fill yourselves full of the cool evening air.
> Feel the warmth of the fire.
> Sit for a while or lie back on the grass.
> Close your eyes and relax.
> List' to the heartbeat of the great drum,
> And let yourself be transported.
> Rise up and out to that most sacred place,
> Beyond Atlantis, beyond time and space.
> Crossing the threshold, higher and higher.
> Ascending through earth, air, water, and fire.
> Arriving at last, transcending
> Into the presence of the Dragon!

Adima looked to see what effect his poetry was having on the crowd. It never failed. They were with him, soaring up and out on the beat of the drum into that willing suspension of disbelief. Parents held children in their arms or on their laps. Some had their eyes closed, others stared dreamily into the fire or lay flat on their backs staring into the milky white canopy of stars that blanketed the night sky. The words and the sound of the drum had transported them out of the mundane world and into the sacred world of storytelling.

Changing the tempo ever so slightly, he shifted himself and continued.

> This is a story about life!
>
> In the beginning, at the time of the creation of the Earth, the Great Creator, Master Alchemist and Maker of All Things, combined all of the elements in the crucible of Matter—and life appeared. At first there was only One, but soon the One appeared as Two—the Lovers—Father and Mother of all living things.

From this sacred marriage, the union of yin and yang, the first living cell was born from the womb of the Great Mother and fertilized by Father Sky with wind and water. Thus sprang forth the fertile seed that was to become the Dragon. Far below, on Earth, a clear pool of water reflected the Heavens in its tranquil surface. Down from the ether the fertile seed fell, landing in the pool with a splash.

Life-giving waters combined with the Breath of Life, and thus the Dragon was born—symbol of the East, the rising Sun, and the spring rain. Serpent and bird, Spirit and Matter...the Dragon stayed forever connected with the water from whence it had come.

Quickly the Dragon grew, devouring everything within its reach, until at last, following the example of its father and mother, the One divided itself into Two.

Behold them—two fabulous beasts—the Dragon of the Marshes and the Dragon of the Mountains. One light, the other dark; one male, the other female; one positive, the other negative. Fierce predators, mortal enemies, they stood ready to devour each other. All of creation trembled before their might, wondering what the outcome would be. In that tense moment before the battle, the world grew quiet, waiting, waiting, as the Dragons drank deeply from the hidden Well, gorging themselves on the Secret Fire of the Salamander who dwells with the Blacksmith in the fiery Heart of the Mother.

At last, sated, the Dragons rose up, blasting forth fire and brimstone. All the world listened to their mighty roars as they clashed in mortal combat, each seeking to destroy the other. Long they raged, scorching the land with their fiery breath as the Earth shook and trembled before their power. Who could win? Neither one, for the power of the Secret Fire was greater than both of the Dragons combined. Each consumed the other in those awesome flames.

For eons, the Earth lay barren and blackened. There was no sound, save that of the mournful wind. Then, from within the destruction, movement! A tiny cry, the wail of a newborn babe. From the ashes, an infant Dragon lifted its head. A Third had been born, child of the Two who had gone before. Up rose the Golden Dragon, towering over all the world. Soaring above the clouds with majestic grace, the great and noble creature sought out the castle and the king, coming before the throne of Uther, bearing a great gift.

"Receive my Name," the Dragon roared with a blast from its nostrils. And so the king received the gift, merging the Dragon's name with his own to form a new name—Pendragon. And as the Dragon had given its name to the king, so now the king gave his name to his son, as yet unborn. "My son," cried Uther, "I name you the Great Bear, the Dragon of Gold. You are the Sleeping Dragon. You are the king who sleeps under the hill, waiting for the time to awaken and claim your kingdom."

The beneficent Dragon watched, seeing that is was good. Then, with a mighty roar, it spread its golden wings and soared forth out into the world, bringing rain, bringing the Life Force, fertilizing the world with its fiery breath. When at last the year drew to a close, the Dragon was exhausted and the vital force was spent. Fertility waned, and winter came upon the world.

For months, the Dragon dwelt underground, resting and renewing itself while the world lay cold and dark and barren. Until the appointed time came 'round, and the Dragon returned to the surface once again, bringing thunder, lightning, and the first rains of spring.

Year after year, century after century, eon after eon, the never-ending cycle continues—fertility and barrenness, life and death, death and rebirth. And so the season comes again, the appointed time, when the Dragon passes overhead along the Straight Paths, breathing fire—the Fire of Life—drawing in its wake the fertilizing powers of life. Invoking the celestial influences, restoring life to the Mother, reanimating Matter, and giving it vital energy. So that, nourished by the virtue stored up within the Mother, trees and crops flourish and bear fruit, and we are sustained.

See the five-headed Imperial Dragon—ruler of wind and waves! The Dragon King issues his commands, moving in all four directions at once, while remaining forever in the center of things. See the Green Dragon at rest. Look to the hills as it wakes! See the Sleeping Giant stirring in the hills. See the Dragon's heart found at a lonely knoll, on a small plain in a valley among the hills. Near the heart, its force is strong and active. At its heart, the Dragon and the Tiger—Male and Female—meet in harmony.

Can you see the Dragon as it comes! From that great heart, the veins of the Dragon Current spread throughout the land, across the meadows, and over the surrounding ridges. Over the high rocky crags and pinnacles where the Trumpeter rules, the Guardian enshrined on the high places sounds the note of each new age.

Who observes the Dragon's passage! Priests and priestesses invoke its presence, astrologers predict its coming, astronomers note its appearance, geomancers mark its course.

Over the lower plains, the warriors watch, standing guard along with the White Tiger and the Blue Dragon over the old Dragon Hills. From center to center, in festive processions, we celebrate along the Straight Paths—the pilgrims' paths that link the holy places.

Behold! Here it comes! Wise Winged Serpent, having celestial power and the power of the Earth. Beyond our ability to conquer or control, the Dragon reveals happiness, the fount of immortality. Receive the gift, the Dragon's gift, the Primal Essence—procreation, fertility, activity, life!

Esopa finished the tale, gently beating a rhythmic cadence as his audience slowly returned from the spellbinding journey that the Bard had weaved for them. The flickering firelight revealed the contented looks on the faces of the people.

It was a peaceful evening, and few, if any, were inclined to move and break the serene mood. Young children curled up to sleep on their blankets. Older children talked animatedly of dragons and magic and the like. Adults chatted quietly in small groups. Lovers lay side-by-side and contentedly looked at the stars in the sky and in each other's eyes.

When it came, the trouble began as an almost imperceptible tremor, an ever-so-gentle vibration under the ground. Almost no one noticed for the first few seconds, or if they did, they paid no attention. But then the tremor grew stronger, and it was impossible to ignore—a powerful shaking of the Earth, accompanied by a deep rumble from far below the surface.

"Earthquake!" a frightened voice screamed. Simultaneously, there was a blinding flash of light, followed scant seconds later by the noise of a tremendous explosion. Beneath their feet, the ground trembled violently as a deep, ominous rumble and the acrid odor of sulphur combined to transform the Dragon Festival into a nightmare of terror. Their joy turned to panic, the revelers screamed in fright as the Great Mother shook herself. Parents stumbled and fell, trampling each other in a frantic struggle to gather their children. Friends and lovers searched desperately for each other amidst a raging sea of writhing, twisting bodies. All was turmoil, all was confusion, all was chaos.

Rushing through the crowd, Adima caught sight of Cybele holding tightly to the twins. For an interminable moment, the family stood still and clung to each other, waiting for the danger to pass. At last, as quickly as they had started, the vibrations began to subside. The earthquake was over in less than thirty seconds, but the sky was glowing a deep orange to the immediate north.

"Explosion at the Pyramid," cried Hu, running up and shouting to make himself heard over the din. "I told you those Sons of Belial were up to something. I think their experiment backfired. There's no telling what's going on over there!"

Cybele inquired as to the extent of the injuries at the festival itself. There were many young children and elders there, all with fragile bones that might easily be broken.

"No one here is seriously hurt," Hu assured her. "A few scrapes and bruises, nothing more. It was a really minor tremor, probably a result of whatever it was they were doing. The best thing we can all do is go home, stay inside, and take care of our families."

And so they did, one by one, each Atlantean family retreating to the relative safety of home, each individual with unvoiced feelings of fear, panic, and dread. Likewise did Adima bring his family to Elysia in silence. Cybele and he put the children to bed, comforting them as best they could, then retired themselves. That night, Adima dreamed.

*****

Transcending the world of conscious thought, spiraling inward and down through the great invisible barrier into the shadowy world of the subconscious, alighting in an alien and surreal dreamscape where past, present, and future occur simultaneously. Moving, always moving, seeing haunting fragments of the Dragon Festival—jumbled images, shadowy faces, cries, taunts, jeers, and whispers. Unseen hands groping at him, pulling him first one way, then another. Unearthly voices bidding him, "Come with me. This is the way. Follow me." Adima follows.

Deep in the Earth, in a massive cavern strewn with huge boulders...

The body of an old woman lies on her bier, an enormous, jagged stalactite pointed straight at her heart. Gaunt and emaciated, her body bleeds from many wounds. Around her, the children weep and grieve as wild jackals and hyenas fight over her possessions, attacking and killing each other in their bloodlust and frenzy to get what they want. As the greedy beasts reach out to devour Adima, the skeleton woman rises and hurls her bones at them, scattering and dispersing the scavengers. Swirling fog and mist envelop him.

On the back of Eagle, soaring on currents of air high above the Earth...

Looking down, he sees Atlantis far below, a tiny speck in a vast blue ocean. Soaring ever higher, until the ocean itself is a tiny, blue-white dot, he realizes that he is looking at the Earth from outer space, close to the Heavens where the Great Creator dwells. Voices cry out to him, carried to his ears on the wind.

"Adima, Adima!" The unseen beings call his name, telling him things, important things, secrets great and powerful. He struggles to hear the words, to understand, but the voices fade before he can discern any meaning. Once again, swirling clouds and mist engulf him.

Within massive storm clouds, surrounded by crackling thunderbolts...

From out of a cloud comes a gleaming, bejeweled Sword, grasped firmly in a woman's hand. Adime drops to one knee and bows his head as she knights him with the glorious weapon, which pulses with power and energy. The nameless woman offers him the Sword. As he reaches out to take it, he is struck by a bolt of lightning and hurled back to Earth.

In the midst of a raging conflagration, surrounded by smoke and flames...

Body quivering from the shock of the blast, Adima sees Cybele. They come together as glowing, molten rock oozes up from every nook and cranny of the Earth and tongues of flame lick greedily at their legs. They embrace for the briefest of moments until the flames come between them, sweeping the lovers apart, sweeping Cybele away in a fiery whirlwind.

From the depths of the black, greasy smoke, Belial's skeleton face shines a ghastly, ghostly white, grinning a death's grin. Face to face they stand, as the Beast's red-rimmed eyes shoot darts of molten lava as it lashes out with a great Spear to impale and devour the man with the Sword.

Floundering in a deluge...

With a mighty roar comes the flood, the onslaught of water immersing everyone and everything in its path. Untold millions struggle to survive amidst the violent rush of the waves. Swept up in the maelstrom, caught below the surface of the water, Adima is drowning. He tries to find his voice, but there is no air. He gasps for breath, struggles to make a sound, any sound. Swallowing water, smothering, dying, he struggles to return from a long way off. He begins to scream.

Adima sat bolt upright in his bed, drenched in a cold sweat.

"What is the matter, Husband?" Still shaken from the events of a few hours ago, there was tension in Cybele's voice. Normally, Adima slept deeply and undisturbed. She was not accustomed to his crying out in terror in the dead of night.

"Just a dream," he said, drawing his wife to him in a tender embrace. But it was not just a dream, not an ordinary dream, anyway. It had been so real, so vivid, so clear, so full of color and sound. He still smelled the stench of rotting flesh, felt the heat of the fire and tingle of electricity. He was still trying to catch his breath, his head even now reeling from his tumble through the flood. What had the voices been trying to tell him? What part of himself was trying to reveal itself? Was it a prophecy? he wondered.

"I need to go out into the woods for a while," he told his wife, forcing a reassuring smile. Cybele nodded silently. She was used to her husband's nocturnal jaunts through the forest. It was where he went to sort things out whenever he was overwhelmed. Tonight had indeed been overwhelming—for both of them.

Dressing quickly, Adima stepped outside into the light of a last-quarter moon. Focusing on his breathing, he tried not to think about specifics as he loped off into the forest. Little by little he increased his pace until soon he was running swiftly. It was warm, and the forest was alive with the sounds of the night—crickets chirping, branches rustling under the soft patter of padded feet. From somewhere off in the distance, an owl hooted. As he ran, he began to feel better. Exercise always made him feel well. The tight, icy ball of fear in the pit of his stomach was beginning to soften and thaw.

He had no real destination in mind, at least not consciously. Still, he was surprised when he rounded a turn in the trail to find himself on a grassy plain overlooking the beach and the Lighthouse. He almost tripped over the black-robed figure sitting on a fallen log and staring out to sea.

"What are you doing here?" Adima cried, amazed at the coincidence that had brought him face-to-face with the one person in all of Atlantis who might be able to help him understand his dream.

"Waiting for you," the Keeper of the Light replied with a grim, wrinkled smile. "I knew you'd be along soon. There are mighty forces at work tonight. I suppose you've come into contact with some of them?"

Adima sat on the log beside his old friend, his teacher and mentor, and looked deeply into his eyes. So this was all planned! Of course! He should have known. Enoch knew about the dream. How was not important. The old man knew, and he had come to help his student deal with it in the appropriate way.

They sat in the silence for several moments, then Adima related the dream. He remembered every detail. Enoch listened quietly, interrupting only occasionally to ask a question or clarify a detail. When Adima finished speaking, there was silence between them again as the old man sat with eyes closed, rocking softly and muttering unintelligible sounds under his breath. Adima knew better than to interrupt when the old man was in such a deep meditative state. He felt better after unburdening himself, and he was confident that the hermit would be able to interpret the dream and give him some insight into its meaning. So he was not prepared for the intensity with which his friend suddenly turned and gripped his arm.

"Prepare yourself, Adima, for what I am about to tell you. For you have not heard words like this before, nor are you likely to hear them again in this lifetime. And what I am about to say is of the utmost importance."

The old man's eyes glittered with reflected moonlight. In the pale glow, Adima could see that he was intensely serious. "My words will cause you extreme emotion," Enoch continued. "They will touch your soul at the deepest levels and inspire in you a fear that heretofore you have only imagined." He paused for the briefest moment, then went on. "Now that fear will be real, and you must control yourself and embrace it and use it to your advantage. Most important, you must not deny its reality. You must gather it in and make the fear a part of your courage."

Adima swallowed dryly. He was used to such strong language from the old man. For almost twenty-five years, they had been student and teacher. Sometimes the lessons had been gentle; other times they were harsh indeed. Apparently, this was one of the latter.

In the darkness, Enoch spoke slowly. "This dream is a prophecy that comes from the Spirits of the Dreamtime," he said, explaining the hidden meaning in the vision. "You are to be their agent in the great work of transformation and cleansing that is about to take place in Atlantis. Through the dream, you were initiated with the five elements—Earth, Air, Metal, Fire, and Water. Each part of the dream is a foreshadowing of events to come. Deep in the Earth, the Great Mother is preparing to cleanse and heal herself. The Sons of Belial will be no more. Indeed, many of the Children of the Law of One will leave their physical forms to assist in this great cleansing, which will come in the form of Fire and Water."

Adima's heart skipped a beat as he listened to the old man. Over the years, he had undergone several initiations as he had grown from boyhood into manhood. He had thought such trials were past. Now another challenge had arisen to confront him. He felt the return of the icy ball of fear in the pit of his stomach, so much bigger now, so much more paralyzing.

"You were lifted up by Eagle and shown the larger picture, the overall pattern of life," Enoch went on, ignoring the fear, refusing to acknowledge it or use it to motivate either of their actions. "Eagle reminded you to take heart, be courageous, and embrace your personal power, which has been offered to you in the form of the Sword—the Hard Lightning. This is your spiritual test, a great opportunity. And as always at such times, there is also great danger."

"What am I to do?" Adima asked, despite his fear. "How can I help?"

"You have your intellect, your words, your gift of speech," Enoch explained. "You are to use them in the Council chamber. You must speak your truth there. You must put the truth forth for all to see and hear."

"What will I say?" Adima persisted.

"The words will be given to you. Sit in the silence and open your heart. When you hear the words, write them down. Then go to the Council chamber and speak out."

This seems easy enough, Adima thought, although he did not relish the idea of saying anything too controversial, too incendiary. There was relative safety in the Council chamber, however, and a speech among many was better than a one-on-one confrontation. Perhaps this would not be as bad as he had first thought.

"Your words will fall on deaf ears, for the most part," Enoch continued, as if in direct contradiction to the younger man's thoughts. "Some will listen as though they are indulging an unruly child. Others will scoff openly. Still others—the ones who are perpetrating the greatest deception—will be enraged, because they will see that you know the truth. Such men will try to silence you. You will make great and powerful enemies on the day that you address the Council!"

The old man paused and shook his head, watching the moon sink lower and lower in the west. "Some, too, will open themselves to the truth," he continued at last, "although they will remain silent out of fear of retribution. Your words will spread like wildfire throughout Atlantis, at which time the people will instantly divide themselves into two camps—one of Love and Truth and Light, the other of fear and lies and darkness. There will be no middle ground, no sitting on the fence. Those who take that course will be swept away in the first cleansing. No," the old man muttered almost to himself, "they must take a stand."

Adima was speechless as he listened to the hermit's dire pronouncement. Many questions were running through his mind, but before he could voice them, Enoch continued.

"Gather to yourself those friends and acquaintances of like mind and spirit. Together, you must prepare for the final cleansing, the time when you are to leave Atlantis. Gather all that is noblest and best of the race—its people and its treasures, its art and its science—that the knowledge may be remembered and preserved."

Adima was even more confused. "How shall we gather all of this?" Was his teacher asking him to play God?

In response, Enoch uttered the words that were to be remembered for so long by so many races and cultures through the millennia, the words that were to form the basis for all of the great deluge legends that were to follow. *"To save the knowledge, carry it in the crystals. To save the people, build an Ark, which the Goddess of Wisdom will tell you how to build, and gather the treasures and the living creatures within its sacred belly."*

Adima started to speak, but Enoch silenced him. "All of your questions will be answered in the days to come. There is much you do not know yet, much even I do not know yet. All will be revealed at the appropriate time, day by day, one step at a time. To try to manage everything all at once would be impossible and overwhelming. We would collapse under the weight of the burden." The old man smiled for the first time, the first gray streaks of dawn lighting up his wrinkled old face. "The first step is to accept and be willing. After that, we shall be told more, and events will unfold to their right and best conclusion, for the highest good of all, according to the Plan."

There were tears in Adima's eyes as Enoch finished speaking. He had hoped for comfort and consolation in the explanation of his dream. Now he was being presented with the greatest and most fearsome news he had ever heard, the embodiment of all his fears, his worst nightmares. He was being presented with a scenario for the end of the world!

He felt his heart racing in his chest, feeling as though it would explode with each beat. With all his strength, he resisted the urge to vomit as the fear within him overwhelmed him and took complete control. He could not catch his breath, and this time he knew it was no dream. He reeled dizzily. Black-and-white spots danced before his eyes, and the ground seemed to rush up to meet him. Adima swooned.

"Breathe deeply and slowly," Enoch commanded, rising to catch the younger man before he collapsed completely. Placing the palm of his hand in the center of Adima's chest and massaging slowly, Enoch demonstrated a breathing technique that was intended to help Adima focus and stay grounded in reality. "In and out, in and out," the old man crooned softly, over and over again. "Breathe in the love, breathe out the fear. Feel the breath of life fill you completely. See the breath fill you with light. See the fear inside you—your fear. See it roll itself into a black, greasy ball in the center of your stomach. Breathe into that place.

"See your fear. See your breath envelop that fear and carry it away. See it turn to wispy gray smoke and leave you with each breath you exhale. See the illusion of fear vanish into the nothingness from which it came."

For a long time Enoch spoke thus, holding his hand firmly over Adima's heart. For his part, Adima, eyes closed, obeyed completely, breathing in and out, visualizing the fear within himself, willing it to subside. Gradually, breath by breath, the panic abated, his heartbeat slowed, and his breathing returned to normal. As he calmed, he felt warmer and stronger. Willing himself to be still, he eventually opened his eyes and smiled wanly at his friend. No words were necessary. A great healing had passed between them, and to try to put feelings into words would have been to demean the experience.

The old man slowly removed his hand and sat once more by Adima's side. He looked at his student as though expecting to continue the conversation, as though there was still some unfinished business, some unanswered questions. "Now that you've crossed over the initial threshold of fear and returned," Enoch said, "what is it you wish most to ask?"

Adima knew what his question was, but the hermit's answer could quite possibly inspire an even greater fear in him. Still, he had to know, and having committed to embracing his fear and making it a part of his courage, he swallowed dryly and asked the question he most dreaded to ask. "What will happen to Cybele and the children and me?"

The old man closed his eyes and was still. After what seemed like an eternity, he took Adima's hand and looked deeply into those dark, kind eyes. "The children will be safe and unharmed throughout the Time of Tribulation and the End Times. Sophia and I shall watch over them. You and Cybele, though, have different roles to play, and you must play them apart from each other. You will be separated at the appointed time. Of her course, I know little. Sophia will show her part to her, as I have shown yours to you."

Adima was so deeply shocked at this prospect that he could not move. How could he be separated from Cybele? What would happen to his wife if he were not there to protect her? How would she survive? This time, however, he remained in control. It was as though Enoch had imparted a new and calming power in him when he had touched his breast. Yes, the fear was there, but it was in its proper place, not controlling and overwhelming him as it had before the breathing lesson. He could barely manage a whisper. "What is my part? How has it been shown to me?"

Enoch looked at the frightened young man beside him, debating whether to answer. For to do so would only bring more fear. Finally he exhaled softly, knowing that the truth was the greatest comfort he could give. "Your spiritual test is to face your darkest fears, stand in your power, and go alone to confront Belial. The two of you will meet face-to-face in mortal combat, the personification of Good versus the personification of Evil, the powers of Light against the powers of Darkness."

Bile rose in Adima's throat. Was he still dreaming? He wanted to wake up and find himself in Cybele's arms, where everything would be all right. He wanted to close his ears and not listen. He wanted to run away, to leave this place and never return. He wanted to go back to the way it had been before this Time of Tribulation. But he remained motionless, held in place by Enoch's firm grip and steady gaze. "What am I to do?" he asked. "How can I stop someone as powerful as Belial? He has ten times my strength and power!"

"You are a skilled warrior, Adima," Enoch said. "Although you have never proven yourself in battle, you are ready and able. And you will have an ally, which will be given you when the time is right."

"Who is to be my ally?" Adima asked in amazement. "There is no one in all of Atlantis strong enough to overcome Belial."

Enoch shook his head. "You do not understand," he smiled at the younger man, quoting from the *Book of Life*. "An ally is not a 'who.' An ally is..."

A POWER IN YOUR LIFE TO WHICH YOU TURN FOR HELP AND ADVICE, AS WELL AS FOR THE COURAGE AND STRENGTH TO TAKE ACTION. YOUR ALLY GUIDES YOUR ACTIONS AND HELPS YOU TO KNOW AND UNDERSTAND.

"You could not get such gifts from another human being," the old man concluded.

Reading the question in Adima's eyes, he answered softly. "Will you survive and be reunited with your wife and children? I do not know. That is not given me to see. I can predict certain outcomes, given the natural course of events. But the future has not happened yet, and so I cannot know."

The two continued to sit together for a long time—master and student, hermit and warrior, father and son—each seeking strength and comfort in the other. They spoke from the heart. They spoke of fears and dashed hopes, of loss and opportunity. They spoke of willingness and commitment and powerlessness in the face of forces far beyond their ability to control. They grieved the loss of peace. They grieved the loss of Atlantis. They grieved the death and destruction and waste. They grieved the end of innocence and the fall from grace of a once proud and mighty Nation-State.

Hours passed, and the day dawned hot and hazy, as if in anticipation of the fiery battle to come. As a blood-red sun rose out of a flat, featureless sea, Adima and Enoch rose and embraced, and the Keeper of the Light spoke one last time, offering hope as he gave his benediction. "Your course is set, Adima. You know this from the great work that we have already accomplished. It remains only for you to accept this request and do your part. We shall meet each day to reaffirm our faith, gather our strength, and continue your preparation. There is much to do and so little time.

"Stay in your higher mind and keep connected to all parts of yourself. Fast, meditate, and pray, seeking your answers in communion with the Creator and the Great Mother. Love your Shadow as well as your Light. There is beauty in both, and you will need both to soar like Eagle. Above all, trust in the Plan. It will never fail you."

They embraced one last time, then went their separate ways.

THE FEMININE

CHAPTER 9

The great Way is easy,
Yet people prefer the side paths.
Be aware when things are out of balance.
Stay centered within the Tao.
When rich speculators prosper
While farmers lose their land;
When government officials spend money
On weapons instead of cures;
When the upper class is extravagant and irresponsible
While the poor have nowhere to turn—
All this is robbery and chaos.
It is not in keeping with the Tao.

—the *Tao Te Ching*

It is written in the *Book of Life:*

GROWING CIVILIZATIONS DISPLAY ENDLESS VARIETY AND VERSATILITY—
CREATIVITY, INVENTION, AND INNOVATION ARE THE DOMINANT THEMES.
NEW PATTERNS OF THOUGHT EMERGE FOR CRITICAL ANALYSIS AND REVIEW,
LEADING TO BREAKTHROUGHS AND PRODUCING BALANCE, INTEGRATION, AND
AESTHETIC FULFILLMENT IN ART, PHILOSOPHY, SCIENCE, AND TECHNOLOGY.
PEOPLE ARE PROSPEROUS, THEIR TIME EQUALLY BALANCED BETWEEN LABOR
AND LEISURE.

CONVERSELY, DISINTEGRATING CIVILIZATIONS DISPLAY ONLY UNIFORMITY,
INFLEXIBILITY, AND LACK OF INVENTIVENESS. SOCIAL STRUCTURES AND
BEHAVIOR PATTERNS BECOME SO RIGID THAT THE ABILITY TO ADAPT TO
CHANGING SITUATIONS BECOMES IMPOSSIBLE. THE INEVITABLE RESULT IS A
GENERAL LOSS OF HARMONY AMONG ALL PARTS OF THE CULTURE. THIS, IN
TURN, LEADS TO SOCIAL DISCORD AND DISRUPTION.

In the months following the earthquake, Atlantis was in turmoil, rocked by civil unrest, political upheaval, and one environmental cataclysm after another. The earthquake had been far more serious than first thought. Damage was widespread, not only in the city but in the provinces as well.

A massive crack had appeared on the Great Plain of Atlantis. The tremor had spawned a series of lesser quakes and aftershocks on the great island. A thousand miles to the west, a series of tidal waves struck Turtle Island, causing massive coastal flooding. Tens of thousands died, and property damage was of inestimable cost.

Weather patterns continued to change for the worse. All of the climate zones were affected. Some geomancers were even predicting a shift in the magnetic poles of the planet, bringing with it a drying up of the land and a return to the ice ages of the dim and distant past. Creatures of the land and the sea were sickening and dying at an alarming rate.

Somehow, word got out that all of this was caused by a banned experiment that had gotten out of control. The Sons of Belial immediately tried to initiate a cover-up and hide their culpability, but to no avail. Groups of concerned citizens circulated a series of petitions, demanding that the Council of Elders institute a full-scale investigation and punish the wrongdoers. When no action was forthcoming, the protestors resorted to even stronger measures, marching and demonstrating for a public redress of grievances. Still, the Elders made no statement and took no action.

Politically, the country was divided. The "armed camp" Council sessions to which Adima had referred several months before had indeed become battlefields—literally and figuratively. Leaders among the Children of the Law of One accused the Sons of Belial with misappropriation of funds, overstepping their authority, and violating civil and human rights. There were even calls for all members of the Sons of Belial to resign from the Council. For their part, the Sons of Belial refused to acknowledge anything positive about the Children of the Law of One. They were most certainly not about to hand over the leading political roles to them without a fight!

In the courts and universities, statesmen and scholars were embroiled in a constitutional debate. The crisis threatened the very political framework of Atlantis, for the words of the Lawgivers had never been challenged since the time of the Orphean Bards. Spiritual leaders called for fasting, prayer, and meditation. Civil leaders called for civil disobedience. Political leaders called for impeachment and new elections. No one called for restraint.

Through it all, the Sons of Belial worked quickly and tirelessly to restore their image and recover their threatened political power. Taking advantage of the extreme emotions being so openly displayed, they capitalized on the general populace's desire for someone to blame. Their greatest orators raised their voices in rebuttal to the inflammatory speechmakers in the public squares, couching their rantings, ravings, denial, and finger-pointing in impassioned appeals for reason, order, and an embracing of their ways— "ways that are for the good of all Atlanteans," they said. Using carefully worded messages and public oratory, they unleashed an incredible barrage of propaganda, pointing the blame for all of the troubles on the Children of the Law of One and their outdated, outmoded ways, accusing them of witchcraft and black magic.

"The Children of the Law of One are the real problem with Atlantis," cried the Sons of Belial. "Eliminate them, and all of our other problems will go away. In fact, they aren't even real Atlanteans, are they? Look at their complexions, their auburn hair, their dark skin color, their small stature. They are genetically inferior, atavistic...throwbacks to an earlier time."

Sadly, the vast majority of the populace believed the accusations, believed the lies. They needed a scapegoat and were glad, relieved actually, to have someone specific to blame.

Frustration, helplessness, anger, outrage, panic—these were some of the emotions fueling the leaders of the Children of the Law of One as they counterattacked, making speeches and urging their followers to action. Actually, they needed little urging. Demonstrations that began peacefully enough soon broke into full-scale riots. The soldiers had to be deployed in several instances. The dungeons were full of political prisoners. For a time, the rioting got so bad that martial law was declared. Healing centers were full of people with serious injuries, not only from the earthquake, but also from the fighting.

Atlantean healers were not used to treating such horrors as those that were inflicted on one person by another. The carnage went beyond broken bones and cuts and bruises. There were second and third-degree burns, massive trauma and shock, internal injuries, organ damage, amputations, hemorrhage, coma, and death. The entire Atlantean social system was being taxed beyond the limits of its endurance and ability to cope. Collapse wasn't just imminent, it had already happened!

*****

From the Lighthouse Keeper's Journal
Morning
Vernal Equinox
Month of the Crimson Gull
Year of the Child

From my observatory in the Lighthouse high above the world, I watch and record as the Atlanteans, for the first time in their long and noble history, attack one another. While the city itself remains relatively stable, out in the country—in the smaller towns and outlying districts where enlightenment is fast becoming a thing of the past—the Children of the Law of One are being set upon, beaten, and even killed. Armed mobs and makeshift militias are rising up under the guise of protecting families and personal property.

Fear rules with an iron hand, so well have the seekers of power, status, and wealth done their work of mass brainwashing. Violence and death are becoming so commonplace that the people—oblivious to where they are being led—are actually getting used to living their daily lives in spite of them, becoming inured to their own misery and the misery of others around them. As society and the environment are being turned upside down, so the people are coming to accept what is happening as perfectly normal, part of the natural course of things.

Yet beneath the surface, very quietly, Atlantean creativity, including our ability to respond to these challenges, is not completely lost. Deeper sociological and metaphysical processes are taking place during this time of disintegration of the Atlantean civilization. Like a great unfolding spectacle whose stage is the bosom of the Great Mother herself, two separate dramas with different plots are being performed simultaneously, side by side, in balance, as the Great Pendulum swings in harmony with a Cosmic Symphony.

On one side, the Sons of Belial and normative culture—static and stagnant, characterized by fixed ideas and rigid patterns of behavior, to which they cling desperately, perpetually rehearsing their own defeat—issue challenge after challenge. On the other side, the Children of the Law of One—idealistic, balanced, and integrated, characterized by their creative ability—rise each time to the challenges being hurled at them like so many thunderbolts.

And always, I remain ever-awake, ever-vigilant, ever in motion, moving smoothly with the rhythms and cycles, the fluxes and flows, the ups and downs, holding the middle course as the Pendulum swings back and forth, back and forth. Challenge, response, challenge, response...the drama continues as I watch the protagonists and antagonists glide across the great stage.

It is a time of preparation. Day by day, the Great Mother continues to prepare herself for the final cleansing. And while the great drama is unfolding, the Earth at its center, so too are the individual dramas unfolding, each with its own cast of characters.

*****

The morning after the earthquake, Belial was in an uproar, out of control, beyond reason. His rage knew no bounds, and the cavernous rooms and dark passageways of the Great Pyramid echoed with his thunderous ranting and raving. Each room had its own acoustical characteristics—one deep, one high, one mid-range—combining to create a sinister, discordant symphony. Pacing back and forth like some malevolent caged beast, the Master made a frightening figure as he stormed and swore, threatened and cursed, kicked and punched. Nothing could assuage or appease him, and his closest advisors knew it was fruitless even to try.

The main object of his wrath, of course, was Shakala, who sat cowering and trembling before the pale-skinned, red-eyed Ogre Tyrant. "Shakala is responsible! Shakala has erred! Shakala is to blame!" The accusations shot forth like poisoned darts, their single purpose—to kill.

"Perhaps not, Master," suggested Draco, most trusted of the Inner Circle. "Perhaps there is a fundamental flaw in the crystals." It was a bold statement, considering the frightful mood of the giant. Many were the broken bones of those Adepts who had dared to contradict Belial when he was under the influence of the Beast.

"It may have nothing to do with the design of the device," ventured another, drawing courage from Draco's lead. "According to our calculations, we need more power, not less."

It was true. The integrity of the design did not appear to be in question. The problem seemed to lie with the power supply. The crystals could not withstand the tremendous energy surges required to power the device at full force. That was where Shakala and his assistants were focusing their efforts in finding a solution.

Belial raised a huge palm to silence the discussion. He was beyond hearing them, having crossed the boundaries of reason, so trying to explain or deny was futile. Fortunately for the Adepts, however, he chose to express his rage vocally instead of physically this day. For several more minutes he continued his vituperations—berating, scolding, and inflicting all sorts of verbal abuse on those closest to him. The Adepts remained silent, eyes averted, waiting for the tirade to be over. The end came swiftly.

In the middle of a particularly obscene outburst, Belial paused in mid-sentence, as though listening to a sound the others could not hear. His head ached, and a dull, throbbing roar filled his ears. He knew what those signals portended. The voices would be starting soon, and he did not want to listen to them this day. He must stop them before they started. Knowing what to do and whom to seek out for help, he placed his hands over his ears, voiced a single, piercing shriek, and dashed headlong from the room. "Hanuman!" The Adepts heard the Master's scream for help, cringing as the dreaded name of the Potion Master echoed through the corridors of the Great Pyramid. No one saw Belial again for thirty-six hours.

In fact, he was quite irrational. His followers knew it, of course. Perhaps they had surmised the state of his mental condition beforehand. This day, though, it was confirmed. Still, they took no action. In fact, they dared not even discuss it amongst themselves. No one dared say aloud, "He is insane," even though they were certainly thinking it.

It was a solitary time for those in the Inner Circle. The best advice a man could give himself was, "Do your duty, keep a low profile, keep your thoughts and feelings to yourself, and trust no one." Belial's insanity was obvious, but the Adepts were too afraid of him to say anything. Too afraid of his anger and retribution, too afraid of the prison camps and other forms of retribution for those who crossed him. Too afraid of just disappearing simply because they had spoken up in disagreement with the Master.

*****

So the days and weeks wore on. Shakala worked in utmost solitude, Belial having thrown an impenetrable cloak of secrecy around the project and everyone involved. Security was tighter than ever before. No one was allowed in or out of the Great Pyramid without specific authorization from the Master himself.

The alchemist felt pushed and pulled from all directions, and the pressure on him was enormous—pressure from Belial to work without rest to perfect the device, pressure from his peers to not fail them, pressure from his conscience to stop the madness because he knew things were out of control. Inwardly, he was a seething cauldron of fear and anguish. Outwardly, he was a model of decorum, choosing to remain silent and painstakingly continue his experiments. To do otherwise would be to invite my own death sentence, he reasoned in the darkness of his own mind.

So he continued his work every day, holding his tongue and keeping his feelings bottled up inside him, his desire for self-preservation winning out over his desire to do what was morally right. So his thoughts and his fear festered within him, eating away at his conscience, just as the cancer within him continued to fester and eat away at his body, cell by cell.

Day by day, the device moved inexorably toward completion. Day by day, the alchemist and the Sons of Belial continued their downward spiral into darkness and madness, out of control and heading toward oblivion, carrying the once-glorious Nation-State of Atlantis along with them.

*****

From Shakala's Journal...
Early Afternoon
Vernal Equinox
Month of the Crimson Gull
Year of the Child

Is the device that I have created another step in a journey from which I cannot turn back? Remember Lus? Remember the earthquake after the Dragon Festival? Am I about to embark on another experiment that unleashes further demons from Pandora's box?

I am a scientist. I am not concerned with debating the morals of my Master. I am interested only in the proper construction and functioning of the device. Or am I?

What is the device? It is an experiment on the sky, intended to change the ionosphere in the ways necessary to create weather and atmospheric effects. It is a weapon of great power—essentially an ionospheric heater—that can be used for constructive or destructive purposes, for good or for evil, depending on the intention of the Master.

The Sons of Belial plan to use the device to manipulate the environment, and to use the environment, in turn, to manipulate Atlantean behavior for their personal advantage. The goals of the Sons of Belial—which I support—will be brought about by producing a controlled and directed society, linked by technology, dominated by themselves—an elite group that maintains control through its allegedly superior scientific and political knowledge. I say "allegedly" because, in truth, we know so very little about the workings of the device. We do not know how it will operate once we overcome the problem of the exploding crystals. (That is, if we can ever overcome it!) Even I, Shakala, do not know, and it is my experiment, my device.

However, that does not seem to matter to the Master. Unhindered by morals or the restraints of traditional Atlantean values, the Sons of Belial will not hesitate to achieve the Master's political ends by using the device for influencing behavior and keeping society under close surveillance and control. Why? Because this technology is of great worth to the Sons of Belial. They can make enormous profits from controlling such technology. Even at low power levels, the device can cause atmospheric disruptions that would confuse or completely disrupt the communications systems of lighter-than-air craft and submarine vessels.

Were the device focused properly, even at its lowest setting, the enemies of Atlantis—indeed, even Atlanteans themselves—would be virtually without communications on land, sea, or air. I could, however, channel our own communications network onto a separate beam, even though the rest of the world's communications are disrupted.

At a somewhat higher setting, I can change the weather simply by altering wind patterns in the upper atmosphere. This can be quite beneficial. As ozone and nitrogen concentrations in the atmosphere are artificially increased, plant growth and food production would also increase. It can also be quite harmful, creating weather effects such as hurricanes, tornadoes, and the like over entire hemispheres, causing devastation to enemy lands on a vast and unprecedented scale.

At an even higher setting, the device can generate electromagnetic disturbances that cause mild to severe physiological disruption, perceptual distortion, even disorientation among living creatures. This as a weapon of war! At this setting, after only a few hours exposure, the enemy's ability to function would be so degraded that they would be virtually helpless. The best part is that the device works quickly, silently, and effectively over a wide range, and as far as I know, not one of the provinces has an effective counteroffensive to combat such a weapon or the adverse effects it produces.

Of course, serious environmental side-effects will occur. Animals will be as affected as soldiers and civilians. At this setting, the device will have profound effects on migration patterns of fish and wild animals that rely on an undisturbed energy field to navigate their routes.

Finally, there is the danger to the environment itself. What are we doing to the air we breathe by unleashing this device? What are the unplanned, unexpected side-effects? We already know, or can extrapolate some things, given the data and our understanding of ionospheric behavior. But there are still many things we do not know.

The ionosphere is a delicately balanced system—a bubble-like sphere surrounding the Earth's lower atmosphere, with movements swirling over the surface of the bubble. It is prone to catalytic reactions. If a small change occurs in one part, a major change can occur throughout the ionosphere.

Belial has suggested that if a beam from the device projects high enough and powerfully enough, it could punch a hole through the ionosphere. If a big enough hole is punched through it, he says, the ionosphere could pop. Then what? I asked myself, examining this possible scenario. I do not like what I find, for Belial has far underestimated the power of the device.

The device will not merely burn holes in the ionosphere, as the Master has surmised. That is dangerous enough, but far less damaging than what will actually happen. A laser burst lasting only a few minutes will slice through the ionosphere like a knife. This produces not a hole, but a long incision, more like a tear.

As the Earth rotates, the beam will slice across the ionosphere and down into the lower atmosphere, cutting huge slices in the magnetic field, creating harsh, out-of-harmony frequencies. These discordant impulses will send all sorts of disruptive vibrations throughout the electromagnetic web that penetrates the atmosphere and covers the entire surface of the planet as well.

At this time, I have no way to estimate the effects of this interference with the normal functioning of the geomagnetic field. I have barely thought about them myself, although I must give myself time to do so. The more I consider it, however, the more it seems that the experiment should be aborted. The device appears to be stable, but the effects are far too dangerous to risk using it.

There are already many imbalances in the atmosphere caused by industrial and nuclear pollutants, especially radiation. If we add the additional high-energy particles generated by the device's beam, the weather disruptions will be so acute and severe, according to my simulations, that the Earth will be forced to take compensatory action. Of course, we all know how that happens. The Earth discharges its buildup of heat, relieves stress, and regains a balanced condition through earthquakes and volcanic action.

The ionosphere is an active electrical shield that protects the planet from the constant bombardment of high-energy particles coming from outer space. Without the ionosphere, we are at the mercy of the radiation of the universe. If the ionosphere is disturbed, so is the rest of the atmosphere below it, in equal or greater measure than the disturbance above.

I am reminded of a story that Grandfather told me about a group of boys playing with a sharp stick. Upon finding a sleeping bear, they poked the animal in the stomach to see what would happen. The bear feasted well that day.

There is a moral there, if we take the time to heed it. Are we performing an act of global vandalism by developing a device that will seriously damage many people and many lands over an extended period of time? Are the risks worth it? Do the benefits outweigh the risks? That is for the Master to decide. I am but a scientist. I will do my job regardless. And may the gods deliver me quickly from his wrath should these words that I have penned ever be discovered.

I shall stop writing now, for the pain in my gut burns sharply, and my head grows heavy with a dull and agonizing throbbing. The voices are beginning to chatter again, and I must silence them before they drive me insane.

I must remember...I am in charge. I hold the key to the device. I build it or I do not. We shall see, we shall see...

C H A P T E R 10

Know thyself.

—Inscription of the Delphic Oracle

In Atlantean tradition and culture, the goal of a teacher was the same as that of a healer—to guide students into the Spirit-world and help them reconnect with their soul. This was the same then as it is now—the sacred art of Transformation. It was the blueprint for growing from a lesser being into a greater one.

As a caterpillar seeks the safety of a cocoon, so the student steps out of the mundane world into the sanctuary of sacred space and time, presided over by the guidance of a ritual elder. As Caterpillar transforms into Butterfly, so Neophyte transforms into Master. Together, teacher and student engage in powerful initiation rites as the student comes to know his own mind and develop the ability to change it. It is the discovery of one's Self!

*****

In the sacred space of Mount Kylene, high above the mundane world, master and student came together once again, as they had done so many times during their long relationship. Day after day, night after night, in quiet groves and on windswept plateaus, Adima continued the work that he had started twenty-five years before and recommitted to on the morning after his dream.

"What is your *intention*?" Enoch asked as they stood beneath the leafy branches of a Hazel tree. "Form an intention, hold it fixed in your mind, and you cannot fail to achieve the results."

Adima stooped and picked up a hazel nut that had fallen on the ground. Cracking it open, he spilled the meaty contents into his palm. Hidden Wisdom of the Mother Goddess, he smiled, recognizing the symbolic message—inspiration, divination, magic. It was easy to form the right intention in the presence of such wisdom.

"It is my intention to come to know my Self."

Enoch smiled. "An honorable intention," he replied, pleased with the younger man's intuition and willingness to learn. "Our task, then, is to help you find the Magician within and transform you into *a strong and peaceful warrior and a master of the ways of Love.*"

Reaching out, the old man picked up a stout limb that had fallen from the tree. Carefully, he peeled off the dead twigs and loose bark as he continued to speak. "Your goal is a worthy one, Adima. It has great worth, great value. No goal can be accomplished, however, unless you have an attitude of willingness. This requires commitment on your part." Enoch held the smooth staff, not quite ready to hand it over to Adima. There was still an important question to ask.

"I ask you now, Adima, in all seriousness and earnestness, for your renewed commitment." Gripping the staff tightly in his right hand, Enoch planted one end firmly on the ground and extended his arm forward. His tone and demeanor were somber. "Do you believe that your goal is so important, so desirable, that it will be worth doing whatever it takes to accomplish it?"

Without hesitation, Adima reached out and gripped the staff with his own hand, entwining his fingers within the old man's in a gesture of solidarity and cooperation. His answer was simple, reflecting the feeling of confidence with which he was beginning this undertaking. "Yes."

And so they began once again. Each day brought a different lesson—lessons in achieving and using one's power, lessons in discovering one's allies, lessons in swordsmanship and martial arts, lessons in the mastering of one's personal demons and fears. Each was a lesson in the truth, the first laying the foundation, each successive lesson building on those which preceded it.

So much to teach, thought Enoch, and so little time. How am I going to impart all of my knowledge to Adima and have him achieve any level of mastery in what little time remains? The old man knew better than to look too far ahead, however. "One day at a time," he muttered over and over to himself whenever he found his thoughts projecting an uncertain future. Alone in the high places, he sat in deep meditation, seeking answers to the questions and doubts that vexed him. Seeking direction for himself even as he was teaching Adima how to do so for himself.

"Do not try to manipulate and control outcomes," an inner Voice whispered. *"Teach the curriculum lesson by lesson, putting forth as much as the student can accept and letting each lesson sink in until it is truly learned. Then, when it is learned, move on to the next one. The agenda is being set by greater forces than you. Your part is to teach. Adima's part is to learn and apply in direct proportion in his life.*

"The course is set. It is fruitless to manipulate the lessons or stall for time. When Adima is called upon, he will take what has been given him and go forth—ready or not. Assume, though, that he will be ready, for as you know, nothing happens in the world by mistake. Trust in the process. Visualize the desired outcome. See Adima as ready. See the teaching complete, for so it is. See the outcome accomplished for the highest good of all. Have faith, trust that it is accomplished, and let go and live accordingly. That is the true teaching, for you as well as for Adima. That is all one can really do. Just do your part and have faith, one day at a time."

So they labored, alone in the silence and seclusion of the high places, without public demonstration or spectacle, keeping their intention to themselves. And so, day by day, lesson by lesson, Adima continued to grow in wisdom and strength and mastery of the forces of Light and Love and Truth, spiraling ever upward toward ascendancy and mastery, and toward his final confrontation with Belial. He continued to be husband and father and councilor. He maintained proper balance, confiding only in his wife, who for her part was doing her own transformative work.

CHAPTER 11

The waters of the sky or those that flow, those that are dug out or those that arise by themselves, those pure and clear waters that seek the ocean as their goal—
Let the waters, who are goddesses, help me here and now.

—the *Rig Veda*

While the men continued their work above ground in the high places, other forces were also at work—softer forces, female forces, playing their parts in the drama and blending their voices into the universal chorus and symphony. I have spoken to you mostly of the Masculine aspect of Atlantis, its male heroes and teachers and villains, the yang side of the culture and society. There is also a yin side, the Feminine, of which you must now be told.

For many thousands of years, the Goddess of Wisdom prevailed and dominated all aspects of Atlantean life—religion, metaphysics, politics, science, and the arts. All of Nature, in fact the very Earth herself, was known to be alive.

The central figure in the yin aspect was, of course, the Great Mother—embodiment of the Feminine, constantly conceiving and giving birth to her many children, nurturing them, sustaining them, feeding them milk and honey, keeping them safe all the days of their lives. All life flowed from the womb of the Great Mother, and all life returned to her when its cycle on Earth was complete.

The Atlanteans recognized and honored the Divine Feminine within everyone and everything. Without the Feminine, the Masculine could not be balanced. Without the Masculine, the Feminine remained ever empty and barren. Each needed the other. This spiritual principle was ideally expressed in the Atlantean science and art of geomancy, which recognized that certain powerful currents, invisible lines of magnetism, ran over the whole surface of the Earth. The task of the geomancer was to detect the currents and interpret their influences on the land over which they passed. The most favorable position was where the two streams met.

This spiritual principle was also being expressed in the lives of Adima and Cybele. Like the yin and the yang currents, each was attuned to a current of energy, each was following a particular path. Just as the yang, or male, current took the higher routes over steep mountains, so Adima and Enoch were preparing to take a steep and difficult course in their interaction with Belial. As the yin, or female, current flowed mainly along chains of low hills, so Cybele was preparing along the softer course under the guidance of her teacher, Sophia.

Within Mount Kylene there was a Cave—feminine, hidden, closed. Both the mountain and the Cave were cosmic centers of transformation. Like the geomantic ideal, where the male and female current met and the energy was strongest, the solution to the problems in Atlantis was synthesizing through Adima and Cybele, complementing their individual power and combining it into the fullness of the balanced male and female Whole.

*****

Nighttime in the forest. A funereal half-moon glowed orange as it traced its path across the star-filled sky. The constellation of the Hunter was still visible in the west, the point of his sword aimed at his ever-faithful companion, that brightest of nighttime lights, Sirius, the Dog Star.

Alone in the night, like a fierce predator of old, the great gray she-wolf padded silently through the forest glade along a secret, tree-lined passage, shaded from prying eyes by the thick branches meeting overhead. Far from the haunts of men, she had been traveling for hours, and now the soft, flickering light deepened the dreamlike trance within which the magnificent beast moved. Like her human counterparts—the geomancers who understood the magic science of invoking the Spirit of Revelation and Ecstasy when they set up their great cathedrals to reproduce the harmonious proportions of the forest—Wolf understood the sanctity and sacredness of the deep woods.

No sound she made, save for the rasp of her hot breath and the brushing of her fur against the foliage. Her coat glinted silver in the moonlight, this great gray she-wolf, hounded and persecuted in Atlantis, she who had lost her mate and her pups to the hunter and the encroachments of civilization, she who padded softly and silently through the forest, howling her anguish to the moon and guarding the secret Cave and the Wild Woman. This night, moving on silent padded feet, Wolf was seeking, for she had a message to relay. Every sense was alert. Suddenly, a vagrant gust of wind brought a familiar scent to her flared nostrils.

She paused, instantly alert. It was the familiar scent of a human being. Breaking into a trot, but still moving silently, Wolf continued onward. Rounding a bend in the trail, she knew immediately that she had reached her destination. She stood in the silence and gazed about her.

A veiled light from an undetermined source somewhere far off in the distance lit the clearing. Overhead, great branches sprang out from the huge tree trunks to form the vaulted ribs of the roof, meeting in knots of foliage. The subtle, broken patterns of the leaves diffused the light and revealed bright, glowing eyes peering from among the thick foliage overhead and underfoot. Wolf recognized them instantly and whined in contentment, for she was in the presence of the Elementals, those magical creatures who dwelt invisibly within the bushes and trees and helped to keep the forest fresh and green and alive.

In the center of the clearing, as if awaiting Wolf's presence, stood an old woman. The two children of the night and the forest and the Earth stood looking at each other for a moment in silence. Wolf remembered how she had first come to meet the old woman. There had been a commotion in the forest—men with "death sticks" had arrived to maim and kill and wreak havoc. In the ensuing chaos, the natural peace and harmony of the forest was shattered. When the noise subsided and the smoke cleared, Wolf found herself lying in a pool of her own blood, seriously wounded. Her mate had been killed instantly, and the pack had scattered to the four winds.

After a time, Wolf knew not how long, the old woman came and took her to a cave and nursed her back to health. It took several weeks, and Wolf was in and out of delirium for much of that time. Of course, the old woman could not possibly have known about the newborn pups alone in their den. And Wolf was too badly hurt to tell her or to leave and attend to them. Yet the old woman sensed that Wolf was worried, and tried to find the den. But Wolf had hidden it too well, and try as she might, Sophia could not locate the lair.

When Wolf was finally stronger, she returned immediately to her den. Expecting to find two dead pups, she instead found nothing! Perhaps they had crawled away, only to die in the forest. Perhaps they had been carried off by larger predators. Wolf never knew. The mother instinct in her was strong, however, and she searched for days, to no avail. The pups had vanished without a trace.

Wolf did not experience feelings of grief or sorrow as humans knew those emotions, but rather a deep sense of emptiness, a sense of something missing in her life, a hole where her mate and her pups should have been. And Wolf did not know how to fill this hole.

Alone she hunted, without family. Alone she ate and drank and slept, avoiding the pack, refusing to take another mate. Alone she roamed the forest, searching...for what? Her animal instinct sensed that things were different now.

She would not return to the pack, not take another mate, not raise a new family. Hers was to be a solitary path. So Wolf did as her instinct told her. She roamed the night and sat under the stars and looked up and listened and waited. She sang her grief and her longing to Grandmother Moon, her keen senses alert to any answer that might be forthcoming. And gradually, the answers did come.

A connection was made, reestablished, actually. A connection to one of those white points of light hanging suspended in the night sky—to the Dog Star, Sirius, original home of the gods—and to her power ally, the Moon. Baying at the moon, receiving the psychic energy, receiving the secret knowledge, Wolf assumed her role as Teacher and Pathfinder.

"Seek out Sophia and stay by her side," Grandmother Moon had told Wolf. "You and she have much to accomplish in the time before you. There is work to be done and much to prepare for." Not in words did they speak, but rather in the Language of Light, where thoughts passing between one and the other were instantly understood. So Wolf returned to Sophia to be her teacher and protector, guardian of the secret Cave and harbinger of new ideas.

"Welcome, Wolf," Sophia said softly. "It is not by coincidence that I am in the sacred grotto at this time. I have been expecting you, for I know you have a message for me. I have been gathering the necessary ingredients and am ready to receive the teaching." The old woman held out her hand to reveal a basketful of herbs that she had been gathering. She was of indeterminate age, how old perhaps even she did not know, and exuded an aura of wildness. Her long gray hair, silver like Wolf's coat, blew in the night breeze. Small as she was, she was not fragile; her thinness belied a greater strength and power. In her deep, piercing eyes—gateway to a mysterious, secretive, and magical nature—glowed an inextinguishable spark of life.

Hers was deep wisdom, an understanding of and kinship with Nature. Sophia was a wild woman, a knower of secrets. And like Wolf standing there before her, she was an endangered species. "The time is almost at hand," Sophia continued. "Will you accompany me to the Cave and stand guard while I traverse the Underworld?"

Wolf approached and nuzzled the old woman, acknowledging the bond between them. Putting her hand on the noble head, Sophia stood silent for a moment. Then she turned and was swallowed up by the forest. Silently, Wolf followed.

*****

The Mountains of the Moon bisected the island continent, rising like a great backbone tens of thousands of feet above the fertile Atlantean Plain, their foothills leveling off and spreading to the very edges of the sea. Part granite, part magma, part basalt, they had been created toward the end of that violent epoch that has come to be known as the Paleozoic Era, when enormous subterranean forces had hurled them upward with tremendous force and speed.

Strong, solid, snowcapped, they presented an impressive and imposing picture. All who came to the island wanted to visit the Mountains of the Moon and scale their vast heights. Young men, eager to prove their mettle, often tested their physical prowess and endurance on their heights. But as impressive as were their forests and rivers and cliffs, far more impressive was that which was not visible to the naked eye, that which was hidden from all but the most discerning of eyes and open of hearts.

Far more impressive than the outer was the inner, that which lay below the surface. For within the living mountains, as within a living body, was a vast network of interconnected tunnels, a living system of arteries and veins through which flowed the energy streams of the Great Mother.

The geomancers ascribed all of this to the actions of volcanism, plate tectonics, and other natural phenomena. The poets and mystics romanticized it as the interplay among the creative gods and goddesses. Legends abounded of this subterranean labyrinth, a place of initiation and second birth. One of the most popular spoke of a wondrous, mystical Cave that lay deep within this vast honeycomb of tunnels, at its very center.

"It has been there for eons," the poets said, "formed when the outer body of the Mountains of the Moon was formed. It was there in the time of Poseidon and the first kings of Atlantis. In fact, it is still there, for those who know where to look. To others, though, those with a denser and coarser nature, it remains secret and invisible and safe from their indiscretions."

> The Cave—the Feminine Principle,
> Womb of the Great Mother and her sheltering aspect,
> A sacred sanctuary, round and dark,
> Sitting atop her very core, her Heart,
> Warmed by the Heart-fire of the Great Mother.
> The Cave—a mystical place
> Where lies the inner esoteric knowledge,
> Place of burial, place of rebirth,
> Place of mystery, increase, and renewal.
> The Cave—home of the Cosmic Egg,
> Where the gods go to die,
> Where saviors are born,
> From which Man and Woman emerge
> And to which they return at death.

Atlantean scholars and adventurers had been searching for the Cave for centuries. Whenever anyone found a new portal, it was hoped that it would prove to be the entrance to the Underworld, that mystical land rumored to lie below Atlantis. But no portal ever did.

For the Cave remains to this day a secret place, a place of initiation, whose entrance is hidden from the profane by a dangerous, labyrinthine passageways and protected by the Threshold Guardian. Entry is only by permission or through overcoming this force, for entering the Cave is like re-entry into the womb of the Great Mother. Passing through the Cave represents a change of state, which is also achieved by overcoming dangerous powers. It is the entrance to the Underworld.

It was here, in this secret place, where Sophia dwelt. It was here, on that night of the funereal half moon, to which she returned with Wolf after gathering the sacred herbs to receive the message from Higher Self.

The trail they walked seemed innocuous enough, unobtrusive enough. It was well-traveled and known to the people of the area. Hikers traversed it constantly, never guessing what lay below their feet, just beyond the fringe of trees and bushes. The old woman paused in the moonlight at the foot of a low cliff. Dense foliage grew at its base. Gently, she knelt and spoke to the friend who walked beside her. "It is time, dear one. I go within to contact Higher Self. How long we shall be in communion, I do not know. Wait here for me and guard the entrance. Allow no one access, lest Higher Self be disturbed and become reticent. When it is finished speaking, I shall return to you here."

Wolf licked the old woman's hand and nuzzled against her, smelling her scent and feeling the deep strength within her. And was there something else Wolf smelled—a hint of fear, perhaps? Wolf could not be sure, and she whined her puzzlement.

Sophia seemed to read the animal's mind. "Yes, there is a doubt, a fear within me. The call from Higher Self is stronger than I have ever known it to be. I sense a great urgency, a message of great import."

As if to confirm her feelings, a chill gust of wind blew through the forest. Bushes and trees rustled in awareness and anticipation. Sophia rose and drew her mantle about her. She walked toward a huge old Willow—tree of enchantment, sacred to the Moon Goddess. In the dim light, the gnarled, misshapen roots seemed to twist and turn, parting before her, revealing a gaping hole in the twisted tangle. Ignoring Wolf's whimpers, Sophia stepped across the threshold and was swallowed up by the blackness. As though conscious of her passage, the roots closed behind her, leaving no trace of the opening for any passing traveler to see. Fumbling in the darkness, the old woman soon found a lantern that she kept hanging from a root growing out of the living rock. Dragging a match across the stone wall, she lit the wick and waited as the glow filled the passageway.

The outer tunnel was chilly and damp, leading directly back into the cliff for several yards. There, the way twisted and turned, with side passages branching off in all directions. The uninitiated wanderer would soon have been hopelessly lost in the twisting, convoluted maze. Sophia, however, walked the way sure-footedly, having made the journey so often that she had lost count years before. The floor and walls were narrow, polished smooth by the passage of countless feet and hands over the ages. She smelled the bat guano and niter on the walls, heard the drip-drip-drip of water trickling along the rocks.

Water! So soft and yet so powerful, a master artist sculpting and painting the limestone into a phantasmagoria of shape and color. Each chamber was different, a series of apparitions of increasing or decreasing size, changing, incoherent, fantastic, otherworldly, and incredibly beautiful. And always the passage sloped inward and down, inward and down. As she walked, Sophia remembered when her grandmother and mother had first taken her to the Cave and told her about Higher Self. She was thirteen, the occasion of her first menstrual flow, her initiation into young womanhood.

She had been brought there by the older women and introduced to various techniques for spiritual transformation—prayer and fasting, chanting, drumming, focused breathing—in preparation for her first vision quest. During her subsequent ordeal in the wilderness, she had received a vision of her role as a spiritual healer and teacher. Fascinated by the possibilities, she fully embraced the ancient ways, over the years developing healing abilities and psychic talents that were considered extraordinary by most Atlanteans. Long ago she had chosen to dwell apart from the ordinary world in order to foster a deep connection with Nature. She had learned well from her elders.

"The Earth is a living community, and all life is interconnected," Grandmother had told her. "The animals, the water, the sea, and the sky—all are your brothers and sisters. All are wise. All have something to teach. All have medicine to offer."

"Be still, listen, and look around you," continued her mother. "See what a wonder you are, what a wonder the universe is. Feel it—feel your power, feel your connectedness, feel your holiness. Let yourself be taught."

"Above all, embrace the mystery," added the High Priestess. "Never forget who you are, where you came from, and where you are going. Always open your heart to your sense of wonder and awe in the presence of the numinous."

Sophia's reverie was interrupted by the sudden leveling off of the tunnel, which had grown gradually wider toward the bottom of the descent. Rounding a turn, the passage suddenly opened into a vast subterranean grotto. She had arrived at the sacred Cave, the center of the Earth, its womb and heart—the place of union of Self and Ego, the place of the Marriage of Heaven and Earth, the meeting place of the Divine and the Human. She immediately stopped and extinguished the lantern. Now the chamber was filled with a natural orange glow, produced by billions of microscopic, phosphorescent organisms. The light revealed a large natural chamber carved out of the living limestone.

The Artist-Mother had done her work exceptionally well here. Huge stalagmites rose up from the floor to mate with huge stalactites hanging down from the ceiling far above her head. Grotesque, misshapen faces seemed to peer out from outcroppings large and small, nonhuman denizens of the Underworld, their features frozen in mute, ghastly shrieks and wide-eyed stares. Silent guard they stood, these spirit sentinels, allowing only the initiated to pass into the chamber and complete their work.

Like arteries and veins in the human body, a series of tunnels branched off in all directions from the outer walls. One led to the surface, another to the Lighthouse. A third ran beneath the Temple of Poseidon, while still others connected to the burial grounds, the beach, and the Dragon Mound. Other shafts there were, too, penetrating deeper into the Earth, below the limestone, ever downward into the bedrock, finally reaching the vast, interconnecting network of tunnels that spread all over, or actually under, the world, connecting the main continent of Atlantis with Turtle Island, Al Khemia, Mu, and even far-off Lemuria.

In stark contrast to the alchemist's lab, this chamber was devoid of charms, fetishes, tools, or amulets. Everything was natural. In the center of the room, a particularly beautiful limestone formation rose up to form a natural altar. Here, Sophia paused and opened her bundle, revealing a small collection of herbs.

The old woman wasted no time in taking the leaves and rolling them into a tight ball, which she then placed between her cheek and gum. Then she paused for the first time since she had met Wolf. It seemed like days ago, not just hours!

Spreading her cloak on the rock, Sophia lay down on the altar, staring fixedly at the rock above her head, clearing her mind and slowing her breath before entering into the Group Mind, comprised of her human ancestors, animal totems, and spirit guides—noncorporeal allies in her quest for wisdom. The Group Mind, where she would make her decisions as to what to do next.

The deep warmth of the room comforted her, the natural light caressed her and soothed her. She lay there, slowly swallowing the juice as it seeped from the wad of herbs in her mouth. The taste was bitter, but she had become accustomed to it. "It seems lately that all of life has a bitter taste," the old woman muttered, but quickly dismissed the feeling. Now was not the time for thinking, it was the time for letting go, for dissolving the ego and allowing it to contact Higher Self, a much larger, much wiser part of herself to whom she turned for counsel in times of extreme crisis.

Gradually Sophia became aware of a sound, a faint thump-thump, thump-thump, first like a drum, then like a pulse, steady and rhythmic. Thump-thump, thump-thump—a heartbeat, *her* heartbeat, the sound of her own heart beating in harmony with the Heart of the Great Mother. Then the colors began to flow toward her from all directions, brilliant, vivid. Blue and green and purple and red and magenta, the colors streamed by, and the hallucinations began to unfold. As the images gradually coalesced, Sophia found herself floating in an iridescent liquid surrounded by a silky veil. She lost all sense of shape and size and self. All of her boundaries floated away, all concepts of time and notions of the outer world.

"I am a fetus in my mother's womb," she realized, "floating in the amniotic fluid and connected to her by the umbilical cord." There was almost no light, and it was comfortably warm and very, very peaceful. After a while, the experience shifted, and she found herself floating in the vastness of interstellar space. "I am still connected to my mother by the umbilical cord," she laughed, looking out into an immense cosmic sea. Millions of stars shone in the blackness, each point of light a living being connected to her, part of her, calling her name. She felt gratitude, gratitude for the miracle of life and the gifts of the Great Mother—rich soil, green pastures, ripe fruits and grains and vegetables, sparkling water.

Now the experience came to life, and she heard a Voice speaking to her, not from without, but from within, from inside her own mind. Not her own voice, not the voice in which she spoke to others, not the voice with which she carried on private conversations in the solitude of the forest. This was the Voice of Higher Self, bringing her information from the Spirit-world...that place beyond her outer self, that part of her psyche which was normally hidden from view, telling her things she could not possibly have known for herself. A sane Voice, a Voice of reason, speaking to her in her native tongue, addressing her concerns, answering her questions, revealing a depth of knowing far beyond that which she knew about herself and the Great Mystery of Life. The Voice of the many—the collective consciousness—so calm, so strong, a source of stability, wisdom, and knowledge of the spiritual mysteries.

"*It will be called Patriarchy,*" the Voice declared, speaking the dreaded word for the first time amidst flashes of lightning and rolling thunder. "*And with its rise will come the end of the Goddess Culture and the suppression of the Feminine.*"

As the Voice spoke, a vision arose, a sensory experience of the future as Patriarchy waxed strong and the Goddess consciousness waned. Sophia listened and watched as the stars began to spin and flash. Within this maelstrom of light and color, she could discern an image. At first it was far away, but then she began to move toward it.

When the motion stopped, she found herself standing at the edge of a great chasm. In her mind's eye, she saw the ancient symbols of the Male and Female Principles standing on opposite sides of the divide. Between them a Great Pendulum hung suspended.

Suddenly, the Pendulum began to vibrate. With a mighty sound that caused the female symbol to crack into many pieces, the Pendulum began to move toward the male symbol. The Voice continued.

"*The time of the fulfillment of the prophecy is now at hand. The Fathers will fall into a deep sleep and dream a great and fearful Dream. Atlantis will be no more, but Patriarchy—grim legacy of the Sons of Belial—will live on.*"

As the Voice spoke, a melange of ghostly images flashed across Sophia's inner vision—skulls, skeletons, bleached bones—accompanied by an onslaught of anxiety that quickly became real panic. Her breath came in short, rapid gasps. She struggled for air.

More shapes—spirals, circles, triangles, and all kinds of geometric patterns. Children being born, growing older, then dying, and through it all moving from one experience of pain, suffering, and death to another. Again the Voice spoke.

"*As Patriarchy rises, the Great Light of the Feminine will be extinguished...snuffed out, suppressed, hidden. So this will be for many thousands of years, as the Pendulum swings far to the other side.*"

Immediately there followed a vision of mutilated baby girls and young women bound in chains. Sophia saw deep dungeons and high towers in which the Feminine was encapsulated and imprisoned. "Aaaaaarrrrrrrgh!" She choked on her outrage and despair, her feelings of absolute hopelessness, her anguish at the sight of so many women living their lives devoid of meaning and purpose. It was all a horrible joke, a vast cosmic joke!

She heard a deep, mocking laugh and turned to see a towering image of Belial with his pale white face and black, red-rimmed eyes. Before him, masses of innocent men, women, and children fled for their lives in panic. But there was no place to go, and they were swept away in the deluge. She wanted to avert her gaze, to flee this place and these visions, but the Voice continued unperturbed "Behold the Great Wounding. The Wound of the Feminine runs deep, as does the Wound of the Masculine."

Sophia felt a spasm of pain, a deep ache in the middle of her chest. She clutched her heart, certain that she was about to die. She saw revealed the *Dark Mystery of the Feminine Body* and its deep wound. She saw men enslaved, too, bound to rigid, limiting, life-draining patriarchal traditions, weighed down by heavy chains and bleeding from a thousand self-inflicted wounds.

"Save the children," she croaked in barely a whisper. "Who will save the children?

To which the Voice responded, *"The children will require a savior, but any attempt at the emergence of the Feminine will be misunderstood and perceived by the Patriarchy as a threat."*

Sophia watched a chained man cower in fear as a woman came forth from her tower prison, only to be impelled backward by other men equally bound. The deep ache in her chest grew worse. And as the pain continued, her feelings of despair and frustration turned to other, darker emotions. She alternately experienced anger and hatred and rage, thrashing and moving violently about, her breath coming in fitful gasps as she pounded the rock with clenched fists. She wanted to rend and tear, maim and kill. It did not matter whom. She was caught up in the throes of primal violence.

"I'll kill you! I'll kill you!" She screamed out her rage time and again, stopping only when she grew too hoarse to voice a sound. For a long time, she lay on her side, heaving great dry sobs, unable to speak anymore. Then the sorrow came, accompanied by the tears. "There is no one to save the children," the old woman keened. "All is lost!"

A wave of abysmal grief swept over her. At first, the grief was for herself and her own losses over the years. Gradually, though, the emotion deepened, and she found herself crying for all mothers and all of their losses. Floods of tears streamed from her eyes, wracking sobs shook her body, and deep sighs and moans echoed through the cavern as she cried for the children. Hers was the grief of a mother, the grief of all mothers, past present, and future—the grief of the Feminine, the grief of the Great Mother. She experienced it all, felt all the anguish and sorrow and pain. It seemed as though her unbearable emotional and physical suffering would last forever. She was trapped in a living nightmare from which there was no escape.

Sophia felt a great weight pressing upon her from all sides. Then she was moving, being propelled forward down a long, dark tunnel. The enormous pressure increased, almost asphyxiating her. She clawed her way forward, fighting for each inch. Then suddenly it was over, and she burst forth into a cool white light. Drenched in sweat, Sophia heard the Voice again.

"Behold the part you will play. Behold the Great Womb in which the Feminine will be saved and shielded during the time of the Patriarchy."

An intensely pleasant feeling of relaxation floated up from the very center of the old woman's being. She was floating again as she had been so long ago, but this time she was not a fetus but a newborn child, surrounded by loving parents and brothers and sisters. From her vantage point in the cradle, Sophia saw a huge ship floating at its berth in a tranquil harbor. A door in its side was open, revealing a great cavity that contained an ornate treasure chest resting in a golden cradle in the center of the hold. All manner of living creatures were seeking shelter in the great vessel.

Suddenly, the wind began to howl and the calm waters of the harbor were aroil. A mighty angel came and closed the door and sealed it with a mighty seal, after which a great tidal wave came and carried the Ark out to sea.

"Behold the new prophecy. Behold the Beastslayers."

The scene changed again. A great Beast had arisen, not the beneficent, life-giving Dragon Spirit who brought energy and fertility to the Earth, but a grotesque monster. Not friend, but adversary, the mighty Beast terrorized the land, the embodiment of evil. Sophia gasped as the dread creature belched forth a great blast of flame, incinerating everything in its path. The Earth lay scorched, black and smoking, littered with the ruins of buildings and the corpses of the masses.

A powerful woman came forth, Shield and Wand in hand, astride a mighty horse. The Beast roared and lashed its tail, causing further devastation. The woman was driven back and knocked to the ground. Before she could be trampled underfoot, however, a mighty warrior joined her and stood at her side, adding his gleaming, bejeweled Sword to her own potent weapons. What the one could not accomplish alone, together they did easily. Through the power of the Two united as One, they destroyed the Beast and drove it from the land forever.

"Behold the wisdom. Behold your place in the life and rhythm of the Great Mother."

Sophia saw herself standing before the Great Mother as she sat at an enormous spinning wheel, gently weaving the passage of day and night, the change of seasons, the cyclic nature of things, and the eternal return. And it all seemed right; it all seemed good.

"So why am I still incomplete?" she muttered.

"I sense your puzzlement," the Voice said gently. *"What is it you would ask me?"*

Sophia replied, "Throughout the great cycles, large and small, there is ever life and death and life again. As this is true for the cycles of Nature, so it is for Atlantis. I know this in my heart, yet I must ask if there is anything I can do to prevent what is about to happen."

The Voice spoke one last time. *"Do not fight your nature. You know when it is time for life, and you know when it is time for death. What must happen, must happen. Let Atlantis die, that it may be born again!"* The Voice faded, leaving the old woman alone on the hard stone slab. Her heartbeat echoed in her ears and pulsed strongly in her chest. Slowly, ever so slowly, it, too, faded into the silence, and Sophia returned to consciousness.

*****

Wolf sat at the entrance to the Underworld, all senses alert. She had been there for a day, a night, and most of another day. In her animal consciousness, she could not anticipate Sophia's return. The old woman simply was not there. That was the way it was, nothing to be done but obey the command and stand guard.

The weather was unseasonably cold, and the sun was hidden behind lowering gray thunderheads. A chill wind blew out of the southwest. Wolf smelled snow, unusual this close to the Vernal Equinox. Pangs of hunger and thirst gnawed at her, but her loyalty to the old woman was stronger than the demands of her body. Wolf would stay where she was until the old woman returned.

The animal laid her gray head on her paws and heaved a deep sigh. A soft vibration in the Earth brought her instantly to her feet. Footsteps below, in the passageway! Then, the almost inaudible rasp of the old woman's breath. Finally her scent as she emerged from the tangled roots of the Willow tree.

Sophia seemed haggard, and there was look of deep sorrow in her eyes. Wrapping a bony hand in the fur of Wolf's neck, she spoke a few hoarse words. "Go and eat and drink and sleep. When you are refreshed, find Cybele and bring her to me. Tell her I have a message for her." Without another word, the Wild Woman disappeared back into the Earth, leaving Wolf alone in the clearing once more.

CHAPTER 12

Don't grieve. Anything you lose comes 'round in another form. The child weaned from mother's milk now drinks wine and honey mixed.

—Rumi

Cybele was depressed. Ever since the Dragon Festival, she had been in a dark and angry mood. Much had happened to her on that day. What had begun in joy and promise had ended in disaster. She'd had a harsh encounter with Lilith just before the wedding ritual and was still smarting from the veiled threats, accusations, and metaphorical slap in the face that the High Priestess had dealt her. Then came the earthquake, which had frightened her at the core of her being, especially when she could not find her children or her husband.

All of her maternal fears about loss, separation, and death had welled up from that place in herself where she had buried them, washing over her in a cold wave. Now, three months later, those fears were with her still. The proverbial "last straw" had come with Adima's dream and encounter with Enoch, which he had shared with her over the next several days. His mood was not much better than her own, and being around him when he was that way was depressing her greatly. Her feelings seemed out of control. She knew what Adima was doing, for he'd been discussing it with her. But what was to be her part?

Her mind was full of unanswered questions and unformed terrors. She wanted to run away and hide, to go to her secret sanctuary deep in the forest and just be alone with her art and her journal. That would have been the easy way, the comfortable old way, and the attraction for it was strong, even after all those years of working to overcome it. Instead, though, she took a different action, calling upon her teacher, seeking out Sophia and asking her friend for help. "As soon as Adima told me of his dream, I sought you out," Cybele explained. "I value your wisdom. I don't know how to sort this out by myself. I haven't the courage, the skills, or the willingness to solve this on my own or determine my own course. But I don't want to be a burden on you, either."

"You do not burden me." The old woman spoke gently, stroking Cybele's hair and looking deeply into her eyes as they sat in the sanctuary of the forest glen just outside the entrance to the Cave. A rich, aromatic blend of pine and eucalyptus filled the air. "Remember how our relationship began, how we made the sacred pact and set out on the co-creative path together when you were but a young girl? I took on the mantle of teacher and healer and embraced you as a student. We joined together in *Holy Relationship* with each other at that time."

Cybele smiled wanly as Sophia continued. "It was not a burden then, nor is it one now. It is never a burden, but rather, a sacred trust that I would never think of abdicating. This is alliance and friendship. This is necessary to our relationship if it is to grow and prosper."

To illustrate her point, Sophia drew a pattern of concentric rings in the pine needles that carpeted the forest floor. "When one enters into a co-creative partnership with another, regardless of the levels of learning of each partner, each has a sacred responsibility to the other. When we started, my part, my responsibility, was to teach and counsel and help you heal yourself. For your part, you agreed to listen and do and practice the teachings in all of your affairs."

"Our relationship is ever growing, ever evolving," she continued, using a bony finger to expand the circles so that they overlapped each other. "As each of us grows, the relationship itself changes. At times now, it is difficult to tell who is the teacher and who is the student. "So tell me," the old woman smiled gently, "what troubles you? Open your heart to me and pour out your questions and your fears and your grief."

Cybele needed no further encouragement. Like a great floodgate bursting at the seams, she was full of emotion. Now it gushed forth in its eagerness to be released. "I don't know what's happening any more," she sobbed, sitting on the lush grass that covered most of the clearing. "I look around me and see everything falling apart. Look at Lilith, look at what's happening in the Temple. Look at Atlantis itself!" She paused to collect her thoughts.

"Is this something new? I think not. It's been going on for a long time, but I just never noticed. How could I have been so blind? Now it's as though my eyes have been opened for the first time and I'm looking at Atlantis in a new light. And I don't like what I'm seeing!"

"What do you mean?" Sophia encouraged her gently.

"The Sisterhood of Priestesses is corrupt," the younger woman explained. "Everything is a secret now, the exclusive property of the High Priestess, who has convinced herself and most of those in authority that she alone can read the Divine omens and interpret the will of the Goddess. With Belial's support, she's placed herself in a position of power, not just over the other priestesses, but over the people as well, whose support she claims to have...although I doubt it."

Cybele wrung her hands nervously, her voice quavering. "So of course, she is now extending her sphere of influence and activities outward, making more and more demands on the population for greater and greater sacrificial offerings. There are even rumors that she is about to call for human sacrifice! Where will it end?"

Sophia remained silent as Cybele continued speaking, but she was not surprised by the younger woman's words. The old woman had been observing these same signs herself. Cybele's observations only confirmed what Sophia already knew to be true.

"We all knew this once," Cybele continued. "The prayers and rituals were common knowledge. There were no secrets, save for the Great Mysteries, which no one tries to explain anyway. Once, we were all more or less linked by a single thread of ancient knowledge and power. Now, though, that thread has become unraveled. There are violations of the Great Mother and other disturbances causing loss of contact with our Higher Selves and the wisdom of the Goddess. Confusion and superstition are spreading rapidly. We are forgetting the old ways."

Sophia interrupted to ask an important question. "What specifically has happened between you and Lilith? How do you stand in the Temple?"

"I've definitely fallen out of favor," Cybele sighed. "I'm not sure how it happened or why, although I imagine it has something to do with Adima and his activities on the Council of Elders. Anyway, just before the Alchemical Wedding at the Dragon Festival, Lilith told the other priestesses and me that there was to be a change in the ritual. She said that rather than the priestesses all participating, this year only she, the High Priestess, would play an active role." Cybele closed her eyes and thought back to that afternoon in the holy chambers of the Temple of Poseidon. Lilith had entered and made a stunning announcement.

"I have been deep in the Spirit all day." The High Priestess had spoken with all of the authority of her rank. "And it has come to me that some of you are not in accord with Divine Will. Some of you have evil intentions. Some of you have lost favor with the Goddess. As a result, she is angry, but not angry enough to mar the festival, *if* we obey her from here on. She has commanded that the Wedding remain pure—that only the purest among us play an active role in the ceremony in order to keep it free from negativity.

Therefore, I shall perform the ritual alone. The rest of you will sit behind me on the podium in silence. The unclean among you know who you are. I urge you to repent your thoughts and actions and do whatever is necessary to purify yourselves before it is too late."

All of the priestesses were shocked, but Lilith had timed her delivery well. There was no chance to protest, no chance to utter a word. For as she had finished speaking, the High Priestess had turned and stepped imperiously out to greet the people. Cybele and the other priestesses had had no choice but to follow.

"I haven't been to the Temple since," Cybele went on, "and to be honest, I'm afraid to return there. What I'd really like to do is hide in the Cave until all of this blows over."

She laughed nervously, thinking Sophia would do the same, but the old woman remained silent for several moments, her eyes closed. The forest was quiet save for the songbirds and soughing of the wind through the pines. Finally Sophia spoke.

"It is not going to blow over," the crone sighed, getting to her feet and walking to the edge of the clearing. "In fact, it is going to get worse. It is not my intention to dishearten you further, but you must know that you are going to be on your own for a while. I won't be with you. I must go away for a while, for how long I do not know. We will have no contact. You will have to rely on your inner strength, your inner guides, your Circle of friends and allies. But most of all, you will have to rely on yourself."

"And so our relationship comes to an end?" Cybele interrupted, jumping up in shock. She was afraid of what the answer might be, but she asked the question nevertheless.

Sophia's answer was most reassuring. "This does not mean that our relationship will end," the old woman explained. "On the contrary, it now evolves into a much deeper and more meaningful relationship, one between friends, partners, equals. With the absorption and integration of wisdom, the student grows up and becomes a teacher herself. You have shifted now from the outer to the inner—from the outer wise ones who have been guiding you to your inner teachers. Now the Inner One guides you. This is a time of completion and commencement, a time of new beginnings. Farewell until we meet again." And then, Sophia was gone, and Cybele was alone in the forest.

*****

Three months had passed, and Cybele had not heard a word from the old woman, although she had tried to contact her. She was used to not hearing from her teacher for long spells and having to make decisions on her own. She did not consider herself to be dependent on Sophia—she was a teacher and friend, not a crutch. But this was different, wasn't it? How could Sophia have gone off like this? Her disappearance had depressed Cybele greatly. She loved the old woman, but now she felt abandoned by her at precisely the time when she needed her most.

Scarcely able to function, the priestess forced herself to continue to perform her duties in the Temple of Poseidon, but her relationship with Lilith was strained almost to the breaking point. The tension between them was palpable. How did it all go so wrong? she wondered, thinking about her relationship with the High Priestess. Once she had been highly favored, her future in the Temple so full of promise.

When Sophia had brought the young Cybele to the Temple for the first time to begin her life in service to the Goddess and the people of Atlantis, Lilith had taken the young woman under her personal tutelage, moving her up from acolyte to initiate in a few short years, bestowing more and more responsibility on the young priestess as she recognized and rewarded her natural ability to heal. For a time, theirs was a close-knit relationship. Gradually, though, things had changed. Lilith spent less and less time with the priestesses and more and more time with Belial, neglecting her duties and obligations and growing ever more aloof, cold, and distant.

"What is she hiding?" the priestesses had whispered among themselves, but they dared not voice their concerns aloud, fearing retribution for questioning the motives and behavior of so pious a figure. Cybele, though, did voice her concerns aloud, confronting Lilith and asking her directly where her loyalty lay. Their interaction had been curt and brief. Lilith's face contorted in rage. She flushed purple, her skin mottled with white patches from which the blood had drained, her lower lip trembling as she struggled to control her temper.

"How dare you question me, you miserable ingrate?" she barely managed to whisper. "I took you in when you were nothing—a miserable pauper wandering in the forest, living with that witch, eating dirt and talking to bugaboos!"

Cybele bristled at the insult to her teacher, but she held her tongue. Lilith continued in a voice that was more hiss than speech.

"Get out of my sight! What was between us once no longer is. You are anathema. Stay in the Temple or leave, I do not care which. But know this—if you stay, avoid me, or face the consequences of my wrath."

Cybele did choose to stay, honoring her oath of service. Life in the Temple, though, became miserable. She found herself continually rebuked and chastised for petty transgressions. She was all but ostracized by her peers because everyone was afraid to associate with her. Her closest friends remained loyal but distant, trying not to put themselves in danger of risking Lilith's disfavor.

Over the weeks, as her mood became more and more despondent, Cybele had turned to her journal to work out her feelings and put her thoughts on paper. Writing always helped her sort through her feelings and get the answers she needed. In the pages of her journal, she recorded all of her emotions, asked all of her questions, and expressed all of her feelings. Sometimes she knew exactly what she wanted to say. At other times, though, the words would not come, and so she would fill the pages with random musings and doodles.

Writing made her feel better and gave her a sense of connection to the Divine. For it seemed to Cybele that as she wrote, Another was trying to express itself through her, Someone with important things to say in a Voice that wanted to be heard. She did not try to resist; in fact, she welcomed this other Voice, whom she had named the Muse. Cybele liked what the Muse had to say and was more than willing to serve as scribe for it. That was how, alone and waiting for her teacher's return, she came to write the *Fable of the Enlightened Serf*, a semi-biographical allegory in which she envisioned herself as a peasant in a faraway land, having been brought to enlightenment by a wise and wonderful crone and then abandoned in a terrible and tyrannical kingdom, powerless to put her new knowledge into practice.

*****

From Cybele's Journal...
Afternoon
Vernal Equinox
First Day of the Month of the Crimson Gull
Year of the Child

The Enlightened Serf
Once there was a Serf who aspired to a better life, although she knew it would never come. Who longed to live in the castle, but resigned herself to the

hovel. Who longed for the queen's blessings but got only curses. Who toiled long and hard but had an empty purse...

This Serf's heart's desire was for enlightenment. So she sought out a great and wondrously wise Crone. "Wise One," she cried to this feminine counterpart of the Sage, "I would like to be enlightened. Teach me what you know."

The Crone agreed and taught the Serf all the secrets and mysteries of life and the universe. The Crone spoke of kings and queens and warriors and lovers and magicians. She showed the Serf how to recognize them and tell the difference between good ones and bad ones. She showed her all of their positive attributes, and she showed her their shadows, too—those darker, negative qualities. Above all, the Crone showed the Serf how to tell the difference between the two...their positive and the shadow. Finally, the Crone had imparted all of her wisdom and all of her knowledge to the Serf, and it became time for them to part. "I shall leave you with one last bit of truth," said the Crone as she stood at the edge of the forest. "The state of the kingdom is a direct reflection of the state of mind of the king and the queen." Then, drawing her cloak about her, the Crone disappeared into the forest.

The Serf was delighted. She was thrilled. She had knowledge. She was wise. She had wisdom and learning beyond what the other serfs had. Through her encounter with the Crone, she was altered somehow...changed, not so much physically, but mentally, emotionally, and most of all, spiritually.

She knew the truth about herself and her place in the universal scheme of things. She understood how things were supposed to work. She had a deep sense of meaning and purpose. She was grateful, she was happy, joyous, even ecstatic. "I can't wait to get home," she thought as she followed the road through the forest. "I can't wait to tell everyone what I've learned and share these truths with them."

At last, the Serf crossed the last stretch of forest and came out onto a high hill overlooking the kingdom. "How long have I been gone?" she wondered. "It seems like only a short time, but much has changed. This isn't the kingdom I left, is it?"

Much had, indeed, changed during her absence. The castle was still there. So were the school and the church. The warriors still rode their great stallions across the fields. Villages, markets, and farms still dotted the landscape. Families still nurtured each other. Babies were born. People got married, people laughed and cried and played, people lived, people died. The serfs still toiled in the fields and lived in their hovels in the shadow of the castle walls.

"The Circle of Life," the Serf mused. Everything was the same, yet everything was different. It was like a veil had been lifted, like her vision had cleared, like she'd gotten a new set of senses through which to view the world.

Now the Serf saw the kingdom in a new light. She saw not warriors serving and protecting the kingdom, but sadists who enjoyed inflicting pain on others. She saw not lovers seeking to merge with each other and the Divine, but compulsives and addicts attempting to find an effective Eucharist but always falling short. She saw not magicians studying and analyzing, but detached manipulators possessing a special esoteric knowledge that they kept secret from the world and used only for their own advantage. She saw not happy serfs tilling the fields, but wretched souls toiling and slaving in abject misery, living in hovels in the shadow of the castle walls. She saw an abject and impoverished kingdom, full of pain, famine, hardship, and suffering. And above it all, she heard the roar of the Ogre Tyrant Queen.

Then she remembered something the Crone had told her about the state of the kingdom...

"What has happened to the kingdom!" cried the Serf. "And what have I done! Is this the reward for my diligence—to be able to see the poverty of my people and to recognize my own plight! What good does that do me! There is nothing I can do about it. I'm powerless, a victim of the system. I'm only a serf—smarter, maybe, more knowledgeable, wiser, but a serf nevertheless."

"Crone, where are you! Help me understand what has happened to the kingdom, what has happened to me." But the Crone was not there. She was gone, remember! She had passed along her knowledge and departed to wherever it is crones go after they impart what they have to teach. Leaving no further learning, no clue, no formula for what to do next, what to do with this knowledge and how to apply it in the world, how to take the next right step.

The Serf was miserable. Everywhere she turned, she saw the effects of her decisions, of her choices, of her situation. And nothing she saw pleased her. She knew there was something more, something better. She had seen it in visions while in the presence of the Crone. But where was it in reality! Certainly not here, not in this kingdom.

The Serf looked at the castle and spat a curse into the dusty soil. "Better to have stayed in ignorance," she muttered. "At least I'd be happy thinking everything was all right. I wouldn't know any better. Ignorance was bliss. And it still would be, because now that I know, now that my eyes are opened, so what! I'm still a serf, and unless there's an accident or chance event, I'm not even going to get close to the queen, let alone teach her or convince her to change her mind."

So the Serf made the only decision she could—to leave the kingdom. But then she paused.

"How can I leave!" she thought aloud. "I need to eat. To eat takes gold with which to purchase food. I need a place to live. To have one takes gold with which to purchase land or establish tenancy. I need to provide for myself and my family. To do so requires that I work and earn a wage, which I must use to purchase the necessities I need to survive—food, clothing, shelter.

"I cannot leave. And even if I could, with the little wealth I've managed to amass, where would I go! From this vantage point on the hill, I can see other kingdoms. They're all the same. Surely there must be other people like myself out there, other kingdoms. But where are they! Are they hidden! Are they far away! How do I find them!

"I have no map, no guidance. The Crone never told me about this. About what would happen after enlightenment, when I returned home and realized the plight I was in...my true state, the true state of the kingdom. She never told me how to deal with life in this kind of kingdom. She never told me how bad I'd feel once I'd recognized the truth. She never told me what to do. She just enlightened me. O cursed day!

"Better that I had never met the Crone. Then, at least, I never would have known how I was living or what I was missing. I'd be ignorant, like my fellow serfs. I'd be ignorant, but I'd be happy—fat, dumb, and happy.

"Why did the Crone do this! Why did she enlighten me and then move on! To what purpose, if I'm powerless to do anything about my plight! To what purpose if I cannot change the queen! To what purpose, if there is no escape! To what purpose...!

"Is the Crone irresponsible? Is the Crone a Shadow Crone herself? Is the Crone interested merely in personal gain or glory? To teach only to a certain point is irresponsible. To point out a problem or expose a wrong without offering a solution or an alternative is irresponsible. Yea, more than irresponsible—frustrating, painful, harmful.

"I am left in despair, hopeless and helpless. I see no way out, no hope, no light. I'm doomed to endless days of drudgery in the service of the Ogre Tyrant Queen, subjected to cruel and taxing laws designed to keep me bound and helpless and crushed under their weight. Left to decide for myself what the alternatives are. Can I pick up and go? How will I survive in the harsh and unfeeling world? Where will I go? Who will show me the way? Will I be all alone? Will I even survive? Am I even in my right mind?

"Crone, you did me no favors by enlightening me and then abandoning me when you did. I need more. I need alternatives. I need salvation. Or else I'm probably going to die—if not by being killed or working myself to death, then from my own frustration and broken heart. You have done me no favors, Crone. Better to have left me fat, dumb, and happy than lean, wise, and miserable.

"I hold you accountable, Crone. Even though you are not here, I expose your culpability, and I challenge you to come forth and take responsibility for your actions. You started this. It is up to you to finish it—one way or another—either by exposing the queen or by enlightening enough others to start a revolution—bloody though that may be—or by providing a new and better way that the queen and her minions will not be able to crush!

"There is my challenge to you, Crone, and to all crones and sages like you. Do not just teach! Do! Act! Build! Take the next right step. Come out of your inner sanctums and ivory towers and go forth into the world and create something new, something better, something safe, something based on the principles and philosophies that you preach and claim to value so highly.

"You can do it. You can lead the way and make the kingdom open and accessible to all who seek entry, regardless of caste or circumstance or wealth. Because that is the only way I see the old order being toppled. If you see it differently, come forth and say so. I challenge you. I dare you. You owe it to us, your students. It is the price of your wisdom—the responsibility and the challenge.

"I will stay at your side and co-create along with you. And I will bring along family and friends and helpers. You won't have to build alone, but you will have to roll up your sleeves and work with the rest of us. You'll have to do your part, and that may involve giving up some things, some luxuries...getting dirty hands and calluses, sweating, and—Heaven forbid!—laboring shoulder-to-shoulder with the rabble.

"Who will rise to the challenge? Who will heed my call? Who will be first? Who are motivated by greed, by the wealth that comes with the selling of spiritual truth, and who are motivated by a sincere desire to be part of the solution? Who are driven by the lust for power, status, and wealth? Who are fueled by love and really want to help?

"Where are the builders, the innovators, the creators? Where is the willingness to walk your talk? Where is the willingness to carry your words and teachings to the next step—action and implementation—away from the cloistered few in their ivory towers and out into the real world amongst the people?

"Which of you will use your great wealth and your great skills and talents to create something new, something that works for everybody—a new world existing, for the moment, side-by-side with the old, using what is right and good about the old to build a solid foundation for the new!

"I'm calling your collective bluffs, great Crones and Sages. Don't give me high and lofty words and then just walk away. Don't give me a little knowledge, take my treasure, and then abandon me for the treasure in my sister's purse. This can no longer be!

"It is time to take responsibility. Who will it be! Who will be first to offer the solution! Come find me. I have been seeking you long enough. Behold, I am right here, perched high on this rock for all to see. I am ready, willing, and able. Are you!"

So saying, the Serf heaved a great sigh, sat down on the rock, and waited.

*****

Later that day, the first day of spring, a day of balance—equal parts day and night—sitting alone on her deck, Cybele reread the story she had written, marveling at the wisdom of the Muse and its intuitive understanding of her situation. Having done her part, her anger was somewhat assuaged, although she was still bitter at having had this done this to her. "Like the Enlightened Serf, here am I with all this knowledge and learning and no one to guide me," she thought bitterly. And who better to blame than Lilith, who was ruled by arrogance and pride, who enjoyed being placed on a pedestal, having assumed the role of crone and believing it was hers to play always. In her mind, Cybele could hear the High Priestess's haughty words ringing through the hallowed halls of the Temple.

"I am the teacher, honor me. You are the pupil, know your place. We can never be friends. We can never be equals. If we were to become equals, then I could not be better than you, could I? I could not hold my power over you. No, I am not your friend!"

The result of such a philosophy of teaching and mentorship was an ever-widening gap between teacher and student and a forgetting of the sacred trust and responsibilities with which such a relationship was imbued. As she experienced these thoughts, Cybele paced back and forth, clenching and unclenching her fists in a series of futile gestures of frustration. Although she did not know it, she was about to move into a higher dimension of consciousness. She was standing on the threshold. And there on the threshold was where Doubt dwelt!

Feeling this potent force rise up to challenge her, Cybele recalled one of Sophia's many teachings. *"Doubt, that inhibitor, shamer, and spoiler who tries to damp out the fires of enthusiasm and hope before they can take hold and build to an unquenchable heat! It takes constant vigilance against this master deceiver, constant attention, constant refusal to give meaning or credence to the lies as they pass through one's mind."*

And so many lies there were! "What good is enlightenment and knowledge if all it brings me is misery?" Cybele asked to no one in particular. "I'm enlightened now. I know what a good queen is and what an ogre tyrant is. I serve an Ogre Tyrant High Priestess and cannot do anything about it. I'm powerless."

"The state of the kingdom is a direct reflection of the state of mind of the king and the queen. And the king and queen are ogre tyrants. So the kingdom is in disarray."

"And where is Sophia? Why has she abandoned me? I'm enlightened and powerless. There is nothing I can do. Why did I agree to be taught? Why did I follow the Crone along the path? Why did the Crone choose me to learn these truths? I can't do anything with them.

"I cannot change the kingdom. I cannot change Gadir or Belial or Lilith. I can only change myself, and changing myself has no effect on king or kingdom. No one notices, no one cares."

Then another thought flashed across her mind, a flicker really, of a forgotten truth...another teaching from Sophia, one of her first teachings, a simple truth, mighty in its effect. A truth that empowered whoever chose to embrace it.

MY THOUGHTS DO NOT MEAN ANYTHING.

THE ONLY MEANING THEY HAVE IS THE MEANING I GIVE TO THEM.

Cybele paused, breathing deeply and letting the truth of those words sink into her mind. She remembered Sophia's teaching. "Your thoughts are like the chattering of many monkeys. They do not represent your real thoughts; instead, they cover them up. Learn to separate the meaningful from the meaningless. See the meaningless as outside you, and see the meaningful within." Cybele had not understood this at the time, but she had practiced the lesson willingly. Sophia had explained that her understanding was not required for the lessons to have a positive effect. All that was required was willingness, and Cybele had plenty of that.

The sun had long since set, and the light was taking on a purplish hue, too dark to continue reading or writing. A few far-ranging sea birds were returning to their nests, having been fishing and soaring far out to sea. The water lapped gently at the edge of the veranda. Cybele sat back, closed her eyes, and let herself relax, recalling more of those early teachings.

"*Acceptance* is the key," she realized, listening to herself as she spoke, being both teacher and student at the same time. "I am disturbed by what I find unacceptable in my life, specifically Sophia's leaving and forcing me to be on my own. I will not experience serenity until I accept things exactly as they are, not as I want them to be." She knew what to do next.

"I let go and accept things as they are," the priestess prayed. "I ask in prayer for the desired outcome, and I believe in faith that my prayer is already answered. I ask for the Grace to receive and accept that answer. And I say thank you in advance for my highest good. For so it is."

Her orisons were interrupted by an eerie howl. The sound drifted down from the high place behind the dome and filled the air, echoing hollowly on the stone beneath her feet. It was a haunting sound, the baying of a she-wolf at the rising of the moon. Cybele turned her gaze to the hills behind her, and a joyous thrill surged through her body. There, silhouetted against a magenta sky, she saw the magnificent animal. The recognition was instantaneous, and Cybele knew instinctively that her prayer had indeed been answered. Wolf was calling her to Sophia!

CHAPTER 13

*Thou art blest among the planets
Blest beneath the feet
Of the dancing circle of women.*

—Lee Henderson

Atlanteans delighted in the telling of a good tale and took every opportunity to tell them and listen to them. Many tried their hand at storytelling, vying with each other to see who could tell the best story and produce an extreme emotional response in their audience, be it love, joy, sadness, or fear. All of this led to a culture rich in story and myth.

As a child in Atlantis, I heard many songs and poems, myths and legends, fables and folk tales. Some were jingles or rhymes, short love sonnets or simple folk tales. Others were parables and allegories—stories that taught a moral lesson and used symbolism and imagery to express truths about the human condition.

Some were pleasant tales filled with humor and joy and happy endings. These were the lighthearted stories, where righteousness triumphed and evil was subdued and vanquished. Others, though, were less pleasant. These were the dark tales, frightening, full of fire and brimstone, destruction and death, where evil ran rampant over a powerless and defenseless humankind.

There was a third category, too—tales of prophecy, superstition, and magic. Once they had been extremely popular, but as science and technology arose, these stories were cast aside and ignored, obscured and forgotten by all but a few practitioners of the occult and the arcane.

Such was the ancient prophecy of the coming of a dark period in the future of Atlantis—*the time when the Fathers fall asleep*—a dire prediction of the end of the Atlantean civilization. The origin of the prophecy was shrouded in the dimmest recesses of antiquity, from the time when giants roamed the Earth and grotesque mutants and aberrations prowled the land.

> And in their sleep, the Fathers will dream a Dream of arrogance, fear, destruction, and death. A Dream of power run amok, in which men rape and subjugate women and the Great Mother in their mad desire for dominance. A Dream in which they forget the complementary balance.
>
> A Dream in which they generate philosophical, social, and political systems that will affect not only Atlantis but also the world, all of civilization for thousands of years. A dream in which men—by force, direct pressure, or through ritual, tradition, law, language, customs, etiquette, education, and the division of labor— determine what part women will or will not play. A Dream in which the subordinate female is everywhere overwhelmed, swallowed up, and consumed by the dominant male.

I know this to be true. I watched the Fathers fall asleep. I saw the beginning of that terrible Dream. I saw it take hold and grow and swell and lead to the great burning and flooding and breaking up of the land.

Throughout the millennia, I have watched the birth and death, rise and fall of thousands of cultures. I have seen the all-pervasive power of the Dream influence our most basic ideas about human nature and about our relation to the universe—*man's* nature and *his* relation to the universe, in the language of the Dream.

How strong the hold of Patriarchy! The one system that, until recently, has never in recorded history been openly challenged. Its doctrines so universally accepted that they have been perceived to be the laws of Nature, and indeed, have always been presented as such.

*****

At the very beginning of the Dream, under the cloak of night, the women came together deep in the limestone Cave under the pine forest. These were the holy women, the keepers of the arcane knowledge. Young and old, they had gathered by the hundreds from all parts of Atlantis, using the straight paths and the tunnels, traveling in secrecy to this most sacred of gatherings.

Coming together from the four winds and the four points of the compass—North, South, East, and West. Gathering in a Circle, the Sacred Hoop, making the connection, establishing the link—one with another. Coming together to make a final stand. Coming together in preparation for the approaching storm. Coming together to gather the wisdom and preserve it through the Time of Tribulation and the long, dark ages of the Dream.

Cybele recognized several of them as she looked around the Circle. There was Eve, High Priestess of Lemuria. Beside her sat Gaia, spiritual leader of Mu. And of course the twins—Suonare, whose name meant *sound*; and Suristes, the Flute Player.

They had been talking quietly for several hours, stopping often to burn incense and meditate. The glow of a thousand beeswax candles illuminated the cavern, casting strange shadows on the walls and filling the room with a warm, ruddy light, which was reflected in their faces. Around them were all sorts of trinkets, amulets, and potions—sage, dried herbs, smudge pots, dream catchers, and natural essences.

At a signal from Sophia, the women fell silent, inhaling deeply and centering their thoughts on spiritual matters. Reaching out, they held hands in the traditional manner of attunement—palms lightly touching, left palm up in the feminine receptive, right palm down in the masculine giving. And so they formed a living, unbroken Circle, allowing the Dragon Current to flow uninterrupted from one to the other.

Softly, Suristes began playing her flute while a child drummed a gentle, steady cadence. Suonare raised her voice in a pure, clear chant.

> *Om mani padme hum*
> *Oma hum*
> *Om tao*

One by one, the others joined in, their voices rising in a hauntingly beautiful and harmonious blending of song in the Language of Light.

> *Hara Hara Gurudeva,*
> *Hara Hara Gurudeva,*
> *Parabrahma parameshvara,*
> *Parabrahma parameshvara,*
> *Hara Hara Gurudeva,*
> *Hara Hara Gurudeva,*

The chanting continued for a long while, sometimes rising, sometimes falling, like the ebb and flow of a great musical sea. Finally, Sophia rose and looked around at the Circle of faces. "Who are we?" she asked the assemblage. The flute and drum continued to play softly in the background.

"We are the seed bearers," Eve chanted in response.

"Why are we here?" Sophia asked the second question.

"We gather to discuss our part in the unfolding drama," Gaia sang from the Circle.

"Not to prevent the destruction, for we know it cannot be prevented," Suonare added. "Rather, to persevere and endure through it all."

For these women understood a great truth—that what seems to be subjugated and die does not die, indeed can never die. The Feminine cannot die; the Goddess cannot die; the Great Mother cannot die. They further understood that, while illusions might seem very real, they are, nevertheless, only illusions. Yet illusion wields great power over the uninitiated. Those who do not understand are caught up in its spell. They think the illusion real, and all of their behavior, thoughts, and emotions flow out of their belief in the reality of the Dream.

"What is our part?" Sophia asked the third question.

"It remains our task to carry the seeds and help the Fathers reawaken when the time comes," Eve replied. "To restore balance by reintegrating the feminine yin with the masculine yang in the sacred marriage."

"And who will guide us in this endeavor?" Sophia asked the fourth and last question.

"You, Sophia," came the unanimous response. "You will guide us, for you are wise and strong and capable of remaining whole and unharmed in the face of danger."

"No," replied the old woman. "I am too old to do this work. It is time to pass the Wand and anoint a younger woman—one of us, of like mind and enlightened consciousness—she who will go forth, seek out others of like mind, and *do*."

"Then let it be Cybele," Gaia pronounced. "She is courageous and pure of heart. She knows and respects the ancient ways. She has power, and she is highly favored by the Great Mother."

"No," Cybele protested, amazed that such an august assemblage would even consider her for such responsibility and entrust themselves to her leadership. "I am not the one you seek! I am weak and full of fear. I have many faults. I would run at the first sign of danger. What strength is there in me to stand up to the likes of Lilith and Belial?"

With each utterance, Cybele imagined all of her fears taking form and flowing out from inside her as wisps of sooty gray smoke. One by one, they built into a greasy black ball that hung suspended in the center of the Circle. The women remained silent and attentive. Cybele waited for a reaction, but none was forthcoming. "Am I imagining this," she wondered aloud, "or do you see it too? What is happening to me?"

As she was asking her question, a deep rumble reverberated throughout the Cave. The floor trembled for several seconds, and clouds of hissing steam rose from the cracks and fissures, which glowed a deep red as the unquenchable fires burned in the Heart of the Mother.

"The sign is given!" Eve declared. "The Mother has chosen you. She approves of you and has selected you to do her work. You cannot refuse."

"I cannot do the work alone," Sophia looked at the young woman whom she loved. "You are the chosen one. You do have the power. You know it in your heart. You can deny the truth if you choose, but it remains the truth nevertheless."

"You must make the choice," Gaia continued. "Are you willing to rise above your fear, above the mundane, and take on this sacred trust? For to you is given the task of confronting the dark side—the Shadow Feminine caught up in the dream of the Shadow Masculine."

Cybele took a deep breath and closed her eyes. This was the moment of reckoning. She *did* know it in her heart. This was what she had been preparing for all of her life. In a flash of insight, everything fell into place and she saw the meaning behind all that had befallen her over the years—her being orphaned, her youth under Sophia's tutelage, her coupleship with Adima and the birth of the twins, her rise as a priestess, her talents in the healing arts, her love of Nature and the Great Mother. Suddenly, Cybele knew Sophia's words were true, and she became quite willing to accept her role and do her part. Thus, with her willingness and acceptance, came the Transformation.

In the center of the Circle, the greasy black ball of doubt and fear burst into flames. The fire burned white-hot for several seconds, then fizzled out. All doubt and fear left her. The dark emotions just melted away, vanished into the nothingness from which they had come. Cybele had crossed the threshold! And in the emptiness left behind came new feelings...new, yet somehow familiar, as of something long forgotten and now remembered. As her heart opened, Cybele became attuned to the feelings of power and courage that rose within her.

"Come forth." Sophia took her by the hand and brought her into the center of the Circle. The women rose and gathered around her. "I anoint you with the Four Attributes of the Heart," Sophia said, dipping her finger in the holy chrism and tracing a circle on Cybele's forehead and overlaying it with two lines crossed at right angles. "I anoint you with Unconditional Love. I anoint you with Compassion. I anoint you with the Healing Presence. I anoint you with Innate Harmony."

A teenage girl stepped out of the Circle, carrying a silken pillow on which rested a golden Wand.

"Receive your allies." Eve placed the Wand in Cybele's hand. "This Wand of yew and hazel wood—gift of the Moon Goddess—contains the power to conduct supernatural forces. It will ensure your success."

A second young girl came forth, carrying a magnificent, shining Shield. Gaia placed it in Cybele's hands. "This magic Shield—gift of the Goddess of Wisdom—will protect you from all physical harm in the presence of the Shadow."

Sophia breathed on her three times. "Receive your new name, your new definition. Henceforth you will be called Latoné—the Swan—because you are at one with the Dreamtime. Trust always in your intuitive ability, in your ability to see the future, in your ability to heal and transform lives, and in the Divine protection of Spirit. For this is who you are."

Three times Eve breathed on her newly anointed sister. "Receive your new purpose, which is threefold. You represent the female side of the balanced Whole. As Adima, your male counterpart, goes forth to wage a mighty battle with Belial, so you must go forth to rescue the sacred Knowledge Crystals from their repository in the Holy of Holies deep inside the Temple of Poseidon. There will be a great confrontation with the Shadow Priestess, but you will prevail if you remain true to your faith."

Gaia continued. "In the time before you, you will direct the building of the Ark and oversee the gathering of the people and artifacts that are to be contained within its sacred belly. Before anything else, however, you must take the time to bring the twins into the mainstream of our culture. They are growing up. They must be initiated into the Mysteries. They also must go into the Temple of Poseidon and see the manifestation of the spiritual as it is encoded in that vast edifice. For the children are the future. They will build tomorrow, so they must have a solid foundation upon which to build."

"How important this is for balance!" Sophia went on. "How important this is to preserve all that is good and wholesome and valuable in Atlantis, to save it through the dark times, until the moment when the ancient wisdom is ready to be brought forth again! For when the time is right, your children's children's children, even unto the penultimate generation, will resow the seeds that have lain dormant for so long."

"Dormant, yes, but not dead," Suonare now spoke, nodding to her sister, who took up her flute and began to play. As Suristes' soft, haunting melody wafted through the air, Suonare closed her eyes and began to sing.

> The Seeds...
>> Lying deep underground
>> Through the cold, dark millennia,
>> Waiting for the right questions to be asked
>> To break the spell.
>
> The Seeds...
>> Waiting for the Sacred Lightning
>> To impregnate the Great Mother
>> And fertilize them once again
>> With the life-giving Dragon Current.
>
> The Seeds...
>> Waiting to be watered and germinate,
>> Waiting to break through their tough outer shells,
>> As the first green buds peek their heads through the black, fertile soil
>> And sprout forth their greenery in the new Golden Age.

It was a moment of deep tenderness. Sophia rose and walked to the mouth of a dark passageway. "And as we have sown the seeds here in the womb of the Great Mother this night, so now let us go forth to the surface and consecrate our work in the light of the moon."

In single file, the women walked up and out of the Cave, through the long and winding labyrinth and into the moonlight, into the sacred grove. Led by Sophia, they passed through the forest, white robes flowing, skin glowing pale in the filtered light, forming a fluid, silken line that threaded its serpentine way beneath a leafy bower of yew and sycamore, willow and pine.

Quiet, ever so quiet. Every creature of the night seemed to sense their passage and remained still, the only sound that of moving water as the trail followed an inland stream. Rising in the high country, it flowed clear and sweet in a long, meandering ride to the sea. The women came to a halt in a wide, grassy meadow beside a quiet spot where the water flowed calm and deep. A pure white Swan glided gracefully over the surface of the pond. Overhead, Grandmother Moon kept a silent lookout, while Wolf prowled the forest edge, all senses alert. No unwelcomed eyes witnessed their presence.

Sophia took Latoné by the hand and led her onto a fallen log that stretched out over the dark water. "Look into the reflecting pool," she instructed. "See your Self in its clear surface. Let the water show you who and what you are."

The younger woman looked at her own image in the calm, clear, dark water. She saw herself in the fullness of her being—woman, priestess, wife, mother.

"Now look below the surface and know your inner Self." Sophia tossed a pebble into the pool. It sank immediately, leaving rings of ever-widening ripples. "Allow your Moon subconscious to rise to conscious awareness."

As she watched in amazement, Latoné saw her reflection change. Suddenly, she was looking not at her self, but at the face of Lilith. Or was she? The light was dim and the differences were subtle indeed. Gaia broke the silence.

"Like the Moon, who has her dark side, her unseen aspect, so, too, Nature has a dark side, the eye of night. In this dark side, there is a dark one whom you must confront, a Shadow Priestess who mirrors for you your own dark side, your own Shadow. You are sensitive, receptive, and passive," Gaia continued, "but sometimes you are given to moments of lunacy. You experience extreme emotional shifts, swinging from great joy to heavy depression. At times, these feelings seem beyond your control, and you have difficulty taking charge of your life and breaking out of old habit patterns and stagnant situations. Through the meeting and the eating of your Shadow, you will complete these old patterns and relationships and move into a new way of being."

The priestess gazed into the water for a long while. Such intense emotion, such deep feeling. A whisper in her ear. She heard someone call her name.

"Latoné."

She looked around, but the women were too far away. There was no one present. Or was there? Like a miniature white moon, Swan floated gently beside the log. Was the Bird of Grace inviting her into the swirling black hole of the Dreamtime?

Closing her eyes, she stood motionless, listening and watching as a vision unfolded before her. She sensed a Presence with her, a mysterious Caller waiting patiently, its arms loaded with gifts, gifts for her. "So full are they, the Caller cannot contain them," she saw in her mind's eye. "They are spilling out and overflowing onto the ground." In a flash of understanding, Latoné realized the truth, and she spoke to the unseen Presence in her heart.

"You are here to deliver the gifts from Another. This is your purpose. But you have not been able to, because I would not open the door all these years."

"Yes," came the response. She did not so much hear the words as feel their vibration within her. *"I have been standing at the threshold for so many years, but you have not heard me knocking, ever so gently. So I knocked louder. When you did hear, you were afraid. You barred the door. You tried to drive me away. You made more noise to drown me out. But I am still here. I am with you now, at the door to your heart. I cannot go away until I deliver the gifts. I must fulfill my purpose, Priestess."*

"What is a priestess?" Latoné asked.

"Priestess is Seer," came the immediate answer. *"From your inner stillness and balance, you know the truth. You are Counselor, Wise One, Oracle. Receive the gifts of the Diamond Vision, which are yours to use in service to those who have been sent to you to care for as the Great Mother cares for you."*

As the Caller ceased speaking, Latoné held out her arms, her eyes still closed. The Dragon Current was strong in this place, flooding over her and filling her with warm, revitalizing energy. She felt different, changed...transformed somehow by this experience. The timid, reticent woman cowering behind the closed door of doubt and fear was no longer there. In her place stood a new woman—calm, cool, stoic, withdrawn...emotionally mature and very, very powerful.

Latoné sensed that the vision was almost at an end. She watched as the Caller sighed and turned its face back toward the east and home, back toward the Source of the gifts. For an instant, only an instant, the Caller remained motionless. Then it smiled and faded from her vision. Slowly, very slowly, Latoné became aware of herself standing on the log above the reflecting pool. Swan still floated beside her, its graceful neck fully extended, listening as the night sounds gently resumed...the crickets and katydids, even the far-off hoot of an owl.

"Thank you," she whispered, raising her head and opening her eyes as she made her way back to the stream bank. Someone had lit a huge bonfire, which burned brightly, making the clearing almost as bright as day. Once again, the priestess stood in the center of the Circle—her Circle—surrounded by the women who loved and supported her. She felt proud and honored to be of service to them and all of Atlantis. She felt a powerful urge to speak to them, a great longing to share her inmost feelings with her sisters.

"I am truly blessed," she said with all humility. "No longer am I a devotee or a follower, but an equal, a partner, a true daughter of the Great Mother. I am raised up. I am spiritually empowered. I accept the responsibility that has been entrusted to me and am willing to do what must be done."

The priestess raised the Wand, which sparkled in the firelight. Turning slowly around the Circle, she pointed it at each of the women while she spoke a prayer to the Great Mother. "Mine is the power of the Moon, for she is my ally, she who controls the tides, the rains, the waters, the floods, the seasons—hence, the span of life. Feminine power incorporates the rhythm of cyclic time. It is the Power of Becoming. Like the Moon, constantly waxing and waning, constantly changing, we are in the process of evolutionary change. It is the end of one cycle and the beginning of another. It is the waning of the Goddess and the Feminine and the waxing of the Patriarchy. Behold the Moon, bringer of change, suffering, and decay—humankind's future condition upon the Earth."

"Great Mother, let me learn from Swan," Latoné prayed. "Help me to be intuitive and feel out the truth. Help me to be aware of my flaws and draw power from that knowing. Help me, O Mother, to complete my work and move gracefully into the next new phase, along with all of my sisters and brothers. I know that feminine consciousness is lunar consciousness. I shall listen to what you tell me in my Moon dreams. I shall strive to think always with my heart, which transcends time. I shall strive to be in all times—past, present, and future. I shall strive to serve well."

Latoné looked around the Circle one more time. She spoke with great wisdom, great knowing, great feeling, great power. She brandished her Shield. A million miniature rainbows sparkled in its metallic surface, sending tiny dots of light forth to dance on the faces of the women. Placing her hands on her heart, she bowed her head and spoke one last word to honor the presence within each of the women. "Namasté."

A shout rose from each throat, joyful, spontaneous, full of enthusiasm. The solemnity of the experience had passed, and the women moved into the passion of the dance. Round and round they danced in the firelight, embracing each other, singing the old songs.

"Now, child, speak to me of anything that has transpired here tonight." Sophia urged gently as she and Latoné sat beneath an ancient sycamore tree and watched the celebration. Overhead, the stars twinkled with their diamond-fire brilliance against a blue-black backdrop of eternal night. The smell of night-blooming jasmine scented the air.

"I have but one question," Latoné replied, reaching out to take her beloved teacher's hand. "When will the Fathers awaken?"

Sophia closed her eyes and spoke softly. "I see a time when the disintegration of the Patriarchy will come, a time when the ability and the desire to practice the gentle arts will be reborn. Like the phases of the moon, the cycle will come full circle, from death to resurrection and rebirth—perpetual renewal and enlightenment. But that time is far in the future.

Behold Grandmother Moon and learn from her. Like the moon, ever changing, so too are the stages and cycles of life. We are moving into the stage of the sinister, demonic Waning Moon, away from the light into darkness of the New Moon. There is much to be accomplished, as individuals and as a race, before we move back toward light, growth, and regeneration during the stage of the Crescent and Waxing Moon. Then, a long time from now, so far in the future, yet only a moment away, with the rising of the Full Moon will come renewal and enlightenment...wholeness, completion, strength, and spiritual power."

COMMUNITY

CHAPTER 14

If there is but one force which feeds the root of pain, it is the refusal to learn beyond the moment.

—Clarissa Pinkola Estes

In the *Book of Life*, it is written that:

COMMUNITY IS A CAUSE WHOSE EFFECT IS HEALING.

It is further written that:

THE MORE RELATED PEOPLE ARE TO COMMUNITY,
THE MORE COHESIVE THEIR SELF IS.
CONVERSELY, THE MORE ISOLATED THEY FEEL,
THE MORE FRAGILE THEY BECOME.

The Children of the Law of One knew this truth and therefore followed a group social process that was grounded in *Community*. If you were to ask them define themselves, they would say, "We are people who are on the path of personal growth—spiritual beings, self-maintained and self-maintaining."

They lived singly and in families, alone and in groups, in the cities or at the seashore or in the hills, in every part of the Atlantean realm. Yet, if you were to ask them where they lived, they would say, "We live in a City of Light that is but one part of a much greater Whole—a vast global community." Not buildings and machines, but something so much more. Their community was a family of people who shared the same Source, were on the same Path, and who were consciously aware of this fact. Theirs was a way of life whose founding principle was Love.

Of course, it had not always been so. The Children of the Law of One had come into being because, centuries ago, the King and Queen of Atlantis—two loving people who measured wealth in gold, jewels, and precious metals—saw scarcity, poverty, and lack everywhere in their lives. But rather than succumb to the illusions of false perception, they had the courage to go forth on a journey to seek a great treasure, which they would bring home to share with everyone. Dressed as Esopa the Bard, Adima liked to tell the tale as a reminder to the Children of the Law of One of the way they had once been and how far they had evolved.

"Lest we forget!" he would begin, taking up his drum and calling the people to gather around him. His voice rang loud and clear, and he smiled deeply, for this was the happiest of stories.

> Once upon a planet, in a kingdom that shone like an emerald at the edge of a sparkling sea, there lived a King and Queen who were feeling rather poor— not "poorly," for this isn't a story about health—but "poor," for this is a story about wealth. There was much about their kingdom by the sea that they loved—the land, the flowers, the fragrant breezes, the salt air, the clear bright sunshine by day, the balmy starry nights, and above all, each other.
>
> But often as they walked through their kingdom, they thought about how lacking it was in substance, especially when they compared it with other kingdoms. The castle walls weren't thick enough; the moat wasn't deep enough; the banquet hall wasn't pretty enough; the coffers weren't full enough; the army wasn't mighty enough; their cloaks, scepters, and crowns weren't dazzling enough;

their resources weren't plentiful enough; their status among other kings and queens wasn't high enough.

Seeing scarcity in all these places, the King and Queen determined to set things right, each in his own way. They made elaborate plans for restoring and revitalizing the kingdom and themselves. They were full of grand schemes. Ideas came one after another.

"If only I can do this. If only I can do that. If only we can do this other thing," they thought. "Then we would be prosperous!"

So they planned and schemed down to the smallest of details. The King sought out allies who would add their vast resources to his meager ones, thus enabling him to fulfill goals he would otherwise not be able to fulfill (he thought). The Queen did likewise, seeking to expand her contacts and increase her skills and resources. Ever restless, they moved throughout the kingdom, scattering seeds wherever they thought they might spring up and bear fruit. Yet one after another, their grand visions fell by the wayside. The seeds they planted began to sprout, then turned brown and withered away. Allies came and went, never staying long enough to make a difference.

"What am I to do!" cried the Queen in despair.

"What am I to do!" cried the King in despair. "I have strong warriors, I have wise counselors, I have loyal subjects, I have a loving Queen, but my coffers are empty. How can I be a good King if I cannot support my kingdom! An Ogre Tyrant would raise taxes or wage war. But I am not an Ogre Tyrant. Therefore, these are not options for me. What am I to do!"

One day, in the midst of their worries, a messenger arrived from an ancient, fabled land far to the north. In this land, in a great Ivory Tower surrounded by a wide moat and a deep forest, there dwelt a wizard. Great was his reputation; powerful was his magic. He had sent his messenger with an offer of a gift to the King and Queen.

"Great King, great Queen," said the messenger, "I bring you greetings from my master and a great and wonderful gift. It is a magnificent jewel, the 'Pearl of Great Price' of which the legends speak."

"Splendid," cried the King in delight, thinking that his problems were solved and that soon the kingdom would be restored to prosperity. "Show me this precious jewel."

"I do not have the treasure," replied the messenger. "It is with my master."

"What must we do to receive it, then!" asked the King.

"Simple," replied the messenger. "My master invites you and your Queen to come and live with him. There, in the innermost recesses of the Ivory Tower, my master will reveal to you the mysteries of the universe and teach you how to unlock their secrets. After that, the jewel will be yours."

When the messenger had departed, the King and Queen went into counsel. Great was the decision before them. The jewel would solve all of their prosperity needs and help them meet all of their goals. But in order to get it, they would have to leave their kingdom and rebuild it in a new land.

They sought the counsel of many advisors, explaining the wizard's offer and describing the grand vision they had seen. So beautiful was the picture they described, so real and exciting did they make it seem, that each advisor was also caught up in the enchantment. Each said the same thing, "It feels right. Do what is in your hearts."

So the King and Queen looked into their hearts, and they made their decision. For such a jewel of great value, they would uproot themselves, leave the kingdom, travel to the north, and abide in the new land. The Queen would learn from the wizard, while the King would follow his bliss and expand his contacts with other kings and wise men. When the learning was complete and the jewel presented to them, together they would build a new kingdom, although where they did not yet know.

And so, at dawn on the third day, they summoned the messenger before them. "We will accept your master's offer," declared the Queen. "We will arrive in your land three months hence. At that time, let the learning begin."

It was a long story whose telling required several hours. First, Adima spoke of the *Preparation*, a time of much hustle and bustle, a time of good-byes and emptying out and closing of the castle. This was followed by the *Journey* itself, a great adventure during which the King and Queen saw many wonderful sights. Each land had its own unique foliage and wildlife. Local villagers turned out to greet them. All along the way, they were entertained by the singing and dancing of minstrels. They were fed and lodged in comfortable wayside inns. All whom they met were kind, friendly, and eager to make them as comfortable as possible.

Then came the *Initiation*, when the King and Queen, having crossed the threshold into the strange new land, learned to their dismay and horror that the wizard wasn't really a wizard after all, and that the treasure wasn't really a treasure after all.

That was a time of great trial and tribulation, in which the royal couple experienced the terrors of the "DARK NIGHT OF THE SOUL," as it was described in the *Book of Life*, and initiated into community. It the cold, gray light of dawn, however, they made the right choices and passed the final test. Instantly, the spell was broken, the enchantment was lifted, and there at their feet, lay a sparkling jewel.

"What enchantment?" Adima was often interrupted by spellbound listeners asking this question.

"The enchantment that caused our ancestors to believe that wealth and prosperity are determined by material possessions and symbols of status," he replied. "When they recognized that it wasn't the jewel that was going to make them prosperous, their eyes were opened. They had been blinded by focusing first only on their lack, and then only on the jewel. They had been oblivious to all of the wealth around them, the wealth they already had!"

So they returned home with their new-found understanding, their minds and hearts having been opened. Calling forth the whole kingdom and convening the Sacred Circle, the King and Queen told their story.

"We thought we were poor, that there wasn't enough. We believed in scarcity. We wanted the outward trappings of wealth and prosperity and status and power. What we had wasn't good enough. We saw lack everywhere. So we abandoned what we had and went in search of a great treasure that would fill our coffers and meet all of our needs and desires, a treasure that would bring us wholeness.

"What we have learned is that we already have the prosperity we've been seeking. It has been ours all along. Wealth is not measured in gold, land, or power. It is measured in family and friends and community, in health, and in peace of mind. It is measured by our love for you and your love for us. With these as our measurements, our kingdom is abundantly prosperous.

"We tried to discard the old and go forth and create something new. We thought it could only be done in the north in the presence of the wizard. Now we know that we are all wizards, we are all co-creators. We need only summon the "Magician Within" with good intentions.

"Sometimes we are offered things that seem to have great value. We're tested or challenged, just to see how we will react to and work with the experience. Sometimes we have to act things out, as we just did. Over the past three months, we and others played many roles—Lover, Warrior, Magician, Wizard, Destroyer, Caregiver, Orphan, Innocent, Sage, Priestess, Fool. In those roles, we had many experiences, and we had to make difficult decisions, even when it meant letting go of a dream or creative venture that no longer served us so we could make room for something new.

"We could have gone into the Shadow World and tried to force things to work out in an unnatural way. But instead, we embraced our inner Darkness alone and sought to find our inner Truth. We stayed with the experience, we had a high spiritual awakening, and we received a great treasure. Now we can share that treasure with you. It is our gift to you, a gift that will never fade, never run out. It is a new consciousness of prosperity, a new view of abundance, a new appreciation of the individual, the family, and the community. It is about supporting and nurturing each other and honoring each other's worth, value, purpose, and walk along the path.

"We began with feelings of loneliness, fear, and deception. Now those feelings have been transformed into feelings of connectedness, calmness, clarity, and confidence. We will be experiencing the effects of this adventure for a long time. More and more will unfold. It is a never-ending process on a journey toward wholeness and completion. We shall keep you informed."

With those final words, the King and Queen arose and walked around the circle, touching each person and looking into their eyes. Not a word was spoken. The only sounds were of soft breathing and the crackle of the bonfire. After a time, one by one, everyone made their way home, each taking a personal bit of the story and the treasure to hold in their hearts."

Such was the myth of *The Founding of the Children of the Law of One* so long ago. Such was their creed, their philosophy, their way of being and living. Such was the solid foundation upon which their community was built—permanent, stable, reliable. Such a community, though, was in direct opposition to another community in Atlantis—that of the Sons of Belial. Seemingly unaware of their spiritual nature, they were more than content to stay at their present level of fragmented emotional and social development.

The destruction of Atlantis occurred for many reasons. One of these was stagnation, an unwillingness on the part of many to continue to search, seek, and expand themselves. For some it was fear and ignorance that kept them thus; for many, though, it was unwillingness. For growth often brings pain and change, and it always requires willingness and courage.

The Sons of Belial were quite proud of their present state of growth. They had made great technological advances. They had social and political prestige. They existed quite happily by exercising the power and control they had achieved. The thought of seeking something spiritual, something higher, never occurred to them. What could be better than complete political and social supremacy?

They ignored the admonition in the *Book of Life*:

UNIVERSAL LAW DICTATES THAT ONE CANNOT STAND STILL. ONE IS EITHER GOING IN ONE DIRECTION OR ANOTHER. WHEN ONE ATTEMPTS TO STAND STILL, HE IS ACTUALLY GOING BACKWARD, TOWARD THE EXPRESSIONS OF NEGATIVITY, DOUBT, EGO, AND PERSONALITY-CONTROLLING THOUGHTS.

As a result, as time passed, their way of thinking and living became increasingly distorted. Not so, however, with Adima and Cybele, who took much delight in learning, viewing it as a treasure of great worth.

"Seek new ideas and experiences," Adima taught the twins. "Relish them. Bite into them. Taste them and savor them for their own sake, for the sheer joy of the experience. For to do so is to move beyond the present moment, beyond the present knowing, thereby becoming, as the *Book of Life* describes it:"

> A VALUED LOVER,
> A VALUED PARENT,
> A VALUED FRIEND.

And so, through myth and ritual and storytelling, the Children of the Law of One never forgot. They continued to grow and evolve toward a higher state of living, a higher state of consciousness. They continued to live in harmony and cooperation, with family and community at the center of their lives. While outside, in the world of the Sons of Belial, the night grew darker and colder, and the wind screamed fiercely.

CHAPTER 15

Tis the gift to be simple, tis the gift to be free.
Tis the gift to come down where you ought to be.
And when you find yourself in the place just right,
It will be in the garden of love and delight.

—Traditional Shaker Hymn

Like the great Atlantean alchemists, philosophers, and geomancers, the Children of the Law of One believed that to know something, really know it, was to be able to express it mathematically. If a thing could not be measured or expressed in numbers, it could not truly be known.

On the first page of the *Book of Life*, it was written that:

AT THE TIME OF CREATION, THE MAKER OF THE WORLD FIRST LAID DOWN A PATTERN OF NUMBER, FROM WHICH ALL ELSE PROCEEDED. NUMBER IS THUS REGARDED AS THE FIRST ARCHETYPE, OR PARADIGM, OF NATURE.

To the ancient philosophers and founders of Atlantis, this knowledge was obvious:

CERTAIN NUMERICAL COMBINATIONS APPEAR EVERYWHERE...IN EVERY NATURAL FORM OF GROWTH AND MOVEMENT, IN ALL THE GREAT CYCLES AND PATTERNS OF NATURE.

"So," they reasoned, carrying the wisdom to its logical conclusion, "those patterns must express essential and fundamental truths. Therefore, we must identify them and set them up as models in the conduct of human affairs."

The Children of the Law of One expressed the essence of their nature and philosophy by using the sacred geometrical symbol of the six-pointed star, formed by joining two sacred triangles that represented the opposites—male and female, lower and Higher Self, Earth and Heaven, microcosm and macrocosm—in the center of which lay a Rayed Sun and a Flaming Heart.

This symbol, then, served as the visual representation of one of the great truths recorded in the *Book of Life*:

WE ARE CREATURES OF DUALITY. WE ARE COMPRISED OF TWO PARTS; WE HAVE A BODY, AND WE ALSO HAVE A SOUL. JUST AS IT IS IMPORTANT TO NOURISH AND CARE FOR OUR BODIES, SO ALSO IS IT ESSENTIAL TO CARE FOR OUR SOULS IN ORDER TO MAINTAIN THE ESSENTIAL BALANCE BETWEEN THE TWO.

To the Children of the Law of One, the human heart was the center of life—the life of an individual and the life of the universe. The heart was the Center of Being, both physical and spiritual. All things radiated out from the Center and returned to the Center. Any thing without a Center was not a complete thing. Any person without a Center had nothing. To be lost was to not know where your Center was.

*****

There was a place in Atlantis, a garden that surrounded the Temple of Poseidon, where the Children of the Law of One came to attend to their spiritual needs—a sacred place—the Garden of the Heart. They believed that this garden was situated on the exact

Heart Chakra of the Earth as it was at that time, having been planted there by the founders of Atlantis in the dim and distant past.

Gardening had special significance for the Children of the Law of One, not only helping them stay connected to Nature and the Great Mother, but also for reminding them of the source and destination of their physical bodies. They believed that a garden was not limited by its physical borders; it's influence extended far beyond its apparent boundaries.

The *Book of Life*, too, stressed the importance of the "garden" metaphor.

> LIKE THE FIRST HUMANS—THE GARDENERS—IN EVERY ATLANTEAN DISTRICT,
> THE LOCAL INHABITANTS ARE REQUIRED TO TEND THEIR PART OF THE EARTH,
> EACH ACCORDING TO ITS ASTROLOGICAL CHARACTER.

Like the Temple of Poseidon itself—indeed, like all of Atlantis—the Garden of the Heart was laid out according to a cosmic scheme that included hidden patterns of sacred geometry. To the Ancients, the number *four* had special significance. It was the basis of wholeness; it was how everything was built. There were four seasons, four directions, four Attributes of the Human Heart—Unconditional Love, Innate Harmony, Compassion, and the Healing Presence.

The garden, therefore, embodied this theme—a circle divided into four quadrants, depicting the vast landscape of Atlantis in miniature, its hills, mountains, rivers, and oceans reduced to small rock clusters, green hillocks, streams, and pools. Poetry in physical form, enchanting the eye with gentle curves, the ear with soft breezes and trickling waterfalls. Thus, as was written in the *Book of Life*...

> THE MIND, SUSCEPTIBLE TO THE HIDDEN PROPORTIONS OF THESE INFLUENCES,
> IS SOOTHED BY THE UNITY AND TRANQUILITY OF THE HOLY CENTER.

From the heart of the garden, a spring welled up from unknown depths to form a pool from which branched four streams, each carrying the lifeblood of Atlantis toward the four cardinal points of the compass. Rooted in the depth of the Earth in the midst of the pool was an ancient evergreen tree, joining the three worlds of Heaven, Earth, and Water and making communication between them possible. Forever green, the tree was a symbol of everlasting life, undying Spirit, and immortality...nourishing, sheltering, protecting, supporting, like the Great Mother herself.

Built by the Ancients as a labor of love, the garden's harmonious influences were immediately apparent to all who visited there, for it had been built according to the Ideal set forth in the *Book of Life*.

> USING THE NUMBERS, RATIO, AND ANGLES OF TERRESTRIAL GEOMETRY, THE
> GARDEN THUS BECOMES THE EMBODIMENT OF THE SECRET RULES OF POETRY
> AND AESTHETICS, WHICH WE KNOW TO BE BEYOND RATIONAL EXPRESSION.

And so it was. There in the Garden of the Heart, the mathematical rules of the universe were made visible to people in the form of beauty. It was a place of strong Dragon Energy!

As often as not, the garden was referred to by its other name—the Garden of Eros. For it was the God of Love who watched over and protected lovers in Atlantis. Eros! So he was named in Atlantis, so he was remembered one hundred centuries later in Greece, so he is still called by children as they learn the myths of the gods and goddesses.

The Children of the Law of One learned to love by calling forth the lover in themselves. Under Eros' tutelage and auspices, they learned how to step out of what they called *"the head-wisdom of reason"* and invoke the *"central wisdom of feeling."* This was a learning that they considered of utmost importance. It could not be denied if they were to avoid a death without rebirth. It was one of the earliest lessons that Adima and Cybele had learned as children, and it was one of the earliest lessons that they taught their own children. When the twins would come to them for advice and ask, "What do you think we should do?" Adima and Cybele would reply, "What do you *feel*? What does your heart tell you?"

And while Adima and Cybele were learning these lessons for themselves and passing them along to their children, they were also learning them for all of Atlantis. Under the protection of Eros, they embraced his teachings, his ways. They were willing to be taught by him. They let themselves be taught by him. The lovers' connection to each other was strong, so close that the thought of losing it brought intolerable pain to them both. As Cybele wrote in her journal...

> Eros wakes us up to feel suffering—our own and that of the Earth, the Great Mother—and enables us to go forth in service to her and to the global community of which we are a part.

In his own journal, Adima added...

> It is love that motivates us to more aliveness, to act in the service of life. Before going out and doing the important work of service, Cybele and I found love.

*****

I am telling you this story of Atlantis because it is, first and foremost, a Love Story—a story of motherly love, erotic love, romantic love, compassion, forgiveness, grace. It is a story of physical and emotional love between men and women. It is a story of the selfless love of people in service to others. It is a story of the spiritual love of the Children of the Law of One for the Great Mother. And it is a story of the unconditional love between Spirit and Matter.

Do not forget this. Do not get so caught up in the excitement and the drama of the characters and their adventures that you forget to look deeper into the story and thus miss the larger picture. For the creation of the universe itself is the greatest of all love stories, the love between the two eternal partners, Father Love and Mother Truth—lovers, friends, co-creators—the parents of the universe. It is the greatest of love stories because from this union comes all other unions, and thus, all other love stories.

Imagine the two lovers together, roaming the universe and the universe of universes—playful, passionate, creative. Experiencing joy and pleasure beyond description. Unlimited by time, for there was no time. Unlimited by space, for they moved with the speed of thought. Creating life where before there was no life.

Listen as I tell you their story. Close your eyes and let the words enter into your heart, for this is the story of your parents. It is the story of your conception and birth.

> In the beginning of all worlds, long ago, yet still, the Eternal One Is. Beyond temporal distinction, above location, behind all manifestation, is the All, the Totality, the Holy Source and Creator of all that later came.
>
> One face of the Eternal One is ever formless and beyond definition, but the other face of the Eternal One appears as Two. These Two, between them, are the source of all created things.
>
> Holy Mother, Truth—
> All Matter is Her body, the Earth is Her eye.
> Holy Father, Love—
> The Stars are His flesh, Spirit His I.
>
> Two lovers, two friends, intelligent partners. Between them, the Universe lives suspended. Through them, all things are created and maintained.
>
> And so it came to pass that the Eternal One knew form and duration through the graceful crystalline structures of Truth that clothe the Eternal Feminine, the Beautiful One, in material form. And it likewise came to pass that the same Eternal One assigned all energy to the suns and brought Love to animate the stars.

And the stars loved Matter. And Matter loved the stars. Great was their exchange, wondrous and pleasurable the times and ranges of their interaction. Together they enjoyed the passionate transformations of Matter into energy that occur on stellar surfaces, and together they enjoyed slower, elongated forms of planetary interaction.

Eons elapsed. And eons again. Enjoyable beyond description, through description. Together they created. Through a body of interwoven galaxies, a body of countless stars, the loving relationships of Love and Truth took many forms.

Through the stars, the Father knew Matter. Together on the surface of her planets, Father and Holy Mother created crystal life, molten lava liquid stone life, snow creatures, smoke beings, mountain and ocean life. On the surface of the stars, they created leaping fire life, gas life, liquid living metal creatures...leaping far into space—exploding, wonderful life.

But where they created together on her planets, the life was excessively material. The intelligence of Spirit could not reside in such life. And where they created together on the stars, the life was excessively stellar, flickering, not long in any form.

Matter enjoyed life most when it was consistent and durable, when Her intelligence could live inside the life and look through it and understand. Spirit enjoyed life that was volatile, animated, passionate, life that Spirit could love within, flow within, from form to ever-changing form.

Animation, Spirit's forte. Duration, the strength of Matter.

And then the Idea came—the Idea! Something between Spirit and Stone, between Starlight and Stardust, a slow form of combustion, fluid flowing structure, blending the natures of them both. Spirit in durable form. Matter inspired. The Idea!

It was on the third planet from a star on one of the outward spiraling arms of the galaxy known as the Milky Way that they first began to work on the new project, there that biological life first appeared in the crucible of their mutual attention. But it was more than biological life that the two eternal partners had come there to produce—it was a Child, a new kind, a third, an equal, one capable of knowing both the intelligence of Matter and the intelligence of Spirit as its own.

And yet, it was more than this. For there was only One who could take up the body of this Child, this biological blending, and make it live.

And it came to pass that the Eternal One spoke to the two eternal partners and said:

"It is right that you should conceive this idea, for I would clothe myself in a body half star, half stone, that through that body, I might commence a Second Stage of Universal Creation.

The Universe you know now is but the egg, the seed. It is right that you should conceive this biological one. You have my blessing. When the time is full, I will arise in the Child."

Creator in Creation, clothed in mortal flesh, birthed of one star and one sacred stone.

One body.

A healthy living organism. Being. Continuously renewed. Matter flowing through. Spirit flowing through. Love continuously crystallizing in the sacred geometry of biological Truth. Cellular. Personal. Planetary. Biological Truth.

Conscious and intelligent. A single Creator, dressed in substance half stellar, half material.

This is the purpose to which the energies of the Universe are—and have been—directed!

Some love stories end in death. Tragedy occurs because the lovers and their surrounding communities are not able to find a way for love to blossom and grow within that community. That is what happened in Atlantis.

It was quite simple, really. For many in Atlantis, love stopped blossoming and growing as it once had. Some simply lost interest, others looked outward for answers and comfort, seeking to get their needs met through their labors, in relationships, on holiday, accumulating possessions, or misusing food, drink, or the healing herbs. They stopped taking the time to love, and so they forgot how. And with the forgetting came a shriveling and drying up of the Love Spirit. They were too caught up in the material side of things, too worldly and out of balance, imprisoned in the physical, ensnared in the Spell of Matter.

How will this love story end, this story of the love between the two eternal partners? Will it produce joy and laughter, ending in marriage that unites not only the lovers, but the whole community? What will happen to the global community? What will be born through the loving union of the two eternal partners, Spirit and Matter, Love and Truth?

Denial of Eros has led, then and now, to a culture that is unable to see the connection between the ravagement of the Great Mother and its own capacity to survive and for its people to live enjoyable, vibrant lives. The Goddess and Nature religions of Atlantis celebrated both death and rebirth. The fertility cycle and the Dragon Festival were about love, death, *and* rebirth.

Learn this lesson well. Learn what Adima and Cybele and the Children of the Law of One knew but were unable to pass along to their global village. Learn it and grow from it, even though the Atlanteans could not. Move forward, even though the Atlanteans could not. Do things differently. Do not make the same mistakes the Atlanteans did. Listen and learn and remember and attend and act.

For if there is one message that Adima and Cybele could pass along through time, it would be this one from the *Book of Life*:

> LET GO OF THE PAST AND YOUR OLD WAYS OF THINKING AND DOING THINGS, AND OPEN UP TO REBIRTH. EMBRACE LOVE. WAKE UP AND MOVE AWAY FROM A DISCONNECTED WAY OF LIVING. EXPERIENCE THE SACRED IN THE MUNDANE. GET CONNECTED. MAKE A COMMITMENT, NOT JUST TO LOVE YOUR OWN LOVED ONES, BUT TO LOVE ALL OF HUMANITY AND THE COSMOS.

CHAPTER 16

Love is the spiritual food of the Soul...To live by love is to accept that all love—however profane or however spiritual—is a gift.

—Carol S. Pearson

They lay together in each other's arms—two lovers, male and female, united as one. Sun Man, Moon Woman, alike and different, individual and couple. "Together again," Adima thought to himself, not wanting to break the silence. "Reborn in each other's arms. We have returned to the comfort and safety of home after a time of trial and ritual and testing in the world."

They had returned that morning, Adima from the high places, Cybele from the Cave. Back from having done their individual work—the work of the man, the work of the woman. Having done this independently, with other men, with other women. As is the Way.

They breakfasted on fresh fruit and muffins, then bathed, changed clothes, napped, and refreshed their physical bodies. It was late afternoon when they came together as husband and wife.

"We have been apart for a long time," Adima sighed as he turned and gently drew Cybele closer to him. "Now we are back in the bosom of family. Two as one again, but only for a time." Her skin was smooth and warm, almost hot as she pressed close to him. Her smell was familiar, comfortable yet highly erotic. They made love passionately and with great power. With orgasm, with the surrender of control and suspension of the ego, came passion, bliss, ecstasy, oneness.

They lay together for a night and part of the next day, speaking but little, reveling in each other in the blissful silence. Sharing a deeper knowing than language could give, communicating through the Language of the Heart. Putting aside their individual identities, putting aside their fears and doubts and questions, the two became one—Adima and Cybele, man and woman, husband and wife.

Each had so many unanswered questions. Each wondered what the other had been doing. Each was concerned for the safety and well-being of the other. Each wanted to hear the other's story. Yet they paused before asking, before speaking, taking time out first to connect with the Beloved, to seek spiritual bliss and union, to care for and feed their souls. In their sexual union, in their physical intimacy, they let themselves be vulnerable and trusting. More than the mere satisfaction of physical desire, each sought something more— closeness, knowing and being known. For just as their bodies needed nourishment, so also did their souls. So, laying armor and defenses aside, undressing and coming together, they let their souls drift gently down to rest upon the Mother's bosom.

*****

Relaxed and refreshed, sipping tea outdoors in the warmth of mid-afternoon, it was time to speak of things unspoken. It seemed so long since their last conversation in that setting, on the day of the Dragon Festival, yet less than a year had passed. Much had happened, and there was much still left to accomplish. Adima was the first to speak.

"So much to do, so little time!" There was a sense of urgency in his tone. "On the one hand, I feel quite confident. For the first time in my adult life, I know who I am and what I'm about. I'm balanced and whole, as much king as warrior, lover, and magician. I'm a man, not a boy masquerading as a man, but a mature man, with real talent and real responsibility."

He looked out at his beloved lagoon and watched the twins frolicking in the water with a pair of dolphins. "That's when I think I'm not ready for this," he sighed, shaking his head. "I'm close, but there's still so much more to do. I don't know quite what Enoch has in store, but he's hinted that it is to be the final stage of my learning before I address the Council." Adima sipped his tea. "He also said that on that day, things will begin to accelerate. From then on, events will happen one on top of the other, many simultaneously."

"Being prepared is the key," he repeated Enoch's words to his wife. "We must have everything ready beforehand, so we can do exactly what we need to do. Timing will be critical. And," he closed his eyes and took a deep breath, "the time is fast approaching when you and I must separate once again."

Cybele drew closer to her husband, gently placing her hand on his arm. On such a beautiful day, with the twins playing nearby and the warm sun shining on them, it was hard to imagine the dark times of which Enoch and Sophia constantly spoke. Yet she knew they were coming, and very, very soon. "How do you feel about that?" she asked Adima the familiar question. It was the opportunity he needed, and he let his innermost feelings pour out, the words tumbling over one another, releasing all of the doubt and anxiety. Voicing the fear, he thereby divested it of its power over him.

"If I let myself," Adima concluded, rising to his feet, "I could become terrified about this. You know, it's funny. Even after all the years I've known Enoch and have been working with him, even after all the things I've discovered about myself and my place in the universe, even after all of that, I don't think I've gotten rid of a single fear. Not completely, anyway," he chuckled.

Cybele smiled with him as he continued. He is so much stronger now, she thought. So much wiser and calmer, even in the face of such pressures and dangers. The boy she had fallen in love with was still there, behind the graying hair, dark complexion, and wrinkles, peering out from those coal-gray eyes. Here, though, was also a man—*her* man, standing straight and tall before her—formed from a combination of the elements of the Great Mother, his body from the Earth with its fiery heat, his blood from the water, his breath from air.

"The only difference," Adima's eyes twinkled, "is that at one point in my life the fears were monsters before whom I trembled, waiting for them to devour me or drive me insane. Now, though, they're just old friends over for tea. And let me tell you," he laughed, sitting once again, "there's a big tea party going on inside my head right about now. It's a conundrum, really. All is progressing nicely and on schedule; I just don't know where I'm going."

Sensing his need for soothing, Cybele reached into a pocket and produced a small, polished stone. "Take this rose quartz," she handed the crystal to her husband, "as a remedy for your heartache and a reminder to move slowly. We only need to worry about today. Yesterday is gone, tomorrow has not yet come. And when the dark times do come, we will divide the labor. For now, though, we must spend as much time as we can resting."

Adima accepted his wife's gift gratefully. He knew the Heart Stone well, having given it as a gift long ago to one whom he would come to love and trust with all of his own heart.

Out in the lagoon, Charis laughed merrily as her brother tried to balance himself on the back of a swimming dolphin. He managed to stay upright for a few seconds, but as soon as the animal began to swim, the boy tumbled into the water. Cybele watched him for a while, laughing with him, pleased by his determination. It is good to laugh, she thought. There isn't much laughter in Atlantis any more. And if her priestess-intuition was any indicator, she doubted that the future held much to be merry about.

Dreams, meditations, the Voice in her heart—all portended a dark and sinister Destroyer looming just below the horizon, jaws agape, waiting to devour them all. And she and Adima were being asked, beckoned really, by forces greater than either of them could imagine, to rise up and challenge the Devourer. With a shudder, she looked at her husband as he clutched the stone tightly in his hand.

"You and I are being called to do something important," she murmured, trembling a bit as she looked into Adima's eyes. "We have been chosen. We are agents of the Divine, like it or not." There! The staggering truth came roaring out, terrifying in its intensity. She had spoken what they were both feeling but had so far not been able to express.

Adima did not have to ask her to explain. He knew exactly what she meant. He looked at his wife in shock, gasping as the full import of her words suddenly dawned on him. Chosen for a sacred task. What task? And by whom?

For a moment, the child in him thrilled at the prospect of going on a great adventure. His imagination soared, just as it had when, as a boy, he had gone off on all those marvelous quests within his young and eager mind. Now it was no longer a game; the challenge was quite real—he was, indeed, being called to go. And he had answered the call. They both had. The mature man thought about what the child could not imagine—danger, difficulty, the real possibility of pain and separation, loss and death.

"So this is my destiny!" He barely whispered the words, allowing powerful emotions to fill him completely. He felt an incredible fear, counterbalanced by an indescribable joy—emotions so deep and strong that he could not help but weep in the presence of truth. This was what his soul had been longing for! He looked at Cybele. She was crying too, staring out to sea as huge salt tears coursed down her cheeks. She made no effort to staunch the flow.

"Why us?" he questioned softly.

"I don't know," she replied, keeping her gazed fixed on the horizon. "Why not us? Someone has to take a stand for truth. We are the chosen ones. That's what being an adult is all about—doing what we must do, allowing ourselves to feel the fear and then doing it anyway."

The tears came faster now. Adima waited patiently for the emotions to pass. At last he broke the silence.

"What is your part?" he asked his wife, a hint of anxiety in his voice. "I've told you of my experiences and feelings over the last several months, but I know so little of yours."

Cybele wiped her eyes and took Adima's hand, hoping to ease his fears. Now it was her turn to recount her adventures in the Cave and the forest. She told her husband everything, about her encounter with Sophia and the women and her acceptance of her new name and new purpose.

"Latoné!" Adima repeated the name over and over again, letting it roll around on his tongue, listening to it as he spoke the sacred sounds. "A name of beauty. A name of grace. A name of power. How appropriate!" He held up his hands, palms outward, feeling her energy. "I sense your new power. It exudes from you. It is all around you. I wish I could partake of some of it myself," he said wistfully, "but I guess I'll get my own name and power in my own way in my own time."

"You shall, husband," Cybele reassured him, "sooner than you think." She paused for a moment, then continued her story. While she spoke, Adima looked at her intently, listening to her instinctual knowing and feeling, which were so opposite of his rational, ordered mind. Her energy was great, the attraction between them strong. He felt it, and he was both sexually aroused and also content, an intoxicating mix of emotions that brought joy to his heart.

It had always been thus, since the time he had first met her. Now, so many years and two children later, that physical attraction was still there, stronger than ever, augmented by the deeper spiritual bond between them.

"I will answer Lilith's challenge," Cybele sighed as she finished speaking. "You will face Belial in the Council chambers. I have accepted my individual role and stand ready to do my part, as you have accepted yours." She spoke with great confidence, unaware of the magnitude of the adventure that was about to befall them and all of Atlantis. Fortunately for them both, the future was hidden from their eyes. Had they been able to foresee the actual scenarios of their respective confrontations, their minds would have recoiled in horror.

For Adima and Cybele were heading toward a primal clash of Good versus Evil, as prophesied in the Book of Mysteries:

> In the time when Good and Evil clash,
> Reason will abandon the world,
> And heroes and heroines will be forced to rely
> On primal, root instinct
> And the intervention of supernatural forces.
> In the time when Good and evil clash,
> Hearts will be pierced and minds will scream,
> And heroes and heroines will call upon
> The gifts of the Divine
> That they might survive and overcome the Adversary.
> In the time when Good and Evil clash,
> The Beast shall lash its tail,
> And sweep a third of the stars from the sky.
> For on that day of wrath and mourning,
> Even the righteous shall mercy need.

As the Ancients had written in the *Book of Mysteries*, so another poet would write again ten thousand years later.

An ominous rumble of thunder echoed hollowly far back in the hills. Cybele and Adima barely noticed, so caught up were they in the intensity of the moment. It was the twins who broke the spell. Knowing better than to be in the water during an electrical storm, they swam ashore, clambered up onto the terrace, and joined their parents. "Why are you crying?" Charis asked, suddenly concerned. It wasn't like her parents to be so openly sad.

"It's nothing for you to be concerned about," Cybele reassured the little girl, wrapping her in a gaily striped towel. "Your father and I were just discussing an adventure that we'll soon be taking." She smiled mysteriously. "But before we take ours, we'll be taking you on one!"

The twins' eyes grew wide with delight. "When, when?" they squealed in unison, delighted at the prospect of an adventure with their parents.

"Tomorrow," Adima winked merrily. "So go inside and get ready for bed. You'll need a good night's rest, because we're leaving first thing in the morning."

The twins were off like a shot, pausing only to kiss their parents before scurrying into the dome. "Where do you think we're going?" Alta asked his sister as they ran upstairs to bed.

Cybele smiled at their youthful exuberance. When they were out of earshot, she took up the conversation once again. "There's one more thing we need to do before we set out tomorrow," she said matter-of-factly. The emotion was not as intense, having spent itself in the shedding of their tears. "We've talked about our individual roles. Now we need to focus on our dual responsibility."

Adima looked at her. "What dual responsibility?" he asked, not really sure what his wife meant.

"The Ark, husband," she gently reminded him. "Our dual responsibility is to plan and oversee the building the Ark." She spent the next several moments outlining her plan. It was bold, brilliant in its simplicity. The question was, would it work?

"Of course, we can't physically construct it by ourselves," Cybele concluded. "That's why others of like mind and intent have to be summoned. I hate secrecy, but we have no other choice. We don't want to start a panic, nor do we want to be stopped by Belial and Lilith before we even get started."

Adima shook his head. Despite the seriousness of what lay ahead, he could not help but chuckle at their predicament. "How do you suggest we approach the others with this information?" he asked. "It's quite a story to just dump on our friends, regardless of their level of enlightenment. Why, they'll have us committed!" He laughed aloud at the image of himself and Cybele being carried away to the healing temple, ranting and raving while their friends and family stood helplessly by, wringing their hands with worry. Cybele laughed with him.

"We'll just have to tell them and trust that their hearts will remain open," she declared, thinking back to the night of her initiation. "In fact, I'm sure that things have been happening to them just as they have been happening to us. The women know it already. They knew it even before they got to the Cave. It was no surprise to them." She paused for a moment as a slow smile lit her face. "I think we're going to be the ones who will be amazed by what the others know and are up to. In fact, I imagine they're already working on solutions to the problem...different than ours, perhaps, but in harmony with what we are doing."

Adima watched the dolphins still cavorting in the lagoon, seemingly without a care. Is there a message there? he wondered. "Perhaps we are not alone," he mused aloud. The thought was comforting. "Perhaps there are others to whom this message is coming. That would make sense. There must be others, each being given his or her part to play in the drama, each having a piece of work to do, a task to accomplish, that, when complete, contributes to the Whole."

He turned to Cybele, encouraged by this realization. "Spirit does not sit idly by. Perhaps they are coming together as much to tell us what they have been doing as they are to hear our stories. If this is true, then it would remain for us simply to coordinate all of the pieces and put them together in the right form."

"Sophia told me to use this time to rest and relax," Cybele reminded them both. "The calm before the storm, so to speak. Our brothers and sisters are coming. They will be here in a few days. That still gives us the time we need for the children. We cannot neglect them on the occasion of their thirteenth birthday. Tomorrow we shall take them to the Temple and then into the forest and up into the high places for this most important of initiations."

Adima leaned back, inclining his face to the sky. It was peaceful on the terrace, there at the water's edge. He did not want the moment to end, although he knew it must. "Latoné," he took the hand of the woman whom he loved and spoke the sacred name once more. A breeze came and carried the vibration inland, toward the high places atop the Mountains of the Moon. "I will hold your name in my heart, where it will be safe from all who would use its power to harm you. I will not utter the holy sound again until the End Times."

*****

Thunder rumbled again, closer this time. Adima glanced at the western sky, where dangerous looking thunderheads were massing, towering high into the atmosphere, their tops illuminated by the setting sun, their underbellies dark and ominous. "A gathering of storm clouds," he observed, "not unlike the storm that is gathering over Atlantis. I think I'll sit here for a while and watch. Who knows, maybe I'll get in touch with my own power!" Rising and leaning on the stone wall that circled the veranda, he looked out beyond the lagoon, far out to sea. The dolphins had disappeared, and the water was becoming quite choppy.

Cybele knew better than to try and change his mind. Her husband had a strange attraction to thunder and lightning. He seldom missed an opportunity to venture forth in a storm. He said the tempest was where he felt most connected to Spirit, where he best heard his inner teacher's Voice, and where he felt the Storm God descend in the fullness of its power. And this is going to be a powerful storm indeed, she thought nervously, judging by the speed and intensity with which it is approaching! As if to verify her apprehension, a gust of wind blew across the lagoon, whipping the sea into frothy whitecaps. The first drops of rain began to fall, large drops, going splat, splat, splat on the stone like so many huge tears. "The Mother is crying, just as we have been," Cybele murmured to herself. She wrapped her arms around her husband and kissed him gently.

"I love you," he whispered.

"I love you, too," came the soft reply. And then Adima was alone in the storm as it unleashed its full fury, covering him in a deluge of wind and water and sound.

He was not afraid of being struck by lightning or swept off the veranda and drowned in the wild sea. Death by electrocution or drowning was not to be his destiny, he knew. In fact, he had been hoping for a storm all day, knowing intuitively that he must stand in it if it came. Now it was here at last, and a long-awaited secret was about to be revealed. A meeting was about to take place, a meeting for which he had been preparing for a long time. An alliance was about to be formed, and alliance that would prove to be both indispensable and life-enhancing. It was time to embrace his ally.

The mist and fog and rain swirled before him, seeming to take shape before his eyes. Adima thought he saw a face peering intently at him through the gloom. Gradually it began to coalesce into a distinct image, lit by a ghostly glow.

"The lightning is your ally!" Enoch's eyes flashed like lightning themselves, his image shimmering and luminescent against the jet-black backdrop of the storm. *"It is your greatest strength, your greatest weapon. Befriend the lightning as it has befriended you. Embrace it, and it will serve you well."*

Adima's skin crawled. He wiped the water from his eyes, but the ghostly image was gone. Had it really been there, or was his imagination playing tricks on him? He felt no fear, only gratitude and joy, for who could ask for a mightier ally than the Dragon Power? He felt emboldened, confident, brave. He felt like a warrior. Suddenly, his hair stood on end as the air around him became charged with electricity.

"Welcome, Ally!" Adima raised his voice above the din and spread his arms wide. As if in reply, a jagged bolt of lightning arced across the sky, its brilliant white flash turning night to day, the thunderclap immediate and deafening. "The Dragon roars with a mighty voice!" he cried again, turning his face into the rain and feeling the vibration throughout his body. "Behold its fiery breath!" Again a terrific bolt traced a ragged path across the sky.

Lightning—the most powerful force in Nature! How much energy in a single bolt! He could recite the scientific facts as well as any schoolboy. Lightning—a dramatic natural phenomenon, building up enormous power and discharging up to a billion volts of electricity in a matter of instants, traveling at incredible speed, taking a fraction of a second to reach the Earth, then moving along the ground at hundreds of feet per microsecond.

Another bolt struck the lagoon in front of him, and another, and another. Time after time they shot out of the sky, each one more fiery and beautiful than the last. "Behold the Dragon Power!" Adima shouted above the roar of the thunder.

The Dragon Power, on which Atlantis depended for life-giving energy. The Dragon Power, bringing fertility and abundance and a bountiful harvest, supplying energy to light the way, dispel the darkness, and dance along the Straight Paths. The Dragon Power, bringing spiritual illumination, enlightenment, revelation—the sudden realization of truth cutting across time and space. The Dragon Power, healing and giving life, yet also capable of wounding and killing.

"How can you who are so beneficial also be so dangerous?" Adima voiced the question to his ally as it danced around him. He had seen its good, and he had also tasted of its destructive power. In reply, the lightning flashed again, presenting him with a vision of the past, reminding him of their first encounter so many years ago. He would always remember.

At a planting festival two days after the Summer Solstice, the storm was still many miles away. Suddenly, from out of the clear sky above him, a rogue bolt had come to Earth, lifting him up and hurling him like matchwood twenty yards through the air. "Bringing instant knowledge," Enoch had told him, although at the time the experience had brought only instant pain and fear.

The only inkling he'd had was a feeling of electricity crawling slowly up his arm. Before his senses could register what was happening, it was over. To this day, he did not remember losing consciousness. All he was cognizant of was a sense of disorientation and an incredible buzzing and ringing in his right ear. His skin tingled all over as he staggered to his feet and looked around in a daze.

Adima had never been the same after that. For a long time afterward, he languished in a state of physical, mental, emotional, and spiritual disarray, experiencing confusion, anxiety, heart palpitations, and loss of faith. Not knowing what to do or where to turn for help, his depression worsened. He sank deeper and deeper into an abyss of despair from which there seemed to be no escape. Then Enoch had come to help him through the Great Void, and everything in his life changed. "Not necessarily for the better, either," he would jokingly say whenever he told the story.

Bang! A tremendous thunderclap rocked the veranda, almost precipitating him into the dark waters of the lagoon. Standing on the edge, struggling to maintain his balance, Adima remembered another time that he had lost his balance and stood on the edge.

And it was true. Enoch had led him up and out of the abyss, out of the darkness and into the light, but he had not made it all disappear as if by magic. Rather, he had led Adima to the edge, where the young man had been obliged to choose for himself whether or not to take a leap of faith and step forward. After that, the old man had led his frightened student through the labyrinthine passageways of his own mind, making him look at much that was shadowy and frightening.

"I cannot lift you out," Enoch had replied whenever Adima pleaded to be rescued. "The only way out is through."

It took a long time, years actually. "In fact, I'm still going through," Adima often acknowledged, although, through Enoch's ever-present teachings, he had come at least to recognize the way and understand the purpose of the journey.

Another bolt rocketed out of the darkness, descending straight down into the sea and seeming to form a ladder connecting earth and sky. "...down which power can descend," Adima exclaimed, "bringing with it fertilization and at the same time the destruction of ignorance." He remembered what Enoch had said when he'd inquired into the purpose of his being struck.

"Why do you want to know?" the old man had chided gently. "Be content to sit in the Mystery." But his student would never be content, Enoch knew, until he understood. The man needed to give the experience meaning and purpose. So, because Adima's learning had advanced sufficiently, it was time for Enoch to reveal the truth. "You were chosen."

Adima thought the old man was joking, but one look at his expression convinced him that his mentor was quite serious.

"The bolt came and carried you up and out, where you were given a message and a reminder of your mission. Then you traveled back along the bolt, returning to do this work and prepare for the Time of Tribulation.

"To those in this world who witnessed the event, including yourself, it was instantaneous in ordinary time, but in spiritual terms it happened in a moment of non-time that stretched into eternity. You cannot consciously remember any of it. All you know is that your life has been changed ever since. In truth, you became a man that day, undergoing instantaneous initiation."

A mighty bolt jolted Adima from his reverie. He looked out into the night, but Enoch's image was gone. No matter, a question still remained. Is this the time for which I have been preparing? It is, he realized. Ever since that day long ago, he had dreaded its coming, and now here it was. The fear of death was strong. Try as he might, he could not shake it. It was the one demon he could not seem to conquer. He felt a strong sense of foreboding as thunder boomed and rolled and lightning flickered across the sky. The storm was abating, moving to the east and out to sea. Yes, this was the time for which he had been preparing, and he was almost ready, but that did not make the journey any easier.

"Do not pretend that you are not afraid," Enoch's face reappeared out of the drizzle, glowing eerily. *"Use your fear. Learn from it and grow from it. Turn your fear into power."*

"How powerful can I be?" Adima voiced his doubt. "I am one man, alone against a mighty enemy."

"Let your ally serve you now as it has already served you when it carried you out into the ether to receive the message and answer the Call. Before long, you will hold the Hard Lightning in your hand, in its physical form. I will give it to you at your Anointing."

The old man's image faded once again. Adima did not quite understand this last cryptic remark, but he had given up asking Enoch to explain himself. It would be made clear to him in its own right time. It always was thus.

"So, it is almost the time of the Anointing, whatever that is." The thought brought him little comfort. "So much left to do," Adima muttered, "and so little time." He stayed on the deck for a long while, listening to the rain and watching the lightning dance and flicker across the night sky. The children came out and kissed him good night, and still he stayed in the rain.

When the day made its transition from the old to the new, Cybele called to him from their bedchamber. He turned without a word and went in to her.

CHAPTER 17

Mirror, mirror, on the wall,
Who is the fairest of us all?
—the Wicked Queen, *Snow White and the Seven Dwarves*

"I want that name!" Lilith slammed her fist on the table so hard that the dishes fell to the floor and smashed into a thousand fragments, which glittered like miniature rainbows in the morning sunlight streaming in through the window. It was a powerful blow for such a delicate fist.

She was alone in her chambers high up in the Temple of Poseidon. She liked being up so high above all of the tedium of ordinary life, where she could observe and judge the behaviors and attitudes of others and then pronounce sentence. As High Priestess of all Atlantis, hers was a vital mission. She saw herself as the appointed Protector of the Truth, guarding it from assault by barbarians such as Cybele and Sophia, whom she judged as naive, incompetent, even dangerous. Like a warrior in one of the lighter-than-air war machines soaring through the clouds over Lemuria, protecting Atlantis by raining death and destruction on the nameless, faceless enemy so far below, so Lilith stood in her Ivory Tower, protecting the sacred light of truth from those who would stamp it out.

From where she stood on this beautiful late spring morning, she could look out onto the main courtyard of the Temple, watching the never-ending procession of pilgrims coming and going from all over Atlantis, caring not a whit for them or their lives. And the pilgrims, for their part, came and went, their thoughts on prayer and healing and faith, never realizing what dark secrets lay hidden behind those massive, gleaming walls. So much spirituality outside the Temple, so much darkness within.

There was a time when Lilith's heart would have gone out to those masses, when she would have felt compassion and love for them, recognizing them as kindred spirits. There was a time when she would have acknowledged her relatedness and oneness and sameness with them. Now, though, she felt only contempt for them. Such peons, such little people, living their miserable little lives! Nuisances, actually, getting in the way of the achievement of her goals. But necessary nuisances nevertheless, necessary for performing the everyday chores that kept Atlantis running and supplied all of her conveniences and luxuries. Doing the physical labor so she did not have to.

How deep her icy frigidity! No tolerance for human feelings and vulnerabilities, no compassion for the individual dramas unfolding below her and in countless homes, alleyways, and byways on the great island and in the provinces. She did not speak aloud, refusing to acknowledge her true feelings of helplessness and paralysis as her thoughts revolved obsessively around and around inside her head. Cold, empty, defensive—feeling at the same time superior, threatened, misunderstood, and even sorry for herself.

"No one understands me," Lilith shouted at the unfeeling walls, barely understanding her frustration and rage as they rolled across the room in waves. "How can they? Their minds aren't capable of grasping what I grasp—idiots! They call me dogmatic and traditional, but what do they know?" she sneered contemptuously. "Why can't they understand me? Why don't they see me as the superior being that I am? Don't they know in whose presence they are? They should be on their knees before me thanking me for all that I do for them!"

She wanted to step out onto the balcony and command the pilgrims to bow down before her and beg her for mercy. But alas, there would be no bowing down this day. One day soon, perhaps, if she had her way, but not right now. It was not the time to be distracted by personal desires. She had other, more pressing matters to which she must attend. Lilith sighed, allowing herself the luxury of a moment of self-pity...she who had sacrificed so much to uphold such high moral standards.

How had she gotten this way? How had she moved away from her once-cherished search for truth toward the protection of her own privileged position, toward using knowledge as a way of showing her superiority over others? Descended from the royal lineage of high priestesses, Lilith had not chosen the work; it had been thrust upon her as part of her birthright. In her youth, she had lived for the joy and the pleasure it gave her to be in service to others. But as time wore on, she became more and more jaded, more and more attracted by the lure of personal gain.

Now greed was her master passion—greed and power. Like so many who worshipped material wealth and status, she once had an open and warm heart, but it was covered now in layers of ice so cold and dark and hard and thick that what tiny spark of light was left within was scarcely enough to melt away the glaciers.

She was a handsome woman, even striking. In her youth she had been beautiful. Over the years, however, her features, once soft and gentle, had grown hard. Deep lines creased her face, and her hair was streaked with gray. Her skin was dry and flaky. She seldom smiled, her face fixed in a permanent scowl, her dark and brooding eyes glaring and penetrating.

Her first meeting with Belial had been an encounter that would forever change her personal course, along with that of Atlantis and the world. For on that pivotal day, they had formed an unholy alliance, a partnership based not on love, but on greed. Each had something that the other wanted and needed. Belial had wealth and government control; Lilith had her royal lineage and the hearts of the masses, along with her strong healing and spiritual power. Together, it was a perfect match. One could squeeze the political side of Atlantis, the other could squeeze its spiritual side. All of the bases were covered.

"The people will be helpless...powerless under this combination!" Belial had cried in glee, rubbing his huge hands together in delight as he ruminated on the full import of their joining. "Although they won't recognize it at first. And even if they do, they will chose to deny it or ignore it. It is safer that way, you see," he chuckled darkly, "safer to deny that they are being slowly crushed to death than it is to admit their predicament and then acknowledge that they are powerless to stop it!"

Belial had a keen understanding of human nature. That was one of the qualities that had so attracted Lilith to him. It was perhaps his greatest gift, and he used it to its fullest advantage. For, true to his prediction, as time went on, the partnership made in darkness began to choke and squeeze the people of Atlantis, thereby growing in power and wealth. And like the proverbial ostrich, the people of Atlantis stuck their heads in the sand and went blindly and blithely about their lives, offering neither comment nor challenge to either of their taskmasters.

Lilith turned away from the window and moved further into her luxuriously appointed bedchamber. She wished they would all go away, all those pilgrims, but they would not. In fact, they kept coming, more and more every day. They seemed to be suffering from some kind of spiritual starvation, crying out for a healing touch and escape from the misery of their everyday lives. Searching for answers, for relief from the stress and sickness that living in Atlantis at this time was causing. Grasping at anyone or anything that might help them, heal them, release them. Listening to whatever prophet had arisen at the moment, the "prophet-of-the-day," as she contemptuously referred to them.

And so many prophets there were, it seemed. Wherever she looked, someone had a teaching, a healing, an angle, a gimmick. Most were charlatans with nothing of substance to offer to the masses, only empty words. A very few, though, were genuine—serious teachers and healers with a new interpretation of the old teachings that presented a direct challenge to Lilith and the status quo.

Cybele, of course, along with Sophia and the others, was one of the real ones. These were the ones to be reckoned with, the ones who posed the gravest threat to Lilith and Belial. Although she wondered sometimes if Belial were capable of being hurt, so mighty he was, so safe and secure behind the Adepts and guardians of the Inner Circle. "Still, Cybele's downfall would make a great gift to my beloved," thought Lilith, "and do much to cement the bond between us."

She had no delusions about her relationship with Belial. What had started out in such excitement and promise had degenerated into something dark and unhealthy. There was little interaction between them. They neither lived together nor consorted in the same circles, except when convenient or necessary—appearing together publicly only for affairs of State; coming together privately to discuss finances, political matters of the alliance, or make love.

"That's a laugh," Lilith chuckled to herself as she realized the phrase that had flickered through her thoughts. For what they did in the privacy of her bedchamber could hardly be called lovemaking. Neither of them was capable of forming a deep, caring relationship. "That would involve commitment to another, and neither of us is about to give up our personal freedom to make such a commitment."

Belial viewed himself as a machine, women as prey, and his penis as a weapon. Lilith found no joy in her sexuality, no miracle in her menstruation or ability to give birth. She had always felt inferior to men and was torn between her pride in keeping her virginity and her fear of losing Belial by not sleeping with him. In the end, her fear won out. Once symbols of the god and the goddess, their male and female genitals degenerated into weapons of conquest.

So theirs was a relationship of perverse non-attachment. When they came together, it was not to make love, but to release pent-up sexual energy. For Lilith, the experience was not pleasurable. It was dark and rough and even frightening, yet that very scariness attracted her all the more—like a moth drawn to a flame, not realizing it is about to be consumed by the fire. There was no talk of ending the relationship, at least not openly. But Lilith felt neither safe nor secure. She existed in her present position because she had something to offer Belial. Should she no longer be able to offer that something, she'd be out in less time than it took her heart to beat a single beat.

"And then what will become of me?" she wondered. "Will I just disappear like so many who have crossed Belial or fallen from his favor?" Thus, it behooved her to continue to have something that Belial wanted. She was a woman who, when met with a threat, confronted it head on. Cybele now presented such a threat, more serious than any Lilith had faced before. This was to be her ultimate challenge, for she realized that, left to her own devices, Cybele would indeed destroy her.

Yet, she could not get inside her enemy's head! Lilith had a talent for looking within people, seeing into their thoughts, reading their character traits and their intentions. She uncannily knew beforehand how a person would behave in a given situation. It was her greatest asset, this ability to predict human behavior. And invariable, she was correct.

Except with Cybele. "I cannot get through!" She slammed her fist on the table again, but there was nothing left to break. "Every time I try, my thoughts seem to bounce back at me as though reflected off a giant mirror." Cybele's mind remained closed to Lilith, and that frustrated her and frightened her. Because if she could not see inside her enemy's head, then she could not tell what her enemy was up to and would therefore have no way of defending against her. That was most important—defending against her.

Lilith needed a way in, and if it could not come from herself, from her own skills, then she would have to find it through another. Lilith needed an ally...a *tool*, actually, she thought. Someone who was expendable, so in case she got caught, it would not be a great loss. Someone capable of getting close to Cybele and earning her trust. Someone gullible enough to be duped into believing that she was acting for the highest good of Atlantis. Someone malleable enough to be shaped to Lilith's purposes—a willing puppet for her manipulation.

Lilith smiled as she recalled her tenth birthday. Her parents had given her a wonderful party, the highlight of which was a puppet show. She remembered clapping her hands and squealing with delight as the puppeteers pulled on the strings and made the gaily dressed puppets dance and sing and behave exactly as they wanted.

"Now I am the master puppeteer," she thought. "I like that image. I hold the strings, I have the power. I dictate behavior. And if I let go of the strings, the puppet collapses. It has no life without me, no power without me. Without me, it becomes merely a shapeless heap—a lifeless, worthless pile of cloth and string and sticks."

Lilith had just found the perfect puppet! A short while ago, she had been visited by a young priestess who was experiencing a crisis of conscience, a young priestess who had been part of a secret women's gathering and who, in the light of day, was having second thoughts about what had happened there.

This young woman, despite her priestess status and training, was a follower of a radical faction of the Children of the Law of One known as the Sun Children. Theirs was an ascetic and austere life, focused more on the *letter* of the Law than the *spirit* of the Law. To the Sun Children, the Law was the written definition of the living truth, unchanged and unchanging, a set of strict, rigid rules that must be followed and obeyed with exactitude. Failure to do so meant bodily punishment in this life and the soul's eternal damnation in the next.

Nabala did not understand, and so she was frightened. And being frightened, she had sought out Lilith in order to get advice, and more importantly, absolution for what her young mind considered a serious transgression—participating in a ritual that was contrary to her religious beliefs and upbringing.

The young priestess had not actually been privy to the events in the Cave. That had been reserved for only a chosen few. Nabala resented that, too, because she did not know Cybele's secret name and could not give Lilith what she wanted most. No, Nabala had only been at the bonfire in the field. And what she had witnessed there had frightened her. Her little world was being shaken, and she didn't like it. She did not like anything that threatened the narrowly-defined structures upon which she depended for her safety and security.

Yet she had wisely held her tongue, biding her time and waiting until morning, when she could go to Lilith and seek her counsel. "Lilith will know what to do," she had reasoned. "Lilith is all wise. She will make things better. She will make things right."

That was how Lilith had come to learn about the secret gathering of the women and why she was in such a rage on this lovely morning. It troubled her that an event of such magnitude had taken place without her knowledge and that she had learned about it after the fact. But there was really no harm done yet, not if she could infiltrate the women and get the information she needed the most.

"Enough of this circular thinking!" Lilith finally said aloud, as if doing so would bring a breakthrough in her thought process. "It is time for action." She reached out and struck a gong that would summon a handmaiden. "Bring the acolyte to me," she commanded. Then she took up a position in the center of the room, arms folded, her face an unreadable mask. Nabala entered in silence, her own face displaying no emotion. She knew her place and would not speak unless spoken to.

"Such a mouse," Lilith thought, sizing up the woman who stood before her in a swift, all-encompassing gaze. "A weakling, not very bright, easily led, easily lied to, gullible. All those qualities which make it so easy to dupe her and mold her into the perfect puppet." But wait! There was more.

"She is ambitious," Lilith realized, delighted with this discovery. "She is vain and wants to rise in the ranks and is probably willing to go to any lengths to get ahead.

"Not that she is evil. No indeed. She is truly loyal and would never do anything to harm anyone intentionally, even if it meant not getting ahead. So she will have to be convinced that what she is doing is for the highest good and that the person to whom she is doing it is evil and a threat to the Goddess.

"Yes," Lilith chuckled, quite pleased with her assessment of the character of the young priestess. "She can be manipulated, if not through reason or guile, then through cunning and fear. She is a mouse. She does not have the backbone to go against authority."

The High Priestess's laughter and bearing reminded Nabala of a fierce and vicious badger just before it was ready to pounce and devour its prey. She had seen such powerful acts of aggression in her adventures on Turtle Island. She shuddered involuntarily. Lilith noticed immediately, not one to miss a weakness in another, be it an opponent or an underling.

"What is the matter?" the High Priestess sneered, immediately establishing her authority and power. "Are you afraid? Who are you afraid of? Not Cybele. She is a weakling, she cannot hurt you."

Nabala's eyes grew wide. She shook her head, remaining silent.

"No?" Lilith pressed, moving for the first time. Her silk robes rustled softly as she drew closer to her victim. "Well, then, it must be I of whom you are afraid."

Nabala managed to swallow dryly. There was not a trace of saliva left in her mouth. "No, Mistress, I am not afraid of you," was all she managed to croak.

Lilith laughed derisively. She made no effort to conceal her scorn and contempt. Nabala felt very small and weak indeed, and her legs trembled beneath her flowing robes. With catlike swiftness, Lilith moved forward, pressing her face so close that Nabala could feel her hot breath. "You are afraid, and well you should be," she hissed. "I hold absolute power over you. I made you, and I can break you. You will either live and obey my command or be consumed in the purifying fires of the Goddess."

Her breath smells sweet, Nabala thought to herself. She's threatening to burn me alive and all I can notice is the sweetness of her breath. Am I insane?

Lilith moved away and stood at the window, looking out over the city. A light ocean breeze blew from the east, ruffling her hair. Her entire demeanor changed, becoming softer, gentler, yet it did nothing to allay Nabala's fears or lighten the mood. "Do you know the Power of Name?" Lilith asked softly, her back to the younger woman as she quoted a passage from the *Book of Mysteries*:

> NAMING A PERSON, A FORCE, A CREATURE, OR A THING IS AN EVENT OF GREAT SIGNIFICANCE. NAMES MUST BE CHOSEN CAREFULLY FOR THEIR MAGICAL OR AUSPICIOUS MEANINGS.
>
> TO KNOW A PERSON'S TRUE NAME MEANS TO KNOW THE LIFE PATH AND SOUL ATTRIBUTES OF THAT PERSON. THEREFORE, THE TRUE NAME MUST BE KEPT SECRET TO PROTECT THE OWNER OF THE NAME SO THAT SHE MIGHT GROW INTO THE POWER OF THE NAME, TO SHELTER IT SO THAT NO ONE WILL EITHER DENIGRATE IT OR DETRACT FROM IT, AND SO THAT ONE'S TRUE SPIRITUAL AUTHORITY CAN DEVELOP TO ITS FULL PROPORTIONS.

Lilith paused suddenly, thinking aloud as she stood almost motionless, oblivious to Nabala's presence. "Beside myself, Cybele is the only other person in Atlantis who has access to the sacred Knowledge Crystals. Not even Belial can get to them. No man may do so, for they are protected by the Great Mother herself. To touch them is to die."

Nabala shuddered as she imagined some poor hapless creature disintegrating into oblivion before the power of those mystical, legendary stones. Will such a fate befall me? she wondered.

"Cybele knows the secrets, she knows the true teachings, and she has great power," Lilith continued, unaware, it seemed, of Nabala's feelings. "I will not underestimate her; I may hate her, but I will never underestimate her."

Lilith paused and turned to face the young woman. "I must know her name!" she repeated her heart's desire for the third time that morning, but now she addressed Nabala directly. "Names are power. I want power over her. And *you* are the person who is going to get it for me!"

The High Priestess smiled at Nabala, but the young priestess felt no warmth, no tenderness in that smile. Moving to the table, slippers crunching the shattered glass on the floor, Lilith opened a great book, which Nabala instantly recognized as the *Book of Mysteries*. It had a look and feel of great antiquity, the leather binding dried and cracked, much like the woman who held it now.

Thumbing through the brittle yellow parchment, Lilith sought a special passage, which she found and read aloud.

> A PRIESTESS IS THE PHYSICAL INCARNATION OF THE LAW OF KNOWLEDGE; SHE KNOWS THE TRUTH. SHE HAS MUCH IN COMMON WITH THE LEY-MAN, ASTRONOMER-PRIEST, DRUID, BARD, WIZARD, WITCH, AND HERMIT. THEY ARE ALL LINKED BY ONE THREAD OF ANCIENT KNOWLEDGE AND POWER.

Lilith looked at Nabala, pausing to let the words sink in.

"Cybele has strong power, and she is protected by Sophia and the others. But I have strong power, too." Lilith's glittering eyes narrowed cunningly, and her voice grew lower. She spoke slowly, wagging her index finger in the air, punctuating each word. "There is a way to learn her name, and that way is through music!" She returned her gaze to the manuscript and continued to read aloud.

> WHEN A PRIESTESS COMES TO UNDERSTAND THE NUMERICAL STRUCTURE OF THE HUMAN MIND, SHE WILL COME TO UNDERSTAND THE POWER OF MUSIC. THE INTERVALS OF MUSIC CLEARLY EXPRESS NUMERICAL RATIOS.
>
> OF ALL THE ARTS, MUSIC HAS THE MOST DIRECT EFFECT ON HUMAN EMOTIONS. THIS ALLOWS IT TO BE USED FOR BETTER OR WORSE TO MANIPULATE INDIVIDUALS AND THE MASSES.

Lilith closed the ancient book and reached for a large crystal bowl resting on a shelf. Her actions were unhurried, belying the intense emotion and excitement she was feeling.

Nabala was now thoroughly terrified. She wanted desperately to leave this place, for she truly believed the High Priestess to be insane. This was not what she had intended, but her legs would not move. She stood rooted to the floor, powerless in the grip of Lilith's frenzy.

"We can manipulate her through music!" Lilith cried triumphantly, eyes glowing like two obsidian pools whose secrets would never be revealed to mortal man. "I will show you." Her breath grew ragged as she produced a crystal wand from beneath the folds of her robe. Rubbing the wand around the rim of the gorgeous cut glass, she soon produced a tone. It was a lovely, soothing tone, clear and bright, a pure vibration produced by the combination of crystal on crystal.

The effect on Nabala was immediate. Her features and body visibly relaxed, and all fear and tension seemed to melt away. Eyes glazed over, she swayed dreamily, and her expression took on a distant look, as though she were seeing and listening to sounds emanating from far beyond the ordinary world. Whatever it was, it was beautiful! Bright pictures and colors floated past her, geometric shapes and symbols danced in her vision, carrying her deeper and deeper into a hypnotic state, opening her more and more fully to the power of suggestion.

Through it all, ever so softly, she heard the voice of the High Priestess talking gently to her. Blending with the pure vibration of the tone, the pure vibration of Lilith's voice moved into the young priestess's mind, taking up residence in her thoughts, telling her things—wonderful things—building her confidence, praising her, restoring order and calm. Telling her other things, too, things about Cybele.

"Cybele is a traitor to the Goddess and a threat to the Temple and the priestesses and the Great Mother. Cybele is evil and must be destroyed. You, Nabala, are the one whom the Goddess has chosen to stop her."

"How?" asked the entranced young woman. The words she was hearing felt so full of energy, so full of life. She was being given a chance to serve her mistress and all of Atlantis. She was being chosen as the instrument through which the Goddess would be saved from the corrupting influences of schismatics, heretics, and blasphemers. It felt so good, so right.

"Get close to Cybele," Lilith continued. "Enter into her inner Circle and gain her trust and confidence. Find out what she is doing and what her plans are. Then report back me. And if you are very, very lucky, learn the secret name and thus gain full power over her. You will go to Cybele as friend and ally. Of course, you are not. Your allegiance always belongs to me. But you will cause Cybele to think that you are on her side. You will tell her that you are with her."

All this Nabala heard and understood, and she saw that it was good. After a time, the words stopped, the tone stopped, and the room grew still. She smelled the essence of lavender and felt strong hands gently massaging her temples. There were tears in the young priestess's eyes, tears of joy at the honor that had just been bestowed upon her. She was enraptured, caught up in religious fervor and ecstasy. For the first time in her life, she felt strong, powerful, and capable.

"Nothing will stop me from fulfilling my mission," she vowed as she knelt humbly before the High Priestess. "I am honored, Mistress, that you have chosen me to be an instrument in saving the Temple and protecting the Goddess. I shall do my best to serve you. I shall not fail you." Rising as though in a dream, Nabala glided softly out of the room, leaving Lilith alone once again.

The High Priestess immediately collapsed onto a sofa and took several deep breaths to relieve tension that had taken over her whole being. It had taken a tremendous amount of focus to maintain her poise when everything in her had wanted to scream out her passion. But she felt more confident than she had an hour earlier.

The puppet had been prepared and sent forth on her mission of betrayal. Nabala would use the truth—or part of it—and mix it with the lie, the great Lie, to deceive and betray. Lilith could anticipate nothing that might stand in her way, nothing that could possibly go wrong. Cybele's downfall was assured. Summoning her handmaiden again, the High Priestess smiled confidently and imperiously ordered tea.

CHAPTER 18

A true cosmology must encompass every created element.
—John Michell

It was the morning of the twins birthday, and the family was coming to the Temple for the first part of a ritual coming of age experience in which the children would lay aside the things of youth and take on the trappings of young adulthood. Adima and Cybele remembered the first time they had carried the children inside the compound walls, on the occasion of their birth thirteen years earlier, when Alta and Charis were consecrated and blessed and welcomed into the community. Now they were returning in the prime of their youth.

It was a glorious morning, one of those rare and beautiful days where the vividness of colors and intensity of aromas combined with the energy of the crowds to stimulate and intoxicate the senses far beyond the ordinary. The streets were filled with people, bustle, and excitement. It was noisier. It was smellier. Bells rang louder. Things moved faster, more aggressively. The city was a place of intensity—electrifying, turbulent, vital. Everyone felt this sensory onslaught, not just the children. It was to be a day of superlatives!

"Pay attention now," Cybele admonished the twins as they stood before the Gates of White Pearl. "Attend to that which you experience around you today. Open your senses. Let your eyes see. Let your ears hear. Let your nose smell. Let your tongue taste. Let your hands feel."

"But hold your voice," cautioned their father. "Keep your thoughts and feelings within and contained. We shall speak later. For now, just take in the experience, the impressions. Be in the moment of the city." And then they stepped within.

The family followed the broad concourse that was the Avenue of the Gods as it crossed the three canals and rose up into the inner core of the city. Along the way, they passed through portals that breached first a wall of copper, then a wall of brass, and finally an innermost wall of orichalcum. "It sparkles like fire," exclaimed Alta in amazement. He couldn't take his eyes off the gleaming metal and wanted to run up and touch it.

"There are the royal residences." Cybele pointed to magnificent mansions of white and black and red stone quarried from the native rock and nestled safely within the embrace of the gleaming walls. Everywhere was grandeur and elegance almost beyond the power of words to describe, for the Atlantean monarchy and aristocracy possessed a wealth so immense that the like had never been seen before in any royal house, nor would ever easily be seen again.

At the same time, at the base of the walls—outside those massive, locked gates, amidst incalculable wealth and splendor—poverty thrived. Beggars and outcasts lay naked and exposed, part of the very dust that covered them. Many years ago, Adima had written in his journal, trying to understand why such extremes could co-exist in such close proximity.

> Somewhere along the way, they have not been able to fit into the rigid patterns of Atlantean society, and so they have become misfits. In all ages and all cultures, they are who they are, choosing to live where and how they do because they know no other way, wearing their anguish and loneliness and despair for all who care to see. And no one seems to notice!

It was true. No one seemed to notice, least of all the twins, so caught up were they in the excitement of the city and the moment. Charis's first impression was that the city itself was alive. People were everywhere...wandering, casual, carefree, aggressive, even violent. "There must be a million people in the streets!" she exclaimed, her child-mind exaggerating amidst the excess all around her.

Indeed, the city was alive, in constant motion by day and by night. It had its music, too, the Symphony of the City, composed from the noise of the crowds, the throaty roar of the Vril engines coming and going from the spaceport, the hustle and bustle of trade and manufacturing, and beneath it all, the beating of each human heart. Alive and awake and alert—but how conscious, how aware of itself?

The city was also a melting pot, a place for the mixing of the races, the mixing of humanity. "Don't just look at the crowds," Cybele instructed, "Look at the people's faces."

The twins did as they were told. So many faces, such terrifying diversity! Such intensity of expression. Unfamiliar expressions...strange, strained. How different these people were from the beggars at their feet—these men and women of power, status, and wealth! What masks they wore to hide themselves behind—masks of power, old age, exhaustion, death. For protection, concealment—so they would not be seen. So they could scurry by or hide unobtrusively or be transformed into something that they were not but wished they were. Not unifying, but separating themselves even more—separate and apart in the midst of a sea of humanity.

The twins held tightly to their parents' hands, not because they were afraid, but because they were overwhelmed by the grandeur and decadence and splendor and hideousness of the city. "It seems like everybody is smiling, but when you smile back, they look away," Alta observed. "No one looks at you. They're only smiling to themselves."

It was true. Life began each morning, the city woke up, and people went about their day. Which was a miracle in itself, considering the amount of energy expended there each and every day. Out in the streets, no one looked at anyone else, caught up as they were in their passionate efforts to carry off their own impersonal roles.

Adima and Cybele looked, though. They looked at everyone. They looked deeply into their eyes, the windows of their souls. No awareness there, only vacant and vacuous stares. They looked, and they saw and felt their despair. "Do you recognize your brothers and sisters?" Cybele wanted to shout from every street corner, but she did not. Instead, she kept her thoughts to herself, as she had instructed the twins, and quietly observed her brethren as they dwelt in their great city.

These are the people who stand on the edge! the priestess realized as her heart opened to the spiritual significance of the moment. On the verge of leaving the Garden, they are experiencing the most negative emotions of the human condition—loneliness, separation, and disconnection from Father Love and Mother Truth—although they are not consciously aware of it!

These are the people who have no hope! Cybele gasped with the intuition. For without awareness, there can be no realization that something new and better is possible! Without awareness, there can be no embracing of the opportunity for re-creation, rebirth, and re-entering the Garden. These are the people who merely go through the motions, not taking the time to pause, reflect, and get in touch with their feelings.

She looked into their eyes, hidden behind those well-placed masks, and saw reflected there the same despair as that which was so overtly manifested by the beggars in the street. No difference! She understood the mystery at last. Who appear to be different are in reality alike, sharing the same experience after all—*that of being separated from their Source!*

The inevitable consequences were frustration, resentment, rage, and, of course, fear. She recalled a time when Adima had lived in a constant state of fear. How unhealthy, how unnatural! Such a state, she knew, had brought him feelings of scarcity and loss. It had been true in his personal life; it was true now in the life of the city. A shift was occurring, and an unnatural world was arising, a world where greed ruled, along with lust, envy, and hostility.

The warrior in Adima sensed the aggression simmering and smoldering just below the surface—the violent nature and aspect of the city…the movement, the agitation. So much violence in the streets, symbolic of how violent the Atlantean way of life had become. A shove here, a jostle there, gestures of impatience, curses of frustration and rage. Mini-aggressions were being played out in the streets even as full-scale aggressions were being played out in Lemuria and the provinces and the Council chambers. "Subdued and controlled now, perhaps, but not for long," he muttered to himself. Fueled by frustration and anxiety and despair and hopelessness, the city was a tinderbox, waiting only for a single spark to ignite a full-scale conflagration.

Alta sensed something, too, although he did not understand what it was. Several times they were jostled and brushed back by nameless people in a hurry to go somewhere to do something important. Peddlers hawked their wares so aggressively!

"Buy this, buy that!"

"Buy from me, I'll make you a fair price!"

A grizzled street vendor shoved an article of clothing in Alta's face. The boy was startled by the ferocity of the man's movements, the intensity of his eagerness. He wasn't just selling, he was *demanding* that the boy buy from him, that the child take the small treasure that was his and give it to the peddler.

Why? Alta asked himself, and knew the answer instantly. Indeed, it was a very simple answer, really. I'm here right now and he wants my gold. His job is to accost me and everyone else who comes into the city and take what is in our pockets and put it in his. No matter that we may not want what he's selling or even need it. "Just give it to me, by the gods! I want mine!" He's afraid that he doesn't have enough.

Silently, the boy wondered when a fight would break out. If it did, would it turn into a full-scale riot? When would the crowds just sweep him away and trample him to death? He voiced his fears aloud. "Is it always so crowded? Are people always so rough with each other?"

Adima looked down at his son, paused a moment, then led the family to the side of the road. Sitting down on a park bench, he took one of each child's hands in his own. "It is always like this when you approach the Center of the World," he said, taking the opportunity to let both twins express themselves and perhaps come to an understanding of what they had been experiencing up until now.

"Why do people live here?" Alta pressed. "No one talks to each other. No one seems to care about each other. They're just jammed in and crowded together."

He is old enough to realize, old enough to sense it for himself, Adima thought as he looked at his son. And he doesn't like what he's seeing and feeling. That is good, he thought. The attraction isn't there.

"I think they enjoy it, somehow," he explained in answer to the boy's question. "Ask any man who lives in the city, and he'll tell you it is a rush, an incredible feeling. There's no place like it. If you can't find what you are looking for here, you can't find it at all. The people who dwell here are very protective about their city. They either love it or they hate it. And even those who hate it still choose to stay. Curious—that they find no reason to leave. That they stay in what bothers them the most and thus perpetuate their feelings of angst."

"And they are so terribly alone," Charis interrupted, displaying a wisdom and intuition that belied her thirteen years. She had been feeling absolutely alone and separate as they walked through the streets. How can that be, she wondered to herself, when there are so many people here?

Now, standing on the side of the road and listening to her father, her eye had wandered off in the distance. She noticed a man, an old man at first glance, but when she took a second look, he did not seem so old, perhaps no older than her father. He was sitting by himself several yards off the road in the grass, cooking a meager breakfast beside a small fire. Their eyes made contact for a moment. Instantly she felt his sadness and quickly turned her gaze away. Such sad eyes, such loneliness!

She knew intuitively that the man wasn't just picnicking. He was different, somehow, outside the mainstream of humanity. Dwelling apart not by choice, but because he did not fit in, because the overwhelming madness and rush of humanity just swept past him and he could not jump into the stream. So the man who ate alone also stayed alone, drowning by himself in a dull and stagnant eddy.

"Why does he hide in the shadows?" Charis asked, waiting until the man's back was turned to point him out to her parents. "There is nothing to be ashamed of, nothing to hide, is there?"

"Certainly not," her mother answered, understanding immediately what her daughter was feeling. It was amazing how many people in Atlantis thought alone, ate alone, sang alone, talked alone, lived alone, loved alone. "Especially not here in this city, not in the midst of so many whose own imperfections are revealed."

Cybele spoke more to herself than to her daughter. "It is curious indeed, that a man would think he was unique and find it necessary to hide." Or, she thought to herself, that his fellow Atlanteans had found it necessary to hide him and cast him out of the mainstream of society, when in fact he was just one of many who were as disturbed, fearful, and alone as he was. He was helpless, perhaps, and so it was easier for those in power to prey on him. So they did just that, because they could.

She remembered something she had written in her journal many years ago.

> The city of Atlantis is, indeed, a city of contrasts—every conceivable manifestation of sublimity and decadence can be found here. Absolute wealth and absolute poverty, absolute power and absolute helplessness, absolute spirituality and absolute materiality.
>
> It is a world of gold and silver and precious metals, of truth and beauty and the manifestation of the ideal in art, music, architecture, poetry. And it is a world completely rotten with wealth, power, indifference, poverty, waste, technological futility, and aimless violence.

"You see..." Cybele turned Charis back toward the great royal palaces they had just passed, to where the homeless and helpless lay exposed and baking in the mid-morning sun, begging their heedless brethren for a crust of bread or a spare coin. "...the man who eats alone is not unique. There are countless more like him, not just here, but all over Atlantis. You just need to pay attention and look. You cannot miss them, really, if you want to see them."

"And if you do choose to see them, ask yourselves how you are changed by the experience," Adima added. "To see them and not have compassion is to remain closed-hearted. To see them and not act is to remain isolated and apart from the human community. To see them and not be changed is to deny the truth. And to deny the Truth is to live the Lie."

The children did not quite understand their parents' last words, but they accepted the teaching in silence, knowing that the whole morning had been designed to arouse extreme emotion and make them think and feel and wrestle with the experience and their subsequent feelings. It would, perhaps, be a long time before they understood the meaning of these events, but this was a beginning that they must remember and from which they must grow.

The family sat together in silence for a long while, each with his and her own thoughts, while the endless stream of humanity flowed by and the innumerable mini-dramas unfolded before them. And while they sat, the sea of humanity whirled and swirled and spun round and round, and the great living city pulled and tugged and sucked at them, drawing them ever inward toward its Center.

CHAPTER 19

A knowledge of the gods is accompanied with...the knowledge of ourselves.

—Iamblichus

Just as the Great Pyramid represented the ultimate achievement in science and technology, and the Garden of the Heart represented the human domain of intuition, feelings, and emotions, so the Temple of Poseidon stood forth as the embodiment of the Divine—the spiritual center of Atlantis, the seat of the society. Like the Great Pyramid, this magnificent edifice in the middle of the Palace compound was situated on the single most powerful meridian line of the Earth, a place where the Dragon Current ran strong and deep.

It was midday. The family rounded a corner and stopped to take in the view before them. As often as they had seen it, the view still rendered the children speechless. It was the Temple itself, indeed a sight to behold for anyone who saw it up close—as magnificent the hundredth time as it was the first.

Rising up from a high hill in the center of the city and dominating the skyline, the Temple sat by itself in a position of honor atop the Heart of the World. Nothing occupied a higher place in the city—not the Palace of the king, not the Lighthouse, not even the Great Pyramid. For the spiritual and the Divine held the highest importance in the Atlantean world, or at least they did once, before the coming of the Sons of Belial.

It was a solemn moment, a proud moment for the parents and an exciting moment for the children as they stood before one of the most magnificent structures ever built. The Temple of Poseidon was dazzling testimony to the metalworking skills of the Atlanteans. Encircled with a wall of gold, the exterior was coated with silver, save only the pinnacles, and these they had coated with gold. An immense golden figure of Poseidon driving six winged steeds dominated the Temple's center court. Statues of sea nymphs gleamed from every shadowed crevice.

Stopping in the shadow of the monumental sculpture, Adima gathered the family into a circle—father, daughter, son, mother—and addressed the twins directly. "Alta and Charis, today you put aside the ways of children and don the trappings of young adulthood. With that comes responsibility."

The twins listened respectfully in silence. They knew there was more to this trip than just sightseeing. Their ritual initiation had just begun.

"You are about to be entrusted with certain knowledge and responsibilities that children cannot know or assume," Adima continued. "Before entering the Temple, before crossing the threshold, your mother will ask you four questions. Think well before you reply, for how you answer will affect the course of your lives."

Cybele grasped her children's hands in her own. "Are you ready to put aside the ways of youth and be entrusted with the ancient knowledge?" she asked the first question solemnly.

"Yes, we are ready," the two answered in unison.

"Are you willing to do your parts as young adults in Atlantis—to serve and learn and grow in knowledge and wisdom?"

"Yes, we are willing."

"Are you able to contain your new knowledge within you as you wait for your life's purpose to be revealed to you?"

"Yes, we are able."

"When you know your true purpose, will you act accordingly and strive to fulfill it?"

"Yes, we will so act."

"Then let us begin," Adima continued. "Henceforth, we will speak to you in the language of adulthood, for you have indicated that you are ready, willing, and able to be adults and to act as adults." He led them out of the shadow of the statue and into the sunlight once again. The eastern wall of the Temple faced them.

"Behold that which you see before you—the Temple of Poseidon. You have seen it before from afar and admired its great beauty. Now you must learn meaning and purpose, for the purposes of the Temple are many. The Temple is one of the seven greatest structures ever built," Adima explained, "and is the heart of a much larger structure that spreads out over the surface of Atlantis. Do you know the others?"

"I think so," Alta ventured. "Of course, there's the Great Pyramid and the Dragon Mound at the end of the Dragon Path. Also, the Lighthouse on the beach and the Obelisk in the center of the Great Plain."

"Don't forget the Garden of the Heart," Charis chimed in, "and the Statue of Poseidon right in front of us."

"Now, what do all of these great structures have in common?" Adima asked, proud that the twins had named each of the seven greatest wonders of Atlantean science, art, and architecture.

Charis thought for a moment before answering. "They're all beautiful," she said. "And big and old."

"That's a start," Cybele laughed. "But you must learn to see more than that. You must learn to look at the interconnectedness of things—how one is related to the other, how each is related to the Whole, and how the Whole is part of an even greater Whole."

"I don't understand," Alta looked quite confused. He wanted to understand, but he just wasn't getting the point of the lesson. Neither was his sister, he realized, looking at the quizzical expression on her face.

"Look at it this way," Cybele explained. "Do you know what the word 'ideal' means?"

"Of course," Charis answered. "It means perfect, the best."

"That's right," her mother answered. "And there you have the first purpose of all of these structures—to express the Ideal in physical form. They are works of art in which all is in harmony, all is perfect. Thus, they are pleasant to behold, and we get a feeling of ease and satisfaction when we look at them."

"And, since art and science are not separate in the grand scheme," Adima went on, "each has a scientific purpose, too. Can you guess what that might be?"

Charis was beginning to understand now. "Could it have something to do with the Dragon Current?" she asked.

"Indeed, it could," Adima looked at her proudly. "The Dragon Current is one of many forces that occur in Nature. Symbolically, the poets and artists name these natural forces after certain gods and goddesses, but they are really natural forces—like electromagnetism, solar energy, gravity, and so forth. Each of the seven structures is built to attract and make use of specific natural forces like the Dragon Current and other forms of energy that benefit the planet. Everything about these structures has something to do with the Dragon Current—their location, the way the windows and doors face, the hills on which they are built—everything."

"How did they do it?" Alta asked, thoroughly intrigued now. He had always been interested in architecture and geomancy, so this was exciting for him.

His father's reply was simple. "They used the sacred numbers. The ancient architects and geomancers knew that certain patterns of numbers correspond to certain patterns in nature," Adima explained. "Have you ever heard of something called a magic square?"

"Yes," Alta replied. "I know what they are. They're rows of numbers that equal the same total no matter which way you add them up—across, up and down, vertically, backward, or forward. I use them all the time. I've even been able to make up magic squares of my own."

Adima nodded approvingly. "Well, that's how the Ancients built all of these structures," he explained. "The ancient mathematicians believed that the magic squares were paradigms of universal laws. Everything they built was laid out according to one of the geometrical designs that are inherent in the structure of the magic squares. Thus, the energy of a particular place could be best utilized. Look!"

Adima bent down and traced several rows of numbers in the soil. "Now, connect the dots according to the pattern in the magic square," he instructed. The twins did as they were told.

"It looks like the Temple," Charis giggled in delight.

"This is fun!" Alta exclaimed, his eyes sparkling.

"It is fun," said his father, "but it is more than fun. The numbers mean something. Remember, everything can be reduced to a number pattern. Number is what is most important. In this case, the magic number is *seven*, which is the number of the universe, representing completeness and totality. Do you know why?"

The twins did not, so Cybele continued with the lesson. "*Three* is the number of Heaven and the soul," she explained, "while *four* is the number of the Earth and the body. Add them up, and what do you get?"

"Seven." The twins did the arithmetic easily.

Cybele smiled in appreciation of their eagerness to learn. "Yes," she said, "Seven. Now do you see the significance? It is a number that contains both the spiritual and the temporal, and it is also the number of the Great Mother. There are seven metals involved in alchemy, seven stars in the Constellation of the Great Bear, seven sisters of the Pleiades, seven major planets, and seven rays of the Sun."

Alta thought long and hard, looking at the magic square they had drawn in the dirt. An idea was slowly forming in his mind. "I think I understand," he said, looking to his sister for confirmation. "Each site is built on a natural energy center, and each one has its own magic number pattern."

"And when you connect the seven sites together, they form a cohesive whole," Charis finished.

Adima looked at the twins proudly. "Exactly!" he smiled. "Now here's what's so exciting, and what gives the deeper meaning and purpose. The pattern on the ground is a reflection of the pattern in the sky. Each building is sited according to its astrological counterpart. When viewed as a whole, they form an earthly representation of the seven sacred objects in the sky—Mercury, Venus, Saturn, Jupiter, Mars, the Moon, and the Sun."

From where they stood, they had a panoramic view extending from the Ocean of Atlas far out across the Great Plain. Using his arm as a pointer, Adima called their attention to several of the sacred sites visible in the distance.

"Again, symbolism is related to function," he said, pointing first to the north. "The Great Pyramid embodies the magic square of Mercury, the Statue of Poseidon that of the Sun. The Dragon Mound is formed by the square of Mars, the Garden of the Heart by the square of Venus. The Obelisk conforms to the numbers of Jupiter's square. And the

Lighthouse embodies the magic square of the Moon. Finally," he finished, spreading his arms to encompass the entire magnificent edifice that stood before them, "the Temple of Poseidon was built according to the magic square of Saturn, and so embodies the Saturnine energy of wisdom. There is so much wisdom here. The Temple is a message in stone."

He paused, giving the twins a chance to contemplate the meaning of his words. They gazed about them for a long time, silently observing, silently trying to grasp the significance of the monumental accomplishment that was the physical city of Atlantis. Finally, given their new insight and appreciation, it was time to go inside.

Cybele took them by the hand and led them to the foot of the wide steps leading up to the entrance portals. "All of the secrets of our knowledge of the world are encoded in the dimensions of our temples and pyramids," she said. "They are monuments in stone— living records of all that we know to be true, living testaments to truth in its highest form. They represent the embodiment of the cumulative wisdom of Atlantis through the ages. You see that wisdom in the physical structure, and you see it in the healing rituals that take place within. Let us go within now and ask the Temple to reveal more of itself to you."

*****

They walked up steps of granite and marble onto a broad terrace. The view was spectacular, offering a 180-degree panoramic sweep of the city and surrounding countryside. But it was not the view from the outside that was so magnificent as that compared with the interior of the structure.

High above them, a series of runes had been carved into the bluestone lintel. "What are they, Alta?" Charis wondered. The shapes were somewhat familiar, but the combination was strange, and she could not translate their meaning. Neither could her brother.

"What you are gazing on is the *Welcome to the Pilgrims*, inviting all who come to the Temple to enter in and be healed," Cybele explained, translating the ancient symbols of the Solara Maru.

> YOU WHO ARE THIRSTY, COME HITHER;
> IF BY CHANCE THE WATER FAILS,
> THE GODDESS HAS, BY DEGREES,
> PREPARED THE EVERLASTING WATERS.

"It is an invitation to step into another dimension, for the world of the Temple vibrates at a higher frequency than our own dense material world. Do you accept the invitation to enter?"

The twins did accept. Entering through massive hardwood doors towering twenty feet high, they stepped into the Grand Hall. They noticed the change in themselves immediately—an exquisite feeling of lightness and airiness, of stepping into a world that was both physical and etheric. The walls and pillars and floors were covered with orichalcum and inlaid with all manner of precious wood, jewels, and multicolored stones of varying shapes and sizes. One hundred feet above, an alabaster and ivory ceiling covered them, decorated with gold and silver and orichalcum.

The family was greeted almost immediately by a white-robed priestess who nodded deferentially to Cybele and smiled at the children. She was an elderly woman who had served for years as greeter and guide. When strangers came to the Temple, her purpose was to make them feel at home and welcomed, and to ask their intent so they could receive what they needed.

The adults chatted for a few moments, making the small talk so common when acquaintances come together—about the weather and the crowds and the twins' birthday. As Adima and the twins moved off, however, the older woman took Cybele by the arm and whispered softly in her ear. "Priestess, a word, if you please."

Glancing furtively around, the greeter assured herself that no one was in earshot. Satisfied that they were not being observed, she moved closer to Cybele and whispered through lips that barely moved.

"Beware those who change shape and form," came the mysterious message. *"You know not their true shape, their true intent. She is he and he is she, changing appearance to deceive and lead you astray. Beware."* And then the woman was gone, off to greet other newcomers, swallowed up by the crowd.

What was that all about? Cybele wondered in amazement. She knew the greeter quite well, not a woman disposed to dramatic displays or covert warnings. But she was evidently frightened and considered this important, judging from the firmness of her grip and the intensity of her words. Cybele looked around to see if anyone was watching, but she saw nothing out of the ordinary. No one had noticed the encounter. Even if they had, they could not possibly have overheard or interpreted its significance. No, the older woman had timed her delivery well. Now it remained for Cybele to receive the message, interpret it, and act accordingly. Puzzled and not a little apprehensive, she went to rejoin her family.

*****

They walked about the cavernous Grand Hall on the ground level of the Temple, their footsteps echoing on the stone floor. Adima served as guide, pointing out various historical and religious items of significance. "Here is where our rulers met to hand down their laws in the old days," he explained, stopping before a raised platform in the center of the room. It was made of polished oak, the wood of strength, protection, durability, and courage; the wood of the Thunder God; the wood of lightning and fire. Ten hand-carved, bejeweled thrones lined the dais, each with its unique spiritual and temporal significance— the Dragon throne, the Lion throne, the Lotus throne, and the rest. In a pit before the thrones, the sacred fires burned day and night, forever.

"What are the thrones for, Father?" asked Alta. "Who sits on them?"

"No one sits on them any more, my Son," Adima sighed sadly. "They are only symbols now, representing the seat of authority and the connection between the Creator and humankind."

He recalled the stories of how it had once been, as his own father had told him.

Atlas—High King of Atlantis—and his nine brothers—Princes of the nine provinces—gathered every six years in this awe-inspiring forum. After sacrificing a bull and offering it to their gods, the dark-robed rulers gathered around the flaming embers and passed judgments, inscribing them upon a golden tablet. Thus wisely governed, the people of Atlantis lived in harmony for many generations, their hearts true and in all ways noble, showing gentleness joined with wisdom.

Not any more, though. How that had all changed! Now the Temple was filled more with the business of finance and politics than with the practice of spirituality. Adima looked away from the deserted thrones toward the outskirts of the room, where the shops and stalls were set up for the sale of sacrificial offerings and tokens of remembrance. So many ghosts haunted that room. Ghosts of dead kings and heroes all around him, crying out to him, "Avenge us. Stop Belial."

The great throne, where once Atlas had sat and ruled so well...empty now, save for the king's ghostly presence. Atlas, whose legendary strength, compassion, and love for the Great Mother and her children were so great that they had become the stuff of legend. It was said that, after having made the transition from this world to the next, Atlas had returned to bear the Mother up and sustain her, carrying her great weight upon his own enormous back.

And Poseidon, his father, and Cleito, his mother, and all the rest...all gone now. Adima shook his head to clear the cobwebs of the past as he looked around for Cybele and the twins. The children had not seemed to notice these things, so caught up were they by the grandeur of the place. They wandered about the Grand Hall for several minutes before Cybele called to them. "It's so beautiful," Charis breathed. "Is this Heaven?"

"Yes, it is beautiful," said her mother. "It was designed and built to express all of the beauty of the world in a single structure. But there is more to the Temple than just physical beauty. Let us ascend to the higher levels." She led them up a marble staircase that wound its way around the perimeter of the Grand Hall. Pausing on a landing that overlooked the crowds below, Cybele continued with the lesson.

"The Temple is a place of healing...a sanctuary, a sacred space, a place where we leave society behind while we go inward to do our work." She led them along a wide passageway that led further into the interior of the building. At the end, a flight of twelve marble steps led upward to a large circular chamber. Twelve alabaster columns, six on either side, flanked the entrance.

"There are no doors, Cybele explained, "because the healing room is never closed and is always available to everyone." In the center of the room stood a table nine feet long and three feet wide, made of an alloy of silver, copper, and ground crystal dust. Its pedestal base was a crystal carved in the shape of a pyramid. The perimeter of the room was ringed by individual healing chambers, tiny cubicles utilized for a myriad of functions ranging from study and meditation to assisting in childbirth, the curing of infections, and the repairing of tissue damage. Through an interlocking grid of multicolored crystals, sunlight passed through the ceiling and was transformed into soft, muted pastels that formed specific healing patterns.

"Why do people need healing, Mother?" Charis asked. "I never get sick."

"Sickness takes many forms," her mother explained. "Physical bodies are delicate and easily injured, especially through physical labor and the waging of war, as has been going on for so long now. And as we grow up, we often start doing unnatural things and behaving inappropriately, such as overindulging in food, drink, and other sensory pleasures. Of course, our thoughts affect our health the most. Whatever we think, that we become. If we think whole and loving thoughts, we remain whole and loving. However, if our thinking is fragmented and fearful, our bodies begin to manifest the effects of those darker, lower vibrational thoughts in our individual organs and systems."

"How so?" Alta asked.

"Well, your mind is a very powerful thing. It is, in fact, the most powerful force in the universe. Things first begin as thoughts. From the Mind of the Great Creator came the *Idea* of Creation, and so the universe was born. From the ideas generated in our minds, all of Atlantean cultural, artistic, scientific, and technological achievements come forth."

"But that still doesn't explain why people get sick," Alta pressed.

"The laws of manifestation are constant," Cybele said. "They work for good as well as bad. All that matters is the intent of the thinker, whether he's aware of his intent or not. Remember what it says in the *Book of Life*:

> THE HEART IS THE CENTER OF LOVE AND SECURITY. A PERSON WITH A CLOSED HEART CENTER LACKS JOY AND EXPERIENCES STRESS AND STRAIN. CONSEQUENTLY, THEY CREATE FOR THEMSELVES INNER HARDNESS. THEIR FLOW IS BLOCKED.
>
> ANGER AND VIOLENCE LEAD TO MANIFESTATIONS OF DIS-EASE WITHIN THE LIVER AND OTHER INTERNAL ORGANS. DEPRESSION, FEAR, GRIEF—ALL BESET THE LUNGS AND OTHER ORGANS AND TISSUES RELATED TO THE ABILITY TO TAKE IN AND APPRECIATE LIFE FULLY AND COMPLETELY.

"Such maladies were rare once," Cybele continued, "but they are becoming more and more prevalent as people vie for wealth and status and let fear serve as motivation for human behavior. In rare cases, the physical organs and systems respond by shutting down, resulting in the physical death of the body. That is why so much of our healing work is focused on the *cause* of the malady rather than on its *effect*. It is one thing to arrest or alleviate the symptoms; it is quite another to eliminate the problem at its source, which is inevitably the human mind."

"How long do people stay here?" Charis asked. "How long does it take them to heal and get better?"

"It all depends," her mother replied, "but they never stay longer than absolutely necessary. As we were met at the door today, so the pilgrims who come here for healing are met by an elder, a guide who monitors their progress while also making sure they do not overstay. They must return home after their time here is done."

She glanced at Alta, who had wandered up the stairs to where rainbow-colored lights shimmered on the alabaster walls. "Come here, Son," she called to him, but the boy made no move. He simply stood in the doorway, eyes wide, staring into the strangely-glowing chamber. Taking Charis by the hand, Cybele came to him. The boy was in tears.

"What is it, Mother?" he sobbed, pointing to a score of men and women lying on marble tables, bathed in the rays of pulsating crystals lit from above by the sun's rays streaming through multicolored glass panes. "What is wrong with them? Are they dying?"

"Do not be frightened, my son," Cybele soothed, stooping to draw the child close. "Does this seem strange to you, this place of healing with sunlight and crystals? It is not strange, and certainly nothing to fear, for it is perfectly natural. Those people are in no danger; in fact, they are quite well and becoming even more so. For they are employing the ancient healing arts, honed to perfection so long ago by the Ancients and serving us now in the forms you see before you. Do you understand?"

Alta sniffed and looked at his mother, wanting to believe but still doubtful. "I guess so," he said quietly, but Cybele knew he needed additional teaching. Drying his eyes with her silk scarf, she led him gently away from the object of his fear. As they walked, Cybele put an arm around each twin and spoke to them.

"My children, you are at an age where you are beginning to recognize the sanctity of your bodies, the interconnectedness of all things, and your place within the temple of your Self and the Round of Life. You must also understand that your thoughts and actions directly affect your state of wellness. As you come to know that your body is a temple, you will learn to open to the guidance of your inner teachers and guides. Let them guide you to begin your healing work. For, as written in the *Book of Life*, they will teach you to:"

ENTER INTO THE INVISIBLE TEMPLE CREATED BY YOUR OWN INTENTION. IT WILL WORK BECAUSE YOU INTEND IT TO WORK. NOW THAT YOU INTEND IT, VISUALIZE IT. CONJURE IT UP, AND SEE IT IN YOUR MIND. FOCUS ON IT.

NOW, GATHER YOUR FORCES AND PROJECT YOUR INTENTION OUTWARD THROUGH YOUR LOWER NATURE, YOUR PHYSICAL BODY. REACH UP AND TAKE IT; FEEL IT IN YOUR PHYSICAL BODY. ALL PLANES OF CONSCIOUSNESS ARE WORKING ON WHAT YOU'VE INVOKED. IT WILL MANIFEST AS SOMETHING YOU'VE RESURRECTED.

Cybele smiled at her children. "This is how you stay well," she explained. "It is also how you heal. You become better and better and more matched to your ideal. Now do you understand?" she asked each of them in turn.

They did. It was that simple. They had listened to their mother and learned more about themselves. It was a lesson they would remember all the days of their lives. Even during the long, difficult years after the destruction, when Atlantis was but a memory, they would recall that day and remember the ancient prophecy in the *Book of Mysteries*:

> WHEN THE TEMPLE IS DESTROYED AND THE RITUALS THEREIN CEASE, THE WORLD WILL FALL OUT OF BALANCE AND DECLINE IN FERTILITY. ONE DAY, HOWEVER, THE TEMPLE WILL BE REBUILT, AND THE DIVINE RAIN OF WISDOM WILL FALL AGAIN TO EARTH, BRINGING IN A NEW AGE OF PEACE AND PROSPERITY.

*****

Continuing their exploration of the inner realms of the Temple, Cybele led them ever upward until they stood on a narrow stone parapet overlooking the Grand Hall two hundred feet below. From this dizzying height, they could reach up and almost touch the ceiling just above their heads. Here, too, they could better appreciate the painstaking detail with which the mosaics had been created to form the hieroglyphs and other images.

"There is a treasure contained within the Temple," Cybele winked mysteriously. "Look around and see if you can find it."

"A treasure!" the twins exclaimed simultaneously, eyes wide with excitement. "What sort of treasure? Is it a magic ring? Or a secret chest? Perhaps a magic lamp?"

"Hush, hush," Cybele laughed at their eagerness. "No, it is none of those things. This is a far greater treasure, more valuable than anything that can be dug out of the soil or conjured magically out of thin air. Look there." She pointed straight down to the floor so far below. It was late afternoon, and there were few visitors to obscure their view of the polished stone floor. From this great height, the colorful slabs and etched lines that they had walked on a few hours before no longer appeared as separate, unrelated blocks. They had come neatly together to form a smooth, seamless, interlocking pattern that covered the whole floor.

"What is it?" the twins gasped as they beheld the enormity of the pattern that lay spread out below them. "Is that the treasure?"

"It is," Adima replied. "It is the geomancers image of the Ideal Cosmology. As is written in the *Book of Life*, what you see below you is:

> THE SCHEME THAT LIES AT THE FOUNDATIONS OF ALL THE TEMPLES AND SACRED CITIES IN THE WORLD; AND INSEPARABLE FROM IT IS THE PHILOSOPHY AND SCIENCE IN WHICH OUR ATLANTEAN CIVILIZATION IS ROOTED.

For in truth, the pattern on the floor was a message in stone...a mystery, actually, the *Mystery of the Atlantean Faith*. The design consisted of twelve etched circles placed in a ring around a central circle, in the center of which was a human form of pure, beaten gold. "The body represents our Atlantean community," Cybele explained, pointing to the figure of a human being at full stretch. "We are one people, united in heart and consciousness, springing from a single Source."

Branching from the midpoint of the body were four paths composed of polished red stone, a perfect complement to the grays and creams of the marble background. Each path radiated outward in one of the cardinal directions. "The paths represent the Four Ways of Wholeness, Totality, Completion, and Solidarity," Adima continued. "See where they intersect to form a cross? The four directions, the four winds, the four rivers of Atlantis and Paradise, the four quarters of the Earth—each of the four elements of the world is united at a fifth point—the center of the world, where Heaven and Earth are joined."

"The cross inscribed within the circle has great spiritual significance for us," Cybele went on. "In the horizontal and vertical lines of the cross, you can see our dual nature. Our active, masculine nature follows the celestial vertical paths of the Spirit and intellect. Our passive, feminine nature follows the rational, horizontal paths of the Earth. The *Book of Life* reminds us that both aspects are necessary to live a full life:"

> IT IS THROUGH THE UNION OF THE OPPOSITES THAT WE ARE CAPABLE OF INFINITE AND HARMONIOUS EXPANSION IN EVERY DIRECTION. IT IS THUS THAT WE ACHIEVE ETERNAL LIFE.

Adima pointed to the great Wheel of Life etched into the stone floor. From each of the twelve circles, lines radiated toward the center. "Surrounding all are the signs of the Zodiac, that everyone might see and understand the mystery of our relationship to each other and to the universe. If you were to measure the dimensions, you would be presented with further truths," he continued. "See how the twelve small circles are arranged in groups of threes? Such an arrangement represents the seasons of the Moon and the months of the Great Year. Each month consists of 2160 years; the number corresponds to the 2160 miles in the Moon's diameter. There are other measurements, too, such as the diameter of the Earth and the circumference of the Moon's orbit.

"You shall learn more at a later time. Your mother and I point this out to you now because we want you to understand that they are important, that they have great value. The message lies plain before your eyes. So it has been recorded by those who came before you, for all time and for all posterity, so that you never forget, so that the Spirit is never lost and the Body never decays."

Yes, Adima thought, there is so much more to be revealed, knowledge that the deluded Sons of Belial ignore; knowledge that a wiser, more realistic generation had found acceptable and recorded in the *Book of Life*:...

> A TRUE COSMOLOGY MUST ENCOMPASS EVERY CREATED ELEMENT. THE COMMUNITY IS NOT PLANNED BY HUMAN ARCHITECTS AND LAWYERS, AND ITS ELEMENTS ARE NOT SELECTIVE, FOR THEY COMPREHEND THE UNIVERSAL SCHEME.

*****

It was time to descend. What was on the surface had been revealed. What was above had been revealed. Now that which lay below the surface would also be revealed. Down they went, ever downward, following the spiral staircase as it wound around the perimeter of the Grand Hall to ground level. It had grown dark outside, and the interior of the enormous room was lit by the glow of hundreds of candles. The family was alone in that cavernous space, the visitors having left, the servants attending to dinner preparations, the priestesses at evening prayers. It was a somber moment as they stood quietly in the flickering candlelight amidst huge, misshapen shadows. More melancholy than eerie, more mysterious than frightening, the silence so loud as to be almost deafening.

Even in the candlelight, the room was dark—hugely dark and mysterious. Alta felt the same chill along his spine as when he had walked into the Dragon Mound at last year's festival. Who is lurking here? he wondered, glancing around into the gloom. There in the corner, did he detect a movement, a mysterious intruder spying on them, waiting to pounce from the shadows? The fear of the unknown. He shivered and pressed closer to his parents.

"We are about to enter a world seldom seen by the surface dwellers...a separate place, an occult place," Cybele said as she led them through a maze of twisting passageways to another staircase, this one leading down into inky blackness. "There is nothing to be afraid of, but this is not a place in which to go wandering around alone."

She reached up and took a flaming torch from its wall sconce. Down they went again, ever downward, into the subterranean passageways and catacombs that honeycombed first the limestone and then the bedrock below it, a vast network of tunnels and caverns that had been created eons ago by natural upheavals of the land.

Following the Hermetic principle of "AS ABOVE, SO BELOW," just as the upper Temple was composed of multiple levels, so also was the lower Temple. About fifty feet down, the stairs opened onto a broad, well-lit hallway.

"Where is the light coming from?" Charis squinted as her eyes adjusted to the sudden brightness.

"From the crystals," Cybele replied, returning the torch to a sconce on the wall. "This is the Hall of Crystals."

They were in a fairly large, rectangular room. The walls on three sides were pockmarked with niches containing all sorts of multicolored, multi-shaped crystals. Some glowed ruby red and emerald green; others were various shades of blue, purple, yellow, and orange.

"Look around you, but do not touch them," Cybele cautioned. "The crystals are bearers of great energy, serving us for as long as we need them. Each has a specific shape, a specific color, and a specific purpose. They are stored here until they are required, then they are brought out and put to use."

"What are those for?" Charis pointed to a cluster of clear white crystals enclosed behind a wire grid in the center of the room.

"They absorb energy that is used for electrical power," Adima explained. "That is where the light is coming from. They can store electrical energy that can be drawn upon at any time. The copper rods run from the crystals straight up through the roof, carrying the current to similar crystals in all parts of the Temple."

"They also serve another purpose," Cybele said, reminding them of the higher, spiritual function of the crystals. "They are used to generate the Father's Light and for healing at the highest levels."

The twins looked silently about them. Each was feeling a vague sense of restlessness, but as to the cause of their unease, they hadn't a clue. "There's more to this than meets the eye, isn't there, Mother?" Alta finally asked. "At school, we learned all about how the crystals work. But this is different."

"You wouldn't bring us here just to show us this," Charis added. "You must want us to see and learn something more."

"Bless you, my children!" Cybele smiled. "You truly are growing up, and your intuition is serving you well. Your father and I were hoping that being here would quicken a new sense of awareness in you, as it has for so many others, and, indeed, that has happened now. Yes, there is something more. Stand beside me and concentrate. Clear your mind. Focus your attention. Give yourselves to the experience."

The twins did as they were told, standing still, eyes closed, concentrating. For a long time, they felt nothing but the warmth of the room and the gently pulsing vibrations of the crystals. Then, ever so subtly, they began to sense something more—enormous energy and enormous power, a Presence, an Intelligence—and it was reaching out to them. Indeed, it was right there in the room with them.

"It's like being inside someone else's mind," Alta gasped. And what a mind it was! Vast intelligence, inconceivable knowledge! Wisdom beyond imagination, beyond their meager abilities to comprehend! They were in the presence of pure Mind—not spiritual mind, but living, mortal, human mind.

"Who is it?" Charis whispered, her eyes still closed, standing motionless and amazed.

"Open your eyes," her mother instructed. Hesitantly, the twins complied. What they saw evoked gasps of astonishment. Before them, the solid rock had dematerialized at eye level, exposing a dark and secret chamber recessed deeply into the wall. Lying within were three clear crystals, each perfectly round and smooth, about twelve inches in diameter, and absolutely flawless.

"These are the Living Crystals of Knowledge," Adima spoke softly, as if not wishing to disturb the living substance in whose presence they were. "You have heard them spoken of in myth. Now see them in reality."

"We thought they were only legend," Alta said, "not something that really existed. How can this be? How can crystals be alive? And why would anyone *want* them to be alive?"

"The idea is quite simple, really," Adima explained, "although the actual technological achievement is vastly complex. In antiquity, before the Earth's magnetosphere became polluted, Athena, Keeper of the Wisdom, conceived a marvelous and highly spiritually evolved idea. 'Let us create living crystals,' she declared, 'capable of containing vast amounts of knowledge. We shall tune their resonance to a delicate pitch, such that we can impress them with the contents of our own minds.'

"The Elders were instantly taken with the idea. Here was an opportunity for virtual immortality; entire lives could be stored in the crystals as memories. So the Ancients set to work, forming globes of silicon combined with certain trace metallic elements that interacted with the electromagnetic field of the Earth. The results were better than even those great minds had anticipated. For the crystals were of such unutterable purity and vibration that they were capable of containing the sum total of all of the knowledge that had been accumulated since the beginning of the human experience on Earth."

"Why are they here?" Charis interrupted. "I know they're important, but why are they hidden here in the Temple and never spoken of or brought forth?"

"Athena created a great many crystals," Adima continued the story. "Then, as now, they were housed here in the Temple of Poseidon with the greatest of reverence. But through the ages, they have become a source of great contention...even violence, bloodshed, and war. Many of the crystals have been lost, others destroyed by floods and earthquakes. Still others have been stolen and hidden away for use at a later time for destructive purposes."

"Why?" asked Alta. "The crystals can't really do anything, can they? They're really just a library, a knowledge repository. Why would anyone want to steal them or fight to possess them?"

"Because knowledge is truth," Cybele answered, "and truth is power. In and of itself, knowledge is neutral, as capable of leading to the accomplishment of great good as it is to the accomplishment of great evil. When knowledge is used in accordance with balance and peaceful pursuits, amazing things can be accomplished. When used with the wrong intention and motives, however, incredible destruction can occur."

"That's why we had to hide the crystals," Adima explained, "to protect them from the Sons of Belial, who wish to use the knowledge for purposes that are not in accord with the Law of One. What once was available to all has now become hidden and separate. Indeed, many have forgotten about these crystals. But here they are, nevertheless. They are real. They do exist. These three have survived intact in this most sacred of sanctuaries. They must be protected at all costs, for they contain all of our knowledge, all that is known. And knowledge equates to enlightenment, for knowledge is absolute. Knowledge is what the human race has come here to gather."

Cybele placed her hands on each of the twins' shoulders, gently guiding them forward into the recess. "These three crystals have been impressed with the conscious awareness of all of our history, all of our knowledge, and what they could hold of our living culture. It is in this sense that the crystal is living. "Experience this life now. Let the crystals speak to you—not in spoken words—rather, let their language ring into your minds, full and complete. Hearken to what they tell you."

Taking a deep breath, the twins obeyed, giving themselves over to the fullness of the experience. Spellbound, they listened, eyes shut, as the Ancient minds reached out to them. The communication began with a warning to all who would misapply knowledge, of the terrible consequences of such an act. Then they learned, through direct experience, what Atlantis was truly about. They experienced for themselves how the ancient Atlanteans perceived their world. They understood the shape of the Great Pyramid, how it worked, and why it was built. They were even given a glimpse into its meaning and purpose, a glimpse into the vast store of sensual impression collected from the dim mists of the Beginning until now.

Of course, it was only a glimpse. Anything more would have overwhelmed their young minds and, if not stopped, cause madness and ultimately death. No, this was only the most infinitesimal glimpse into Consciousness of a magnitude far beyond theirs or anyone else's ability to absorb fully.

"Are these messages from the Creator?" Charis asked when it was all over. She felt an overwhelming sense of sadness and loss at being disconnected from conscious contact with the crystals. The wall had closed up, leaving only solid stone where the crystals had been but a moment before.

Adima smiled at the question. It was so innocent, so simple, so typical of the kind of thinking among many of the Children of the Law of One and all who thought so limitedly. "Of course they are Divine," he said. "But the most important thing for you to remember is that the 'Divinity' of which you speak is not outside yourselves, not separate and apart from you, as so many believe."

"We shall speak much more about the use of the crystals as you progress in your learning," Cybele said softly. "One day, as we continue to evolve, we will no longer need them. But for now, they serve us well."

She was interrupted by the sound of footsteps coming from the exterior passageway. A young priestess entered the room. When she saw the family gathered there, she stopped. "Forgive me, Priestess," she bowed humbly. "I heard that you were in the Temple, and I have been searching for you. May I have a few moments of your time?"

It was not unusual for younger priestesses to seek advice from Cybele. She always tried to help and give where she could. And this young acolyte was well known to her, having been with her in the forest on the night of her naming. "Certainly, Nabala," she replied. "Adima, take the children and continue. I will join you in a little while."

*****

The two priestesses sat together in a small meditation room in an antechamber of the Hall of Crystals. "I feel so out of place, Priestess," the younger woman was saying. "I want so much to belong to the group. I believe in what you stand for and what you are trying to accomplish. Yet I don't feel that I fit in. Every time I try to get close to the other women, they cut me off. They never include me. I am alone within a whole community."

There were tears in Nabala's eyes as she spoke. Cybele looked intently at the younger woman, listening as the words tumbled over each other in Nabala's eagerness to express her intense feelings. "What can I do?" she continued in apparent earnestness. "How can I make them like me? How can I fit in? I know I don't fit in here any more. The High Priestess's ways are not my ways. I cannot continue to serve here with no hope for rescue or salvation."

Nabala wrung her hands, summoning up the lie that would conceal the truth. "I want to run away, but I know that's not the answer. I can't think straight any more. What am I to do?" The acolyte dropped to her knees, burying her face in the older woman's lap.

"Please let me help! Please give me a role to play! I have so much to offer, if only you'd let me. I love and honor the Great Mother. I am deeply spiritual. I am able to serve."

None of what I am saying is a lie, either, Nabala thought grimly to herself as she sobbed the words of deceit through the muffled folds of the priestess's robe. I *am* telling the truth about myself. I *am* spiritual. I *do* love the Mother. That is why I am about to betray you, Cybele, because I do love her so. For you and your kind are going to destroy her. You have put your own ways above hers. And I will not have her inflict punishment on the rest of us because of the actions of a corrupt few!

"What is she thinking?" Cybele asked herself. She could usually perceive thoughts and feelings with a keen sense of accuracy, but there was no such reading from this woman. It was as though a wall had been put up—an impenetrable barrier through which Cybele could not see.

It is working, Nabala thought smugly to herself, careful not to let her facial expression betray her true thoughts. My mirrors are up. She cannot see through me. Everything is reflected back. I am protected. Continuing to couch the lie within the truth, she said, "I know you are the true and chosen spiritual leader of our people, Priestess. I am willing to follow you and obey your commands. Tell me what you would have me do. Rescue me from this evil place, I beg you."

She sobbed and fell to her knees, clutching desperately at the hem of the older woman's robe, crying real tears. She had only to think of the Mother, helpless victim of Cybele's wiles, and those tears came easily enough. Cybele was flooded with feelings of tenderness and compassion. She knew what it was like to be an outcast. She was one herself within the Temple precincts. And she knew the importance of having friends and a sense of purpose.

Beware those who change shape and form.
You know not their true shape, their true intent.

The ominous warning echoed suddenly in her ears, and Cybele jumped like a child who had been frightened by a monster under the bed. Was this the danger of which she had been warned but a few hours ago? Was Nabala not what she seemed? Did this young acolyte have a covert, malignant purpose in coming there? Or were her words true, and could she be trusted?

Cybele just did not know. She had no way of knowing, except through her skills at judging human nature, and they weren't working just now. This was a dilemma indeed. It didn't feel quite right, yet there was nothing wrong...was there? Why was she suddenly doubtful? Frowning, she made her decision. "I will help you, Nabala," Cybele resolved. "Sit up now and dry your eyes."

Hastily removing her diamond pendant, she handed it to the younger woman. "You will leave here at once. Take this gemstone, go to my home, and show it to one who will greet you there. She will feed you and give you a place to rest. Then she will take you to a safe place. Wait there until I send for you. In a few days hence we shall all gather to make further plans. Now dry your eyes and go."

Cybele paused, still not sure where the real danger lay. "Speak to no one. Take no belongings. Just leave here at once. You know how to exit the Temple without being seen, as you know how to travel through the city unobtrusively. Go, and may the Guardians be with you."

Cybele sat alone for a few minutes. "Have I done the right thing?" she wondered aloud. The young woman was in obvious distress. What could she do but help her? As for it not feeling right, well, perhaps that was just imagination. It had been a long day, and she was tired. Her reasoning and intuition weren't as sharp as she would have preferred. With proper rest, she'd be back to her normal, perceptive self.

Of course, she could always ask Sophia about it, but she didn't want to do that. She had accepted a leadership position, and she should act as a leader. Someone had come seeking help and inclusion in the group. She had indicated a genuine desire to serve and a deep spirituality. Who was Cybele to judge or exclude her? This was not about specialness. This was about the good of all. No one was special, no one deserved to be excluded.

Beware. She is he and he is she.

Again the cryptic warning rose to the surface of her consciousness, only now it was not Nabala whom she doubted, but the messenger herself. Was the old woman just being overly dramatic? She had a reputation as an alarmist, often overreacting and predicting dire outcomes to trivial affairs. It was a standing joke among the priestesses that she would condemn anyone to everlasting damnation for the most minor slight. "She enjoys the drama," they said. "We should be thankful that the Great Mother does not have her personality, or we'd all be roasting in the fires of perdition by now."

Too, Nabala's gratitude had been quite real. Her embrace had been heartfelt, her relief genuine as she had taken her leave. "You will not regret this, Priestess," she had said, kissing her cheek. "I am in your debt." And then she had been on her way.

Of course, Cybele had no way of seeing the corners of her mouth twist ever so slightly in a malicious smirk. Nor could she know what was in that naive and confused heart. For Nabala's emotions had, indeed, been genuine—relief that she had fooled the priestess into letting her into the inner Circle, gratitude that she was well on her way to serving and saving the Great Mother. For in her own heart, she did not believe herself to be evil. Her intentions were honorable, and the goal was worthy. She honestly felt she was doing the right thing. Her cause was noble, she knew, because it was declared so in the *Book of Mysteries*:

THE ENDS JUSTIFY THE MEANS.

"Well, I have been forewarned, and so I will be prepared," Cybele said aloud. "I will let Nabala into my home. I will give her the benefit of the doubt. I will also watch her and observe her and not make her privy to all of the details. She will have to earn such trust. But for the moment, at least, she will be welcome." Taking a deep breath and smoothing her gown, she went to rejoin her family.

*****

"What is this?" Adima wondered aloud as he and the twins walked along a gently sloping corridor. He had glanced into one of the lit rooms along the hallway and noticed something so out of place that it immediately caught his eye. A scientific apparatus had been partially set up over a gaping hole that had been chiseled in the floor. It was a strange-looking device, employing a technology with which he was not familiar. This was not something that belonged to the priestesses, of that Adima was sure. It did not have the look of a spiritual tool. No, this was an alien device, not part of the natural accoutrements of the Temple. "So who could have put it here, and for what purpose?" he asked aloud. "And why is it hidden away so far underground?"

"That's easy to answer, Father," Alta replied. "To be sure no one discovers it by accident, of course."

"And why would that be?" Adima questioned his son further.

"Because it has a sinister purpose." This time it was Charis who supplied the correct answer.

"It's a simple enough device, composed of wire, crystal, and metal," Adima mused, examining the apparatus from all angles. "It cannot be complete. There is no substance to it, not even a power source. Someone must be building it even now." He was interrupted by a sound behind him. A man carrying an armful of copper rods entered the chamber. Taking one look at Adima, the newcomer gasped in astonishment, dropped the rods, and dashed from the room, the grating clang of metal on stone echoing after him.

"I recognize that man," Adima said evenly, although his mind was racing with possibilities. "He's an alchemist at the Great Pyramid, actually a well-respected man in his field. I think his name is Shakala. What is he doing here at this time of night, alone in the Temple?"

The name of Belial instantly flashed across his mind. Of course! This must be some sort of experimental device with which Belial was involved. It probably had something to do with tapping into the subterranean energy currents beneath the Temple...and it would have no beneficent purpose, of that he was sure. "Have I stumbled onto something important here?" Adima wondered. "It would seem so."

"What are you going to do, Father?" Alta wanted to know. He was trying his best not to be frightened, but his lower lip trembled ever so slightly.

"I'd report it if I thought it would do any good," Adima laughed, trying to lighten the tension, "but there's no way Shakala could have gotten in here without the permission of the High Priestess. And it's common knowledge that she and Belial are in league with one another. No, I'll keep this to myself for a while." He winked slyly at his son. "They already know that I know. Maybe that will be enough to stop whatever is going on."

I doubt it, though, he thought to himself. It has never stopped them before. Still, there's no sense in frightening the children or letting this mar their birthday. They're growing up, but they don't have to become responsible adults all at once. That's still my job. "Never mind them anyway," Adima said cheerily, putting his arms around the twins and walking out into the corridor. "It's growing late, and there is one more revelation awaiting you. Your mother should be catching up to us momentarily. We'll wait for her below."

* * * * *

"Here she comes now!" Adima pointed back along the passageway they had just exited. He and the twins were standing at the very lowest level of the Temple in a cavern that had been hewn from the solid bedrock. Massive pillars of iron and stone soared out of the floor and pierced the roof, forming the foundation upon which rested the entire weight of the colossal structure.

They no longer needed the torches, for the room was awash in a soft red light. A light breeze ruffled their hair as they clung to a carved wooden railing that circled the perimeter of the chamber. Very softly, as from a great distance, a dull roar could be heard. Like the breeze, it seemed to rise up from a wide, gaping hole in the center of the floor. The air was quite warm and charged with energy as miniature lightning bolts snapped and crackled through the ionized atmosphere above the fissure in the Earth.

"These catacombs are very deep down," Adima whispered as Cybele joined them, "and through these underground channels the magnetic currents of the world flow." He pointed around the mysterious chamber. "This is the center of a vast web of tunnels and caverns. Some lead to various points on the surface of our island. Others, though, have not been explored in modern times...deeper, darker tunnels leading to places we only know about in myth and legend."

He paused a moment, sensing the hidden power waiting just below the surface, ready to spring forth when the word was given. "The red glow you see and the sound you hear is caused by the Secret Fires of the Earth. The Temple of Poseidon was raised over an epicenter of magnetism, and that which is located here is continually churning underneath. Stand patiently and observe. Perhaps you may see something."

The twins did as they were told. Never in their wildest imaginings had they expected to see anything such as that which they were witnessing here in the bowels of the Temple. The vast mysteries that had already been revealed above them were wondrous enough in and of themselves. But those had been man-made, and they paled in comparison to the awesome presence and power of the Dragon Fire.

"Can you feel the ground shaking?" Alta whispered to his sister.

"Yes, I hope it doesn't cave in..." Charis started to reply, but was instantly silenced by a gentle touch from her mother, who pointed into the shadows far across the cavern.

From the dim recesses of the earth, several black-robed, hooded figures made their silent way to the edge of the smoldering pit. They stood together in a semicircle, hands joined, staring into the fiery depths below. Man or woman, it could not be told, just dark, human shapes coming together for a great and sacred purpose.

"They are the Holy Ones," Cybele whispered softly, bending close between the twins so that the sound of her words did not carry beyond their young ears as she quoted from the *Book of Mysteries*:

> LIVING SEPARATE AND APART FROM THE WORLD, DEEP IN SECLUSION WITHIN THE GREAT MOTHER, THEY UNDERSTAND THE GREAT MYSTERIES OF HEAVEN AND EARTH, AND THEY HAVE DEVOTED THEIR LIVES TO PRAYING FOR THE PEACE OF THE WORLD. THEY DO THIS BY PROJECTING THEIR THOUGHTS TO THE SEETHING UNDERWORLD.

"If you have any prayers you want to say or petitions you want to ask, now is the time," Adima stooped to join them. Together the four joined hands and prayed in the silence of their hearts. For prayer among the Children of the Law of One was understood to be a deeply personal thing. It followed no prescribed form or formula, being much more preferable to allow the feelings to flow from within one's own heart in a personal conversation with the Great Creator as they understood their Creator to be. And so the family prayed, opening themselves and asking according to their heart's desire, spending a Holy Instant in personal communion with the Divine.

It did not take long for an answer to come. As the family watched and prayed, the fire glowed ever redder, the breeze blew ever warmer, the roar grew ever louder. As if in response to their petitions, a mighty tongue of flame shot up from the depths with a thunderous roar, showering the cavern with red-hot sparks, which cascaded slowly down upon the stone floor. By the time that the last of the sparks died out and the yellow, sulphurous cloud of smoke cleared, the Holy Ones had vanished, leaving the family alone once again.

CHAPTER 20

Surrounded by nature, we discover our spiritual selves, our natural selves, our real selves.

—Henry David Thoreau

They stayed overnight in the city, and before the next sunrise had climbed aboard "the Way" and were soon zooming westward at supersonic speed. Mid morning found them walking through a dense, old-growth forest on the western side of the island continent. The twins were used to traveling great distances with their parents at a moment's notice, and had often done so during their young lives. This place, however, was new to them.

"You've seen the city and explored the Temple," Adima said as they disembarked. "Now you are about to step into another community and another temple—the sacred space of Nature—where you will learn to attune yourselves to the natural way."

It was raining, and they walked through dense fog and mist, their breath curling into little wisps of vapor in the damp air. Visibility was poor, the gray light revealing nothing more that a few yards in any direction. The path rose steadily upward, winding among moss-covered trees and huge, jumbled boulders. The twins were not particularly happy about this part of the adventure, but they trudged along stoically, each bundled inside a waterproof parka to keep out the moisture and chill air.

"I hope that wherever we're going has a warm fire and hot drinks waiting for us," Alta grumbled to his sister.

"Me too," came the disgruntled reply. "I hope Mother and Father know what they're doing. Look at them! They don't seem to mind the climb or the weather!"

Indeed, Adima and Cybele were blissfully unaware of the dank weather or the arduous trail. To their attuned senses, the forest had come alive in the rain. The droplets of water on the evergreen trees sparkled like tiny diamonds. The green leaves had a phosphorescent glow. The smell of the damp earth, the cool, moist fog caressing their faces...they saw abundant life and beauty everywhere. As they walked, each took the time to point out interesting things about the living forest. "Look at the trees," Adima instructed. "Feel the living presence of the living planet. Everything is alive."

The twins looked around, searching for signs of life in this enchanted wonderland. Visibility was poor here in the deepest part of the forest. At such a low elevation, fairly close to sea level, the light had a dim, greenish glow, for the trees were so tall and the branches so dense that almost no sunlight filtered through to the ground. Ancient monarchs of spruce and hemlock, perhaps two hundred and fifty years old or more, soared hundreds of feet into the air, their massive trunks dotted with mosses, lichens, and ferns.

"Listen to the forest song," Cybele urged, calling their attention to a symphony of birdsong—the mating call of the grouse, the percussive rat-a-tat of the woodpecker, and the tiny chirps of sparrows and chickadees as they flitted quietly through the branches along the forest floor. Far overhead, gentle breezes sighed through the uppermost boughs. Overall, the feeling was one of serenity and repose.

On either side of the trail, if indeed it could be called a trail, massive slabs of stone lay piled one upon the other, perched at precarious angles. To the twins, they appeared to be so delicately balanced that they would come tumbling down at any minute. Yet when the

the last ice age, carried along by the moving frozen mass, then left stranded in their new home when the glaciers had receded. From within the cracks and fissures of those rocks, piercing, nonhuman eyes peered furtively at these aliens who were passing along this sacred trail. "Who are these strange creatures?" curious voices whispered to each other. "What are they doing here on Mount Kylene?"

"They are human. Beware!" came the reply from the ancient wise ones. "They are not like us. They bring only death and destruction wherever they tread."

Of course, these denizens of the forest did not speak in the language of the human Atlanteans. Theirs was the first language, the language of the animals and plants and Earth spirits, understood only by those who are one with the forest community. These were the people of the forest—four-legged creatures, many-legged creatures, crawlers and burrowers, winged ones, rooted ones, those who roamed by day, and those who prowled by night. All part of a vast, complex, harmonious community. Perfectly balanced, perfectly ordered, they acted on instinct and natural law, manifesting the Circle of Life, the Eternal Return.

"Stay hidden," a blue-eyed elder spoke up. "To let them see you means the end of our existence here. Beware the two-legged creatures who walk upright and bring only death and destruction wherever they tread. Their ways are not our ways. Their ways are not in accord with the Law of One."

"Wait," an orange-eyed elder interrupted. "What you say is true. But listen to what the large ones are telling the small ones. Those are not the words of the outworlders. The large ones speak the words of truth, words that are in accord with the Law of One. Could these be the ones? Could they be the ones of whom the prophecy speaks, those for whom we have been waiting?"

"Of course not," the first Elemental snorted, blue eyes glowing brightly in the dark recesses under a huge slab of basalt. "Everyone thinks the prophecy will come to pass during their sojourn here. But it never does. There's no reason to think it will now. "Besides, they don't look like prophecy-fulfillers. I know what the prophecy says. I've been studying it for ages, and I'm an expert, as was my teacher and his teachers before him."

"Don't smell like them, either," Yellow-Eyes sniffed and wrinkled its nose disdainfully. "I say get rid of 'em. Push a boulder over on 'em. Cause a landslide and bury 'em, the deeper the better!" The tiny creature danced up and down, eyes sparkling in excitement and anticipation at the thought of wreaking havoc on the humans who dared to encroach upon the sacred forest.

"I say wait," Orange-Eyes spoke again, calming his more obstreperous companion. "Who are we to interpret the prophecy or to decide in what form it should be fulfilled? Who are we to try to make Spirit conform to our definition of it?"

Had this been a human company, perhaps there would have been a long and bitter argument, ending with hurt feelings, violence, or a divided community. But this was a community of Elementals, with no human egos to bruise, no unnatural motives or feelings to adversely influence their behavior. True, they were fearful, but for such as the Elementals, fear served its natural purpose of protecting them from harm. Fear was not, as is the case in the human world, a motive for their behavior.

"Your words are wise and true," the group agreed, each colorful pair of eyes glowing brightly. "We shall observe these strangers who have so suddenly come into our midst before we take any action. Look, they have stopped in yonder grove. Let us listen. Shhhh!"

"Look at the nurse tree," Adima stepped from the underbrush into a small clearing and pointed to a huge bole that had crashed to Earth at some unknown time in the past. "Nowhere is the cycle of life and death, decay and rebirth that perpetuates the forest better illustrated than here," Adima explained in reference to the fallen tree's ability to nurture life. The trunk was in a state of partial decomposition, one of many fallen sentinels decaying by degrees into a carpet of mosses, mushrooms, and ferns. Sprouting in rows along the top of the parent log, tiny green seedlings poked up their heads, fertilized and nurtured by the moisture and nutrients in the rotting wood.

After so many years, it had become home to ants and termites and all sorts of wood-boring creatures, bugs, and beetles. Assorted mushrooms and other fungi bracketed the sides of the rotting log like scalloped sculptures. Emerald-green moss grew along the top side of the fallen trunk and spread onto the ground for several yards. Small round holes like dark eyes had been burrowed into the moss at various places in and under the log.

"Those are Elementals' houses," Cybele pointed out. "Be careful where you step. You don't want to disturb their beautiful carpet. The Earth spirits take very good care of their homes. We're guests here, so remember to tread very carefully."

The twins stayed at a discreet distance. They were no strangers to the elf houses, as they called them, having seen them since early childhood on excursions with their parents. From infancy, their parents had told them tales of the Elementals—elves, fairies, devas, and other Earth spirits who inhabited the old-growth forests and helped things grow.

"Will we get to see one?" Alta wondered aloud, letting his imagination soar as he conjured up images of fairy faces peering out at him from among the leaves and flowers. These spirits of trees and plants were creatures with which every woodland traveler was familiar, described in the *Book of Life* as:

...THE FOREST SPIRITS—AN INSEPARABLE PART OF
THE VISIBLE QUALITY OF EVERY BUSH AND TREE.

"No," Adima laughed, "this isn't like the Dragon Festival, where you can catch a glimpse of the green flash if you're very alert and conditions are just right. The Elementals don't reveal themselves to humans. They're very shy, and rightly so, having suffered much devastation to their homes and communities at the hands of the human race. The best thing we can do is to honor them by respecting their right to privacy and leave their belongings and their community undisturbed. Besides, we have to be moving along if we're going to reach our destination before nightfall!"

In the darkness under the rocks, naturally bright eyes began to glow even brighter. One by one the Elementals looked at each other, heads nodding in approval. Still they listened and waited.

"It's so foggy," Charis waved her arms, trying to disperse the gray mist that swirled all around her. "It's not a very nice day here. Are we lost?"

"You can never get lost in the forest if you understand its ways and speak the language of Nature," Adima told her. "Look around you. Do you see a trail? Do you know in which direction to go?"

Charis looked. Try as she might, she could not discern a path through the impenetrable growth that seemed to surround the tiny clearing. "We're lost," she shrugged helplessly. She wasn't really worried. Her parents seemed quite calm, so they probably knew exactly where they were and which way to go to reach their final destination. As usual, they were trying to teach her something.

"Why not ask the trees to show you the way?" Adima suggested. "That's what I do when I'm in the forest and can't find my way."

"The trees?" Alta raised his eyebrows in an expression of sincere disbelief. His father had some strange ways, to be sure, but this one seemed particularly implausible.

"The trees are the elders of the forest," Adima explained. "This is their home, their community. They can never be lost, being so firmly anchored to the Great Mother. Of course they know where they are, and they are always willing to show a lost traveler the way."

"If that traveler is one with the forest and intends no harm to the forest community!" Cybele added. "Trees are among the gentlest and most unconditionally loving creatures on the planet. Consider the ancient proverb in the *Book of Life*.

> BE LIKE THE TREE, WHICH OFFERS SHADE EVEN
> TO THE WOODSMAN WHO WOULD CUT IT DOWN.

The twins mulled this over for a moment. Neither of them had ever thought like this before. Their mother was offering them a whole new way of looking at trees, a whole new understanding of this living creature that they were so used to, yet knew so little about. So they asked.

"Which way do we go?" Alta addressed a stately blue spruce. He did so with all earnestness and seriousness. To do otherwise would have displeased and dishonored his father and mother, and he had no desire to do that, even if he really did not believe it would work.

"Look, even now the way is opening before us," Adima pointed to a gap in the foliage. Stepping through, the underbrush instantly seemed to thin out and grow less dense. So they walked on, and the way cleared before them. There were rocks and branches on either side, but in front of them clear passage was readily discernible. Even when he turned around, Alta could not figure out how they had come through, but there they were, walking through the fog and mist, apparently on the right path.

On and on they went through an ever-changing forest, here in a thicket of evergreens, there under a canopy of broad-leafed maples and bushy cottonwoods festooned with vines and colorful orchids. And ever the way led steadily and gently uphill. And as they walked, others traveled with them, silent and unseen...creeping on padded paws along the ground, gliding like a whisper through the upper terraces, or sailing invisibly on the currents of the wind. There was an air of great excitement among the forest community. These humans could be the ones for whom they had been waiting! It felt right. They were here at the right time. They were going in the right direction. They seemed to understand the natural ways and speak the natural language.

So, following the guidance and wisdom of the trees, the Elementals and the others allowed the family to pass, showing them the right way to go to reach their final destination. And as if in agreement, the weather, too, began to help the travelers. The rain stopped, and a warm breeze blew gently down from the heights above. Gradually, the fog began to lift, and a soft orange glow lit the western sky above them.

*****

As the family passed through the two thousand-foot elevation, the air became perceptibly cooler, although not chilly enough to be a particular burden. The lush, moist lowlands, with their moss-hung limbs, nurse logs, and giant spruce, had given way to stronger, tougher trees such as fir, pine, and hemlock. On the steep mountain slopes, huge, moss-covered logs lay tumbled across each other, and streams fed by torrential rains boiled over cliffs and through narrow ravines and chasms.

"I defy anybody to cross without falling in or breaking their bones!" Alta declared, as though translating the torrent's challenge to travelers to dare traverse its icy waters and slippery rocks. Yet cross they did, continuing their steady ascent.

At last, above five thousand feet, beyond the last windfalls and dense stands of fir, the confining world of the forest finally fell away to reveal a vastly different ecosystem indeed from those which lay below. This was the harmonious and beautiful world of the high meadows, nestled almost a mile above the rain forest and coastal plains, at the topmost edge of the tree line, yet still below the barren, rocky peaks above.

Parents and children felt it immediately—the definite sensation of a difference in quality between this wild, elevated world and the quiet, secluded forest below. In the same way, there was no comparison between the comfortable, intimate atmosphere of their home at the edge of the sea and that of the elemental high country, where the Dragon ran strong and wild and free.

"Shhhh!" Cybele cautioned, not wishing to disturb the furry marmots cautiously searching for succulent stems, the black-tailed deer grazing quietly among the gentle slopes, and the elk lazing in the warmth of the mid-afternoon sunshine. They passed quietly through fields of wildflowers that seemed to leap up from beneath a sea of long green grass like multicolored jewels and stars.

"They're so beautiful!" Charis exclaimed, inhaling deeply of the fragrances. "And there are so many. What are they called?"

"Those are paintbrush," Cybele pointed to a cluster of delicate red-orange wildflowers. "The blue ones are called lupine, and the white are peaceflower."

Tired from their long climb, they rested themselves on cushions of soft grass and ate the lunch that Cybele had brought along. On such a clear, bright afternoon, after the dampness of the rain forest, the meadow even *smelled* warm, the fragrances of firs and flowers combining with the sunshine to quicken the life forces. Before long, they napped. And while they slept, the Elementals kept careful watch, confident now that the time of the prophecy was about to be fulfilled. The animals sensed it, too, grazing peacefully and undisturbed in the presence of the humans whom they had allowed to enter their private world.

*****

I watched, too, present there on the high places even as I was present in the deep forest. As the family slept, I stood and listened to the hills as they called to each other across the valleys, listened to the sacred harmonies of the Earth rhythms, felt the ancient beat of the Dragon's mighty heart. Letting my mind conjure poetic images of the forest, the high places, the natural, untamed, primitive world, I gave myself fully to the highly evocative experience of Nature.

Slowly at first, then ever more quickly, I felt myself sloughing the thin veneer of civilization in which I was cloaked, releasing my natural, unspoiled Self beneath. As though I were caught in a whirlpool, I felt myself spinning round and round, slipping further and further backward through space and time. Coming to rest at last in the Beginning Time, in the wild places where the first humans practiced an ancient way of being, more than religion, more even than spirituality. A way of being that was grounded in natural law, a way of being so alien to your own that you can barely conceive of its power, its potential, its benefits. A way of being whose implications are now unimaginable to you who have forgotten the natural way.

Such energy all around me, such power. An almost fluid force, I felt it wash over me, a substance both material and spiritual, natural and Divine. Vibrations of motion and form—intelligent, alert, and alive. Realization dawned on me. I understood. I was in the living presence of the *Imagination of Nature*.

How shall I describe it, this palpable, tangible Life Essence? It has been called by many names in the *Book of Life*.

> THE THREAD THAT CONNECTS THE LIVING WITH THE WORLD OF THE DEAD.
> THE LIFE ESSENCE—THE PREVAILING FLOW WITH WHICH, AT DEATH, THE
> SPIRIT BECOMES MERGED, AND FROM WHICH ARISES THE VITAL SPARK THAT
> STIMULATES BIRTH AND NEW GROWTH.

This was the foundation for the whole primitive existence—as it was for Atlantis and as it is today—for it both creates the universe of which we are aware and also determines the ways in which we perceive it. And perhaps without fully understanding it or knowing why, this was the reason that Adima and Cybele had brought their children to the high places—to spend some time apart from the ordinary world in order to find and connect to the Life Essence.

I felt vibrant, strong, renewed, refreshed, in touch with an energy force of enormous strength and power. All senses alert, attuned to the natural rhythms and harmonies, experiencing beauty beyond anything the man-made world can give. Ready to receive a truth that once was commonly known but is now forgotten. In that state of being, from my vantage point at the top of the world, I heard the soft, gentle Voice of the Hills calling to the Spirits of the Four Winds, asking them to grace me with their message and teaching.

A bitter wind blew out of the North, bringing with it a change of seasons. I turned, and it was winter. In the Land of the Dead, in the darkness of the night, I had become an old man, and I was cold and afraid. From out of the primordial chaos, I beheld a Black Tortoise. Opening its mouth, it spoke to me in a voice that echoed of the grave.

Long ago, before there was an Atlantis, before there was a civilization, before there were roads or houses or any of the trappings of civilization, still there were the hills and the forests and the sea and the high places. It was a different time, a time so unlike your own as to be inconceivable to you. In those early days, the places where you now live—the plains and the valleys—were uninhabited by humans. For in those days, the people dwelt on the high places, the inaccessible wastes that today you find so inhospitable and incompatible with life.

Behold this wild, untamed, natural place! No houses as you know them now, no shelters, no roads, no stores, no modern conveniences, no electricity, no mass communication. Nothing between the inhabitants of the land and the elements themselves. Raw, unspoiled, pure. No roads or paths gouged in the rich, black soil. No living trees cut down and their lifeless bodies reshaped into shelters. No stones unearthed and carved and placed in circles and monuments. No bits of paper and metal to exchange for goods or services. None of the modern conveniences of the world in which you now live. By today's standards, primitive, even savage.

In those days, the people dwelt in harmony with the land, for they knew a great truth—that their lives were enriched by the Life Essence which flowed strong and deep on the high places. They could tap directly into this force, and as a result, theirs was a way of life so different from yours, so alien, as to be completely misunderstood.

For ages, life was simple, harmonious, and complete. And then, a Shift occurred. Not in a single day, not in a week or a month or a year, but gradually, over the course of centuries. The aborigines began to drift down from the mountains and the high meadows and take on the trappings of civilization. They stopped hunting and gathering and began instead to plant crops. And while the crops grew, they began to settle in a particular place for longer periods of time. They stopped wandering with the cycles of the moon and the seasons of the year and the roaming of the great herds upon whom they depended for so much. As a result of staying in one place for longer periods of time, they began to gather more and more things to themselves—livestock, clothing, goods, food supplies, and all manner of possessions. And they began to experience the effects of weather, too.

Poor, fragile humans—so out of place in such an inhospitable environment! Many froze to death, many starved, many drowned in the sea, swept out of their boats as they tried to navigate the waters that they did not understand. Partly to protect themselves from such inhospitable climates, partly to communicate with each other, and partly to store their grain and supplies and animals, they built shelters and roads and storehouses. Eventually, cities were born, and with them, civilization.

Throughout this process, a few remembered the old ways and the benefits of life in the wild places, but their voices were drowned out in the clamor of the new vocabulary of commerce, industry, and civilization. So the old knowledge gradually faded from the common memory and consciousness, relegated to poems, songs, myths, and certain healing practices. As a way of life, the old days were gone!

Of course, there developed new knowledge and traditions to replace the old—knowledge of how things grew and how the tides worked and how to trade and barter goods and services and how to build things. The city-dwellers set up an elaborate system of roads and towns and villages. And to control it all—something that they found to be extremely more difficult than they had ever anticipated—they enacted a social structure far more elaborate than any system they had employed on the high places.

Now they needed governors to keep law and order. Now they needed rules and regulations to control trade and commerce. Now they needed boundaries and fences to protect that which was theirs from others who wanted it. Now they needed weapons not just to hunt, but also to protect themselves from human predators. Little wonder that, not long after the building of the first city, the first murder was committed.

The Black Tortoise vanished, leaving only echoes ringing in my ears. Knowing that there was more to come, I waited. A warm wind blew out of the South, bringing with it a change of seasons. I turned, and it was summer. In the Land of Life, in the light of day, I had become a youth, and I was full of strength and vigor. From out of the fire, I beheld a Red Phoenix. Opening its mouth, it spoke to me in a strong, masculine voice.

Thus it was that modern civilization came into being, as the first people migrated from the high places down into the valleys and plains, where crops grew in lush abundance and the way was easier to accomplish what they had set out to do. Forgetting the old ways, the old places. Coming even to fear them as not being conducive to life. Coming to view the high places as wild and dangerous, where one could be torn apart by wild beasts and suffer grievously from exposure to the elements. Coming to believe the Lie that those who dwelt in the forests and on the hilltops were benighted savages, forced to cower in fear of wild beasts and predatory neighbors.

In a relatively short time, these confused souls came to view the natural world—their former home—as a place of great danger, and they began to fear it greatly. They came to believe that they could only be safe in the company of others who dwelt in the new communities they had created.

Thus it was that the Shift occurred—a shift from a natural state to an unnatural state. A shift from conscious contact with the Life Essence to a forgetting of its life-giving power and potential. Their whole minds were affected, their whole way of being and living. Losing conscious contact with the Life Essence, the quality of life decreased, and the humans suffered greatly. So, too, did the animals and the land.

They did not know it at first, did not realize the harm they had done to themselves and their world as an effect of their incorrect choices. A few did, and they chose to leave the lowland cities and return to the wild and natural state. They were scoffed at and ridiculed and viewed as demented and dangerous, but these few went on to became the stuff of legend—the wild ones, the hermits...so feared by those who do not understand their ways.

The Red Phoenix vanished, and a deep sigh floated through the hills. Knowing that the story was far from complete, still I waited. A dry wind blew out of the West, bringing with it a change of seasons. I turned, and it was autumn. In the Land of the Setting Sun, in the twilight, I had become a middle-aged man, and I was full of sorrow. From the Home of the Thunderer, I beheld a White Tiger. Opening its mouth, it spoke to me in an unearthly, metallic voice.

In the civilized world, the fear grew ever stronger, ever more entrenched. And soon, the whole reversal was complete. The human race had shifted from a natural, tranquil state to an unnatural, unhealthy one. Disease, sickness, and all manner of unwellness and depravity abounded.

Where once there had been a conscious, loving relationship with the Goddess and the Great Mother, now there was Patriarchal religion, replete with dogma, strict rules, and a horrible system of punishments in this world and even after death. Innate, natural freedoms gave way to alien concepts of sin and guilt and death and decay. The old songs of light and love and joy and freedom were replaced with fear-based songs of sorrow and misery. The inevitable results were dissolution and decay, belief in sickness and suffering and death, and toil and pain and misery.

As with all things, regardless of whether they are recognized or not, the great, eternal cycle spins round and round, following the natural laws of Cause and Effect. The Pendulum is always in motion, swinging first to one side, then to the other. And now, the turn of the Pendulum was bringing with it other horrors—poverty, slavery, famine, pestilence, and war.

Did the people see it? Did they realize what was happening? A few did. Slowly and subtly, they began to sit up and take notice. Soon, more and more followed. It did not take more than a glance around them to realize that their world was changing. They could see it, they could hear it, they could feel it. On a global scale, things were changing that they thought would never change. Everywhere they looked, walls were coming down, empires were toppling, fallen giants were lying by the wayside in their own ashes. In their personal lives, they were confronted with change at every turn—in their labors, their homes, their relationships, their communities.

Each had a personal story to tell. How they worked hard, yet after years of labor and commitment were told they were no longer needed or wanted. How they had spent years in marriage only to find that it no longer worked. How they had visited a healer for a routine treatment, only to discover a serious illness. How a loved one had died, and they felt sad and alone. Some were not fitting in too well with their usual groups anymore. Some were beginning to lose interest in what most people still found quite entertaining. Their ordinary routines had become just that—too ordinary, even painfully so.

The goals they'd been striving for no longer seem to exist. What they thought was real was no longer real. The whole world was changing, their personal worlds were changing, and they didn't seem to be able to do anything about any of it. One by one, their Sanctuaries disappeared, leaving no refuge from the dangers of the world.

Little wonder that their first reaction was to be confused and afraid. Wiping the sleep of centuries from their eyes, they asked themselves, "What is going on around here! Is nothing permanent anymore! Everything is topsy-turvy! Everything is out of my control! What am I going to do! I'm trapped. Help!"

The truth was frightening, frightening indeed. These people were as frightened by the truth as their ancestors had been upon leaving the high places. Many of these newly awakened ones concluded that to stay in such a world would mean certain death—their own as well as that of the Great Mother, who they were coming to recognize, if only vaguely, as a living being. Not a quick and relatively painless death, but a long and agonizing one—dying slowly but inexorably of poisons that were the lethal by-products of modern civilization and closed minds.

The only solution was to return to a more natural way of life, but they had little idea of what such a state might be like, let alone how to search for it or where to find it. In their competitive, fast-paced, technological world, they had no means of expressing, other than in aesthetic terms, what it was that made one part of the country seem different from another. They spoke vaguely of a certain spot being picturesque, powerful and stimulating, or peaceful and soothing. They dreamed of what a new world might be like. Yet an all-pervasive fear paralyzed them. In their misunderstanding and forgetting of what was once perfectly natural, they were too terrified to act. So entrenched were they, so stuck in the ways of civilization, that to abandon them, they believed, would mean certain death. What were they to do!

"Mind change," a bold few realized after a time. "We've got to change out minds. We've got to reverse this. Regardless of how afraid we are. Regardless of the consequences."

But others, more powerful in the new culture, said otherwise. "No," they said. "Mind change is not the answer. Heart openings are not the answer. That, in fact, is a lot of magic and witchcraft and mad babbling. The real solution lies in technology. For it was technology that created the problems that we have, and it will be technology that will fix those problems and raise us up to new levels of greatness."

"No!" the awakened ones cried, and so the debate raged full tilt. Back and forth they seesawed, first one side winning, then the other. And all the while, the decline worsened.

The White Tiger vanished, and an unearthly silence enveloped the hills. Wrapping my cloak tighter about me, I waited for the final chapter. A gentle wind blew out of the East, bringing with it a change of seasons. I turned, and it was spring. In the Land of the Rising Sun, in the dawn of a new day, I had become a child, and I was full of hope and new life. From out of the Heavens, I beheld a Green Dragon. Opening its mouth, it spoke to me in a soft, feminine voice that was alive with promise.

One fateful day, the sky darkened, the wind blew fiercely in mighty gusts, lightning crackled, and a strange and powerful Prophet appeared in the midst of the land. Everyone rushed to the mighty City in the Center of the World to see this strange apparition who had come apparently from out of nowhere.

All eyes were on him—a wild figure indeed. Eyes glowing fiercely like an avenging angel from the farthest reaches of the Heavens, he extended a bony finger and proclaimed a great truth and a dire judgment.

"Look at your civilization," he rumbled in a deep and hollow voice. "You think you are a proud and mighty people. You think you have developed a civilization and a technology that has surpassed anything the world has ever known. You fancy yourselves masters of the world and the highest life forms in the universe. Silly, arrogant mortals," he laughed derisively, not bothering to hide his contempt, his scorn unmistakable. "You could not be further from the truth. You could not be more wrong." As if to punctuate this last remark, a bolt of lightning lit up the sky, and a thundrous roar shaking the buildings and the very ground on which they stood.

"For indeed, you are not the masters of the universe. In truth, the civilization you have miscreated is not the greatest the world has ever known. Far from it. Just the opposite. All these thousands of years, you have been moving steadily in one direction, it is true, but that direction has not been forward. It has been backward. Backward, I say!" His voice rose to a shrill pitch, and he laughed maniacally while the sky grew ever darker and the gale intensified. He was hovering on the brink of madness, it seemed, but just as he was about to fall over the edge, he regained his composure and steadied himself.

"Yes, backward," his deep voice softened once again. "You have been in a great and downward spiral ever since you shifted from the natural ways. And now you have produced a world that is so broken, a system so self-perpetuating and negative, that it is bordering on the brink of annihilation. "Annihilation, do you hear!" The madness had returned. "Annihilation!"

The crowd grew ever more restless. Men and women looked at each other nervously, frightened in part by the violent weather, in part by the strangeness of the Prophet, but mostly because they did not understand his words. To some, however, to a small few, these words were strangely comforting. At last, here was validation for what they had been thinking and experiencing in their own lives. "What must we do to save ourselves!" an eager voice shouted from the crowd.

For the first time, the Prophet smiled. It was the question for which he had been waiting. It was proof that the old memories had not been completely forgotten, that the ancient light had not been completely snuffed out. Even the elements seemed pleased. The lightning ceased, and a soft yellow glow—the light of Hope—lit the eastern sky. The Prophet's whole demeanor changed, becoming softer, gentler, and more tolerant. His words, though, were still sharp, still keen, still held a cutting edge.

"You need a mind change," he said simply. "To save yourselves, to avert an approaching crisis so great as to be inconceivable to beings as arrogant as yourselves, you need a mind change—as does your entire world. But this mind change that you need to so radically alter your present social structure is so great that, from a rational point of view, it is beyond achievement. Therefore, you need a Miracle!" From beneath the folds of his robe, he produced a glowing rose-colored crystal, pulsing with energy.

The crowd shrank back in fear, muttering and fidgeting restlessly. "What sorcery is this!" they demanded. "How dare you come here and attempt to destroy all that we have worked and struggled for, all that is dear and valuable to us!"

"What is so dear and valuable to you!" the Prophet asked, genuinely perplexed. "What is this strange attraction for the unnatural—for the fast-paced life of cities and technologies and business and governments! What is this strange aversion to the wild, the primitive, the natural!"

He shook his head sadly, muttering to himself. Ignoring the crowd, he walked through the streets to a grassy knoll just outside the city's eastern gate. Clambering onto a large, flat rock, he raised his eyes skyward, from whence he had come, and addressed the eternal Heavens directly.

"These are strong words, these truths that I am telling them. Some choose to discount them, scoff at them, ignore them. Those who do listen are frightened indeed. Now is not the time, now is not the time." He shook his head, and a great wave of sorrow seemed to emanate from him.

The soft yellow light dimmed once more, and again the wind intensified. After a period of silence, the Prophet turned back toward the crowd. "There is much to teach you, much you need to learn. How to open your hearts, how to reconnect to the Life Essence, how to properly perceive yourselves and your real place in the living universe. How to understand the universe itself. But your minds are closed. You cannot hear my words. What you knew once, but have now forgotten, frightens you too greatly."

He pointed to a group of young children clinging to their parents' hands. "And this is why you fear, because you have lost your connection to the Life Essence. You cannot keep it in the cities. There is too much noise, too much confusion, too many limitations and restrictions placed upon you by unnatural laws—rules, and regulations designed not to enhance life but to limit and curtail its growth.

"Be not discouraged, however. I do not tell you this to leave you afraid and hopeless. There is a solution, and it lies in your own minds, in your own hearts, in the memory of and recognition of the truth, in a realization that transcends human agreement, politics, business, and government."

The Prophet placed the glowing stone on the ground before him. It was almost midday, yet the sky was as dark as twilight. Heavy, roiling clouds obscured the sun. He glanced skyward, then addressed the crowd one final time.

"I am going away for a while," he said. "So I leave this gift with you, the gift of the Heart Crystal. If you use it properly, it will help you, for it contains great truths. If you do not use it now, so be it. It makes no difference. You can act now or wait. The choice is up to you. That you must act is inevitable. The only question is when.

"Let yourselves feel. Be open to the truth and to the experience. Abandon your arrogance, which no longer serves you. Open your hearts. Take a long, hard look at yourselves and your world. Be honest. Above all, be as truthful with yourselves as you can possibly be. Do not lie, even to yourselves, as you are wont to do even in the privacy of your secret writings and conversations, for lies will do you no good. If there is to be any chance for the miracle, you must be open to the truth.

"To you, this cannot seem natural, for what you have done to hurt your mind over the ages since you fell from the high places has made it so unnatural that you do not remember what is natural to it. And when you are told what is natural, you cannot understand it. The recognition of the part as Whole, and the Whole in every part, is perfectly natural, for it is the way Creation thinks, and what is natural to Creation is natural to you.

"It is stirring in your memory even now. Some of you hearing my words are saying, yes, I remember. It feels so right. I do remember. Of course. It does not have to be this way. It does not have to be thus. There is a better way."

This was more powerful sorcery than the crowd could stand. Words and ideas far too frightening to be tolerated here in the City at the Center of the World. No thoughts of gratitude. Only the desire to silence this mad, grim messenger of doom. "Stone him," came the cry from the terrified, bloodthirsty masses. "Stone him. He is evil. He is dangerous. He must be destroyed."

Inevitably, someone cast the first stone. In the ensuing melee, the rose crystal disappeared, and those who had been moved by the truth of the Prophet's words scattered to the four winds. The storm raged for a long time, and the Center of the World was deserted, the only sounds the wind and thunder and driving rain. But in each crash of thunder, the echo of the Prophet's voice rang loud and true, echoing hollowly off the stone walls, hardened hearts, and closed minds.

There were tears in my eyes as the Four Winds finished speaking, for I knew their tale was true. I knew who they were talking about. I knew from the past, and I knew from the future.

"Thank you," I whispered, bowing in turn to each of the four directions, remembering to be grateful, remembering to show the proper respect to my teachers. From out of hiding, the Elementals came and sat beside me and comforted me. We exchanged no words, content just to sit in the high meadow in the late afternoon sunshine. Finally their leader spoke.

"Are these the ones?" His orange eyes glowed brighter even than the sunlight. "Will the prophecy be fulfilled through them? Will they be the ones to bring about the reversal? Will they be the ones to carry the Life Essence back, to unblock it and restore its flow all across the world?"

"I do not know." I shook my head, looking at the sleeping family as they lay in the soft grass. "I just do not know. The choice is not up to us. We can only remind and whisper and guide, gently and unobtrusively leading them in the right direction. If they choose to come, wonderful. If they choose a different path, so be it. The choice is up to them. We cannot choose for them. They have free will. They have to want to do this. Willingness, acceptance, and understanding are the keys."

"Their minds are awakening," Blue-Eyes sparkled. "Will they stay awake?"

"I think they have already chosen the truth in their hearts," I replied. "That is why they are here today. The Seed has been planted. Now it remains for it to be nurtured and tended and cultivated until it grows strong."

"The Seed must be carefully tended," Orange-Eyes warned, "so that weeds and vines and insects do not choke it or eat it."

"So that extremes of temperature do not freeze it or burn its leaves," Green-Eyes added.

"So that the reaper's sickle does not cut off the stalk at ground level and cast it into the fire," Blue-Eyes admonished.

"And while it is growing, the Seed must be pruned and watered and fertilized, so that, at the appointed time, it will bear strong fruit," Yellow-Eyes concluded.

I looked at the gentle creatures around me. So innocent. So eager and willing to help. "You are the Elementals, the keepers of things that grow," I said. "As you cultivate the Mother's garden, so I charge you now with helping to cultivate the Seed which has been planted here today. By human standards, many thousands of years will pass before it grows strong and bears good fruit. And much will happen In-Between.

"First will come the destruction and fall into ignorance. Isolated groups of survivors scattered about the world will forget their former unity and the sublime science of Atlantis. False and diverse ideologies will arise, vying for supremacy. A few will attempt to rebuild, of course, but they will be frustrated and thwarted, ever at the mercy of those rival idealists.

"Human history will be a series of continuous defeats for those groups and individuals who attempt to reverse the tide of ignorance, superstition, and arbitrary violence. Until the time when the next reversal takes effect. When the progeny of Adima and Cybele and Alta and Charis awaken and remember the true nature of Creation:"

A SINGLE LIVING UNIVERSE, A VITAL ORGANISM WHOSE EVERY PART IS SUBTLY RELATED TO EVERY OTHER...THE SUPREME MANIFEST IMAGE OF THE NUMBER ONE!

"When they view themselves as a part of the Whole:"

EACH ONE LINKED TO EACH OTHER AND TO THE GREATER BODY THROUGH THE SEASONS AND CYCLES COMMON TO BOTH AND THROUGH NATURAL SYMPATHY BETWEEN THEIR CORRESPONDING PARTS.

"When they recognize who and what they really are!"

Orange-Eyes reflected on my words for several moments, nodding his head in agreement. Rising to his feet, he gathered the Elementals about him and addressed them. "A long time to accomplish indeed," the tiny being said, "this journey out of Darkness back to the Light." His huge eyes were aglow with enthusiasm. "Yet by the reckoning of the immortals and the Mother and the Great Creator, it is already accomplished. We have waited a long time. We can wait a little longer still. The time is coming. It is only a moment away. We will help the humans!"

*****

Alta dozed lightly for barely an hour, then he could stand it no longer. In his eagerness to reach their final destination, he ran on ahead, across the meadow and back into the trees, full of the exuberance and boldness that come with being thirteen and in Nature. After his experiences of the past few days, he thought he was prepared for almost anything. But nothing in his wildest expectations had prepared him for the experience of stepping out of the last fringes of forest onto that windswept plateau for the first time.

He gasped in astonishment, drawing in his breath through his teeth and standing perfectly still, just wanting to look, to let his senses drink in the experience of this place. Leaving the world of the forest behind, he had stepped boldly out onto a broad expanse of rock just below the summit of the most sacred of Atlantean high places—Mount Kylene.

Before him, like a window into Heaven, lay an incredible panorama. Behind and to the east were the forest, cliffs, and waterfalls. Several miles to the south, a silky white ribbon of beach bordered a deep blue sea. To the west, the setting sun filled the horizon with its brilliant yellow glow. Due north, the naked pink rock receded for an unknown distance into a blue, opaque mist. And above everything, the snowcapped peaks rose upward into the vast, open sky.

The light took on a golden color, the sounds of birds, wind, and water filled his ears, the breeze caressed his bare skin, and time seemed to be suspended. "We are in the presence of the Guardians," Adima spoke softly as he, Cybele, and Charis came up to join Alta in the experience.

It was enough. He need say nothing more. For this was a place of choice treasures, blending in countless elemental forms, especially those of Earth and water. As old as the Great Mother herself, this was *The Place Where the Mountains Meet the Sea*. From a deep natural spring at the very top of Mount Kylene, the River of the Setting Sun was born, along with its three brothers and sisters—the four great rivers of Atlantis. Nothing more than a wide stream at this altitude, the blue-green water tumbled down over the pink granite cliffs, coursing through a series of three waterfalls on its gorgeous, adventure-filled journey to the Sea of Peace many miles to the West.

Where it tumbled over the rocks to form a deep, clear pool at the base of the cliff at Alta's feet, the watery spray had painted the adjacent pink cliffs a bright, glowing red. Against this vermilion background grew maidenhair ferns, stream orchids, and a wealth of foliage almost surrounding the pool in coat of lush greenery.

"I've never seen water this color," Alta exclaimed, splashing his hands into a pool of the most brilliant turquoise imaginable. Indeed, the water was of a color like no other Atlantean river—a delightful blend of reflected blue skylight, blue-green algae, and billions of white mineral particles suspended in the icy flow.

Stretching in a line along both banks of the river, yellow monkey flowers, stalks of blue monkshood and lupine, red columbines, and a rainbow of other blossoms grew in profusion, while bees bustled and butterflies flitted about in the drowsiness of late afternoon. In their midst, flashing colorfully in the sunshine, blue jays, black grosbeaks, golden finches, orange orioles, and red summer tanagers danced in and out through the foliage like winged fairies searching for delicate morsels to eat. And ever-present in the background, soft and subdued, could be heard the musical play of the falling water.

The blue-green pool, the pink and red granite, the green plants, the colorful blossoms, the birds and bees and butterflies, the icy spray, the waterfalls...all were lovely in and of themselves. Together, they formed a near-mystical experience. Ages ago, before even the terrible lizards had roamed the Earth, the Island of Atlantis had come into being, and with it, the sacred slopes of Mount Kylene. The *Book of Life* recorded it thusly:

> IN VIOLENCE ATLANTIS WAS BORN, IN VIOLENCE IT LIVES. YET OUT OF THAT VIOLENCE IS CREATED A GREAT AND BEAUTIFUL PLACE—A PLACE OF COMPROMISE, CONFLICT, AND ETERNAL CHANGE. A PLACE WHERE MIRACLES HAPPEN ALL THE TIME. A PLACE WHERE LIVES THE DRAGON!

And standing guard over that fragile pocket of beauty, and, indeed, over all of Atlantis, were the Guardians, spiritual watchkeepers of Atlantis and protectors and allies of the Great Mother. Ages ago, they had come from far across the universe to set up their bold experiment. Great winged beings with multicolored light bodies, they landed in their crystal ships, appearing as gods to the aboriginal inhabitants.

Every schoolchild knew the story as it was written in the *Book of Life* and told around the holiday fires—of how the Guardians had met the early humans and given them the gifts of fire, language, music, metallurgy, "cold fire," and flight. How they dwelt here with the First Man and the First Woman, teaching and informing them until that great day when Poseidon was born to raise up the Kingdom of Atlantis. This was the Guardian's sacred place, and as an eternal reminder of its extraordinary qualities, all manner of remarkable events occurred here—lightning struck, meteors crashed, nobles were born, and strange visions took form. Adima pointed to several huge symbols that had been deeply etched into the living rock.

"These etchings tell the story of the creation of life," he said, pointing to each of the sacred carvings in turn. "The undulating serpent beneath our feet is a symbol of the current of life energy. Those drawings farther up on the cliff depict family life and moral lessons. And there, closest to the edge, is a map of the Dragon's route across the countryside."

The air was warm with the passing of the early-morning storm. It was a lovely, balmy summer evening. Adima led them to a fallen log that served as a bench on which to sit and admire the view. Reds, oranges violets, blues, pinks...the sunset was a riot of color, warm and pure and all-embracing. From behind huge thunderheads, the great rays streamed out in all directions, emanating from a single source, spreading out over land and sea and air. Arcing across the heavens, a rainbow formed a sacred bridge between Heaven and Earth. Far below, the Mother's voice whispered softly, the wind soughing through the trees.

"How silent, how ordinary," Cybele mused aloud. "This sunset has happened every single day since the First Day, regardless of who is here to watch it. Regardless of clear skies or cloud cover. Alchemists and geomancers can describe it and tell exactly why it happens and reduce it to mere scientific facts. But there is more to a sunset than that, something far beyond the ordinariness of it. Something even beyond the beauty of it. There is a sacredness about it, a sacredness in the ordinary." She put an arm around each twin and spoke directly to them.

"Learn this lesson well, my children. Even in the most ordinary circumstances, even in the most mundane places, even in the most commonplace events, like seeing a sunset or saying hello to a stranger or watching a rainbow or petting a dog, be conscious, be aware. Experience, *feel*, the sacredness of the encounter, the holiness of the moment. Do not squander the opportunity, for you will never have it again. Each instant is all there is. Each instant is sacred. Each instant contains the opportunity for a miracle."

The twins listened in rapt attention, their twin minds and twin thought processes in perfect accord. They had heard various forms of this lesson for most of their young lives. Over the years, in lessons such as these, they had assimilated various bits and pieces of facts, some related, some not, or so they thought. Now, though, after their experiences in the city and the Temple and the forest, they were beginning to develop a new understanding. An inner Voice seemed to be saying, "Wait a minute, all of this is related! All of it combines to form a Whole greater than the sum of its parts. Now that we know enough facts, our parents are trying to instill in us a concept of the Whole."

"For it is thus that you become adults," Adima continued. "If you can carry the feeling of sacredness into the ordinary, everyday actions of life, if you can attend to that which is going on around you and that of which you are a part, then you cannot help but know your place in the scheme of things and recognize your interconnectedness to the great unfolding life process of which you are a part. And you must be a part of it by your very nature...not recognizing it doesn't mean it's not true.

"You are still a part of the grand design, even if you are ignorant of the fact. So why stay ignorant? It's so much more exciting and fulfilling to know your part and accept it and embrace it fully. That's the gift, that's the beauty, that's the Sacred in the Mundane!"

"And that's how we change the world, heal the world, and transform the world," Cybele concluded. "We achieve redemption by liberating and intensifying the bodily senses, by an improvement of sensual enjoyment, and by attaining and sustaining that mode of vision that does not deny the fallen world, but transfigures it. Quite simply, we literally change our minds! And in changing what is in our minds, we change what we create. The effects of what we create ripple outward and affect everything else. By changing how we *see* the world, we change the world itself."

They paused to watch the Master Artist paint the sunset—silently, with no noise or fanfare, only a blaze of color. No words were spoken until Charis voiced the questions that reflected not only the inner struggle in her own young self, but also that of so many Atlanteans, young and old alike.

"How do we change the world, Mother?" There were tears in her eyes as she spoke. "There's so much wrong, and so much that needs fixing. How can we do it? There aren't enough like Alta and me to do it by ourselves."

"Yes, what *is* our part?" Alta chimed in. "What are we supposed to do? We can't change the world by ourselves. We're only thirteen. We're small and insignificant and powerless in the face of the likes of the Sons of Belial. The system is too entrenched for us to have any effect."

"Shhh," Adima patted each of them on the back. They have strong passion, he thought to himself. They will be strong adults. They will need such strength in the time to come. "It is not your task to try to change the world." Adima gave the answer that was so simple, yet so hard to understand and accept. "You are not in charge of changing anybody but yourself. You only have to change, heal, and transform yourself. That is a big enough job in itself."

"Isn't there a great deal of relief in knowing the rest is not your responsibility?" Cybele asked.

"But why isn't it up to us?" Alta clenched his fists spasmodically in frustration. Like his sister, he was feeling rather powerless in the face of the likes of the Sons of Belial. "Where did it all go wrong? What happened to the grand experiment of the Guardians? What happened to make the Sons of Belial so powerful and corrupt? And what happened to make the Creator punish us by expelling us from of the Garden?"

"Yours are ageless questions," Adima smiled. "Be comforted in knowing that you do not struggle with such thoughts alone. I have them, your mother has them...we all have them from time to time. Everyone has doubts and fears and frustrations. But it is in how we learn to deal with those feelings and emotional states that we overcome them and so heal and transform ourselves. Let me answer your questions by telling you a story."

> When the Guardians first arrived and Atlantis was new, there was a release of energy—experimental boldness and creative power were in full bloom in the world. We were a people with a deep understanding of the nature of the universe. But that went away as we became ever more engrossed in the material realms, forgetting who we were and where we had come from. Forgetting our true identities and natures. For you see, we did not fall away from the Creator. Just looking at the sunset tells you that."

Adima pointed to where the sky had taken on a purplish hue.

> No, we fell away from our oneness, our One Self. We fell into division, into a collection of fragmented, separated, isolated beings, running around living separate, isolated lives, not in tune any more to the other lives around us, the other lives of which our life is and must be a part.

> In division, there is suffering, tyranny, static negation, and isolated selfhood. In unity consciousness, there is relaxed innocence, without the clash of contraries.

> We did not "fall from grace" or get expelled from the Garden. The Garden is all around us. We got expelled from our own minds, from our own psychic awareness of the truth about ourselves. And who could have expelled us but ourselves!

"So it's going to be your own imagination that will redeem you from this 'fallen' state," Cybele continued. "Recognize in your imagination that you create the world you see and that you are capable of changing your mind about that which you see. Then indeed you can create exactly the world you want. For it has been done. The Guardians and the Ancients did it. The Sons of Belial are doing it now. In their worldview, they hold that the ultimate reality is a mechanized world consisting of physical particles in motion, and so we have the world order that we do—sickness, war, greed, pollution, and scarcity consciousness."

"But Nature proves the opposite to be true," Adima pointed out. "The outer universe is a living entity that shares the feelings of the observer. The world is sharing your feelings even as you look at it. You are watching the sunset, you are experiencing it, so the sunset is feeling what you are feeling. It is as happy to show itself to you as you are to observe it. And as a way of saying thank you for noticing, it gives you food for thought—a memory, a provocation to stir something in you to think about."

He pointed to the landscape all around them. "That's why the great nature poets come to places like this—to look at a rock or a tree or a butterfly or a moth or a daffodil. Not to describe the daffodil for its own sake, but rather to let the daffodil invoke something deeper in them. Natural objects are symbols that have a natural correspondence to the spiritual world. Roses, sunflowers, mountains, caves, and clouds are objects that possess a significance beyond themselves. Our great romantic poems often begin with an aspect or a change of aspect in the natural scene, which serves as a stimulus for thought. The scene raises an emotional problem whose development and resolution constitute the organizing principle of the poem."

Adima paused and smiled at his children, remembering what it was to be so young and have so much to learn. "That's the secret—for the poets and geomancers, as well as for you and me and everybody, even the Sons of Belial. Imbue the landscape with human life, passion, and expressiveness. For you see, unlike the city, unlike the Temple of Poseidon itself, the physical universe gives us direct access to the Creator, even itself possessing the attributes of Divinity. The landscape has attributes associated not only with God, but with Father, Mother, and Beloved. In the *Book of Life* it is written:"

> SEEK IN WHAT YOU SEE THE LIKENESS OF SOMETHING BEYOND THE
> PRESENT AND TANGIBLE OBJECT.
> THE MIND IS ITSELF THE CREATOR OF THE UNIVERSE IT PERCEIVES.
> THE MIND ITSELF CREATES ITS OWN EXPERIENCE.

They were interrupted by a rustle in the underbrush. A magnificent antlered elk leapt from the forest and trotted across the bare rock. It stood motionless for a moment in full view of the family, poised, every sense alert. Then in a flash, the animal was gone.

"Great Spirits now on Earth are sojourning," Adima whispered. "There is something Divine about this time in which we are living—a pervasive climate—the *Spirit of the Age*. Let us stop and watch."

He ceased speaking. They all watched as the sun, now a huge, flaming orange ball, sank lower and lower toward the horizon. Alone with their thoughts, they let the experience enfold them and take them where it would, transform them as it may, imbue them as it may.

And then the sun was gone. The family sat in silence for a while longer, until the first stars began to shine in the darkening sky.

*****

It was completely dark before the campsite had been set up and the fire blazing. "No moon tonight," Adima murmured. "That is good. It is better to look at the sky in compete darkness, with no white light to interfere with and affect our night vision." Calling the twins once again, he led them a short distance along the cliff to a spot beyond the glow of the fire. "You've looked at the world around you. You've looked at eye level; you've looked below. Now it is time to look up.

"Indeed," he continued, "that is the most important place of all to look. For it is in looking up that we are reminded of our true nature, from whence we came. It is in looking up that we gaze into the Eye of Spirit and see our own spirit reflected back to us in the twinkling lights in the sky."

Adima pointed into the night, his arm tracing the path of the ecliptic across the heavens. A soft, milky white cloud floated above them in the blackness, the glow of billions of stars as he and the twins looked out into the galaxy from their position at the edge of one of its outward spiraling arms. "All of the stars are alive," he said, sweeping his arms through the air, as if such a gesture could encompass the entire heavens, "and intelligences live in them.

"There is the Archer," he pointed to a cluster of stars far to the East. "See how he aims his bow and shoots his arrow at the giant Scorpion? Each group of stars forms a pattern. Each pattern is a reflection of some aspect of our human natures."

"You, Charis, and you, Alta." Adima stood between his children, an arm around each of them. "Sister and brother. Conceived in the same place at the same moment in time. Twins. Look up, and see yourselves in the sky!" He directed their gaze to a cluster of stars far out on the western horizon. Indeed, as they looked, they could detect the pattern of the Sky Twins standing together, linked arm in arm.

"What do you see as you look at the Sky Twins?" Cybele asked as she joined them.

"Two people holding hands," Charis exclaimed, taking hold of her brother's hand in imitation of their celestial counterparts. "A brother and a sister, tall and strong, standing watch over us."

"Interesting that you noticed their strength," Cybele was pleased at her daughter's intuition. "What makes you say that they are strong?"

"They look strong," Alta was frustrated at his inability to be more descriptive. He knew the answer was deeper than mere appearance, but his youthful mind could not quite grasp the metaphor for which he was searching. "They're big and powerful, looming over us in the sky. That must make them strong."

Charis nodded her head in agreement, but words failed her, as they did her brother. Yet there was a tantalizing realization floating just beneath the surface of her awareness. She tried in vain to bring it into expression.

"You're close to the truth," Adima encouraged, sensing their struggle, "but the Sky Twins' strength has nothing to do with their size. Observe them once again. What else about them could make them strong?"

The twins peered intently into the sky, but the insight they sought was still tantalizingly out of reach. Finally, Adima pointed to them. "Look at yourselves," he instructed. "What are you doing that the Sky Twins are doing?"

"Looking at them as they are looking at us," Alta answered quickly. "How does that make them strong?"

"What else are you each doing that is the same?" Adima ignored the last part of Alta's question.

"Holding hands?" It was more of a question than a statement. "But that can't be a source of strength, can it?" Charis asked doubtfully.

"Indeed it can," Cybele stood up and took her husband's hand in her own. "The Sky Twins are showing the two of you how to behave, how to be strong, how to make your way in the world. Look at them, and learn from them." As she spoke, she pointed to the sky, and with her index figure, slowly traced the human figures, separately first, then joined together.

"Each twin is a separate person. Each is a unique being in his own right. Each maintains his individuality. Each has his own power and talent. But when they join their individual selves together, their individual powers and talents are doubled. The two become as one, retaining their individuality but functioning perfectly together as a single being."

Adima stooped and drew a yin-yang symbol in the soft dirt at their feet. "Each may be quite opposite from the other, as are the two of you," he said, referring to the symbol that depicted the opposites encased within the Whole. "One may be dark, the other fair. One may be outgoing, the other introspective. One may be male, the other female."

"Like the Sky Twins, you, Alta, and you, Charis, share a unique relationship that most brothers and sisters do not. You are opposites—one yin, the other yang, always alike, yet always different. Each of you is whole. Each of you is a complete person.

"And," placing his hands on each twin's head and looking at them with a father's deep love, Adima uttered the sacred, defining words, "*you share the same soul!* You are the unified Duality—twin children of the Swan, unified Fire and Water. This is your true nature. This is what it means to be a twin. This is your strength, which can never be broken."

He paused to let the full weight of his words sink in. A light breeze wafted up from the valley floor so far below. Simultaneously, Alta and Charis felt that delicious light chill of awe in the presence of truth as it ran along their spines and over their skin.

Cybele joined in the embrace and blessing. "This is the lesson that your sky teachers are sharing with you and that your father and I have been leading up to for these past few days," she said. "You each possess a dual nature—a human nature and a wild nature. Neither one alone is enough. Your power comes when you recognize the opposite sides of yourselves and bring them together. As it is written in the *Book of Life*:"

THE POWER OF THE TWO IS IN ACTING AS ONE.

The twins sat in silence, each thinking the same thoughts about their relationship to each other, their love for each other. They were so very close. They always seemed to know what the other was thinking, always were able to sense the other's feelings, even anticipate the other's behavior before it happened. Now they knew why. They also knew why their parents had gone to such lengths to nurture their twin natures and twin relationship over the years, not neglecting either side of the duality. Such attention—never devoting more or less time to one than to the other, ensuring that everything the twins shared was of equal measure, value, and balance.

"Thank you," they whispered together. Forgetting for the moment that they were young adults, they kissed each of their parents as they had been wont to do as children. A single tear welled up in Cybele's eye, and she grew reminiscent. Sitting cross-legged on the stone, she motioned the others to join her. "When you were born," she said, stroking Charis's hair gently, "your father and I knew the special soulfulness you would bring to the Atlantean community, for we knew that which is written in the *Book of Life*:"

TWIN ENERGY IS THE MYSTICAL ENERGY OF THE SOUL.

"At your Consecration, our teachers, Enoch and Sophia, named you *The Mystical Pair*. It is thus that they have always referred to you."

Alta and Charis looked at each other in the darkness, sharing in each other's astonishment. They had been given a name, not separate and unique names; rather, a single Name, which they shared as one.

"In those days," Cybele continued, "they charged us as your parents and givers of life with our mission as Guardians of the Mystical Pair, charged us with ensuring the integrity of your staying together. All of your lives, your father and I have been preparing you for the time when you would make your way in the world. That time begins here and now, as your childhood dies this night on Mount Kylene and your adult selves are born."

Adima removed two eagle feathers from his pouch and handed one to each twin. "If these were ordinary times, each of you would now embark on your separate vision quest," he said. "For it is in the practice of such rituals that you learn your connection to the cosmos and the community. But these are not ordinary times. You will not embark on the ritual vision quest tonight. Yours is to be a different experience. The coming upheaval will serve as your initiation. While in the future others will be initiated in ritual form, the two of you will walk *the Path of Direct Experience*."

He paused, heaving a deep sigh. The twins sensed their father's emotions—sadness at letting his children go, joy at their entrance into adulthood. "You have heard your mother and me speak of the End Times. You have heard strange talk, rumors and whisperings not intended for the ears of children. But this night marks the end of innocence. This night you are adults, and so your ears must be opened, and you must listen well if you are to serve in your appointed roles and put forth your gifts in the coming transformation."

Alta and Charis nestled closer to each other as their father spoke. Strange words, indeed; strange attitude. Where was the kind and loving protector who had always watched over them and kept them from harm?

"Some of this may frighten you," Adima seemed to be unaffected by their fear, "but you must be told. There is nothing at all to be frightened about." He pointed to the sky, then drew his arm across the heavens, following the plane of the ecliptic once again. "You have the greatest of allies, the greatest of teachers, the most protection and support that you could possibly have. Your safety is assured, not matter what might appear to happen.

"And that is a most important word to remember—*appear!* Be not deceived by appearances. Be not deceived by that which you do not understand. All will be revealed as it unfolds. You will be shown the way, shown your part in the Plan, and protected throughout its unfoldment."

Alta peered intensely at his father, but in the gloom could barely discern his features. If only he could see his face! If only he could reassure himself that this strange man was indeed his father. But there was only blackness where that familiar countenance should have been.

"What are you talking about?" the boy blurted out, his fear disguised as anger. "Your words are strange. What is it that we are to be protected from?"

"There will be upheaval," came the voice from the darkness. "There will be a reshaping and a reshifting of the land and of the Atlantean culture. But if you do not resist, if you go with the natural rhythm and flow, all will happen as it is supposed to happen. The old will fall away of its own accord, and the new will rise up gently in its place. Both will happen in accordance with the Plan."

Charis tried to ask more questions, but her mother's voice was firm. "We will talk no more of this now. Over the next few days, more will be revealed to you." As with Adima, Cybele's tone and demeanor had subtly changed. There was a serious edge to her voice, a sense of urgency in her manner. Under the shroud of night, her lovely face appeared only as a featureless, dark oval in the surrounding blackness.

"On this occasion of your thirteenth birthday, your father and I give you the gift of the past few days." Cybele and Adima rose to their feet as she spoke, drawing the twins up with them. "Take with you in your hearts this single piece of advice—keep your Center amidst the pull of opposite forces. As you are continually faced with choices, remember who you are, and see yourselves in others."

Adima spoke, too. "Belial will try to break you, so be strong," he counseled, walking a few paces away and looking back at them. "You are strong when you stand together. When you are with each other, you cannot be torn asunder."

A brilliant streak of light arced across the sky, lending emphasis to Adima's words. "Behold the shooting star," he continued, now only a voice in the blackness. "It travels incredibly swiftly, its fire shining brightly. But only briefly. All of its energy is consumed in its fierce-paced run across the heavens."

"Learn from its mistake. Receive the gift of stamina from Elk. You will need this gift before long. Pacing yourself will increase your stamina, so that you accomplish your goals and reach your destination with strength and energy to spare, without burning up, as does the shooting star."

"Now we retire for the night." Cybele, too, began to move away as she spoke. "We leave you alone on the sacred slopes of Mount Kylene, without us, your parents. Alone for the first time, but not alone, for you have your individual selves, and you have each other. As you spend the night on Mount Kylene, be awake and watchful. Remember the experiences and lessons you have shared during these past few days. Attend to the new, as well—that which you experience this night. Above all, be alert, for something will come if you are aware of it."

Adima and Cybele looked back at their children from the edge of the woods. "Good night," they called in unison. Then, holding hands and softly humming an Atlantean lullaby, they were swallowed up by the forest, leaving the twins alone in the darkness.

*****

They were alone, they were tired, they were overwhelmed, and they were afraid— terribly afraid! They tried not to show it, but it was useless to pretend. The tears came, softly at first, then in great, wracking sobs. Wailing out their fear, their sorrow, their confusion, their anxiety, their grief, their lost youth.

How long they wept, they could not remember afterward. But after the tears, after the release of emotion, came the catharsis. Was it Alta who remembered the teaching, or was it Charis? Which of them, thrashing about on the ground, looked up through tear-filled eyes to behold a watery vision of the Sky Twins holding hands and looking silently down on them?

Each reached for the other's hand. Finding it in the darkness, they drew closer to each other until their bodies touched. With the drawing together, a curious thing happened. The feeling was comforting. It was reassuring. The touch of his sister's hand; the feel of her brother's skin. The texture of each other's clothes. The sound of each other's breathing. These were things they knew, things with which they were familiar, things that gave them comfort.

In the familiar, they were soothed. And once they were soothed, they began to notice something else. Sitting there on the rock, listening to the night sounds, watching the stars, they were not so afraid any more. Why not? each wondered silently. They were still alone. The future events had not changed. They were still about to be faced with the fearful terrors to which their parents had alluded. But the fear was not there. Or at least, it was more tolerable.

"Maybe we aren't going to die after all," Charis whispered to her brother. His answer was a tightening grip on her hand. That was when they heard the groan for the first time.

"Mooooooooaaaaannnnnnnnn!" The mournful sound floated eerily on the night breeze. The hair on the napes of their necks bristled. Alta jumped to his feet, dragging Charis with him. Neither had any intention of letting the other one go.

"Mooooooooaaaaannnnnnnnn!" There it was again, followed this time by an audible cracking sound.

"It seems to be coming from right around here," Alta whispered as softly as possible. "Do you see anything?"

"Nothing," came the frightened response. "But I thought it came from farther away."

"Let's start walking," Alta suggested. "Maybe there's a bear or some other wild animal around."

"That was no bear," Charis chided. "That was not an earthly sound. That was a ghost. I know a ghost when I hear one, and that was a ghost!"

As if to confirm her conclusion, the eerie wail sounded a third time, almost at her elbow. She broke into a run, dragging her brother behind her as she dashed along the rocky plateau.

"Wait a minute," Alta exclaimed, finally slowing her down, gasping for breath. "Remember what Father said about not wasting our energy. I can hardly breathe. The air is thin up here, and if I'm going to have to fight, I'm going to need my wind. Besides, I can't see all that clearly. We might run into a tree or fall off a cliff. Then we'd be in a real fix."

"You're right," his sister agreed. "I'm sorry. But I'm really scared!" The tears started to flow again.

They sat down on the rock and huddled close together, each seeking comfort in the other. Each waiting for the monster to spring from the shadows, pounce on them, and devour them. Each surrendering to a fate they were powerless to avert. But the monster never came. Even as the sounds continued, no wild animals loomed up before them, no ghosts or demons appeared to haunt them. Yet the incessant wails and clicks continued. It was Charis who finally discovered their source. Lying on her side, one ear to the ground, she heard the sound and at the same time felt a subtle vibration in the rock beneath her head.

"It's coming from inside the rock!" she exclaimed in astonishment. "Listen, the rock itself is making the sound."

Alta placed his ear to the granite and listened. He did not have long to wait.

"Mooooooooaaaaannnnnnnnn!" The uncanny sound drifted up from deep within the living rock beneath them. Again and again the sound was repeated, and suddenly, Charis started to laugh. At first it was just a giggle, but then she laughed out loud, happy laughs of relief.

"What?" Her brother looked at her in amazement. "What's so funny? What's going on? Are you crazy?"

Finally Charis regained her composure long enough to catch a breath. "It is the rock, silly," she told him. "Don't you remember what we learned in geomancy class when Teacher took us on that excursion to the Pillars of Atlas?

"No, I don't!" Alta was angry at his sister. What was she getting at?

"Of course you do," Charis went on. "Remember that she told us how the warmth of the sun heats the rock all day long, then after dark, when the air cools down, the rock cools down, too? And when it cools down, it creaks and groans and makes a lot of weird noises. We've just been listening to them." Charis beamed a smile of glib satisfaction. She was quite pleased with herself at having remembered that particular scientific fact and applying it as a solution to their plight.

"You're right," Alta grinned sheepishly. "I forgot all about that. I'm glad you remembered, because I wasn't looking forward to staying awake all night keeping a lookout for demons."

The twins laughed happily at themselves for a while. After a time, listening to the rock creak and groan as it cooled, Alta grew reflective. "The voice of the rock," he mused. "How is it like us? What do I think as I listen to the rock sing? I think of my own song. I think of my own voice."

Charis looked at her brother but did not interrupt his reverie. She was the mathematician-artist. He was the poet-musician, and when he found his voice, as he was doing now, something wonderful always came forth.

"The Voice of the Rock," Alta sang, the light, impromptu melody drifting across the darkened plateau. *"My own voice."*

> *"The rock speaks its truth.*
> *I speak my truth."*
> *"The voice of Nature.*
> *The Imagination of Nature.*
> *The imagination of myself."*

"How like the rock am I?
The rock—pink and smooth and strong.
Firmly anchored to the world."
"How like the rock am I?
Myself—young and growing strong."
"Not like the rock,
Or so it seems."
"Perhaps I am.
Perhaps a deeper part of me
Is very like the rock."
"The rock shares our fear,
Shares our pain,
Shares our feelings,
Shares our experience.
As we cry, so cries the rock.
As we grieve, so grieves the rock.
Even the mighty one weeps,
Yea, the mighty rock,
Firmly anchored to the Great Mother.
Lying on the Bosom of the Mother
As we lie on the bosom of the rock.
The rock grieves, grieves for the Mother,
As we grieve, grieve for ourselves.
The rock grieves for the loss of the Earth
As we grieve for the loss of our childhood.
The rock shows us it is okay to cry.
Okay to be afraid.
Okay to grieve.
This is part of life.
This is part of the Way.
It is okay, it is okay, it is okay...

Lying there, looking up at the Sky Twins, Alta sang his soul song, not just for himself, but for his twin sister, with whom he shared the same soul. "It is okay, it is okay, it is okay..." he intoned over and over again, until the gentle gift of sleep embraced him.

A shooting star blazed across the heavens, and Charis instinctively made a wish for each of them, as they had been taught as little ones sitting on the veranda at Elysia. Tears welled up in her eyes again, and she lay her head on her brother's shoulder. A soothing peace enveloped her as she listened to the great pink rock sing its lullaby of grief. Soon, she followed her brother into sleep under the watchful eye of the Guardians in the sky.

CHAPTER 21

For now we see through a glass darkly; but then face to face: now I know in part; but then I shall know even as also I am known.

—*1 Corinthians 13:12-13*

There were three opposing philosophies in Atlantis occupying three different points on the Pendulum's arc, each with its own distinct set of values and beliefs. Far to one side were the *Sensates*, espousing a value system which held that Matter alone was the ultimate reality, and that spiritual phenomena were merely manifestations of Matter. "All ethical values are relative," they argued. "Sensory perception is the only source of knowledge and truth."

Thinking this way, the Sensates could justify all manner of "civilized" evils—the Divine right of kings, manifest destiny, slavery, racial supremacy, and the curious belief that the Earth was a nonliving, nonfeeling storehouse of inexhaustible riches that were there for the taking, there to be exploited by the dominant species for their personal gain, regardless of the cost in suffering or loss of freedom, even unto the extermination of all life on the planet. Thus were birthed two dangerous and destructive ideas that have survived in various forms throughout the long cycle of recorded history:

The needs of the few outweigh the needs of the many.
The ends justify the means.

Far to the other side of the Pendulum, diametrically opposed to the Sensates, were the *Ideationalists*, representing a value system that was profoundly different. "True reality lies beyond the material world, in the spiritual realms," went their argument. "Knowledge can be obtained only through inner experience." Theirs was a world of absolutes—absolute ethical values and superhuman standards of justice, truth, and beauty, thus laying the foundation for future representations of the concept of spiritual reality.

In the center of the Pendulum, representing the Ideal, holding the Tension of the Opposites, were the *Idealists*. Their value system was a synthesizing stage, harmoniously blending of the best of the Sensate and Ideational expressions of human culture. "True reality has both sensory and supersensory aspects that coexist within an all-embracing unity," taught the Idealists. Thinking and acting accordingly, they at one point attained the highest and noblest expressions of both Ideational and Sensate styles, producing balance, integration, and esthetic fulfillment in art, philosophy, science, and technology, planting seeds that would sprout up and flourish on more than one occasion over the next several thousand years.

Over time, from within these three very different philosophies, two separate and distinct communities emerged. Like yin and yang, they were in direct opposition to each other, in direct contrast to each other. At opposite poles, on opposite sides of the Pendulum. One light, one dark; one spiritual, one material. One following the left-hand path of the soul, one following the right-hand path—the ego's way. The best of Atlantis, the worst of Atlantis. One relatively at peace within itself, one full of dissension, discord, and strife. One moving forward toward enlightenment, the other standing still, even moving backward into chaos.

Each was convening its leaders. Belial called together his henchman and thugs and soldiers—strong, oppressive men, dominant and domineering, tyrannical, dangerous killers. Adima and Cybele called together the leaders of the Children of the Law of One—wise, sober men and women, not leaders so much as trusted servants.

As the family made their way home from Mount Kylene, so too these leaders made their way to the great city. From all over Atlantis they came, these few men and women of power. Summoned by Belial, the Dark Ones made their way to the Great Pyramid. Summoned by Adima and Cybele, the Light Ones made their way to Elysia.

Both groups traveled in secret—the Dark Ones because it was their intent to sneak up on their prey and pounce and kill, attacking by surprise; the Light Ones because they were concerned for the safety of the masses should word of their gathering get out. From far and wide, along many roads, they all converged, following the spokes of a great wheel that lead from the outer rim inward to a central hub. Coming into the center for a great gathering. Making ready. Some with focused intent, others barely conscious of what they were doing. All of the diverse and polarized groups were gathering together.

Moving throughout the Atlantean realm, silent and unseen, I saw all, I felt all, I shared the experience with all. I watched a once proud and mighty people cower and tremble, huddling together for safety and protection, looking skyward, casting fearful, furtive glances to the heavens or backwards over their shoulders.

Politicians convened in the Council chambers. Priestesses and pilgrims gathered at the shrines and in the temples. Wanderers returned home, adventurers did not veer too far off the beaten path. Parents drew their children nearer. Watching and waiting—for what, they did not know. Nor did they realize, although all of the signs were there—in the land and sea and sky.

The wind blew more fiercely. The birds sang less often. Fewer and fewer turtles came ashore to lay their eggs. Whales and dolphins beached themselves and died. The Earth trembled more violently every day. Lightning flashed and struck with ever-increasing frequency.

Many chose not to stay in their bodies in such fearful times. There was much sickness and dis-ease, as well as widespread transition. Those who did not understand remarked that there seemed to be a lot of trouble in the world at the moment. They could never remember times being like this. Those who were even partially awake, however, knew that something was coming—a great, mysterious Unknown, slowly and inexorably spreading widespread unease and anxiety before it, bringing with it troubled minds and restless spirits. Permeating the land was an air of expectancy.

"Soon," a Voice whispered on the morning and evening wind, *"but not quite yet. There is still much to be done. But soon nevertheless."*

"Gather yourselves," it cried to all who would listen. *"Gather your families and friends unto yourselves. There is strength in numbers."*

But they would not attend. Poor Atlanteans. They would heed neither the warning nor the advice. They heard and ignored. They saw and closed their eyes. Had they hearkened and acted, many more would have survived. Such a stubborn race, such a proud race! Perhaps it never entered their consciousness that they could be brought low.

So only a few, a very few, endured—those who knew, those who listened, those who were willing and committed. Gathering together, confronting evil, building the great Arks, enclosing themselves and their treasures within, floating on the turbulent waters to another place and time, floating toward a date with destiny.

*****

Even as Belial and the Adepts met in the Great Pyramid to discuss their future plans, so, too, the Children of the Law of One gathered together at Elysia, invited there by Cybele to discuss the future. As Belial had issued the challenge, so Cybele had put the forth the Call—summoning others like herself, those wise in the ways of the Mysteries, schooled in the knowledge of the Law of One. From all over Atlantis they came—the Poet, the Artist, the Scribe, the Physician, the Farmer, the Teacher, the Lawyer, the Musician, the Architect, and the Scientist. From Poseidia, Amaki, and Sus—large cities and small villages—gathering at the request of one among them whom they loved and respected.

Elysia was the perfect location—secluded from the city, with easy access by land and sea, close to "the Way." And the time of year was perfect, too—early fall, just as the leaves reached their peak colors. The day began in reunion, with Cybele greeting each guest warmly, like an old friend. Indeed, these were the friends of her youth, those with whom she had attended school in the Temple, with whom she had been instructed and initiated into the Mysteries. While she had chosen to stay and serve as priestess, however, the others had chosen more secular lives.

Most of the morning was occupied with the small talk associated with a gathering of old companions, many of whom had not seen each other in several years. They had grown up together, played together, learned together, lived and laughed together. Then adulthood had come, and they had scattered to different parts of the island, each according to the dictates of his or her own Inner Guide. Always, though, they stayed connected in heart and mind, communicating frequently, exchanging news of each others lives—of marriages, births, deaths, and the like. Now here they were together again, the original ten plus herself—eleven to take on such a seemingly insurmountable task. Of course, they would be ably supported by Adima, Enoch, Sophia, Alta, Charis, and Nabala. But the Eleven were the ones who would, Cybele hoped, answer the challenge and respond to the Call.

The Eleven, plus one more. In her heart, she knew there were to be twelve. The missing one, however, remained unknown to her. Who else is there? she wondered, trying unsuccessfully to picture who was missing. The answer would not come. She would have to wait for the twelfth one to be revealed.

They spent the first hours just chatting and reminiscing, catching each other up on their lives. Reminding each other of things they had forgotten—joking, laughing, relishing each other's company, reveling in the joy of being together again. After a light midday meal, they gathered together in the shade of the veranda to talk of more serious things. Cybele spoke first, Sophia by her side. "I am going to ask you to open your minds and hearts," the priestess began, "for I have something amazing to tell you. Something that you might find difficult to accept at first. Something so unbelievable, so frightening, that you probably won't want to believe it."

She looked at her old friends. Some of them fidgeted nervously or looked out at the lagoon. No matter. They were deeply spiritual men and women. She could be open and honest with them despite the strangeness of the truth. That was why she had summoned them. "Some of you might doubt what I am about to tell you. Perhaps you will call me a liar or tell me I am crazy." She smiled, knowing that her friends would do no such thing, even if they absolutely could not find it in their hearts to agree with her words.

"Some might choose not to listen at all. That is your privilege. You may stay or leave as you wish. But I ask you to consider this. You all know me. I would not have summoned you here if I did not think this was important. Nor would you have come if you did not love and trust me. Please, I beseech you in all humility, hear me out. Give me a chance to tell the whole story. Then and only then, make up your minds. Fair enough?"

Heads turned back and forth, eyes met, tacit agreements made. "Fair enough," each one nodded. And so Cybele began, starting out by reminding the Eleven of that which they already knew—how the quality of life in Atlantis had degenerated under the rule of the Sons of Belial.

Lawyer interrupted her. "Cybele, we already know all of this. We live it every day. Have you called us here to state the obvious?" It was a subtle, gentle prodding for her to stop beating around the bush and come to the point.

She got the message. "You do know this," she agreed. "You know that something is terribly, terribly wrong with Atlantis. But do you know what the *effect* of these actions will be?" She looked each one in the eye as she asked them to consider her question. "Have you ever really considered what is going to happen if this keeps up?" She paused, knowing it was time to reveal part of the Goddess's message, although she did not reveal its source. *"Absolute destruction of Atlantis,"* Cybele spoke slowly, emphasizing each word, *"the end of our way of life!"*

There! She had said it. She had spoken the unspeakable. Startling news indeed. Unbelievable news. Heads turned, friends glanced at each other.

Poet spoke up, her face ashen, filled with fear. "Why do we have to talk about this?" she asked, pleading with her eyes to not have to listen any more. "Why can't we just talk like we were talking this morning? Why do we have to discuss politics and the Sons of Belial anyway? Let's just have a nice reunion. It's so lovely here, why let them spoil our fun?"

She spoke for the whole group, Cybele knew, and perhaps for all of Atlantis. Knowing there was a problem, they did not wanting to face it or acknowledge it in any way, choosing, instead, to deny or ignore its existence in the hope that by doing so, it would go away.

"Trust me," Cybele answered," I do not enjoy talking about this any more than you do, but I feel there is no choice. Whether we choose to look at the problem or not, it nevertheless exists. And because it does, someone has to address it. I feel that someone is the collective 'we.'" She paused, letting the group reflect on her words for a moment. While they were still thinking as individuals, each was experiencing a particular aspect of the group mind. That's why she had summoned these particular friends.

As children, whenever they had a problem to solve or a challenge to face, they had come together in a group to work it through. Each of them would assume a particular role, often without even knowing it. In that role, they would express individually what the collective was experiencing. One might express the doubt and fear, another the powerlessness. In response, someone would speak with courage and optimism, suggesting that they investigate the situation further before giving in to the fear and panic. And so the process of creative problem-solving would begin.

Soon, the group consciousness was immersed not in the problem, but in the solution, gathering information and marshalling their resources while remembering to care for and nurture each member of the group, each individual that needed emotional support. It was why they had always worked so well together. Each brought a unique creativity to the group, each loved the others, and each always remembered to have compassion for the others. That was how and why they worked so well together. That was why they would work so well again this time.

"I do not want to deny the possibility of this danger looming over us like some malevolent cloud," Cybele continued. "I want to assume for a moment that the danger is very, very real. That there will be a great conflagration. That the Sons of Belial will destroy all up. That there is nothing we can do to stop them. So, you ask, then what? We'll all be dead and Atlantis will be gone." She laughed nervously. "That is, if you haven't already made up your minds that I'm crazy."

Her friends laughed with her, calming her, letting her know that they loved her, crazy or not. That offer of emotional support was all the encouragement she needed.

"It is not my purpose to dwell on the *problem* this day," she said in her most optimistic tone. For in truth, she was optimistic, and she wanted to share that feeling with the group, too. "I have invited you here because I want us to talk about what we can do about it. I want to focus on the *solution*."

It was Artist's turn to voice the feelings of the group. Before they could be optimistic, they had to express their powerlessness and pain at the effect of her words and the truth of their situation. "What solution might there be?" she asked. "If what you say is true, there is nothing we can do about it. We are far too weak to stand up against the Sons of Belial. They would cut us down in a moment. In fact, they're just looking for an excuse!"

Cybele nodded her head. "You are absolutely right," she agreed. "We cannot challenge Belial."

"So then what?" Teacher asked. "Have you gathered us here just to frighten us?"

"Yes," said Farmer. "What do you want us to do, jump into the ocean and swim away?"

Cybele smiled. In jest, her friend had come quite close to the truth. "That is exactly what I want us to do," she laughed, pointing to the edge of the veranda as though she were about to dive into the inviting waters of the lagoon. Then she grew more serious. "But not helter skelter, not one by one, with no rhyme or reason. I want us to do it as a group—a collective exodus from Atlantis, taking our loved ones, our treasures, and our culture with us."

So she revealed the whole truth, beginning with the prophecy of the Goddess and the directive to gather the treasures against the dark times and concluding with the directive to build the Ark, leave the island, and carry the essence of Atlantis with them. As she spoke, incredulity spread across the faces of her friends. Cybele thought it was because they were surprised to hear the prophecy. But it was something so much deeper.

As they listened to her words, each one felt a strange feeling inside, a sense that somehow all of this had been planned, that they were players in a much larger game, a much larger set of events. There was no surprise at her words. Each one already knew exactly what she was talking about. Why? *Because each one had received the same message from the Goddess!*

To some, the message had come in dreams and meditations. To others it had come through artistic expression. The problem was that, in every case, no one knew what the message was, who it was from, or how to interpret it. All they knew was that it had been extremely vivid, very real, and constantly in their thoughts. Try as they might, they could not get rid of that "something" buzzing around inside them. And there they had sat with it, some for weeks, others for but a few days, trying to figure out how to deal with it or even to understand what it was that they were dealing with.

Each one felt the same thing. Something momentous was trying to break through, but they did not know what. So they had kept their thoughts and experiences to themselves, as was their wont. No need to go off sharing that which they did not understand until they understood it a little better. Now it had surfaced again, here at Elysia, in the most unlikely of spots, as they listened to Cybele relate their experience back to them.

How amazing! Teacher looked at the others, thinking she was unique, that she alone shared a similar experience with Cybele. Little did she know that this was a collective message—that each had been given a piece to share and a part to play. She stood up and looked at her friends. "I hear your words, Cybele," she said, nodding also to Sophia, "and I honor you for your courage in speaking so boldly to us. Now I, too, must be courageous and speak my truth. You saw the look of surprise on my face as you spoke. I am surprised by your words, it is true, but not by what you say. Rather, I am surprised by the fact that you have spoken aloud what I already know to be true in my heart."

Her friends looked at her, intrigued. "For you see, I, too, have come to believe what you believe." She thought for a moment, deciding within herself whether or not to reveal a personal secret. "I may be laughed at and ridiculed for saying this, but I have no choice. Not now, not in light of what I have just heard.

"For many months now, I have had a recurring dream in which I see a terrifying darkness sweep over the land. A loud voice cries out to me, pointing me toward the South, where a huge vessel lies at anchor. On board are hundreds of people, but they cannot sail until I arrive. For I am their captain, and only I know the way that will lead them to safety. In my dream, I stand at the water's edge, not knowing what to do. The voice urges me forward, the people call out for me to embark, but I just stand there, powerless to move, confused."

She paused, obviously shaken by the secret she had revealed. "Each time I dream it, it is the same. Each time I awaken, I try to rationalize the dream away. But it will not go away. It is always with me. Now I know, having heard your words, that the dream is a message, an assignment from Spirit directing me to fulfill a great purpose. I shall stand with you and support you in this, although I have no idea how we are ever going to accomplish it. But if Spirit says we can, we can. I have faith."

There was silence after Teacher spoke. A few of the friends looked at each other, but mostly they kept their heads down. What are they thinking? Cybele wondered, letting them take all the time they needed to digest this powerful news.

Artist stood up timidly. "You aren't going to believe this," she said, almost apologetically, "but I, too, have had a similar experience. Not a dream, but a vision, almost identical to your dream, Teacher. I didn't know what to do about it or how to interpret it, so I turned to my art and painted what I saw. Look!"

She reached into her bag and produced a small water color in which she had depicted herself lead a group of pilgrims away from the destruction of Atlantis in a great floating Ark. "I have shown no one until today," she said, "not even you, my husband." She patted Poet's shoulder. He squeezed her hand reassuringly.

"You mean to tell me you painted Teacher's dream?" Poet asked, astonished. "I wrote a poem about it."

"I wrote a song," Musician announced.

"I drew a map," Lawyer declared.

"I carved a boat, and I never even knew I had any talent for sculpting!" exclaimed Scribe.

"I built some kind of an engine for a machine that I don't even think exists," Architect revealed. "It's sitting on my porch because I don't know what to do with it."

Heads nodded in agreement and confirmation as one by one, each of the Eleven spoke, sharing a common experience, a universal Call from the Unknown, warning them of a great deluge that would come upon the land and inviting them to board a huge ship and float off to safety.

So each one shared their personal experience of how they had expressed, through their craft, their encounter with the Unknown. Some had used art forms that were familiar and comfortable; others, much to their amazement, had discovered talents they never knew they had. Now that they had revealed their secrets and learned they were not alone—and, more to the point, not crazy—they turned to each other for emotional support. "When did you have your dream?"

"A fortnight ago. I remember it well, because the weather was so terribly rainy. I remember thinking the next morning that the rain and flash floods probably influenced my dream. Then I put it out of my mind until now."

It was the same for each of them. First had come the encounter, followed by vain attempts to rationalize it and explain it away. They had tried unsuccessfully to forget about it, delving into the creative experience, and trying to deal with it all alone. Until now, when the call from Cybele had come, and they had journeyed to Elysia. Who would have imagined it was on account of this! They had always known they were close, linked by bonds of love and friendship. Now, it appeared, they were linked by another bond, one that they did not quite understand yet.

"What does this mean?" Lawyer asked, reaching out to the group for emotional support. She was quite shaken and tired of feeling alone. Her friends were here, and she was glad for their support as they shared this experience with her.

Sophia had been sitting quietly off by herself, silently observing and listening to all that passed among the friends. Now she spoke for the first time, answering Lawyer's question. "It means," she said, explaining the purpose behind the Calling, "that we have all shared a common spiritual experience, including myself." The old woman went on to speak at length of her own encounter in the Cave. "You are deeply spiritual people. You are all Children of the Law of One. You know your Source; you know your purpose. Don't you find it at all interesting that the common theme underlying each of your experiences is not fear, but creativity?"

No, they had not realized that, but now they paused, struggling to grasp the significance of what was happening. "So what do we do with this common experience?" Scientist asked, voicing the uncertainty for them all.

Sophia's answer was simple and direct. "We draw together. We come closer, forming an alliance, accepting the will of Spirit, doing as we are asked. We will divide the labor, each according to his and her skills and uniqueness. Some of us will gather resources and make plans. Some will be Seekers, going out and gathering information. Others will serve as Destroyers, helping all of us let go of illusions and false hopes. Still others will assist with embracing change, maintaining the commitment, and creating the new. And always...from answering the Call, to preparing for the journey, to taking the journey and coming out the other side...we must remember what is most important—to care for ourselves and each other, to have compassion for ourselves and each other, and to attend to our own needs and the needs of each other."

Artist was incredulous. "So we build an Ark?" she asked, eyes wide as saucers.

"Yes, we build an Ark!" Scientist exclaimed enthusiastically, not waiting for Sophia to answer. "We employ all our skills, all our artistry, all of our Atlantean technology and science, and create the most perfect vessel ever to sail the waters of the Great Mother."

"But how will we fit everyone into a single Ark?" Physician asked. The questions were starting to come faster now as they became more enthused, caught up in the spirit of the adventure, responding to the crisis in a novel and more appropriate way.

"We'll build more than one," Poet replied. "We'll build several, one for each of us. In fact, there's probably one built already. I've seen a rather strange-looking vessel cruising around the harbor in Poseidia."

Poseidia—the great seaport and shipbuilding center on the southernmost side of the island. About half the size of the city of Atlantis, Poseidia was situated a few miles inland, along the banks of the River of Many Waters, which ran deep and clear and smoothly to the sea. It was a perfect harbor—deep water, protection from the elements, access to inland waterways, and the great docks.

"I know that ship," Teacher said. "It belongs to Nuah and his sons."

Everyone knew Nuah, or at least knew of him. He and his family had been shipbuilders for generations, for as long as anyone could remember. Shipbuilding was of utmost importance in Atlantis. A seafaring people, they prided themselves in their great skill as shipbuilders, plying their trade across the world's oceans in their huge, magnificent ships. Of all the Atlantean shipbuilders, Nuah was the best. His were more than mere ships. They were works of art. From cargo vessels to yachts to simple pleasure craft, everyone wanted to own a vessel that Nuah had built.

The old man liked nothing better than to open his shipyards to the public, speaking at great length of his knowledge of ships and his great love for and understanding of the sea. If he did not know you by name when you approached him, he certainly would after a few minutes. And even if many years went by before you saw him again, he would still remember your face and your name, and the occasion of your last visit.

"Well, then, let's call upon Nuah to come up here and speak to us."

"We'll send for him tonight," Cybele exclaimed, delighted by this response. "If he is willing, he can be here by midday tomorrow." Of course! she thought to herself. Nuah was the missing one. He made the Circle complete. He was the twelfth—the Sailor!

*****

So a few among the Children of the Law of One were called to perform a great service for the many. So they answered the *Call*, beginning in optimism and innocence, learning first to trust their own intuition, their own inner Voice, as also they trusted each other. They would need that trust in order to move through and beyond their feelings of disappointment, abandonment, and betrayal by the Sons of Belial.

"We trusted them," Farmer cried, angry now at the people who were supposed lead and protect them. "We went about our lives as carefree innocents, thinking everything was fine because our trusted leaders said it was so. And they let us down. They abandoned us—the very ones who were supposed to care for us." There was not only disappointment in his voice, but bitterness as well. He was voicing the feelings of orphaning and betrayal that they all felt.

"We must learn from this," Sophia replied soothingly. "We must learn that we have to take care of ourselves and stop trusting the Sons of Belial to provide for our every need, because they won't. They've proven that once and for all. In spite of how badly it hurts to think so, in spite of how afraid we might be to rely on ourselves, this it exactly what we must do."

The old woman stood up, stretching her ancient back and throwing a few crumbs of bread to the ever-present birds hovering over the veranda and lagoon. "But we don't have to do it completely alone. We can band together for mutual support. We can form a nurturing community in which we all cooperate with each other."

And so they did, on that very day, sitting on the veranda at Elysia. They took charge of their own lives. The *Time of Preparation* was underway.

For the rest of the afternoon they talked, dividing the responsibilities, developing their strategy, setting goals, making plans. In a single day, they became again as they once had been—a community, caring for each other, helping each other remain courageous whenever the fear and doubt crept up, as they often would, especially at night and when things did not seem to be going as smoothly or as quickly as they expected. Reminding themselves about the danger of expectations. Keeping focused on Divine Order and the Plan.

The gifts that would come would be fourfold. First of all, they would be optimistic. They would stand together as one, as a single community. They would develop the courage to face the Beast...as frightening as it appeared to be. And most importantly, they would learn compassion—for themselves and for others.

Such were the ingredients for the Community of Love, which they were going to have to begin building this day and re-establish at the journey's end. They were setting a strong foundation now. The answer was given, the commitment made. It called for a level of willingness and bravery and courage the likes of which the world had never seen.

It would be a while yet before the full import of what they were doing would dawn on them. Better that way, Cybele thought, so as not to dampen their enthusiasm. When the time came for the actual embarkation, they would have had lots of time to get used to the idea, and perhaps it would not be so traumatic. The reality, she knew, was never as bad as the anticipation of the reality. Her mind could generally conjure up much worse images than the actual events brought. So this was acceptable for now.

Thus began the movement through the cycle along each stage of the journey—the *Call*, the *Preparation*, the *Journey*, the *Initiation*, the *Return*. It would take a long while as they responded to the challenge and moved from the beginning through the cycle and back to joy and innocence, but eventually they would get there.

*****

That night, as Adima slept peacefully beside her, Cybele lay awake, thinking about her first meeting with Nuah. She had been a young girl, just into her fifteenth year. Having grown up in and around the Temple, she had never actually been on the sea. The closest she had come was when she swam at the beach and floated on her friends' rafts in the lagoons. The experience of sailing over the waves on the high seas, however, lay before her.

Then the occasion came for Sophia to have business in Poseidia. "Would you like to come?" the old woman had invited her. "I think there might be a surprise for you there," she winked.

"A surprise!" Cybele wondered excitedly. "What could it be?" But Sophia was not saying, even though the girl bothered her the whole length of the Way. When at last they got to the city, she could stand it no longer.

Poseidia sparkled like a jewel in the morning sun. There was water everywhere, far more than there was in the city of Atlantis. But this was a different kind of water, not the turbulent, salty sea, but vast expanses of smooth, clear, fresh water on which the boats floated—boats and ships of all shapes, sizes, and colors. From all over the world they came, from the provinces and from far distant lands. Flying the flags of their nation-states, bearing the colors of their homelands. Large and small, trading ships and pleasure craft, powered by great Vril engines or rigged with sails that caught the Mother's breath, there they floated on the river or rocked gently at their moorings.

It was a new and unfamiliar world, and Cybele was a bit nervous until she walked into the streets. Then everything was the same—the same familiar crowds and faces of strangers she was used seeing in the city of Atlantis. Like Cybele's own city, Poseidia, too, played host to visitors from all over the world.

"I'm going to take a boat ride, aren't I?" the girl guessed as they approached the docks. Clapping her hands in glee, she looked at Sophia for confirmation. The old woman could keep the secret no longer.

"Yes, you are," she said. "I've arranged a wonderful excursion for you. You're to spend the day with Nuah out on the sea. Now let's get there before he leaves without you!"

Nuah greeted her with all of the warmth and enthusiasm and love of an old friend, inviting her to join a group of other boys and girls about her own age as they boarded his boat—a beautiful, hand-carved sailing vessel, a work of art of which Nuah was particularly proud. "I built her myself, carved her with my own two hands," he declared proudly to the young people. "She's the finest ship in all of Atlantis, in all of the world! And today, she welcomes you aboard, anxious to take you on the ride of your lives."

Cybele kissed Sophia good-bye and off they went, drifting down the river, past the docks and wharves and houses, waving to the people on shore as they waved gaily back. At the river's mouth, the ocean flowed in to greet them, and the water took on its familiar, characteristic deep blue-green color.

On a signal from Nuah, two of his sons set to work raising the sails. Up and up they rose, adorned with brilliantly colored paintings of flamingos, parrots, and other tropical birds. The sails flapped sluggishly at first, until the wind caught them. It was like magic. With crisp snaps they filled out, growing taught, bellying out like the proud birds painted on them. The party was off, sailing out onto the Ocean of Atlas.

Cybele never forgot that day—the thrill of speeding over the waves, watching the enormous flocks of sea birds flying overhead, Nuah and his wife and sons singing songs and telling stories of the sea and pointing out all of its creatures. It was one of the richest sensory experiences of her life. Nuah even let her navigate.

Dolphins danced and frolicked in their wake, racing the ship, leaping in and out of the waves. Cybele marveled at their speed and agility, but most of all she marveled at the fun that those most sleek and graceful of sea creatures were having.

"Look over there!" Nuah shouted above the wind, pointing off the starboard bow as a herd of humpbacked whales spouted. "They're heading north for the summer," he cried, explaining how the great mammals migrated with their calves and their families several thousand miles twice each year, from warm water to cool and back again, following the change of the seasons according to the rhythms of the Mother.

It was a wonderful day, and when it came time for the sun to set, they dropped anchor and waited. That setting sun—larger than any she had ever seen before or since—was as beautiful as anything she had ever experienced. As the great flaming orb sank into the ocean, she thought she could almost hear the sizzle. And then, of course, the quick green flash, while Nuah clapped his hands delightedly as the Dragon made its always-welcomed appearance.

"Thank you, thank you, thank you," she had cried when they docked and disembarked, first hugging Nuah, then his wife, then each of his sons, then Nuah again. "I had the best time of my life."

"Well, you come back any time, young Priestess," Nuah said warmly, kissing her gently on the top of her head.

Cybele was startled. How did he know she wanted to be a priestess? She had told no one of her intention to dedicate herself in service to the Goddess, not even Sophia. But there was no time to ask. Nuah was quite surrounded by the other children as they, too, gathered around to thank him.

"Let's go home," Sophia said as they waved good-bye one last time. On the way back, Cybele asked her why the old man had addressed her as priestess. "I'm not a priestess, at least not yet," she said, somewhat confused.

Sophia smiled. "Nuah knows things," she explained. "He is a very holy man, and he has lived a long time. He holds fast to the Law of One, and he is an excellent judge of human nature. He looked at you, spent the day with you. So he knew your true nature. Addressing you as priestess was a great honor, a sign of respect and love."

Cybele sat quietly for the rest of the trip, reliving the events of the day, but mostly thinking about Nuah and his family. First thing next morning, she wrote them a letter of thanks, ending with a promise to visit with them again.

Now that promise was about to be kept.

*****

"Yes, I have built the boat to which you refer," Nuah said quietly after the group explained what they wanted and why they had summoned him. He had remembered Cybele right away, and was only too eager to come when her plea for help arrived. "I built it because I, too, have received a spiritual message."

The circle of friends looked at the strange little man sitting before them. Barely five feet tall, thin as a rail, the old shipbuilder appeared to be as ancient as the sea he loved so well. A shock of snow-white hair crowned his head, and his piercing blue eyes twinkled from beneath bushy white eyebrows when he smiled.

How old he was they could not guess. His face was a patchwork of lines and wrinkles, his leathery skin baked brown by years of exposure to sun, salt, and wind. He could have been fifty or five hundred. Small and old as he was, however, there was a ruggedness to this man who dwelt so close to the lifeblood of the Great Mother—a deep strength, both physical and spiritual. Strength and wisdom, too—a deep knowledge of things both revealed and hidden.

Cybele realized what it was right away—love coupled with humility, an overall gentleness of spirit that was manifested in everything he thought, said, and did. There was no doubt that the stories about him were true—Nuah walked with Spirit!

The friends were intrigued. So Nuah was part of this too! "Tell us," they pressed around him, "did you also have a dream?"

Nuah shook his head, lighting his pipe as he told his story. "Not a dream," he said, "an encounter. One day, a Voice spoke to me from the Heavens. Actually, it was not out loud, but within my heart." The old seafarer patted his chest as he puffed contentedly. "The Voice told me of a time of darkness and chaos that was about to overtake the world, and it asked me if I would be willing to do my brethren a service.

"When I agreed, it was pleased. Again and again it spoke to me over a period of many weeks, telling me what I must do, giving me instructions on how to build the Arks, opening my mind to new shipbuilding knowledge, to new mathematical formulae, and new principles of navigation.

"I listened carefully, repeating what I heard to my sons, who recorded my words lest we forget. Compiling all of that information and teaching, we then drew up plans and built the first model. It is floating in our harbor even now, a simple prototype of a much larger vessel." He paused to refill his pipe.

"So you can build it?" Scientist asked eagerly.

"Of course I can build it!" Nuah smiled, exhaling a perfect ring of aromatic blue smoke. "In fact, I *must* build it. I have been commanded to do so. One does not refuse such a request as this." He settled back again, looking down the river and out to the sea he loved so deeply. There was one more part of the message to reveal.

"All in all, there are to be twelve ships," he said, gazing at each of the Eleven, "each with its own unique cargo, its own captain, its own destination, its own navigational system. I was told that when the time was right, I would meet others who would provide me with additional details. I guess I've just met you—eleven of you. Eleven plus one— now we are Twelve!"

*****

It was past midnight. Cybele and Sophia knelt in prayer in the deserted sanctuary of the Great Temple, communing with the Goddess of Wisdom, asking the important questions that were on their minds and the minds of the Twelve. And in her love, the Goddess answered them, reminding them of the spiritual significance of the Ark even as she instructed them on how to protect the physical treasures against profanation in the hands of the uninitiated.

"*The vast body of Atlantean knowledge is invaluable,*" the Goddess spoke from within the sacred fires, appearing as tongues of flame and wisps of smoke. "*It is part of your duty and purpose to preserve the Sacred Truths for which so much will sacrificed. For the Knowledge Crystals and other treasures are dangerous in the hands of those who seek to use their power for darker intentions. Thus it is that the treasures are to be stored in the Arks and then hidden where no one can find them until the appointed time. There will the wisdom of this greatest of all cultures lie, preserved against profanation by coming generations until such time as humankind might again comprehend their significance.*"

The eyes of the Goddess glowed like two fiery coals in the surrounding gloom. Cybele lifted her veil and looked directly into the glowing embers. "When will that happen, Wise One?" she asked.

"*It will happen when the Mother shifts her position on her axis for the second time.*" As the Goddess spoke, the embers glowed hot, their fierce red light illuminating the Grand Hall and casting long shadows around the vast room. "*At that time, the knowledge will be brought forth again for the benefit of a new generation yet to come.*"

It was Sophia's turn to speak. "How shall we succeed, Wise One?" she asked, adding more coals to the brightly burning flames. "How shall we guard the secrets and keep them from being revealed too soon?" The old woman had always known that there was more to guarding the treasures than simply hiding them in a secluded cave in a foreign land. She had come this night in search of particulars, asking the Goddess to reveal her Plan in more detail.

"*You will be guided to the land wherein the treasures are to be safely stored,*" the Goddess explained, sensing the old woman's uncertainty. "*As you are being told how to build the Arks, others of you will be told how to build the great stone monuments that will house the treasures. There in Al Khemia, in the heart of the Sphinx, you will place the Knowledge Crystals and the other treasures of Atlantis, where they will remain safe until the time of the Great Awakening, ready to be brought forth again and used for their true purpose, which is the creation of a new earthly garden as the Great Mother is reborn.*"

"All well and good," Cybele thought, "but when our generation is all gone, who will be left to remember the legacy of Atlantis and guard it through the ages? When our descendants are ready, how will they know where to look and what to look for?" She voiced her questions aloud.

"*They will know,*" the Goddess replied, "*because you will have told them. You will have left them a marvelous, magical map that they can use to find the treasures.*"

"A map?" Cybele asked, surprised at the simplicity of the answer. "Is that not dangerous? What is to keep such a map from falling into the hands of the uninitiated and wrongfully-motivated?"

The embers glowed even redder as the Goddess acknowledged the priestess' wisdom. "*You ask wisely, Priestess,*" she approved. "*Such danger would be very real, were it not for the nature and structure of the map. For the map that you will make is to be a treasure map indeed, decipherable only by those who are awake and know the truth. Understandable and readable only by those whose hearts are pure and attuned to the vibrations of Unconditional Love, Compassion, Innate Harmony, and the Healing Presence.*"

In the semidarkness, Cybele and Sophia looked at each other as understanding of the full import of the Goddess's Plan dawned in their minds. They were to initiate a vast and intentional deception upon their posterity, painting a picture of confusion around the deluge and the Ark, hiding the truth in stories and myths so as to conceal the true nature and true location of the treasures of Atlantis. They listened as the Goddess explained the details.

"Let the people think that the Ark contained two of every kind of living creature, when in truth it contains the yin and yang, the Duality, the sum of all Atlantean knowledge. Let the people think that the Ark was made of wood and capable of rotting and decaying over time, when in truth it is an indestructible vessel of Spirit. Let the people think the Ark came to rest high on a mountain, where the winds and rains and sands and fires of time have moved and covered it, when in truth it lies where you placed it after the flood.

"Leave them clues, clues that can never be destroyed by the ravages of time. Draw not your map on parchment, nor etch lines in bits of metal or stone, lest they wear away or be lost or stolen. Use, rather, the living rock of the Mother. Place the clues in your stone monuments and circles. Place them in the geometry of the Great Pyramid, the Sphinx, and the other megaliths that you will rebuild. Use the eternal and universal language of mathematics, as well as the aesthetics of poetry, to provide the clues and pinpoint the location.

"Conceal the map and its most sacred information in the very landscape itself, spread out across the globe, visible only from above, visible only when their technology and intuitive wisdom develop to the extent that they can rise above, see the larger picture, and decipher its meaning. Thus will you create the map. Thus shall the Great Mother and I guard the map until the time comes for them to remember."

The coals glowed a soft red as the Goddess finished her instructions. The two women knelt in silence for a long time, contemplating the task that lay before them. Their part was relatively easy, they realized. The Mother's task, however, that of guarding the map and the treasures, seemed daunting indeed.

"Goddess, will you help the Mother?" Cybele and Sophia asked the favor in unison.

Again the embers burst into flames as the Goddess spoke from the heart of the fires of truth. *"Of course I shall never abandon you or the Mother,"* she reassured them, explaining the part that she, herself, was to play in the Plan. *"You will succeed because I shall help you. I shall divide myself in two halves—one dark, the other light. My Light Self will remain with you always— gentle and loving and kind, instructing you and your descendents in the ways of love and truth and wisdom.*

"That other aspect of myself—the Dark Goddess—shall I transform into a Gorgon, having the power to petrify. In that form, I shall assume a hideous face, turning to stone all who seek the secrets without proper initiation. But fear not. For you will always know that behind the mask, it is I. The hideous face I wear is simply a persona with which to frighten away those who are not meant to have the knowledge that is related to the secrets hidden in Nature."

Now the sacred fires burst into a great sheet of flame, burning but not consuming the coals and embers that were its source. In those mystical, magical flames, the women could see a dark and fearsome image gradually taking shape and form. It was the Gorgon, its hideous serpent-hair coiling and hissing, eyes glowing like two golden coals. Opening its mouth, the fearsome Guardian spoke to them, voicing a prophecy of death and rebirth.

"Atlantis is falling under the Spell of Matter," the Gorgon's words hissed from its mouth, each word dripping liquid fire, *"sinking into spiritual oblivion and drowning in its own self-centeredness. That powerful and potent Spell will weave its sinuous threads through Time just as a river wends its way through hills and valleys and fields to reach the sea.*

"Humankind will ride the currents, ebbs, and flows of the tide of that river until the stream carries them to the time of the Great Awakening, when they will be given the opportunity to break the spell and shift back into the Light of the Spirit. However, before the spell is broken, the right question must be sought, found, and asked."

The Gorgon's image lingered before them, waiting for the questions it knew would come. Cybele spoke for all of Atlantis, asking the Dark Goddess to reveal the name of the Redeemer.

"Who will be the Seeker, Goddess? Who will ask the right question and set the human race free at last?"

Within the fire, the hideous Gorgon seemed almost to smile. They still knew so little, still did not understand who it was that must ask the all-important question. As one teaching a very young child, she explained the truth to them.

"After a time, one will rise up among your descendants, one in whom the Light of Spirit burns brightly. That one will be a Knower and a Wayshower who will teach them the right questions to ask and remind them of the truth about themselves—that which they will have long since forgotten.

"Then it will be up to them! They will either reject the Wayshower or learn and wake up. The choice will be theirs. If they choose correctly and ask for themselves, *they will be led to the great treasures and the knowledge contained within."*

Slowly the image faded and the fire died down, reduced once again to glowing coals and burning embers. Relaxed and confident now, calm and reassured, there was but one question left to ask. Cybele spoke boldly, asking for clarification of one last piece of the Plan that she did not yet fully understand. "But if you guard the treasure, Goddess, how will you know when the Seekers are ready?"

It was almost morning, and the acolytes would be arriving soon to rekindle the sacred fires. Softly, the Goddess completed the last part of the picture.

"I shall know by how they come to me. If they approach in loudness and anger and ignorance and arrogance, I shall know that they are not yet ready. If they approach in strife and greed, I shall turn them to stone. But if they approach quietly, map in hand, following along the Grail Path that you will have laid down, I shall know that they are, indeed, ready. Then I shall transform my Dark Self once again.

"The snakes in my hair will transmute themselves into ringlets of gold, and my Dark Self will merge with my Light Self once again. The Goddess of Wisdom will be reunited and whole at last, and the treasure will be brought forth for the benefit of a shining Age of Awakening and Discovery."

There were tears in the women's eyes as they made their way back to Elysia in the predawn light, tears of joy and gratitude for the roles they would play in the forthcoming drama that was about to unfold. So the purpose of the Ark was indeed spiritual—a symbolic vehicle for navigating the river of time during the Dark Age of Patriarchy and Anarchy.

Within that symbolic Ark, the Truth would live, completely contained and safe. The Truth—represented on the Earth in its dual nature, yin and yang, whole and complete, forever changeless—waiting only for the right time to emerge—the time of the Great Awakening.

*****

In the Temple, when the acolytes came to tend to their morning duties, they were astonished to find the sacred fires burning brightly, the coals hot, the wood largely unconsumed.

THE MASCULINE

CHAPTER 22

Alas, sweet Spouse, what fate pursues us?
Thy fearful vision betokens a terrible prophecy;
By it, the child in thy womb is overshadowed.
It will love nothing, it will sunder blood relationships.
At length with passioned words
It will breed dissension among citizens
And will rage like fire in the hearts of the righteous.

—Echempertus, Ninth-century Chronicler of the Landwulf of Capua

There is no moral authority above and beyond the State, there is no moral or legal principle that transcends the State. Beyond the State, there is no spiritual truth, no philosophic principle, no higher court of appeal.

Such was the Sensate value system and philosophy espoused by the Sons of Belial during their reign of terror in Atlantis. Theirs was a totalitarian regime, with no tolerance for creativity or free thinking outside of a narrow, rigid set of ethics and beliefs.

Based upon the primitive consciousness that only the one is free—the despot, Belial—they suppressed every social and political institution that did not serve their definition of the Nation-State. The Atlantean citizen was scarcely differentiated from the plants, animals, and minerals, having neither spiritual individuality nor individual worth within the caste structure of the society. Religion and custom were set aside and forgotten.

The law was redefined and reinterpreted according to the Sons of Belial's fundamental premise, their first tenet, as recorded in Belial's journal by his own hand:

The Nation-State, which includes our government and our culture, is the great organism to which everything human belongs. This organic totality, which is the Nation-State, is the source of all our culture, all our morality.

The ethical life of an individual member of society is defined by the culture itself, by the Spirit of the People, as it is embodied in the institutions of the society—the legal, political, economic, religious, and educational institutions of the society.

According to the Sons of Belial, what served the purpose of the Nation-State—that alone had value. Therefore Belial, as moral and spiritual guardian of Atlantis, was perfectly justified in discarding that which no longer served him. Gone were the ways of the Ancients, the ways of the Children of the Law of One, the ways of Spirit, the ways of the Great Mother.

It was the inception of the consciousness of *"I am the State, the State is I,"* which would weave its terrible legacy down through the ages of the *Slaughterbench of History*. It was the beginning of an ongoing struggle in which proud and noble nations would rise and fall; freethinking paragons of morality and virtue would be wiped out; and human misery would assume a most fearful aspect. It was the birth of the principle in which tyrants and dictators—of whom Belial was the first—would come to see themselves as great leaders whose destiny was to rule on a global scale. Such "innovators" believed themselves justified in destroying all people and institutions that stood in their way. You know their names—

the tyrants of the terror of history—Alexander, Caesar, Charlemagne, Atilla, Napoleon, Hitler, and hundreds of lesser demagogues—wielders of so mighty a force that it would trample down the innocent flower and crush to pieces any object that stood in its path.

Of what worth was the individual Atlantean citizen? What rights did they have, what freedoms? "Your moral life can only be moral if it embodies the culture's values," Belial decreed. "It is the only morality you have. Whatever is not for the good of Atlantis— any new ideas, or even existing ideas, thoughts, or philosophies—is wrong, immoral, and worthy of suppression."

Of course, this doctrine of oppression was openly challenged by the Children of the Law of One, who maintained that the numinous—the spiritual, the Divine—were both source and fulfillment of all values—all spiritual reality.

"The culture provides the only morality you need," the Sons of Belial responded. "The Nation-State is the All. No individual can separate himself from the beliefs and values of his society in his own time."

"What if the Spirit of the People goes demoniacally astray?" countered the Children of the Law of One. "Or a government becomes corrupt?"

Long and hard raged the debate. Bitter the verbal assaults, even more bitter the violence and bloodshed that inevitably erupted when two such strong opposing paradigms collided. But the argument of the Children of the Law of One was doomed to failure. They were suppressed, forced to submit to the dominant will of a power far greater than theirs.

The change did not happen overnight. It took years to evolve. It took the right combination of people, socioeconomic conditions, synchronicities, and magic. It also took one more thing—the ever-present, guiding hand of Spirit as it led the human race along the Grail Path toward its final goal—the achievement of the *Consciousness of Freedom* in which, at last, the Human Spirit would learn that all Human Souls are free.

*****

The story of Belial is a story for the ages, for it the story of all great dictators in world history. Their stories, however, are but reiterations of the original. Belial was the first of the world-historical figures to rise up and embrace the Spear and change the world. The first to set the human race upon the path toward the Consciousness of Freedom.

Belial's story begins before his birth, as an embryo within his mother's toxic womb, poisoned by chemicals and smoke and all manner of toxins. The semiconscious fetus, struggling to maintain its tenuous hold on life, lay helpless and trapped in a hot, noxious, blood-red sea. His was a never-ending struggle, never-ending agony. Day after day, month after month, he was assaulted by horrible dreams and visions, terrifying beyond description—images of decapitation, blood, and devouring demons and monsters swimming through his developing awareness. There was no exit, no way out.

Far in the distance, dull and muffled, he heard the incessant screams and thuds, the dull poundings that coincided with the spasms of pain that rocked through his tiny, half-formed body. Until one day, this world, horrible as it was, grew even more so, closing in around him until he began to smother. Struggling to escape, the fetus began to move forward, as though down a long tunnel. Struggling, ever struggling, fighting for oxygen, fighting to fend off the suffocating darkness pressing in on him from all sides.

And then it was over. The man-child emerged from that imprisoning and toxic world into a blinding light. The air was chilly, and the newborn child felt strange. The oppressive weight had been lifted. There was a sense of expansiveness, and all manner of new stimuli were impinging upon his consciousness.

Those far-off screams were louder now, ringing in his ears, hurting the tender tympanic membranes. There were other noises, too—deep, guttural noises, animal grunts, and bestial roars. Foul and noxious odors assailed his nostrils—the stench of blood and filth, disease and decay. The terrified newborn did the only thing he could do. He opened his mouth and roared out his fear and anguish to the world. His tiny voice filled the chamber with plaintive cries for help and comfort.

But there was to be no succor for this newborn babe, no tender mother's touch, no soothing father's strong yet gently cradling arms, no warm breast at which to suckle, no greeting or welcome outpouring of love from joyful parents. No welcome to the world, no gratitude to Spirit for sending this lovely child. No blessing or thanksgiving for his arrival, only a coarse blanket and a withered, sour nipple.

*****

They named him Bel, in honor of the Earth energies that they so deeply worshiped, and, conversely, abused. Nature herself shared the infant's anguish. The planets had aligned themselves in such a way as had never been seen before. A comet streaked across the heavens. The moon eclipsed the sun, the Earth shook, and there was a mighty storm. The tragedy that had begun in the womb continued after birth and into childhood. Bel had been born on the cusp of the War God and the Bull, at the conjunction of the sign of the God of Restriction and the Lord of the Underworld. And so his early life began.

The son of royal, erudite, drunken, and lascivious parents, his was a world of paradoxical extremes—a family of enormous wealth and education that often chose to live in incredible filth and squalor. He experienced moments of great pleasure in which he heard the sweetest music and saw the finest art forms. He also witnessed equally extreme orgies and rituals of utter depravity and degradation.

Through this insane, topsy-turvy world roamed the boy—highly educated, well-read, and emotionally sensitive. He had a huge capacity for warmth of heart and unselfishness, and a deep earnestness and devotion to things spiritual. Yet his earliest memories were of experiences and feelings of isolation, rejection, and blame. Beaten, shamed, broken—he was irreparably damaged by an energy of rigidity and unforgiveness that would help give rise to an ogre-tyrant nature that would continue to manifest itself for thousands of years into the future.

Inevitably, the child who had come in whole and perfect soon began to fragment, and it was going to take the rest of his life to put himself back together, if he chose to do so. Bel did not so choose. Instead, he began to act out the energies that he did not understand. He withdrew into a fantasy world peopled with powerful giants and wizards and heroes. He was extremely imaginative and devoured everything he could about the legendary Atlanteans of old. They became his heroes now. How he longed for them to come to his rescue, to lift him up and out of this terrible dungeon and carry him off to live happily ever after in their mountain aerie. But the heroes never came, except in dreams and fantasies. A deep and overwhelming pessimism enveloped him like a blanket. Pale and thin, he gazed out from huge, hollow black eyes upon a world filled with unutterable pain and fear and loneliness.

Perhaps the greatest wounding came at puberty. With no father to guide him through the powerful changes taking place within his body, the young boy turned to expressions of schizophrenia, violence, and rage. He began to hear voices inside his head, soft, gentle voices, speaking soothing words, telling him what a good boy he was, that he did not deserve this kind of life, that he was destined for greatness, that he was destined to be the savior of his people and lead them in an archetypal war against the evildoers of the world. Starting with his father, he hoped.

Of course, he did not understand this at first, but the voices were friendly and warm, and they came to him at the times when he needed them most, when he was most alone, locked in a dark closet nursing cuts and bruises inflicted by a malevolent and abusive sire. The voices made him feel safe and no longer alone, and they confirmed what Bel had always known—that he was destined for greatness. The voices also promised enlightenment. "Follow us," they said, "and we shall illuminate for you the bridge between the two worlds."

"What worlds?" asked the boy.

"The worlds of outer and inner space, earthly and supersensible," came the enigmatic reply. "You can cross this bridge if you choose."

Bel so chose. Thus began his indiscriminate experimentation with mind-expanding herbs and potions—voyages into altered states of consciousness. But without guides, without a safe and sacred space in which to contain the experiences, he traveled a perilous and illicit path toward a revelation for which he was totally unprepared.

In his obsessive desire to escape and seek a better world, he sought out others like himself, joining cults, embracing the dark side, moving from one seamy counterculture to another. Slowly, he became as one possessed. Forces beyond his control got the better of him, and, because of his upbringing, or lack thereof, he embraced them to make up for the loss of what he never got from his parents.

*****

In his fifteenth year, his mother grew gravely ill. Bel nursed the dying woman with patience and tenderness, if not love, but the progression of the disease was not to be stopped. Lying on her deathbed, she was overwhelmed with feelings of guilt and remorse. A strange pain burned within her—not the familiar agony of the wasting disease, but an anguish deep within her soul. "I must tell him," she muttered incoherently. "I must warn him. The demons hover over him. I must protect him."

Her nurses tried to calm the dying woman, bathing her in cool water and covering her with light satin sheets. Still the pain continued, a constant burning agony, until she could do nothing but scream out her son's name.

"I am here, Mother," Bel said at last, standing by the bedside. "What is it that I can do for you?" He spoke with a detached calmness. He knew that his mother was about to leave him, but there were no tears to shed, no feelings of loss for the woman whose love he had never known.

"My son, I am dying," came the almost inaudible whisper. Bel had to bend close to hear the words. His mother had a strange smell, the smell of death, he realized later.

"I have given you nothing in this life other than sorrow and pain, for which I have paid and will continue to pay a dear price. I can never atone for the wrong I have done you, never repay you for the loss of your youth and your innocence. But this I can give to you—a final warning before I go to my cold and lonely grave."

The emaciated woman who had been his mother grimaced in agony as a spasm of pain swept through her wasted body. Drawing a tortured breath, she continued. "Soon you will face the most important choice of your life, whether to walk the Light Path or the Dark Path. Right now, both are open to you. The quick and easy successes are shallow and fleeting. Heed my warning, my son, and choose not the Dark Path. Beware the black magic. For once you have embraced its oppressive evil, it will dominate your destiny. It will hold you captive."

Bel listened dispassionately, the woman's words having little effect. What does she know? he thought to himself. I have freedom of choice, my will is my own.

His mother seemed to sense this, and she struggled to sit up and make her final, desperate plea. "There lies before you the power over a realm of pure spirits." She gripped his arm fiercely, her fingernails digging into his flesh. Bel tried to pull away, but he could not break that viselike grip. "Do not allow yourself to be led away from your true path by Earth-bound spirits," she screamed, staring sightlessly at some strange apparition beyond physical space and time. "They will rob you of your creative power." The dying woman collapsed on the bed, her eyes burning with fever. They were the last words she ever spoke.

After his mother's death, Bel left home, vowing never to return, vowing to become a great hero and destroy all of the bad people of the world so that he and everyone else would never be hurt again. He traveled alone, far from his former haunts, seeking somehow to function within the psychosis that was already well-formed and in full bloom within him.

The cults weren't helping; his mind wasn't expanding. The people he was with were interested more in the thrill of the drug-induced hallucinations rather than the enlightenment they were purported to bring. They were as aimless as he was, so there was no need to stay with them. They could not give him what he needed.

Then came the first of the countless synchronistic events that were to follow him all of his life, a coincidence so unusual and so psychologically meaningful that it could not possibly be the result of chance alone. He met Nebo—"the first and most important of the masters of darkness who were to groom me for my meteoric rise to power," he would write in his journal years later. And thus was Bel's life changed forever.

"You will attain higher levels of consciousness," the wizard had promised, "and under my tutelage, you will make a penetrating study of ritual magic."

Bel was excited beyond his wildest expectations. His dreams were about to come true, although he had no way of imagining their extent and scope at his young age. Occultism was to be the way, the missing ingredient that would lead him up and out of the dark hole of ignorance toward enlightenment. And Nebo was to be the wayshower.

> This was the single thread throughout my life that was to give a central meaning to all of my diverse activities—a deep and earnest pursuit of occultism. My years with Nebo have proved to be the most vital and formative of my life. I have learned all I need to know to assume leadership.
> I am ready.

It began thusly. It was cold and damp, one of those bone-chilling fall nights so common in late November at the northern tip of the island. Bel tried to make a fire, but it was no use. The leaves and twigs were saturated. Nothing was going to burn on this damp, raw night. He would have to seek shelter, in hopes that within the gloomy interior of some cave would be a few scraps of dried grass and twigs.

A noise behind him startled him. He turned to see a hooded figure standing at the edge of the clearing, observing him. The boy started.

"Do not be frightened," said the strange figure. "I mean you no harm. I am Nebo. You are wet and cold, and I have much to offer...a warm fire and a dry place to rest. Meat and drink. Secrets to be revealed. And the answers to all of your questions."

There was a tantalizing intimacy about this mysterious stranger. Odd, yet also familiar. Bel took to him instantly, deciding to trust this herald of promises soon to be fulfilled.

Together, they passed through the dank undergrowth until they came to a nondescript hovel. A fire was burning within, and the room was warm. Strange shadows danced and flickered across the walls, but Bel was not frightened any longer. I'm home! he thought to himself. At last, I have found my place! The boy was full of questions, but Nebo made it clear that he would entertain no queries this night.

The wizard lit an oil lamp and began attending to necessities—getting the boy dry and fed and rested. Bel could not remember ever having eaten a better meal. It was a hot, pasty gruel with strips of dried animal flesh, but to the famished boy, that dinner far surpassed any of the sumptuous feasts of his parent's house. The repast made him drowsy, and he yawned mightily.

"The hour grows late," Nebo noted, draping a soft, sweet-smelling fur over the boy's shoulders. "You must rest now." So, wrapped in the warm skins of the forest creatures, Bel lay back and closed his eyes. He slept for several hours—a deep slumber, undisturbed by dreams. When he awoke, he found his strange new companion staring at him.

So he had not imagined it! This was, indeed, real. He was to have a mentor who would teach him all of the wonders of the universe. Highly excited, the boy stepped outside to relieve himself and wash his face. The rainwater was cold, and his breath steamed in the early morning chill, but Bel barely noticed, so eager was he to begin his training.

"Tell me your story," Nebo invited, offering a boiling cup of hot broth to the boy as he came back inside. It was more than a invitation. It was a command.

Bel could not help himself. He began to speak. As though the floodgates of a mighty dam had been opened, so all of the pent up emotions came pouring out. All of the pain, anguish, bitterness, fear, aloneness, sorrow, grief, shame, and guilt. All of those dark and bitter feelings that had built up inside the boy over the years...they all came pouring out in a torrent of self-pity, rage, and tears. As Bel spoke, a strange thing happened. His very words began to take shape and form in the still air within the room. Drifting from his mouth in wisps of gray smoke, they coalesced into an almost palpable ball of black grease and soot in the center of the room, growing with each utterance, with each release of all of those black, pent-up emotions.

Bel stopped speaking and stared in amazement. The greasy black smoke just floated there, hanging suspended in the midst of the room. Nebo spoke not a word, but rose and approached the strange, dark essence. Removing the hood of his robe, he closed his eyes and intoned a strange, singsong chant, after which he turned his gaze directly upon Bel.

"This ball of smoke represents all of your fears, all of your pain," he said. "Look at it there before you. Do you want to keep it, or do you want to let it go? The choice is yours. But know this. If you choose to keep it, I cannot help you, and you must depart from this place, never to return."

"I choose to let it go," came Bel's instant reply. He was already feeling better from the cathartic release, and he certainly did not want that scatological mass back inside him.

"Good," Nebo's eyes glowed a dull red. "Then behold as your troubles vanish before your eyes, vanish into the nothingness from which they came, back into oblivion, gone forevermore, never to torment you again."

Nebo inhaled deeply, creating a vortex through which the smoky blob was sucked directly into his lungs. The boy sat wide-eyed, completely entranced as the wizard's eyes burned fiercely redder. Then, with a mighty exhalation, he breathed out a stream of pure white light, brightening the entire cabin.

Bel knew exactly what had happened. He had seen this mystical rite performed by the High Priestess of the Temple at his mother's deathbed. His mother had been in terrible pain, her body consumed by the effects of years of dissolute living. The priestess had commanded her to speak out all of her pain and anguish, which had taken form within the room. The priestess had then inhaled the smoky glob and transformed it through the flame of her own compassion into pure, healing light. All of his mother's pain had been removed, and she had slept peacefully until she died a few hours later.

Now, Nebo had done the same thing for young Bel. Transformed by the power of the light, his heartache and anguish had dissipated, evaporated. They were gone forever. He felt better, but he was still afraid. "Will I die now?" he asked, anticipating the same fate that had befallen his mother.

Nebo smiled soothingly and laid a strong hand on Bel's shoulder. "No, you will not die," he reassured the boy. "You will live a long and extraordinary life. Now tell me about your hopes and dreams."

He does not ask, Bel noticed. He commands. He has great authority. I have no choice but to obey him. His mind seemed to be caught by a powerful magnet, drawing it open and pulling him toward a strange, hazy light. "What power is this that compels me?" he wondered aloud.

Bel stood before Nebo, grasped both of the older man's hands, and gripped them tightly. He was in a deep trance, and his eyes were feverish, as much from the excitement of the moment as from exposure to last night's cold and damp. Even his voice had changed— from boyish soprano to a hoarse and raucous bass. It was as though another being were speaking through him, having taken possession of his mind and body and using him as a means to achieve some sinister end. Bel himself seemed astonished, listening with amazement to that which burst from within him with such elemental force. Like floodwaters breaking through their dikes, the words poured forth.

"I have a vision of a great and historic destiny that lies before me. I see the Slaughterbench of History spread out over the millennia. And I am to be the first. The first of the great men of the ages. The first to own the world and change it and mold it through the force of my will, and mine alone.

"The spirits have charged me with a holy mission—to bring Atlantis greatness and glory such as the world has never seen, nor ever will see again. No one and no thing will stop me from achieving this end. I shall crush to pieces everything in my path that might stop me from fulfilling my grand destiny."

There, in the cold and fog and rain at the extreme northern tip of the Island of Atlantis, on the last day of the twelfth month of the Year of the Emperor, with none to witness save Nebo, Bel uttered the words of doom. Grim words, prophetic words, words that were to be fulfilled with staggering concreteness, not only in Atlantis, but throughout the long, dark course of human history. A strong feeling swept over the boy, a feeling of some mighty Presence within him, nodding in approval and supporting him in his mission. It was a warm feeling, the same warm feeling he had felt as a child trembling in the dark closet when the disembodied voices had come and comforted him.

"Good, good," Nebo smiled as the boy collapsed on the bed in exhaustion. "So you are the one. I knew it was so. I have been waiting for you for a long time." He rubbed his hands together gleefully. "I have been charged with searching for the one who would be the first—the first of the Men of Destiny. The first of those who will come after you, the first to receive the Spear and thereby change the world."

"Who are you?" Bel whispered through dry lips, staring up at the gaunt creature towering over him.

"I am to be your teacher," came the simple reply. "You have seen the white magic and the powers of the Light. Now I shall show you even greater wonders. Now I shall show you the powers of the Darkness!"

*****

Hanuman, the Potion Master, was a frightening figure indeed...short of stature, with a hunched back, huge paunch, and amazingly long arms. "He looks like a surrealistic toad," Bel whispered to Nebo, trying to break the tension of the moment.

"Shhhh!" the wizard cautioned. "This is a serious time. There is no room for levity here."

They were still in the cabin. Several weeks had passed since Bel's arrival, time that had been spent preparing him for today's ritual, in which he would drink the Elixir of Initiation. Nebo had prepared the boy well, showing him all sorts of wonders in preparation for the inner experience that was about to come. The boy had asked a thousand questions, and the wizard had answered every one with patience and understanding.

There was much to be learned—incantations, spells, and charms to be spoken or sung; names of spirits and demons, as well as prayers and invocations for petitioning their aid. Each day added to the previous day's teaching.

At first, Bel thought he would never be able to master all of the intricacies of ritual black magic, but he plunged into the lessons with relish and eagerness, devouring all that was set before him. Nebo was an expert teacher, and Bel was an excellent pupil. The knowledge came easily.

Each night, the boy lulled himself to sleep anticipating the great initiatory event that lay before him. Finally the day had arrived. For hours, others had been arriving at the cabin—strange, dark men, robed and hooded. "Your allies and supporters," Nebo had explained. "Each has passed along the way you start today. Each has taken the inner journey and been initiated into the Dark Circle of Adepts. They come today to honor your initiation."

Each man greeted the boy with deference and respect. Bel felt honored and flattered by all of the attention. His thoughts wandered to a time, far in the future, when he would stand at the head of these men, leading them to power and glory as they shouted his name and sang praises to his greatness.

It was time. Hanuman lumbered forward, carrying a smoking goblet, which he handed to Bel. "Drink, drink!" The loathsome creature smelled of rot and decay...a familiar smell, awakening a long-dormant sense memory in the boy, which now came roaring back to conscious awareness. Bel staggered under the full import of the realization.

This was the first smell that had assailed his newborn senses on the day of his birth. Had this foul creature been there on that bygone day, somehow officiating in the delivery? Was the Potion Master responsible for the strange thuds, screams, and curses?

Bel was frightened, but he dared not show it. He looked around at the Circle of Adepts that surrounded him. They were encouraging him. He could not show fear before the men whom he would one day lead. He looked into the cup. In his trembling hands, he held the key to enlightenment. This was what he had been waiting for, what he wanted so desperately. The decision had been made; there was no turning back. Putting the cup to his lips, the boy performed his last act of Innocence, drinking deeply of the blood-red liquid.

*****

Thus began young Bel's initiation into the mysteries and arts of black magic. There, in the quiet and solitude of the woods, isolated from the noises and distractions of the city, he made the first incursions into mind expansion. Under the expert but misguided tutelage of his spiritual mentor, he began his journey toward the attainment of transcendent consciousness.

Was the boy prepared and ready? By no means. There is no easy way to spiritual illumination, no fast track to the attainment of transcendent consciousness. Rather, it is reached by following a much more arduous and morally demanding path.

Bel had not trod that path. Therefore, he had neither the temperament, mental faculties, nor general life habits to appropriately deal with the energies he was about to access.

Instead, he sought and achieved enlightenment through highly illicit means—a secret potion brewed in a shadowy alchemist's lab, a potion that was to bring about a shortcut to the most high knowledge.

There was no doubt that the potion he was about to swallow would open the gateway to energies from the Collective Unconscious—the primary energy force that informs both the physical world and the human psyche. Incredibly powerful energy, hard to contain, difficult to appropriately access, even for those who were physically, mentally, emotionally, and spiritually prepared.

Here, however, was a child, with no healthy ego, brain, or central nervous system to function as a protective barrier against what was to be an overwhelming intrusion of Total Mind. The Innocent stood open and receptive to the full nuclear force fire of the formative energies of the universe. In the presence of such energies, he stood naked and exposed, completely vulnerable and unprotected.

At this juncture, the boy had not consciously chosen to tread the Dark Path over the Light Path. He was, however, incapable of distinguishing between them. And there was no one to intervene on his behalf.

*****

The effects of the potion were instantaneous. Bel's schizophrenic personality, coupled with a near-starvation diet and psychotic condition of inner stress, had created the kind of body chemistry that offered little or no protection from the devastating impact of Hanuman's powerful hallucinogen. Terror swept over the boy as he felt his soul rudely ripped out of three-dimensional space and time with shocking brutality.

"Aieeeeeeeeeeeeeeee!" His scream filled the room, falling on deaf ears. There was to be no rescue from this incredible madness. Alone and lost, he continued his headlong plunge, spiraling and shrinking as he sped through shimmering, pulsating, preternatural colorscapes, coming to rest at last in the dimensions he had sought for so long, those higher dimensions of Time and Consciousness.

In this highly charged world, with no boundaries and no barriers to protect him, the energies came swirling in and captured him. There was no transformer to step down the fire as it came roaring forth at full voltage. Young Bel had taken hold of a live wire, had stepped within and embraced a nuclear explosion. These were forces that needed to be respected and properly accessed; the boy could do neither. He was entirely consumed, losing all sense of self and personal identity. Now he heard the full sound and fury of the voices, felt their full power.

"We want you!" the voices screamed. "We want to possess you...all of you!"

How long in ordinary time he spent there, he had no way of knowing. He was held captive, forced to listen as the orders and directions that would serve to guide him to his sinister goals of personal power, tyranny, and world conquest were channeled into his subconscious mind. And he was powerless to stop the experience. Like a game fish snagged by the fisherman's barb, he was hooked, he was caught, later to be fried in the fire and consumed.

Nebo and the others looked on, unmoved, as Bel twisted and writhed madly about the cabin floor. How could they do otherwise? They knew no way save the way of the dark powers. Their mission was to initiate and prepare the chosen one for the role he was to play. Bel was the one. They held his head while he vomited, retching up great, steaming gobs of bilious goo. They held his tongue to keep him from swallowing it and choking to death. They surrounded him with pillows lest he dash his head or suffer a broken bone. Other than that, though, they did not interfere.

*****

It took months for young Bel to recover. For weeks, the boy could not even speak. Thin as he had been, he had grown even thinner. Strangest of all, his skin had been bleached a pale and ashy white at some point during the encounter, giving him a ghastly, skeletal appearance.

He lay on his bed, barely breathing, heart fluttering, his expression vacant, lifeless, as though the very spark of consciousness had been extinguished, staring with blank, sightless eyes at some internal vision that only he saw. Nebo and the others brought him food and drink, but he took nothing save the few drops of liquid that they forced through his parched, cracked, and swollen lips.

Yet Bel was far from lifeless, floating through the labyrinth of his own expanded mind—a dreamlike world of molten, colorful images—with a sense of awareness so concentrated, so sharp, so vivid as to be excruciatingly painful. Magically, the barriers of sequential time and three-dimensional space had slipped away, and his soul was transported on a journey through past, present, and future.

He saw himself as he had once been—weak, puny, and trembling. He saw himself as he was now—full of confusion, doubt, and hope. And he saw himself as he would one day be—Master of the Adepts, absolute ruler of the world.

As water changes shape to conform to its surroundings, so Bel's fluid soul melted from form to form as he saw himself in one life after another. Life after life, form after form, it was always the same—his soul being driven inexorably toward a final destiny that he could not quite grasp. Something was there, far in the future, behind a black, shimmering mass, hidden from his eyes. Beyond the boundaries of his inner vision loomed a mysterious object, a talisman of incredible power, waiting for him, waiting to be taken up and carried forth, yet never to be possessed by any man.

"What is behind the veil?" he cried aloud to the cosmos, sensing a vast, dispassionate intelligence guiding his every move, his every experience. Echoes of his voice reverberated across the hollow dreamscape. The only reply was a deep, palpable silence. The more he insisted, the further the veil receded, until at last it was hidden completely from his eyes. "It is over!" he cried sadly, feeling himself being drawn back into his physical body, to which he was attached by a slender, silver cord.

It had been an extraordinary transcendent experience, a sudden lifting of the Veil of Time, full of wonder and mystery. And through it all, over those many months, he still had retained his present-day identity as Bel, initiate of Nebo. At last, one day a few weeks after the Winter Solstice, the boy turned his head, looked directly at the wizard, blinked his eyes, and said, "I am hungry."

It was the beginning of his return to the ordinary world. From that day on, he grew stronger and healthier. Slowly at first, he began to take solid food and sit up in bed for short periods. Soon he was walking in short circles about the room. After that, things started happening even faster. He dressed himself and went outside into the fresh air. As winter cycled into spring and the Earth turned green again, so day by day the boy grew ever stronger. The transformation was incredible to watch. His boyish frame was disappearing virtually before the astonished eyes of Nebo and the Dark Circle. He grew several inches in a matter of months and added even more inches to his girth.

And how strong he was becoming! At sixteen, Bel had the endurance, stamina, and strength of ten ordinary men. He seemed tireless in his physical activity, rarely needing to rest or pause in any way. A fierce energy impelled him. A strange light glowed in those coal-black eyes. An internal fire fueled him, unquenchable and all-powerful.

His personality, shaky at best before the initiation, was now thoroughly schizophrenic. The budding man inside the ever-growing body suffered from extreme mood swings. Sometimes he was quite calm and collected—introspective, musing, even poetic. At other times, however, he was completely out of control—moody, dark, malevolent, even violent. Woe to any of the Circle who crossed Bel when he was in one of those moods! Many were the Adepts who felt the effects of his foul and irrational temper. Many were the bruised and broken bodies that were slowly mending.

Nebo alone was safe from his wrath. Nebo alone could manage him, control him, approach him. They would spend hours together, Nebo teaching, Bel absorbing like a sponge all that the wizard was capable of giving, all of the secrets and mysteries of the universe.

They spoke of magic potions and amulets, spells for suborning a man's will and making him subservient to the will of another. Nebo showed him how to use the power of his voice and eyes to mesmerize entire crowds, manipulating their very thoughts and instilling their minds with the visions he wanted them to see. Bel learned how to project his aura and essence for good or evil, at his whim.

"…to protect whoever needs protecting," Nebo explained, "or to kill whoever needs killing." They practiced on the woodland creatures. The forest floor was littered with the rotting carcasses of rabbits, squirrels, even birds that had been halted in mid-flight by the power of Bel's mind. For a while, the carrion-feeders had feasted well, until the forest denizens, through silent communion with the Great Mother, trotted, flew, or slithered away, seeking safer, hallowed ground.

Each of these lessons was designed to instill confidence and audacity in the future tyrant. For Nebo knew the young man's inner thoughts, knew the secrets that Bel kept tightly locked within the vault of his own ever-darkening heart.

"I see great fear inside of you." Teacher and student were sitting in their accustomed spot on a high cliff overlooking the sea. "Even after all that I have given you, that fear is still there. Tell me, what is it you fear most?"

Bel did not respond at first. When he did, his tone was boastful and haughty. "I fear no man or beast," he thundered, rising to his feet and thumping his great chest.

"Be silent and sit." Nebo's command crackled through the air like a whip. Instantly, like a beaten puppy, Bel grew placid and sat at his teacher's side. "I shall ask you the question again," Nebo hissed through clenched teeth. "Do not make me repeat it a third time. What is it you fear the most?"

The boy took a deep breath and looked down at his feet. "It is not what," he whispered softly, "it is who. I fear the one who would vanquish me. I fear that my power will be taken from me, at the cost of my life. I fear humiliation, I fear shame. But most of all, I fear pain and the loss of my life."

The wizard nodded in agreement. "Good, very good. Admitting your fear, owning it, is the first step toward mastery. Bring that which you fear out of the darkness and into the light. Expose it, and you will see in the light that it is not the powerful demon that you had convinced yourself it was. Heed this lesson well, for it will serve you faithfully if you remember to avail yourself of it."

Bel looked at his mentor with mixed feelings. Part of him loved the man who had brought him to enlightenment and taught him so much. Another part of him, though, hated Nebo for having such power over him. The hating part was stronger than the loving part.

"Now let me tell you something that you are ready to hear." Nebo rose, aware of his student's love-hate dilemma but caring not a whit for such trivial things as emotion. "Kneel before me."

A wave of anger surged through the boy, his pride recoiling at the thought of bending his knee to any man. Still, he complied, too afraid of his mentor do otherwise.

The wizard placed his shriveled palms on the head of the initiate kneeling at his feet. "From this day forward, you are no longer Bel. Henceforth, your name is Belial—*The Angel Who Keeps Hell.*"

A deep rumble echoed ominously through the forest. The boy glanced up apprehensively. The sky was clear, yet the thunder pealed. Why? His thoughts were interrupted as Nebo continued to speak.

"Through the power of your new name, you will rise up and rule the world. None will oppose you, none will threaten you or cross you or harm you in any way. To all you will be invincible...save for one."

Belial reacted as though he had been slapped in the face. He started to speak, but Nebo quickly cut him off.

"One there is who waits for you. One there is who has the potential to vanquish you. If he makes the right choice."

"How will I know him?" Belial asked, afraid of this faceless, formless man, yet even more afraid to show his fear to his teacher.

"You will know him when you meet him," came the ambiguous response. "You will recognize him instantly, as he will recognize you. The repulsion between you will be strong, for you each carry the same electrical charge."

"How will I vanquish him?" Belial asked.

"You will not vanquish him," Nebo replied. "Your enemy cannot be harmed by you, nor can you be harmed by him, until the appointed time, when you meet each other in mortal combat upon the Plain of Armageddon."

Armageddon! The name was pregnant with virulent power. Belial knew of no such place in Atlantis, indeed, in all the world. Yet why did the mention of the name send a shiver of fear along his spine?

"Until then, however," and now a wicked gleam came into Nebo's eye as he continued, "you can prey upon his weaknesses, his fears. For, like you, he suffers from phobias and obsessions, and his demons, like yours, are very strong."

"Tell me what I must do," Belial licked his lips in anticipation. Although he had not even met his antagonist yet, already he was delighting in visions of his enemy writhing in agony, impaled upon a pointed stake, withering in the hot sun under Belial's malevolent stare.

"You can threaten him and frighten him by harming those whom he loves," Nebo smiled evilly as he read the thoughts in his pupil's mind. "You can break him and demoralize him and inflict psychological harm on him. So that, when his time comes to choose, he will choose the safe path and leave you alone. And you can mark him, so that he carries with him an eternal reminder of your power."

Nebo withdrew his hands and walked down the trail that led to the cabin. "Rise up now," he spoke with his back toward the initiate. "Be by yourself to reflect upon my words and the power of your new name. Dwell apart and remember. You are the one. You are invincible. You need not the company of others. You are content in your solitude, growing stronger, ever stronger as you dwell apart from men."

For three years they were thus, three long years in which Belial saw no other men, had no other human companionship his own age. Saw no cities, only the solitude of the forest and northern hills. Preparing, ever preparing—body, mind, and soul—to be the standard-bearer of the forces of Darkness.

And so the years passed. One day, as Belial was again sitting on the steep cliff looking out over the northern sea, Nebo came to him in the usual manner. The surf crashed on the black, wet, jagged rocks below. "It is time for you to leave this place," Nebo said softly. "You have completed your training and are prepared. I have arranged for you to go forth into the city, to the university, where you will meet others who are waiting for you. They will show you what to do. From this day forward, you will see me no more."

Belial made no reply. He simply stood up, turned his back to the sea, and walked off into the forest. He did not stop at the cabin, did not stop to pack his few meager belongings. He just walked to the south, ever to the south, toward the great and gleaming city that lay at the heart of the island. A city oblivious, for the time being, to his presence, but soon to come to know and fear the name of Belial.

Nebo watched the black-robed giant disappear into the forest. "What have I done?" he asked aloud, spreading his hands and facing the sky. There was no answer from the silent trees, no voice to justify his mighty transgression...no sympathy, no comfort, no consolation, no forgiveness. The wind sighed through the evergreen boughs as if to say, "You know what you must do." And he *did* know...

The wizard sat for a while, enjoying the warmth of the mid-morning sunshine. After a time, he went to the cabin. Taking a log from the fire, he touched the flaming tip to the window hangings and floor coverings and dry cabin wood. Then he calmly seated himself in the center of the room and watched as the all-consuming flames licked toward him.

In no time, the cabin was an inferno. Nebo made no outcry. He quietly sat in his chair and was consumed in the raging fire. The heat was intense, the fire almost alive, burning with a preternatural intensity and ferocity. Not the simple fire of burning wood, but a passionate, all-consuming fire of purification. Purging the ground, purging the site, burning up all of the contamination and impurities of that unhallowed place. Consuming the cabin, the artifacts, the amulets, the clothes, and the master perpetrator, Nebo himself.

In less than an hour, the cabin was a black and smoking ruin, and the charred body of the wizard was reduced to sizzling ashes. The greedy flames looked elsewhere for more to consume. They began to spread beyond the blackened circle of the clearing. Soon the whole forest was ablaze. Fire leapt up the trunks of the great old trees, who seemed to utter a great moan of thanks that they were being released from that fetid and festering nest of iniquity. One by one, the forest giants crashed to the ground. The few remaining forest creatures took flight, some to safety, others only to be caught in the fiery whirlwind. For miles in all directions, the fire burned, until the sky darkened, and the Mother sent the blessed water of her tears in the form of rain to quench the angry flames and sweeten the ground.

From a vantage point high on a hill several miles away, Belial turned back to look at the conflagration. No emotion passed along that mask of a face, that ashen white countenance gleaming beneath the black hood. No remorse, no sadness, no questioning of any kind. It was simply gone.

The cabin was gone, Nebo was gone, everything was gone. He was orphaned once more, but he was not alone. The voices started within his head again, speaking the words of comfort to him, reminding him of his greatness and his destiny. Making him feel safe and sweet and warm. Belial turned and continued to walk toward the south.

*****

In the city of Atlantis, the Earth shook, the waves roared, and the wind blew in great gusts of rage and fear as a hurricane roared out of the east. Above the pandemonium of the storm, the Voice of the Mother spoke her warning to all who would listen, saying...

"Beware, ye proud and mighty people, for the time of your undoing is at hand."

CHAPTER 23

The Beast does not look what he is. He may even wear a comic moustache.

—Soloviev, *The Anti-Christ*

Belial entered the city by night. There was no one to observe his passing, no one to ask, "Who is that?" No one to exclaim, "What a strange figure, shrouded in that black robe!" He had no map, no names, no directions of any kind, yet he knew instinctively where to go...which streets to traverse, where to turn, at which door to knock. Many from the Circle of Adepts dwelt in a house on the outer ring of the city, those who had been with him on that long-ago day when he had drunk the potion. The shock on their faces was intense and overt, but Belial took no notice.

They made him comfortable and offered him meat and drink, which he gladly accepted. Hurriedly, they made preparations. In a matter of days, all was in readiness for the appearance of Belial in the world—for his enrollment in the university and his grooming for a meteoric rise to political greatness.

The university was a marvelous place, a city in itself, a microcosm of the greater Atlantean empire. It was a bustling, vital community, as well as a most sacred institution. From all over the world they came, men and women of all ages, shapes, and colors, attracted toward the center of learning and knowledge like iron filings to a magnet.

The most highly regarded studies were those which were considered particularly numerical and thus closest to the essence of things. These were arithmetic, music, astronomy, and geometry. Of special interest was the art and science of stereometry, in which students explored the shapes of geometric solids and the structure of the universe.

The intervals of music, the ratios of geometry, astronomical periods, and the cycles of time—all were measured by the same standards of number. It was with great excitement that Surya, the ancient philosopher-priest, had discovered that these same numerical patterns were also somehow inherent in the structure of the human mind.

"HUMAN NATURE," Surya had written in his now-famous treatise, "LIKE THE NATURE OF THE ENTIRE UNIVERSE, IS ESSENTIALLY AND FROM THE BEGINNING A CREATURE OF NUMBER. THE SIGHT OF DAY AND NIGHT, OF MONTHS AND THE REVOLVING YEARS, OF EQUINOX AND SUNSET, HAS CAUSED THE INVENTION OF NUMBER, FROM WHENCE WE HAVE DERIVED ALL PHILOSOPHY."

Thus, the priests and priestesses who established and taught the curricula drew no distinctions among these subjects, applying the same sacred canon of number to all of them. Theirs was a sacred charge, to ensure that all who sought advancement in life studied and worked according to the ancient canon of number and proportion. Nothing was beyond the scope of these numerical principles, especially that most sacred and profound of all of the academic disciplines—statecraft. For as it was written in the *Book of Life*...

THIS HAS THE EFFECT OF MAINTAINING THE LEVEL OF CULTURE FOR AT LEAST TEN THOUSAND YEARS.

Belial was captivated instantly, his thirsty mind eager to soak up ever more knowledge to add to his already vast storehouse of occult lore. Applying his vast intellect to the study of the arts, science, and statecraft alike, he delved deeply into the principles of *Dynamic Equilibrium* and *Fusion*, by which opposite tendencies are reconciled, and the ordering principle of *"like attracts like,"* which underlies the phenomenon of coincidences.

Reading the works of Surya and other master philosophers, he came to understand the complementary and reflexive nature of the universe. Thus was the foundation laid for his philosophical views, so subtly different from the truth of the Ancients—that the world was essentially a structure of number, and so being, *could be manipulated as such!*

Under the guise of an insatiable thirst for knowledge, Belial began his obsessive quest to understand the numerical patterns underlying the dynamics of atomic, solar, and galactic systems. Within those hallowed walls, he formulated the first rudimentary plans for the building of a device that could harness such power and bend it to his will. Of course, he kept his true intentions and his true personality to himself, not wishing to become to conspicuous or be branded as a nonconformist, or worse yet, a heretic.

Entering the mainstream of Atlantean society, he altered his appearance ever so subtly so as not to stand out completely as an alien figure. He removed the sinister black robe and donned the traditional student's garb—loose-flowing tunic, sandals, and knotted waist cord. He even tried his hand at expressing emotions—smiling and grinning, although what passed for a smile was more like an evil grimace. Were he not such a sinister figure, it might have been comical to watch the giant practice before the mirror each evening, trying to feign warmth and interest and friendliness.

His efforts succeeded well enough. No one looked too closely at the young man or his actions, which was exactly his intent, *for now.* There would be another time, coming soon, when he would reveal himself as he truly was. But for now, it was best to blend in.

The university years passed quickly—a whirl of activity and opportunity. Belial worked hard, learned much, and grew in wisdom, experience, and popularity. His teachers were impressed by his intelligence and eagerness to learn, as well as by his astute observations and innovative ideas about government, science, economics, and politics.

Outside the Circle of Adepts, he gave no voice to the dark and ominous thoughts that lurked in his mind, no inkling of his true intentions. To all who knew him, he was the epitome of genius, unusual in physical appearance, perhaps, but brilliant of mind. Belial's professors arranged for him to meet many of the greatest minds in Atlantis—philosophers, scholars...even members of the Council of Elders. Each vied with the others to be the young man's mentor and advisor, offering scholarships and invitations to join in research projects of the highest caliber.

"Study philosophy with me," one would offer. "Together we shall do great things."

"No, mathematics is your forte," counseled another. "The world of measure and number is a world of great wonder and amazement. Let me show it to you."

"Politics! You have a genius for politics," encouraged still others. "You owe it to the world to step up and govern wisely."

It was not long before the name of Belial was widely known, not just within the academic community, but also within the political ranks of the city all the way up to the Council of Elders. Belial accepted all of this recognition with a great show of humility. Here was the opportunity to begin the work of spreading his ideas and gathering others of like mind to himself.

He had an enthusiasm and charisma that were both intoxicating and irresistible. It seemed to Belial as though he was the agent of messengers from the spirit world, those higher intelligences he had encountered on his journey into the realms of higher consciousness. When he spoke, he issued forth a magical flow of words, delivering them with spellbinding effect. At such times, he believed that one or another of those spirits had temporarily possessed his soul and was delivering its message through him.

All who heard him marveled at his speaking voice, at the power of his words and the strength of his message. One of the Elders remarked in an address to the Council:

He is a mesmerizing and captivating speaker with a fantastic potential for leadership. His voice rings with strength and power, and he holds his audiences spellbound, gazing at them through eyes that have the mystical look of a prophet. Men and women alike are excited by the power that exudes from him.

Belial began to travel amongst the upper crust of Atlantean society, receiving invitations to teas, dinner parties, balls, even Council sessions. "Watch that young man! He will go far! The gods have greatness in store for him!" Such were the exclamations of dozens of hosts and hostesses as they held one successful social affair after another. Then one day, toward the spring of his last year at the university, Belial's path crossed with that of an obscure first-year student, also of noble birth, yet relatively unknown, having yet to distinguish himself in the academic or political worlds.

Belial had heard that the son of a noble family had been enrolled, one whose seat on the Council of Elders had been assured from birth, one whose ancestry dated back to the original founders of Atlantis. Why have we not met? Belial wondered as the months went by. Where is he? We must be introduced. It would be of great help to me if I were to enlist the support of the son of such an influential family!

For his part, the young student knew of Belial only by reputation, having heard stories of the popular student and catching fleeting glimpses of him from far across the lawns. Try as he might, however, he could never seem to get close enough to make the other's acquaintance, being jostled away by the crowds or called to other appointments. "I'll meet him tomorrow," the young man would say after each failed attempt. "I'll seek him out and stand my ground and make myself known to him."

But fate was to decree otherwise. The two were not to meet yet. Many months would go by—fall would turn to winter, then winter would turn to spring, before the fateful meeting was to occur. The first encounter between Belial and Adima would come at the Vernal Equinox, during the Season of Rebirth, when the first rains came to sweeten the soil and give drink to the newborn sprouts.

*****

Accidents, chance encounters, random events...such things do not exist in truth. Within the vast consciousness of Universal Mind, there are no coincidences. Everything is intentional, everything has a purpose. Every Cause produces an Effect. Every action results in an equal and opposite reaction. Every journey has a beginning and an end, every road a starting point and final destination. Long ago, before either soul had ever taken form, the meeting place had been set, the date and time appointed. What way could lead but to the meeting place?

Along their respective paths, Adima and Belial walked, unaware of their relationship to one another, unaware of the role each would soon play in the unfolding drama of the End Times. Aware only of a slowly-building tension in the air. Each felt the energy, the dynamic flow of charged electrical particles dancing in space around him. Something incredible was happening, an event of enormous scope and magnitude was being born here and now, at this first coming together between them. So Belial and Adima trod their seemingly separate paths, converging on a single point in space and time, a place known in the eternal Heavens as the *Difficult Passage...the Sword Bridge!*

On that fateful day, an early afternoon thundershower precipitated a flash flood, preventing Belial from taking his usual route after class. "Go that way!" an old man pointed toward the mouth of a narrow alley between two buildings as Belial tried to traverse a wide, muddy puddle. He was a very old man, stooped and bent, his flowing beard hoary with age, certainly out of place on that crowded university street corner.

I've never seen him before, Belial thought as he followed the stranger's directions. It never occurred to him to wonder how the mysterious stranger knew where he was heading or that this detour would take him where he wanted to go.

On the opposite side of the campus, Adima was facing the same problem. Although the sky had cleared, there was water everywhere. He really wanted to stop and frolic with some children who were cavorting in the mud, but intuition seemed to say, "Not tonight. Another duty calls you." As the sun began to set behind the ivy-covered walls, Adima approached the alley from the opposite direction, having been guided there by an inner Voice that whispered, "Go this way!"

It was quite gloomy within the long, narrow passageway. Windowless brick walls rose several stories on each side, to where the sky shone golden blue overhead. As he entered, Adima's fertile imagination conjured up all sorts of fanciful scenes. He pictured himself stepping into the gaping jaws of a coiled serpent, and that the passage led between two clashing millstones, waiting only for his entrance before rushing together in a thunderous roar, crushing the life out of him. He smiled at his childlike fantasies, but he did cast a wary glance around him as he walked.

Each entered at the exact same instant, casting long shadows as he walked, footsteps echoing hollowly on the cobblestones. Even from a distance, they recognized each other instantly. For a brief moment, each was elated at having the opportunity to meet the other at last, but their joy was quickly replaced by almost overpowering feelings of revulsion and distress welling up from within.

They slowed their pace, becoming cautious, wary. As they approached each other, a bolt of electrical energy passed between them, a crackling charge that arced and flickered like blue lightning. Both recoiled from the shock, as do like poles of magnets when they repel each other. They stopped dead in their tracks, facing each other from ten feet apart— hero and antihero, protagonist and antagonist. In an obscure byway out of sight of the world, on the sharp edge of a razor with but a hairsbreadth to separate them, the bipolar opposites came together for the first time.

"You will know him when you meet him...the repulsion between you will be strong." Belial remembered Nebo's prophecy. So it was true after all, although the wizard was not there to see the fulfillment of his dire prediction.

"The Dark One!" Adima gasped, "the one who will lead Atlantis into the abyss!" This was no child's fairy tale, this was real. He knew the prophecy, but he hadn't thought it would be fulfilled in his own time, with himself starring in a central role. Could this really be he? Adima longed for wise counsel, but that would have to wait.

The silence was deafening, the tension think and heavy. They exchanged no pleasantries, no cursory words of greeting that would customarily pass between strangers encountering each other at close quarters. Nor did either one move, each standing firm, each staring at the other, sizing up his adversary. It was Belial who spoke first.

"Did you feel it?" he asked in his deep, booming voice. He knew the answer; it was obvious from the other's whole demeanor. Nebo's prophecy had come to pass.

"Of course I did," came the unnecessary reply. Adima looked at the giant before him. A slight shiver of fear crept along his spine. Is that a smile on his face? Does he sense my fear? Adima wondered silently.

As if in answer, Belial responded, "I am Belial. Who are you?" It was not a request, it was an order.

"I am Adima," Adima replied, amazed that a stranger would offer his name completely without fear, and even more amazed that, in spite of his own fear, he had offered his own name in return.

"Well, Adima, it would appear that you and I are to have intercourse together. Our paths have not crossed by accident." Even in the shadows, Belial's dark eyes glowed deeply black against that pale background of skin.

"It would appear that fate wants us to meet," Adima replied coolly, trying to hide his growing anxiety. He felt uncomfortable around this giant, hulking man, yet he was strangely drawn to him, too. "Perhaps we should spend some time together and try to find out why."

"As you wish," the giant replied, "although I already know who you are and why we have met. That is why I gave my name to you, to show you that I am not afraid of you. And that is why you have been shown to me, to show me that I have nothing to fear from you. You are weak, you are puny, you are good."

Adima's mind was racing. With each word, he wanted to flee, wanted to run and hide and never look on Belial's hideous face again. He hoped it was all a dream. Oh, how he hoped he would awaken in his own bed! Even the screams of a nightmare would be welcome in lieu of the living nightmare before him.

"I am strong and powerful," Belial continued, flexing his bulging muscles. He stooped to pluck a large black beetle from its nest between two bricks, holding the creature gently between a thumb and forefinger. With a swift movement, Belial closed his fingers. The bug popped sickeningly as it died.

"The time will come when we shall meet as mortal enemies," Belial continued his menacing tirade. "On that day, I shall crush you, and you will be as worthless as dried dung that burns in the sun and is blown away in the desert wind." He flicked his fingers, dropping the carcass on the stone and crushing it beneath his sandaled foot.

"Before then, our paths will cross many times, this being but the first. I shall smile in your face and greet you as friend. But know this, puny one..." Belial did not even use Adima's name, so contemptuous was he of this cowardly weakling who presumed to stand in his way.

"...I am not you friend. There can never be friendship between us. We are opposites. We have been placed at opposite sides of the Pendulum to serve a larger purpose. We shall always be in conflict. We shall always challenge each other. And I shall always win."

Confidently, Belial took several steps forward, while Adima shrank back into the wall in terror. "So that you will always remember me and this first meeting between us, I shall mark you as my own."

The giant raised his arm and traced a line in the air with his right index finger. Adima felt his cheek grow hot. Searing pain burned across his face from his jaw to the top of his head, and he staggered and screamed in fear and anguish. Great gouts of his own blood flowed into his open mouth, causing him to gag and choke as he collapsed on the ground in a pitiful, soggy heap.

"Piece by piece, I shall eat you," The Beast loomed darkly over the now thoroughly cowed man-boy. "I shall take what is yours and devour it. I shall take from you all whom you love. And in the end, I shall take your very soul." The Dark One rose to his full height and continued on through the passageway. As he was swallowed up in the gloom, his mocking laugh came floating back on the cool evening breeze.

Young Adima sat for a long time in a growing pool of his own blood, numb with terror and agony. Finally he struggled to his feet and made his way home, using a wide strip of cloth ripped from his ruined tunic as a cowl to hide his shame and disgrace. That night, alone in his darkened room, he cried himself to sleep. His face ached fiercely, and he was terribly afraid. He did not understand any of what had just happened. He wished his father were here. His father would know what to do. But of course, his father was long dead, and he knew no other wise men to talk to.

I have no one! Adima realized, and that brought even more fear. Not only did he suddenly have a new and powerful enemy, but it also appeared he was going to have to deal with that enemy all by himself. And he did not want that. He did not want that at all.

What can I do? Panic seized him. He needed advice, but to whom could he turn? Certainly not to his mother, nor his younger brother. And his older brother was halfway around the world, fighting in the Lemurian War. No, there was no one to help him, no one to protect him from this frightful new menace looming before him. With that realization, he broke down and cried. He was alone, alone in all the world, and it felt like he was going to be alone forever.

"Help!" he screamed, burying his head in his pillow so that no one would hear his anguish. "Won't someone please help me? I cannot go through this alone. I do not understand. I do not know what to do! Who can teach me? Who can show me the way? Come to me, please. Please show me the way. Please tell me what to do!"

On and on he cried, wailing out his desperation, pleading for succor, pleading for someone, anyone to help him. At last, drenched in perspiration, physically and emotionally spent, he got up and went to the window.

Has my prayer been heard? he wondered as he leaned on the sill and looked out into a warm, moonless spring night. Is anyone listening? Is there a teacher out there somewhere, even now being sent to me in answer to my request? "I am willing," he whispered to the distant stars, his voice hoarse, his face wet with tears. "I am so very, very willing." For a long time he lay thus, hugging his pillow as he stared out into the darkness and listened to the silence, until finally he fell asleep.

CHAPTER 24

Swift, swift, you dragons of the night, that dawning
May bare the raven's eye! I lodge in fear;
Though this a Heavenly angel, hell is here.

—William Shakespeare, *Cymbeline*

The Atlantean calendar followed a twenty-two-year cycle, corresponding to the twenty-two universal principles of life. Each year, in turn, was divided into thirteen months of twenty-eight days, with a single day left over.

That day was ruled by the Hawthorne tree, sacred to the Goddess, and considered to be a non-day, falling between the old year and the new. On such a day, no work was undertaken, neither started nor finished, because the day was considered unlucky...a period of potential disaster in which nothing new or important was begun.

On that day, in the thirteenth year of the twenty-two year cycle, the Year of Death, Belial wrote thrice in his journal.

*****

From Belial's Journal...

Morning

    We shall talk with the people on the streets and in the squares and teach them to take the view of political questions that at the moment we require. For what the ruler says to the people spreads through the country like wildfire; the voice of the people carries it on all four winds.

    We—the Beast always says "we," for he is legion—shall create unrest, struggle, and hate in the whole of Atlantis and thence in the provinces. We shall at all times be in a position to call forth the new disturbances at will, or to restore the old order. Unremittingly, we shall poison the relations between peoples and states. By envy and hatred, by struggle and warfare, even by spreading hunger, destitution, and plagues, we shall bring all peoples to such a pass that their only escape will lie in total submission to our domination.

    We shall stultify, seduce, ruin the youth. We shall not stick at bribery, treachery, or treason, as long as they serve the realization of our plans. Our watchwords are Force and Hypocrisy. In our arsenal we carry a boundless ambition, burning avidity, a ruthless thirst for revenge, relentless hatred. From us emanates the spectre of fear, all-embracing terror.

From Belial's Journal...

Midday

    We are the chosen, we are the only true men. Our minds give off the true power of the spirit; the intelligence of the rest of the world is merely instinctive and animal. They can see, but they cannot foresee; their inventions are purely corporeal. Does it not follow that nature herself has predestined us to dominate the whole world?

We shall not submit the greatness of our ultimate plan—the context of all its particular parts, the consequence of each separate point, the secret meaning of which remains hidden—to the judgment and decision of the many, even of those who share our thoughts. We shall not cast our gleaming thoughts before the swine, and even in the most intimate circles, we shall not permit them to be carped at.

We shall paint the misdeeds of Lemuria in the most garish colors and create such an ill-feeling toward them that the people would a thousand times rather bear a slavery that guarantees them peace and order than enjoy their much-touted freedom. The people will tolerate any servitude we may impose on them, if only to avoid a return to the horrors of war and insurrection.

Our principles and methods will take on their full force when we present them in sharp contrast to the putrid old social order.

From Belial's Journal...

Evening

Outwardly, however, in our "official" utterances, we shall adopt an opposite procedure, and always do our best to appear honorable and cooperative. *A statesman's words do not have to agree with his acts.* If we pursue these principles, the elders and people that we have thus prepared will one day accept us as benefactors and saviors of the Atlantean race. If any province dares to resist us, if their neighbors make common cause with them against us, we will unleash a world war... By all these methods, we shall so wear down the provinces that they will be forced to offer us world domination. We shall stretch out our arms like pincers in all directions, and introduce an order of such violence that all people will bow to our domination.

CHAPTER 25

*He issued his commands to kings and tyrants, and his
relation with them was as authoritative as though he were
the ruler of the whole Earth.*

—Regino of Prune, Chronicler of the Ninth Century

If there was one thing that disturbed the peace and well-being of Atlantean society, it was the ongoing war with Lemuria. Ever present in people's lives, the war had been raging for centuries. So many lives lost, such carnage and destruction on both sides! The best and brightest of the youth maimed, captured, killed, missing. Such incomprehensible waste, such incalculable expense!

The politics of war had divided Atlantis for decades. At first it had been a holy crusade. Fathers and grandfathers who had served were only too happy to boast of their heroic exploits, proud to entice their sons and grandsons to follow in their footsteps. With age came a softening of memory, a dulling of the sharp horrors that the real-life experience of war had brought. Now, however, the consciousness of the people was changing. Returning soldiers were openly expressing their dissatisfaction with the war, telling horrific stories of all manner of atrocities. Try as they might, the militia was powerless to silence these disillusioned young men. All efforts to assuage them proved futile.

The exposé had two immediate results, the first being the raising of the consciousness of the citizens of Atlantis. With that heightened awareness came another benefit, the realization that the war was not a holy crusade to be perpetuated. Rather, it was a frightful leech, sucking the lifeblood out of Atlantean society. The cost was becoming far too much to bear, especially in the minds of the families of the young men who were laying their lives on the line for the cause. Bitter debates raged, rallies and demonstrations. Children turned against parents, respect for old institutions and authority was flouted. There were riots in the streets.

Into the midst of this chaos strode Belial, fresh from his university years, brimming with ideas and visions of a better world, a world where a new order had been instituted and structure and discipline dwelt...a world, too, where he ruled in absolute power over the masses, although that part he kept hidden unto himself.

Belial was well aware that his difficult apprenticeship was finally over. Now he was ready to embrace that long-awaited role which destiny had begun to enfold for him. With amazing powers of intuition, he knew at a glance how to recognize the people and the opportunities that would take him along a direct path to the pinnacle of power.

"I have already effectively dealt with the one threat that could harm me," he wrote in his journal. "By marking Adima, I have made him visible and thereby have rendered him powerless." Now Belial could turn his attention to more important things—the drawing together of the men who would compose his Inner Circle and the establishment of the political cult that would bear his name.

So continued the strange rise to power as he spoke tirelessly in one public forum after another. His message supplied exactly what a tired and war-weary populace craved. People flocked to hear him. Through a series of synchronicities, offers of power and opportunity were thrust into his grasp from all directions. Strange men appeared from out of nowhere, positioned appropriately in the right place at the right time.

Belial grew ever more visible. He began to speechify and orate publicly, outlining his vision for a new and even more glorious Atlantis. Now the Elders were filled with even greater praises:

"A light appears in a darkened window. A hulking giant with brooding black eyes and bleached white skin becomes as an archangel. Listening to Belial, one suddenly has a vision of who will lead humankind to glory."

Many on the Council of Elders were impressed by his innate knowledge of statecraft and his apparently all-consuming love of Atlantis. It was not long before the whole country was captivated by the almost magical charm of his personality. Within, however, in the secret chambers of his mind and heart, that childhood fear had never left because the childhood wounds had never healed. Now that fear was deeply hidden, but it was still there, nevertheless. Oh yes, deep inside, it was still so very much there!

He—Belial—was a weakling. He had always been one, and he had always been ashamed of this tragic flaw. It was the one secret he dared not reveal, even to himself. He remembered Nebo's admonition and warning. "You are horribly weak. To get power, you need a strong Inner Circle. Gather them unto yourself. Surround yourself with strong men."

Slowly and methodically, Belial began to gather the future members of his cult together. As to a great magnet, so they came together from all over the world—dark allies drawn to the Dark Lord—attracted by the magnetic force of his personality and his mission, forming a new political party as well as a spiritual cult.

To draw them in, he drew on the principles of attraction that he had studied so diligently at the university, particularly the principle of *"like attracts like."* Thinking as they thought, feeling as they felt, he knew exactly the lures to throw out, knew exactly how to entice them with promises that would appeal to their egotistical desire for power. "I do not offer the same old form of government," Belial declared to each of the dark Adepts who entered his Inner Circle. "I offer something fresh, something new, something that works."

Belial did, indeed, offered something new. His were new ideas, ideas not previously talked about openly in Atlantis. "Think about it," he hissed in the privacy of his inner chambers. "You know it is true. We are the enlightened ones. We are superior."

The Adepts nodded their heads in confirmation, and Belial was pleased. Whenever he saw heads nodding, he knew that his words were having their desired effect. It was amazing how easy it really was. All he needed was the hook and the lure. Once the bait had been taken, it was simply a matter of reeling in the intended victim.

"We few, we elite!" he continued. "*Our* desires, *our* needs are what really matter. What care we for the rabble? They are a necessary annoyance. We must tolerate them, keep them able to scratch out a meager existence. So that they can serve us."

It was the planting of a philosophical seed that would take root, grow, and spread throughout history, surviving the great flood and destruction and rising—like the phoenix from the ashes—thousands of years later in its new forms.

The needs of the few outweigh the needs of the many.
The majority of the population exists to serve the few, the State.

For the few who desired power at the expense of the many, Belial's words were like a welcome draught of fresh, cool water. "We will serve you, Master," each declared with eagerness and hope as Belial placed his hands palms down on their bowed heads. One after another, each pledged his undying loyalty, his life, his fortune, his very soul in service to Belial and his unholy cause.

Publicly, however, Belial espoused a subtly different philosophy. "We are people," he exclaimed to the vast throngs assembled to hear his message. The bunting fluttered gaily in the breeze while the crowds jostled for position around the podium. "First, we are individuals. Second, we belong to our families and our communities. Finally, at the highest level, we are citizens of Atlantis.

"Each individual is part of the larger Whole," he would declare, pounding his clenched fist on the dais for emphasis. "You have no independence apart from the Nation-State. You are parts of Atlantis like the tiny cells of a larger organism.

"The Nation-State! You are part of its life. You share in its culture. And you exist as the parts of an organism exist, to serve and maintain the Whole, which has more importance than you or any of its parts."

Again the heads bobbed up and down in agreement, and Belial was pleased. Human nature was the same everywhere, it would appear. From the Inner Circle to the filthy rabble, they were all the same. It was all he could do to hide his contempt, but he managed quite successfully.

"The State must go on," an impassioned Belial spoke in the piazza surrounding the Great Pyramid. "Atlantis must continue to survive. Atlantis must continue to grow strong. In order for a nation to exist and maintain its greatness, it is justified in imposing its will on the people. In exchange for this, the people are free to pursue their lives within the predefined limits of what the Nation-State deems to be right and appropriate."

Many arose and said, "Yes. He is right. Absolutely! We are tired of war, tired of this constant struggle. Belial has a better way. Let us join him."

Few were the voices raised against him. Those that were came mostly from the youth, who presented themselves as an angry, unorganized mob, full of unrest and discontent, with little of value in the way of ideas to offer as a better solution. Had they been better organized, had they had an eloquent and charismatic leader such as Belial, perhaps the young people of Atlantis could have posed a more effective challenge to the burgeoning tyrant. But alas, such was not the case.

So the innocent yet ignorant masses listened to Belial, came to believe the Lie, accepted his vision, and were swept up and carried away by the hypnotic appeal of his mania. Day by day, his power and influence grew, as did his cult following, growing in strength and numbers until they reached critical mass at last. He had even given them a name. "...a most effective name," he thought smugly, "a name that implies family and community, while at the same time placing me in position of parent, to be respected and obeyed."

The *Sons of Belial* became a force not only to be acknowledged, but also reckoned with. Belial was everywhere, a dynamo of energy, quietly forming alliances with Elders, priests and priestesses, and of course, the military. Offering favors, making enticing and alluring promises, dangling carrots before them—dangerous carrots, with sharp barbed hooks concealed within their sweet orange flesh. "Side with me. Step up as I step up. Rise as I rise. I shall not forget you."

Surrounding himself with the best and the brightest, he surreptitiously instituted a complex web of spies and informants, asking for and getting the information he needed. Overtly, though, everything the Sons of Belial did was aboveboard, for Belial insisted that the group activities be able to pass the closest of scrutiny. Everything was legal and moral; there was nothing to be afraid of—at least not on the surface.

At last, the Sons of Belial were a political force powerful enough for the Elders to notice. "They have the ability to overthrow us," came the warnings in the Council chambers. "They have the sympathy of the people, and, most importantly, they have the votes!"

"What are our options?" Tiwaz asked. The Chief Elder seldom spoke first, preferring to reserve judgement until his subordinates had presented all of the facts and expressed their opinions.

"We can fight them." suggested one Elder.

"We can try to expose them and hold them up to ridicule," suggested another, "but the expense would be great, and the chance of success slim."

"We could wind up looking like fools." Tiwaz scoffed at this plan. "Then Belial would be able to portray himself as victim of the terrible tyranny of the Elders. The people would flock to him more than ever, and we would become ineffective and powerless, a mere puppet government." This was, of course, something the Elders dared not risk. So they tried another way, sending a representative to approach Belial with a compromise, a joining of forces.

The Master was a charming host, receiving the emissary with great deference and respect. He made tea, serving the steaming liquid in delicate china cups, hand-painted with intricate floral patterns in soft pastels, then listened to the proposal attentively, interrupting once or twice merely to clarify a point of information. "I am delighted and only too eager to accept the compromise," Belial said as the envoy finished speaking. "Of course, I have one small request that I would humbly ask."

"Name your terms," the representative said.

Belial smiled and whispered a few words in the man's ear. "I am sure that can be arranged," the emissary said, rising to take his leave. "The Council will contact you with its decision."

Thus were established the Sons of Belial as a new political power in Atlantis. And of course, their first representative on the Council of Elders was their founder, Belial.

*****

Appearances can be deceiving. "All that glitters is indeed not gold," as the adage goes. All promise and hope and optimism on the outside, within the order of the Sons of Belial there dwelt a dark, aggressive, oppressive evil—an evil so encompassing, so pervasive, that it was capable of bringing total annihilation of all that Atlantis valued and held dear. And it would not come to the surface until it was far too late for anyone to stop it.

Belial's chief joy seemed to lie in instilling fear among the members of the Inner Circle. Disappearances, injuries, accidents...there were all kinds of strange and unexplainable happenings. "Cross Belial, and get hurt or disappear." That was the consensus, although no one spoke the words out loud.

Why did they stay? Why would men of such power in their own right become subservient to the will of another, at the risk of their own well being, their own lives? The psychological reasons were varied and complex. There was nowhere else to go. They knew no other way, and the lure of power was great. Add to that the fear of retribution, and Belial had an unassailable stranglehold on all who had vowed to follow him. Once a member of the Inner Circle, they were members for life.

To men who walked each day with death riding on their shoulders, the rewards far outweighed the risks. Belial could give them what they so desperately craved. If the price was their lives, so be it. Power was worth such a price.

*****

It was not long before Belial made his presence felt on the Council. His ways were not their ways, and try as he might, he could not conceal his true nature, his true intent, any longer. He had one altercation after another with senior Council members. Fortunately, he had enough allies to protect him, so there were no repercussions outside the Council chambers. He had already swayed many of the Elders to his side through the power of his voice and personality. Still, there was a solid core group whom he could not win over.

"...so I shall have to do something about them in a different way," he raged, pacing back and forth before a huge fire within an abandoned stone temple, where he had taken up residence. Outside the city walls, the dwelling offered a perfect place of concealment for the various cult rituals and secret meetings that Belial loved so well.

It was a desolate place, standing at the end of a rugged box canyon overhung by a beetling cliff. When the wind blew in ragged gusts through the box canyon, it was said, you could hear the wail of the ghosts who haunted the area. Hikers and passersby always commented on how devoid of life the place seemed to be—no songbirds, no playful woodland creatures, no colorful wildflowers. Only scrubgrass, jackpine, and the ever-present wind.

Legend had it that the building had once been a prison, not for men, but for caged beasts, the terrible aberrations that had been produced during the years of genetic experimentation. Long since banned, the memories of such creatures lived on in fanciful tales of multi-headed beasts, one-eyed giants, and hideous mutants. Older siblings delighted in torturing their younger brothers and sisters with tales of monsters lurking under the bed or in dark closets.

For Belial, though, the stories were not legend. They were fact. Ever so surreptitiously, he had rekindled interest in the genetics projects and was supporting research in those very ruins. He had just returned from a conversation with his master alchemist, where the news had not been good. There was a problem in the genetic code, whereby the mutants could not survive for more than a few hours after birth.

"We require more funds for our research, better equipment, better laboratories and working conditions," Shakala said. "In short, we need the facilities that only the Great Pyramid can provide."

Belial knew that this requirement was impossible to meet as long as Tiwaz and the Children of the Law of One represented the majority on the Council of Elders. Thus, it was in a foul mood that he had convened the Inner Circle that evening to discuss ways to get and hold even more power, and thereby move his experiments closer to the mainstream of Atlantean science. "I shall have to win them over through fear," the diatribe began. "I shall have do something so terrifying, so hideous, that they will cower at my feet and proclaim me their absolute master, just to keep themselves alive."

The Adepts listened in silence, knowing better than to cross their Master when he was in such a black fury. His tirades and abuses were becoming notorious. Such men learned well. Many carried the scars from those times, so many years ago, when the young Bel had inflicted his wrath on them in the cabin far to the north. How much more terrible were the beatings now, with his great strength augmented by the power of Hanuman's magical potions, which the Master still drank each week during the occult rituals.

A newcomer, however, one who had not yet tasted of Belial's wrath, could not hold his tongue. "Perhaps you could try to reason with them," he suggested innocently. "Perhaps you could show them how they might benefit from such experiments."

Belial turned on the young man with a demonic fury that frightened even the most hardened of the Adepts. Lashing out with an incredible torrent of vituperation that bordered on hysteria, he screamed and spat abuse. The verbal violence lasted for several minutes. None dared come to the newcomer's defense, none dared offer him a consoling gesture, a comforting glance. The young man stood alone, reduced to a shocked and resentful silence. Then, as though nothing out of the ordinary had taken place, Belial returned to his chair to sip wine and resume his quiet reading before the fire.

Such occurrences were common within the Inner Circle. Careful not to be on the receiving end of Belial's wrath, most had developed a kind of hopeless resignation, becoming inured to the sufferings of whomever Belial chose as victim. So, as they had done so many times before, the Adepts remained silent as Belial went through his manic gyrations from thought to rage to uneasy calm. They had no doubt that he would accomplish his goal of winning over the few remaining Council members. He did not need their suggestions.

The evening ended with a ritual convocation, after which the room grew dark and quiet. Belial and most of the men retired, but a few of the most senior advisors gathered around the dying embers. "He will devise the perfect plan, he always does," they whispered among themselves. "And he will do it in such a way as to seem perfectly natural. There will be no overt show of force; the decision will come from the Elders themselves."

*****

Deep below ground, in a squalid stable that passed for a laboratory, an unclean beast cried out in agony as she delivered her grotesque, misshapen child. Shakala took the creature and placed it on a bed of straw inside a small cage, expecting it to be dead within a few moments. Such was not to be the case, however. With a display of agility and strength that belied its deformed shape and tender age, the creature stood up on its hind legs, shook itself convulsively, and voiced a weird, bloodcurdling howl.

Shakala stepped back in astonishment. This had never happened before. This was not supposed to be. The creature should be dead by now, according to all of the other experimental results. But this newborn seemed to be growing stronger, not weaker. Man and beast eyed each other from opposite sides of the cage. A fierce, intelligent light gleamed in those baleful yellow eyes. The creature licked its lips and growled softly. Shakala put his hand to his mouth to stifle a scream.

CHAPTER 26

Again, the Devil taketh Him up into an exceeding high mountain, and showeth Him all the kingdoms of the world, and the glory of them.
And the Devil saith unto Him, "All things will I give Thee, if Thou wilt fall down and worship me."

—*Matthew 4:8-9*

Watching Belial plan his attack was magnificent to behold. Very quietly, week by week, month by month, he sowed the seeds of his plot, ingratiating himself with the military as well as with the most influential Elders. The Chief Elder, however, would have none of it. He did not trust Belial. He was not convinced. He despised the strange giant with the bold and dangerous ideas. And he was openly outspoken, denouncing Belial within the Council chambers and in public.

"THE BEAST DOES NOT LOOK WHAT HE IS," Tiwaz warned, quoting from the *Book of Life*.

HE IS YOUNG AND VIGOROUS AND HIS VOICE RINGS OUT WITH MAGICAL POWERS THAT, LIKE THE SEDUCTIVE TONES OF THE MASTER SEDUCER, CAN LURE GREAT LEADERS INTO A TERRIFYING CONDITION OF DIMINISHED MORAL RESPONSIBILITY, AND AT THE SAME TIME EXCITE THE MASSES TO RISE UP AND TURN A VIBRANT CULTURE INTO A HEAP OF RUBBLE AND ASHES. BENEATH A BANAL AND CHARMING EXTERIOR IS CONCEALED A BLOOD-HUNGRY TYRANT, A MIGHTY DEMAGOGUE.

"Be careful, Tiwaz," his advisors warned. "Belial has powerful friends. To challenge him invites danger. He will not stand idly by and let you so besmirch his name. He must strike back, and with the power of the military behind him, there is no hope that you can withstand him."

"The truth must be told," the old man insisted stubbornly. "We cannot let a demon like Belial rule Atlantis. He will bring ruination on all of our heads." He laid a trembling hand on his advisor's arm. "Thank you for your concern. But I am an old man, and my first duty is to the people whom I serve, not to protect this ancient and decrepit body, which has served me well these many long years.

"If I do not challenge Belial, if I do not rise up and serve as an exemplar, no one will. I cannot expect the young to do what I am unwilling to do. Leadership must come from me. Tomorrow I shall openly challenge him in chambers. I shall call him out and open everyone's eyes to the blackness within him. Then we shall see. Then we shall see..."

No one paid any attention as one of the soldiers quietly slipped out of the Council chambers, exited the building, and headed for a ruined temple on the outskirts of the city.

*****

"Perfect!" Belial was beside himself with delight as he stood in his bedchamber with Dakinis, Captain of the Atlantean Guard, a loyal member of the Sons of Belial and high-ranking member of the Inner Circle. "The Chief Elder wants to challenge me."

The Master was careful to maintain a serious expression, however. This could not have happened better if he had planned it. "Tomorrow, I shall assume control of Atlantis," he declared confidently. "Atlantis is mine now. Atlantis is mine. Mine!"

His deep voice bellowed throughout the chamber, which was lit by dozens of candles. A huge fire roared in the stone hearth, while outside, a full moon glowed yellow in the eastern sky. Perhaps it was the heat and the suspense, perhaps it was real magic. Dakinis never knew. Something was happening, however. They were no longer alone in the room. Another had joined. Another was making its presence felt. Belial cocked his head to one side, as though listening.

Is that a smile of recognition on his face? Dakinis wondered to himself. He looked around, but there was no one there. Still, he knew that they were not alone. Something had joined them, Something huge, Something powerful, Something invisible, Something not of this world...

The emotion was overwhelming. As Belial's excitement waxed, his face seemed to melt and twist, shaping itself into a hideous mask. His nose elongated into a snout, his ears grew into satyr's points, horns sprouted from his head, his skin grew dark and leathery, and his teeth became pointed fangs. The Beast within had revealed itself, turning its glowing red eyes on the Captain of the Guard.

"Agghhhhhhhhhhhhhhhhhh!" The man sank to his knees in fear and disgust. "Mercy, Dark One, mercy."

"I rule," the Beast spoke in a voice from the Netherworld itself. "I own Atlantis. I am your king. Bow before me."

Dakinis, Captain of the Atlantean Guard—a powerful warrior, no stranger to violence, death, and the horrors of war, having known battle for thirty years—felt a warm, wet stickiness in his crotch as he lost control of his sphincter. Trembling so violently that he could not stand, the man prostrated himself before the thing that Belial had become.

The Beast roared a mighty roar, its face contorting into a hideous, perverted grin of conquest. Towering above the cowering mortal, it extended a hairy foreleg and drew the man erect, lifting him as easily as a child might lift a pillow. It exuded the foul stench of decay, and its voice had quieted to a guttural growl.

"You did well, Captain, in coming to me. Your loyalty will not be forgotten. You will sit at my right hand and have charge over the Atlantean host. Go now," the Beast pointed to the doorway, "and speak of this to no one, for on the day that you reveal what you have seen this night, you will surely die."

Dakinis wasted no time in letting himself out of the room, glad to be away from the house and back in the relative safety of the streets. He shuddered as he looked back at that frightful place. He could still hear the screams, could still see the monstrous shadows behind the silken drapes.

Standing on a low rise, Dakinis looked out over the city as it quietly slept, unaware of the danger looming so close. He wanted to pray but dared not. The Beast was still about, and he had no desire to taste of its certain wrath should it catch him petitioning the Spirit-world for succor. It was only an hour later, in the relative safety of his quarters, that release came—first tears, then nausea as he choked, gagged, and vomited up blood, bile, and all manner of filth and corruption. At last, Dakinis drifted off into a fitful sleep, where he dreamed of mutilation and gore and depravity.

On the outskirts of the city, Belial slept well that night. He rose early and got to the Council chambers on time. He did not want to be late for his first day as Chief Elder.

*****

No one really knows how rumors get started—where they are born, how they take on a life of their own and spread like wildfire through dry timberland. Suffice it to say that word had spread quickly about the imminent confrontation between Tiwaz and Belial. "If you are loyal to Atlantis, be there." The message was cryptic, but clear. And so they came.

The dome glistened like a stainless steel beehive in the morning sunshine. Multicolored glass panels were interwoven throughout the gridlike structure, flooding the interior of the chamber with myriad shades and colors. For it was the light that was the focus of attention in that sacred circle. Light—which to the Atlanteans was synonymous with knowledge. Within those hallowed halls, the Council of Elders sought illumination—not from the gloom of night, but rather from the darkness of ignorance.

Everything was circular—walls, tables, the vast, ribbed dome overhead. Rising from floor to ceiling, a wall of glass spread in a 180-degree arc from south to north along one side of the structure. To the south, the Avenue of the Gods, with its magnificent palaces and shops, ran straight and true. To the north, the Palace and Temple formed the centerpiece of the three concentric rings that formed the city. To the east and west, straight paths led respectively from the Council chambers to the sea and the Great Plain along broad, grassy fields, offering a gorgeous, uninterrupted view of the Ocean of Atlas and the Mountains of the Moon. Ordinarily, everyone would have paused to admire the view. But this was not an ordinary day. It was a morning like none that any of the Elders could remember.

To young Adima, sitting there for the first time, there was mystery in the air, a sense of expectation and intrigue. He watched in tense anticipation as, one by one, the Elders filed into the Council chamber, exchanging a quiet word or two, heads nodding in greeting. There was not a vacant seat.

The challenge came quickly. After the opening prayers and traditional ceremonies, Tiwaz rose to address the august assemblage. He wasted no time with introductory remarks or circuitous dialog. "I shall come straight to the point," he said, his thin voice high and reedy with excitement. "There is danger amongst us. There is one in our midst who is not as he seems."

Elders turned to look at each other, casting furtive glances around the room. Several shifted uncomfortably in their seats.

"I censure you, Belial!" The old man rose and pointed a bony finger at the black-robed giant. "I condemn your ways, I condemn your ideas, I condemn your philosophy and your intentions and your mad blueprint for the future of Atlantis!"

His voice softened as he continued. "However, I do not condemn you. I recognize the beauty and Divine inner spark that lies within you as it does within all men and women. Therefore, I order you to stand down, to cease and desist from your terrible course. I further order you to divest yourself of the trappings of office, doff your frightful black robe, and enter the Temple of Poseidon for healing and cleansing.

"You have great and wondrous gifts, but your mind is deluded. You follow a Dark Path. Within the Temple, through the power of prayer and the cleansing crystals, the priestesses will heal you and restructure your mind, removing your demons and evil thoughts and returning you to the Path of Light."

Sitting in the assemblage, young Adima listened and watched with amazement. "How brave this old man is!" he thought to himself. "I could never do it. I could never challenge Belial." He fingered the terrible, half-healed scar that ran like a jagged bolt of lightning along his right cheek. He shuddered as he remembered that fateful encounter with Belial. He still had nightmares. He still was so very much afraid.

Now it was Belial's turn to speak. "Be silent, old man," he thundered. "How dare you denounce me! You are the deluded one. It is you who are weak. Your body no longer functions, and your mind itself has grown soft and confused. In your senility you see monsters and demons everywhere.

"Look around you, and ask yourself this. Why is it that you are the only one who sees this insensate evil within me? Are you the only one who can see? Are all of these great men and women blind to the truth, save you? Are you the only one who can think and reason and save all of these poor wretches from the terrible plight of being consumed by the monster Belial?" He laughed, and several of the Elders laughed with him, if only to break the tension of the moment. Several others shifted uncomfortably and coughed nervously.

The Captain of the Guard, too, stood uneasily at his post. He was dreadfully ill and experiencing strong feelings of anxiety. He could remember nothing of the past twenty-four hours, only that he had awakened this morning in a puddle of his own vomit. He vaguely remembered having set out to visit Belial the night before, but whether they had actually met he could not recall. That troubled Dakinis exceedingly, as did the faint memories of frenzied, disturbing nightmares.

"No, old man, it is not I that you fear," Belial continued. "It is the fear of death, which lies heavily upon you. It is the fear of dying without leaving a legacy for which you will be remembered. So you invent one here today. You invent a threat where there is none. You create a demon where there stands but a man. You sow the seeds of doubt and mistrust for one who would but serve. And thus do you create a place in history for yourself. I do what I do, I say what I say, out of my all-consuming love of Atlantis. If there are any who disagree, let them reveal themselves now, for they are the true traitors."

Belial sat down smugly and confidently. A few of the Elders glanced approvingly at him, nodding encouragement and offering smiles and gestures of support.

It was Tiwaz's turn once again. He had lost, and he knew it. The Beast had won, and the minds of the Elders were ensnared in the web of lies and deceit. Nevertheless, he had no choice but to utter one last prediction—a single dire prophecy—in the faint hope that the words would ring true and penetrate but a single heart within the room open to receiving the truth.

"I denounce you, Belial." Tiwaz could barely stand, so great was the effort he was expending. He felt the paper-thin tissue of his heart bursting within his chest. Somehow, he managed to find the strength to continue. "I denounce you, and I warn the rest of you. Beware this demon who is even now lusting for the leadership of the Council of Elders. For he will prove himself to be a false prophet.

"Assuming total power over the nation, he will one day be responsible for reducing the whole of Atlantis to rubble and its people to defeat and moral degradation hitherto unknown to history!"

A murmur of astonishment ran through the assemblage. They had expected censure, perhaps, but nothing like this. This was total condemnation—and total challenge! Had this been the old days, the two men would have settled the dispute with swords. All eyes looked to Belial to see what he would do.

The Master's reaction was swift...so swift, in fact, that no one was prepared for it. He spoke not a word, but rose to his feet and stared intently into the old man's eyes. The silence was deafening. They locked gazes. Neither one wavered, neither one blinked.

Suddenly, Tiwaz clutched his chest and staggered backward, gasping for breath. He sagged to the floor, already turning blue. He was dead before his body touched the ground.

Instantly, the Captain of the Guard and several soldiers formed a phalanx around Belial. "Who else dares to question my authority to rule or my motives for the good of Atlantis?" The giant let his gaze travel around the room, locking eyes with each of the Elders in turn. One by one, each lowered his head, not wishing to share the same fate as old Tiwaz.

In the deafening silence, Belial at last turned to Adima. He paused for a long time, as if listening to some inner voice delivering a message to him. Adima tried to lick his lips, but there was no moisture. His mouth had suddenly gone bone dry.

"I have disturbing news for you, young Adima," the terrible figure boomed in an incredibly bass voice that had grown even more powerful in the few seconds since the Chief Elder's death. "Word has reached us this morning of a terrible loss in our ceaseless struggle with the Lemurians. Many of our bravest young men have been lost in battle." Belial glanced around the assemblage, then returned his gaze to Adima once again. In a voice that echoed of the grave, devoid of all compassion, all sympathy, all human emotion, he said, "Adima has just lost a brother."

Like cosmic arrows of doom, the words penetrated Adima's soul, bringing a depth of pain he had never imagined possible. Images of his brother's rugged, handsome face coalesced in his tear-filled eyes, replaced by images of a torn and broken body, lying in a pool of blood on a nameless, foreign battlefield.

Adima remembered a time when, as boys, he and his brother had been fighting. Grandmother had chastised them both, forcing them to sit facing each other while holding hands and making amends. "The day will come when you will weep bitter tears because you will not be able to see each other," she had predicted melodramatically.

The children had laughed at such foolishness then. They loved Grandmother, in spite of her morose and melancholy nature. Their young minds had not yet tasted of separation and loss. They could not conceive of a time when they would not be together. Now Grandmother's words had come true, and Adima's regret and guilt were excruciating.

"You have my sympathies, little one," Belial continued, showing no trace of the rancor he had displayed in the alley. "I promise you that I shall do all in my power to end this carnage and bring all of our brothers home. This war stops now."

The blood drained out of Adima's face, and he swooned. Were he not sitting, he would have slumped to the floor. Silent tears welled in his eyes, and he sobbed gently. Belial's words kept repeating in his head. *Piece by piece I shall eat you. I shall take from you all that you love. And in the end, I shall take your very soul.*

Pandemonium broke out in the Council chamber. Some rushed to the aid of the fallen Chief Elder. Others sought to comfort Adima in his hour of loss. The majority, though, gathered themselves around Belial. Amidst the confusion and hysteria, someone had the presence of mind to sound the alarm. Bong! Bong! Bong! From high atop the Temple belfry, the deep, muffled tones of the gong pealed forth, sounding the call, summoning all of Atlantis to stand ready to receive word of dire news.

From every doorway, every byway, every nook and cranny, people poured forth into the streets, converging on the Temple grounds. For hours the bell tolled; for hours the people waited for the news they had been summoned to hear. Finally, the Captain of the Guard stepped out onto a balcony overlooking the square. "Tiwaz, the Chief Elder, is dead," he announced simply. "We grieve the passing of a great man. A time of mourning is declared. May you all be blessed."

Thus it was that Belial rose to absolute supremacy in Atlantis. Thus began the End Times.

CHAPTER 27

Over the realm of all Spirits that live between Heaven and Earth, whether good or evil, [his] power dominated them all: God alone could protect them.

—Richard Wagner, *Parsival*

There was one final act to complete in order to firmly establish Belial in a position of power and authority. One final step to remove the last remaining vestiges of doubt and fear that still clung to him, deep within his soul.

It took little effort to enthrone himself as Chief Elder. He did it carefully, making it look as though it were their idea, even though it was really his.

"Me?" He feigned shock and surprise when a delegation from the Council of Elders approached him with the idea. "How can I lead you? I could never fill the shoes of Tiwaz, with all of his years of experience and his deep, abiding wisdom." There were tears in his eyes as he spoke.

"You are too humble, Belial," the delegates insisted. "It must be you, for you know the people's heart. You have their ear and their sympathy. There is a great wisdom and assurance about you, despite your young age," they assured him. "With your wisdom and knowledge of statecraft, coupled with your burning love of Atlantis and her people, we would consider it an honor if you were to serve us in this capacity."

What could Belial say? Too much modesty would have been unseemly and might have worked against him. Grudgingly he accepted, while inwardly he beamed with satisfaction and delight. "Chief Elder!" His spirits soared each time he repeated the words. It had happened, all according to plan.

He had no trouble keeping control of the Adepts and those within the Inner Circle. He ruled with an iron hand, having taken Nebo's admonition to heart.

"Because you are weak, surround yourself with powerful men who can place you in power and keep you there. But remember the paradox and beware, because they are strong and you are weak. Because they are so powerful, they can wrest power from you, who are so vulnerable. They can break you and take control from you. Therefore, you must rule with an iron hand. Make them fear you. Keep them constantly alert, ever vigilant, looking over their shoulders, ever watching their backs."

He insisted on each Adept's participation in ritual magic and enlightenment, forcing them to drink Hanuman's strange brews and journey into the depths of their own minds in search of enlightenment. For, unbeknownst to them, the potions had hidden side effects. Combined with the occult rituals, they had the effect of turning the Adepts into puppets. Little by little, they lost their powers of free will and came more and more under Belial's subjugation.

Yet even being fully ensconced in power as Chief Elder, even having instilled fear within the Inner Circle, Belial was not content. That old, secret fear was still very much present within him. "How can I keep and hold power?" he asked the voices. "Who will show me the way?" he asked as he swallowed the vile brew he had come to love so well, the magical potion still prepared for him by the Potion Master whenever the moon was full.

It was during one such experience that he had a vision. Nebo appeared before him, not as he had been in life, but horribly disfigured, his face scarred and burned almost beyond recognition. But it was the wizard, nevertheless. Belial recognized the spirit of his old mentor immediately.

"I am still frightened," he told his teacher. "What more must I do to retain my hold on power and fulfill my mission?"

Nebo's cracked and disfigured face displayed no emotion.

"You will have one more weapon at your disposal, a weapon that will make you invincible if you use it properly. A weapon forged by the Fire God deep within the Heart of the Great Mother—the Spear of Destiny."

Belial awoke with Nebo's words ringing in his ears. Where was this Spear? How could he get his hands on it? He had neither long to wait nor far to search for an answer. In fact, the answer came to him. It was in the third week of his reign as Chief Elder that a messenger approached the ruined temple, carrying word of the arrival of a stranger.

"My master is a powerful sorcerer who dwells in a far country," the messenger began. "He desires an audience with Belial, for he has a valuable gift to bestow on he who is to be ruler of the world."

Recognition! Belial thought. He recognizes me. He has been sent by Nebo to give me the Spear. This is what I have been waiting for!

The sorcerer's needs were few and simple, the messenger explained. He required no food or drink, no bed in which to rest. All that was necessary was for Belial to willingly accept both the gift and the ensuing responsibility. "Come to the obelisk in the center of the Great Plain at midnight on Midsummer's Eve," the messenger said, "and yours will be the world." And with that last cryptic message, he departed.

Belial wasted no time in preparing. He was like a child awaiting the arrival of a parent bearing wonderful presents. He summoned the Adepts, a sizable body of men now, their ranks having swollen since his impressive conduct in the Council chambers. This was to be an elaborate ritual on a grand scale. What better setting than the flat Atlantean Plain, with its standing stones and megaliths? He would stand on a raised platform, the Inner Circle surrounding him in full regalia, and accept the gift in full view of the Atlantean populace.

He would put forth a display of magic and ritual such as had never been seen before. He would make the people gasp in awe. They would honor him and love him. And subtly, very subtly, through the power of the Spear, he would inspire fear. He would brandish the weapon before the eyes of the entranced masses, and they would know—the Spear of Destiny was the ultimate capstone of power.

They would know, and they would fear the might of the great god Belial. He imagined his reign of terror. As long as he had the Spear, he would rule. Then, at the appointed time, he would pass the Talisman of Power along to his son. So the dynasty would continue, from father to son, generation after generation, forever.

*****

Belial thought he was doing this for continuity—to keep the power in his lineage. He did not surmise the higher purpose behind the Spear—a talisman of power, yes, but also an instrument of Spirit. A tool to bring about the true Will of the Divine—awakening within the human soul its natural consciousness and state of freedom, where there is no need for tyranny, no need for rigid and limiting rules, no need for the suppression of new ideas, no need for fear.

It pains me to speak about Belial and the destruction of Atlantis. Acknowledging the scene of such ruination of the noblest of nation-states and the finest of people is mental torture.

The story of Belial begins at the time when the fathers fall asleep—this long sleep of human history. The story of Belial is the story of the beginning of the terror of history. History—a Slaughterbench where victims are tied down and killed as a sacrifice at the whim of some great dictator.

The story of Belial elicits extreme emotions of the most profound and hopeless sadness. For the innocents of Atlantis and the ages, there can be no consolation, no release from pain.

Belial was the greatest villain the world has ever known, responsible for the death of millions and the ruination and destruction of an entire civilization. He was also a man of great passion—one of the great individual agents of change in history—motivated by his desire for power and greatness in his own time.

In talking about Belial, it is easy to stop with the assumption that he is the personification of the greatest of evil. On one level, this is true. Yet on a deeper level, Belial was, in fact, so close to the Truth. He was on the verge of illumination, which he wanted so desperately, but never quite got. He became the greatest of evildoers, when he could have become the greatest of gift givers.

Belial's philosophy stated that the individual was part of the larger Whole, that they had no independence from the Nation-State. They were parts of the State like the tiny cells of an organism. In his own words, he stated...

> The Nation-State—you are part of its life. You share in its culture.
> And you exist as the parts of an organism exist—to serve and maintain the
> Whole, which has more importance than you or any of its parts.

It is here, in this most important philosophical statement, that Belial makes his fundamental reasoning error. So close to the Truth—but not quite there. This is the fatal flaw!

Belial was content to stay at his present level of growth and development. He did not feel the need to go further, having become enraptured with his position of power and deluded by his own false beliefs. By not continuing the thinking and reasoning processes, he never took the next step, and so he never carried through to the final, inevitable, logical conclusion.

Of course, he had no one to show him his error, no enlightened teacher to help him see and learn. Oh, he would have learned, to be sure, for Belial was extremely intelligent and gifted. But there was no ritual elder for him, so he continued to perpetuate the mistake.

And the mistake is this. True, the individual is part of a greater whole. True, the individual shares in the national life and the national culture. True, the individual exists as parts of an organism exist—to serve and maintain the whole. False—the whole has more importance than any of its parts.

There, in that last sentence, is the faulty reasoning, the irrational logic, and the root of the problem. And, because the concluding premise—that the whole is more important than any of its parts—is wrong, then everything that follows must be equally invalid.

On whose authority can it be stated that Belial's conclusions are incorrect? On the highest authority—the authority of the Great Mother, whose principles of Truth are manifested in Nature.

Observe the natural world of the Mother. Take a good, long look at her laws and creations. Such observation of Nature would tell you the Truth, if you took the time to observe in the long term rather than the short term, say a mere few thousand years or so.

There is symbiosis everywhere—within the rain forests, within the intestinal tracts of termites; among the plant kingdom, among the mineral kingdom; throughout the hydrologic cycle, throughout the organs of the human body.

Create an imbalance in but a single one, and the whole organism suffers. Chop down the rain forests, the world cannot breathe. Tear a hole in the ozone layer, everything eventually burns up. Clog up the arteries and veins so that the blood cannot flow, and eventually the body dies.

In Truth, the Whole cannot survive without all of its Parts. The Whole is the sum of all of the Parts, which, by definition, complete the Whole. Therefore, every single individual Part is of vital importance to the Whole.

Without a single Part, the Whole is not Whole, it is incomplete. No Part is indispensable. No Part has greater or less value. All Parts are equal, all Parts are valuable, all Parts are crucial to the continuity of the Whole.

Thus, the worth of each individual Part is immeasurable, for should a single one be damaged, lost, or destroyed, then the Whole becomes incomplete. And the more this happens, the more fragmented the Whole becomes.

If only Belial had recognized this! If only he had had a mentor who could have taught him this great Truth. Would he then have pursued the path he did? One can only guess. One can only shake one's head sadly and wonder what might have been. Would there then have had to have been the Slaughterbench of History, or could the lesson have been learned there, in Atlantis, for all time?

If only he had taken the time and spent the effort and been willing to go where the next step in his thinking would have inevitable led him, as it has led us here today. How much they could have saved, how much could we all have benefited.

Alas, however, he did not, and so humankind fell into history. Repeating and learning each time another dictator rose up to follow Belial's paradigm and embrace the Spear. Learning the hard way, by walking the Path of Direct Experience.

Until now. Now you know. You have finally gotten there—to the place of Truth. Where you need no longer continue to repeat the same mistakes. You can now rise above, go beyond, and create something new and better.

The Whole cannot exist without the individual parts. The Part cannot exist without the Whole. It is truly a *Symbiotic Universe*, in which the Universe exists for Life, and Life exists for the Universe. It is perfectly natural! Hurrah, hurrah, hurrah!

*****

Singly and in groups, the people of Atlantis had been gathering all day. It was a festive atmosphere. The war was coming to an end—reason enough to celebrate—and there were high hopes for a new era of peace and prosperity. Amid joyous shouts and laughter, blankets were spread, food and drink were consumed, games were played, naps were taken.

In the center of the Great Plain, facing east, a wooden platform had been erected to serve as the focal point for the evening's ceremonies. The stage was bare except for a tiered platform and a few elegant wooden chairs...not quite thrones, but beautifully hand-carved and covered with soft purple cushions. Matching purple bunting adorned the guardrails and edges of the stage. In the background, huge, gaily-colored banners rose thirty feet high—the flags of Atlantis and the provinces serving both as background and as symbols of unity.

From the middle of the stage, a flight of steps led down onto the grass. These steps had been overlaid with a brilliant red carpet that stretched for three hundred yards due east, where it merged with another coming in from the northwest. It was hard to miss the significance of this carefully crafted three-part symbology. The flags of unification combined with the color purple—traditional color of the royal family—and overlaid the confluence of the crimson straight paths, which represented the lifeblood of Atlantis flowing through the veins and arteries of her people.

By the time darkness fell, tens of thousands of people had gathered around that central point, forming a great semicircle that spread for hundreds of yards out onto the Great Plain of Atlantis. It was an assemblage the likes of which had never been seen before. Dignitaries, priests, priestesses, noblemen, laborers, soldiers, parents, and children stood shoulder to shoulder. Tonight there were no class distinctions, no separations. All were Atlanteans! All were Sons of Belial!

Everything was in readiness. The night had come. Spotlights bathed the stage and its surrounding precincts in a soft yellow glow. Huge floodlights arced across the sky, illuminating the bottoms of massive thunderheads that had been building in the west all day. The conical beams of light soared up into the Heavens, as though calling out to the gods themselves to witness this spectacle.

Around the perimeter of the stage and along the eastward-flowing path, huge bonfires had been lit, tended by several of the younger priests. A huge, blood-red moon had risen through the shimmering haze on the eastern horizon and was now rising toward its zenith. Outside of this circle of light, all was blackness. A few twinkling stars shone dimly through a hazy, overcast sky. To the north, south, and west, heat lightning flickered sporadically, and an occasional rumble of thunder drifted across the Plain.

"What is going to happen tonight?" friends and strangers asked each other in eager anticipation, while musicians played soft music.

"Don't know," came the vague replies. "Belial has promised something wonderful, and he's never let us down yet. Whatever it is, it will be quite spectacular."

Spectacular indeed. Belial had been careful to plan every last detail. All of the elements of ritual magic were present—bonfires, the full moon, talismans and amulets, the symbols of pentagram and hexagram, the familiars, the shadows. Visual images, auditory stimuli, the elements of light and dark, insignias of initiation—all were designed to evoke an extremely powerful sensory and emotional experience in the Atlantean people. Even the hour itself was carefully chosen—midnight, when the old day dies and the new day is born, when spirits walk abroad and the human mind is most malleable.

Belial was extremely excited. He himself did not know what was coming, only that it was going to bring him much goodness. He was to receive a magical and marvelous Spear. More than a Spear—a Talisman of Power that would make him invincible. Tonight was the night when the fear would go away. It was the final step. From this night forth, the debilitating, immobilizing, burning inner fear would be a thing of the past. He would be free at last!

An hour before midnight, the trumpeters rose and burst forth with a mighty fanfare. From the east, in full dress armor, the members of the Inner Circle marched two-by-two into the circle of light. Parents hugged their children as the parade went by. Lovers tightened their grips on each other's hands. Children's hearts thumped in time to the booming of the bass drum. The crowd was caught up in the spirit of the moment.

Straight as an arrow the column moved, looking neither to left nor right. Focused, alert, they assembled on the stage, standing at full martial attention, lined up in full dress armor according to the various degrees they had attained in their quest for enlightenment.

Under the counsel of Hanuman, Belial had instituted an elaborate pecking order within the Inner Circle. Each man's uniform was symbolic of his current level of spiritual awakening. Each wore his insignia with pride, a sign of his rank and station within the group. Along the lowest tier stood the Aides, wearing the sign of the black Raven, symbolic messenger and wizard's familiar. A row behind them were the Early Initiates, men who were developing new capabilities of inner vision and mental acuity. Their armor was imprinted with the many-splendored plumage of the Peacock, signifying their multicolored imaginative and picture building powers.

The Swans stood in stately elegance along the next highest tier. The Novice who sought to attain this third degree of initiation had to sing his swan song. That is to say, he had to die to his own selfish desires and weaknesses to serve the higher aims of his cult.

Those Adepts who had attained the fourth degree were few, indeed. Three men stood at this next level—Shakala, Draco, and Dakinis—their breasts adorned with the symbol of the Pelican, the bird that wounds its own breast to feed its young. These were the Teachers, charged with fostering the well-being and instruction of the younger members of the cult. "You live for the perpetuation of your own people," Belial had said as they were initiated. "You hereby dedicate yourselves to nurturing our youth."

Alone at the top of the pyramid, Hanuman, the Potion Master, wore the Lion's image. "I am the vessel of the Folk Spirit of Atlantis," he had cried in a loud voice as he attained this penultimate degree of initiation. "Our consciousness is one; our will is one; our words are one." The "surrealistic toad" had quietly risen up to become the highest and most trusted advisor to the demonic leader of the Sons of Belial.

It was time. The clip-clop of horses hooves on cobblestones signaled the arrival of the stranger. Riders were approaching. On a prearranged signal, the spotlights and floodlights were darkened, leaving only the bonfires to light the area. These were immediately stoked by the attendants until the flames hissed and crackled and emitted spectacular showers of sparks as bone-dry wood fed red-hot coals.

All eyes looked out across the Great Plain to the northwest. The lightning and thunder were growing stronger now, flickering and rumbling louder and more frequently around the perimeter of the assemblage. Off in the distance, just within the edge of the circle of light cast by the enormous bonfires, an eerie caravan came into view. Two roan-red horses drew a black carriage trimmed with silver. Following close behind came a procession of six hooded figures. Between them they bore a long, coffin-shaped box.

"What do you see? Are they male or female?" The whispered queries passed through the crowd.

"It's too dark to tell," came the replies. "We're too far away." Already the enchantment was working. Jostling for position, the crowd pressed forward, swept up in the excitement of the occult drama that was unfolding on that muggy summer night.

All of their attention was focused on the strange box. Its otherworldly shape, its mysterious contents—all served to enhance the sense of mystery and wonder. Made of acacia wood from the sacred Tree of Shittah, the box was polished and buffed to a lustrous sheen and adorned with white and red roses, the flowers of life and death, death and rebirth. Inlaid across the lid was a crescent moon of pure, beaten gold, its curved tips rising like the horns of a mighty beast.

The procession stopped before the assembled Sons of Belial. The coachman alighted and opened the door of the carriage. An old man emerged from within—a very old man indeed. The assemblage gasped in awe. It was as though a legend had just sprung to life. Before them stood a stooped, wizened old man, his face as creased as a gnarled oak. Peering out from beneath a cascade of flowing white hair and beard, his eyes twinkled with a dark mischievousness. He was the personification of a malevolent dwarf, leaping to life from the colorful pages of an Atlantean fairy tale.

He was obviously delighted to see the vast assemblage and the extent to which preparations had been made to welcome him. He let his gaze roam slowly over the Plain, taking in the whole expansive view. Countless thousands of faces glowed in the flickering firelight. A waving sea of humanity, multiple facets of a single living being pulsing with life...these were the heartblood of the community, the living Soul of Atlantis. With his glittering eyes, the stranger caught them, held them, mesmerized them.

"A Puppetmaster!" Adima realized suddenly. He was standing close to the front of the crowd, and from his vantage point he had an excellent view not only of the dais, but also of the people gathered with him. He looked at the faces closest to him—men and women whom he knew and loved, with whom he lived, worked, and played. This was no longer the gay and carefree crowd of late afternoon and early evening. The nature of the gathering had changed indeed. This was a crowd that had been whipped to a frenzy of passion.

Emotions were running high, people were tense and anxious. Eyes glazed, breath coming in short, ragged gasps, each seemed to be staring at some personal inner vision, very real to them, yet invisible to Adima's uncaptured eye.

He had a sudden crazy image of the huge crowd as a single entity entangled in the strings, limbs flailing crazily as the master puppeteer put them through their gyrations. "They are under the control of the Puppetmaster. He has this all planned, and they do not even see it." Adima was thinking of the stranger, but he might as well have been referring to Belial. "Strange that I am not affected. I watch, but I retain my wits, my senses." He tried to understand but could not. He simply knew that he stood alone and apart, even in the midst of the many.

"Why am I different?" he wondered. "What is it about me?" He could not explain. All he knew was that he was grateful, very grateful, to have his sanity and his wits about him . At that moment, he caught sight of a face in the crowd—a bold, strong man, staring not at the dais but intently at him. There was a flash of instant recognition.

"I know him!" Adima exclaimed. "The Keeper of the Light! This must be an important night if even he has ventured forth to witness this grand spectacle. And he, too, seems to be unaffected by the Puppetmaster." Adima nodded his head in greeting, a gesture of courtesy to a prominent figure whom he'd never met but nevertheless knew by reputation.

Enoch continued to hold Adima's gaze—not a rude stare, but a frank, open look of assessment. To the young man who had lost his elder brother but a few short months ago, whose father had died many years earlier, there was warmth and comfort in that face. Adima felt an immediate attraction, an affinity that he did not understand. It was then that he heard the voice.

Adima! It called. He turned, startled, but there was no one there. "I'm just skittish," he laughed, trying to calm himself.

Adima! Again his name was repeated. He looked at the Keeper of the Light. Could it be he who was calling. The old man's gaze had not wavered, but neither had his lips moved. Besides, he was too far away to make his voice heard above the restive crowd.

Adima! He heard his name a third time. Now he was sure. The Lighthouse Keeper was addressing him, calling him by name. He turned to face the man.

Come and visit me. He heard the words in his mind, loudly and clearly. There was no mistaking their reality or their intent. Still the man's lips had not moved. *Come and visit me. You are invited.*

Confused, not really knowing why, Adima nodded in the old man's direction, acknowledging that he had, indeed, heard. For the first time, Enoch smiled, a warm, heartfelt smile of genuine affection and appreciation. Then he put his finger to his lips, winked one eye, and turned to face the dais.

"Belial, come forth," the Puppetmaster commanded in a strong, deep voice that belied his diminutive size and advanced years. The blue velvet drape that had been hung as a backdrop rustled in the warm night breeze. There was a moment of tense anticipation. Then, with a flourish of sound, the trumpeters burst forth with another fanfare, and the giant figure of Belial appeared from behind the curtain and stepped out into full view of the people.

"Belial!" they cried. "Hail to Belial!" Arms outstretched, chanting his name, the crowd surged forward, pressing in upon the stage. It was oppressive, overwhelming. Adima felt as though he were being crushed and smothered at the same time. Were it not for the presence of the soldiers, the crowd would have swept over the dais in an overwhelming frenzy of passion.

Belial raised his arms in a call for silence, revealing a golden Eagle emblazoned on his coat of armor. Eagle, sign of the highest degree, signifying that the initiate now had developed the loftiest powers and faculties attainable to man. The message was clear. Such a man could now assume a destiny unique in the history of the world. Such a man was Belial!

The Puppetmaster ordered the bearers to lay the mystical box horizontally at Belial's feet. The old man spoke not a word, for there were no words that could convey the feelings that were being expressed. Straightaway he opened the lid. The crowd strained to see, but most could only rely on the whispered remarks of those nearest the dais, who, having the best vantage points, could pass the word back through the ranks.

Looking within, Belial laid his eyes on the object of his desire for the first time. "At last!" he breathed, trembling with excitement.

His immediate experience was one of complete bafflement. He hadn't known what to expect, but he hadn't expected anything even close to this. Lying in its red velvet case, the Spear was incredibly beautiful. Its wooden shaft was studded with diamonds, emeralds, and rubies—the *Jewels of the Gods*. It was carved with all sorts of intricate, mysterious runes—the *Secrets of the Gods*. Its highly polished metal tip glinted in the firelight, emitting tiny sparks of light—the *Essence of the Gods*.

With great pomp and ceremony, the dwarflike stranger gently lifted the Spear from its red velvet cushions and held it in his outstretched arms. "Belial, I offer you this gift of the gods. It is yours for the taking. What say you?"

Belial needed no second urging. He reached out and pulled the weapon from the old man's hands, taking it forcefully, with great determination and strength. Now he stood before the people, grasping the Spear with both hands, exuding confidence and courage.

"Know this, Belial," the Puppetmaster said solemnly, his voice drifting clearly across the plain on the warm night air. "Now you hold the Spear. *Whoever possesses it, whoever understands the powers it serves, holds in his hands the destiny of the world—for good or evil.*"

A great shout rose up from the crowd. "Hurrah, Belial!" they cried with one voice.

"At last!" Belial thought as he listened to the shouts of praise. "The Talisman of Power!" It was his, all his. No more fear, nor more insecurity. He, Belial, would rule the world—safe and unchallenged—forever.

The weapon was heavy, far heavier than its slender shape indicated. Belial could feel a strange and powerful energy emanating from the iron spearhead, an energy that he could not readily identify. He stood there for a long minute, perplexed by its inscrutable riddle. Hefting the Spear, he minutely studied every physical detail of its shape, color, and substance, all the while trying to remain open to the all-important message he knew was about to come.

The night was drawing to a climax. One most important thing left to do—a demonstration of the talisman's power. Raising the weapon high above his head, Belial lifted his eyes to the black velvet sky. "Behold the Talisman of Power!" he cried in a loud voice that carried clearly to every ear. "The Spear has been given and received. I have taken it. I shall use its magical powers to make us a great nation, respected and feared throughout the world. But first, I shall use its restorative powers to heal us—to bring us to wholeness and completion."

He turned to Hanuman, who was standing ready at his side. "Bring the infirm one forth." It was a masterful plan, all carefully arranged. The healing of the sick, a miracle to demonstrate the awesome powers of the Spear, the weapon that he—Belial—controlled, to wield for good or evil at his whim.

From behind the backdrop, a young child was carried out on a stretcher. She was well known to the people, having lived all of her short life with a strange, debilitating malady of mind and body. All efforts at healing in the Temple of Poseidon had failed, so mysterious a disease was this. Now it was time for a new cure.

Belial made a great show of attending to the child, touching her fevered brow, seeing to her comfort, stroking her hair. "Child, you are sick," he addressed her in a clear voice. "Do you desire to get well?"

"Yes," she said in a soft, childish whisper that immediately tugged at the heartstrings of the compassionate crowd.

"Do you want to run and play with the other children?" Belial swept his arms in an expansive gesture at the crowd, who were straining now to see and hear.

"Yes, I do," the child nodded again, barely lifting her head off the pillow.

"Do you want to grow strong and wise and serve your people with your glorious gifts?" Belial asked the third and final question, toying now with their emotions as a cat toys with a mouse.

"Yes." The child looked confused. She did not know what was happening to her.

"Then rise up and do so!" Belial commanded in a voice more forceful than the thunder that was pealing ever more frequently. He reached down and gently placed the point of the Spear on the top of the child's head. Lightning flashed and danced around the perimeter of the circle, and thunder boomed ominously as the elements indicated their displeasure at this act of mass manipulation. The crowd, however, was completely unaware, their attention totally focused on the unfolding drama before them.

Without a word, the child suddenly sat bolt upright on her pallet. With a look of astonishment, she jumped to her feet and stood alone for the first time in her life. Not knowing how to walk, she would have fallen had not Belial caught her in his strong arms, lifted her gently up, and handed her lovingly to her grateful but disbelieving father and mother.

The miracle was complete, the deception was accomplished. Belial stood triumphant and all-powerful. The fear was gone, and for the first time in his life, he was completely at peace. He turned, Spear in hand, and walked to the edge of the stage. In a single swift motion, he grasped the weapon in both hands and raised it high above his head, standing in the traditional posture of emperor and conqueror.

The crowd went wild. There was no containing their exuberance as they shouted forth their praise and joy and pleasure. The ovation continued for many minutes, and all the while, Belial basked in the glow of their appreciation and good wishes.

It was a sight that would live in the sense-memory of the human race for eons—the crowds, the noise, the firelight, the emotions. All the while, the thunder and lightning continued to intensify. Mountainous thunderheads rolled and boiled across the sky. People glanced apprehensively above them. Atlanteans were used to Nature's electrical displays and had little fear of the weather. The standing stones would attract the lightning and prevent anyone from being struck. But still, it was not a good idea to tempt fate by being out in the open during a storm of such intensity.

A brilliant flash of lightning arced across the sky, followed by an instantaneous thunderclap heralding the arrival of the Shapeshifter. The crowd was startled into a restless silence. No one moved a muscle. All eyes were riveted on the man who held the Talisman of Power. Slowly, they began to sense something.

Belial felt it, too...a mighty Presence around the Spear. With the awareness came a dawning realization—this was the same awesome Presence he had experienced inwardly on those occasions in his life when he had sensed that a great destiny awaited him. Once again, he was in the presence of the Voices. Belial stood beside the Puppetmaster like a man in a trance, like a man over whom some dreadful magic spell had been cast. His face was flushed—if that were possible for such pale white skin—and his brooding eyes shone with an unearthly emanation. He swayed on his feet as if caught up in some totally inexplicable euphoria.

The very space around him seemed enlivened with some subtle irradiation, a kind of ghostly light. His whole bearing and stance were transformed, as if some spirit now inhabited his very soul, creating within and around him a kind of evil transfiguration of its own nature and power. It was a sight to behold. Everyone watched, each person having his or her unique vision. The crowd saw a blessed man, a hero who would save and heal Atlantis. In their collective mind's eye, they saw Belial surrounded by the warm, ruddy glow of angelic light. In that aura, he was transformed into the beautiful avenging angel of legend, who stood guard at the gates of Paradise, lest any evildoers enter therein.

The people watched in awe as Belial unfolded for them a glorious vision of the future of Atlantis. They saw a time of peace and prosperity, a time of tremendous scientific and technological achievement when all of their needs would be met. A time when all dwelt in harmony under the wise rule of Belial, the reincarnation of the great Guardian, Quetzalcoatl. A time when they all willingly bowed down and worshipped this demigod who had come to save them from themselves.

But it was not for the rabble that Belial had transformed himself and projected this illusion. It was for another. Let the rabble project their angelic images onto him. What did he care! Like a great psychic mirror, he would reflect those images back to them. If the people beheld him as their messiah, so much the better. They would see his real self in good time. Tonight, he would reveal his true self only to one other.

Belial looked out on that waving sea of humanity as they experienced their mass hallucination of his blessedness. The fires were burning low, and the crowd shifted restlessly in the smoky haze, each lost in the trance. Amidst all of that crowd, he was searching for someone, a single someone for whom he had planned this final demonstration of power. There! Adima, standing but a few yards away. So tantalizingly close, close enough to reach out and crush. Patience, Belial reminded himself. Not yet. There is so much more of him to take.

Their eyes met, their gazes locked, and Adima's third eye was opened. He saw Belial as he truly was, as Dakinis had seen in the ruined temple in the box canyon. He saw the man transfigured into the Beast...the leathery skin, baleful yellow eyes, cloven hooves, monstrous grin. Shutting his eyes, Adima tried to block out the images, but he could not. He was not seeing with his physical eyes, but with an inner vision that could not be averted by simply closing his eyelids.

Stay with it! Enoch's voice spoke clearly in Adima's mind. *Behold what you must behold. This is the real man. This is that which lurks within. Look on it and see—so that you will always recognize the Beast and come to know it well.*

For a moment Adima stood his ground, unflinching. But only for a moment. He could not stand the sight of those horrible fangs dripping blood, could not listen to the hissing, venomous breath. His knees shook, his legs grew weak, and he had to steady himself on the shoulder of the man beside him to keep from falling.

The exchange was brief and personal, between himself and Belial. The crowd had not noticed, had not even seen what Adima saw. Once again, the old message of fear had been sent. This time, however, there was a subtle difference. Try as it might, the Beast could not invoke the lightning, which it desired for one awesome, grand finale. Brandishing the weapon, it invoked the rain and thunder gods, commanding them to strike this puny figure down. Try as it might, however, it could not make the Dragon obey.

The Beast roared in frustration and rage, brandishing the Spear and cursing the elements, the crowd, and the Great Mother herself. But all of its efforts proved fruitless. *You see, it is not all-powerful*, the voice whispered in Adima's ear. *The elements do not obey it. The lightning does not come when the Beast summons it. For the lightning brings only good. The lightning serves another.*

Adima looked up, steadying himself. The Keeper of the Light was staring at him once again. While all other eyes were on an angelic Belial who showed them a vision of a gloriously renewed Atlantis, Enoch and Adima looked only at each other. Now a new message had been sent—sent and received!

*****

And as the people watched, as Adima and Enoch watched, I watched, too. I watched, and I wondered. *"Am I witness to the incorporation of the Spirit of the Darkness in this deluded human soul? Has this poor boy from an obscure but wealthy family momentarily become the vessel of Spirit known as the Tempter, whom the Ancients described as leading the evil hosts that had been cast down into the soul of humankind?"*

No time for such questions now. The answers would have to wait until I could ask them of the One—the One who knew. The vision was finally over. The crowd was enraptured. Some collapsed on the ground, others held tightly to each other to steady and support themselves. The people returned to ordinary consciousness, and they were greatly changed.

That night, on the vast alluvial plain of Atlantis, using his uncanny power to bewitch an audience, Belial succeeded in communicating his passion to his followers. The people watched and saw. Those who had come out to witness lived through a powerful, emotional experience of sight, sound, smell, taste, and touch. This outpouring of emotional stimuli had its desired effect—sensory overload, mass hysteria, mass hypnosis.

"Belial!" they cried as the Adepts followed their Dark Lord in a recessional march along the Pathway of the Blood. "Blessings on Belial! Long live Belial! Praise Belial!" Caught up in the spell of powerful emotions, all restraint had been removed. Men groaned and shouted, women sobbed openly...anything to relieve the pent-up tension. There was no containing them, nor did Belial and his cohorts have any intentions of trying. The crowd had taken on a life of its own...a mad, frenzied song and dance.

On and on they chanted, on and on they sang, on and on they danced to that maniacal, monstrous tune of a people run amok. Long after the Puppetmaster and his retinue were swallowed up in the darkness, long after the legion of initiates had paraded back across the Great Plain and into the city, the crowd went on, until the fires were reduced to glowing embers. Then, and only then, their voices quieted and their frenzy abated.

Individually and in small groups, the people of Atlantis slowly made their way home. Physically exhausted, emotionally spent, they left behind the wreckage of their mass gathering—dirty rags and blankets, scattered bits of garbage, and the torn and broken bodies that had been trampled into the mud by an unconscious and unfeeling mob. What they experienced had a profound impact on them. They saw, they felt extreme emotion, and they were changed. Changed by a "truth" that was not quite true—in Truth.

"This is what the people really want." My Teacher's Voice spoke within my heart as I sat alone on the now empty Plain. The first light of a damp, gray dawn was just beginning to silhouette the city skyline as I asked my single question.

"Why?" I asked.

"Through the power of the spoken word, Belial brings to consciousness what in other human beings is unconscious," spoke the Counselor. *"His thoughts, so openly transparent, are the same thoughts that are a part of their inmost souls. He brings to light their baser instincts, proclaiming the most secret desires and sufferings of a whole nation."*

"He is doing what the people themselves unconsciously want and approve of—that is why they will follow him. They feel unconsciously that he is on the right track."

I heard, and I understood. This was the psychology behind his leadership. Belial had hurled the firebrand of his word into the hearts of the people. Like an arrow to their target, his words had touched each one's secret wounds.

Hearing what they wanted to hear, the people of Atlantis, unwilling to take responsibility for themselves, were projecting their shadow thoughts outward onto Belial, who was more than happy to take on the role of Ogre Tyrant. Belial was giving them what they secretly wanted but were incapable of admitting, even to themselves.

I shook my head sadly. If it were possible for me to weep, I would have. But there could be no tears from me, only from the Great Mother. So I sat in silence as the gentle rains soaked the ground, washing away all traces of the dreadful ritual. I sat beneath the Mother's tears as she wept for her children, wept for herself.

The people of Atlantis would never be the same, I realized. Atlantis itself would never be the same. The world would never be the same. The human race would never be the same!

CHAPTER 28

> *She [Athena] assumed the appearance of Mentor and*
> *seemed so like him as to deceive both eye and ear...*
>
> —Homer, *The Odyssey*

In the twenty-five years since Belial's appointment as Chief Elder, much had happened. Atlantis was no longer the paradise that the Ancients had worked to hard to create. It was, rather, a decaying and dying world, a corrupt world, a hell on Earth. Belial had succeeded in putting all of his scientific, social, and economic programs into place. There was a rise in a new kind of science. The Sons of Belial took over the Great Pyramid, where they placed a new emphasis on technology, separating that field of study from the rest of the arts.

At first, the professors and scholars had raised their voices in protest, but there was nothing they could do. And they soon learned that it was neither prudent nor healthy to openly criticize the methods or motives of the Sons of Belial. Those who did had a nasty habit of disappearing, either into the oblivion of banishment or, worse yet, into the labyrinth that was rumored to lie deep beneath the Great Pyramid.

The Sons of Belial controlled every aspect of life in Atlantis, from the arts to religion to education to fashion, leisure, and recreation. They had huge wealth and huge resources at their disposal. It did not take Belial long to realize that, in his world, wealth was another form of power. He amassed an obscene fortune in gold and jewels and art treasures, often at the expense of the rest of the population. And he used it to buy whatever he needed—loyalty, scientists, thinkers, scholars...all who could help him further his aims of conquest and power.

Yet, as with all things, these actions had their inevitable consequences. While the Sons of Belial continued to rise and grow more powerful, Atlantis continued to decay from within, the result of abuse, overload, toxic shock, and a forgetting of their connection to Nature and the interconnectedness of all life.

No longer recognized as a living being, the Great Mother Earth was now perceived as a lifeless mass of compounds, chemicals, and elements that existed for the sole purpose of exploitation by the dominant species. Not enlightened and benevolent stewardship, but raping and pillaging. It was the Earth's first experience with the consciousness of Manifest Destiny; it would not be the last.

In the midst of Atlantis, a dark presence festered, a cancerous disease that no amount of surgery would be able to cut out. Extending its roots deep into the very fabric of society, it grew and spread until it had affected every aspect of the culture. Against such a foul and loathsome presence there was no defense. Like Shakala's disease-ridden body, decaying from within, so the entire social and political infrastructure was collapsing.

Suffering from the effects of a systemic immune deficiency, whole systems began to erode and collapse. Some shut down completely. Arteries clogged. Poisons filled the air, breathing grew labored. Even the vast planetary defense systems of the Great Mother were powerless against this most unnatural invader. The Children of the Light decried the situation in a public orations:

"Social structures and behavior patterns have become so rigid that Atlantis and its people can no longer adapt to changing situations. A general loss of harmony is ensuing, appearing in various

forms as pollution, scarcity, drought, famine, and mental and physical disease. If this does not stop, the inevitable result will be disruption and loss of the Atlantean way of life."

To no avail. While the traditional form of government still endured in the form of the Council of Elders, the real government remained aloof, hiding from the light of day and prying eyes. This was the occult government of the Sons of Belial, less enlightened individuals in the grip of the forces of Darkness. So very secret they were, so deeply hidden, that the sinister practices in which they engaged were not known even the Elders or the King. Dark, mysterious, and occult—hidden away and protected behind great stone walls and high fences were the secret places in which the Sons of Belial formulated their secret plans to meet their secret agendas of power, status, and wealth.

And what terrible secrets they were! Genetic experiments that produced horrible mutations—one-eyed monsters, creatures half human, half animal. Fortunately, most of these aberrations died soon after birth, but a few lived to maturity. Some, too, escaped into the wilderness, where they were occasionally glimpsed by unwary people who did not know what they were looking at. Scarcely able to believe their eyes, with no frame of reference for what they were seeing, these travelers to the wild places brought back strange tales of even stranger creatures.

"Guess what I saw! A flying horse with the head and shoulders of a man! Right up there on Mount Kylene!"

"Me too! I saw some really weird things up on that mountain. Once I even saw the footprints of the one-eyed giant who lives there."

"One-eyed giant?"

"Yes, there's a whole family of strange beasts up there—three-headed dogs, multi-legged men and women, and a one-eyed giant who carries a great big club and can kill you just by looking at you."

And while the people invented the legends that are remembered even to this day, perverted and misguided alchemists and geomancers continued their secret and evil experiments deep in their labs. What egos! Did they know what they were doing? Were they aware of what would happen if one of their creatures escaped? Of course they knew; they just did not care, else they would have stopped or never have started in the first place. Too interested in technology for its own sake and the role it could play in their plans, they refused to take time to confront its possible consequences.

"Besides, we are safe," they declared in their arrogance. "The aberrations cannot hurt us, for we are protected behind our walls. The only people who can get hurt are the commoners, the rabble, and what does it matter if a few hundred thousand or a few million or even all of them, for that matter, die? The sperm and egg banks are full. We can clone a few men, seed a few women, and pretty soon there will be more than enough new slaves to meet our needs!"

Such was the thinking of the Sons of Belial! Such massive misuse and abuse of power and the Mother's gifts! Such pride, such hubris, such wanton arrogance! Thinking they could do anything they wanted. Placing themselves above the Law of One, their egos became so bloated that they fancied themselves as gods, having the power of life and death, joy and sadness over the masses.

As far over to one side of the Pendulum as ever there was in the history of the world—until now, when the Pendulum has returned to the far side of its swing. It is all happening again, just as it did once before in Atlantis—viruses running rampant, all manner of plagues visited upon man and beast. Created by a technology run rampant—out of control, wild in the streets.

In Atlantis, the end result was inevitable. In their hubris, the Sons of Belial created a device that even their great intellects could not control—a machine of such absolute power and destructive potential that it was capable of splitting the very planet in two. Capable of destroying not just all life on and in the planet, but the life of the Great Mother herself—disintegrating, pulverizing, turning the living Earth to dust.

Did they know they could not control the device? One did and was afraid to speak up. As for the rest of the secret government—an extensive network spread through the great island and into the colonies—they could not quite grasp in their convoluted brains that they had built the ultimate doomsday weapon.

"We built it, we can manage it," they boasted in their ignorance. "We are in control. We'll just use it enough to get what we want, then we'll turn it off. We never have to unleash its full potential. Of course, even if it does get out of control, we will have time to escape in our flying machines. We'll have plenty of time to set up energy vortices into which we can enter for protection, jumping out to other colonies on other planets and in other dimensions." Such was their theme song, their credo, their way—break everything here, go to a new place, start over there, and repeat the same mistakes all over again. "The only thing we'll lose is a little time."

And so, over a period of twenty-five years, Atlantis was transformed from a garden into a wasteland, from a heaven into a hell. And as this amazing transformation of a civilization was taking place, so an equally amazing individual transformation was taking place. Adima was being transformed from a boy into a man!

*****

The day after the Spear Ceremony, Adima went to the Lighthouse and knocked on the door. There was no path to follow, and he was quite nervous as he carefully picked his way over the rocks. He was afraid, but curious, too...one of his many admirable traits. No matter how afraid he was, he never let fear stop him from accomplishing what he really wanted to do. Fear might slow him down, might immobilize him temporarily, but eventually he achieved his desired aim. "Feel the fear and do it anyway," Grandmother had reminded him over and over again until the words were etched firmly in his consciousness. It was a tenet that would serve him well in the future.

He could not stop thinking about the strange events of the night before. He had slept fitfully, tossing and turning as replays of the experience churned over and over in his mind. He wanted an explanation, needed an explanation, would, in fact, *demand* an explanation from this mysterious stranger who had invited him for a visit. What had happened out there on the Great Plain of Atlantis in the dark of night? Who was the Puppetmaster? For that matter, who was Belial? Did he really see a monstrous Beast baring its fangs at him, desiring to devour him? In the clear light of day it all seemed rather silly, almost like a bad dream. But it had been quite real last night. The ensuing nightmares had proved that only too well.

So many questions on this lovely morning, so much that required an explanation. Why had he been unaffected by the events? Why had the Keeper of the Light invited him to visit? And most curious of all, what had the old man meant by his strange remark about the lightning serving another Master? Adima was a young man who wanted to know...needed to know. He was as distressed as ever he had been, more so even than when his father had died.

Day in and day out he experienced a profound, gut-wrenching anxiety that gnawed away at his insides like voracious rats chewing through old burlap. He had tried everything he knew to make the feelings go away—exercising, keeping busy, drinking ale, even praying—but there was no respite from the obsessive thoughts and fearsome emotions churning within him. His back hurt, his head ached, his heart fluttered and pounded, his mouth had a dry, metallic taste. He couldn't eat, couldn't sleep. Everywhere he went, he found himself looking over his shoulder, fearful of encountering his enemy, fearful of another attack.

Attending Council sessions was agony...so close to the man who wanted to kill him, who had probably killed his brother. And there was nothing Adima could do about it. He had to sit on the Council. It was part of his duty; the responsibility had been passed along to him and his brothers at the time of their father's death.

Adima was afraid, and angry, too. Angry at his father for having died and left him alone. Angry at his brother for going off to war and getting himself killed. Angry at the war itself. "My duty," his brother had said when they bade each other farewell. Well, damn that duty! And damn the war! He was angry at Belial for despising him so. Why? What had he ever done to deserve such venomous hatred? Damn Belial, too! And he was angry at his mother for not being his father and helping him through this. Angry that he couldn't even tell her what was troubling him, let alone expect her to fix things. Damn her weak and simpering femininity!

Then, too, he was angry at the Divine for abandoning him and taking his loved ones away. Angry that his prayer for a mentor had been answered with an emphatic "No." Damn the Ogre Tyrant gods. And finally, he was angry at himself for being a coward and not taking a stand against his antagonist. Oh, how he wanted to! How he wanted to hurt Belial as the giant had hurt him!

In his imagination, Adima saw himself accosting his enemy, walking up to him, taking hold of that ridiculous black robe, lifting him bodily off his feet and beating him within an inch of his life. This was his fantasy every night as he fell asleep, but alas, he knew he'd never do it. He had neither the strength nor the courage. And that made him angry, too, angry that there was no strong man on his side to attack Belial for him. Damn himself for being a weakling and a coward!

Yet maybe there was. Maybe this mysterious summons was about meeting the ally he craved. Maybe it was the old hermit himself. "No," Adima shook his head, muttering under his breath, "it can't be him. He's too old. He's frailer than I am. I need a powerful man, a giant like Belial himself."

Then what are you doing here? a voice whispered in his head. Adima stopped, suddenly confused. What *was* he doing there? He didn't know. He actually didn't even remember much of the walk he had just taken. All he knew was that upon rising that morning, he had dressed and set out, determined to find his way to the beach and demand answers of the mysterious old man who had spoken to him in his mind the previous night.

The door to the Lighthouse was open, but there were no signs of life. Adima looked around, even walked around the base of the huge structure. It was amazing just how large it was, how long the distance around its perimeter. Above the lintel, cut deeply into the stone, was a strange monogram—two Ds and an H interlaced, surmounted over a triple crescent moon, beneath which was inscribed a single phrase...

I N YOU REPOSES ALL POWER.

In time, he would come to learn the significance of Enoch's crest—the two Ds representing, in the Language of Light, the *Gifts of the Divine*; the H representing the *Unknown Principle*, so important to the success of alchemical work. At the moment, however, the symbols had no meaning at all to the uninitiated young man who gazed upon them.

It looks like no one is home, he thought with disappointment. I came all this way for nothing. That made him even angrier. Damn the Lighthouse Keeper! Damn me for getting my hopes up! Then another thought struck him. Why would the hermit go out and leave the door open? He must be nearby. "Hello," Adima called out. "Is anyone here?"

"Welcome," a voice floated down from high above him. "Come up."

It was a strong voice, a gentle voice, but Adima did not want to go. He almost turned back, so insistent was the fear. But then something even more compelling than his fear took hold of him, seeming to pull him gently but firmly within—his curiosity. He could not resist. The young man entered the Lighthouse and stood in the relative darkness of the interior. The room was empty save for some machinery and a spiral staircase that wound its serpentine way from a hole in the stone floor upward into the gloom. "This is very strange," he muttered, but again the intense pull of curiosity won out over fear. He started to ascend the ladder.

Up and up it wound, around and around in almost total blackness, even though the sun was shining brightly outside. Adima felt as though he were in a vertical tunnel, not climbing so much as being pulled upward. He could almost feel an invisible but powerful magnetic beam that had latched onto his heartstrings and was drawing him into a patch of white light far above his head.

After what seemed an eternity, the long climb came to an end. Winded, he poked his head into the upper room, which was brightly lit by the midday sunshine streaming in through the glass walls. The sweet fragrance of citrus blossoms wafted up from the orchards far below, borne on the gentle currents of the sea breezes. Blinking and squinting, he clambered into the center of the room and looked around him. For a moment, he forgot all about his fear and anger, so enthralled was he by this enchanting haven high above the city.

Glass...everything was glass, from floor to ceiling. And what a vista! The whole of Atlantis lay spread out below him in a 360-degree panorama. It was like standing on top of the world! He could see everything.

The furnishings were sparse—a few overstuffed chairs, pillows and cushions, a large wooden table, and books everywhere. All kinds of books—new, old, thick, thin...story books, text books, histories, biographies, almanacs, encyclopedias. Some, like *The Book of Mysteries*, Adima recognized instantly from his studies and from his own small but growing library. About others though, he had not a clue. There they were, with mysterious titles such as *The Seven Secret Folios of Kiu-ti*, *The Stanzas of Dzyan*, *The Commentaties for Initiates*, *The Book of Golden Precepts*, *The Book of Tao, Light and the Path*. Such books had he never seen before or even heard of.

His eye was attracted to a gorgeous illuminated manuscript of the *Book of Life* resting on a hand carved oak lectern in the middle of the table. Next to this was a highly polished crystal ball. Adima knew better than to touch the crystal and contaminate its energy field with the sweat from his palms. The book, though, was different. He reached out for it, running his fingertips lightly over the beautifully painted pictures, being careful not to smudge or tear the paper.

He had his own copy of the *Book of Life*, but it was nothing like this. This edition must be immensely old, perhaps the first one written. He conjured up an image of an ancient priestess sitting hunched over the manuscript, drawing each letter painstakingly by hand. Applying paint with meticulous love and care, she drew the figures of Atlantean folklore and mythology, bringing them to life on the page through the cunning of her art. Adima read the inscription on the page:

LIFE TAKES REFUGE IN A SINGLE SPACE.

He did not understand the meaning of the words, did not understand the reference to the safe haven from catastrophe, where death could not enter in. He determined to ask the Lighthouse Keeper about the meaning. By the way, speaking of lighthouse keepers, where *is* my host? he wondered. The room was empty. There was no one there.

Adima heard sounds from another chamber above him. Craning his neck to look, he saw an old man moving about, tending to his plants, putting things on shelves, straightening up...going about the everyday business of keeping house. He seemed oblivious to the fact that there was a guest in his parlor or that he himself had invited this guest.

It's as though I'm not even here, Adima thought, the anger returning in a flash. He asked me to come, and now he is ignoring me. Why is that? He waited, but still there was no sign of greeting from the Lighthouse Keeper. This is ridiculous, he chafed impatiently. Perhaps he's changed his mind. Maybe I should go. After all, I've got things to do, too.

He almost did leave. His hand was on the railing, his foot poised to take that first downward step. But something stayed him. "No," he said with determination. "I am not going to leave. I was invited, and I am going to stay and wait until my host comes to welcome me, no matter how long it takes for him to notice me."

As though reading his mind, the old man immediately descended the spiral staircase and stepped into the room, extending a wrinkled brown hand in greeting. "Welcome to my home," he said. "I am Enoch. I'm glad you have arrived."

"I've been here for almost half an hour," Adima was about to say, but again something stopped the words from coming out. "I am Adima," he said instead, remembering his manners. He was, after all, a guest in someone's home.

The old man gave him a strange smile, as though he had somehow heard the thoughts but chose not to be offended by them. "Sit." Enoch offered a chair. "I've made tea."

Adima accepted the scalding liquid with some trepidation. Was this to be merely a social visit? That was not why he had come. Nevertheless, he took the proffered seat and put the cup to his lips. The tea was really not very good, but he sipped it politely as he looked at the old man seated before him. Enoch said nothing, letting Adima enjoy the view while he just stared at him for several moments. After a while, the silence grew uncomfortable. The young man fidgeted nervously in his seat, waiting for his host to say something, anything.

"The view is great," Adima said at last, not knowing what else to say. Enoch just nodded his head.

"Those stairs are a killer," Adima pressed. "You must get pretty sore legs climbing up them every day." This time, there wasn't even a nod from the older man.

"Does the Lighthouse ever sway in the wind?" Adima tried again, feeling very uncomfortable and helpless. The silence was terrifying, that "fear of the vacuum," of being alone in the silence with one's self and one's thoughts. The two continued to stare at each other.

"Who are you?" Enoch finally broke the silence. It was a strange question. Adima did not quite know how to answer. Was the old man senile? Did he not remember the invitation? Did he not even remember his greeting of a few moments ago? The doubts had returned.

"What do you mean, who am I?" Adima answered the first question with a question of his own. "My name is Adima. You should know who I am, you invited me here last night. Don't you remember?"

He was beginning to be more than uncomfortable. He was afraid. Was this old man insane, as the stories said? Ever since he was a boy, rumors had abounded about the crazy old hermit who lived in the haunted Lighthouse. Telling the stories was a favorite pastime of any child who wanted to scare a younger sibling, or any adult who wanted to create an air of mystery for a visiting tourist. Now Adima was on the receiving end of a direct experience with the mysterious recluse, sitting there in the Lighthouse itself, high above the ordinary world.

Have I walked into a place I should have stayed out of? he wondered. No one knew where he was. He had left home early, without telling anyone of his destination. There could be no rescue if it were needed. Adima set his teacup on a table and started to get up to leave.

"Who are you?" Enoch asked a second time, raising his palm in a gesture that indicated that Adima should remain seated. "It is not so difficult a question. Surely you must know who you are."

Adima was getting angrier by the minute. Is this why he had been invited here, to take a test? What a disappointment. He shook his head sadly, trying not to let his feelings show. Better to humor the old man, answer his questions, and leave as quickly as he could. "I am Adima, the son of Themis and Rama," he replied matter-of-factly, the words belying the emotion he was feeling. "I am 22 years old and on the Council of Elders."

He paused, thinking about what more he could say. What else was there? That was about it. "I, er, am a student of the, um, arts and sciences," he was struggling now. "I, uh, enjoy..." The words drifted out in a mindless babble of inane phrases.

Years later, as a mature man, Adima always laughed whenever he recalled his hesitation and nervousness. How little he had known about himself! How insecure he was, how immature! It was reflected in his answer, in which he painted a fragmented portrait of an almost invisible man.

As the young man spoke, Enoch nodded his head in approval, a broad smile creasing his wrinkled face. The smile did nothing to make Adima feel more at ease. In fact, it made him even angrier, and at last, unable to control his feelings any longer, he let that anger out.

"Who am I?" he blurted out, surprised at the intensity of his feelings. "I'll tell you who I am. I'm the one who stood in the middle of that confounded field last night and watched some lunatic transform himself into a monster and try to kill me." Pointing to his face, he stood up, towering over the still-seated old man. "I'm the one who met this same madman a few months ago and let him cut my face and give me this lovely scar to wear as a reminder of how much he hates me."

Bang! He smashed his fist into the oak table, then paced about the room as the rage took hold and swept him up in its mindless embrace." I'm the one who came here looking for answers because you invited me, damn you, and instead of you telling me what in the name of Atlas is going on around here, all you want to do is ask me questions!"

He paused, trembling as he loomed over the old man once again. "I'm the one who's afraid and alone and came here for help, and all you can do is make tea? You think a lousy cup of tea is going to fix everything? Well, old man, you know what you can do with that tea, and what you can do with yourself. I don't want tea. I want answers. Like who, in the name of all that's holy, are *you*?"

Adima was angry, really angry—at his father and mother and brother and Belial and the Divine and life and himself. And now he was angry at the Keeper of the Light, and he told him so. "I'm the one who gets to experience this lovely life in Atlantis with a homicidal maniac breathing down my neck while you hide out up here in your ivory tower and watch. And then you have the nerve to laugh at me?"

His tone was derisive, but he didn't care. The old man had started this, and he, Adima, was going to finish it. If he could not lash out at Belial, at least he could lash out at this weak old recluse who couldn't do anything to stop him anyway.

"Tell me, old man," he ranted, letting the rage fill him with an intense red light, "you're so smart, you've got all the answers. Who is this Beast with the Spear? Who is this demon ruling the Council of Elders? Why does he want to kill me? Why does he hate me so? Why is this happening to me? You're a wise man. You've got spell books and a crystal ball and who knows what else. Why are *you* letting this go on? Why don't *you* put a stop to it once and for all?"

Adima paused, trying to catch his breath. His heart was pounding, and his chest felt like a great anvil had been laid on it. Suddenly, his head grew light, and he swooned dizzily, collapsing onto the cushions as his legs gave out. And then the tears came. All at once, without warning, the frightened boy who wanted so desperately to be a man broke down and sobbed, letting all of his darkest, most secret feelings out.

Tears and tears and more tears—nothing seemed able to stop the flow of water. He cried out his fear, screamed out his rage, sobbed out his sorrow and grief over all of the traumatic events of his life, one after another, until there was nothing left hidden and unexpressed. The more he cried, the more he wanted to cry. The more he expressed his own sorrow, the more he felt a deeper, all-encompassing sorrow—the sorrow of the Great Mother crying for her children, for all of Atlantis. Now he could cry with her, sensing her mighty pain even as he came to embrace his own.

Enoch let him weep, not bothering to staunch the tears. Neither did he offer a comforting embrace, a tissue with which to dry his eyes or wipe his nose. The hermit just sat there, holding the sacred space, observing and attending, but otherwise leaving him alone to wrestle with the intense emotional experience. He would keep Adima from hurting himself, but other than that, he let the younger be free to explore the dark feelings as deeply as he needed to.

Finally it was over. Adima had cried for almost an hour, and there were no more tears to shed. He lay back, exhausted, resting his head on a pillow and staring up at the ceiling. He was embarrassed. He had had no intention of doing what he did...venting his anger on an innocent, helpless old man, then exposing himself to a complete stranger. Yet even as he experienced shame and remorse for his actions, so also he felt better, as though a great weight had been lifted from his chest and shoulders.

"I'm so sorry," he whispered, trying to make amends for something he knew could never be atoned for. "I have insulted you and disgraced myself. Please accept my humblest apology for hurting you. I will go now and leave you in peace."

Before he could rise, Enoch was at his side, placing a strong arm around his shoulder. "There is no need for shame," the old man said soothingly, "no need to apologize, and certainly no need for you to leave, unless you want to. You are still my guest. I invited you, and I want you to stay, at least until you understand the meaning behind these events."

Adima let the old man hold him, wanting to flee but feeling more comfortable in that loving embrace. He sniffled and wiped his nose on his sleeve.

"Do you know what just happened?" Enoch asked, reaching into a pocket of his robe and producing a soft piece of flannel. Handing him the cloth, he walked over to the *Book of Life*, where he quoted an ancient proverb.

WHEN THE STUDENT IS READY, THE TEACHER WILL APPEAR.

Adima looked at him questioningly. He had no idea what those words meant. "How does that relate to me?" he asked, not arguing, but truly trying to understand.

Enoch was only too happy to explain. "You've lived your life, going through all of the experiences that have combined over the years to make you a unique being—from your birth and early childhood, through your father's death, up to your encounter with Belial, and everything in between." He made a sweeping gesture with his hand, as though to encompass all of the experiences of Adima's young life. "Good and bad, peaceful and traumatic, loving and fearful, you've lived through life's lessons—until here you are today, in your twenty-third year, sitting with me in the Lighthouse. You prayed for help. You want to know what your life means. You want to know why such incredible, terrifying things are happening to you."

The hermit paused, shaking his head as he thought of how many times such questions had been asked and would continue to be asked over the ages. For these were the questions of all who presented themselves as candidates for initiation into the Mysteries, whether they knew it or not. "But before you can get what you have asked for," he continued aloud, "you have to be ready for what the asking brings. Now you are."

Adima was about to protest, but Enoch held up a silencing hand. "This is about *trust*," he explained gently, not wanting to incite another emotional outburst. "You want what you want, the way that you want it. I am offering you answers, but not in a form that you expect. That does not make what I offer any less valuable, however. But in order for you to come to realize that value, you first have to be able to trust. Trust yourself, trust your own intuition, and trust me and the truth I have to offer. To do this requires courage. So allow me to make it easy for you." He reached out and placed a warm hand on Adima's shoulder, looking directly into his eyes, offering a kind, loving smile. "Allow *yourself* to make it easy for you.

"You do not have to make any life-altering decisions today. You do not even have to trust me for a long time. All I ask is that you trust me for one hour. One single hour. Listen to what I have to say, answer my questions, decide if you like what you hear and feel. If you do, fine. If you do not, that is also fine. It is up to you. What do your heart and intuition tell you? What do you say? One hour?" The Keeper of the Light leaned back on his couch and waited, allowing time for his guest to digest the words and make his decision.

For a long moment, Adima was silent. What am I feeling about all of this? he wondered. I came here of my own free will. I have already exposed myself by losing my temper and crying as I have. I have prayed for help, and this old man is offering it, so it seems. So the help isn't in the form that I want. So the old man is not a physical match for Belial. So this wise one is not going to transform me into a mighty warrior overnight. He is, however, the only person in all of Atlantis who has presented himself to me. So why not? What is the worst that can happen? If I leave, I won't know any more than I did before I came. I still won't have any answers or know where to get them. I will still have to figure things out all by himself. So really, what do I have to lose? I'll spend the hour and see where this goes. I can always say thanks, but no thanks.

Adima looked at the old man sitting across from him. "I'll stay," he said simply.

"Good," the old man exclaimed, genuinely pleased at the young man's answer. All seemed to be forgiven and forgotten as he leaned forward in anticipation. "Let us begin again. Let us begin with the same question I asked you previously."

"Who are *you*?" Enoch asked a third time, this time emphasizing the personal pronoun. "Do not parrot back to me someone else's definition of you. Tell me *your* definition of you. Tell me who you *are*?"

Adima looked intently at the man sitting across from him. What is really going on here? he asked himself. The old man did not appear to be crazy. In fact, he seemed quite rational and in complete control of himself. Part of Adima regretted the decision he had just made, but another part really wanted to stay and see what this was all about and where it was going. As he remembered his promise to trust for one hour, something inside seemed to calm him. Taking a deep breath and relaxing somewhat, he thought long and hard about the question. Who was he, really?

He had always been a "people-pleaser," as the phrase had come to be known, trying to make everyone like him, trying to be on his best behavior, trying to excel, trying to do exactly the right thing at exactly the right time. It was exhausting, but that's who everyone wanted him to be.

But what about the real Adima? The child with the fanciful imagination who had all sorts of imaginary friends and who talked to people and animals who weren't "really there." Who would rather be by himself within the universe of his own rich and fertile imagination than playing with a lot of noisy children. Not that there had been a lot of playmates in his neighborhood. In fact, there had been none other than his older brother. And his older brother had been absent a lot of the time.

The one who liked to run and play and get dirty and wander through the forest. The one who liked to make music and explore new ideas and travel to new places. The one who read every piece of prose and poetry he could get his hands on. The one who thrilled to seek out new places, meet new people, learn new things.

The one who remembered, albeit vaguely, another time, a better time, a long-gone time in the dim and distant past. The one who liked to roam through the imaginary lands of the Atlantean fables dressed as a proud and mighty warrior in shining armor—rescuer of damsels in distress, slayer of terrible beasts, bold doer of deeds. The one sitting astride his mighty charger, cantering along a golden road leading to a shining castle.

Such behavior, however, was not condoned. It wasn't seemly for a boy to be so fanciful, so aloof. That was not what was done. Such a boy was displeasing to his parents, who wanted him to follow a far different path, a path that would lead him to prominence in the public eye. A path that would lead to fame and stature. A path that would make them proud of their son and his accomplishments in the world.

So Adima had stuffed away that other self, hiding it deep inside his being. Why? Because he was a good son, because that self was displeasing to his parents, and because it was a self of little worth or value in the world around him. In fact, he stuffed that other self so far inside that, after a time, he forgot all about it. Until today, with the third asking of the question.

Where had that other person gone? More to the point, who was the person inhabiting this body in which his consciousness was residing? "I don't know," he replied at last, openly admitting his confusion. These were questions without answers, and nothing in his considerable education had prepared him for dealing with such perplexities. "I guess I don't really know who I am."

"Excellent," Enoch said, smiling broadly. "Confessing one's ignorance is the first step toward knowledge. Now let me ask you a different set of questions as we come to get better acquainted. Do you know who I am?"

"Yes, you're Enoch, Keeper of the Light."

"Do you know what I do?"

"Yes, you tend the light and keep the ships from dashing themselves on the rocks. You shine the light and guide seafarers to safe passage. You rescue wounded animals and tend to lost travelers."

"Yes, yes, yes, that's all well and good," Enoch waved his hand abstractedly, as though hearing himself praised was quite dull and boring. "Those are some of the things I do. But I do other things as well."

The old man rose and walked over to the table, where he placed his palm on the shining crystal globe. "I am, first and foremost, an observer—a watcher and a knower," he said as he peered intently into the glass. Adima almost expected to see images of tiny people floating about within the crystalline structure.

"I have a keen eye, and I observe all that comes within the range of my vision. I see both the outer and the inner—that which is visible on the surface as well as that which remains hidden within." Slowly, almost lovingly, the old man's hands caressed the sphere as he paused to look at the young man seated before him. "I have been watching you for many years," Enoch said, rising up and standing before Adima. "Long ago I noticed you, and I have been waiting for you to be ready. I know more about you, perhaps, than you know about yourself, or that you remember about yourself."

Adima sat very still. The rage and grief were gone, replaced now with fascination at what he was hearing and seeing. Were it not for the bright sunshine streaming in through the glass windowpanes, he would have thought this was a dream. But it was no dream, it was very, very real. He listened as the old man continued.

"I see how you carry yourself, how trustworthy and upright you are. I see your kindness and compassion. I watch you feed people who are hungry. I watch you teach. I watch you treat all living things with respect, not wishing to kill even a pesky mosquito that is biting you. I see that you have a good heart."

"How do you know all of this about me?" the young man asked in amazement. It was all true. Enoch was describing him perfectly. But how did this mysterious hermit know so many of the details? He had never spoken to the man before today, having seen him but once or twice in all of his life. Their acquaintanceship was by reputation only. Or was it? "It's really nothing," Adima said deprecatingly. "It's how my parents raised me. They always taught me to respect all life and treat others with kindness and compassion, as I would want them to treat me."

"You may think that it is nothing," Enoch replied, standing at the windows, looking first toward the east and the Ocean of Atlas, then turning back to face Adima, an easy smile lighting his features. "But it is everything."

He smiles a lot, Adima noticed. He wanted to acknowledge his host's kind words of praise. Wanted to thank him for affirming what he already felt was true about himself. Wanted, too, to jump for joy with the knowledge that his way was, indeed, worthy and valuable. That's when he remembered the gift.

"Oh, I almost forgot," he interrupted eagerly, slapping his palm to his forehead in a gesture of forgetfulness. Reaching into his coat, he produced a small package wrapped in brightly colored cloth. "I brought you a gift. My grandmother always told me honor my host with a gift. You invited me to your home. Please accept this small token of my appreciation." Adima handed the package to Enoch.

Without a word, the old man unwrapped the gift and held up a small, pink crystal. It was encased in a thin wire net and suspended from a golden chain. "Rose quartz," he murmured softly. "The heart stone."

"I don't know anything about a heart stone," Adima answered. "I just know that I saw it and liked it and wanted you to have it."

"You may not know this stone now," Enoch replied, placing the bauble around his neck, "but you will come to know it intimately, for it will serve you well over the years each time your own heart cracks open a little wider. Thank you for this gift, Adima. I receive it in the spirit in which you give it."

The old man placed a warm hand on the younger man's shoulder. His touch was surprisingly light, yet Adima sensed a deep strength beneath the surface. Almost palpable, it felt like a warm electrical current coursing through the old man's entire body. "Now let me get to the reason for which I have invited you here today," Enoch said as he sat back on the couch. "I, too, have a gift to offer. But first you had to pass a test so that I could see if you are indeed ready to receive it."

Adima looked puzzled. He raised his eyebrows quizzically.

"You passed that first test," Enoch went on. "You made up your own mind about staying when you wanted to leave. You swallowed your pride at not being greeted according to the way your ego wanted to be greeted. You emptied yourself out, let all of your negative emotions go, and made a decision to stay. When you made that decision, you arrived. I'm glad you are here!"

"I'm glad, too." Adima was beginning to feel more comfortable. He was starting to like this strange old recluse with the mysterious ways and the kindly smile and the great library and the house with the magnificent view. He thought of his own father, dead these many years. Perhaps Enoch was a lot like him. He would like to think so, anyway.

"I see everything," Enoch interrupted Adima's reverie and continued speaking, nodding toward the crystal ball on the table. "And what the ball does not show me, I see in my mind's eye, at those most sacred times when the Akashic Record is opened up and the Mysteries are revealed."

Out on the window ledge, a large bird landed, alighting with barely a flutter of its wings. "An osprey," Adima was about to say, but he sensed that the old man was already well aware of the bird, even though he did not turn to acknowledge its presence.

"From my vantage point high up here in the light, I have been observing you," Enoch continued as the great bird gazed intently at Adima. "Everywhere I look, it is you that I see. You keep coming into my line of vision. I see your finer qualities, your strength of character. And I see your Shadow side, too—your fear and anger, your childish stubbornness and pride. Those qualities no longer serve you, and will, in fact, lead you astray if you continue to indulge them."

The raptor continued to stare, its gaze fixed, its white headdress feathers sparkling in the sunshine. Adima returned the stare, as he knew he should, while at the same time listening intently to the words of the Lighthouse Keeper.

"You are the one, Adima. You have always been the one. I have been waiting for you, waiting until the time was right. That time is now. Belial has the Spear. We cannot wait any longer. You must be prepared, if you are willing."

Enoch paused and reached out through the window. Ever so gently, Osprey stepped onto his arm, letting the old man draw him into the center of the room. Adima admired the magnificent bird, noting its soft colors and markings, the sharply-angled curve of its hooked beak, the graceful way it held its head, the smooth flowing lines and symmetry. He had never been so close to such a wild creature. He sensed the bird's presence...an alien presence of power and majesty, for this winged creature belonged to an alien world, the world of the sky.

What he knows I could never know, the young man thought wistfully. Where he has been, I could never go.

"What I propose is this," Enoch held his arm steady while Osprey continued to stare. "I would be honored if you would let me teach you, if you would let me pass along my knowledge to you. All of Atlantis would be honored if you would accept your true purpose and fulfill your destiny."

Adima thought long and hard. There was no doubt of Enoch's sanity. He was a rational, thinking being, not the crazy old coot he was rumored to be. Something was stirring in Adima's soul, a faint memory of an ancient song once known but long since forgotten. It was there, tantalizingly close, but not quite within his grasp. A feeling of warmth and peace flowed over him. He had not felt such a feeling since he was a boy when he had held onto his father's hand and walked through the world by his side. Holding onto his father's hand he had felt safe and warm, grown up and strong.

"I'm going to be like him someday," Adima had vowed. But then his father was gone—too soon, before his time. With a single scream in the night, the man Adima loved had expired, leaving the legacy of an anguished cry still ringing in his son's ears, drowning out the old songs, raising in their place a new and fearful clamor.

Now, sitting here in the Lighthouse with Enoch and Osprey on this warm spring afternoon, the good feelings were returning. They hadn't left after all. They were still there, and now they were coming to the surface.

"I am honored that you have chosen me," Adima replied, truly grateful, not just to Enoch for being his teacher, but to Spirit for answering his prayer, and to himself for being willing to trust for just one hour. Now that hour had passed, but he would continue to trust for a long, long time. For that he was even more grateful, and he said so.

"You are giving me a wonderful gift, the gift of your wisdom and the knowledge of the Ancients. I am honored to learn your ways. I will do my very best to take care of your gift and use it for the highest good."

"Creeeeeeee!" Osprey's shrill call rang throughout the room, startling Adima so that he knocked the half-empty teacup off the footstool on which he had set it over two hours before. The china cup crashed to the floor, shattering into a hundred pieces.

Enoch seemed not to notice. He was looking at the bird, silently communicating with it, it seemed to Adima, like two old friends who were completely at ease in each other's presence, not needing to exchange words. Walking to the window, the old man extended his arm. Man and bird exchanged a last silent look. Then, with a rush of its mighty wings, the bird was airborne.

Higher and higher it soared. Adima hurried to the window and watched until it was floating effortlessly on the currents of the wind high above the world. He imagined himself on the bird's back, soaring with it, seeing what it saw, feeling what it felt as it looked down upon the world from above. It was with great effort that he brought his attention back to the room and his host.

This was exciting. He was about to embark upon a bold new adventure with a grand master teacher. He would become like his father after all. He would do all the things he used to dream of doing but never thought possible. New worlds were going to open up for him. "When do we get started?" he asked with all of the enthusiasm of youth. "How long will this take? What is the first lesson?"

"Patience, patience," Enoch laughed at his contagious eagerness. "So many questions cannot be answered all at once. You must take the time to let the journey unfold before you. You are about to embark on an adventure. Do you really want to spoil the surprise and know the ending before the beginning?"

Yes, I really do, Adima thought to himself. I want to make sure it ends all right and that everything will turn out for the best. I want to be sure. I want to be secure. But he kept his thoughts to himself. Whether or not Enoch sensed them, he never said.

"Attend for a moment to Osprey's message." The old man leaned out the window and looked up at the bird, now a tiny brown speck against an azure sky. "It was a call to pierce your state of unawareness. It was a request that you go forth and seek the truth. It was also a cry to beware, or rather, to be aware. You are being asked to heighten your awareness and attune your senses to receive a message. You now have the power of Hawk. You will come to see the larger view, recognize signs and omens, hearken to messages from the Spirit-world, and pay attention to details."

Adima was skeptical. "How have I suddenly received this power?" He sensed no new skills, no special new abilities within his repertoire of talents.

Enoch smiled that easy smile that would become so familiar over the next quarter of a century and beyond. "Now you have the power to learn," he said, "because you have admitted your ignorance. You have owned up to the truth."

Adima looked puzzled, but Enoch continued, putting his arm around him and leading him back to his chair. Then he crossed to the couch, nestled himself comfortably into the cushions, and spoke a great truth. "In fact, my dear young friend, you are quite right. You have no idea who you are or where you came from."

"You have forgotten who you are and what the Will of Father Spirit created you to be. You have forgotten your true identity."

"You have no definition of Self, no sense of your true nature and reality. Thus, you are not whole. You are fragmented and perceive yourself as weak and little." Enoch leaned forward, a twinkle in his pale blue eyes. "Would you like to find out who you are?"

This time Adima knew the answer. "Yes," he said confidently.

"Excellent choice," Enoch responded. "A worthy goal for a worthy man. Not many have the willingness to undertake what you are about to undertake. I must warn you now that the path to the answer may be a long one, with lots of twists and turns and peaks and valleys along the way. The goal is noble; it shines like gold in the sun before you. Sometimes you may think that you will never achieve it. Always remember, though, that life is a *journey*, not a *destination*."

All the while the old man was speaking, Adima nodded his head softly. Enoch's words had a true and familiar ring, reminding him of that which he had once known but had now forgotten. Nodding in agreement, he started to remember. "What will the journey be like?" he asked humbly, not in search of a happy ending, but because he really wanted to know.

"It will be marvelous," Enoch declared happily, clapping his hands and sitting on the edge of the couch. "Let me tell you what it will be like."

The old man reached into his robe and produced a clay pipe and tobacco. Taking great care, he filled the bowl, lit the sacred herb, and drew in the pure white smoke. Then, offering the pipe to Adima, he settled back into the cushions, closed his eyes, and began to speak.

> One day, a brave and noble Warrior was walking along a trail in the woods. He was headed home to a gleaming castle in a fabled kingdom deep within the forest. He had been gone a long time, and his memory of the way was dim. But he knew that the castle lay before him, for he had seen it from afar at several times when the trail rose up and crossed the high places.
>
> At such times, the kingdom and the castle sparkled like jewels in the morning sunshine, lying tranquil and still in the distance, shimmering in the mist. At such times, the Warrior stood long and still, fixing his gaze on his goal, burning the image into his mind's eye, renewing his singleness of purpose, his single desire to reach the kingdom. Then, feeling refreshed and renewed, he pressed on, taking up his sword and his cloak and moving forward once again.
>
> These sightings always encouraged him, always gave him hope and strengthened his faith. For each time that the trail rose up to the high places, the castle was a little bit larger, a little bit closer, a little bit brighter that it had been before. Thus he knew that he was indeed headed in the right direction.
>
> But the trail did not always stay on the high places. It dipped and dropped along the cliffsides to the forest floor far below. Sometimes, it descended into deep valleys, dark and mysterious and foreboding. At such times, there was no view of the great kingdom, no clue that it lay somewhere before him, no sign to indicate its presence. The wild animals howled, the wind moaned, the branches creaked and sighed.
>
> At such times, drawing his cloak tighter about him and gripping his sword more firmly, the Warrior drew on the vision in his mind's eye—the vision of the great kingdom sparkling like a jewel in the sunshine—and he kept moving forward.

Enoch finished the tale and looked at young Adima.

"Who are you?" the Keeper of the Light repeated the question a fourth time. This time, Adima remained silent.

"When you can answer my question," Enoch said, rising to signal that their meeting was drawing to a close, "you will know that your training is complete and you are ready."

Thus it came to pass that there in the Lighthouse, which was to become a second home for Adima, a friendship began that was to last a lifetime. Under Enoch's expert tutelage and guidance, Adima would make the transition from boy to man, from darkness to light, from sleeping to waking. And he would do it not through black magic, but rather, by walking the Path of Direct Experience.

Slowly, as one in a trance, Adima descended the spiral staircase and walked out onto the slippery black rocks at the edge of the Ocean of Atlas. All the way home, the old man's words kept ringing in his ears, while high overhead, a great sea bird soared majestically, crying shrilly "beware, beware, be aware" as it kept careful watch.

*****

Under cover of darkness, teacher and student picked their way carefully through the forest. The path was dark and narrow, the way illuminated only by the faint light of a first-quarter moon. Enoch seemed quite sure of himself, walking surefootedly, maintaining a steady pace that was neither too fast nor too slow.

Adima, however, was not comfortable at all. Branches slapped his face, he stubbed his toes on rocks and tripped over roots. Thorns and briars pricked at his clothing and bare skin. The mosquitoes were biting, he was bruised and scratched, his feet hurt, and he had no idea where he was going.

Why did I agree to this? he chided himself. I have been duped, that's why, he reminded himself. The old man had dropped by his home earlier that evening, just after sunset, and invited him to go for a walk. He had not mentioned either the purpose or the destination of the journey.

Having nothing better to do, Adima had agreed, for it was a lovely night. The moon shone brightly, a few fleecy clouds drifted lazily along on the currents, and the ever-present stars twinkled overhead. Now here they were, groping their way through almost impenetrable blackness heading to who knows where, with unseen dangers lurking around them, ready to pounce.

"I can't see a thing," he complained to the old man leading the way. He didn't much care for the nighttime, especially not night in the forest. Although it was a fine place to be by day, the deep woods had an ancient aura of mystery about them, and Adima was not comfortable in a place he did not understand or appreciate, a place that he actually feared. Every sound startled him, every shadow appeared as a lurking monster. "Why didn't you bring a light?"

Enoch made no reply, but kept doggedly to the trail, plodding steadily forward. At last, rounding a bend, he held up his hand for silence. Adima did not see the old man stop and so bumped right into him. Enoch ignored him and put a finger to his lips. "Listen."

There was no sound, just the quiet night breeze and the smells of the forest. All new sensations to Adima...new smells, new sounds, new everything. It was then that the owl hooted—a low, deep-throated call from the invisible world all around them. Adima shivered and pressed closer to his guide. At that moment, he felt something brush his face. It was a soft touch, a gentle presence, barely a flicker against his skin. It startled him out of his wits. "Ahhhhhhh!" he yelled, jumping closer to Enoch. "What was that?" He brushed at his face and hair, flapping his arms and making a lot of noise.

"Quiet," Enoch said sternly. "You're making a spectacle of yourself. Your behavior is most unseemly. That is not the proper way to receive a gift." The old man bent and picked up something from the forest floor. Holding it close to Adima so he could see it in the dim light, Enoch brushed a silky soft feather against his face. "Owl has just given you one of its tail feathers to help you get started on your journey. Take it with gratitude and appreciation."

Adima reached out to take the feather. He could not see it, but he could feel its silky smoothness. It had almost no weight. He felt silly now, having completely overreacted. "I'm sorry," he said. "I did not understand."

Enoch made no comment, continuing on through the night. A short distance later, they came out of the forest into a broad meadow. The light was brighter here, and Adima was able to discern individual trees, rocks, and background hills.

A few deer, grazing peacefully, lifted their heads at the stranger's approach. Nostrils quivering, ears pricked straight up, they stood stock still, assessing the situation, deciding whether to stay or flee. They chose to flee. As one, they wheeled and broke for the cover of the woods on the opposite side of the clearing.

"One day they will not flee from you," Enoch said, sitting down on a flat rock. "One day, the forest creatures will come to accept your presence as a kindred spirit among them. But you have much to learn before then." He patted the smooth surface of the rock. "Come, sit beside me. Begin to learn Nature's wisdom."

"Why do you think I brought you here?" Enoch asked when Adima was comfortable.

"I haven't the faintest idea," Adima answered truthfully. "I won't even try to guess."

"I'll accept that for now," Enoch said, "but henceforth, I want you to start paying attention to the details of life—to the events, people, places, and things going on around you—so that you can eventually learn to answer such questions."

Adima nodded his head to show that he understood. Enoch continued speaking.

"Everything has a purpose. Everything happens according to a master Plan. There are no accidents or chance events. You may think so now, but that is not really the case."

The old man walked out into the field, stooping to feel the grass, opening himself to the warm night air. "Take this clearing, this forest, this night, for instance. You think it just an ordinary clearing in an ordinary forest on an ordinary night. I ask you why you are here, and you cannot answer. In fact," Enoch laughed, "as we walked, you complained because you could not see. *And that is both the problem and the solution.* You cannot see, and you need to be able to see if you are going to get anywhere on your journey and appreciate the things that happen to you along the way."

"Come on, Enoch," Adima said. "How can I see in the dark? There are no lights out here. This isn't exactly the Avenue of the Gods, you know. It's the middle of the night in the middle of the forest. Can you see out here?"

"My vision is not in question. Yours is. Take a look around you and tell me what you see." Resuming his seat on the rock, the old man waited patiently for his student to observe their surroundings.

Adima looked. He looked for quite a while. He saw the rocks sitting fixed in their place. He saw the waving grasses and smelled the fragrance of the wildflowers and night-blooming jasmine. He saw the silhouette of the treeline forming a jagged border against the lighter background of sky. He saw the clouds and the stars, and above it all, the silvery moon. All of this he told the old man.

"Very good," Enoch commended him. "So you do have a keen eye for details, when you take the time to attend to them. Now here comes the hard part. Try to give some meaning to what you see. Why are you here? What are the particular qualities and attributes of this place that make it of special value to you at this moment?"

Again Adima paused. At first, he could think of nothing, and he was about to say so. He turned to Enoch, then stopped, realizing that he could not actually see the features of man sitting next to him, just the shadow of his shape.

"Darkness," Adima thought out loud. "That's the biggest thing about this place. It's dark. I can't see anything, only shadows and outlines. I have to guess at what's really there."

"What else?" Enoch urged him to continue.

Adima looked around, listening to the night sounds. "The quiet and solitude. There's a different kind of noise here. Everything is peaceful. There are no distractions. It's perfectly natural."

"What else?"

For a third time Adima looked. What else could there be?

"The animals?" It was more a question than an answer. Of course, that was it. He had heard of the ancient belief that the animals possessed certain healing properties which, if properly understood, could be of great benefit. Perhaps that was it.

"One more thing," Enoch urged. "Turn your attention outward for a moment. Do not look down. Look up."

Up. Of course. There in the sky—the silvery orb of the moon. It was his birth sign. That had to be the symbol Enoch had in mind.

Enoch pointed to the stars. "Do you know that shape surrounding the moon?" A pattern of lights sparkled in the sky, forming the giant image of a scorpion, its tail poised to strike.

Adima recognized the constellation instantly, for it dominated the summer sky like its victim, the Hunter, dominated the winter sky. Having stung and killed the hunter, the two enemies were set in the Heavens and separated by the gods, destined never to appear together in the sky. "But I still don't understand how it all fits together," Adima said. "How are all of these separate elements related to each other, and how do they apply to me?"

"Let me put the puzzle together for you," Enoch said. "First of all, you were born under the sign of the Moon, the first quarter Moon, to be exact. Thus, your consciousness has a lunar rather than a solar character. Add to that the sign of the Scorpion, which represents your warrior nature. Like them, you are a distant star. You will always be aloof and stand apart from other men, never being completely understood.

"What better place for you to do your work, then, than in the quiet and solitude of the forest? What better time than the darkness of night under the light of the moon? Who better to teach you than the animals, who know the natural order of things and can help you learn to see in the dark? For that is your first challenge, learning to see in the dark! Not so much the physical darkness of the night around you, although that will be a big help to you, since this is the first of many such nocturnal adventures we will be taking.

"Yes," Enoch nodded his head in agreement with his own thoughts, "you'll do most of your work in the dark because you are a creature of the night. But the real darkness to which I am referring is the darkness within you." The old man gave Adima a gentle poke in the center of his chest. "There is where you need to go and look. There is where you need to learn to see. For the better you can see in there, the more you can learn, the more light you can shine, the more you will come to know yourself, and the easier your journey will become."

Enoch reached into the folds of his robe and took out two small objects. "Two stones— one black, the other white; one day, the other night; one male, the other female." He handed them to Adima. "Keep them where you can see them. Let them serve as a reminder of the dual nature of things and your own dual nature, as well. For you are a creature of duality, Adima. Your entire life is duality—what you have, what you do not have; what you know, what you do not know; what is, what is not."

Adima fingered the smoothly polished stones and thought about Enoch's words. Is he giving me a definition of who I am? he wondered, hoping that here was an answer to Enoch's first and foremost question of him that afternoon at the Lighthouse.

As if reading his mind, Enoch spoke again. "A second ally entered your Circle tonight, joining with another. Do you know who it is?"

"Owl!" Adima knew at once. He found all of this fascinating. Enoch was so enthused by his teaching and so skillful in presenting his knowledge that Adima could not help but share in the excitement. It was intriguing to look at the larger view, thrilling to picture himself in the larger sense that Enoch had painted him—a creature of the night, ruled by the Moon; a distant shining star; an aloof warrior.

"The medicine and gifts of Hawk and Owl complement each other," Enoch continued. "These birds share the same territory, one hunting by day, the other by night. Theirs is not necessarily a friendship, but more a peaceful tolerance of each other's presence. In the daylight, Osprey—the Fish Hawk—came to you at the Lighthouse and gave you its Spirit-message, cautioning you to be alert and pay attention. Now, under cover of darkness, Owl comes to give you the first of its special gifts—*the ability to see in the darkness.*

"Their gifts balance each other and so can help to balance your solar and lunar aspects, balance the male and female energy within you, balance your duality. When Osprey gives you her feathers, tie them together with Owl's to help stimulate your dreams and assert your will over your dream state.

"You walked along that trail in despair because you did not know where you were going and could not find your way in the darkness. Owl offers to teach you how to do that, being more at home in the dark forest at night than you are in the bright city by day."

Enoch pointed in the direction of the crescent moon shining brightly overhead. "Know your nature, Adima. You are a creature of the dark, born under the first quarter moon. The nighttime is symbolic of the darkness within each of us, the place where we hide our secrets. Use Owl's feather to help you uncover secrets about yourself. Since Owl is a creature of the night, it can teach you the secrets of the night."

Again Enoch reached into his robe, this time producing a small vial filled with a clear liquid. "As Owl uses its third eyelid to cleanse its eyes and clear its vision, so, too, will you cleanse your old vision now and open your third eye to a new one." Enoch tilted Adima's head back and squeezed a few drops into both eyes. They watered and burned as the cleansing fluid did its work. He started to rub them, but Enoch stayed his hand. "Do not spoil the magic," the old man whispered. "Be still and let the drops do their work."

Eyes smarting, Adima complied, blinking rapidly to clear his vision. Was it his imagination, or was something happening in that moonlit glade? Where before there were only dark shadows, now there were sparkling colors. Static shapes were changing form and coming to life, emerging out of the ground, materializing out of the surrounding forest, out of the very air itself. The moon spun round and round within a glowing halo, shooting pale moonbeams down to Earth, bathing the center of the clearing in a silvery glow.

It was marvelous and magical, and Adima could feel the deep lunar influence on the entire scene. Reflecting sunlight from far out in space, the moon released special rays of occult solar power, transforming the ordinary forest into a garden of otherworldly beauty and light. He realized that he was being given a glimpse of something special, not ordinarily seen by humans. He was looking at the invisible world of the Nature-spirits, in which they played and cavorted in harmony with the hidden and mysterious properties of the Great Mother.

Two elves danced and cavorted in the moonlight. Hand in hand they played, leaping high in the air, twirling each other in their arms, spinning dizzily. Adorning themselves with garlands of wildflowers, they tossed bouquets of posies in the air and let them shower down around them. Rolling in the grass, feeling the sensuous pleasure of the Earth and the night air on their bare skin, their laughter filled the air like tiny musical chimes blowing gently in the wind.

"The play of invisible forces in life," Adima whispered softly. As he spoke, one of the sprites turned her gaze upon him. Catching his eye, she smiled, waved, and blew kisses in his direction as her breath became a stream of silvery flecks, wafting toward him and settling gently all around him. Millions of silver sparkles danced in the air, landing on his hair, his clothes, his bare skin, lingering for a moment, then evaporating like snowflakes on a warm surface. Adima felt as though he had just been blessed with another gift, some unusual good fortune in appreciation of his recognition of the elusive play of the underlying forces in nature and his intention to cooperate with the invisible world.

Into the midst of the dance, a great horned owl flew. The beautiful bird alit on the ground before him, its huge penetrating eyes motionless, staring at him. Adima was mesmerized by their yellow coloring. "The sun shines in the nighttime," he whispered. "The sun lives through Owl at night."

Owl opened its mouth to speak to him. He heard the bird's words in his mind, just as he had heard Enoch's words on the Great Plain. In silent communication with his night guide, Adima listened.

"I am the eyes of night. I know what transpires when the sun is gone. I see what is not in the open. I have secret knowledge to share. Will you accept it?"

Adima could only nod his head softly in agreement. The acknowledgment was enough. Without a sound, the bird flapped its magnificent wings and flew off into the night.

Back in the moonlight, the elves continued their playful dance. Adima realized that he was being presented with a powerful teaching about duality. In his creative imagination, he was being shown the contrast between the inner and the outer, the visible and the invisible, the known and the unknown, the idyllic dream and ordinary everyday reality. He was looking at the play of the invisible forces, being asked to recognize and acknowledge his invisible helpers and cooperate with his natural instincts.

As soon as he realized this, the vision began to fade. Holding hands, the elves waved good-bye and ran lightly into the forest. The moon stopped spinning, and the moonbeams vanished along with the silvery halo. The flowers, grass, stones, and trees lost their sparkle, reverting back to their shadowy forms.

"It's all over," Adima said sadly to Enoch. But the old man was not there. Adima sat by himself in the now-darkened meadow. "Enoch, where are you?" No answer. Adima was alone in the dark. He knew that now. With the realization, a wave of panic swept over him. Then he heard Owl hoot, and the fear left him.

Smiling to himself, he realized that he was still grasping the black and white stones, to which he had clung throughout the vision. Slipping them into his pouch, his groping fingers brushed against the Owl feather. Fingering the gift, he called out to the darkness. "Thank you, Owl. I shall strive to make wise use of your gift. Help me to see my way clearly in the dark and find my way home."

CHAPTER 29

I was going through the hardest thing, also the greatest thing, for any human being to do; to accept that which is already within you, and around you.

—Malcolm X

That was how it started so many long years ago, how Adima came to begin his long walk along the path to enlightenment and the development of inner vision.

FOR THEY SHALL WALK THROUGH THE AGES
ALONG THE GRAIL PATH,
AT THE END OF WHICH
LIES THE LAPSIS EXCELLIS—
THE PRECIOUS STONE, THE HOLY GRAIL.

"Nothing will remain secret to the man who has the key," Enoch said as they began that most wonderful of relationships, a Holy Relationship based on mutual affection and respect, in which two people would come to know, love, and trust each other. Each teaching the other, each learning and growing from the other. This was to be a relationship for a lifetime, perhaps many lifetimes.

For Adima, it was a coming to believe; it did not happen overnight, nor in a single lesson, a few days, weeks, months, or even years. Rather, the process was gradual, unfolding one piece at a time over two and a half decades.

GRADUALLY DEVELOPING
THE INNER LIFE OF THE SOUL,
STEP BY STEP,
DEGREE BY DEGREE.

As with all learning, Adima's education was divided into several distinct periods in his life.

BEGINNING IN DULLNESS AKIN TO SLEEP,
WALKING THROUGH DOUBT AND FEAR,
ARRIVING AT A SINGLE POINT IN TIME—
AT THE MOMENT OF SPIRITUAL AWAKENING.

And always, shining brightly in the sun, the Grail—that magnificent goal for which he was striving—lay before him.

WHEN THE THIRD EYE OPENS
TO A MARVELOUS AND GLORIOUS VISION. BEHOLD—
THE HIDDEN SECRETS OF THE UNIVERSE ARE REVEALED,
AND THE MEANING OF HUMAN DESTINY.

*****

Having accepted Enoch's gift and making a decision to embrace a new way of life, there was much to do, much to learn, much to discard. Had he known at the outset the staggering the amount of work, effort, and energy that would be involved, Adima probably would have refused the gift. But fortunately for Adima, as for all who make similar decisions, the future was hidden from his eyes. He saw only the immediate situation at hand, and, although it appeared formidable, it also appeared possible and manageable.

First came a *Period of Undoing*, a time of clearing out and letting go of all of those learned behaviors and misperceptions that had resulted in negative thoughts, emotions, actions, and misperceptions. A time of making room for the new, it was not really painful, although Adima perceived it as so.

"It seems as if everything is being taken away from me," he complained to Enoch as they sat together one rainy evening along the bank of a small, swift-flowing stream that wound its way down from the high places on its journey to the sea. It was late fall, and the weather had turned cold. Already there was a thin layer of ice along the edges of the stream where the water ran still and clear. Adima had spent the day in anger, arguing with his friends, and he was nursing a cold. He did not feel much like learning anything new tonight, which was why Enoch had summoned him to the woods southwest of the city.

"That is because you do not yet know how to distinguish between that which has value and that which does not," Enoch replied. "You do not yet understand that many of the things you value really have no value at all."

"There is so much change all around me," Adima persisted in wallowing in self-pity. "I don't understand what it's all about."

"Regardless of your understanding, such changes are always helpful," came the seemingly unsympathetic response. "Do you know what the most important qualities are for you right now?" Enoch seemed to be changing the subject.

Adima thought for a moment, then answered hopefully but hesitantly. "Responsibility and achieving higher wisdom and enlightenment?"

Enoch laughed. "Absolutely not," he said. "You could not be more wrong. It is about play, my boy," he thumped Adima resoundingly on the back. "Remember the elves at play? Didn't you learn anything? It's about imagination, spontaneity, enthusiasm, playfulness. You've got to lighten up and release some of that nervous energy you carry around inside you. It does you no good at all. That is why you've got that cold."

Adima snorted and blew his nose in some leaves. He had a cold because he was spending too much time outdoors in this lousy weather. It had nothing to do with nervous energy.

"Learn a lesson from the stream." Enoch picked up a handful of leaves and twigs and tossed them into the water. Their combined weight was not nearly enough to crack the light skin of ice that had formed. "Your problem, if it can be called that, lies in your attachments to persons, places, things, and ideas," Enoch explained. "You seek safety in that which is familiar, regardless of whether the form still serves you. Like the water in the stream, which stands still because it has frozen into ice, so the flow of the life force within you is blocked. You need to break up the ice within yourself so you can flow freely once again."

"How?" Adima asked. He had a vision of an ice sculpture of himself. Standing before it, he hammered away at the ice with a pick axe, chipping and hacking until it was reduced to a pile of ice chips, each indistinguishable from the other. Of course, he knew Enoch was speaking metaphorically.

"Through dreaming and meditation," came the answer. Enoch poked lightly at the ice, tapping it with his staff until it had cracked into many pieces. The miniature icebergs floated listlessly for a few moments, then the current caught them and swept them downstream. "It is through these twin practices that you will become like the undammed water, flowing freely, changing shape and form with each twist and turn of the streambed. For it is in your ability to flow freely that your true safety lies. Do you still have Owl's feather?" Again, the old man seemed to be changing the subject.

"Right here," Adima patted his pouch, which was growing quite full, containing not only the feather, but the black and white stones and numerous other objects he had collected over the past few months.

"Take these and add them to it," Enoch said, handing two Osprey feathers to Adima. "Tie the three feathers together and hang them over your bed to aid you in your dreaming. Before you go to sleep tonight, lie in the darkness and use your natural ability to send an image forth as a question. Dream about the details, and thus release your frustration. Ask the Dreamtime to show you what you must let go of. Ask your dreams to help you understand your place and function within the larger picture."

"I don't dream," Adima pointed out. "I sleep deeply and well, but I very rarely dream."

Enoch was silent for a moment, debating whether to continue. Adima did not interrupt, waiting respectfully for the old man to continue. Together they sat on the stream bank, their warm breath turning to vapor in the chill night air.

"Belial." For the first time in the months since the Spear Ceremony, Enoch spoke the dreaded name. "Like your shadowy counterpart," he said, making the first of what would become many allusions to the strange relationship between the two adversaries, "your goal is the attainment of *higher consciousness*. Each of you is faced with the same baffling challenge—to awaken dormant powers in the soul that will lead to genuine Spirit-vision. For each one, the end is the same; you just have chosen different means to achieve it."

"He has already achieved it," Adima said somewhat disgustedly, pulling his cloak tighter about him. "Even if I tried, I could never reach his level of achievement or compete with his occult skills. His power is far greater than mine and will always be so. And dreaming about it isn't going to change anything."

Again Enoch laughed. "Let me tell you something," he said lightly. "Belial, with all of his enormous power, is not even a tenth as prepared as you are now. Although he seeks the same thing as you, he does not know where to look. In fact, he is not even looking because he thinks he has found his Grail. But he has not. In fact, he is going to be very surprised when he finds that you have."

"I haven't found anything yet," Adima sneezed and blew his nose again. His cold was getting worse, his head ached, and he was starting to shiver in the chill night air.

"Yes, but you have the willingness," Enoch explained as they sat together. A milky white fog had risen from the forest floor to envelop them, adding an air of isolation to their conversation and surroundings. "And you know where to look." He leaned close to Adima and lowered his voice, as though about to reveal the solution to a vast, universal mystery. *"Such powers can only be achieved by meditation."*

"Meditation!" Adima exclaimed in disgust. "What kind of meditation?" This was not the excitement he had expected. He wanted action...signs and wonders like visions in crystal balls, ospreys flying in through the window, elves cavorting in the moonlight. Of course he had heard about meditation as a form of spiritual discipline, but he had never bothered to apply it in practice or principle. That was for priestesses, mystics, and the like. All he knew was that meditation took a lot of time and effort just to find a quiet place and spend half an hour doing nothing.

"Where and how am I going to find time to meditate with all the things I have to do in my life?" The resistance was there, overt and obvious. So, too, was the anger. Adima was no stranger to such emotions. They had always been within him, simmering just under the surface of his persona, ready to burst forth in an explosive display of physical energy. Not one to suffer in silence, he had learned at a very early age that the crying and screaming that accompanied his temper tantrums would lead to the rewards he craved.

He had seen the same behavior in his parents. His father's rage was met with passivity and silence from his mother...his father, whom he idolized; his mother, upon whom he looked as a model of decorum and appropriate behavior. *Such behavior is both appropriate and acceptable.* So the child had received and misinterpreted the message. It was inevitable, then, that his life be filled with all of the tension, drama, and negative excitement of misplaced and misdirected anger.

How frightening those dramatic emotional displays had been, scaring the object of his wrath as well as himself. Intending to silence the other rather than eliciting meaningful communication, Adima would lash out with all the power and invective at his disposal. And it was considerable—violent, punitive, derisive, out of control.

As he grew older, repressing his true feelings and ignoring the feelings of others, Adima directed his anger outward, blaming others rather than taking responsibility for his own feelings and behavior. These bouts of anger were not brief encounters, momentary flare-ups quickly let go of and forgotten. Rather, he held on to those negative feelings, nursing grudges small and large, which continued to endure for days and even weeks as bitter, festering resentments. Now it was time for this to stop. Now it was time to learn a new way, a better way. Now it was time to wrest control of his behavior from the neurotic child and let the responsible adult nature of his personality take charge.

"Tonight you begin to learn how to dream," Enoch instructed him. "Beginning on the morrow, I want you to meditate three times a day, following a prescribed ritual that I shall show you." Again, Adima cocked his head to one side, pursed his lips, and looked askance at Enoch. This time, the old man laughed right in his face.

"Boy, you are a piece of work! Your arrogance is superseded only by your ignorance." Adima started to say something, but Enoch held up his hand to stop him. "You have an ego the size of this great island. You think you know it all. You think you are always right. You think you can do whatever you want because of who you have set yourself up to be." There was no anger in Enoch's voice, no attack or ridicule. The words were true, and Adima knew it. Enoch had read him so well, and now he felt resentful and ashamed.

"These are the first steps in the process of transforming your avoidance of your true feelings into an appropriate expression of them." The old man seemed to sense his student's self-contempt. He smiled and playfully tousled Adima's hair. "It takes heroic work to drop the drama and express oneself appropriately. Until you learn how to get in touch with, express, and then release your true feelings, however, you cannot make further progress.

"Tonight you begin the process of letting go. Tonight you begin to empty out your mind, clearing out all you think you know. Admitting that you really know nothing, you approach this new process of meditation with *Beginner's Mind*." Enoch thumped Adima resoundingly on the back. "Congratulations, son, it's the first day of school!"

Adima could not help but smile, even though he did not really feel very happy. The old man's energy and enthusiasm were stronger than his own feelings of anger and self-pity. He remembered his promise to receive and honor the old man's gift. If this was to be the form it was to take, then so be it.

"Well, then," he said resignedly, "let's get started." It was his first experience with practicing a principle that he would come to know very well over the years, although then he did not know that principle's name. It was his first experience with *Surrender*.

"You will find a place where you can be by yourself," Enoch wasted no further time getting to the heart of the lesson. Now his tone grew serious. "At first, it should be a dark, quiet, and isolated place where you will not be distracted by light, noise, or other sensory input. Your first task is to let go of any impressions that come from your five senses. You want to replace that kind of thinking with a new kind that does not come from that brain of yours." Enoch tapped his head with his index finger. "Yours is to be a sense-free experience." He handed Adima an obsidian cross and seven red roses. The young man just looked at him, waiting for an explanation.

"Add these objects to your pouch. They will be the symbols upon which you will begin your meditations. These separate symbols never appear together in the sense world. They symbolize the inner significance of the Blood—which gives life to your Body—and Water—which gives life to your Spirit." The old man arose, stretched his stiff limbs, and began the long walk back to the city. "This will be the central theme of your search."

*****

For someone not used to the practical application of spiritual practices, it was a lot to ask to put forth such an effort in a sustained period of concentrated meditation. That Adima managed to accomplish it in the face of such odds against him—from friends, family, responsibilities, and especially, his own persistent and resistant ego—was quite an achievement, speaking volumes for the strength of his character and the depth of his willingness and commitment. At the age of twenty-three, he was a young man caught in the tension between two conflicting worldviews—the world of the Ego and the world of the Heart. At first, Enoch's teachings were hard to accept, for they went against everything his reason had warned him to avoid...against all of his schooling, too.

Oh yes, Adima knew the ways of the Ancients. His mother and father had schooled him in the ancient ways. Until his eighteenth birthday, he had held fast to those ways and knew them so very well. Adima could quote chapter and verse from the *Book of Life*. He was thoroughly familiar with it all—ideas, philosophies, and the wise sayings of the Ancients from Quetzalcoatl to the current High Priestess.

With his entrance into the university, however, he had been exposed to a new science and a new philosophy, and his thirsty mind had soaked up the knowledge like a sponge. Thus was he caught in a net of intellectualism and rationalism that would leave no room for affairs of compassion, humanities, or the occult. Although his body did not change form, the distance from his mind to his heart had expanded from a mere few inches to an ever-widening chasm, an insurmountable gulf that was impossible to bridge. Not that he wanted to.

"The old ways are pretty much worthless," he had told his mother one evening at dinner. Having just completed his first semester at the university, he was brimming with new ideas. What began with her innocent observation about the changing times soon turned into a rancorous argument.

"I just want you to be sure you know what you're doing," she had said, feeling genuine concern for her son's safety.

Adima was incensed and highly indignant. Did his mother think him a gullible fool, incapable of thinking for himself, of looking out for himself? The more he looked at the petite, pretty woman sitting across the table from him, the angrier he got. How dare she reject him like this? What did she know about changing times or new ideas? She had wasted her whole education and her whole life. He knew that now.

"Look at you," he fairly bristled, his voice loaded with contempt. "How could you have attended the university and been exposed to such knowledge and truth and wind up a simple housewife, slave to the demands of an uncaring husband and children?"

His mother reacted as though she had been slapped across the face. She was not prepared for his sarcasm, nor was she used to it. Tears welled up in her eyes, but she made no comment. Seeing the tears only enraged her son more. She was choosing to live the lie. How could she do that? He was angry with her for not treating him with the love and loyalty to which he felt entitled. He wanted to punish his mother, and he let her know it.

"Too bad you didn't pay more attention when you were in school. How could you have let such an opportunity go by? You're forty-five years old and have wasted your life. And what have you got to show for it? Nothing." Adima slammed his fist down on the table with such force that the plates rattled. His mother jumped involuntarily but made no comment.

"We'll talk later, when you're more calm," she said softly, wiping her mouth with the corners of her napkin. "Excuse me, please." Very quietly, without a word, the older woman stood up and walked from the room. It was an act of grace, a lesson in poise and willpower. Adima saw neither. What he saw was further punishment, a refusal to acknowledge his feelings and worth as a man.

"You have been exposed to the highest of truths and have not been changed by them," he called as her bedroom door closed softly behind her. "Well, I'm not going to make that same mistake. Most of all, I'm not going to listen to anything you have to say, because what do you know?" Bang! He slammed his fist into the door and stormed out of the house.

It was sophomoric behavior, and it might have ruined their relationship were it not for his mother's patience and understanding.

He'll come back around, she had told herself, expressing her mother's love and fear as she wrote in her journal. He is caught up in the excitement of new times and new ideas. Everybody at the university has something to offer. Everybody he's coming into contact with now appears to have a brilliant mind. He gets a piece here, a fragment there, and he thinks he knows it all. He doesn't see the big picture yet. Hasn't put it all together and formed his own hypothesis based on knowledge and experiences of his own. He's spellbound. I just have to hope and pray that he won't get led down a twisted path and get lost in the morass of false thinking.

That incident had occurred during his first year at the university. Now, five years later, here he was, a young man in his early twenties, just starting his work with Enoch. His whole way of thinking and philosophy of being were being challenged again, not just by his mother this time, but by a relative stranger who seemed to know lots more than himself, his mother, or most of the people at the university combined.

On the one hand, Adima's mind was dominated by the world of modern Atlantean scientific thought and method as espoused in the new thinking of the Sensate philosophers who would mold the thinking of the Sons of Belial.

"*Man cannot be explained or understood except within terms of the physical world in which he lives,*" these alchemists and geomancers declared.

Having much influence within the university, they had devised and proffered an entire curriculum that taught Adima and others like him about a world devoid of Spirit—a godless world of measurement in which human beings were reduced to insignificant specks. "The Earth itself is no more than a speck of cosmic dust in a dying galaxy," these Sensate philosophers continued.

Now, five years later, Adima was learning another curriculum. Away from the influence of the university, a year into his practice of meditation, another world was revealing itself, a Spirit-world where perception was akin to knowledge, and intellectually derived thought had no place. Three times each day, he sought the solace of his private sanctuary. It was easier than he had first anticipated. He just closed his eyes, tuned out the outer world, and focused on the images of the black cross and the seven red roses. It took a while, but gradually, as the months went by, he began to experience a change in his thinking. When it suddenly dawned upon him what was happening, he could scarcely believe it.

There are strange new forces churning within me," he wrote in his journal,
that are not part of my everyday thought processes. Indeed, they are far stronger.

How shall I describe the meditative experience? As I lay my body down,
my translucent soul rises up, shining brightly, filling my inner vision with pure,
white light. It seems almost overjoyed to be free of the confines and restrictions
of its corporeal prison. After a time, my body sleeps, yet my consciousness
remains awake and alert as I move out into the ether. After a time, I cross the
threshold into another realm of existence, where I find myself floating serenely
in a heightened state of awareness.

I am first of all frightened that such powerful forces—which I barely
understand—reside within me. Yet at the same time, I am thrilled to realize that
I can call them forth almost at will from the depths of my own soul.

It took tremendous perseverance, but now he was excited and gave willingly of his
time and energy. As the months continued to pass and the meditations intensified, he
continued to record his experiences, seeking always to understand that which was
happening to him. From deep within his soul, the Voice of the Muse sang to him,
encouraging him to pour his feelings forth as often in prose as in the language and imagery
of poetry.

It is a highly personal experience that I find difficult to describe in language.
If there is another world beyond the physical, and if it is from that world that
Spirit fashions Matter, how are they sustained? So many questions, so few
answers!

I am thrilled, but I am also confused...part skeptic, part visionary. I do not
feel complete. And I cannot reconcile my conflicting thoughts.

> I am a Walker of Two Worlds,
> Standing on the Razor's Edge,
> Walking the fine line
> Between the world of Matter
> And the realm of Spirit.
> Understanding neither,
> Belonging to neither.
> I come to my dreaming with new questions now.
> Where is the bridge that joins the two worlds?
> What path will carry me across?
> Show me the way. Show me the way.

*****

Within two years, Adima achieved the first milestone that Enoch had set for him—
the ability to see things not visible to normal human sight.

"Congratulations," the old man complimented his student as they sat in the
Lighthouse discussing this new talent. "You have begun to grow and nurture within
yourself that which is called by many names—intuitive sagacity, second sight, clairvoyance.

The old man walked over to the crystal ball resting on the polished oak table. "I
prefer a different name, though, one more suited to the truth behind the mighty forces into
which you are tapping and to which you have staked a claim." Gently, almost lovingly, he
caressed the flawless globe. "I call your new and heightened perception of the Spirit-
world the *Knowing of the Imagination.*"

Of course, it was not always easy or enjoyable. There were obstacles, too, times of
great stress and trial. Emptying out was much easier said than done, and Adima had to

practice the principle of surrender on an almost daily basis. For with the decision to "stake his claim," there came the experience of the *Second Force*, that powerful energy of resistance which rises up whenever one makes a decision to do something new and better. For Adima, the resistance came in many forms, often from unexpected corners.

"You're not the same any more," his friends told him one night as they sat in an inn drinking ale and listening to music. "This is the first time you've been out with us in months. We never see you any more. If we don't contact you, you certainly don't contact us."

"Explain yourself," Tyr's voice had an ugly tone to it. He had been drinking a good deal of ale, and he was spoiling for a fight. If not with someone in the tavern, then it might as well be with Adima. It didn't matter, as long as it was a fight. "You're a real toadstool," he sneered at the one he called friend. "You think you're better than us now. You've got other things to do. You've got a fancy teacher who's showing you great secrets. So to hell with us."

He paused, expecting a response. When none came, his frustration spilled over into rage. "Well, to hell with you." Tyr stabbed an accusing finger in Adima's chest. The blow was surprisingly strong, and it hurt. Adima said nothing, however, rubbing the bruise and sipping his water.

"Take a drink, damn you!" Tyr's speech was slurred, his vision blurry. "Take a drink of ale. What's the matter, don't want to get drunk with your old friends any more?"

"No," Adima said quietly. "I will not take a drink. I don't want to." He raised his arms and forced a light smile. "I just want to sit here and talk and listen to the music. Drink all you want. Don't worry about me."

"You'll drink, damn you," Tyr retorted, grabbing him by the collar and forcing him to his feet. "We'll make you drink. Hold him."

Four strong hands immediately pinioned Adima's arms behind his back, while a fifth grabbed his hair from behind and yanked his head backward, forcing his mouth open. Another friend poured a tankard of ale down Adima's open throat, splashing it all over his blouse and tunic, causing him to choke and sputter. The group of young ruffians laughed with delight. The anticipation of a good fight was far more exciting than their original purpose in coming to the tavern that evening—to meet and seduce women.

Through beer-soaked eyes, Adima looked at the bawdy, randy, physical men around him. Were they men, or were they boys masquerading as men? They had all the physical characteristics of men, they functioned physically as men. But their thinking and behavior were, nevertheless, those of boys—unruly, misbehaved, belligerent boys. Boys with no self control, no sense of right and wrong, no moral values or guidelines to uphold them. Boys smarting from dozens of nameless wounds inflicted upon them by their own wounded fathers.

These are my friends, Adima thought in amazement as he looked around him. Or at least they were. What had he ever seen in them? What had attracted him to such relationships? "You disgust me," he choked and sputtered when they had let him go. The laughter was all around him, but he did not care. "Grow up," he raged, lashing about with clenched fists. "Behave like men. You're a disgrace." The more he yelled, the angrier he got, but his fists struck only empty air.

They danced tantalizingly close, laughing at him, ridiculing him, taunting him. Adima lunged forward, landing a fist squarely in the middle of Tyr's face. Blood spurted from his nose, and there was the sickening crack of bone. I've broken it, Adima thought smugly, but his satisfaction was short lived. Again he was grabbed from behind. Again he was held tight, but this time there was no beer poured in his face. This time, fists pummeled him, heavily booted feet kicked him. He sagged to the floor, knees buckling. He would have passed out had not someone thrown a pitcher of cold ale over him.

"Hear this, Adima." Tyr's bloody face loomed an inch from his own. The smell of alcohol and stale tobacco filled Adima's nostrils. "Our friendship is over. You take your new ideas and your fancy teachings and whatever else you call them and get out of here. Don't ever come back." Heads nodded in agreement, while murmurs of assent punctuated each stinging barb.

"We don't want to see you, we don't want to hear about you," Tyr continued, speaking now not just for himself but for the entire group of comrades. "We don't care if you live or die. You're no friend of ours, not any more. You can drop dead, for all we care." He stood up and looked at the beaten man lying in a filthy puddle on the cold tavern floor. "Get him out of here," he jerked a thumb in the direction of the door.

Adima's head was spinning. He could barely see straight. A million bees were buzzing in his ears. He felt himself being lifted and carried through the air. The lights suddenly dimmed, and there was a sensation of flying. He landed with a thud, all the wind knocked out of him. But he never lost consciousness. Rolling over on his back, he looked up and out from behind a wall of pain at his former friends, now ghostly black silhouettes in the doorway of the inn. For a few moments, curses, taunts, and mocking laughter rang in his ears. Each one carried its own emotional pain to add to the weight of his physical pain. Then the door was slammed shut, leaving him to lie in the street alone.

"I'll teach them," he growled when he could gather his wits about him. "If I can't reason with them, I'll let my sword be their teacher." Slowly he staggered to his feet, using a lamppost for support. A few passersby stopped and stared, but no one offered a helping hand. No matter. In his foul black mood, he would have refused any offers of succor, especially from strangers. It took almost an hour, but he eventually reached home and dragged himself painfully up to his room. "Where is it," he muttered. His left eye was swollen shut, having turned a ghastly red and purple. He groped around the room, knocking over books, lamps, even toppling a nightstand, until at last his fingers closed on the object of his search—his father's sword, the weapon he loved so well and wielded even better.

"The point of a sword will teach them to respect me," he muttered through pain-clenched teeth, gently touching his bruised and swollen face. "I'll teach them the error of their ways." He smiled a horrible, frightening smile. His reason had escaped him; he was caught in the dramatic frenzy of ego-centered, manipulative theatrics. Teach them he would! What Adima could do with a sword few others could even think about. He had no equal in all of Atlantis.

He had first picked up the weapon at an early age, after watching his father practicing in the gymnasium. The little boy promptly cut his finger, but that could not dampen his enthusiasm.

"So, I see you have found my sword and it has given you a taste of its power." His father stood above him, toweling the sweat from his face. Rather than scold the child for disobeying, however, the adult made a surprising offer. "Would you like to learn how to use it?"

Adima nodded with relish. He proved to be an apt pupil, with an incomparable skill and talent. His father was an excellent swordsman, but the student soon outdid even the master. The sword became an extension of his own arm. Yet never before tonight had he thought about raising it in anger against another human being—let alone friends. Now, as he buckled the scabbard about his waist, that was all he could think about—drawing blood, making them hurt as he was hurting. Vengeance! A holy and righteous vengeance, a justified vengeance. How dare they strike him! Didn't they know to whom it was they were doing this?

"I'm Adima," he screamed into the night as he staggered through the dark streets, his rage-filled ego impelling him to voice his darkest, most prideful feelings of arrogance and resentment, feelings that he had been carrying inside himself since he was a child. "How dare you treat me this way! You should be on your knees before me thanking me for befriending you and doing the great work that I am doing."

Approaching the inn, there was murder in his heart, not forgiveness. The streets were deserted, which suited him just fine. There would be no one to interfere with the lesson he would teach to those who had crossed him. Adima started at a noise behind him. So, he was not alone after all! Someone was standing just to his right, leaning quietly against a lamppost. Even in the darkness, he recognized the shadowy figure instantly, and his anger flamed more brightly.

"Where are you going?" Enoch asked softly.

"Stay away, old man." Adima was in no mood for lessons this night. His rage had taken him too far. "This has nothing to do with you. This is my fight, and I'll handle it my way." He was about to brush past the older man, when he felt himself held by an invisible force in the center of his chest.

"*Stop!*" The single word boomed like thunder in the stillness of the night. Adima stood motionless, held in the grip of some unknown force.

In a single bound, Enoch crossed the intervening space between them. Standing before the rage-consumed young man, he gripped his shoulders in strong hands. "What are you doing?" Enoch demanded an answer. "There is murder in your heart. You are not a man; you are not even an animal. You have sunk lower than the dust."

Adima tried to pull himself away, to no avail.

"Look at yourself," the old man shook him roughly. "Your reason has left you. Think. Open your mind."

Adima swayed unsteadily in the damp night air. The murderous thoughts had not left him. They felt so good. How he wanted to hold on to them! How he resented Enoch for interfering! But then a new realization dawned, and he began to see this night of blind rage as a microcosm of all of his rage over the years. His throat opened, and all of his resentments began to spew forth, not just against Tyr and the boys, but against all who had wronged him over the years.

"Why do people treat me this way?" he sobbed, collapsing into Enoch's comforting arms. "Why is everyone jealous of me? My life is nothing special. Why do they think it is? Why do they begrudge me wanting to better myself? Why do they want to keep me bound in the same chains that bind them. I hate them for that!"

He slapped his open palm against his forehead in a gesture of futility, helplessness, and despair. It was an immature act, one he had learned to do as a child when he wanted to lash out in anger at his parents but knew better than to strike them. Having no one else on whom to vent his rage, he had vented it upon himself. As then, so now.

"I chose to follow this path of my own free will," he continued, letting the needy child speak through the angry man, "knowing it would lead to great changes in my life. But I never thought people would hate me for it. I thought at least that they'd acknowledge it in some positive way.

"Part of me knows I'm not doing this work for personal glory and honor or to get put on a pedestal and revered. Yet there's a dark part of myself that wants that, and when I don't get it, I turn into a feel-sorry-for-myself spoiled brat!" Again he made a move to strike himself, his trembling hand pausing just before it reached his tear-streaked face. "Except I'm no longer a five-year-old having a temper tantrum and throwing my toys. I'm an adult with a sword. I don't mean to get so arrogant and so prideful and so angry, but I can't help it. I can't control it."

There! At last he had allowed himself to acknowledge his true nature. He had been hiding and protecting this shadow Adima for years, not willing to allow it to reveal itself except in the privacy of his own home. Now, however, it had burst forth in a blaze of glory, appearing not just to himself and his family but to Enoch as well.

The truth was difficult to accept. Now Enoch knew what Adima had known all along but had refused to admit—that he wasn't the kind and loving young man he pretended to be; he was, rather, a spoiled, selfish, angry child. Ashamed and afraid, Adima wanted to run and hide from that self. Instead, he sank deeper into the consoling embrace of the old man's arms.

He sobbed long and hard—great wracking sobs—alone with his teacher in the middle of the night on a dimly lit street corner. It started to rain, and while the tears of the Mother sweetened the Earth, Adima's tears came pouring out, carrying with them all of his resentments and guilt and shame and anger and fear. At last, there was no more left inside.

"It would seem that you are now ready to learn about *Forgiveness*," Enoch said softly as they sat on the curb in the lamp's soft glow. The rain had slackened to a fine mist, and a yellow fog hugged the ground all around them.

"Forgiveness!" Adima shook his head in disgust, not at his friends this time, but at himself. "I can never forgive when I get into moods like this. Instead of forgiving, I sentence my so-called enemies to death for what they did to me. It has always been thus, starting with my brothers and my parents when I was a little, little boy. And I certainly can't forgive myself for succumbing to my feelings!"

The child came out again, pacing back and forth on the cobblestones, pounding his thighs with clenched fists. "I'm judgmental, arrogant, conceited, unforgiving." The words were bitter, recriminating. Each time the boy-man thought about it, the frustration and rage came welling back up from deep within.

"Why is this happening to me?" he sobbed again, looking deeply into Enoch's eyes. "I gave up those old ways. I don't do what my friends do any more. I don't want what they want any more. I've committed to something new and better. Yet I still feel the pain. I still have the fears and resentments and all the other stuff I used to try to make go away in that tavern. Look at me!" Adima stood before Enoch, arms outstretched in a gesture of openness. "What is wrong with me?" He threw back his head and screamed his inarticulate anguish into the unfeeling night. There was no response, only empty silence.

"Why are you so angry with yourself?" Enoch asked quietly.

Adima paused, startled. His teacher was confused. The anger was directed at his former friends, not at himself...or was it?

For several moments, he just sat on the damp curb, breathing in and out, thinking long and hard, taking a rigorously honest look at himself. It was a turning point. There in the night, on a deserted street corner in the city of Atlantis, the boy who wanted to be a man started to learn a lot more about himself. Looking at himself in more and more detail, he began to admit to a lot of things he did not like about himself but that were true nevertheless.

"All of the rage I've projected onto others I'm feeling toward myself," he confessed. "I realize now that I'm quite capable of hurting myself and others. That's what I'm afraid of now and what I've been afraid of all these years."

The old man made no comment, save to nod his head encouragingly, as if to say, "You're right; go on."

"Inside me there's a beast...alive and well and waiting to be unleashed," Adima continued his confession. He closed his eyes and imagined himself a vicious beast, a horrible man-eating monster quite capable of destroying anything that stood in its path. "This beast always came unleashed when I was with my friends in that tavern. Every single evening ended in the uncaging of the beast. I'd let go all the stops and out it came, wreaking havoc on whoever was in the way, including myself."

Adima shook his head in disbelief, amazed to hear himself speaking these truths about his character. "I punched things, broke things, threw things, screamed my rage, insulted people, cursed, swore, condemned. And you know what?" He looked at Enoch, about to reveal the most incredible truth of all. "I expected people just to take it and to accept me for who I was. After all, wasn't I Adima? Weren't people always jealous of me? Wasn't I better than everyone else? Wasn't I special? Wasn't this acceptable behavior for me because of who I was? That's what my mother always told me. So that's what I came to believe."

Enoch nodded his head and spoke, his observation couched as a question. "So you're afraid of yourself?"

"Yes," Adima agreed. "I am afraid of myself, and I do not like myself. I'm ashamed of myself and probably even hate myself, and I have felt this way for a long, long time. As I said, there's a monstrous side to me, and I don't want to ever see it again, yet I always get into situations that seem to unleash it."

"Like tonight," Enoch said, stating the obvious.

Adima nodded in agreement. He wasn't sure where this conversation was leading, but he did know that as he unburdened himself he was beginning to relax. The anger was flowing out of him in a cool wave, and in its place, the light of insight was filling the void. Now his fear was becoming understandable. He could sense that he was close to a great discovery. He wanted to talk longer, *needed* to talk longer.

"I keep having these thoughts that at the next moment, the beast will come out and I won't be able to control it...that the next time, the 'beast me' will devour everyone I love and destroy all that I have, and I'll become a deranged killer, or worse, they'll find me, put me in a straight jacket in a padded cell, and there I'll stay in misery until I die, after which I'll continue in eternity as a madman."

"In other words, that you will become like Belial!" Enoch uttered that single missing bit of truth. In nine words, he provided the key to Adima's whole understanding of his fear and anger and shame.

"Yes, that's it exactly!" Adima exclaimed, amazed at his teacher's insight. "That night on the Plain two years ago, I saw Belial's beast, and I knew it was my beast too."

"What are you afraid of, really?" Enoch asked. Adima was much calmer now, and the conversation was approaching its deepest level. The truth was close now, very close indeed.

"I used to think that I was afraid of the Creator, but I am not afraid of the Creator. I am afraid of myself. That's why I don't like being alone."

"Of course," Enoch pointed out. "It all goes back to the fact that you do not know who you are. You have no definition of yourself, so you must rely on others to tell you who you are. When others are around, you see how they respond to you and how they perceive you. When they offer love, you feel loved because you accept their definition of you. When you are alone, there is no one there to love you or judge you differently and not condemn you, so you must accept your own judgment about yourself, which is loveless."

Enoch led him over to a puddle of rainwater glistening in the lamplight. "Look at your reflection in the puddle," the old man instructed. "What do you see?"

"I can't," Adima drew back in fear. "I never look at my reflection, even at home in the mirror."

"Why not?"

"Because I know that if I were to really look at myself for a long time, if I were to stare long enough and hard enough, I'd see the beast."

The tears started to flow again, as the words came out haltingly between the sobs. "And...I don't want to see it...I really don't."

Gently, Enoch placed a strong, warm arm around his student. It was time for him to step out of his role as detached observer and become the compassionate teacher. Time to gently but firmly teach the man-boy the difference between the cold, unfeeling stone hero on the pedestal and the warm, heroic human being living a life of love and compassion.

"Let me tell you something about this inner beast that you fear so much," the old man said, handing Adima a snowy piece of damask on which to wipe his face. "What you are describing and experiencing here tonight is surface emotion...drama, for want of a better word. Yes, you have chosen the Light Path, and it is proving to be a better way for you. But that does not mean that *you* are better than anyone else, or that their ways do not also lead to Home and Source.

"Stronger, faster, better, more enlightened—these are the adjectives that your immature ego uses to describe yourself, hoping that somehow the words themselves will mold the personality and the man accordingly. Such a person may be 'loved' by himself, but rarely is he loved by his brethren."

So much truth in those words, so much wisdom from the all-knowing sage! Adima felt Enoch's compassion flow toward him, wrapping him in a soft, warm blanket of love. He listened peacefully as the old man continued.

"Your true nature is not vengeful, my young friend. Were it so, I would not have approached you with the offer I did. However, the temptation to give in to the baser instincts in your nature is strong within you." The old man stared directly at his student, inviting him to take the next higher step along the path.

"This is the challenge you must now overcome—to know your Shadow, not as an enemy, not as a part of you to be denied or removed. Rather, you must face your Shadow and eat it." Enoch smiled again. "And you will, with my help and the help of all those who love and support you on your journey."

Adima made a mental note to ask who those others might be. He wasn't sure exactly how one went about eating a shadow, but the metaphor conjured up all sorts of exciting images in his mind. For the first time in his young life, he finally understood how his anger and shame and vulnerability and ego and pride expressed themselves. He had not mastered them as yet. That would take many more years and many more lessons. But now he had a solid understanding from which to begin, and a solid foundation on which to build.

"So your next task is to embrace forgiveness," Enoch instructed him, seeming to read his thoughts as he quoted from the *Book of Life*:

> FORGIVENESS IS THE KEY TO ALL PROBLEMS,
> FOR IT IS THE KEY TO TRUE HAPPINESS.

Enoch helped Adima rise to his feet, continuing to speak as he brushed off his student's clothes and straightened his hair. "You will always be a distant star—a watcher—never really understood. By your nature, you do inspire extreme reactions in people...good, bad, sometimes both."

Adima fingered the scar on his cheek, remembering the extreme reaction he had inspired in Belial on the occasion of their first meeting.

"I speak to you now of your grandeur, of your kingly nature," the old man went on. "Before, I could not speak to you of this, because your undeveloped ego would have turned grandeur into grandiosity. Now, however, you have progressed far enough in your learning to hear this truth about yourself."

Adima remained still, listening intently to his teacher's words, hearing himself described in a way he had never heard before. Rather than swell with pride, however, this time he experienced a far different feeling—*Humility*.

"Your job is not to get hurt by other people's reactions to you, nor to take responsibility for their feelings." There was gentleness in Enoch's voice and touch. "Merely be sensitive to that which is occurring around you."

The old man's voice grew ever softer, barely audible in the silence of the night. Closing his eyes, he whispered another quotation from the *Book of Life*. Adima had to strain to make out the words.

Flow not toward conflict, but toward Blessing and Forgiveness.

Adima remembered that cold night in the forest when Enoch had broken up the ice and first spoken to him about flow and safety. Was the ice within himself finally starting to melt? He listened as his teacher continued.

"Henceforth, when faced with an extreme negative reaction, do not close up within yourself. Open totally to the experience. You already know what is wrong. Like the king, however, you have to be able to bless the perceived wrong, forgive it, and totally relate it to the common human experience. For in truth, whatever is wrong is merely a symptom of the human condition. Remember what is written in the *Book of Life*:

Imperfections are inevitable in a world in progress.

It was growing late. The lights in the tavern were out, the last of the rowdies long since sleeping off the effects of the evening's revelry. The street lamp was sputtering, almost out of oil. Morning was nigh.

"You are going to be in charge of powers that can hurt people." The lesson was drawing to a close. "If someone slights you, you must not be tempted to use your power for revenge. That is the old way; it is also Belial's way. That way no longer serves you."

Adima just shook his head. Impossible, he thought to himself. There is no way it can happen, not in this lifetime or in a thousand lifetimes. The unforgiving Shadow is too strong.

As usual, Enoch read his thoughts. "Forgiveness is not always easy, because you are a human being," he agreed. "You have feelings that can be easily hurt." For emphasis, he pointed a long, crooked finger at Adima's chest. "But hurt feelings are no excuse."

"So then, how do I do it?" Adima truly wanted to know. He did not like the drama. It was exhausting. He had been struggling with it all of his life, and he was very tired and ready now to release it in exchange for a better way. "If forgiveness is really the answer, and it's really possible, how do I forgive?"

Enoch's answer was simple and direct, and at the same time very deep and complex. "Look to a Higher Being who has wisdom. You and I have small knowledge, but that Being has knowledge beyond ours because that Being, having total vision, sees all. Let that Higher Being take care of acts against you."

He's speaking of another form of surrender, Adima realized. There was nothing new here, merely an elaboration and clarification of the original teaching. That was when Enoch taught him the prayer.

"To turn things over to the Higher Being, say... *You know better. Please take care of this for me.* To do this is actually the greatest warfare in which you can engage. It takes great character to be able to say this prayer and mean it." Enoch arose, patted Adima's arm, and started to walk off into the fog.

"Wait a minute," Adima called to the receding figure. "Is that it? Are you just going to leave me here, sword in hand? Aren't you even going to take the weapon away from me?"

"You have the truth now," Enoch's voice came floating back out of the night. "You can accept it and live accordingly, or not. The choice is yours." And then he was gone.

"By the Beard of Poseidon!" Adima exclaimed in amazement. For several minutes he just stood there, shaking his head. Then he went home to bed.

Standing in the bath that night, Adima washed his face, anointed his wounds, and prepared for sleep. And for the first time in many a year, he took a good long look at himself in the mirror. What he saw did not frighten him; in fact, it pleased him very much.

*****

The Second Force continued to make its presence felt over the next few years as Adima continued to grow and discard the old and take on the new. Now, though, he had a third ally with which to combat it. Whenever the Second Force rose up and challenged him, he simply enlisted the aid of the *Third Force*—the all-wise Higher Being about whom Enoch had taught him.

It worked, and with far less pain and drama than he imagined. One by one, old friends and old habits dropped by the wayside, some in bitterness, others laid gently aside. At the same time, one by one, new friends and new ideas were rising up to meet and greet him. So enthused was Adima by all of this that he wanted to tell everyone he could about his new found way of living and being. He started with those whom he loved best...his mother and younger brother.

They did not understand what he was saying, neither his ways nor his words. They had envisioned greatness for him as he followed in the footsteps of his father and sat on the Council of Elders. All of Atlantis would admire him, and they would reap the benefits that his power, status, and wealth would bring. Now, seeing that their expectations were not to be fulfilled, mother and brother grew angry and resentful. It was all Adima's fault. He was responsible for their predicament. He was both cause of and solution to their problem.

"I don't know what's wrong with you," his mother said one evening at dinner, having decided to confront her son once and for all. "You don't eat what I cook for you any more. You don't wear the clothes I lay out for you. You're never home. I never see you." On and on she went, ticking off an endless litany of his flaws and faults. Then the questions began.

"Why don't you ever go to the Council sessions? Why aren't you more interested in the affairs of State. Why don't you use that wonderful education of yours for the good of Atlantis?"

"I still love you, Mother," he said, trying to comfort the woman. "I just have other interests right now."

"Hmmph!" She snorted through a mouthful of food. "Do you know how many young men would give everything they have to trade places with you? Do you know how fortunate and blessed you are? Yet you choose to throw your life away on fantasy and occult nonsense!"

"You're ungrateful," his younger brother chimed in. "You don't care about us any more. You never stay around here and do anything with us any more. You've abandoned us."

Adima suffered in silence. He wanted so badly to shout and defend himself, but he chose a silent response.

How the roles have reversed! he wrote in his journal that night, remembering his last argument with his mother when he had returned from college for the first time, so full of himself. Now I am witness to the drama rather than an active participant. Perhaps I am learning something after all.

Over the next several days, his family relationships grew ever more troubled. Mealtimes were strained affairs. His mother did not say much, picking at her food, playing the role of martyr-victim that she knew and loved so well. His brother shouted, accused, and placed blame, giving voice to his fear and resentment. "If I could do it, I would. I'd take care of us. Then you could go away and never have to worry about us again."

It took a while, but eventually it worked. Torn between what he wanted to do and what he felt obligated to do, Adima lost his appetite and couldn't sleep. Barely able to focus on his meditations, he was a man consumed by guilt. *Poor Mother,* he thought to himself. *What am I doing to her? She needs me. I have no right to be so selfish. I'm her sole means of support. I've got to stop wasting my time in the woods and start taking care of my responsibilities.*

At last he could stand it no more. Succumbing to the feelings of guilt that were pressing in on him, Adima put his own affairs on hold to spend more time with family and focus on his public responsibilities.

It's just for a little while, he wrote in his journal, trying to reason with himself and justify his decision. *Until they get more used to the idea of my being on my own more often. I'll just help them get settled and able to fend for themselves, then I'll get right back to my training.*

It was to be his last journal entry for quite some time. The intention was there, perhaps, but not the action. Falling back into old patterns of caretaking, months went by, and he made no progress. He did not pray, did not meditate, did not walk in the forest.

CHAPTER ♂ 30

Everybody wants to be somebody; nobody wants to grow.
—Johann Wolfgang von Goethe

It was the beginning of the second great period of his learning—the *Period of Sorting Out*. These were difficult times for Adima. He knew about change now, and even how change brought blessings and benefits. But his attention had shifted from the inner to the outer. He was completely focused on the material world.

Still, the opportunities for learning presented themselves. Adima was faced with conscious decisions about whether or not to accept and receive changes that were being offered to him. That which he once thought had value was now getting in his way and actually keeping him from doing what he really wanted to do. Yet what other choice did he have?

"I must take care of my family. I must make my way in the world." Obsessed with these responsibilities, placing them as his highest priority, he concentrated on his duties, sat in on Council sessions, attended meetings, traveled. It wasn't long before the sweet smell of success caught him with its enticing aroma. He fell off the Grail Path and back onto a path of materialism and worldly success. Yet through it all, the Third Force—the Higher Being—kept careful watch, presenting life experiences designed to teach the difference between that which was valuable and that which was valueless. Over the next several years, he was faced with many decisions and many opportunities to discard what was valueless.

To Adima, however, all such opportunities to follow his bliss involved a lot of fear. What would happen to him if he were to just go off and live in a cabin in the woods? What would happen to his mother and younger brother? How would they eat? Where would they live? What if they got sick?

"Someday I'll do it," he promised himself each time he lay awake in the night tossing and turning, burdened by the stress of the life he had chosen. "After I'm a success, I'll retire and be able to do everything I used to do. Once all of my responsibilities are met, I'll be able to take care of me. Someday, someday, someday..."

Drifting off to sleep, he had the best of intentions, but always on the morrow the fear was there, and so he continued to follow the safe path, the known path, the comfortable path. It took a long time and a lot of learning before Adima understood that all persons, events, encounters, and circumstances contributed to his learning and the definition of who and what he truly was, thereby making him complete.

Fortunately, his foundation was solid, and he did not let go of everything that he had learned. He still held to a once-a-week meditation, still fasted occasionally, still practiced the lessons when he remembered them. It was not a total loss. The new had just gotten shoved aside temporarily in favor of a more comfortable and familiar path—the way of fame and success. It took a long time for Adima to return from his detour. But inevitably he was led back. It took time, and it took a powerful nudge to get his attention. It was the beginning of the third major period of his life—the *Period of Relinquishment*.

CHAPTER 31

*What would life be if we had no
courage to attempt anything?*

—Vincent van Gogh

At first, Adima perceived the *Period of Relinquishment* as a time of sacrifice, of having to give up what he desired most, including his sanity and life itself. There was much conflict between the old and the new, a lot of stress and tension until he learned that he was actually giving up nothing in exchange for a new sense of freedom and lightheartedness as, one by one, the shackles of his limiting thoughts were removed. Before he could arrive at that realization, however, he had to answer a giant *wake-up call* from the universe.

*****

The thunderbolt came out of a clear, azure sky as he was standing in a field of wildflowers. Striking him down, lifting him up, tossing him through the air, filling him with an electrical charge—shocking him, jolting him, deafening him.

He had been sitting in the field meditating, as he had been instructed to do so long ago. Several miles to the south, thunderheads were building, but they seemed to pose no immediate danger. So he had closed his eyes and let the vision come. It was a very strong meditation, an overwhelming sensory experience. "This is no ordinary reverie," Adima realized almost immediately. Never had he experienced anything quite like this violent barrage on his senses. He could not only see images, but hear them and feel them as well.

Part of him wanted to open his eyes, so terrified was he of the vividness of the experience. But another part of himself would not allow it, for the journey promised to be far too incredible, far too fascinating. So, summoning his courage, he kept his physical eyes shut and continued to experience the vision through his mind's eye.

A fiery whirlwind descended toward him...huge, almost a mile wide, kicking up great clouds of dust and debris. Adima raised his arms, trying to protect himself, but he was powerless against such titanic forces. Spinning counterclockwise, the tornado caught him in its viselike grasp, lifting him up like a rag doll and bearing him off—unwillingly—into the unknown. Instantly, the immediate surroundings of the field melted away as time and space lost all meaning and the laws of physics and the material world evaporated.

He felt himself moving at incredible speed within the vortex, spinning round and round as the hands of time turned ever backward toward an age before the beginning of the world. Then he was falling, plummeting downward in inky blackness, screaming and screaming in absolute terror, until, with startling abruptness and equally startling gentleness, he landed in the midst of an astounding scene.

The sky was red with fire and black with soot. The acrid stench of sulphurous flames filled his nostrils. Black smoke boiled upward, forming billowing clouds, blocking out a blood-red sky. The ground itself, if indeed it was ground, was on fire—seething, boiling, and buckling under titanic forces of heat and pressure. The noise was deafening, a great cacophony of sound—the boom of terrible engines of destruction, the clash of primal forces coming together in conflict, screams of rage and pain, the wails of the suffering, the death rattle of the mortally wounded.

"It is the War in Heaven—the legendary battle between the spirits of Light and Dark," Adima realized. "And I, Adima, am witness to it all!"

A mighty trumpet blast smote his ears. Trembling, he looked up to gaze upon an awesome sight. "The Archangel of the Grail!" he gasped, the recognition instantaneous. Above him in the distance, enveloped in swirling mists of light, a mighty winged figure led an array of angelic hosts as they descended upon a pack of fierce, howling demons. Formed of molten gold in the consecrated fire of the Blacksmith's forge, the angel's helmet sparkled and shone in the light. White raiment fell in shining folds of living beauty from that mighty breast.

"Absolute purity of heart," Adima breathed in awe, beholding the majesty and power of this heroic being. Such was his joy and wonder that he found it impossible to avert his gaze from that translucent Spirit, whose countenance, he would describe later, was like the countenance of the Great Creator.

In his right hand, the Angel grasped an incredible Sword—a Blade of Light—which he smote across the Heavens with immeasurable purpose and Divine Will. Flashing forth from the blade, lightning forked down to strike clusters of demonic spirits who sought to re-enter the celestial worlds from which they had been cast out.

Adima had heard tales of the horrors and carnage of war, but nothing in his limited experience had even remotely prepared him for this incredible scene in which the evil spirits were thrown back in desolation before the uncompromising might of this Guardian of the Threshold of Heaven.

As the battle came nearer, like the approach of a terrifying cosmic thunderstorm, Adima, too, felt himself within the range of that purging sweep of the Spirit-Sword. He was tempted to flee in panic along with the grotesque creatures surrounding him on all sides, who seemed to have come alive from the nightmarish paintings of Atlantean fairy tales and myths. Somehow, however, he found the courage to remain.

"Open yourself to the purifying flame!" The angel's voice rang in his ears.

"What does this mean?" Adima wondered. "Is the angel going to smite me with his Sword?"

He tried to run but could not. His legs were as lead. There would be no escape from the swift and terrible approach of the Archangel of the Grail. Adima could hear the rush of wings, could feel the enormous heat of the Light Blade.

Lifting his eyes, he saw the winged warrior hovering above him. "No use," he muttered to himself as he stopped trying to resist the inevitable. "I cannot fight this power greater than myself. I surrender," he cried, opening his arms wide. "I willingly reach out and open myself to the purging fire."

The lightning struck, and Adima gasped as the enormous bolt penetrated his body, bringing with it incredible, searing pain and anguish. He felt as though he was being hollowed out as the enormous energy burned into his very soul. When he could withstand the agony no longer, he swooned into unconsciousness.

As suddenly as the transcendent experience had overcome his physical senses, Adima now found himself back with an equally breathtaking abruptness in the field of wildflowers. His right hand was fully extended as though he was grasping at something, his fist clenched so tightly that his fingernails had drawn blood in his palm. Enoch was standing there, reaching out to him. Adima crawled into his teacher's arms.

The sun was shining through billowing white clouds, illuminating the multicolored field of flowers. A gentle breeze was blowing, and butterflies flitted on the gentle currents from one colorful blossom to another. Bees hummed, gathering pollen and nectar with which to make honey. The contrast between the peaceful field and the wrathful energy of the War in Heaven from which he had just emerged stretched his mind to its utmost limits.

"How long?" he barely managed to gasp. But Enoch made no answer. Adima never knew if he had been lying there for hours, minutes, or just a few brief seconds.

*****

Adima languished for months, not alive but also not dead. Physically he was very much in the world, dressing himself, eating, and moving about as though nothing out of the ordinary had happened. Emotionally and spiritually, however, he was in a transitional state, hovering on the border between two worlds. Each moment of each day he was faced with the decision of whether to stay or go.

"I can't make up my mind," he told Enoch as the old man sat by his bedside. "I don't like this world anymore, of that I'm sure. But I also don't know what the other world is like, and I'm sure I don't want to go there. I'm so depressed." And he was, sinking deeper and deeper into the abyss of his own negative thoughts and fears.

One day, from out of nowhere, the terror came. Not the ordinary fears that he always felt, this was something different—vastly larger and more powerful, a force from outside himself, a nameless, shapeless dread, as of impending doom.

"He has entered the Great Void," the High Priestess explained to his mother, who had requested healing for her son. "Pregnant with all possibilities, it contains both the questions and the answers." The two women looked down on Adima as he lay huddled under the blankets, staring with sightless eyes at some terrifying vision. "He is in there alone. Whether he chooses to come out depends on him. It is the next step in his journey and learning."

It was true. Alone in the Void, Adima was experiencing what the *Book of Life* described as...

THE GREAT ENIGMA OF THE ANATOMY OF EMPTINESS, IN WHICH THE SOUL MUST SEEK IMMEASURABLE FULLNESS IN AN APPARENT VOID.

"How can I accomplish this?" he wondered, not really understanding the meaning of the words as he read them. He determined to seek out Enoch and ask his advice.

"You must learn to empty your mind of all thought and desire," Enoch explained the passage in simpler terms. "For it is only by reconciling your will to the one *Higher Will* that you will eliminate the fear and resolve the tension."

There were tears in Adima's eyes as he listened to his teacher. "I don't know how," he said humbly in a final act of surrender. "I want to learn, but I'm so afraid. Help me, please."

Enoch came and sat beside his student, stroking the young man's head and speaking softly. "Serenity is God kissing the Soul," the old man whispered in Adima's ear. "Allow yourself to be kissed." He placed the palm of each hand on either side of Adima's head in a gesture of benediction. Closing his eyes, he breathed deeply in and out three times. "Empty out now," Enoch guided. "Use the power of the breath to cleanse and heal. Breathe out the stale vapors of contagion and death; inhale the life-giving breath of Spirit."

Adima felt a deep sense of peace sweep over him. For a moment, the fear was gone, and he felt perfectly safe and healed and whole. Doing as he was told, he made deep, slow inhalations and exhalations. It was not long before his body began to tingle, his senses heightened, and he moved into a higher level of awareness.

"Tell me what you are experiencing," Enoch urged, knowing that a vision was in progress.

From that faraway place of peace, Adima saw himself as a child in bed waking up in the morning. "I see Father Love reaching out to me as I sit up and reach out to him." He spoke the words reverently, with awe. "As he takes my hands in his, I realize that my bed is Mother Earth, and she is gently releasing me into my Father's arms. As I stand up, my

Father and Mother stand on either side of me, holding my hands. I grow into adulthood between them as they hold me, and when I am grown, they turn their faces to me and kiss me, one on each cheek." Adima held the vision as long as he could, feeling the serenity.

"Return now to your vision of the War in Heaven." Speaking softly, Enoch continued to hold Adima's head between his palms, gently leading him back to the vision in the field of wildflowers. "Behold the mystery in which the Imagination of Nature clothes itself as a thought within your mind."

Swirling patterns of colored light danced before Adima's eyes. One by one, beings both good and evil swam in and out of his field of vision. The thought occurred to him that, even though they were only thoughts, they were, nevertheless, quite real in the truest sense of the word—more real, indeed, than the very ground upon which he walked.

THERE ARE NO NEUTRAL THOUGHTS.

The words of the *Book of Life* echoed in his mind as he watched the Spirit-thoughts come and go before him.

"See the angelic hosts, the demonic spirits." Enoch's voice was guiding him through the experience. "Look around yourself with heightened awareness, with a new understanding. *For all of those angels and demons you see in your vision reside within you!*"

Adima started in amazement, but Enoch held him firmly in his grip. "Let the Light of Truth dawn in your heightened awareness. Each grotesque being that was cast out is a symbolic representation of your own Shadow nature. The Archangel of the Grail is you, yourself, casting out the demons of negative thought from your own mind before they can manifest as all of the deadly sins of the human condition.

"It is to the purging of such thoughts from the heaven of your own being that you dedicate yourself now. Clear your mind of all of the demons of negative thought and desire. Let go of guilt, shame, fear, rage, hatred, envy, jealousy. Then, in the void that is left behind, sit in the silence...a reverent and humble soul who awaits the Grace of the Divine."

Enoch paused to let the images float freely through Adima's inner vision. Gradually, a figure began to coalesce out of the shimmering patterns of light, taking shape and form before him. "Behold once again the Archangel of the Grail and remember, too, the Higher Being." Enoch's voice was small and far away. "For you know him well...the sublime, eternal aspect of your very Self."

The angel opened its mouth to speak. Strange words they were, reminding Adima of a vague, mysterious thought lingering just beneath the surface of his consciousness, a dim remembrance of an event of utmost importance, something that happened long ago and far away, before he was born.

"Remember your solemn oath in service to this Spirit of the Most High. Remember the pact between you both, made in the time before you came to Earth. This is what it really means to be a man, dedicating your whole life on Earth to the fulfillment of the aims of Spirit. Strive now to prepare yourself for the tasks that lie ahead, whatever they may be."

Enoch finished and released his hold on Adima's head. Slowly, the translucent figure of the angel receded into the swirling, luminous mists. Reluctantly, Adima opened his eyes.

"Continue this practice for a while," Enoch instructed as he departed. "See where it leads you."

Adima was only too glad to comply, for he found speech troublesome and action strangely disquieting. Thus, he entered into the *Silence* with a great deal of willingness. And therein an understanding of the workings of the Spirit-world—the world of the angels and Heavenly hosts—was born.

What are they doing? he wondered as he watched the magnificent beings moving through the Great Void at will, fashioning from their own intentions the physical world of the senses. And how might I do the same thing, focusing my own thoughts, intentions, and desires so that they take form and manifest for good in the physical world?

The spirits were more than willing to show him. Thus it came to pass that gradually, step by step, Adima acquired the gift of being able to empty his consciousness at will so that he could enter the invisible world of *Intention*. Once there, he would listen to that still, small Voice within the silent place in which Creativity was born. And, unlike Belial, he was learning it all by walking the Path of Direct Experience, without the aid of artificial stimulants, spells, potions, or black magic.

*****

From then on it was much easier, and Adima's learning progressed far more quickly. The time of transformation was upon him; he had emerged from the chrysalis and was ready to take on the new mantle of manhood that was waiting for him. Part of the spell had been broken.

During the months that followed his first vision of the Archangel of the Grail, he plunged into his daily meditation with new heart and resolution. He sought to move beyond mere visions of the Spirit-world, seeking now to make personal contact. He felt a deep sadness, an ineffable longing and loss at being disconnected from the angel. How he longed to see that mighty being once again, to stand in its presence and enter into direct communion with that sublime Spirit who served the purposes of the Divine.

"To achieve what you desire demands strength of will," Enoch told him, picking up a knapsack and beginning to stuff a few random articles of clothing into it. They were preparing for the first of many excursions to Mount Kylene. Adima had never been there, but he had heard many tales of the sacred mountain—a holy place of great beauty and wonder, marked with the footprints of the Guardians.

"Your goal is worthy because you desire to know yourself and become aware of the real nature of your individual spirit." The old man paused to see whether his student was paying attention. Whenever he did that, Adima knew, the next words were important and should be attended to very carefully.

"What you find may startle you at first. Indeed, it may even upset you, as it has so many others who aspire to ascend to this ultimate realization of the Grail."

"What can be upsetting about coming to know myself?" Adima asked in open amazement. "I mean, that's the goal, isn't it? If that's what they're striving for and that's what they achieve, then why the shock?"

Enoch shook his head and sighed. "Expectations, my boy, expectations. They don't find what they expect to find. And when they don't, for many the center of their world collapses."

"Why?" Again Adima did not understand. "What's the big surprise?"

Enoch put down the knapsack and scratched his chin, as if deciding whether or not to reveal this secret bit of truth. At last he spoke a single phrase. *"The discovery that they are not their earthly egos."*

Adima let the words simmer a while in his brain before responding. "I think I understand," he said at last. "The key to understanding this lies in taking that realization one step further. As it says in the *Book of Life*:"

> THE CENTER AND CORE OF ONE'S BEING IS NOT THE EARTHLY SELF.
> IT IS THE ETERNAL SELF REFLECTED THERE.

He looked proudly at his teacher, pleased at having reasoned this through on his own.

"Excellent," Enoch shared his delight, overjoyed at his student's intuition and skill in drawing this further conclusion. "Because you have reasoned this out so well, let me give you something else for your active mind to chew on. *The day will come,*" Enoch hinted mysteriously, *"when you will see your true name inscribed in the cold steel of the Hard Lightning. When you can read that name, you will know that you indeed have achieved Inner Vision."*

The old man snapped shut the clasp on the knapsack, slung it over his back, and walked out the door. "Bring the tent and supplies," he called over his shoulder. Those boxes are too heavy for me to carry."

Adima wanted to ask more about the mysterious name, but Enoch was already halfway down the road. By the time he caught up, the old man was engrossed in another topic.

"I give up," Adima said to himself. "He's not going to tell me, so I'll just have to live with it and wait and see."

*****

"Over the next several months, you have two goals," Enoch explained as they were returning from the high places, where Adima had experienced his first vision quest. *"First, to further your capacity to create vivid mental images. And second, to learn to wield your thoughts as if they were things."*

Their seven days in the wilderness had been mostly uneventful, except for a single conversation. Looking out over the Earth from the barren rock of Mount Kylene, Adima had grown philosophical and introspective.

"What do you see out there?" Enoch was whittling a piece of pine, attempting rather unsuccessfully to carve a face in the soft wood. A small pile of shavings was collecting in his lap.

"I see the Creator," came the reply.

"Tell me, what does this Creator of yours look like?"

Adima looked straight out into the sunset, its brilliant red and purple hues streaking the sky with cold fire. "I see the Creator as an all-powerful being," he said, "an old man who dwells apart, high in the Heavens." He swept his arm in an arc across the sky. "He is a powerful Creator, a strict Creator, a demanding Creator."

Enoch frowned and raised one eyebrow, but kept silent. Adima continued.

"He lives by a strict moral code, and therefore he has imposed a rigid set of rules upon me. I have no choice but to obey those rules, more often out of fear than out of love."

"This is a very limiting Creator." Enoch did not look up from his whittling. The pile of shavings was growing, but the image in the stick was no closer to being recognizable. "He is as restricted as you are, as limited as you are."

"Well, that's the Creator I've always known," Adima replied, as though there were nothing he could do about it. "It's the Creator my parents introduced me to, and the Creator I've seen working in my life all of these years."

"Why don't you do yourself a favor and let your old definitions of things go," Enoch said without looking up. "This night, add a new practice to your daily routine."

"What's that?" Adima wanted to know.

"Look at everything around you in a new way, with a fresh eye. Just observe, like you are doing now, but do not judge anything. Simply let your experiences teach you, whatever they may be. Most of all, do not try to define the Creator, because you are facing an impossible task. Many have tried before you, and many will try after you. Your energy will be much better spent in trying to *experience* the Presence of the Divine. Don't try to give it a name. Live the experience!"

It was good advice. Adima took it, and so his fullness had developed.

*****

As his awareness and consciousness expanded each time he had a new experience or a new understanding, another shackle slipped away. Another chain was loosed. Another bar in his prison cell was removed. As he dropped the limitations within his thought processes, things grew larger, life grew larger, *he* grew larger. Whatever was happening to him was extremely personal. He could not explain it even to himself, let alone to family and friends, or even to Enoch. The transformative experience was so personal, so deep, that it was beyond words.

His fullness, however, was reflected in his actions, in his bearing, in his whole way of being. One had only to look at him to realize that here was someone who was different. Not unusual, not peculiar, but very, very different.

"Be bold in direct action and truly cooperative in your intention," Enoch said, quoting from the *Book of Life*.

Adima took that advice to heart, and it was reflected in his life. Building, always building, his way was a practical, worldly way, settling first the personal parts of his life, then turning his energy and power outward. Always and everywhere he was cultivating new relationships...not relationships based on fear, shifting and changing with the wind, but rather genuine relationships based on mutual love, affection, and trust. Even his relationship with his family improved.

Sitting in Council, his decisions were wise and just, his thinking clear. He made mistakes, it is true. He sometimes chose the wrong course. But his motives and intentions were pure, and he was able to recognize a wrong decision almost at once and take steps to rectify it. This honesty, integrity, and easy-mannered lifestyle earned him the respect and admiration of many a senior Council member. "What does he know? How does he do it? What is his secret?" These were the questions they bantered back and forth amongst themselves as they tried to understand this strong new personality who had risen up amongst them.

Adima had something that they wanted, although they did not know what that "something" was. All they knew was that he seemed less troubled by life than they were. He had an easy way of dealing with the quirks, vagaries, and unknowns of life as they arose. There was very little drama, and a lot of peace of mind.

"I don't understand it," he told Enoch during one of their innumerable discourses in the Lighthouse. "People come to me for advice. They look to me for leadership and counsel. It is as though they are my disciples."

Enoch nodded his head in agreement. "You seem surprised by this," he smiled. "Why is that?"

"Because I have given no special teaching or made any great orations. I've done nothing to promote my philosophy of life, nothing to..."

"Wait." Enoch raised his palm to interrupt the conversation. "This isn't about your words or beliefs or teachings. This is about your *actions*!"

"Actions?" Adima repeated the word, not understanding where Enoch was taking the dialog.

"Actions!" Again Enoch emphasized the word. "It is time you realized that there are going to be others who are inspired by what you do and how you behave. Therefore, you must take full responsibility for your actions. You can no longer use ignorance as an excuse, because you are no longer ignorant."

To Enoch, this principle was quite simple, as matter-of-fact as any other of the physical laws to which the material world conformed. Thus, it was easy to understand, and therefore, easy to accept. Adima, though, was not so readily convinced.

"Hold on," he interrupted. "This is too much responsibility for me. I don't want a following. I don't want to be responsible for influencing other people's behavior. I've got enough trouble taking care of me!"

"Again you misunderstand," came the patient reply. "You have no choice in the matter, because of who you are and what you have embraced. People *will* follow after you, not because you have tried to convince them, *but because they are attracted to the truth that they see reflected in you.*"

Adima paused to reflect on these last words. Here was a new insight, a new truth to digest. "I don't know," he said doubtfully. He seemed almost frightened. Sensing this, Enoch went over to the *Book of Life*, opened to one of his favorite passages, and began to read.

THROUGH THE EFFECTUAL USE OF HIS WILL,
A CONSECRATED MAN CAN BECOME A SYMBOL OF COURAGE
FOR ALL THOSE WHO FOLLOW IN HIS FOOTSTEPS.

"It is about courage," he said, marking his place and closing the great book. "Courage and willpower. You must allow yourself to be a consecrated being. You must begin now to develop a fearless faith in yourself."

It was another beginning, the embracing of a new insight upon which Adima would reflect and meditate and dream, eventually coming to integrate the teaching into his life and thinking. It was to be the point of his greatest development—the journey out of timidity and fear into courage. It would not be an easy challenge, and it would take many years to achieve the goal. But eventually, he would rise to a level of achievement that few in history can claim to have reached.

*****

Always throughout this period, Adima was confronted with his dual nature as reflected in his magnetic personality. People were not lukewarm around him. They had extreme reactions to his presence, either for good or for bad. Many respected him, admired him, were drawn to him. So too, there were others who neither liked nor respected him. Without even knowing why, without even knowing the essence of the man, there were those who hated and feared him. These were the Adepts of the Sons of Belial.

"He must be a sorcerer," Draco declared. They were assembled in the Lair, as they had come to refer to the ruined stone temple that Belial had appropriated some years earlier. It was a most intimate gathering, reserved for the Inner Circle alone. The subject of the evening was "dangerous Atlanteans," a most serious topic, because any name mentioned during such discussions was soon to be named an official enemy of the State. And enemies of the State had a disconcerting habit of disappearing without a trace. This night, the name most often mentioned was Adima's.

"He has a strong connection to the Keeper of the Light. Perhaps he is a practitioner of black magic." Even the dim and flickering candlelight could not hide the shock, fear, and hatred on the faces of the members of the Inner Circle.

"If it is black magic, we need to know," a deep, muffled voice sounded from beyond the room. All heads turned as the hooded figure of Belial loomed in the passageway. "We cannot have practitioners of the black arts on the Council of Elders."

Instantly, the atmosphere in the room changed, becoming tense, strained. "Yes. Absolutely. Agreed." Each vied with the others to ensure that his was the loudest voice of assent. Each cast suspicious eyes around the Circle, looking to see who was in agreement with their leader and who dared to raise a challenge.

Such hypocrisy! The newcomer, Balor, scarcely dared even to think the words. The greatest of the Adepts in the forbidden black arts is the Chief Elder himself. Or am I experiencing mass denial? he wondered. For to admit the truth about Belial was to admit that their Circle was flawed, that they were following a dark and dangerous path to extinction, led by a Shadow magician.

Belial strode into the room, throwing back his hood as he walked, revealing that demonic, bone-white face. The Adepts knew that look. He was deep in the throes of one of Hanuman's potions. There would be no reasoning with the Master this evening. In fact, they would be lucky to leave the room unscathed.

"It is sorcery," he declared vehemently, pounding a giant fist on the table. Goblets of water spilled, dishes clattered to the floor, but the Adepts remained motionless, their faces blank and expressionless lest they be accused of displaying an emotion that might lead to a most hideous death. "No one can have such good fortune without sorcery. He must be stopped and punished. He must become an example!"

"You are absolutely right, Master," Draco warned, "but we must proceed carefully. It will not be so easy to accuse Adima of sorcery. He is very popular, and he has powerful friends. If we make unsubstantiated accusations against him, we will have an uprising on our hands as sure as the sun rises."

Belial's rage poured forth like an erupting volcano. Grabbing his closest advisor, he hurled the hapless man across the room, where he crashed into the stone wall, a broken and whimpering mass. No one moved. To have rushed to Draco's aid would have been to invite the same fate.

The insanity seemed to leave as quickly as it had come. "Draco speaks truly and wisely," Belial said calmly, helping his victim to his feet as though the violent episode had never happened. "Therefore, we must ensure that our accusations are not unsubstantiated, that, indeed, they are provable beyond any reasonable doubt." Gently, he helped the wounded man take his seat at the table once again.

"We shall appoint one from among us to observe Adima and catch him in the act." Belial chose his words carefully, making it clear that this was to be a covert act. "If we have proof, there is nothing his bleeding-heart allies can do. When we have proven that he has broken the ancient commandments, then we will be justified in putting him to death—publicly, as an example."

The leader of the Sons of Belial fixed his gaze on each man at the table in turn, staring into his eyes, reading his very thoughts. "Decide on the details, then put the plan into effect." He wheeled and left the room, leaving the Adepts to plan Adima's demise and soothe their broken comrade.

*****

Alone in his private chambers, Belial rubbed his hands in glee. It would be a glorious spectacle. First the arrest. All of Atlantis would be in an uproar. Then the public trial and the display of the incontrovertible evidence proving that Adima had defied the ancient laws against spiritual manipulation of the occult arts. The verdict would be swift and merciless—death by slow torture, followed by rending the body to pieces and throwing it to wild dogs for consumption. Disgrace and banishment for his family. Destruction of his heirs. Assumption by the State of all of his assets and fortunes.

At last, his dreaded enemy would be gone, once and for all. Belial's would be the final victory. Having hounded Adima mercilessly all these years, first marking him, then taking his brother, now Belial would take the most precious things of all—Adima's life, his fortune, and his future—all that he held dear, all that he loved. Oh, it would be glorious...

*****

The Adepts selected Balor as their spy. He was both a member of the Council and a secret member of the Sons of Belial, not having declared his party loyalty openly. This was intentional. It had been Belial's idea. "A spy will serve us in good stead one day," he had prophesied. It seemed that prediction was about to come true.

"You know Adima better than we do," the Adepts said, explaining the reasoning behind their choice. "Perhaps he will let his guard down in front of you and inadvertently reveal the secret. Approach him under the guise of friendship," they instructed. "Put on an air of desperation. Tell him you need help. Get him to trust you, then get him to reveal the secret...the magic behind the man."

Balor accepted the assignment reluctantly. He did not relish the idea of being a spy, but if it were true that this man was an enemy of the State and a threat to Atlantis, then it was certainly his duty to find out all he could and report the truth to his superiors. He planned carefully, choosing the early afternoon, when most of the Elders were resting. At such times, he knew, Adima sat in the Garden of the Heart in silent reflection and meditation. Often during such times, he would engage in long conversations with friends.

The day was warm, the sun was shining, and the birds were singing as Balor took his place in a concealed alcove behind a thick covering of flowering shrubs. The niche afforded perfect concealment as well as an excellent view. He did not have long to wait.

Hardly had he concealed himself when Adima entered the garden. Sitting on his favorite stone bench, he paused to peel some fruit while watching a colony of ants busily attacking a morsel of food that had been dropped by a picnicker. A man approached, another Elder.

"May I speak with you, Adima?" he asked somewhat hesitantly. "I know you are busy, but I need someone to talk to."

From his place of concealment, Balor grinned smugly, pleased with his good fortune in being able to overhear one of Adima's private conversations. This was too good to be true! Perhaps Adima would reveal himself without Balor having to take any action at all. In his excitement, the spy tried to position himself for a better view. Gently parting the foliage, he was careful not to rustle the leaves or make the slightest noise. He did not see the dried, brittle branch lying just beneath his boot.

The twig broke with a soft snap, not loud enough to startle anyone. Just loud enough to be noticed. Adima hesitated. Something was not quite right. He felt eyes upon him, prying eyes. Someone was watching, but who?

"I have problems, and they don't want to go away," the Elder went on, not waiting for permission to continue. "Life is wearing me down. I'm getting sick. I'm at the end of my rope."

"Why do you come to me?" Adima asked, still looking casually about him, trying to spot the object of his unease.

"What is your secret, Adima?" the man asked. "How do you handle life like you do? You seem to have the key. You seem to know the way. Can you show me? How can I be like you? What must I do?"

There it was, behind a gorgeous lavender bougainvillea—a glint of sunlight reflecting off polished metal. Careful not to stare directly at it, Adima watched from the corner of his eye. He was being observed, of that he was sure. But why, and by whom? he wondered. What was the motive behind this? And *who* was behind it?

His intuition enlightened him in a flash. Of course! This was Belial's doing, as it always was. Adima decided to take no action until he could find out more. I'll have to play along, he thought to himself. I'll have to be careful. But I also will hold to the truth. There can be no danger if I just hold to the truth.

He turned his full attention to the man seated beside him. "Of course I'll tell you," Adima replied with a twinkle in his eye, compassion in his heart. "I'll be glad to tell you, if you really want to know."

"Yes, I do" came the eager reply.

"Then let's take the next few hours to sit down and talk about it. "Here in this lovely garden, where we won't be disturbed, I shall tell you how it works for me."

"The next few hours!" came the chagrined reply as the Elder rose to leave. "I don't have that kind of time. I am a very busy man. I have important things to do, appointments to keep, people to see."

"I understand," Adima called to the retreating figure, not surprised by the man's reaction. It was always thus. It was human nature to want to know the secrets of life, but people were seldom willing to take the time to hear the details. "If you change your mind, I'll be here whenever you are ready."

Alone once again, Adima decided to have a little fun with the spy who was still concealed behind the thorn bush and completely unaware that he had been found out. Getting up, Adima meandered slowly through the garden, pausing now and then to smell a flower or watch a bird.

Balor remained motionless. He was disappointed in not having heard anything incriminating, but at the moment he was more afraid of being discovered. Cowering behind the bushes, scarcely daring to breathe, he watched as his enemy drew nearer and nearer to the hiding place. Perhaps he won't notice me, he silently hoped.

One butterfly in particular seemed to have captured Adima's complete attention as it flitted from flower to flower. First to the roses, then to the tulips, coming to rest at last amid the flowing bougainvillea thicket. "Hello there, little one," Adima whispered to the delicate creature. "Drinking the sweet nectar on this fine day? Let me help you find the tastiest flower." He reached his arm into the bush and pulled back the branches. It worked. The spy was exposed, sitting hunched within the tiny stone alcove, blinking in surprise.

"Hello," Adima smiled gaily. The man was so startled he almost fell into the thorns. Adima recognized the spy immediately. "This is a surprise," he continued innocently. "I didn't mean to disturb you. I had no idea I had company in the garden."

"No problem," Balor mumbled. "I, er, had come back here to, um, get out of the hot sun. It was so comfortable, I fell asleep."

How nervous he was, hands trembling, palms sweating. He can't even look me in the eye, Adima thought in amazement. How afraid he is! Yet Adima's first emotion was not anger. Although he sensed trickery and deceit in the man's heart, knowing he had been put up to this, Adima's own heart opened in compassion. Balor's mind was an open book. Belial's sinister plan was revealed in complete detail for Adima to see. Now that he was forewarned, he could defend himself. The first thing to do was to send a message back to Belial.

"It is good that you've had your rest, Balor," he remarked casually. "You'll need all of your energy when you report that you have learned nothing. Imagine how angry Belial will be when you tell him that there are no secrets, no mysteries to reveal."

Balor blinked in fear. How did Adima know? He had read his mind. It was sorcery after all! His jaw dropped open in amazement, and he shivered as a cold chill of fear swept over him. "You misunderstand," he stumbled to apologize, not wishing to offend a sorcerer who could read his very thoughts. "It was an accident. I mean you no harm. Please excuse me." The man turned on his heels and hurried away, glad to be out of the presence of one who had the power of life and death over him.

Adima stood for a long time, lost in thought. "I have not heard the last of this," he told Butterfly. "Like the fish in yonder pond, I shall be watched from now on. I shall have to be very careful to make sure that my actions are in accord with my principles."

*****

It was a time of cat-and-mouse. Everywhere he went, Adima felt those furtive eyes upon him, peering from behind corners from under half-closed lids, quickly looking the other way if he happened to turn his gaze in their direction. At the same time, more and more people came to him for advice. Some he knew, some he did not. Always, however, the questions were the same. "What is your secret? How do you deal with life as easily as you do? Can you help me do the same?"

Unlike the Elder who had approached him in the garden, some of these others took the time to inquire further. Were they spies? Adima did not know. He did not even bother to try and find out. For various reasons of their own, they had approached him, and he felt obligated to speak his truth to them. As Enoch had shared with him, so now he shared with others, regardless of their motives. Listening for those few hours, they were amazed at the scope and depth of the process.

"I could never do that," they would say. "I don't want to give that up or change that behavior."

"If a goal is important to you, you must be willing to do whatever it takes to achieve it," Adima would reply. "And if it has any worth or value at all to you, you will want to do whatever it takes and focus only on that goal."

He smiled, realizing how overwhelming the Path seemed to be when viewed from the beginning. "You don't have to do it all at once. Take your time. It's a lifelong process, one step at a time, until one day you look back and realize that all of those steps have combined to form a journey, and the journey is you—the whole Self that you now are. That's when you realize that the very next step you take is the beginning of the next journey. It's an upward spiral; it just keeps going round and round, and you keep ascending with it."

After such words, even fewer were willing to embrace the way, engage the process, and do the work. They wanted the quick fix. Adima's way took too long and required too much time and effort.

"Can't I just take a course or read a book? Better yet, can't I just swallow a potion? Maybe I really don't need that or it doesn't need fixing. Maybe if I ignore it, the problem will just go away." Human nature was already starting to shift. Stuff it, hide it, deny it, ignore it, and it will go away. Hear the truth and try to change the truth. Or worse, hear the Truth and live the Lie.

And all the while, month after month, the spying continued. At last, Adima could stand it no longer and approached Enoch seeking a solution. "I don't know how to stop it." He was exhausted from the constant stress and tension of always being on display. "It's a constant struggle, almost a war. I turn one way, they follow. I seek solitude, they're always there. I try to ignore them, they make their presence felt even harder. I lash out in anger, they deny my accusations. I can't win."

He threw up his hands in despair, sinking into the soft cushions of Enoch's couch. High up in the Lighthouse was the only place in all of Atlantis where he felt safe any more. Knowing his frustration and weariness, Enoch let him talk for as long as necessary.

"I sense a conflict coming," Adima continued, "a time of confrontation between Belial and me. We are going to come together face to face in direct confrontation, with the ability to do each other great harm. I sense battle."

"How do you feel about going into battle?" Enoch asked.

"My whole life has been a battle or a struggle in one form or another," Adima replied. "I'm no stranger to battle, but I'm not fond of it, either."

"Well, then, perhaps it's time for you to exercise more discernment before doing battle."

"What do you mean?" Adima was confused.

"I mean that you've chosen to see these past few months as a time of battle. You've created a very real enemy out there," Enoch waved his arm expansively. "You've struggled against that enemy. You've set up elaborate defenses, and now you are exhausted."

"What else can I do?" Adima asked. "I have to defend myself. They're setting me up to accuse me of being a sorcerer. Do you know what that means?"

Enoch's reply was to quote from the *Book of Life*:

THE ONLY MEANING IT HAS IS THE MEANING YOU GIVE IT.
IF YOU DEFEND YOURSELF, YOU ARE ATTACKED.

"Do you understand these truths?" The old man raised one eyebrow quizzically.

"I guess not," Adima laughed, "but I'm sure you'll explain them to me."

Enoch laughed too. "Am I that transparent," he asked, "or are you just getting to know me better?" The old man lit his pipe and settled himself deeply into the cushions. "By setting up defenses, you must perceive a real enemy, otherwise you would have nothing to defend against. Since you now perceive a battle, you devote all of your energy to fighting it."

"Well, aren't these men my enemies?" Adima asked. "Isn't there a constant battle being waged between Belial and me?"

"I don't know," Enoch answered, puffing contentedly. "That may well be, but for our purposes today, the battle is not the point. The lesson for you is how well you see the place that this particular battle has in the overall evolution of your life. If it does not have a significant function, do not waste time and energy engaging in it."

Adima paused to digest his teacher's words. He walked over to the windows and looked down upon the countryside. From this great height, Atlantis seemed so peaceful and calm. There was no sign of the turmoil within.

"Worthy or not, I'm quite afraid," he said at last. "I don't know if I can stand up to him. Even with all of my learning over the years, I'm still afraid."

"Courage," came the one-word response. "That's your point of greatest development." Enoch walked over to join him at the window. "You are afraid and you are not afraid. You are timid, yet you are also brave. It is a mighty paradox...a reflection of your duality, actually. On the one hand, you will do anything to avoid a confrontation and seek peace at all costs. Yet you will fight to the death to protect home, security, and family."

"What's your point?" Adima asked. Enoch was not telling him anything he didn't already know about himself.

"My point is this," Enoch snorted. "When doing battle, the key is to resolve the conflict, even if it means taking the hit and withdrawing from the field..." he paused, gesturing for Adima to complete the sentence.

"...to fight another day," Adima finished, the light suddenly flashing in his mind.

"To preserve something better and more noble," Enoch corrected. "That's the key—*retreat*, not flee. Through singular acts of resistance, make it difficult for your opponent to do more than just hold his own, even as you retreat from the field where you don't need or want to be."

Adima looked through the windows once again. It was hard to imagine enemies somewhere out there lurking in wait for him. "This is wonderful, and I'm grateful to you for teaching me," he said, "but I still don't understand how this insight will help me develop courage."

Enoch arose and went over to face his young student. He placed a warm palm on the power chakra in the center of Adima's chest and pressed forcefully on the solar plexus. "Courage and power are within you already," he revealed. "You don't need to 'develop' them, as you say. You merely need to keep them from being overpowered by the timid part of yourself, the one who is afraid all the time. You are most timid when you've gotten seduced off your path, when you've lost sight of your goals and become confused by the goals of other people. And that is how Belial is trying to lead you astray, by getting you to abandon that which you hold dear."

"So he can lead me into a morass to get me lost and entrapped and swallowed by quicksand." Adima was enthused. Why hadn't he figured this out for himself?

"So the point is..." Enoch urged him toward the moral of the lesson.

"Don't get sucked in. It's that simple." Adima was quite pleased with himself.

"Yes, it's simple," Enoch warned, "but it takes a great deal of understanding and spiritual development to realize that the battle need not be fought right now. It may be fought one day, perhaps, but not today. And if and when the time does come for the two of you to meet, you will know it is the right time, and you will be ready and well-prepared."

Adima grew somber as he thought about what might transpire between himself and Belial one day. He found it difficult to imagine what an encounter between them would be like. All he could think about was the outcome.

*****

The Sons of Belial could never understand the relationship between Enoch and Adima because, in their arrogance, they were not willing to even entertain the possibility that such relationships might exist, or if they did, that they would have anything of value to offer. They could not have been more wrong. For the nature of the relationship and the effects it was causing were subtle, so subtle that Adima himself wondered sometimes if they were really happening or if it was all in his imagination. It was so quiet, too, without fanfare or drama. So that on the surface, at least, his life seemed calm, even dull and boring.

What Belial perceived as a war—a constant struggle with victory and conquest as a goal—Adima came to see as a natural, inevitable process...a continuous journey that was at the same time part of a larger event, a single event—the awakening within the human family of the Consciousness of Freedom and the return to unity of purpose and being.

"*This is a required course,*" Enoch had told him when they had begun their work so many years ago. "*That you take it is inevitable. Only the time you choose to take it is up to you. You can do it now, or you can delay it. The choice is up to you.*"

Of course, Adima had chosen the now, and that had made all the difference. What had once so amazed him was now becoming familiar; he was getting used to miracles. He was getting used to talking to angels and having supernatural and spiritual events occur all around him.

"I don't get it," he told Enoch one day as they were walking along the Avenue of the Gods. "Nothing exciting happens to me any more."

"How so?" Enoch raised one eyebrow quizzically. It was a busy morning, and crowds of people hurried to and fro. The weather was warm but cloudy, and the sky glowed with a strange, silvery light. There would be a summer storm before the day was out, Adima remembered thinking later.

"I haven't had an exciting dream, meditations have been dull, no coincidences have occurred, no animal sightings. Life is becoming dull and ordinary."

Without a word, Enoch plucked at the sleeve of Adima's tunic and brought him over to a storefront, where their reflections appeared in a plate glass window. That old lesson he had tried so long ago in the puddle under a street lamp was about to have a different result.

"What do you see?" the old man asked.

"I see myself."

"Now be still and listen. What do you hear?"

"I hear the crowds walking by."

"Besides that. Attend, and listen more deeply."

Adima paused and cocked his head to one side. Below the surface noises of the street there were other sounds—subtle, steady rhythms. He felt the vibrations coming in through his feet and mingling with those within himself. "I hear my heartbeat, mingled with the pulse of the city," he replied.

"Now look down and around you. What do you see."

"I see ants dragging crumbs to their colony. I see the primrose blooming and the bees sucking nectar. I see people walking by."

"Now look up. What do you see?"

"I see a blue sky and fleecy white clouds. The sun is shining and some birds are flying overhead."

"Hmph," Enoch snorted. "No miracles, eh? Nothing unusual happening to you? Nothing out of the ordinary? Guess what, my boy!" Enoch slapped him on the back, a wide grin stretching from ear to ear. "You are absolutely right. It's all ordinary! You get up every day, your heart beats, the flowers bloom, the birds and bees go about their work, the sun moves across the sky. And you take it all for granted. You've gotten so used to it that you don't even pay attention to it." The old man shook his head and laughed heartily.

"Pay attention to what?" Adima asked, grinning in spite of himself.

"*To the miracle of life!*" Enoch continued walking along the street, smiling as he spoke, nodding to passersby. "To the sacredness all around you. To the fact that you are standing here in that perfectly functioning body in this perfectly harmonious world. You want a miracle? You try it. Go ahead, create yourself a body and a world. Then sustain it and maintain it and keep it all working in perfect order and harmony."

Adima looked around him, suddenly realizing that they were standing in the courtyard of the Temple. The magnificent columns and spires soared upward, a metaphorical reminder of the Atlantean aspiration to reach ever-greater heights of physical, mental, emotional, and spiritual achievement. He did not remember walking there, but here they were, a huge crowd milling all around them.

"Every instant is a miracle," Enoch was saying. "Every instant is precious. Every instant is so incredibly awesome and grand and magnificent and sacred that if you were to really pay attention to it, you would gasp in awe at the magnitude of what it truly is.

"But you want excitement. You want fanfare and drama." Enoch pointed to a particularly ominous-looking thunderhead looming over the Temple. "You want the Heavens to part and the sky to grow dark and the lightning to strike and a voice from the Spirit-world to cry out in a loud voice and speak to you. *Adima, I am the Lord. I want to talk to you.*" Enoch's tone was light, not mocking, but gentle and teaching. "But it doesn't work that way."

The old man looked at the vast, surging crowd—people from all over the world, making their pilgrimage to the holiest of holies. "You want a miracle? You want to hear the Voice of God and have a conversation with Spirit?" Enoch pointed to the marble steps leading up into the Temple. "Go and stand on those steps, stop the first person you meet, look into his eyes, and talk to him. There's your miracle. This is who you are—greater than the sum of all your parts."

Adima listened, and he understood. Of course! How perfectly natural and right! The face of the Divine peering back at him from the faces of everyone he met. The One Voice of Spirit talking to him through the many voices of all his brethren. He took a long look at the people around him. How different they all were, yet how alike...diversity in the midst of sameness. He heard the sweet melody of Cybele's voice singing softly in his ear.

> *The Divine in you, the Divine in me.*
> *Makes us whole, makes us see.*
> *Who we are, what to be.*
> *The Divine in you, the Divine in me.*

Now he understood the meaning behind the words of his wife's poem. "Thank you," he whispered in gratitude, both to the woman he loved and to the nameless throng who walked beside him on his journey. Then it suddenly occurred to him that he was not married! And who, indeed, was Cybele?

The next thing he knew, they were in the Garden of the Heart. It was Adima's favorite spot in the city. He could relax here, unburdening himself in the idyllic setting, stepping behind the garden walls and leaving the cares of the workaday world behind for a while. Sitting on a bench, they watched the birds flitting from one bush to another. Families strolled along the paths, children played on the soft green grass. Neither man spoke, content just to sit and enjoy each other's company.

It was a lazy afternoon, almost timeless. Adima felt his head nodding. Colors faded in and out, sounds mixed and merged into a steady, monotonous drone, his senses dulled, and he drifted in and out of sleep. He awoke with a start as a bony finger prodded him in the ribs. "Look over there." The old man pointed down a gently sloping hill, at the base of which lay a quiet pond. It was surrounded by azalea bushes in full bloom—reds and pinks and whites. Their subtle fragrance mingled with the honeysuckle and lilacs to create a most pleasant perfume.

"How can the azaleas bloom at this time of year?" Adima wondered, but there was no time for an answer. He looked in the direction in which Enoch was pointing. There at the pool's edge he saw a young child. The little girl could not have been more than two or three years old. She was playing by the water, and she was naked. "I wonder where her parents are?" Adima thought, looking around for any adult who might be missing a child. But there was no one there. He started to get up.

"Where are you going?" Enoch asked, holding his arm.

"To bring the child away from the water's edge."

"Why?"

"Lest she hurt herself or fall in and drown."

"Why not just wait and see what happens." Enoch's eyes were full of play. "You wanted a miracle. You wanted excitement. Well, don't go squandering an opportunity now that it is being presented. Just sit back and watch. You may learn something."

Adima looked at Enoch, his mouth hanging wide open. The old man gently pushed his chin closed, put his finger to his lips, and pointed in the direction of the child.

The little girl was running happily along the water's edge, laughing and pointing to something in the pond. Adima strained to see but couldn't quite make out what it was. Suddenly she stood quite still, then lay down flat on her belly, arms poised. For a moment, she was as still as the rocks around her. Then she reached out, plunging her hands into the water as though trying to catch hold of something.

"She's trying to catch a goldfish," Adima realized, laughing at the little girl's repeated efforts to catch the elusive creature. Time after time she plunged her hands into the water. Time after time she came up wet, but empty handed. "She's persistent, I'll say that for her," he commented to Enoch.

"Yes, she is," came the offhanded reply. "Why don't you go down there and talk to her?"

Adima looked at the old man.

"Go on," Enoch urged. "Maybe you can help her!"

But it was not about helping a child catch a goldfish, of that Adima was sure. There was another lesson here. Slowly, he approached the child. "What are you doing, little one?"

"Trying to catch something in the water." Her tiny, melodic voice reminded him of wind chimes.

"Do you know what it is?"

"It's pretty and has lots of colors and it moves very fast and I want it."

The fish darted in and out among the rocks and lily pads, making its way to the far side of the pond. The child followed gleefully as Adima watched.

"Do you know what you are witnessing?" Enoch whispered at his elbow.

Adima nodded his head but did not speak. It was all so strange.

"Am I dreaming?" he mumbled to himself, suddenly not sure whether he was awake or asleep. Looking around, the experience seemed real. Enoch seemed real, the child seemed real, he himself felt real, and the surroundings were quite familiar.

But this could be a lucid dream. He had been having more and more of them lately—sharp, crystal-clear images and experiences so lifelike, so impossibly real that he was certain at the time that he could not be dreaming. Yet always the visions faded, and he awoke in the familiar surroundings of his own bedchamber, the memory of the experience fresh in his awareness. "I know I was not asleep," he had said to himself, time after time. Yet the mystery remained. Where had he been, if not asleep?

Enoch was speaking again. "When you are confronted with a symbol," he said, "take the time to attend to its meaning, for therein lies a gift of great value. Empty yourself, and reach out with a pure and unconditioned mind to embrace these most elementary experiences which natural life offers to you."

Adima shook his head in perplexity. "What in the world does that mean?" he wondered. Enoch often spoke strangely, but he usually understood what his teacher was saying. Now, however, he had to attend very carefully to understand the meaning of his words.

"Come here, child," Enoch called by way of explanation. The little girl ran over to them. "Tell this man who you are and what you are doing."

"I am the Innocent reaching out for understanding," the little girl spoke with a wisdom far beyond her years, "trying to satisfy my curiosity about what seems mysterious and fleeting."

Adima gasped in astonishment. Her form and actions were those of a child, but her voice was that of a mature woman. Now he knew he was dreaming, or if not dreaming, at least in some sort of altered state of consciousness. The naked child, the goldfish, the pond—everything was symbolic, with a deeper significance and a hidden meaning. There was a message here, he knew, and it was his task to decipher it.

"What is in the pond that you want?" Adima questioned the delicate creature before him.

The child-woman clapped her hands over her mouth and giggled happily, taking Adima's hand and leading him to the water's edge, squealing with glee as the goldfish jumped, glistening in the light. Again the startling contrast of the woman's voice speaking from the child's body.

"The pond represents my Infant mind," she explained, wading out into the water, "which has a very limited scope of consciousness. The goldfish symbolizes the Innocent's first awareness of the greater meaning of life. It is that awareness—that swift and elusive realization—which I eagerly reach out to catch." The child looked deeply into Adima's eyes, wanting to make sure he understood.

He nodded as the symbolic message became clearer. He almost had it. One last question to ask.

"Why are you naked?"

The child whirled and spun around faster and faster until she tumbled dizzily to the ground. Giggling and waving merrily, she started to run across the lawn, calling back over her shoulder in a strong, mature voice. "My mind is innocent and spontaneous, unclothed by cultural rules, unrestrained by do's and don't's." Then she was gone, skipping gaily down a bark-covered trail.

Adima shook his head and looked at Enoch. "I think I'd better sit down," he said when he could collect his thoughts. The old man just laughed.

They returned to the bench. "So tell me," Enoch urged. "What have you learned?"

Adima spoke slowly, trying to sort out the exact meaning of the experience. Somehow, his unconscious mind had understood everything he had just seen, and now he heard himself explaining the symbolism to himself. "I think I just witnessed the first spontaneous quest for knowledge, for that ever elusive understanding of life," he said. "The child showed me the first curiosity of being—untiring eagerness, unsocial, perhaps even infantile cravings." He paused to look at Enoch. "What I can't figure out is how to relate this to myself."

"The child was showing you both the present and the future," Enoch explained. "The most important symbols here are Purity and Understanding. The Child-Innocent is the true wildness—unsophisticated yet also non-judgmental."

"Remember when I stopped you from approaching her too soon?" he reminded. "You would have said 'don't' to her, restrained her. That would have been too bad, for then she would not have been free to indulge her nascent curiosity about life, which makes her child's mind reach out in spontaneity rather than in the mere imitation of elders."

"And I probably would have awakened from this most incredible dream," Adima said to himself.

Enoch nodded his head in agreement. "Because you would have refused to give yourself permission to play in the dream," he said. "How many times, day in and day out, do you say 'don't' to yourself?"

Adima made no answer. He knew the dream's meaning now. It was a reminder to play and explore and be free. It was an exhortation to allow himself the freedom to not be limited by the beliefs of others or of the society in which he was raised.

The scene shifted once again. They were standing before the Great Pyramid, looking up the sloping sides toward the apex, which gleamed brightly in the late afternoon sunlight. "Not only did the child show you yourself as you are now," Enoch continued as the sun sank rapidly in the west, "she also pointed out the evolutionary process you will follow as you continue on your journey."

The light was growing brighter. As he listened to his mentor, Adima had to squint to avoid being blinded by the sun's rays shining directly into his eyes.

"Yours is the innocence of the tiny being rather than the Elder." Enoch's disembodied voice seemed to be coming from a dark shadow in front of the Temple. "In order to evolve and mature, however, that innocence has to undergo additional transformations. You must move through the nobility and kingliness of the Lion to become the Servant—the

Priest-Shaman who will help his people move out of one way into another, out of one world into another, out of one life into another through a symbolic death, place, and time..."

As he was speaking, Enoch's words grew slurred and dull. Adima strained to hear, but he could not make out the rest of the teaching. At the same time, the bright afternoon light suddenly faded, the image of the Great Pyramid faded, and he found himself alone in total darkness.

"Where am I?" he cried out, sitting up and looking about him. It was his own bedchamber, and he was in his own bed. Had the whole day been a dream, from his early-morning walk along the Avenue of the Gods to the late-afternoon encounter with the child in the Garden of the Heart? It would seem so. Time had moved swiftly throughout the day, changing from early morning to midday to late afternoon, each with its own distinct weather pattern and natural setting.

His conversations had been strange, too. The language was formal, the vocabulary stilted and obtuse rather than the typical conversation of two people engaged in an ordinary chat. Then, of course, there were the symbols—the Avenue of the Gods, the crowds, his reflection in the glass, the Temple, the Garden, the pond, the goldfish, the Great Pyramid.

And the Child-Woman! He lay awake for a long time, thinking of the tiny little girl and their interplay. She had brought joy to his heart, and now he missed her, he really did. And most of all, he wanted to play some more.

Vowing to take time to play each day, no matter how busy he got, Adima wondered about Enoch's last words, those he hadn't quite heard. What had he missed? What was his unconscious mind trying to tell him about the next stages of his journey? Try as he might, he could not remember. At last he gave up trying. So it all had been a dream. Or had it?

"I wonder," he said to himself as he drifted off to sleep. His last waking thought was of the faceless woman whose poetry had so touched his heart—Cybele—she who was to be his wife.

CHAP♂ER 32

Where love reigns, there is no will to power; and where the will to power is paramount, love is lacking. The one is but the shadow of the other.

—Carl Jung

Back in the Light, feet firmly planted on the Grail Path, Adima walked with confidence, and whole new worlds opened up to him. He could not have gotten off or changed course now if he had wanted to, and he certainly did not want to.

It was the fourth stage of his learning—a *Period of Settling Down*—and it was to last from the time of his first meeting with Cybele, through their courtship, wedding, and birth of their children, and through the next fourteen years, culminating with the Dragon Festival on the Winter Solstice in the Year of the Child.

*****

The most significant event of the Period of Settling Down was the kindling and cementing of the relationship between the man and the woman—Adima and Cybele. For many years, each had been working to balance opposing forces within themselves and so consummate a mystical marriage within themselves as individuals. Now, in marriage, they sought to accomplish the same thing together, thereby birthing a third—the *Relationship*, in which the separated duality would again become one.

Early in this period, although relatively late in their lives by Atlantean standards, Adima and Cybele met, fell in love, and got married. Each was thirty-three years old; each was ready.

They met quite by accident one afternoon in the Garden of the Heart. He was lost in thought, paying scant attention to either the weather or the people around him. Thus, he did not notice the laughing group of priestesses come strolling into the garden from the Temple precincts. Nor did he notice the change in the weather. It had been threatening to rain, and the sky had turned a slate gray. There was no thunder, just the oppressive heat and humidity that often presaged a summer storm in Atlantis. The rain started without warning. His first indication that anything was amiss was when a large drop struck him squarely on the nose. Then another, and another. Within seconds, everyone had been caught in a teeming downpour.

Amidst happy shrieks of distress, people scrambled for shelter. Not that there was any danger. It was more to avoid the inconvenience of spending the afternoon in wet clothes. Adima made a mad dash for the shelter of an overhanging alcove. Others had already crowded within. "Hurry," they cried, beckoning to him as he ran toward them. The rain was torrential now, with sheets of water cascading down on him. Running was really pointless. By the time Adima got to the alcove he was saturated, as were most of the people who had crammed themselves into the tiny niche.

"Got room for one more?" he cried as he squeezed under the overhand. He pressed in as tightly as he could, just out of the water's flow. Laughing heartily in spite of his bedraggled condition, he apologized for adding to the crowd.

"You might as well stay out in the rain," a woman's voice teased. "You can't get any wetter." That voice—familiar yet not familiar! He turned to look at the speaker, and suddenly he knew. It was the woman from his dream, whose poem he knew so well. Their eyes locked. "It was a moment of instant recognition," each would say later. "We were complete strangers, yet it was like seeing an old friend. That's when we knew that this was the one."

Old friends indeed, one from whom he had been separated for a long, long time; one for whom she had been seeking far and wide. Adima looked at the woman, not realizing then that she would present him with the opportunity to confront his *Anima*, the unrecognized feminine and intuitive parts of his own personality.

Her long auburn hair was tied back in a gentle sweep off her face. The white of her priestess robes contrasted nicely with her dark skin, gently cooling the blush in her cheek. He scarcely noticed her figure and could not remember later if she was tall or short, thin or heavy. It was her lovely face that caught and held his attention—the large dark oval eyes, high cheekbones, and straight nose. And that smile! A smile of perfect light and joy. She's smiling at *me*! he realized, thrilling to the feeling. There is Heaven in that smile. I could be forever content in that smile. I could get lost in that smile.

Cybele looked at the man who would reflect the *Animus*, the masculine power of reason and assertion that Atlantean society had told her to hide. Strong and handsome, yes. But his most striking feature was not his rugged good looks; rather, it was the gentle air of confidence and serenity that he seemed to exude. He's different! she thought to herself. There's a calm Center within him.

They spent the rest of the afternoon together, talking and getting to know each other. The rain stopped as quickly as it had started, so they sat in the sunshine while he dried out, talking about those things that young people who are attracted to each other talk about when they first meet. He told her about himself, she told him about herself. Their conversation was casual, relaxed, and most pleasurable. They parted company reluctantly, promising to see each other again soon.

That was how it all started. Falling in love was easy. It required no effort at all. It happened without being forced or manipulated...the next right part of the natural unfolding of their lives.

"How can you be so sure?" Enoch asked when Adima told him the good news.

"I just know," he replied. "My heart told me. I feel it inside. It's funny. The first time I saw her, I knew we would be married one day."

Their wedding day dawned clear and bright. Much of Atlantis turned out to witness the joining of these two popular young people. Family, close friends, acquaintances, even strangers...they all gathered together within the Temple of Poseidon to witness the exchange of vows.

"Look," the celebrity-watchers exclaimed. "There are the King and the royal family."

It was a colorful ceremony. The Grand Hall was filled with bouquets of fresh flowers—lilies, roses, carnations, daffodils, bird-of-paradise, orchids, and a hundred other gorgeous blossoms. The air was perfumed with the aroma of jasmine and mint and citrus. Children had strewn rose petals all over the floor and out into the courtyard.

Strains of a harp filled the cavernous chamber with soft music. The happy couple walked arm in arm down the long aisle toward the altar, which was adorned with the symbols of duality and fertility—wine, bread, corn, and water in various forms and combinations. On either side stood the opposites—the Virgin Corn Goddess, manifestation of the Great Mother; and the Sun Hero, adorned with corn and surrounded by hummingbirds. Friends and loved ones lined the way, smiling and beaming, wishing them well, wishing them luck, wishing them health and good fortune.

Suddenly, a shadow flickered across the room, just a flicker, so subtle as to pass almost unnoticed by the throng of revelers. Adima saw it, however, as did Cybele—an aspect of fear and death that had come to haunt the wedding.

Cybele looked at the man—the stranger, actually—walking beside her. *What if the part of myself with whom I am walking to the altar turns and overwhelms me?* she wondered.

What if it does not work out? Adima wondered as he looked at the woman whom he barely knew. *What if the joy and promise of the day turn to sad and bitter tears on the morrow?*

Instinctively, they moved closer to each other, each squeezing the other's hand more tightly. It was to become the hallmark of their relationship, the keynote that would serve them well and help them grow ever closer—their willingness to *move together* in times of crisis and doubt, acknowledge their hidden qualities, even their shadows, and join with them in sacred marriage.

It was a simple ceremony, yet one with great spiritual, symbolic, and metaphysical significance. They had carefully planned their wedding to coincide with one of the most solemn of Atlantean rituals—the summer Marriage of Heaven and Earth. One of the most sacred and festive occasions in the world, this was a time when the people openly acknowledged the living nature of the worlds of Matter and Spirit, honoring the living Presence in both. Using metaphors and symbols that all could understand, the alchemists followed an ancient ritual alchemical formula based on natural law.

Twice a year, on the Summer and Winter Solstices, they ceremonially fused together the elements of mercury and sulphur, not in their laboratories, but on a far grander scale. At these times, the Atlantean alchemists worked within the retort, or womb, of the Great Mother herself.

The winter ritual—the Dragon Festival—took place at the Temple of Poseidon. The summer ritual—the Marriage of Heaven and Earth—took place at the Great Pyramid, within whose rocky mass the terrestrial, female, current was contained. High above, at the golden tip, the crystal caught and distilled the Divine spark of celestial masculine fire from the ether.

The formula was simple. Mercury represented the receptive, female principle in Nature—the *Spirit of the Earth*. It was animated by sulphur, the positive, male force radiating from the Sun. From this union was born the Life Essence, the *élan vital*, the *Spirit of the World*.

This was the Child of the two eternal partners—Holy Father Love, Holy Mother Truth—described in the mythology of the Children of the Law of One. A spiritual child, referred to in the *Book of Life* as:

THE ANIMATED MERCURIUS, FERTILITY-BEARER,
REVEALER OF KNOWLEDGE,
AND GUIDE BETWEEN LIFE AND DEATH.

So, while the Marriage of Heaven and Earth was being consummated at the Great Pyramid, Adima and Cybele spoke their vows of love to each other in the Grand Hall of the Temple of Poseidon.

"Today I join with you.
Reuniting Self with Self,
Male and female,
The two become one flesh.
In Spirit—the two are one."

Now it was time for the High Priestess to perform the ceremony. Taking the three symbols of the marriage ritual, she held them up for all to see. "Wine," she intoned, lifting a golden chalice, "Liquid of life, revelation, truth, and vitality."

Setting down the cup, she took a golden loaf of freshly baked bread. "Bread—visible and manifest life." She held the loaf high, displaying it for all to see.

"Corn." She showed the third element, a freshly-picked ear, its perfect seeds shining golden within its sheath of green husks. "Abundance and fertility, the awakening of life."

Taking a pitcher of water from the altar, she poured the crystal clear liquid into a goblet of new wine. "May the wine and water ever help you blend your Divine and human natures." She offered the cup, from which each drank.

Placing the chalice beside the ear of ripe, golden corn, the High Priestess continued. "May the corn and wine, representing warmth and youth, always remind you of your Solar and Divine natures inextricably intermingled with your humanity."

Taking the bread, she explained that it was the symbol of union, having many grains in one substance. "Bread is the sustainer of life, providing food for body and soul. Break and share the bread." The High Priestess handed Cybele the loaf, which she broke in half and gave a portion to Adima. "As you eat, as you partake in this Communion, remember always that yours is a shared and united life."

The High Priestess lifted her gaze to encompass the wedding guests, spreading her arms as she included them in the ceremony. "Behold yourselves within this sacred ear of corn, with all its seeds as myriad as the people and all things in the universe. I invite you now to come forward and partake of the bread and wine, the balanced product of Atlantean skill and work in agriculture." One by one the people came forward, participating in the ritual, partaking of the masculine wine and feminine bread.

When the last guest was seated once again, the High Priestess addressed Adima and Cybele once more. "You have drunk the sacred wine and experienced Divine ecstasy. You have eaten the sacred bread, visible manifestation of the Spirit that rises again. Now the Masculine and the Feminine are united, the Liquid and the Solid are united, Divinity and Humankind are united."

She handed each one a perfect grain of corn. "Place the grains in the garden that will surround your home," she instructed. "Water them and nurture them so that they may spring from the ground, germinating and growing in the light of the sun, bringing you the abundance of the universe. Year after year, forever increasing and multiplying, for as long as the Great Mother remains fertile, the corn will return with the Season of Awakening Life. For golden ears of corn are the offspring of the Marriage of the Luminous Sun and the Virgin Earth."

"Now therefore go, and be happy in your new relationship, remembering that love alone can give you full stature, and only the Spirit can give life its highest meaning. Because Love needs the Spirit and the Spirit needs Love for their completion."

Thus, the two, now one, followed in the footsteps of Father Love and Mother Truth, repeating the eternal process, "CONSTRUCTING THE IMAGE OF THE INCARNATE GOD," as it was written in the *Book of Life*.

As with all aspects of their lives, Enoch and Sophia were there to help them give meaning and purpose to their relationship. At the celebration in the Garden of the Heart, the old people addressed the newly married couple.

"As you are wed this day and you begin your new life together, we urge you to consider the meaning and purpose behind your joining," Sophia began. "Have you come together simply to follow the traditional path, setting up house, raising children, achieving material success, growing old, and eventually passing from this life to the next?"

The newlyweds shook their heads. "We think not," Cybele replied for both of them. As a couple, they had thought long and hard about how to evolve their relationship beyond the traditional concepts and confines of Atlantean marriage, where men and women were expected to play specific roles as providers, caregivers, and parents. Far from being idealistic and starry-eyed lovers, Adima and Cybele wanted to bring new meaning and purpose to an institution that was rapidly stagnating and decaying. Fewer and fewer of their friends were choosing to join. Those who had already done so were less than happy.

Many relationships that had begun in much hope and joy were devolving now into loneliness, bitterness, and loss of self. Hopelessness and despair had replaced optimism and enthusiasm as the primary life emotions. Some of these couples had separated completely. Others, though still living together, found themselves emotionally further and further apart, aimlessly adrift in relationships that had no meaning or purpose. Hiding behind a mask of respectability and faithfulness, theirs was a shadow world of neglected love—characterized by negligence, procrastination, suppression, and repression—in which they gave their vital energy to everything except the relationship between themselves.

"Home, family, wealth, success—what you have described are the results of following the old forms of joining," Adima said as they munched the traditional honey cakes and sipped new wine. "These serve neither us as individuals nor the higher purpose to which we have directed ourselves. You have taught us that there is far more to the joining of a man and a woman. We know that there is a better form that a loving relationship might take. We seek your help now in setting the proper direction."

It was no small honor that the newlyweds had just bestowed on their mentors. Adima and Cybele were acknowledging the value of the elders' experience, wisdom, and truth. And in that acknowledgment, they were affirming that theirs was a better way, and that they—the couple—would continue to be guided by these wise old teachers.

"The most important thing for you to remember is to retain your individuality," Enoch said, accepting the gift in all humility. "That is first and foremost. Each of you will serve in your respective familial roles as parents and caregivers. Your spiritual responsibility, however, is threefold—to be good custodians of resources within the community, to find the higher cause, and to become teachers."

Now Sophia leaned forward, a happy smile on her face as she offered her wedding present. "Your collective purpose as a couple, Adima and Cybele, is to teach the transcendence of the old form of the Genesis mystery."

The newlyweds looked at each other in amazement. Genesis—the First Ones—who had lived in absolute bliss in the Garden until succumbing to the wiles of the Tempter. It was the most well-known of all of the Atlantean myths. Every nursery-school child could recite the story "by heart."

"You look confused," Enoch laughed at their perplexity. "No, you do not have to go off and live in a garden and never eat apples again. Remember, this is about transcendence, about moving out of the old into the new."

"That's good," Adima grinned. "I don't think I could go without apples for very long."

The banter was light and pleasant. The guests mingled with each other, dancing, eating, making merry. Amidst the beauty of the Garden of the Heart, in that most sacred setting, Enoch and Sophia helped them understand the truth behind the myth, retelling the story of the First Ones in a bold new way, giving it a bold new meaning and purpose.

"Originally the two were one," Enoch began, *"until the time when they split into two, losing the recognition of their spiritual identity. The First Ones accepted the presence of the Individualizer. They accepted knowledge. They were born out of passivity to Nature's god. They became aware of their ability to choose, to act differently from the plants and stones and animals."*

Now Sophia took up the tale. *"The individualization experience frightened them."* The old woman waved her arms in excitement, her tone somber, her look intense. *"They had to hide. And so they 'clothed' themselves in Matter. They 'hid' in the material realms of three-dimensional experience."*

Adima and Cybele sat with mouths agape, listening to this new version of the ancient tale. Noticing the looks on their faces, the old woman broke out in a hearty chuckle.

"What's so funny?" Cybele asked.

"You are," the old woman continued to laugh. "You take things so seriously. I wish you could see the expressions on your faces. So somber, so grave...just like the First Ones when they went into hiding."

"Don't you see?" Enoch broke in. "It's time to lighten up, to take things less seriously, to move out of the shadow of the grave and soar lightly through the air."

They nodded, beginning to understand as the old man continued to speak. "The challenge of individualization—the 'original sin,' if you will, has nothing to do with accepting a devil. It has to do with overcoming fear."

"Fear of what?" Adima asked.

"Don't you know?"

They each shook their heads. The answer, when it came, was so simple, so easy to understand. They wondered why they had not thought of it themselves. They knew the words were true.

"Fear of the individualization process itself. Fear of using your self-conscious awareness and knowledge in a loving, natural, non-fearing way. And fear of acknowledging your spiritual identity." Enoch handed goblets of the new wine to everybody. Raising his own, he proposed a toast to the couple.

"This is the primary purpose to which you dedicate yourselves today. It is living with Nature, as a cooperator with Nature, not fearing *your* individuality or anyone else's. Let us drink and feast in joy and gratitude for the noble purpose that you assume today."

They raised their glasses and sipped the wine—wisdom drunk from the cup—initiates partaking of the spiritual and vital powers of the Divinity. Each saved a last portion, pouring the deep purple liquid onto the ground as a libation to their Ancestors and to Mother Earth herself.

*****

And so Adima and Cybele came to know each other in a deeper, richer, fuller way—each finding a proper counterpart in the other. As they shared romantic love, their feelings of unity and identity grew stronger.

"When two personalities meet, it is like mixing two chemical substances," Enoch told them during his first visit to Elysia. "If the elements are compatible and able to be combined, both are transformed. He looked at them with all seriousness. "The question remains—what do you want to be transformed into?"

Of course they knew. There was never any doubt. Their mutual desire was to attain a state of complete harmony, that "GREAT HAPPINESS" extolled in the *Book of Life*, in which the couple has become "ONE HEART AND ONE SOUL."

In the exuberance of youth, they conceived children. "Eros thrives because Spirit and Instinct are in right harmony," Sophia exclaimed when she heard the news that Cybele was pregnant. The twins had been a surprise. Having expected only a single child, the new parents' joy was doubled when suddenly there were two. But it went far beyond merely reproducing their own kind, or even having a love affair. It was deep, so very deep. A journey...not individual journeys now, but a combined journey in which the two walked their separate paths—together.

When the first crisis came, they were surprised, and not a little terrified. Seeking out their teachers, they described a time of drama and unrest, punctuating their conversation with threats and accusations. Listening with care, patience, and understanding, the elders offered them wise counsel, presenting their young charges with a map for journeying through and out of such crises.

"Seldom does a marriage develop into an individual relationship smoothly and without crises," Enoch explained. "There is no birth of consciousness without pain."

"Yes, but this pain is terrible," each sobbed in anguish. "I never knew I could hurt this much!"

Sophia pointed to an illustration in the *Book of Life*. It depicted a dark warrior, sword in hand, striking at a shadowy, naked female as she danced seductively around him. "When animus and anima meet," she said, emphasizing the drawing with an explanation, "the animus draws his sword of power and the anima ejects her poison of illusion and seduction. The outcome need not always be negative, since the two are equally likely to fall in love, as you did. But remember, yours is not a love affair, which inevitably ends in failure. Yours is a marriage, a lifelong relationship."

"That's right," Enoch added. "Marriage is not a simple love affair. You are no longer in this alone. Your individual identities are now embroiled in a relationship. You are undergoing an *ordeal*...a trying experience, a test of character and endurance."

Adima and Cybele looked at each other, beginning to understand now. Reaching out, their hands touched, and they held tightly to each other. Each was flooded with an all-embracing warmth. Marriage was an ordeal, they realized, one in which they were sacrificing their egos for the sake of a relationship in which the two have, indeed, become one. It was not about giving in to each other, or about being right or wrong, or about being caught up in a power struggle. It was about unity, the interplay and interaction of the primordial pair of opposites—good and bad, light and dark, male and female, conscious and unconscious—the yin and yang, which symbolize every conceivable duality that can occur.

"Understand something," Sophia reminded them. "Just because you have chosen to join, nevertheless you still represent irreconcilable opposites. When activated, as they are now, there is always a danger that they can degenerate into deadly hostility. But herein also lies the gift. The greater the tension, the greater the potential. Great energy and creativity spring from a correspondingly great tension between opposites."

And so they returned to Elysia and took up their lives. Gradually, over time, Adima came to see his female nature reflected in his wife; Cybele came to see her male nature reflected in her husband. And so the years passed. Balanced, centered, and not easily dislodged or upset, they used all of the tools that had been given them to create a sacred marriage in which both partners had equal value. Embodying the interplay of the duality, retaining their own individual identities, they created a third—the identity of the *Relationship*.

The united couple now did together what each continued to do as individuals—they took the journey toward wholeness, following the Grail Path through the initiations, joys, and sorrows, feeling the tension of the opposites, each seeing and experiencing the opposite in the other. The alchemical stage had been reached. The transformation was taking place as the two experienced that they were one.

*****

During those quiet years after the wedding, Adima rested a while in reasonable peace. Belial went about his business without getting in the way. Their paths seldom crossed. Relaxed and confident, it was time to consolidate his learning and apply it fully and completely in his life.

"Keep what you want, discard the rest." This was the theme of Enoch's easy lessons. How simple it was now, and how obvious. Adima wondered why he had ever found life so difficult, and why others still found it so.

Metaphorically, it was Harvest Time—time to rest and reap that which he had sown. He hadn't come as far as he thought yet, of course, but Enoch wisely waited to reveal that little tidbit of knowledge. To do so would have been discouraging, unfairly denying him the pleasure of his accomplishments to date. Besides, in this time of ease, without interference from Belial and the dark forces, there was much that Enoch was going to be able to teach to his eager young pupil.

Adima's ways were not Belial's ways. He chose another path. Like the mythical anti-twins, the two opposites walked their separate roads, alone yet together, seemingly apart, but each heading toward a future time when their destinies would come together at the appointed place. While it might seem like Belial's life was far more exciting, the truth was just the opposite. Belial's way was full of fear, rage, danger, pain, and the most negative of emotions.

"He may be able to cast spells and wield a magic Spear," Adima told Enoch one day, "and that may be exciting and have great appeal to a lot of people. But I play with angels."

While Belial focused outward, Adima fought the inner battle, slaying the inner demons. Where Belial had stopped when he had received the Spear, thinking he had reached the pinnacle of enlightenment, Adima kept going deeper and deeper, and paradoxically, higher and higher. Where Belial experienced confusion resulting from his illicit and unprepared forays into transcendent awareness, Adima experienced mastery over his thinking, feelings, and personal will. Belial's life was chaotic; Adima's was ever more ordered.

Belial used sorcery, magic, spells, and incantations. Adima tapped into the innate power within himself, developing natural capabilities, honing physical and mental skills and abilities. Belial was becoming ever darker and uglier. His mind grew ever more stagnant and ever more closed. His huge body, once a mass of muscle and sinew, was beginning to show the deleterious effects of a wasteful and dissolute lifestyle. Muscle tissue was breaking down, deep lines and wrinkles were etched into his perpetually scowling face, and his internal organs and systems were beginning to succumb to the strain of the constant assault of the noxious potions.

Adima, on the other hand, was growing far more beautiful. Although far past maturity, his physical body had experienced a new spurt of growth in the past year. He had added much bulk to his muscle and body mass. Always unusually strong, now his great strength and agility had increased tenfold. Toning, shaping, and conditioning, he was the epitome of the Atlantean athlete—a fine physical specimen, an imposing heroic figure.

For Belial, the drug-induced awareness ever-channelling through his consciousness drove him ever more deeply into the insatiable depths of personal power and ambition. For Adima, opening to the *transcendent awareness known as Grace*, came the experience of an inner knowing, which served as balm and healing for his aspiring soul.

Belial surrounded himself with an Inner Circle of powerful, wicked men. His court was filled with noise and drama. Adima worked alone, quietly and patiently, under Enoch's tutelage and guidance. Yet he who appeared to be alone was never really alone. Indeed, Adima had allied himself with a vast Circle of physical, archetypal, and spiritual beings. Powerful allies, they wielded a kind of power that Belial and his ilk could never understand, let alone tap into or have a relationship with.

In the physical realm, there were the animals. Osprey brought him messages on the breath of the wind. Owl brought him wisdom and helped him see in the dark. Turtle reminded him that he carried his armor and his home on his back while helping him stay grounded and connected to the Great Mother. Deer taught him gentleness. Horse brought him power. Bear reminded him of the importance of introspection. For help with dreams and visions, he turned to Lizard. For prayer, abundance, and connection to Spirit, he had only to seek out Buffalo and Eagle. Hummingbird brought joy.

On the archetypal level, there were, of course, the energies of Father and Mother. Learning to be both father and mother to himself, Adima had then been able to embrace the loving parental energy of the father and mother within his own nature, as well as his Spirit Father and Earth Mother. He gained new appreciation for the famous commandment in the *Book of Life*:

HONOR THY FATHER AND THY MOTHER,

THAT THY DAYS MAY BE LONG UPON THE EARTH.

Then, too, there were his Ancestors—those who had gone before him, helping to pave the path and make it ready for his time in the world. Obeying the Law of Cause and Effect, their actions and experiences had a direct impact on his genetic code. Through their work, through their experiences and choices and actions, they had helped to make him what he was.

His Ancestors were part of him. Their blood ran in his veins. Their genes were part of his genes. Their experiences were part of his experiences. Their thoughts and feelings and perspectives about the world had formed the very foundation upon which he was built and upon which he continued to build. And he was part of them. "For time does not only move forward," Enoch explained. "It is possible to move in either direction, for Time is really an illusion. So it is quite easy to travel in whatever temporal direction you want. You just need to learn how."

The spiritual part of his Circle was led by the ever-present Voice within his heart—the Comforter, the Inner Teacher—that still, small Voice, as it would come to be known to all who were willing to quiet their thoughts and listen—really listen.

Of course, there were the angels—the Winged Ones, the Light Beings. He remembered his first angelic encounter when he had actually spoken to the Archangel of the Grail, asking the Spirit *to go before him with his flaming sword to clear the path and light the way.* Adima had asked, and the angel had complied. Now he began every day by asking.

Yes, it was a vast Circle—all who wanted to help, as well as all who wanted help. All who could give, and all who needed to receive. For Adima had come to another profound realization...

TO GIVE AND TO RECEIVE ARE ONE IN TRUTH.

CHAPTER 33

What we're seeking is an experience of being alive, so that our life experiences on the purely physical plane will have resonances within our own innermost being and reality, so that we actually feel the rapture of being alive.

—Joseph Campbell

The *Period of Unsettling* began on the day of the Dragon Festival, when Adima had discovered the footsteps of Belial's spies and the first of the explosions had occurred. Although it was a time of great unsettling for the Children of the Law of One and the people of Atlantis, it did not seem so for Adima and Cybele and their children. Indeed, it seemed more like a period of accomplishment. The two years following the twins initiation had been a good time for the family. They grew in wisdom and knowledge and love for each other.

Cybele had been given her new name and had taken up the Wand and the Shield, stepping into her role as Guardian of the Crystals. She had found a new friend in Nabala. Work on the Arks was progressing under the guidance of the Spirit-Teacher's Voice. Yet something else was there, below the surface, intruding on all aspects of their lives—the tension, the turmoil, the unsettling. Things were falling apart, breaking up. The structures of the past were crumbling, the established norms were crumbling, outmoded forms were giving way. Breakage and wreckage were everywhere.

The Dragon Festival had ended with the first of the explosions, the result of the aborted crystal experiments using the forbidden sciences. After that, events had followed one upon the other, for time seemed to be speeding up in a mad, headlong dash toward an inevitable catastrophe. Then had come the twins birthday and initiation in the Temple and on Mount Kylene.

*****

After the twins' initiation, Adima had begun the final phase of his learning. The terror following his nightmare after the aborted experiment at the Dragon Festival had passed, and he plunged into his work with heightened enthusiasm and vigor.

There was so much to learn—so much greatness and vastness in the universe. He learned about the power of the animals and about the medicine of herbs, trees, leaves, and flowers. He learned about the cycles of the sun and moon and the various powers of the different seasons and their relationship to health and wellness and thought and feeling.

He learned about the power of prayer and fasting, and the wisdom of asking for help, guidance, and advice from Above and Within. Many were the nights he spent alone and shivering in the forest or high up on Mount Kylene, hungry and thirsty, awaiting a vision or message from the Spirit-world.

He learned the songs and chants of the Ancients, carrying messages of power and healing from far back in time, from the dim and distant past, from the Beginning. Gift of the Guardians, taught by the Ancients to each succeeding generation, these were the old words, spoken in the first language, the Solara Maru—the Language of Light. Even though he did not understand their meaning, just saying them—intoning the sounds of the syllables, the vowels and consonants—had an immediate effect. For the power of the spoken word was great.

"Greater than any sword you carry," Enoch told him. "You think the sword a mighty weapon. Wait until you see what the spoken and written word can do! You already have an inkling, having seen how Belial uses words to get what he wants. But there is so much more. After a time, you will lay your sword aside in favor of the gift of language. Not the sword, but the pen will be your greatest weapon, words your greatest artistic tool!

"You will tell stories, you will paint glorious, beautiful, descriptive pictures with words. You will open your mouth to speak, and people will listen to you spellbound. You will bring them joy with you words, laughter with your words, delight with your words, knowledge with your words. Your songs and stories will reveal to them places to which they could never have taken themselves. Your words will open whole new universes to them."

Adima learned dangerous things, too. Along with the good, Enoch insisted that he learn the ways of those who, like Belial, worked with the dark side. "This is so that you will be able to help the victims of their attacks and be prepared for such attacks upon yourself," Enoch explained when Adima protested that he did not wish to know such things.

That was when Enoch taught him about the power of Thought—how there are no idle thoughts, how each thought is a cause that ultimately leads to an effect. How thoughts are meaningless in themselves but can lead to good or evil depending on the *intention* of the thinker.

THE ONLY MEANING ANY THOUGHT HAS IS THE MEANING YOU GIVE IT.

Enoch reminded him, quoting from the *Book of Life*. "So be careful to give each thought a meaning in accord with the highest purpose and intent."

Thus, Adima learned how to heal himself and others. Not just through natural remedies, but also through the practice of the spiritual principles of love and forgiveness, through the changing of his mind and the release of thoughts that caused sickness and harm.

He enjoyed everything, amazed at the depth, complexity, and diversity of the universe and the universe of universes. Most of all, though, he liked learning about the four powers that comprise a complete man—the archetypal energies of King, Warrior, Lover, and Magician.

*****

"These are the inner guides who will help you find yourself and transform your world," Enoch explained when he first introduced the four figures. It was midnight in early spring. More than two years had passed since the twins' initiation. They were standing in the shadow of the most magnificent structure the human race had ever built—the Great Pyramid of Atlantis. Usually there were guards everywhere, but tonight the Pyramid seemed strangely deserted.

"Isn't it dangerous for us to be here?" Adima asked, casting furtive glances in every direction. He shivered, imagining Belial's guards lurking in the shadows, waiting to pounce on trespassers and cast them into the dungeons beneath the Pyramid, never to see the light of day again.

"Do not worry," came the reassuring reply. "No one will see us tonight. "We are safely concealed in the light of the first-quarter moon."

Adima relaxed, knowing that Enoch had the power to render himself invisible to any whom he did not wish to see him. However, that still did not explain why they had come to a place that was so dangerous for any of the Children of the Law of One.

"Do not be deceived by changing forms," Enoch explained in answer to Adima's doubts. "On the surface, this place appears to be the seat of power of the Sons of Belial. Such as they, however, can never usurp the true meaning and function of the Great Pyramid. What was intended in the design of the Ancients still holds true, regardless of the intentions of the unenlightened inhabitants who swarm through its interior trying to use its mighty power for their own misguided ends."

They stopped before the south face, its polished surface reflecting the moonlight even as the moon was reflecting the light of the sun. "Look at it," Enoch said. "Remember your dream, in which I told you the Innocent had to progress through the stages of Kingliness to become the Servant of all?"

Adima nodded.

"You did not understand then, but you are ready now to understand the larger purpose of the journey you have undertaken. Behold the Great Pyramid." Enoch pointed to the magnificent edifice. "See the four sides rising upward toward Heaven. Have you ever wondered why the Ancients constructed a four-sided figure—not counting the base? They could as easily have constructed three sides, or even five. Yet they chose four. Why?"

"I don't know," Adima mused. "There's probably a very sound architectural reason with which I am not familiar. And I'll bet there are also very strong symbolic reasons, too."

"Right on both counts," Enoch congratulated his pupil. "The key is the number *four*. Psychologically, four indicates the basic archetypal structure of the Self, as illustrated in the geometric shape you see before you. Among its other unique and fascinating attributes, the Pyramid represents you, yourself. If you study the Pyramid in detail, it will provide you with a blueprint of the human journey toward wholeness."

"On a symbolic level," Adima added.

"On a symbolic and *mythic* level," Enoch continued. "Mythologically, it's a journey, a journey through the Kingdom of the Self. You have been taking the journey for quite some time now."

"This intrigues me," Adima exclaimed eagerly. "Tell me more. Tell me about this kingdom. Who inhabits it?" He loved the study of symbols, myths, and metaphors and their relationship to each of the fields of human endeavor. Now, in the presence of the Great Pyramid, under a blanket of stars, caressed by a scented breeze, he was about to see his own life elevated to a higher level, taking on a higher meaning and significance within the mythos of the Atlantean race.

Enoch smiled, as eager to teach as his student was to learn. "As with any land," he began, "there are many denizens of the Kingdom of the Self. The four that we will concern ourselves with are the King, the Warrior, the Magician, and the Lover—or rather, the archetypal energies that inform those qualities within each of us."

"I'm familiar with them," Adima exclaimed. "I've encountered these characters ever since I was a child. They've appeared in myths, dreams, fantasies, art. Why, they're even present in our religious and spiritual beliefs!"

"That's right," Enoch agreed. "They are everywhere...common across cultures and across space and time. No matter the story, the motif is the same. Which means," the old man was about to reveal the point of the lesson, "that these archetypes are inherent in the human psyche."

Adima was fascinated. He barely noticed the sweet fragrance of jasmine in the air, paid scant attention to the pale moonlight outlining the fleecy clouds in a tracery of silver light. "How do these energies work?" he wanted to know, oblivious to the beauty of the night.

"They reside in the inner world of your subconscious and work like a magnet," Enoch continued. "We are attracted to them, as you are now while I speak of them. And they are attracted to us. They come through from the subconscious, where they manifest as Good King, Warrior, Magician, and Lover; or as dark, sinister, shadowy forms.

"I welcome them," Adima interrupted enthusiastically. "Especially Warrior..." Enoch raised his palm in a cautionary gesture. "Be careful, my friend," he warned. "You do not want to go and jump into an archetype. It is far too dangerous. These are powerful energies, akin to the incredible nuclear energy contained within the atom. Each archetype wants to possess you totally—and *will* if you let it!"

"How?" Adima asked. He could not imagine anything wrong with being "possessed," as Enoch put it, by the energies of King or Warrior, or any of the archetypes, for that matter.

"The only way to explain it without direct experience it is to liken it to your own encounter with the lightning. Remember how you felt when you were struck?"

Adima remembered only too well. "I was fried," he said grimly.

"So, too, this psychic energy will fry you immediately," Enoch confirmed. "No, you don't want to get possessed by an archetype, *as Belial has!*" He shook his head sadly.

Now Adima understood. Realization swept over him in a sudden flash of illumination. Of course! Belial had been totally overwhelmed by these energies. It explained exactly why his nemesis was the way he was. It also explained tonight's lesson. How one uses archetypal energy was the extent to which he was psychologically healthy or ill. With the Great Pyramid as a backdrop, Enoch was providing him with practical, metaphorical guidelines to help him figure out where he was and where he needed to work. He took a deep breath, inhaling the perfumed air as he paused to enjoy the evening and reflect on his teacher's words.

"Is there an appropriate way to understand these energies?" he asked with some trepidation. The thought of becoming like Belial was appalling, while at the same time he wanted to understand the positive aspects of working with these tremendously powerful forces.

"They need to be contained...stepped down and transformed," Enoch explained, "just as the electrical energy from a lightning bolt is stepped down to a safe level for lighting a home in the dark." The old man pointed to the Pyramid shining in the pale moonlight. "Just as the Great Pyramid transforms the energy of the Dragon Current into useful and usable energy, so your healthy ego provides you with a safe and appropriate way to access the archetypal energy. The key lies in the taking of the journey."

Again the reference to the mystical journey. "Tell me about it," Adima asked. He felt like a child once again, caught up by the fantasies he had spun in his own imagination when he was just a boy, before he had learned that such behavior was not appropriate or pleasing to his parents. "When did my journey start, where am I now, and where am I headed?"

He pictured himself in a magical kingdom in the prime of his youth. The sun was shining, and all of the villagers had turned out to bid farewell to this heroic young man who was about to embark on a great adventure to save the world from oblivion.

"Farewell! Good luck! Godspeed!" One by one, family and friends bid him farewell. At last, he faced his new bride. Taking her gently in his arms, they came together in a final embrace, kissing each other tenderly. Then, with a wave of his hand and a gladsome smile, he climbed astride his mighty steed. The great beast whinnied and reared up on its hind legs. Sword in hand, shield flashing in the brilliant sunshine, he urged the animal forward.

Through the streets they raced, villagers flanking the route on either side. "Open the gates," someone cried. The huge portals were swung wide, and amidst thunderous cheers, man and beast flashed through the gates, the clatter of the horses' hooves mingling with the shouts of encouragement and blessing from the crowds.

His bride rushed to the parapet, straining her eyes for one last sight of her beloved, visible now only as a cloud of dust on the distant horizon. She put a pale hand to her lips, remembering her lover's touch. "Be safe," she whispered, blowing a kiss into the wind, "and return to me soon."

Out on the road, the kiss sped straight and true. Topping a rise, the hero stopped and turned for one last glance toward home. The village lay like a glistening white pearl in the center of an emerald valley, ringed by amethyst mountains and covered by an azure sky.

"Farewell, my True Love," he whispered. "I shall return to you." And then he was gone, disappearing behind the hill, off on a glorious adventure into the unknown, the touch of her long and tender kiss still lingering on his lips, the memory forever safe within in his heart.

"Do you want to hear my story?" Enoch interrupted, a twinkle in his eye, "or are you having a better time entertaining yourself with your own fantasy?"

"Sorry," Adima laughed. I guess I got carried away. I went away for a while, but I'm back now. Please, go on."

"It has been a multistage journey," Enoch began, setting into his best storytelling voice, "actually not unlike the adventure you just created in your own imagination."

"The *Call* came in your eighteenth year, when you entered the university and encountered Belial for the first time. Standing on the threshold of adventure, you entered a *Time of Preparation*. Remember how you felt?"

Adima remembered. He would never forget that time, those vague, uneasy feelings of wanting something more, yet not knowing where to look. The fear during his first encounter with Belial, in which he had received the mark he still carried, ever reminding him of the enmity between the two and of the day when they would meet again in mortal combat.

"There you stood, both Innocent and Warrior, embracing your dual nature and overwhelmed by it, marked by your enemy, paralyzed by fear. Yet even then you were in touch with your greatest gift-weapon—that willingness to rise up, let go of the old, and embrace the new, as frightening as it might seem."

Enoch paused in the story and began to walk along the marble piazza that flanked the perimeter of the Pyramid's base. It was a long distance, perhaps half a mile, and they walked for several minutes in silence.

"*Answering the Call*, your world broke apart," Enoch continued at last, stopping as the great stone face of the west side of the Pyramid loomed before them. "You encountered the Beast in Belial, and you confronted the Beast within yourself."

Adima remembered only too well each of the trials and tribulations of those years of *Encounter*—from the demonic Belial roaring forth his challenge to the searing pain of the lightning as it surged through his body. How grateful he was that somewhere along the way, before he had gotten completely lost, Enoch had appeared to help him.

"You are the Magus who was sent to help me," Adima realized happily. He was starting to understand the functions of each archetype now—how they had helped him during various stages of his journey, and in what form they had appeared.

"Yes, I am the Magus," Enoch replied, "but I merely showed you how to embrace the Magus within yourself as you fought the inner demons of fear and anxiety and lay in the darkness of the Great Void. I guided you through many deaths and rebirths, many spiritual initiations, as you became a Seeker of the Truth, Destroyer of the old forms that no longer served you, Creator of something new and better, and now a Lover who has taken on a life partner."

On they walked in silence, continuing their stroll around the perimeter of the Pyramid. "The final stage of the journey lies before you," Enoch broke the silence once again. The north face rose up and out of sight into the night. "Tonight you begin the *Return*. The hero recrosses the threshold and finds himself once again in ordinary space and time. The King returns from the Encounter, a 'MONARCH OF EMPOWERMENT, MATURITY, AND SELF-AWARENESS,' as it is written in the *Book of Life*. Do you know who the allies are who return with you?"

Adima thought a moment. "Of course!" he exclaimed. "The Magus, the Sage, and the Priest—the Magicians within me, the Wise Counselors."

"Do not forget the Wise Fool," Enoch said, "who offers the gift of humor so that the King is able to laugh at his own foibles, taking neither himself nor the world too seriously."

A sudden thought occurred to Adima. "Now that I embody each of the archetypes, does this mean that you are leaving me?" he asked somewhat nervously. "I still have need of you; I still value our friendship."

Enoch placed a warm hand on Adima's shoulder. "I am always your friend," he reassured him. "From now on, though, our relationship changes. No longer an acolyte, you step up now and take your place beside me as one who is about to be *anointed*."

There would have been a time, not too long ago, when Adima's ego would have soared to hear such words of praise. Now, though, listening to his mentor, he experienced not pride, but humility. It was to become another of his great resources.

On they walked, coming at last around to the east. The stone figure of the Guardian watched over the main entrance to the Pyramid, silent and deserted at this hour of night. "Behold the Great Pyramid!" Enoch pointed to the magnificent edifice once again, repeating the phrase he had used at the beginning of the lesson. Then he pointed to Adima. "Behold the man!"

"What do you mean?" Adima asked, a sudden chill sweeping over him as the energy of his teacher's words enveloped him.

"You are the Pyramid, the Pyramid is you," Enoch replied. "You carry within you the energies that the Pyramid was designed to express in monumental form. You are the living expression of those energies."

"Behold the man!" He pointed to the statue of Quetzalcoatl, which loomed larger than life. He reached into his pouch and drew forth a shining white flower. It was the bloom of purity, peace, resurrection, and royalty. "You are the King." He handed the lily to Adima. "The King brings order. Every Kingdom must have a Good King, whose purpose it is to bless. In the Kingdom of Atlantis, Belial is the Shadow King—the Ogre Tyrant who rules with an iron fist."

Delving into his pouch once again, Enoch produced a second flower. It was the Flower of Light from the Time of the Beginning, the perfection of beauty. "You are the Warrior," he said as Adima took the lotus blossom. "Every King needs a Warrior, whose purpose it is to protect and serve. Without a Good Warrior, the King is powerless, and the Kingdom is defenseless. In the Kingdom of Atlantis, Belial is the Shadow Warrior—a sadist who enjoys inflicting pain on others."

A third time Enoch rummaged in the pouch. A third time he produced a mystical bloom, the plant of enchantment, the power of magic. "You are the Magus." The mandrake was added to the bouquet. "There must be a Magician, whose purpose it is to analyze and transform. Without a Good Magus, the King is a bit stupid. In the Kingdom of Atlantis, Belial is the Shadow Magician—a detached manipulator, using his knowledge only for his personal advantage."

For the last time, the old man reached deep within the pouch. It was the flower of Time and Eternity, the flower of Love and the Heart. "You are the Lover." The crimson rose was a perfect complement to the green and white of the bouquet. "The Lover's purpose is to merge, bringing sexual joining as well as communication and eventual communion with the Divine. In the Kingdom of Atlantis, Belial is the Shadow Lover—an addict-adept attempting but never quite able to find an effective connection with the Source of his own being."

For a long while neither man spoke, each enjoying the silence and the beauty of the night in the presence of the Great Pyramid. They walked in an easterly direction until they stood on a small hill that afforded a full view of the whole edifice. "This is who you are," Enoch told him, "Don't you see that?"

"Yes, I do see it," Adima answered, wanting to show his teacher that he really did understand. "Together these four archetypes form a four-sided pyramid, which, by the way, is one of the strongest geometric structures."

"A *balanced* Pyramid," Enoch added. "The archetypes balance each other because of their opposition. The Warrior has boundaries; the Lover has no boundaries. The King is blessing, order, being seen; the Magus is hidden, occult. Together, there is balance." The old man turned and looked directly at Adima. "The same is true of a man—*properly balanced, the four archetypes become the expression of the mature man.*"

It was growing late, and the moon was approaching the western horizon. "We must be leaving," Enoch concluded, wrapping his cloak about him in preparation for the long walk home. "The moon will not be able to conceal us much longer. Make no mistake. Tonight marks but the beginning of your Return. You still have much to embrace, assimilate, and integrate before you come back to the place where your journey began. Go home now," the old man dismissed him with a loving embrace. "Make love with your wife, then bid her farewell for a while. We leave tomorrow at sunrise. As always for those who travel this path, there are more adventures ahead of you."

"The first awaits you on Mount Kylene tomorrow evening when the moon reaches its first quarter phase. If you are successful there, you will meet your wife thirty days later, at Kuneware."

CHAPTER 34

It is like the grain of mustard seed, which, when it is sown in the Earth, is less than all the seeds that be in the Earth: But when it is sown, it groweth up, and becometh greater than all the herbs, and shooteth out great branches; so that the fowls of the air may lodge under the shadow of it.

—Mark 4:31-32

The Great Pyramid of Atlantis was arguably the most awesome and magnificent physical structure ever to grace the surface of the Earth. Oh, that you could have been there to see it gleaming white in the sun—sublime, awesome, awe-inspiring. Rare was the visitor to the city who could stand in its presence and not be moved. The physical Pyramid is gone now, along with all of Atlantis. Gone, but not forgotten, living on in scores of replicas across the globe. Living, too, in the sense memory of the collective consciousness. A most familiar shape, an ancient shape, symbolizing the highest spiritual and physical attainment of the human race.

To modern architects and scientists, it is a structure of precision, an engineering marvel whose truths are unfathomable by modern standards, an instrument designed for a type of spiritual, mystical, even magical science that today is no longer recognized. Such is the conundrum for those willing to admit that the extent of their knowledge might have limits, and that those who came before them may have possessed a technology that is now barely conceivable.

To Egyptologists, it is a tomb wherein once lay shrouded mummies of the dead kings of a dead race. Designed by the dead, built for the dead, inhabited by the dead, its only value is that which is contained within its stone maw—precious gems, art, and artifacts originally intended to ease the soul's journey to the afterlife and, once there, attend to its comfort.

To metaphysicians, it is an occult place—mysterious, foreboding, sinister. A place in whose dimensions occur symbolic numerical patterns connected with rites of initiation, magic, and mysticism. To others, more thoughtful and observant, it is a structure that represents the encapsulation of the highest of ancient knowledge, whose dimensions were apparently designed to symbolize the dimensions of the Earth.

To the Ancients, the original builders, the Great Pyramid was called by many names—the Fire, the Flame, the Solar Force, the Fifth Sun of Quetzalcoatl. It also served many functions. On a symbolic and metaphysical level, it was an enduring monument depicting the entire code of ancient scientific knowledge—to those who knew how to decipher the secrets stored in its structure of measure and number. On a spiritual level, the numbers in its dimensions and proportions were intended to procure the invocation of that aspect of cosmic energy which those numbers symbolized—in this case, the god variously known as Hermes, Mercury, and Thoth. On a mundane level, its numerical properties also had a practical purpose in relation to the form of science that the Great Pyramid was designed to serve. On the highest level, it served as an accumulator and transformer of cosmic energies.

The Great Pyramid was the great transformer—stepping down the nuclear fire of the universe and making it manageable, containing it within that vast body of stone. Serving the same purpose for the cosmos as a healthy, developed ego serves for a human being—stepping down the archetypal fire of the collective unconscious and making it manageable and useful. The Great Pyramid was an ego made of stone; the ego is the Great Pyramid of the psyche.

It was there, at those most sacred seasons of the year, that the Marriage of Heaven and Earth took place. The union between the terrestrial current accumulated in its rocky mass and the Divine spark of celestial fire distilled from the ether at the point of its gold and crystal apex. From this union was born the Life Essence, known to the Ancients as the *Spirit of the World*.

To Shakala, master alchemist and fourth degree initiate of the Sons of Belial, the Great Pyramid was the place where he went to work every day. He paid scant attention to the fact that within the monumental structure's fabric were encoded the most sacred of scientific laws and formulas. For Shakala—a man of concrete, practical, and precise thinking—there was no mystery, no sense of wonder, no sense of awe as he approached the Great Pyramid.

Such emotions had long since absented themselves from his psychic repertoire, replaced by rational thought and jaded cynicism. There was no respect for the symbology, no appreciation for the works of the Ancients, no awe at the scope of that which he entered into every morning and emerged from every night, no feelings of insignificance in the presence of such a monumental structure. This was due less to arrogance than to the fact that he had become inured to the Great Pyramid's wonders through years of mind-numbing devotion to only scientific and physical pursuits. The alchemist did not glance up, as did the numerous visitors marvelling at the whiteness of the stone. He was completely unaware of what it was he was missing.

So many tried to get his attention, in so many ways did they try to show him the wonders of the day. A gust of wind carrying the essence of newly-blossoming rose buds. A songbird flying close, chirping a melody of joy and delight. A close encounter with a passerby, a friendly nod, the bright, enthusiastic grin of a child.

On he walked, with bent head and furrowed brow, deep in thought, oblivious to the sights, sounds, and people around him. A man obsessed—mulling over and over in his mind the dilemma of the exploding crystals and what to do about them. His scowl was not one of anger or contempt, it was one of perplexity and frustration mingled with fear—fear of Belial's wrath should he not be able to solve the problem. He had been concentrating on this for so long, and yet he was no closer to a solution than he had been on the morning of Lus's disappearance over two years ago.

So this morning, following his familiar routine, Shakala approached the Great Pyramid with the same indifference with which he had approached it every day for so many decades. Little did he know that this was a day of destiny, that someone was about to come into his life and alter its course forever.

*****

Entering the piazza, Shakala was surprised to see Nargal, Belial's scribe, standing with arms folded in earnest conversation with a young man. "Unusual," he grunted to himself. "He never leaves the Great Pyramid unless it is extremely important. I wonder what he's up to?"

Shakala did not like Nargal, nor did he trust him. The man was not a high-level Initiate, but the simpering fool had Belial's ear and never hesitated to whisper into it whenever he thought that doing so would serve him.

"This is Kafar," the scribe waved to Shakala as he walked across the piazza, motioning to him to come over and meet the newcomer.

Shakala glanced quickly at the young man standing before him, sizing him up in a single, all encompassing glance. He was in his early twenties, tall, thin, athletic, with average looks. An up and coming scientist, Shakala thought to himself. Very bright, very ambitious. But too personable, too moral ever to be a man of greatness. His must be a special skill, and they're going to use him as a means to achieving an end.

"He has tremendous potential as an alchemist," Nargal was saying, as if to confirm Shakala's character assessment. "His is a brilliant young mind. Already he has achieved much, and I see more greatness in him. That is why he is going to be assisting you in your experiments with the crystals."

Shakala was surprised, but he did not allow his facial expression to betray his thoughts. An assistant! At last, some relief from the long hours and tedium of endless experimentation. But more than an assistant, he realized as the ever-obsessive voice of his own insecurity and lack of confidence began to chatter inside his head. A rival who has Nargal's favor, who is being groomed to replace me. I must be careful what I tell him. I need to observe him and see what he's about. I don't trust him, and I certainly don't trust Nargal. Yet I dare not show my true feelings or tip my hand.

"Welcome," Shakala extended his right palm forward in the traditional Atlantean greeting. Long had he played this game. Years ago he had learned to keep his face an emotionless mask lest his enemies read his thoughts and pounce on his weaknesses.

In complete innocence, unaware that Shakala harbored any doubts or misgivings about him, Kafar returned the greeting, beaming with pride. Shakala—renowned as the leading thinker, scholar, and alchemist of the day. To be in the presence of such a great man, to be chosen to be apprenticed to him! How Kafar wanted to be like him, and here was his chance.

Shakala smiled politely. Through years of constant practice, he had mastered the art of outwardly expressing a completely different emotion from that which he was feeling within. "Come with me, and I'll show you around," the older man said, moving out to the fringe of the piazza. Turning around, he extended a hand and pointed forward. "There it is," Shakala said, as though it really meant something to him, which of course it did not.

Kafar stood in front of the Great Pyramid for the first time. It was like he had died and gone to Heaven. There it was, in real life—the Great Pyramid, the object of his dreams. He'd read about it, spoken about it, seen pictures of it, even dreamed about it, and now he stood in its shadow.

He devoured the edifice with his eyes. A shape so familiar...its four triangular sides rising up at an impossible angle from a huge, flat base, its eastern face bisected by a golden stairway that led to a miniature golden capstone hundreds of feet overhead. And the capstone itself crowned by the tiniest of crystals—an ultra-pure diamond. Massive blocks of stone perfectly shaped and fitted together on a scale of perfection so grand as to be almost inconceivable.

Gleaming white in the brilliant sunshine, the whole structure reminded Kafar of a mountain covered in hieroglyphs. Such markings, such strange and beautiful letters and symbols, expressing the entire knowledge of antiquity. Now it was real, and he had nothing with which to compare it. In the presence of such an incredible technological achievement he felt childlike, dwarfed, consciously aware of his insignificance, awed by the presence of something so mighty and so wonderful.

He was an Innocent, trusting life, trusting himself, trusting others. He knew it, he felt it. He was not ashamed to admit it. For having been nurtured in a safe and loving home, Kafar had an optimism and enthusiasm that were contagious. "I'm like a kid again," he grinned boyishly at Shakala. "I feel like I'm two years old and don't know what to do."

Shakala laughed indulgently in spite of himself, in spite of his doubt and misgivings and mistrust. He remembered his own feelings the first time he had seen the Great Pyramid up close. This young man was no different. Maybe he's not so bad after all, Shakala thought. The voices inside his head were quieting. Perhaps I misjudged him, as well as Nargal and his motives. Maybe Kafar is okay. Maybe I can take him under my wing and mold him into a great alchemist.

Shakala was beginning to experience something akin to actual enthusiasm. The voices had started again, but different voices this time...friendlier, more hopeful. Maybe together we can build this confounded device and actually get it to work. "Go ahead and ask your questions," he said as they stood before the mighty structure. "Let yourself be a child again, for the Great Pyramid has that effect on people. To resist it is to fight a battle that cannot be won. You never get used to it, really. Perhaps you build a tolerance for it, as I have," the older man shook his head. "But you never really *get used* to being with the Great Pyramid. You can't. It just doesn't happen." He seated himself on a stone bench, motioning Kafar to sit beside him.

Kafar took a deep breath. It appeared that the Master Alchemist liked him after all. That was good. Now he could pose all of his questions. "There's so much I want to ask," he exclaimed. "I know all about this from my books, but now that I'm here with such a great man as yourself, I want to ask these questions all over again."

He remembered his manners. He was, after all, in the presence of greatness. Shakala had a renowned reputation. Kafar's was a great and singular honor. No one else in the entire world was Shakala's protégé; only he could claim that rank. Be grateful, be grateful, be grateful were his thoughts. And he was! "I want to learn from experience. I want to learn from you. Teach me, Shakala, tell me, show me the wonders of this Great Pyramid."

"Ask your questions," the alchemist said, beginning to warm to this likeable young man. Beginning to feel faint stirrings of emotions he had thought himself incapable of feeling. Beginning to feel—dare he even think it—like a parent! "As a child asks a father, so you can ask me. I will answer as best I can." He placed his hand gently on the young man's arm.

With the touch, Kafar visibly relaxed. What a nice man, he thought to himself. So easy to talk to! I can ask with impunity, and Shakala will have all the answers. "I guess my first question is, 'What is it?'" He spoke aloud. "What is it really?"

Shakala thought about the question, knowing it to be a rhetorical one. Kafar was not stupid; he was a scientist, too. Therefore, he needed a different answer, a nontechnical answer, a poetic answer. So Shakala gave the best kind of poetic answer that a non-poetic, scientific mind could give. "What is it?" he repeated the question. "A machine. A power source. A tool. A work of art. A monument in stone. All of this and more."

Kafar nodded his head in agreement. Yes, the Great Pyramid was indeed all of those things. And so much more. Mysterious. Other worldly. *For* Atlantis, but not *of* Atlantis. Magnificent. Awesome. Gorgeous. His mind was working in superlatives.

They rose and walked in silence along a promenade of polished terrazzo that extended in a huge square around the exterior base of the Pyramid. In the center of the square stood a huge statue carved of solid marble. Larger than life, towering thirty feet above the promenade, it was visible to all who approached.

"I know who that is." Kafar recognized the figure instantly...human yet not human, Atlantean but not Atlantean, a man strongly built with a broad forehead, large eyes, and flowing beard. He was dressed in a long white robe reaching to his feet, and on his head he wore a mitre. In his hand he held a sickle. It was the great Guardian, Quetzalcoatl.

Kafar had seen replicas of the statue, but nothing could depict the sheer beauty of the real thing, its enormous size, the smoothness of the lines. Larger than life, it was a thing to be admired, and so much more. For it was the face and eyes that drew and held Kafar's gaze. Even though this was a figure carved from stone, the essence of the Guardian—that kindly, loving face and those deep-set eyes burning with great intellect, spirit, and love—was revealed for all to see.

"What do you know of him?" Shakala asked, remembering a day so many years ago when his grandfather had taken him to see the Great Pyramid for the first time. How he had thrilled to its wonders and marvels and been caught up in the mystery and magic of the place! Since those early days, Shakala had been obsessed with the power of the Great Pyramid and what it was capable of doing. Obsessed, too, with the story of Quetzalcoatl, the feathered serpent god, greatest and most beloved of the Guardians.

From out of the sky in the direction of the distant East, this mysterious being had come and been enthroned as the patron demigod and High Priest of the Ancients of Atlantis. His habits were ascetic. He never married and was most chaste and pure in life. He asked for no sacrifices except those of fruits and flowers, and was known as the God of Peace.

Skilled in many arts, Quetzalcoatl was revered as the first and greatest of the Atlantean teachers—having given the gifts of gem-cutting and metal-casting, as well as originating and inventing the Atlantean calendar. For uncounted years the Guardian dwelt amongst his people, until one sad day—a day whose memory was still honored in Atlantis—he returned to the sky. Embarking in a Sunship, he soared away to the East from whence he had come, vowing to return one day and create an even greater empire for all the world.

Shakala remembered the legends that his grandfather had told him. How Quetzalcoatl had created the grand design for the Great Pyramid. How the Ancients, under his direction, had followed the mystical blueprint, using the gift of cold fire to cut and shape the stones and the gift of levitation to transport them and set them in place.

"I want to be like him," young Shakala had whispered as he sat enthralled on his grandfather's knee.

"And so you will, my boy, so you will," his grandfather had replied, stroking the child's head and smiling assuredly.

"How did the Ancients build it?" Kafar wondered aloud, interrupting Shakala's reverie. "How did they actually erect such a structure? And to what purpose? Surely they could not have built it for the same reasons it is being used today."

"Of course they didn't," Shakala replied. "They built it for the sheer pleasure of building it, as though playing a game, because it was enjoyable," he explained simply. "First, they positioned the crystals and created the energy fields. Then, they projected their thoughts and moved the stones. They were very pleased with themselves and took great pride in their achievement."

Kafar nodded. "You know, I can recite all of the scientific facts about the Great Pyramid," he said. "I understand the dry, textbook reasons behind why it was built, but tell me again. I want to hear the living words from you, the Master Alchemist. Please, if you're willing, tell me about the Great Pyramid from your point of view."

Shakala was more than willing. He was pleased beyond description. His heart soared. It felt good to have someone lean on his every word. It assuaged his ego, but more importantly, it made him feel as if he were talking to a son—his son—the son he had never had. He peered intently at Kafar. Here was a young man who looked up to him and was honored to be in his presence. Shakala appreciated that and so was more than willing to teach.

"The Great Pyramid was built as a receptacle to hold the consciousness of the Ancients," he began. He spoke not as an alchemist, not as Belial's right-hand man, not even as a mere user of tools. Rather, he spoke as one who loved science and technology for its own sake.

Somehow, in having spent just a few short moments with Kafar, Shakala had been changed. He had experienced an emotional and intellectual shift, had been lifted up out of his ordinary, technical world and transported to a higher level of thinking and teaching.

From this elevated place, he began to remember the true purpose of the Great Pyramid. From this higher level, he taught the concepts that had come from the higher minds of the Ancients, concepts he had learned at the Academy of Science but had long since forgotten. Forgotten, perhaps, but not lost. For on this clear, fresh morning with Kafar, they stood out vividly in his mind, bright and new and true.

"The Great Pyramid was designed to monumentalize the entire code of Atlantean scientific knowledge," Shakala explained. He spoke as one with great authority, knowing his words were true. "Within the Great Pyramid's fabric are encoded all of our records— scientific laws and formulas. And its overall dimensions were made to symbolize the dimensions of the Great Mother Earth.

"Building it was to be a daunting task, even with the help of Quetzalcoatl. How would the Ancients express all of the significant formulae capable of being encoded in the measurements of the Great Pyramid? Each had a different idea, a different plan from which to approach the task, and each thought his plan to be the best. The discussion raged long and hard, while Quetzalcoatl remained aloof, letting them debate among themselves.

"Yet after many long years, the Great Pyramid was still only a vision. At last, eager to begin the actual work of construction, the Guardian proposed a brilliant solution. Even before his coming, the Ancients had already developed a refined science of geodesy, as was evident in their use of geodetic measures. 'Therefore,' the Guardian said as he addressed the Elders, 'you will use the Language of Number to achieve your goal.'"

Of course, Kafar realized. How simple! Number was the universal language; it was how they built things. From then on, it had been easy. But there was more to the story, wasn't there? "Yet the preservation of such knowledge can scarcely have been the only motive of its builders," he interrupted, asking his question aloud. "Don't the Pyramid's numerical properties also have some practical purpose in relation to the form of science that it is designed to serve?"

"Of course they do," Shakala replied. "Along with its traditional use in connection with initiation, magic, and mysticism, the Great Pyramid is also an accumulator and transformer of cosmic energies. You have been brought here to help us understand and harness those energies."

Kafar was intrigued. He had not been told the nature of the work he would be doing, only that it was vital to the future of Atlantis. He listened as the alchemist continued.

"We have improved much of the Ancients' technology. We know how everything works, and we have given the Pyramid a new purpose, a grander purpose, one that will improve the world and make Atlantis even greater than it already is."

Shakala merely hinted at this. He did not reveal all of the truth, that the original intent of the builders had long ago been put aside in favor of a more sinister, evil intent. He did not reveal how the Sons of Belial were transforming the original Pyramid of the Ancients into a weapon of death, destruction, and control. That would be for Kafar to figure out for himself, if he proved worthy of entering the Inner Circle.

"What does the future hold for the Great Pyramid?" asked the eager young man. "What good things are we going to do here to help improve life for every Atlantean and for the whole world?"

Shakala looked at Kafar. Here was an extremely intelligent and eager young man. That was obvious. There would be questions. Lots of questions. Already here was one for which Shakala had no answer. So idealistic, so full of innocence and hope and promise, Shakala thought. He shook his head and smiled.

"Yours are the eager questions of youth. Be patient, Kafar, and let the Great Pyramid reveal itself to you. There is much to be learned. Let us go inside now and see more of its secrets."

*****

What Shakala did not tell Kafar, in fact, what Shakala had probably forgotten, was the true nature of the Great Pyramid, a nature both Spiritual and Divine, that had practical, human, worldly ramifications. Its first and true purpose, the reason for which the Ancients had built it, was to produce the Alchemical Wedding, serve as a connecting rod to cement the Marriage of Heaven and Earth, and thus bring the life energy of the Dragon Current to the world.

According to Quetzalcoatl, the Great Pyramid would demonstrate the laws behind the pure growth of life. Therefore, he had instructed them to build a miniature golden pyramid at the very tip of the gigantic structure, fastened by a stainless steel rod set into the upper course of stone, extending deep within the Pyramid and rising a few inches above its surface. On that rod was a diamond point, the purest and finest crystal, casting the finest possible shadow. Serving, like a cat's whisker, to concentrate the energies for the Great Pyramid's main function.

This crystal, to which Quetzalcoatl actually referred as a "seed," was placed on the apex of the Great Pyramid to distill the solar spark, the element of fire by which the Life Essence was fertilized.

The first gift that Quetzalcoatl gave the Ancients was the gift of fire. This does not mean that he invented fire; rather, he gave them an awareness of fire—its existence, purpose, and function. Speaking in symbolic language, the Guardian explained fire as...

THE GERM OF ENERGY, THE ACTIVATING PRINCIPLE
THAT INSTILLS LIFE INTO FORM.

So the words were recorded in the *Book of Life*.

The ancient geomancers, always eager to express things numerically, immediately set to work to create a geometric shape to represent this element and first gift of Quetzalcoatl. They would place it in the center of the world for all to see—the Great Pyramid, whose very name means *Fire*.

Quetzalcoatl admired their artistry and instantly realized the benefits of the pyramid shape as the first, lightest, smallest, sharpest, most acute and mobile of solid figures. His words of praise were legendary.

THAT SOLID THAT HAS TAKEN THE FORM OF A GREAT PYRAMID
WILL BE THE ELEMENT AND SEED OF FIRE.

Lest they forget, the Ancients recorded these and all of the Guardian's teachings, for they were dealing with enormous forces and knowledge that was new to them. Here was a world that they never knew existed. At first, they were confused by his words, but they trusted in him to help them understand.

It was not easy for Quetzalcoatl to explain. He was trying to instill in the Ancients an understanding of the potentially unlimited power latent in the atom, as illustrated in solid form by the Great Pyramid. To do so, he had to teach them all of the particulars of quantum physics, mathematics, and engineering.

It could not be done all at once; it was accomplished over time. He proceeded slowly, speaking to them first in parables using metaphors with which they were familiar and only later expounding upon all these things.

*****

Are you familiar with *The Parable of the Seeds* as it is written in the *Book of Life*? Perhaps the favorite of all the Quetzalcoatl parables, because it is an expression of scientific truth couched in beautiful poetry. As Quetzalcoatl said as he began the story...

> Learn from the many symbolic and magical number series, which the Great Pyramid will show you and you will construct. The structure of Humankind is like the structure of the Great Pyramid. As the Great Pyramid is oriented to the four cardinal points of the compass, so human beings must orient themselves to the four aspects of the human psyche. As the Great Pyramid has five sides— East, West, North, South, and Base, so a person has five natures—King nature, Warrior nature, Lover nature, Magician nature, and Spirit nature.

> Consider this Spirit nature for a moment. It remains hidden—out of sight— just as the Pyramid's base lies hidden—out of sight beneath the visible parts of its structure. Yet it is the invisible—the Spirit side—that provides the base upon which everything else rests. Without a solid base, there can be no Pyramid. Without a spiritual foundation, there can be no human being.

> Both the Great Pyramid and Humankind contain sacred patterns of measure and number that can be expressed outwardly or inwardly. Both are limitless. Where distance and dimension are expressed outwardly, both the Great Pyramid and Humankind can extend far into the Cosmos, expanding ever outward, measuring distance on planetary and stellar intervals, measuring time in the cycles of the Grand Orb—the circle described by the Great Mother's path around the sun. So too, both the Great Pyramid and Humankind can express themselves inwardly, shrinking from miles to inches to mere specks, smaller and smaller, deeper and deeper within, until finally into the world of the atom and beyond, to that smallest of universes, the world the subatomic, the world of Heaven.

> And both the Great Pyramid and Humankind are crowned with crystal and gold, representing their whole structure in miniature. Crystal and gold—the Sacred Water and the Sacred Element, ever pure—through which will be transformed the energies required for the Alchemical Wedding and the Transformation of Humanity.

> Thus will the Marriage of Heaven and Earth be consummated and the Sacred Seed be planted—containing within itself all the numbers and ratios for its potential growth. It is like the smallest of all seeds, a grain of mustard seed, the germ from which all else grows. It is the Seed of Fire—the vital element. From the invisible speck grows the Tree of Life, encompassing the whole universe.

This story has not been told this story for a long time. It is so beautiful. The Ancients heard the Guardian's words and never forgot. Thus informed and inspired, they set to work and accomplished their task. Long stood the Great Pyramid as the symbol of their philosophy and science, indeed their whole civilization, the symbol of their recognition of the unity that links both the macrocosm and the microcosm with the patterns of the visible universe. The symbol of their understanding that the mathematical laws to which all natural growth conforms were known to prevail in both the greatest cycles of celestial motion and in the development of life from the smallest germ of a cell.

The physical Pyramid was destroyed on the final day, in that terrible instant when the Spear and the Sword came together in a clash of Earth, Air, Metal, Fire, and Water. That the stone edifice, though, was merely a representation in physical form. The real Pyramid was and *is* a construct of energy—pure energy. Therefore, it can never be destroyed and will continue to function until its purpose has been fulfilled.

The Ancients housed the original blueprint in a crystal and hid it away in anticipation of the time when the true purpose of the Pyramid would be forgotten. On receipt of a prearranged signal, the crystal was programmed to make itself known and let itself be found by those who would remember how to use it. That time is coming. Soon, now, very soon...

*****

Kafar's last question was still ringing in Shakala's ears as they approached the entrance to the Great Pyramid. It was a question for which the alchemist had no answer. He really could not say how the Great Pyramid was improving life in Atlantis. As he thought about it, he realized that there was no answer. Worse yet, the truth was that the Great Pyramid was not being used to improve life in Atlantis. It was only improving life for the Sons of Belial, and Belial in particular. Theirs was not the technology of improvement, it was the technology of the dominant species. It was the technology of power.

Kafar was a Seeker, a gatherer of information, one who asked questions. He had made that quite clear in his first half hour with Shakala. So many questions, about everything, it seemed. They had come like a cannonade, one after another, as the two men walked to the entranceway. Why did Shakala do things the way he did? How could they change that which needed changing? How could they improve upon an already perfect system of scientific inquiry and experimentation?

At first this had frightened Shakala. Why so many questions? They seemed innocent enough, innocuous enough, but were they? Suddenly, he was beginning to feel light-headed and shaky, oppressed and burdened. He knew the symptoms, realized what was happening to him. All of the old feelings were returning. Here come the demons again! he thought to himself in panic, referring to the uncontrollable anxiety that welled up and smothered him from time to time. Doesn't he know when to stop? Shakala screamed within himself. I don't want to hear this. He's making me look at things best left in darkness, making me question, making me think. And as a member of Belial's Inner Circle, that is something I do not want to do.

Then came the anger. It was his only recourse, his only defense, unless he wanted to spend the next several days in a state of near helplessness. "Enough!" Shakala finally lashed out, putting his hands over his ears to stop the incessant chatter. "How dare you interrogate me? Who are you to come here and question the methods of the masters? What right have you to ask what you ask? What have you accomplished that makes you such an authority that we should abolish all that we hold true, all that we hold sacred, and embrace your ways?" The older man was quaking with rage, his face shocked and pale, his lips a deep blue.

"I'm sorry," Kafar was taken aback by the change in Shakala's demeanor. "I did not mean to offend you or overstep my bounds. I ask a lot of questions, I know." He smiled gamely. "My father says that I'm a pest, I talk too much. Yet I've always been curious. I want to know. I really want to know. Sometimes my enthusiasm gets the better of me and overpowers my ability to restrain myself and stay in my place. Once again, I apologize. It will not happen again."

This expression of humility seemed to calm the older man. He stood before the entrance to the Great Pyramid, lost in thought. "Your questions show that you are wise," Shakala finally conceded, "and that is good. But you must learn that sometimes it is better to keep your wisdom to yourself. Sometimes it is better to observe in silence. For to be inquisitive within the Great Pyramid is to make oneself noticeable. And a noticeable person invites scrutiny, which is something I know better than to want." Shakala put an arm around Kafar in a fatherly gesture, having made the decision to accept his protégé and take him into his confidence.

The young man felt better almost immediately. He believed in Shakala's authority, just as he believed in his parents' authority. He had erred grievously through his own fault, of this he was convinced. But now, with the touch of an arm, all was forgiven. He was not to be abandoned after all. Kafar remembered all of those times when, as a boy, he had been chastised by his father. First had come the tears and feelings of abandonment, followed by an almost overwhelming desire to be rescued. Then finally, receiving the soothing comfort of his father's touch—an expression that said, "I still love you"—came the return of safety.

"Heed my advice, Kafar," Shakala warned his young protégé. "Draw no attention to yourself. Stay within your chambers and laboratory. Do not go exploring or let grand ideas tempt you to aspire to heights you cannot possibly scale. Simply do your job."

Kafar opened his mouth to say something, but Shakala placed a finger on his lips, as though silencing a noisy child in a museum. "Silence. We shall speak no more of this. There is work to be done. Let us go inside."

Shakala turned and disappeared within the dark opening, leaving Kafar with all of his unattended feelings, all of his unanswered questions, all of his shattered fantasies. For his part, the protégé accepted the advice and admonition without question, believing that he was entirely dependent upon Shakala for survival in this strange new world into which he had so suddenly been thrust.

*****

The two scientists stepped into the cool, dim interior of the Great Pyramid. As they crossed the threshold and entered the tunnel, Kafar felt the change instantly. There was a feeling of inconceivable weight over his head and on all sides—the weight of enormous blocks of stone pressing down on him from the apex to the base, immense weight coupled with immense age. How old the Great Pyramid was he could not even guess, for it had been built in an era before they measured time.

They passed along a polished passageway hewn out of solid rock. Kafar reached out and ran his hand along the walls. What was he expecting? Certainly not the silky texture that he encountered...stone so smooth as to be almost soft. Surprisingly warm, too, considering the temperature of the air. He felt a vibration when he placed his hand on the stone, almost imperceptible but there nevertheless. Kafar stopped and put his ear to the wall and listened.

"Ah," Shakala smiled. "I see you've discovered one of the secrets already. It did not take you long."

"Secrets?" Kafar raised one eyebrow quizzically.

"Yes, the warmth of the stone and the vibration. The Great Pyramid is, you might say, alive. It has an almost human temperature, and the energy running through the stone courses as do blood and *Chi* through the human body."

"How is this possible?" Kafar asked in amazement. He thought he knew everything about the Great Pyramid, but here was a new discovery.

"When combined, the shape, the natural design, and the stones themselves gather, conduct, and transmit the Earth's electromagnetic current. Those energies are coursing through the whole structure even now." Shakala began a long theoretical discourse on how the Great Pyramid formed an instrument of fusion between the elements from above and those of the Earth beneath to bring about the fertile union of the two elements of sulphur and mercury.

But Kafar was not listening. He was tingling with excitement, reveling in the newness of the experience. Enthralled by the sights, sounds, and smells, he silently reminded himself that this was really happening, just as he had hoped. Thoughts of his departure from home and his parents' final words of advice brought a warm smile to his lips.

"Son, today you become a runner in the long-distance race of life," his father had told him as he boarded the Way. "In that competitive world, always strive to achieve success, for you will be measured by that which you accomplish. Be steadfast like the runner, disciplined, industrious, strong-willed, competitive. Be bold! Produce goods in abundance, build magnificent structures, develop powerful allies and resources, amass great wealth, set new standards of excellence, discover new worlds."

His mother held his face in her hands and gently kissed his cheek. There were tears of joy and pride in her eyes. "May all your dreams come true," she had whispered softly.

This was a dream come true! He had wanted this all of his life. He had worked hard to achieve this goal, and now it was here. He was to work directly with Shakala, a master alchemist and brilliant mind. He was to have a great mentor. And he was going to change the world by making new discoveries and inventions for the benefit of all Atlantis. He would rise up quickly in the ranks of the scientists, growing in skill and prestige and renown, making one discovery and contribution after another.

Then one day, when Shakala grew old, Kafar would become Master Alchemist and be revered and rewarded for the greatness that he knew was his. He would have fame and wealth and live in one of the beautiful red stone mansions that lined the Avenue of the Gods on the way to the Palace and Temple of Poseidon. He would have servants, too, and a wonderful wife and loving children and all of the best things that Atlantean society had to offer. All of Atlantis would honor him for his magnificent deeds and accomplishments. Perhaps one day his statue would stand in the piazza next to the statue of Quetzalcoatl. Oh, Kafar was willing to work hard for this most noble and enticing ambition. And he knew that once he could show everyone what he could do, they would recognize his potential, reward him, and put him on the fast path to success.

His thoughts were interrupted as they rounded a corner and entered a small, gleaming chamber. The room was well lit and arrayed with scientific instruments and equipment.

"You will work here," Shakala walked over to a stone slab and picked up a strange black object. "I want you to spend your time examining this and others like it. They are the power source for a most important new technology that Belial is developing. You are the expert. How do these black crystals conduct energy? How might we improve on their energy conducting and transmitting capabilities."

Kafar took the crystal from Shakala and examined it. In all his experience—and it was considerable, despite his youth—he had never seen its like before. He would enjoy getting to know its properties and capabilities.

"Our problem is that they explode when the current reaches a certain strength," Shakala went on. "We need them to retain their integrity far past the temperatures and pressures that they are currently able to tolerate. Examine them, and see if you can figure out why they shatter as they do. And once you determine why, devise a solution to the problem.

"If you can do that," Shakala winked paternally, not really expecting Kafar to succeed, "you will please a lot of people and be well on your way to making a name for yourself. Of course, it will not be as easy as it sounds. We have been struggling with the problem for months and are no closer to a solution today than we were when the first explosion occurred more than two years ago." So saying, Shakala left the younger man to begin work.

Kafar was somewhat disappointed. The black crystals were intriguing, to be sure, but he had hoped to be assigned to a far more exciting and visible project than this. Nevertheless, he refused to let his spirits be dampened. Little did he know that he was working on the solution to the problem of getting Belial's ultimate weapon to work without exploding. Little did he know that he was only days away from discovering the secret to perfecting a device that would destroy the entire Atlantean civilization and alter the course of human history and evolution.

Rolling up his sleeves, he put on a white lab coat and picked up one of the crystals. He plunged in with enthusiasm.

CHAPTER 35

Hear now how those who are called to the Grail are made known. On the Stone, around the edge, appear letters inscribed giving the name and the lineage of each one, maid or boy, who is to make the journey.

—*Parsival*

With each new learning, Adima was faced with new tests...challenges, actually, designed to measure his character and his faith. The night after learning about the archetypes, while Kafar worked late in his laboratory within the Great Pyramid delving into the problem of the exploding crystals, Adima slept peacefully in the great western forest that blanketed the steep slopes of Mount Kylene in verdant splendor.

"Wake up," Enoch roused him from a sound sleep.

"What's the matter?" Adima asked groggily, wiping the sleep from his eyes and yawning mightily.

"Put this on and come with me." The old man tossed him a robe and walked into the forest. "The first quarter moon beckons you."

"Where are we going?" Adima shouted to Enoch's retreating back, stubbing his toe on a root as he tried to dress and follow at the same time. He caught up with the old man at the edge of a gurgling stream that tumbled down from the hills high above.

Enoch handed him a little white stone and said, "Go and stand in the middle of the river. When you are there, swallow the stone. That is your staying power. Regardless of what happens, whatever you see, stay put. Do not move. Stand your ground. However, as always, you have a choice. If the water is too cold, or the fear to great, or you do not like what you see, you can swim away and return to dry land. But then that is as far as your training can take you. So if you want to learn something, stay put. It's up to you."

Without a word, Adima doffed the robe and waded out into the river. Needles of icy cold water pierced his skin, constricting the flow of blood through his veins. He inhaled and exhaled several times in rapid succession to balance his temperature and adjust to the shock of the temperature change.

The bank dropped off sharply, and the current swept him out into deeper water. He was a strong swimmer, though, and reached the middle of the stream without any difficulty. Treading water, his feet brushed against a sand bar. He could stand. Imagine that! But he was really not surprised. He was sure that Enoch knew all about this submerged islet. Adima stood waist-deep in the swirling current, popped the stone into his mouth, and swallowed. Although he had no idea what was about to happen, he was determined to stand his ground.

Overhead, the stars twinkled, and fleecy white clouds drifted by. Off in the distance, a great horned owl hooted its mating call. Adima stood perfectly still and gazed upstream, waiting. Even in the darkness, he could sense the swirling patterns in the current forming little pools and eddies as the water swirled over the submerged rocks.

Was that a movement below the surface? He could not be sure. Straining his eyes, he looked harder. Sure enough, there it was again, a serpentine flicker under the water, moving toward him. Now it was joined by another and another...dancing patterns of light like phosphorescent water snakes streaming in colorful bands all around him.

One of the snakes moved toward him, swimming rapidly and rising out of the depths. It broke the surface and reared up directly in front of him—a huge, full-bodied snake, its five heads waving tentacle-like before him. As the fearsome serpent swam in circles around him, Adima stood his ground, determined to discover its purpose. The monster opened its jaws wide, seeming to smile a pleasing smile at him. Poison dripped from its gleaming fangs. Slowly, almost dreamlike, each of the heads extended themselves toward him in turn, biting him in the center of his chest. There was no pain, but he felt the fangs sink deeply into his flesh, squirting great gobs of hematoxic poison into his bloodstream.

It was over in a moment. The snake seemed to enter his body and melt within him, vanishing along its companions, leaving him alone in total darkness once again. Adima clutched his chest in terror. He knew he wasn't poisoned, for there had been no pain, and he knew that the pain of a real poisonous snakebite was excruciating and brought almost immediate paralysis, often death. No, this had been a test, which he had passed by standing his ground. As a result, he had been given a gift and initiated into a higher level of achievement. But what gift? he wondered as he swam slowly back to shore.

Enoch was not there, but the smell of smoke drifted through the woods. Adima arrived back at their campsite just as the flames were taking hold and a cheerful fire was burning. "Now you are a Snake-Man," the old man said casually. "You know, such medicine is very rare. Living through multiple snakebites allows you to transmute all poisons, be they mental, physical, spiritual, or emotional.

"Snake has entered within you this night, first to teach you to how to find your heart's joy and how to be faithful to your personal truths. And from its place of honor wrapped along your spinal cord, it will protect your sacred space."

"My sacred space?" Adima asked.

"There is a place within each of us that is ours alone, sacred unto ourselves, where only we go," the old man explained. "Each of us has it, but not many consciously acknowledge its existence any more, although at one time we all did so openly. The place is never shared except by invitation. Of course, you have invited another to share that place within you, as she has invited you to share hers."

Adima smiled as he thought of Cybele—his wife, the mother of their children—home at Elysia.

"But there is another who wants to enter your space," Enoch said, suddenly serious, "and that cannot be, for to allow him to do so would be to invite disaster."

"Is it Belial?" Adima asked, knowing that it almost certainly was.

"It is," Enoch replied. "But now you have another ally—the multi-headed Snake who looks in all five directions at once, protecting your sacred space, keeping it yours and yours alone."

Adima sat and warmed himself by the fire. "Would I really have had to stop my training if I had not stayed in the river?" he asked.

"Of course not," Enoch laughed as he handed his student a steaming mug of tea. "I just told you that to give you an added incentive for staying. You might have had to postpone some new adventures for a while and go back and revisit some others. But you can never really stop the process once you get on the path. The universe will not let you.

"But none of that matters anyway, because you stood your ground, which means that, when the moon returns to its first quarter phase a month from now, you will face the Dragon that guards the Well of Kuneware."

*****

"What is that?" Adima asked, pointing to a strange object glinting in the sunlight. They were walking through an unfamiliar part of the forest on this bright, cool morning. It had been almost a month since his encounter with Snake. The deep woods were quiet after the previous evening's storm. There had been a torrential downpour during the night, with thunder, lightning, and driving rain. The wind had been cyclonic, whipping the grasses, filling the air with a whirlwind of leaves, twigs, and small objects, bending and breaking even the oldest and mightiest trees.

Now, with the dawn, the air was fresh, clean, and sweet smelling. Signs of the storm's ravages were everywhere—fallen limbs, uprooted shrubs, flowers, grasses, and debris of all kinds littered the forest floor. In many places the rock lay bare and exposed, the topmost covering of soil, leaves, and moss having been blown away.

It was to one such area that Adima now pointed. A huge oak had been partially uprooted and was leaning at a precarious angle. Were it not for the support of a larger forest brother, the tree would have fallen and died. As it was, however, it would continue to live, its vast root system only partially exposed, forming an extensive and almost impenetrable maze, at the center of which lay a man-made object.

Approaching carefully, Adima saw that it was a weapon, an ancient, rusty sword. So old and rusty, in fact, that it must have been dropped there ages ago, when the Ancient Swordsmen roamed the countryside. Over the centuries, it had gotten covered by falling detritus and eventually been buried.

Slowly, Nature had done her work, deoxidizing the outer surface of the iron blade and turning it to rust. At some point ages ago, judging by the size of the tree, a tiny acorn had sprouted and grown over time into the mighty forest monarch before him. In their constant search for water and nourishment, the roots had spread out, digging deeply into the soil and entwining themselves around the sword. There it had lain for ages, until last evening when the storm had uprooted the giant and exposed the ancient weapon to air and sunlight once again.

It took a while, but Adma was finally able to extricate the sword from the tangle of roots. Enoch said nothing, merely sitting on a rock, an interested observer. "It must have been a fine weapon once." Adima held up the blade, admiring the strange and unknown craftsmanship. A closer examination showed it to be in remarkably good shape. The edge was still keen, and there was only the thinnest coating of rust on the surface of the metal. Rubbing a bit of dirt off the handle revealed precious stones set into the hilt...strange stones, also of unknown origin. Whoever the blacksmith had been, he was certainly a master craftsman, an artist of great skill and cunning.

"I wonder who could have made it?" Adima mused. The sword was enormous and very heavy. It would have taken a powerful man to wield such a weapon with any skill. "And who could have owned it?"

He spent the next several minutes looking around for a scabbard and armor, any clues to the identity of the former owner of the sword. He even looked for a skeleton, thinking perhaps that the warrior might have been killed nearby, with this sword and his bones being all that were left of the man. The search proved fruitless, however. "It's a mystery," he said at last, joining Enoch on the rock.

"Not such a mystery," chuckled the old man.

"Well, then, at least a coincidence."

"A coincidence indeed!" Again a light chuckle. "Imagine the odds against your finding this sword at this time on this day. First, the storm had to uproot exactly the right tree just before you entered the forest. Then, the wind had to blow the tree in the perfect direction.

It could have been blown to the north instead of the south, burying the sword even deeper. But it was not. It was blown so that the sword was exposed to you as you walked past."

"Of course, there had to be somebody to find the sword. Of all the paths you could possible have taken, you chose this one and walked to this spot. You could have been looking above or to the left, but instead, you were looking to the right, and so you caught sight of the blade. And all of this would have been for naught had the original owner of the sword left it in a completely different spot. Suppose he had..."

"Enough!" Adima cried, laughing at the old man's rambling monologue. "I get the picture. Okay, so it isn't a coincidence. There are no coincidences. Everything happens for a reason. It's all part of a Master Plan."

He parroted Enoch's teachings back to him, not with animosity or rancor, but with love and affection. Indeed, he knew the old man was right. Time and again over the past twenty-seven years, he had lived the *Mystery of Synchronicity*. Now he was living it again, having chanced upon this sword entangled in the roots of a fallen tree uprooted by a storm.

"Maybe there is no coincidence, but there is still a mystery," he repeated. "Who put it there? Why was I supposed to find it? And having found it, what am I to do with it? Adima stood up and brandished the sword, the blade whirring as it cut through the air. He held the weapon easily, despite its great weight. It seemed to fit his hand as though custom-made for his grip.

"Now you begin to ask the right questions," Enoch said. "What do you think you should do with it?"

"I suppose I could bring it home and try to restore it," Adima said. "It would take some effort, but I imagine I could wash away the dirt and grime of centuries and bring out some of its original luster. Of course, it's too unwieldy to use in tournament competition, but it would make a marvelous trophy for display."

"It is not a trophy for display," Enoch said. "There is a deeper meaning to the sword than this. Nor will it be restored by a simple cleaning and polishing. It has been presented to you for a far greater purpose, not a worldly purpose, but a spiritual one." The old man took the ancient relic in his hands and examined it closely. "Its power is gone," he said matter-of-factly. "You may only swing it once, and that is all. The weapon will withstand the first blow, but at the second it will shatter."

Adima looked at the heavy iron blade. "Shatter!" he exclaimed. "Why, I couldn't shatter this sword if I tried for a thousand years. It would take the strength of Atlas to shatter it, if indeed even a Titan could do it."

"If you doubt me, try it," Enoch suggested. "Yonder lies a tree stump. There is no life in it, so you will not cause it any pain. Go ahead, strike the stump with your new-found weapon."

Adima did as he was told. He had unquestioning faith in the old man, but he could not believe that the sword was as fragile as Enoch said. How could a sword lose its power? Wasn't the power in the swordsman rather in than the weapon itself? Standing before the stump, which rose about ten feet out of the ground, Adima flexed his muscles and hefted the weapon. Grasping it in both hands, he swung with all his strength.

The blade bit deeply into the lifeless wood. The stump quivered under the force of the impact. And the sword held, solid and unharmed.

"A mighty blow," Enoch applauded. "You do have a fine skill, coupled with great strength. Try again now."

Again Adima prepared himself. He was excited by the adventure, and his adrenaline was pumping freely. This would be a bold stroke indeed, far mightier than the first. He walked back several paces and stood facing his target. Raising the sword high in the air, he threw back his head, voiced a bloodcurdling yell, and charged, bringing the weapon crashing down with such force that the blade was torn from his grasp and he hurtled headlong to the ground. Stunned from the fall, the wind knocked out of him, he lay still for several seconds. After a moment, he felt Enoch's arms helping him to his feet.

"What happened?" he asked groggily.

"Behold," Enoch pointed to the broken pieces of the sword lying at the base of the stump. "As I foretold, it shattered at the impact of the second blow. Now it remains for you to make it whole again."

Adima could not believe his eyes. The weapon was not even recognizable. "I guess I must have hit my head harder than I thought," he looked at Enoch. "I thought I heard you say I now had to restore the sword."

"So I did," Enoch answered.

Adima snorted. "Restore it! I'll be hard pressed just to find all of the pieces." He knelt on the ground, fingering a few of the larger fragments.

"They are all there," came the mysterious reply, "and you will find them. Here." The old man handed him a mildewed burlap sack. "Place each piece in the sack. It will make them that much easier to carry."

"Carry where?" Adima looked up at the old man, never stopping to wonder how his mentor had happened to have a smelly old bag in his possession. "Aren't you going to help? I'll never be able to find all of the pieces."

"Focus," Enoch instructed, having by this time returned to his perch on the rock. Adima knew that tone. It was time to get serious and concentrate, for an important lesson was at hand. "This is the only task you have. This is the only time there is. This is the only place there is. This is your only purpose. Focus on the task at hand. When it is complete, you will know."

Unquestioningly, Adima obeyed, long since familiar with Enoch's method of teaching. He let go of his doubts and questions, let go of the frustration and need for answers. Surrendering to the conditions of the moment, he set about the task. He concentrated on finding each fragment of what had once been the sword. Working on his hands and knees, he placed the broken parts in the bag, piece by piece. Time seemed to stand still, although the sun continued to climb higher and higher toward its zenith.

As he worked, Adima sensed a new relationship with the forest, and with Nature in general. He felt the living Presence of the Great Mother reflected in every living creature around him. He felt them blessing his endeavor and sensed their cooperation as he labored. The children of the Father and the Mother were bringing him their gifts, offering them in gratitude and gladness.

The flowers gave him the gift of their scent, blessing him with their sweet fragrance. The trees extended their arms to shield him from the heat, spreading their leaves upon the ground as a soft cushion upon which he might kneel. The shrubs offered succulent berries to help him break his fast. The birds sang their happy songs to ease his mind and gladden his heart. The Angel of Sunlight lit his way. The Angel of Air whispered sweet poetry in his ear. The Angel of Water quenched his thirst and brought him strength. The Angel of Earth provided him a firm foundation upon which to do his work.

Under Enoch's watchful eye he labored. Under other eyes, too...nonhuman, brightly colored eyes, sparkling blue and orange and green and yellow from their place of concealment within the trees and bushes and under the rocks and ledges. At last, when the sun was directly overhead, he stood up, stretched his back, and sighed deeply. "I think that's it," he said. "I'm exhausted."

"Are you sure you found them all?" Enoch asked.

"As sure as I can be," came the tired reply. "But I have no way of being certain." A thought suddenly struck him. "Unless you do..." Adima turned to his teacher.

"Sit down," Enoch said, handing him a gourd of water. Adima drank gratefully, feeling the cool liquid flow down his throat and quench the hot fire in his stomach. "I can't be any more sure than you are. But there are others who inhabit this realm who have better eyesight than we do. What remains hidden to us, they can see clearly."

Adima looked around. He knew exactly to whom Enoch was referring. "The Elementals?" he asked. He felt a thrill of excitement quiver through him. Was a lifelong dream about to come true? Was he going to make contact with an Elemental?

"Be very still," Enoch instructed. "Think peaceful, loving thoughts. Open your heart to Unconditional Love, Compassion, Innate Harmony, and the Healing Presence."

Adima did as he was told. It was remarkable how easy it had become to settle into such a peaceful state. What had once taken a lot of physical and mental effort now came as naturally as breathing itself.

"Now ask them to come and show you what your eyes cannot see."

Adima was about to close his eyes, but Enoch stayed him. "Keep them open," he said. "Your heart is pure, your thoughts are just. You have earned the right to look upon the Elementals without artificial aids." The old man was referring to that night so long ago when he had used the magic drops to open his young student's eyes to a vision of the fairies.

Together they sat and waited, blending in with the forest community. They were one with the forest now, not aliens from an alien world, but one with the flora and fauna around them. As it was in the Beginning... Adima thought, feeling the harmony and unity of life all around him.

It did not take long. There was a rustle in the bushes as the tiny creatures presented themselves. They seemed to emerge from the very leaves and twigs and bark, taking shape and form from within the living foliage.

First the eyes appeared—two glowing orbs of color within the structure of a bush. Then a three-dimensional face formed where before there had only been a jumble of leaves, peering out with those enormous eyes, observing and checking to make sure it was safe. Then the body emerged, forming out of the bark and limbs of the plant itself.

There were four of them. How their eyes sparkled! Adima smiled his widest smile as they approached, each carrying a piece of the sword in their tiny, delicate hands. He was thrilled and honored that such gentle creatures felt safe enough to be in his presence.

They trust me, he thought. I must do everything I can to protect and preserve that trust.

Approaching slowly, Blue-Eyes carried a piece of the hilt. "Thank you." Adima held the sack open as the Elemental dropped the fragment within. Then came Yellow-Eyes and Green-Eyes with scraps of the blade. At last the largest of the four approached. Dropping his fragment in the bag, he looked at Adima with those sparkling orange eyes. The tiny being stared at him for a long moment, as though considering whether or not to speak. Then he did so.

"Take the fragments to the Well of Kuneware," Orange-Eyes instructed in a voice like water flowing over smooth, round pebbles. "There in the Spring, the sword will become whole again, restored in the flow of the sacred liquid."

There was no communications barrier, even though the creature had spoken in the First Language. Adima understood the meaning of the words as clearly as though they had been spoken in his own tongue. Rising, he extended his right palm in blessing. The little people of the forest, so solemn only a moment ago, broke out in delighted peals of joyous laughter. Returning the gesture, they danced and skipped happily about the clearing, tumbling over each other in their exuberance.

For several minutes they cavorted. Then, on signal from Orange-Eyes, they returned the blessings and made signs of peace, then melted slowly back into the foliage from which they had come. The forest returned to its pristine state. The bushes looked like bushes once again. Try as he might, Adima could find no trace of hidden faces or figures within the leaves and bark. But they were there. He knew that now as surely as he knew his own name. The Elementals were there, and they had presented themselves to him.

"What an honor!" he exclaimed when he could find his voice.

"An honor, yes," Enoch replied, "but more than that. They have charged you with a mission. Have you forgotten?"

Of course—the Spring! "Where is this Well of Kuneware?" Adima asked, "and what did they mean that I was to restore the sword?"

"Before I answer your questions, let me ask if you understand the symbology of the sword itself." Enoch replied. "Do you understand that this is not an ordinary sword?"

"I realized that the moment it broke," Adima replied. "I was thinking a lot about it while gathering the pieces. I seem to recall a legend in the *Book of Mysteries*, something about a powerful man with a sword in his mouth. I wish I had the book here so I could read it."

"No need," Enoch said. "I know the legend well. You are right, as far as you go. The sword proceeds out of the mouth of the man. But there is more to the legend." The old man closed his eyes, reciting from memory.

> THE HUMAN WORD IS ALSO A SWORD
> THAT PROCEEDS OUT OF THE MOUTH OF A MAN.

"The legend describes it as..."

> ...A WORD-SWORD THAT HAS GROWN OLD,
> ATROPHIED, SHATTERED, AND LOST ITS POWER.

"As has happened to the sword I found," Adima understood.

"The legend goes on to say that..."

> ONLY BY DISCOVERING THE ORIGINAL SOURCE
> OF ITS POWER CAN THIS WORD-SWORD BE RENEWED.

"And the Elementals have told us where that source lies," Adima finished, "the Spring that feeds the Well of Kuneware."

"Yes," Enoch answered, glancing at the sky, "and we had better be getting started if we are to get there before dark. We have a long walk ahead of us."

He headed off in an easterly direction. As they walked, the old man quoted more of the legend, explaining the challenge that lay before Adima and how it would be his task to solve the puzzle and restore the sword.

> THE SPRING BUBBLES FORTH FROM BENEATH A HUGE ROCK, FORMING A CLEAR,
> SPARKLING POOL OF THE PUREST, FRESHEST WATER. IF THE PIECES ARE NOT
> LOST AND THE INITIATE FITS THEM TOGETHER PROPERLY, AS SOON AS THE
> SPRING WATER WETS THEM, THE SWORD WILL BECOME WHOLE AGAIN. THE
> JOININGS AND EDGES WILL BOND STRONGER THAN EVER BEFORE, AND THE
> SIGNS OF THE CONSTELLATIONS ENGRAVED UPON THE BLADE WILL REAPPEAR
> IN THEIR ORIGINAL LUSTER.

They continued their trek throughout the afternoon. For the most part, Adima remained silent, lost in thought, wondering how he would accomplish this most difficult task. He could think of no way that would lead to success, yet he was sure that the Elementals would not have presented him with an impossible challenge.

"Time will tell," he muttered under his breath. He gazed behind him at the western sky.

*****

The sun was just setting as the two men approached their destination. The forest had thinned out several miles back, giving way to prairie and meadowlands. Large herds of deer, antelope, and buffalo grazed on the tender grasses and drank from the numerous watering holes that dotted the landscape. There was the Well, marked by a huge rock that rose out of the ground. Even from this distance, it appeared much larger than an ordinary well.

"Why is it so big?" Adima wondered. Then, as they got closer, he realized that he was not looking at just a well. There was something on top of the rock, something large and green and very much alive. "It's a Dragon!" he exclaimed in shock. "I thought they were extinct."

"Not quite extinct," Enoch answered, looking at the fabled creature, who returned their gaze with baleful yellow eyes from its perch on the rock. "Just hiding out, like the Elementals, knowing the price of revealing its presence to those who do not understand."

"There is magic here." Adima shivered, drawing his cloak about him as a chill wind swept across the meadow. The air grew cold, and leaves and dust blew in the swirling eddies of air currents all around him. He could sense the power of the place. It was not difficult to understand for one who had been initiated into the Mysteries. The Well of Kuneware was fed by a magic Spring. Therefore, it was only natural that the waters be guarded by a Dragon, lest the shadow Adepts of black magic usurp and pervert their potency.

"Here at the Well of Kuneware, you face a twofold challenge," Enoch said, revealing more of the Legend of the Word-Sword.

> BEFORE THE SPRING WILL YIELD ITS VIRTUE—THE CREATIVE HEALING POWER OF THE WORD—THE INITIATE MUST ONCE AND FOR ALL OVERCOME HIS DEEP-SEATED EGOISM AND PRIDE, TRANSFORMING THEM INTO SOMETHING ELSE.
>
> ONLY THEN MUST HE ATTEMPT THE SECOND PART OF THE TASK—TO FIT TOGETHER THE BROKEN PIECES OF THE SWORD. EACH PIECE GOES INTO ITS RIGHTFUL PLACE TO MAKE UP THE SIGNS OF THE ZODIAC. THE FIXED CONSTELLATIONS MUST APPEAR IN THEIR RIGHT ORDER AND POSITION. NOT ONE PIECE MUST BE LOST.

*****

"Greetings," a female voice hailed them. Adima turned to see two women beckoning to them from beyond the Well. A happy smile of recognition lit his face, and he rushed to embrace his wife. "What are you doing here?" he cried in delight.

"We came to support you in your challenge," Sophia said simply. "It is not right for you to have to undertake this great task by yourself. Some things you must do completely on your own, as you have done many times. Others, though, such as this one, can be done with help."

"Does that mean you will all help reassemble the sword?" Adima asked, unslinging the musty sack from his shoulder and throwing himself on the ground. He was exhausted, and it felt good to take the weight off of his legs.

"None of us can actually assemble the pieces and restore the sword," Sophia shook her head. "That can only be done by you. We are here as your allies, though, to encourage and support you, offering you whatever aid we can."

"I am grateful," Adima said humbly, "and I'm so glad to see you." He squeezed Cybele's hand tightly, overjoyed that she was there to share this adventure with him.

"Let us eat something," Sophia said. "We've prepared a small repast. You will need all of your strength, for you must labor long into the night in order to complete your task before the light of day returns."

"What do you mean?" Adima asked. "Don't I just put the pieces in the water and let the Spring do the rest?"

"Not quite," Sophia smiled. "The restoration of the sword requires the recitation of a magic incantation. If you knew the magic words, then of course you could do just that, and the sword would be restored easily, with no effort on your part. But I'm afraid you forgot to learn the spell."

"What spell?" Adima asked. He could not remember ever having had to memorize anything in the nature of a magic spell, although he had learned several songs, prayers, and incantations over the years.

"That is for you to find out," the old woman winked mysteriously. "You have been given all of the clues over the years. If you paid attention and interpreted them correctly, you already have the answer. You already know the spell. And if your mouth ever does speak the words, the power of fortune will sprout and grow forever."

"I'm quite tired," Adima said, feeling more than a little bit overwhelmed by the events of this most unusual day. "We've been walking for hours. I was hoping for a good night's sleep before trying to put the pieces of the sword back together."

"That is not to be," Enoch answered, "for time is of the essence now. You must place the sword in the water at its source beneath the rock before the light of day has shown upon it. Otherwise, all will have been for naught."

*****

They ate dinner and chatted quietly, each recounting their adventures to the other. After the meal, Adima fell asleep for a while, resting his head in his wife's lap. Enoch awoke him when the first quarter moon was high above them.

"Take the sack and go to the Well," he said, handing him the bag full of the broken pieces of the sword. "We shall await you here. If you are successful, you will return in the morning with the sword fully restored."

"And if I'm not?" Adima wanted to say, but he kept silent. He had his doubts, but always before he had managed to find the right way. He hoped he'd be able to find it again. "Good night," he said, walking out of the circle of firelight toward the Well and its mighty guardian. The three stood and watched him disappear into the night. After a few moments, they heard a powerful roar. Adima was at the well, and the Dragon was acknowledging his presence.

"Will he succeed?" Cybele asked.

"That remains to be seen," Sophia shrugged. "He has all of the tools, all of the allies. He is ready."

The old woman looked at Enoch, who nodded in agreement. "Now it's just a matter of consolidating his learning and putting it all together to come to the realization that he already knows the spell," he said.

"Before dawn," Sophia added.

"Yes," Enoch agreed, quoting again from the legend.

> THE INITIATE MUST ACCOMPLISH THE TASK IN TRANSCENDENT AWARENESS, UNILLUMINATED BY THE LIGHT OF WAKING CONSCIOUSNESS IN THE THREE-DIMENSIONAL WORLD OF THE SENSES.

"What is the spell?" Cybele asked. "Can you tell me?"

"It is so very simple," Sophia answered her. "It is both cause and effect, beginning and end, source and goal of all there is. It is the single unifying principle and force underlying all of Creation."

The old woman turned to Enoch for confirmation. "Yes," he said softly. "It is so very simple."

> FOR THE MAGIC SPELL THAT WELDS TOGETHER THE SHATTERED WORD-SWORD IS *LOVE*—THE UNCONDITIONAL LOVE OF SPIRIT. AND ONLY THROUGH SUCH LOVE, WHICH TRANSCENDS ALL PREJUDICE OF RACE, COLOR, NATION, CREED, AND GENDER, CAN THE INDIVIDUAL HUMAN SPIRIT COME TO BIRTH IN HUMANKIND.

*****

The initial roar of the Dragon frightened him. Adima drew back, instinctively reaching for his sword. But of course, there was no sword, nor any other weapon with which to defend himself. Perhaps it is not a challenge, Adima thought. Perhaps it is just a greeting, an acknowledgment that I am here and about to do something important. We'll soon find out, either way.

He approached the Well and stood before the great stone from beneath which the stream bubbled. He could see quite clearly in the moonlight, and the softly flowing water added a sense of tranquility to the scene.

The Dragon watched him from its perch atop the globe, its huge head weaving from side to side. He's guarding me! Adima realized in amazement. He's another ally, keeping watch so that I am not disturbed. The thought of being under the protection of a Dragon, coupled with the knowledge that his dearest loved ones were only a few hundred yards away, calmed him. With a sense of purpose and determination, he settled into the task at hand.

Sitting cross-legged at the edge of the pool, the moonlight reflected in the inky black water, Adima spread the pieces of the sword on the ground before him. He was perplexed. The shape of each piece stood out clearly, and it would not be a problem to match up the larger pieces. But there were so many tiny ones that were not placed so easily. And what would he use as glue to cement the entire structure together?

Hours went by, or so it seemed, as he struggled to fit each piece into its proper position. A low growl from the Dragon was the first intimation that he was no longer alone.

"What are you doing?" a strange male voice asked. Adima barely glanced up to look at the man, so engrossed was he in the puzzle. "I say, sir," the stranger asked again. "What are you doing? Can I sit and watch? I'm lonely and need someone to talk to."

"Sorry, but I'm very busy and must be by myself right now," Adima waved his hand in dismissal. The last thing he needed was a pesky stranger to distract him from the task at hand. The man stood there, just looking at him. "I don't mean to be rude," Adima looked up for a brief instant, barely noticing him, "but I must ask you to leave me by myself."

"As you wish," the stranger acquiesced, leaving Adima alone with the puzzle once again. "Don't let anyone else bother me," Adima spoke jokingly to the Dragon. "Do your job and keep the pests away." The Dragon snorted a little puff of steam and lay its head on its forepaws.

The night continued to pass, and he was no closer to a solution. Each time he thought he was done, the sword crumbled or he found an additional piece for which there was no place. Adima glanced at the sky. The moon was rapidly approaching the western horizon. He sensed someone standing behind him. The stranger had approached once again.

"Sir," the stranger hailed him.

"What does he want now?" Adima grumbled in frustration. "And how is it that he escapes the notice of the Dragon?" He looked at the mighty beast. Its head was tucked into its folded wings. It was fast asleep. "Some guardian," Adima grunted. He turned to take a closer look at the stranger. What he saw astonished him.

The man was a Lemurian, sworn enemy of the Atlanteans. And judging by his appearance, he was not well. A bloody rag was tied around his head, his clothes were but tattered rags, and he was barefoot. Thin and emaciated, he leaned on a single crutch for support...homeless, hungry, and alone.

Adima knew that look and recognized that odor. He had seen such men lying in the street before the Palace walls. He had smelled the sickness and filth, the stench not only of physical disease, but also of poverty, misery, and ignorance. Now here the man stood, not even an Atlantean, but an enemy—the epitome of the homeless Everyman, making his way through the world alone, forgotten, unrecognized, and unloved.

Adima wanted to care, he really did, but there was no time just now. "Sir, if you come back tomorrow, I will try to help you," he spoke kindly, but he chafed at the amount of time the stranger was taking. "If you like, walk several hundred paces yonder. There you will find food and drink. I cannot help you here. I must accomplish my task before the break of day." Which is approaching ever more rapidly, he thought, watching the moon disappear below the western horizon. There was so little time and so much to do that he could not afford to get sidetracked by helping this pitiful stranger.

"As you wish." The man vanished into the darkness. Far in the distance, a wolf howled, its long, mournful dirge floating on the wind. Adima barely noticed. The Dragon's ears twitched, but otherwise it slept undisturbed.

Time continued to pass; Adima's frustration continued to mount. "This is impossible!" He scattered the pieces of the sword in the dust, standing up to stretch in frustration and exhaustion.

The stranger was standing at the edge of the pool. Silent this time, the man spoke no word nor made any move to approach him. "There are bread and water in my pouch." Adima tossed him the sack, hoping this would satisfy the man long enough for him to complete the task. The stranger accepted the food hungrily, crawling off into the darkness to eat and drink.

It was almost dawn. In desperation and near panic, Adima gathered the fragments of the sword and plunged with them into the pool. The water was shallow at the edge, and the bottom was smooth and sandy. Vigorously he began to scrub, attempting to wash away the grime of ages and somehow fit the pieces together. He had sung every song he knew, said every prayer he knew, muttered every incantation and healing remedy he knew. Nothing. The sword was as shattered as ever.

"I've failed!" he cried aloud to the darkness. The Dragon opened one eye to look at him. Filling its cavernous chest with air, it heaved a great sigh of disappointment. A thin wisp of smoke curled upward, barely noticeable in the dim light. "I cannot do it," Adima spoke his frustration to the Dragon. "I know neither the way to mend the sword nor the magic words to utter. I give up." The mythic beast made no reply, remaining atop the rock, staring at him with those huge, intelligent eyes.

In the gray light of early morning, the stranger appeared once again. Adima was about to chastise him and walk away, but then he paused. Is something else going on here? he wondered, looking first at the man and then at the Dragon. There must be. It was too much of a coincidence for this man—a wounded Lemurian enemy—to have shown up in this desolate spot at just this time. Could the stranger be part of the puzzle, or, better yet, part of the solution?

With new hope and a clearer vision, Adima paused to look at the man as he approached. At first, all he could see was his pitiful state—the open sores, filthy rags, matted hair, and hollow eyes. The Lemurian was quite ill, swaying unsteadily, barely able to support himself on his feeble crutch.

What has brought him to this lowly state? Adima wondered. Obviously the man was suffering from exposure, fever, and who knew what else. It was then that a thrill of recognition swept over him. All of those adjectives he had applied to the man—homeless, hungry, lonely, sick, Lemurian—mattered not. The man was not the adjectives he had attributed to him. *He is a man, just like me!* Adima realized.

Now the Dragon was fully alert. Perched atop the rock, it stood poised in tense anticipation, pacing restlessly back and forth. Wings spread, head thrown back, it voiced a thunderous roar. Adima sensed that the Dragon was aware of his thoughts and was encouraging him to continue.

"He is a man, just as I am a man," Adima exclaimed. "Underneath the surface differences, we are exactly alike. We have our hopes and dreams, our loves and fears, our secret desires."

Compassion flooded his heart, and he felt an overwhelming desire to help. Forgetting the sword now, forgetting everything but the plight of this pitiful stranger who was so like himself, Adima waded out of the pool and rushed forward. His only thought was to reach out and embrace the man, kiss his wounds, and help him heal. Ignoring the fever and the filth, the dirt and the stench, Adima caught the man in his arms just as he was about to collapse. Tacitly acknowledging their kinship and kindred spirit—their sameness—he carried the sick man to the water's edge. Calling him by the name he shared with all men, he asked the only question that could break the spell.

"Brother, what ails thee? How can I help?"

With a tremendous rush of wind that almost knocked him off his feet, the Dragon spread its wings and leapt into the air, taking joyous flight. Great sheets of fire shot from its nostrils in an awesome display of power. Huge, hissing plumes of steam billowed in the air. A mighty bolt of lightning struck the ground around the Well. The Earth shook from the impact as a deafening thunderclap reverberated across the hills. From deep within the echoes, Adima seemed to hear Enoch's voice speaking to him, reminding him.

"The lightning serves another."

Adima stood rooted to the spot, unable to move even if he had wanted to, so overwhelmed was he by the awesome display of natural and spiritual forces in cooperation with each other. Another bolt struck close beside him, the electrical current standing his hair on end as it danced along his skin.

"The lightning is your ally. It is your greatest strength, your greatest weapon."

Finding its mark in the center of the Well, a third bolt squarely struck the sword fragments. It was the moment of transition. Instantly the spell was broken. The stranger vanished, and the ancient sword lay whole and gleaming in the shallow water, while beside the pool, the rotting burlap sack had been transformed into a gorgeous bejeweled scabbard.

"Take your personal power, which has been offered to you in the form of the Sword—the Hard Lightning."

Dirty, cold, wet, and completely exhausted, acting purely on instinct, Adima stooped to pick up the magnificent weapon—now fully restored to its original, otherworldly splendor—just as the first light of dawn broke over the horizon. This Sword was exquisite and flawless, the blade reflecting the first rays of morning sunlight while also emitting powerful rays of light from within the shining steel itself. The twelve signs of the zodiac were etched deeply into the metal. He could make out a thirteenth symbol, too—one with which he was unfamiliar, its shape and message predating even the Ancients. "It is the symbol of Transformation!" he exclaimed, overwhelmed by the immediate sense experience of the weapon that had been crafted on the Forge of the Gods.

Adima knew the Sword's name immediately. This was the *Hard Lightning*—his old ally newly transformed, just as he himself had been transformed. As the physical lightning had filled him with fire so many long years ago, so now a current of healing warmth flowed through his body, connecting Mind and Heart, opening the channels of love, filling his breast with powerful emotions of reverence, humility, and gratitude. A final bolt flashed across the sky high above his head, while Enoch's words drifted slowly down to him on the currents of air.

"The day will come when you will read your name written in the cold steel of the Hard Lightning."

In the morning light, Adima read the inscription on the beautiful jeweled hilt:

THROUGH COMPASSION TO SELF-KNOWLEDGE

Inscribed in the Language of Light, it was a message from the Divine, a call of compassion from the Archangel of the Grail. Knowing intuitively that life itself was a gift of Grace from celestial powers, Adima dropped to his knees and uttered a simple prayer.

"This day I am renewed and reborn as a complete human being. For the very first time in my life, I know the meaning of compassion, joy, and spiritual release. Thank you for bringing the light of awareness to shine away the darkness of confusion and self-doubt within my soul."

For some moments he was almost overcome by the chastening experience. High above his head, the Dragon soared, its thunderous voice proclaiming its approval and appreciation for all to hear. Adima looked up, scarcely able to comprehend the full impact of his accomplishment. A wave of dizziness swept over him, and he would have fallen had not Enoch caught him in his strong arms.

"It's all over," Cybele whispered in his ear as they lowered him gently to the ground. "You did it. You broke the spell."

Adima had a brief glimpse of the faces of his loved ones standing over him. "I love you all," he whispered as the events of the past thirty days finally caught up with him. His eyelids fluttered, his body grew limp, and he fell into a deep, restful sleep.

"We love you, too," they murmured, covering him with a blanket so that he would not catch a chill in the cool morning air.

CHAPTER 36

My father broke the seal—
He sensed not the breath of the Evil One
But set him free to roam the world.

—Albrecht Haushofer

"Of course!" Kafar sat back and smiled a wide smile of satisfaction. There were dark circles under his eyes. He had barely slept since entering the Great Pyramid only a week ago. He had become so interested in his first assignment that he could not stop working. What he had discovered was a simple flaw deep in the atomic structure of the crystals. When subjected to certain stresses and temperatures, they just could not take the strain. They exploded.

Finding the problem—the flaw in the atomic structure—had been relatively easy. Now for the trickier part—how to solve the problem and ensure that it would not happen again when the new crystals were grown. He thought he saw a way, but it was so simple that he could not believe Shakala and the others hadn't thought of it. Yet when he checked their notes, that was indeed the case. So Kafar set to work, and lo and behold, this night he thought he had found the solution. But he wanted to be sure; he had to be accurate. There would be no point in failing the first week because of overconfidence. He needed to test his newly created crystal.

But where? It was very late, and there was no one around, or so he thought. He walked through the dark corridors of the Great Pyramid in search of a laboratory that might contain an appropriate power source. "Why didn't I ask for a better tour?" he chided himself. "I really don't know my way around here. I don't even know where Shakala's lab is. And I certainly don't want to wait until morning. I want to know now, so when daybreak comes, I'll be able to spring the solution on him when he arrives." On he walked, talking aloud to himself for company, hopelessly lost within the maze of passages within the vast interior of the Pyramid. "Oh, I'll make points for this one, to be sure. I'll just have to be careful how I tell Shakala."

He remembered something his mother had told him as a child. He had come home very upset because his schoolmates had ostracized him after he had bragged about how smart he was for winning first prize at the science festival. "Kafar," she had said, "you are so very smart, but you have to remember that others may not be so. They may not see and understand things as easily as you do.

"Remember, therefore, to reveal your discoveries gently, not with arrogance and pride, but with compassion and respect for others. If you want to succeed and make friends and have others like you, make them feel as though they are a part of your work and your life. Share your success with them. Do not lord it over them that you are smarter than they. Be humble. It will serve you well."

That was good advice, he thought as he walked further and further through the maze of corridors. His footsteps echoed hollowly on the stone floor. It was late at night, it was dark, he was alone with a vivid imagination, and he succeeded in frightening the wits out of himself. He shuddered involuntarily, half expecting a monster to pounce out at him from the shadows.

"I'm a grown man," he chided himself. Yet still he cast furtive glances behind him and approached each intersection with great care.

At last he stopped before a set of double doors, behind which a flight of stairs led down into the darkness of the lower levels. Having explored every room on this level, he decided to descend. But first, he peered carefully through the windows to make sure the way was clear. "No one there," he muttered to himself. "You foolish man." Throwing caution to the wind, he bravely pushed open the doors and entered the stairwell.

The monster reared up from the shadows, fully nine feet tall, its waving tentacles lashing out at him, fangs dripping cold, noxious saliva.

"Aieeeeeeeeeeeeeeeeeeeeeeee!" Kafar screamed and lashed out at the black, misshapen mass, stumbling over the creature's body in the darkness and falling down half a flight of stairs in a mad dash to escape. He landed with a thud as the creature clambered after him, filling the narrow passageway with a deafening roar. A small light illuminated the landing. Kafar clambered to his feet, ready to defend himself. There was no one there, just a damp mop, water pail, and trash barrel.

"I guess I deserved that," he laughed at his gullibility and foolishness, rubbing a bruised shin. "I'm lucky I didn't break my neck."

Limping slightly, heart still pounding, he continued his quest, walking for a while in almost total darkness, the way being marked only by small glow bulbs at each corridor junction. At one such juncture, he saw a dim light and heard the hum of a generator far down an adjoining hallway. "Ah, perhaps someone is here after all," he muttered. "Maybe they can provide me with a place to work."

Turning to his left, he walked down the corridor and approached the door. It was unlocked and opened into a dimly lit room, the sight of which astonished him. It was a laboratory, but one so different that at first he did not know what he was looking at. Rows and rows of cages lined the walls. Inside each one, dark shapes huddled in the blackness. The first thing he noticed was the smell—heavy, cloying, sickening. The overpowering stench of decay and putrefaction mingled with the strong scent of urine and feces, and beneath it all, the odor of blood.

"What is this?" he muttered. Genetic experimentation was the first thought that came to mind. He had heard rumors of such practices, how evil scientists had created mutants and projected their life energies into them, crossbreeding species to produce all sorts of horrible aberrations. But those were just rumors, weren't they? Such things did not exist in fact. The Great Pyramid was a place of science, a place of honor. Or was it? Were magical forces being misused now to satisfy some baser instincts, passions, and desires?

Cautiously, so as not to disturb anything, he peered into one cage after another, being careful to tread ever so softly and make no noise. It was too dark to see anything, and the odors were offensive and overpowering. What was that? There, in a large cage in the corner, did he discern a movement at the back of the cell? Leaning closer, he put his face to the bars. The gold chain around his neck gently brushed the metal, making a tiny, almost inaudible click. But it was enough. What happened next occurred so quickly that he was completely taken aback.

"Roarrrrrrrrrr!" The creature in the shadows leapt forward and crashed into the cage with a force that sent him reeling. Staggering backward, he banged headlong into a surgical cart, crashing both the tray and its contents to the ground. The clatter of steel on stone was deafening. Kafar lay sprawled amid a ruin of broken glass and medical instruments. As he fell, he banged his head on the stone floor and saw stars. A cavernous void of blackness reached out to enfold him, and he had to struggle to remain conscious.

Pandemonium had broken out in the laboratory. Every creature in every cage began to shriek and growl and hurl itself at the bars in a frenzy of agitation and rage. Groggily, he tried to sit upright, but he was too dizzy. Looking about, the room seemed to spin all around him, while strange and horrible creatures reached out to grab him.

Half human, half animal they were—altogether monstrous and grotesque in shape and size. How deformed they were—stooped, misshapen, hairy creatures with grotesque limbs and beetling brows. Kafar blinked stupidly, not comprehending as a huge caricature of a man stared at him from a single unblinking eye in the middle of its forehead. "This cannot be happening," he cried aloud. "This cannot be real!" He tried to continue, but his head hurt too much, and he felt faint. His vision blurred, and the stars flickered across his field of vision once again.

Now the most hideous beast of all loomed above him, its face a grotesque and pasty white. Moist black eyes looked down on him from a sallow, bloodless face. The creature seemed to exude evil, growling and rumbling in a deep bass voice. What was it saying? His stunned brain could not make out the words. "I didn't know," Kafar cried, raising an arm to protect himself from the blow he was sure was about to fall. "I meant no harm. I was just looking for a place to test my new crystal discovery."

He wanted to say he was sorry, that it had all been a mistake. He wanted desperately to wake up from this hideous nightmare. He wanted to go home. But then the giant reached out for him, and all he could do was scream as the blackness enveloped him and he fell deeper into the void.

*****

"There, there, you had a bad fall." Shakala gently placed a cool, moist cloth on Kafar's forehead.

"Where am I?" the young protégé mumbled. He tried to sit up, but his body would have none of it. His head throbbed with a fierceness and intensity he had not thought possible. His skull felt as if it were going to burst apart. "Like one of the defective crystals," he thought ironically as he imagined his head exploding and splattering all over the white stone walls of the lab.

"Just lie there and relax," Shakala soothed him. "You've had a terrific blow to your head, but you are going to be all right. The healers have done their work well. You will be fine soon. You just need to rest now."

"There were monsters..." Kafar tried to say, "...and a one-eyed giant. It reached out for me..." Confused images swarmed through his head, and he knew he wasn't making sense. Was he dreaming? What had happened to him? It was all so confusing. He could not remember. The pounding inside his skull took on a new intensity, and he heard a roaring in his ears as the black void came spinning back up to swallow him one more time.

*****

Hours later, Kafar awoke far more refreshed and relaxed. The pain in his head had been reduced to a dull and distant throb behind his left ear. Opening his eyes, he gazed about a small rest chamber. The room was amazingly sterile—white walls, white floor, white ceiling. The only furniture was the cot on which he was lying and a straight-backed chair. A man was sitting with his back to him, reading from a book. Kafar turned to get a better look.

"Oh, you're awake," Shakala said, coming toward him. "How do you feel."

"Like an idiot," Kafar admitted sheepishly. "What happened to me? What did I do? Where am I? Did I damage anything? Am I going to be all right?"

"Shhhh," Shakala soothed him gently. "You're fine. Nothing is wrong with your head, and I think the experimental monkeys you scared will recover nicely enough." He laughed, a thin, high-pitched, nervous sound. "It's a good thing Belial was there to rescue you, though, because you did get a bad concussion that needed immediate attention."

Kafar looked at the older man. The alchemist was trying quite hard to be earnest, but the friendliness in his voice was forced. And was that a trace of fear there, behind his eyes, as he spoke the name of Belial?

"Tell me," Shakala said, gently adjusting the bandage on Kafar's head, "what made you go wandering around alone so late at night? Didn't I tell you not to go off on your own? Didn't I tell you certain places were off limits?"

"I know, and I'm sorry," Kafar apologized, "but I think I've found a solution to the energy problem, and I needed a place to try out a new crystal that I grew. So I went looking for a power source to test my theory. I didn't think I was doing anything wrong. I stumbled into that weird lab completely by accident. What was that, anyway?" he asked, trying to remember.

The memory of the previous night was all a blur now. He could remember nothing clearly. Vague impressions lingered tantalizingly close to his awareness…shadowy images of caged animals and getting scared and a white face peering down at him. A lot of noise and bad smells. He closed his eyes and shuddered. "I can't remember," he looked at his mentor appealingly, wanting to know, needing to know.

"It's okay," Shakala reassured him. "That blow to your head must have really confused you. As best we can figure, you went into one of the genetics labs and tripped over a surgical tray. You got a pretty good knock on the head. That accounts for your hallucinations and bad dreams. But let this be a lesson to you. Do not go gallivanting around by yourself until you know your way around better. This is how accidents happen.

"Fortunately, Belial was nearby and heard the commotion. It was the Master himself who found you crawling down the hallway, bleeding and raving incoherently, and administered first aid. You owe him a debt of gratitude. He will be coming round soon enough to see you. Remember to thank him and apologize for your misguided eagerness and enthusiasm. He is a very understanding man. There is nothing to worry about."

Kafar looked at Shakala. What is he hiding? the young man wondered. The words were not what they seemed. Shakala was trying to send him a message, but what was it. His thoughts were interrupted by the older man.

"Now, tell me about this discovery of yours." The alchemist sat on the edge of the cot and smiled warmly at his protégé. "I want to know what was so important that you have not gone home for days and have slept in your clothes in your lab."

Kafar sat up in bed, his headache and the events of the previous night all but forgotten. "I've found the key to maintaining the integrity of the crystals," he cried, grabbing Shakala's arm with an irresistible enthusiasm. "All we have to do is test my theory, but I know it's going to work. I just know it!"

*****

Shakala and Belial sat alone in the Lair. "There is nothing to worry about," Shakala said. "He is convinced that it was merely a genetics lab."

"For his sake, that had better be true," Belial rumbled. "Because the next time he goes wandering about without an escort, it will be his last. It matters not how great his scientific accomplishments may be. I will not be disobeyed." The giant was working himself into a lather of rage, pacing back and forth before the ever-present fire. Shakala knew he had to focus the great man's attention on the topic at hand.

"The good news is that Kafar has discovered the solution, Master. Now the device can be built and the experiment completed." It was not necessary to provide the technical scientific details. Belial was interested only in the final outcome.

He stopped his restless pacing and stared into the roaring fire, his back to Shakala. "I am pleased," he said, giving voice to a rare compliment. "How far is the device from completion?"

"A matter of days, Master."

"Excellent." Belial's voice was almost a hiss. "My astrologers tell me that there will be an eclipse of the sun in ten days. We shall test the device at that time."

Belial turned to face Shakala. "Until then, keep a sharp eye on the boy and keep him out of trouble. I shall hold you responsible if he gets into mischief again." Belial glowered, and the old alchemist knew what had been left unsaid.

"If the experiment works, the destruction will be devastating," Shakala spoke almost to himself. He shuddered to think of the imminent attack about to be unleashed on an unsuspecting population.

"No matter," came Belial's emotionless reply. "This time it will work. This time we are ready. This time, let the people of Atlantis beware!"

CHAPTER 37

Seeker, enter the Inmost Cave and look for that which will restore life to the Home Tribe. Suddenly, you...find yourself face to face with a towering figure, a menacing Shadow composed of all your doubts and fears. Here, in this moment, is the chance to win all or die...it's Death that now stares back at you.

—The Writer's Journey

"I thought I had learned willingness," Adima said to Cybele as they prepared for bed. It had been several days since their return to Elysia, and they had spent most of that time resting. "But now I don't know what that willingness is for.

"I'm so judgmental. I know what Belial is up to, I know what's in store for us and Atlantis, and I hate it. I want to take up the Sword and go out and stop him. I want to stand on the street corners and grab people as they pass by and tell them to wake up and attend to that which they see all around them."

His wife let him speak, knowing that he did not need answers, but rather a safe place in which to voice his feelings. He would not abuse the privilege, she knew.

"Enoch keeps telling me to wait, that it is not time yet. 'Almost,' he keeps saying. 'Almost.' He has been saying that for three years. When is *almost* going to be *now*?"

There was a knock on the door. "Who can that be at this time of night?" Cybele asked. There was a note of panic in her voice, so crazy were the times, so much unrest was there in the city.

"Adima," Enoch's familiar tone drifted up from the courtyard. "I must talk to you. Please come down and let me in."

"Of course," Adima called down. He had not seen his teacher since their return from the Well of Kuneware.

"What can he want?" Cybele wondered nervously. She put on a soft silk robe and followed her husband down the stairs to the front door.

"Come in, Enoch," Adima welcomed his friend. The old man shuffled into the room, followed by Sophia.

"Surprise," the old lady winked, hugging each in turn as Adima and Cybele gasped in astonishment. The two old people looked tired and drawn. There was an air of worry about them.

"What is the matter?" Cybele asked, taking each by an elbow and leading them to the soft cushions of the sofa.

"Bad news, I'm afraid," Enoch came straight to the point. "Belial has discovered the secret to the integrity of the crystals. The construction of the weapon is in its final stages. It will be ready in a matter of days, a week at the outside."

"What can we do?" Adima asked softly. The old familiar ice ball of fear had just come back, right there in the pit of his stomach, at the center of himself.

"We must challenge him," Enoch said tersely. "I wanted more time, but apparently Spirit thinks we are more ready than I do. Either way, ready or not, the time has finally arrived." The old man turned to his friend. "You must make one last attempt to reason with them, Adima. You must address the Council, tell them the truth, and hope that they accept it. Your efforts probably will be in vain, but you must try."

Adima felt a lump of fear well up in his chest and rise in his throat. So, the time had come at last.

"You knew this day was coming," the old man said evenly, sensing his emotions. "I have done my best all of these years to prepare you. Now there is one more thing I must do to help you. I'm glad you are both here, because this is something you should do together. That is why Sophia is here too."

Sophia smiled at Cybele, who looked anxiously at her old teacher and friend. "You need do nothing now, for your time for action still lies before you. For tonight, sit by your husband's side while we reveal to him and to you a terrible secret."

Adima and Cybele drew closer to each other on the couch. Whatever was about to happen, it would be life-changing, of that they were sure. They reached out and held each other's hands, waiting for their guests to reveal what they had come to reveal.

Enoch drew a deep breath and exhaled slowly. "We've kept a secret from you, Adima," he confessed, "a great truth that we have known these many years. It is a truth that we have known since before your birth, since before your very conception."

Adima tightened his grip on his wife's hand; otherwise, he displayed no emotion. His confidence in Enoch was absolute. Whatever was coming, he knew it was necessary and for his highest good.

"It was not our decision alone to keep this hidden from you. There were others involved, both in this world and not."

"This was done for several reasons," Sophia took up the explanation. "First, for your protection, because the truth would have brought you certain death had it been known by another."

Belial! Adima and Cybele exchanged meaningful glances. Neither had to speak the name aloud to know to whom Sophia was referring.

"Second, the secret was kept from you because of the fear that the truth would have brought you. You have grown beyond that now, for you know that fear is an illusion of your own making and cannot harm you unless you choose to let it. So the decision was made to keep the truth hidden, burying it in a deep, dark place, safe from prying eyes, hidden from all the world until the time was right for it to be revealed. That time is now."

Adima and Cybele drew even closer to each other and held hands tightly. What was about to be revealed? What dark truth was about to come to light, and how would it change their lives and the lives of their children? They waited in tense anticipation, looking first at Sophia, then at Enoch. The room was still, save for the ticking of the timepiece on the mantle. Outside, the waves lapped gently at the deck. An owl hooted.

It was time. The old man sat forward, took Adima's hands in his own, and looked deeply into his eyes.

"Belial is your twin brother," Enoch said simply, holding his hands in a viselike grip, adding his strength and resolve to the younger man's. *"You were conceived of one egg and one sperm, separated into two, and shared the same womb for the first nine months of your lives!"*

Cybele drew in an involuntary gasp and reached out to grip Sophia's arm. The old woman put a comforting arm around her. At the same time, Adima's face softened and relaxed. He was not surprised. Relieved would have been a better word. Of course he had known, he had always known. Perhaps he had not wanted to admit it to himself, but at some level, he had always known.

"Would you like to see?" Enoch asked.

Adima nodded, speaking not a word. There was no fear, no anxiety. He was far past that. It was enough that he was willing. So, sitting safely in Elysia with their two beloved teachers and friends, Adima and Cybele allowed Enoch to take them backward in Time, opening their third eye to a vision from the *Cosmic Chronicle*—that eternal tapestry of events in which past, present, and future are inseparably woven—revealing the circumstances of Adima's birth and the events of his early life.

*****

Back in the womb—that toxic womb—there is another. Smaller, quieter—what started as one has become two. Not one, but two. The zygote splits, and the one becomes two.

Quietly, the tiny "other" floats in the amniotic fluid, feeling the same smothering sensations, the same noxious poisons. Feeling, too, the resentment of his larger twin. Such hatred, such animosity from one so like unto himself, from one who is, in fact, himself!

Quietly, the other remains hidden, hiding from the violence of his larger brother. His brother lashes out, kicking and clawing, trying to force him from the womb, wanting all for himself. Competing, struggling, fighting to survive, but there is no place to go.

The other resigns himself to his fate. To protect himself, he stays quiet, passive, submissive. He stays small, not growing, trying to find a quiet place where he can find some peace in that small, wet world. This seems to placate the larger twin, and he grows calmer. As long as the other is quiet, there is no danger. As long as the other remains small, there is no threat. As long as the other does not encroach upon him, there is no violence.

The time comes to leave that dark, watery world. The twin goes first. Somehow, as the two are twisted and turned by the spasms and contractions of labor, the cord gets entangled around the other's neck. How does it happen? Has the twin, in a desperate attempt to kill his brother, placed the cord around his neck? Or is it done by Another, with a different intent—as a means of protection?

Is that laughter the other hears, the laughter of satisfaction? He cannot be sure. All he knows is that he cannot breathe. What was already difficult is now impossible. Consciousness dims, sensation diminishes as he claws at the cord with tiny, powerless fingers. Vaguely, he feels himself moving down a long tunnel. Then everything fades to black.

*****

The birth is not easy. There is agony and blood. The mother cries out—long, deep screams of anguish. Difficult, so very difficult, to deliver this first large child.

At last it is over. In the birthing room, the midwife places the infant in the crib and awaits the passing of the placenta. "Here it comes," she mutters. But it is not a placenta. It is a second baby. It is the other.

"How is this possible?" she wonders. "I sensed no other presence in the womb." No time for questions. The cord is wrapped around the baby's neck. It is already blue and not breathing...a boy, a twin brother.

"Dead," the midwife mutters.

"Good," replies another, a foul-smelling, hunchbacked man. "You know what to do. Dispose of it quickly."

The midwife reacts as if slapped in the face. "This is a child, a living being," she cries. "We must try to save it."

In a rage, the hunchback slaps her across the face. "Destroy it," he hisses, his face contorted into an evil leer.

His fetid breath assails her senses, the shock of the blow stings her cheek. Fearing for her life, she wraps the stillborn child in a heavy blanket, carries it from the room, and places it outdoors on a pile of rubbish. "I am sorry, little one," she whispers, taking a last look at the tiny, lifeless bundle, "but you are better off dead."

Discarded, abandoned. Cold and alone. Unloved, unwanted, unknown. Without an identity, without even a name. Ignominious end for a life that had barely begun. The midwife returns to the mother and the living child. The afterbirth comes, and she attends to them. Only later, after they are asleep and the hunchback has gone, does she return to the stillborn child to give it proper burial. There is nothing there. The other is gone. Fearing the consequences, she utters not a word, keeping the secret in her heart.

*****

Outside in the cold and the dark, the child who was abandoned and given up for dead stirs. Within that tiny body, a spark still burns. There is still the strength to draw breath. A mournful wail goes out to any who would hear. In the forest, a great gray she-wolf prowls the night. What is that she hears? A baby's cry? She approaches a clearing, sensing danger. Danger and evil.

What is that she smells? The scent of the dreaded humans, mingled with the scent of blood, and the scent of death. Instinct warns her to avoid this place, but then she hears a woman's voice—the old woman whom she loves and obeys, telling her to stay. Cautiously, the she-wolf creeps through the dense foliage and looks about the clearing. She sees nothing but a pile of trash and a bloody lump of cloth.

"Bring the child to me," the old woman commands.

Gently, ever so gently, so as not to harm its delicate skin, the she-wolf lifts the bundle in her mouth and disappears into the forest. In the Cave, the old woman waits to receive it. There is another there, too, an old man. Wolf senses no danger. The man is known to the woman. There is nothing to fear.

Gently, they remove the blankets and attend to the child. Warming it, washing it, holding it in their arms. Offering it love and affection and the warm milk from the breast of the she-wolf whose own cubs had so recently disappeared.

"We love you," they croon softly. "We are glad you are here. You will grow into a good man—wise and strong. You will bring great joy to people's lives. You will do much to serve your people," the old woman predicts.

"And one day, at the appointed time, you will save your world," the old man concludes.

*****

Under cover of night, the old man and the old woman approach the Palace, carrying their precious bundle. Entering by a side gate, a servant leads them through a maze of passages and rooms. The prince and princess await them.

"Behold the child," Sophia hands the baby to the young woman. "Yours is a great gift—the willingness to share your love and your lives with this orphaned boy. See how he thanks you." The infant is already nestled comfortably into the woman's soft bosom.

"We are honored to do our part," the Prince replies. "As long as my uncle, the King, reigns, the boy will want for nothing."

"We shall speak of this to no one," the old man cautions, "until the day when the secret is to be revealed. For his own protection, the boy must grow up apart, sheltered from the knowledge of his true identity. For if another were to find out the truth, he would do everything in his power to destroy him."

"We understand," they reply. "We shall carry the secret to our graves."

"Meet your brother," they say, laying the infant in a cradle next to the royal couple's own son. The two infants take to one another immediately, snuggling closer and cooing contentedly.

"His name is Adima," Sophia said softly as they left.

*****

Returning to ordinary space and time, the four looked at each other in silence. What was there to say? No words could express their innermost feelings. Together they sat, drawing strength from each other as the fire burned and the candles cast their flickering shadows.

Enoch was the first to break the silence. "Adima, your spiritual enlightenment and the revelation of this truth has in no way changed your personal destiny. Everything continues as before."

"Only the *motive* for your action has changed," Sophia continued. "Do you understand what that motive is?"

Adima nodded his head grimly. "Belial's unholy crusade to vanquish the free spirit of Atlantis must be stopped," he said. "And now it's personal." He had a dark look, the look of one betrayed and who now seeks revenge.

"I was afraid you were thinking that," Enoch said, shifting in his chair. "Let me try to explain to you why you must not think the way you do."

"You can go ahead and try," Adima retorted, "but there is nothing you can say that will change my mind. My only brother my greatest enemy! My only living blood relative responsible for the destruction of an entire race! The other half of myself wishes me dead, unless I destroy him first. How is my thinking wrong?"

Enoch lit his pipe and puffed contemplatively, deciding where to begin. "There are far larger and more potent forces at work here than mere sibling rivalry or maniacal lust for power," he began. "The reign of Belial in Atlantis is not a solitary event to be reckoned with; it is part of a much larger process. What is trying to be birthed here is a new concept of freedom within the evolution of the human race."

"How so?" Cybele asked, intrigued by Enoch's words. She had not spoken since before he had begun the flashback.

"A great sleep has descended upon Atlantis in the materialism of Belial's rule," Sophia answered her, "and our spiritual origins have been forgotten." The old woman paced back and forth before the fire, warming herself in its ruddy glow as she spoke. Adima and Cybele listened in rapt attention.

"Unable to find the path back to the recognition of Spirit, the masses have been tricked by Belial into believing that patriotism—the Nation-State—is the highest ideal. It is out of such misplaced reasoning and attention that the forces of darkness are mobilizing even now.

"Picture it if you will—sleeping men in power are preparing to unleash a cataclysmic chain of events upon other sleeping men. Both are in the grip of forces that they can neither understand nor control. They are deep in the nightmare. As was predicted of old, this is the time when the Fathers fall asleep."

"Well," came Cybele's inevitable response, "why can't we wake them up, enlighten them? Surely there has to be somebody who will listen to reason."

Now Enoch spoke. "People under the influence of fear are unable to reason. They are not thinking. They are letting their emotions determine the course of their lives. Misguided science, inappropriate technology, negative human emotions...those are the causes that have brought Atlantis to this sleep state. And underneath it all is the fear. It is the single biggest reason for the sleep and the coming disaster. Fear has become the motivation for all of human behavior, and that is not how it was intended to be."

"Why?" Cybele wanted to know. "What is it that they fear?"

"They fear their own awakening and the revelation of the truth—that all of their cherished ideals are no more than a tissue of dreams and illusions."

"There must be some way to awaken them, to bring them to their senses," Adima threw up his hands in frustration.

"Alas," said Sophia, "the sleep is already too deep, the Dream too entrenched. To awaken them now would no doubt instill but more fear, and that would lead to even more tragedy. No, I am afraid that only a long, drawn-out period of unprecedented suffering and loss will awaken the human race to the falsity of its beliefs and values and return them to a recognition of their spiritual identity."

"So Atlantis will not be the last race to experience this?"

"The last?" Sophia laughed mirthlessly. "Hardly. Atlantis is but the first in a long series of rising and falling nation-states. Countless civilizations will come and go, countless Belials will live, rule, and die, each with a different form and a different name."

"Others will follow in Belial's footsteps?" Adima could not believe what he was hearing.

"The power is not in the ruler, it is in the Spear," Enoch affirmed, repeating the words of the Puppetmaster. *"Whoever has the Spear holds the power to shape human history for good or evil.* Thus, it remains for whoever holds the Sword to rise up and stand against him. So, too, there will be a long succession of heroes."

"Is there any hope?" Cybele wondered, addressing the question to no one in particular.

Sophia's answer was far from comforting. "Not until long after Atlantis has been reduced to moral degradation and a heap of smoking ruins, finally to be obliterated from the face of the Earth and the memory of humankind, lingering only as a legend and not a reality."

"Then they will recognize the utter futility of it all?"

"No, not even then. Not until the End Times, after millennia of evolution. Only then will millions of men and women begin to experience within themselves a new sense of awareness of their true identities. As you and Adima already have, as a few individuals will do in various lifetimes and civilizations across the globe, so it will happen on a mass scale then. For in the End Times, the masses will begin to reawaken as they learn to let go of the shackles of fear that no longer serve them, assuming instead the mantle of love."

"So what do we do now?" Adima was too frustrated to talk of re-awakenings and love and true identities. Jumping to his feet, he paced back and forth in anger and frustration. "This is terrible. It is awful..."

Enoch made no move to stop him, letting him express his feelings in the safety of home and family. Adima knew the truth. So did Cybele. That was enough.

"Both of you have to act on the basis of what you believe to be good and just and right, to combat whatever needs to be combatted," Enoch said after a few moments. "But do not make the mistake of judging anything or anybody, because it is not necessary to label things as good or bad, right or wrong, better or worse."

"Why?" Cybele did not understand.

"Because the real enemy, the real struggle, is within the mind and its attachment to outcomes."

"Are you saying that we needn't bother to take a stand against Belial?" Cybele was incredulous. She must not have understood him correctly.

"Those who choose to combat the Darkness are still spending all of their time, energy, and consciousness combatting that which just *is*," came Sophia's strange response. "It is only 'wrong' or 'bad' or 'dark' because of your perception and attachment to outcomes, matter, and forms—even understanding.

"On one level, everything exists by the Grace of Divine Intelligence. By shedding light on anything, however you perceive it, its true nature is revealed, and harmony is achieved. Therefore, you need not fear it, you need not deny it, you need not change it, you need not even destroy it." The old woman was about to reveal the simple, perfect solution.

"Because if you shed enough Light, it will flee. It recedes. The Darkness recedes as the Light is increased. And the Light is increased," the old woman pointed to each in turn, "through you. That is the formula, that is the motivation, and that is the task—*to bring Light to the Darkness so that the Truth is revealed.*"

The old people stood, signifying that it was time to leave. As they walked through the garden, Enoch turned for a last word.

"As you come to the end of this Period of Unsettling, you must do as the *Book of Life* teaches:"

LEARN TO LAY ALL JUDGMENT ASIDE AND ASK ONLY
WHAT YOU REALLY WANT IN EVERY CIRCUMSTANCE.

"We will be with both of you whenever you need us, as will all of your allies in each of your Circles. Be at peace."

The old ones went off into the night, leaving Adima to contemplate the discovery of his new-found brother and Cybele to hold all of these matters in her heart. As they clung tightly to each other in the darkness, each wept for a world in which only slaughter on a global scale could serve to awaken humankind to the recognition of Spirit and end the Dream of sickness, separation, scarcity, suffering, and death.

CHAPTER 38

There's a hero,
When you look inside your heart,
You don't have to be afraid of what you are.
There's an answer,
When you reach inside your soul,
And the sorrow that you've known just melts away.
And then a hero comes along,
With the strength to carry on,
As you cast your fears aside,
And you know you can survive.
So when you feel like hope is gone,
Reach inside you and be strong,
And you'll finally see the truth,
That a hero lies in you.

—Mariah Carey

At last began the *Period of Achievement*, in which all of the learning was consolidated and Adima stepped forth transformed, in the fullness of his power. Having been taught in the sacred temples of the wild places and the Lighthouse, he now stood ready to bring his learning and talent forth into the world. Above all, he had learned to see—truly see—not with the body's eyes, but with the clarity and truth of inner vision. Already a man, now he was also a Master in the truest sense of the word.

The night before his address to the Council of Elders, Adima, Cybele, and the twins spent a most pleasant evening in the city at the gala opening of the brand new Center for the Performing Arts. The inaugural occasion was the premiere of a vibrant new theatrical performance by a multi-talented group of Atlantis' most prominent artists. It was a unique event, combining for the first time the individual arts of music, theater, and dance into a single performance, not as individual acts, but as a cohesive whole. The idea had sprung from the creative vision of a single man.

Kallista, the mastermind behind the whole effort, had long held that music, especially singing, would intensify the dramatic effect of other elements such as dance and spectacle. Such a collaborative effort had never been attempted before, but here it was—a combined work by scores of the most recognized talents in the world. Each had merged his and her particular art into a single, cohesive presentation.

In a burst of enthusiasm, famous artists, used to wild adulation and sumptuous theaters, had flocked to the great city from all over Atlantis and the provinces. All of them were giving freely of their time and talents to produce what they hoped would be an event of epic proportions—a masterpiece of light, sound, color, and motion—for the sheer joy of creating it.

The composer had written a musical score. The dramatist had developed a plot. The lyricist had penned dialog in the form of song. The choreographer had added dance. Finally, singers, actors, dancers, musicians, and designers put it all together under Kallista's watchful eye and superb direction. The result was sweeping and romantic—a drama set to music. They called it *Opera*.

The city had been abuzz for months, not just the aristocracy, but most of the populace. Now the night had arrived, and most of the city had come to see this wonder of wonders. There were the Elders in their silk capes and robes mingling with lawyers and judges, merchants, shippers, farmers, teachers, healers, laborers, parents, and children.

For in Atlantis, the arts were appreciated by and available to everyone. Funded by the State until recently, the performances were open to all who wished to attend. If there was not enough room on a particular night, no matter—there would be another performance the next evening, or the one after that.

"Isn't it beautiful!" patrons exclaimed. "You have to give them credit. I never thought it would get built."

Many had predicted that the controversial theater and production were doomed to failure before ever ground was broken, so much dispute had there been over what constituted "proper" and "acceptable" art these days. It seemed that everyone had become a critic. Every special interest group had an opinion, from artists to audiences to sponsors and patrons. The opinions that held sway, however, the ones that counted, were those of the Sons of Belial. They controlled the purse strings. As well, they controlled who saw what, when, and where. Until now, that is. Against all odds, using his vast personal resources and enlisting the cooperation of all who loved the arts, Kallista had accomplished an amazing feat.

The Theater of the Muses had been designed and built as the perfect place to stage the event. It was a gorgeous structure. The man-made edifice and natural landscape of the Great Plain combined harmoniously to form a visual and acoustical masterpiece. "I want a brand new design," Kallista had explained to the Master Architect. "Forget everything you know about architecture and give us something new, something bold, something brilliant."

And so he had. Researching the classical Atlantean theater design, the Master Architect discovered that it was merely a mirror of the social history of Atlantean performing arts. What had begun as a democratic recreation available to all, with row upon row of identical tiered seats, had blossomed into a microcosm of contemporary Atlantean society, with tiers of boxes clustering around a central Royal box where the cultural elite vied for favorable positions nearest the King. Alas, what had once been available to all was rapidly devolving into a purely aristocratic recreation.

"Not if I can help it!" the Master Architect had exclaimed. And so he had set to work to produce his masterpiece and make it available to all, a showcase for the world's best performers. "In my theater, the focus is on the performance, not the aristocracy."

And so it was. Designed as an open air arena, built into the side of a white limestone cliff, the Theater of the Muses faced southwest toward the Great Plain. In the center was the stage, its view completely unobstructed. There were no reserved seats, except for the King's box high atop the summit of the cliff. Everyone else gathered and sat where they wanted—either in tiered aisles etched step-like into the cliffside or on the grassy Plain itself, which had been gently sloped toward the stage, a perfect lawn on which families could spread blankets and enjoy picnic baskets or lovers might share a bottle of wine and listen to music under the stars.

The amphitheater was an acoustical masterpiece. The rock cliffs caught the sound and echoed it back in clear, flawless harmonics. "Listeners will be able to hear every single note," the Master Architect had said proudly.

Walking through the crowd, the family stopped numerous times to say hello to people they knew. The twins naturally had to endure the "my how you've grown" comments from adults they could barely remember. The plight of children everywhere, they persevered as their shoulders were thumped, their heads patted, their cheeks kissed.

"Won't they ever realize that we're grown up?" Alta whispered to his sister, his expression disdainful and annoyed. She just shook her head, a pained look on her face as another of their parents' friends complimented her on her "cute little smile."

But it was fun. It was exciting to dress up and attend such a gala event. "Creativity is part of our nature," Cybele explained to the twins. "We cannot lock it up inside; we must express it and bring it forth—either as a solitary artist or as part of a collaborative effort." She pointed to a row of portraits. Each was a recognized talent, a virtuoso performer and artist, yet now they were acting in harmony as a single unit. "What strange new art form is this?" Cybele mused. "It would seem that in the opera you are not just a lonely performer, you can be the star in a collective effort."

The family settled into their seats amid the general murmur of the crowd. "What will the musicians perform, Father?" Charis asked. They could not help but notice the huge orchestra assembled in a hollowed-out area below the stage. The tips of their instruments were just visible above the edge of the pit.

"I'm not sure," Adima replied. "This is as new to me as it is to you. I would imagine that they will provide instrumental accompaniment for the singing and the stage action."

A distinguished-looking gentleman in dark robes leaned forward in his seat. "Begging your pardon," he interrupted with a pleasant smile. "The orchestra plays a far more important role in the opera than mere accompaniment. The drama itself develops within the orchestral framework, which provides background and continuity for the story and prepares you—the audience—for the drama to come."

"The essence, however, is found in the singing. The high points of the drama are set to wonderful musical pieces called arias, duets, and trios. Always, the emphasis is on the music." The man spoke most eloquently, pleased to pass along his knowledge to an appreciative and attentive audience. "During the performance," he winked at the twins, "listen carefully to the music and see how it supports the singers, underscores the climaxes, changes mood, provides interludes, and rings down the curtain at the evening's end. Notice, too, how even though the voices remain dominant, the orchestra acts as a partner with the singers rather than an accompanist."

"Thank you," the twins replied, slightly star-struck as the stranger excused himself. They recognized him from the portrait they had just seen. It was Kallista himself, creator of the opera, and he had just taken the time to teach them how to better understand and appreciate the performance.

The orchestra continued to tune up. Arpeggios from the horns and woodwinds mixed with runs and cadenzas on the strings, punctuated by cymbal crashes and assorted drum rolls. It as a cacophony of quiet discord, the melody always the same no matter the performance.

Anxious to see more celebrities, Alta and Charis looked around at the glamorous couples. "There are Hia and the emissaries from Turtle Island," their mother pointed to several tall, red-skinned men with straight black hair flowing almost to their waists. "And there is Isis, Princess of Al Khemia," she pointed to an olive-skinned woman with large, dark, almond-shaped eyes.

"Look up there," Charis directed their attention to a closed area high above the last tier of seats. Just entering the royal box was Belial, with Lilith at his side; the King and his newest consort, however, were singularly absent. A group of fawning sycophants clustered around the couple, vying for their attention as goldfish in a pond wait for a morsel of bread to drop from a child's hands.

"Interesting," Adima commented, "I never knew them to be patrons of the arts."

Before he could comment further, the lights dimmed, the musicians ended their warm-up, and the crowd began to settle themselves into silence. A pin spot lit up the far side of the stage. All eyes turned to look. Springing like a benevolent jinn from behind a red velvet curtain, the maestro appeared to thunderous applause. Walking to the podium, escorted by the light, he bowed once to the audience, then turned, picked up his baton, and stood poised before the orchestra.

A hush fell over the vast assemblage, a pregnant moment of anticipation. Then, in response to a wave of his right arm, the timpani rolled, and the overture began. The opera was set in motion—an auditory and visual experience, not merely music, but a story, a mythos that embodied some of the most basic images and emotions that characterized the Atlantean culture which gave it birth.

Remembering Kallista's remark that the opera was concerned with unity of mood and theme, Adima paid special attention to how the musical motifs from the introduction would lead directly into the action. Rumor had it that this was the story of the rise of an unknown boy to become ruler of the Forces of the Universe, from his apprenticeship under the tutelage of the sages, through his initial efforts at creativity, to the achievement of true Mastery.

The twins sat in rapt attention on the edge of their seats, listening to every note of the music. The overture ended, and the curtain rose on Act I. Dark and somber were the sets, the heavy walls and gloomy rooms of a mysterious castle. Like the sets, costumes, and lighting, the music was morose and ponderous. The crowd gasped as a sorcerer, apparently a man of great power, age, and wisdom, emerged from within a cloud of smoke in the center of the stage. He sang the introductory recitative, describing in a strong baritone how a newcomer had appeared that day at the Castle of the Ages.

> *"A frightened, helpless boy,*
> *Brought to the Master*
> *To have that great Sage*
> *Undo his early training and beliefs."*

Adima liked the style immediately—rapid syllabic singing in free tempo, accompanied by simple chords and following the natural inflections of speech. What a unique way to articulate the plot and carry the action forward! He glanced at Cybele, who nodded her head appreciatively, realizing that such recitative was all-important to the narrative structure. The language was simple and easy to follow. Thus, she could concentrate on the dramatic aspects of the music, noticing how the melody line was perfectly suited to the words it was meant to carry.

But recitative alone would never carry the opera. A brief musical interlude ensued, followed by a suspension of the action as the dancers whirled and gyrated across the stage, paving the way for the evening's first aria. Now the sage appeared, his strong tenor revealing the boy's story to the assembled congregation.

> *"So much of his training, upbringing, and beliefs have been shrouded in*
> *darkness,"* he sang to the circle of wizards, magicians, and courtesans who
> had assembled on stage.
> *"In the shadow—hidden, secret, occult.*
> *Unknown, unfathomable, mysterious.*

The Master's task—our task—
Is to help the boy understand the Great Mystery."

It was a powerful and intentional interruption of the action in order to dwell on particular emotions. Music and voice soared, freely repeating themselves, flowering on one point after another. Act I continued for almost an hour, full of passionate, dissonant harmonies. Voices and orchestra combined in an artistic attempt to convey to the audience the performers' feelings of agitation and fear.

It worked. Chaotic emotion and action, higher registers of voices and instruments...the effect was strong, dramatic feeling, art imitating life. Watching the performance, Adima could not help but see the similarities between the boy and himself. He felt his own emotions welling up inside him. This opera might not have the verbal richness of a play, he thought as the tears flowed, but in its music it gains the richness of a language that speaks directly to my emotions—directly to my heart and soul.

When the curtain closed at the end of the act, the applause was thunderous, praising the performers' vocal virtuosity as well as the orchestra's masterful techniques of harmony and instrumentation. "The boy reminds me a lot of you, Father," Alta remarked as the lights came up.

"He does, does he?" Adima laughed, but he knew his son was right. There was an uncanny similarity between the opera's plot and his own story. Of course, it was purely coincidental, wasn't it? He glanced at Cybele, but she just smiled sweetly back at him before continuing a conversation with the lady seated next to her.

He felt uncomfortable, as though he were being watched. Glancing up to the royal box, he saw Belial staring down at him, his deep black eyes peering intently at him. Does he sense the similarity, too? Adima could not help but wonder. Of course he does. He would have to be deaf and blind to not recognize it.

There would have been a time when that look would have disturbed him immensely, but this night it mattered not a whit. If the similarity bothers him, then it bothers him, he shrugged. Too bad he's going to let a coincidence ruin what could be a beautiful experience for him. The lights blinked, and he turned back to the stage, putting Belial completely out of his mind. It was so very easy to do now. What had once seemed impossible was now second nature. He barely gave him a thought.

Again the pre-act ritual was repeated. The house lights dimmed, and the audience settled back into their seats, applauding as the maestro stepped up to the podium once more. Surprise! The Act II curtain rose on a brilliantly illuminated stage. Gone were the dark and heavy costumes, the melancholy mood, the frenetic yet somber music. It was time for the sopranos.

The audience applauded the appearance of a strikingly beautiful woman, perhaps the most famous of all Atlantean virtuosos, known for her utmost achievement in range and flexibility. Her voice had been declared to be more powerful than a trumpet, and it was said that she could sustain a note longer than any singer who had ever lived. Bursting forth in a voice of great clarity and beauty, she sang a pure, melodic aria, describing the moment in which the darkness was brought to the light.

"And now the darkness stands ready to come into the light.
To let itself be illuminated.
No longer hidden."

"Exposed, open,
Brought forth from the invisible to the visible.
To be transformed by the Magician's Wand."

Alta leaned over and whispered in his father's ear. "See, it is your story," he declared knowingly.

"Shhhhh," Adima hissed, poking him playfully in the ribs. "Watch the show."

For another hour, the women dominated the stage. The voice of the dramatic soprano was full and powerful. The coloratura was vibrant, her light and extremely flexible voice executing virtuoso passages featuring rapid scales, trills, and other ornamental displays. Again the act closed to a thunderous ovation. As the lights came up, several of the operagoers rose to stretch their legs. Conversation resumed, polite chatter about the quality of the music, the singers voices, even speculation about what the third act might present.

"Belial is gone," Cybele observed quietly, nodding her head in the direction of the royal box. It was true; the seats were empty.

When did he disappear? Adima wondered to himself. Sometime during the second act, to be sure, but why? Could he have disliked the performance that much? Once again he put thoughts of Belial out of his mind. He would be seeing him soon enough. Best to spend as little time thinking about him as possible. He'd enjoy the opera and the evening so much more.

Act III began with a triumphant fanfare, followed by a processional in which the former boy, now grown into the Master of Worlds, paraded with his entourage onto the stage in a riot of light, color, and sound.

The music was airy and light, not weighed down by gravity, but ethereal, almost angelic. Adima and Cybele could not help but marvel at how easily the rhythms varied among impetuous declarations, stately ceremonial ensembles, and love duets and arias, providing pace and coloring as the situation demanded, while maintaining a continuous musical texture. What would have been gibberish if two or more actors had spoken at the same time was, instead, a masterpiece of musical complexity. For the composer had discovered the secret of such dramatic presentation—only a group of singers joining in ensemble could express more than one point of view at the same time.

Slowly, with considerable repetition of words and phrases, bass, baritone, tenor, and soprano voices soared in grand, magnificent, harmonies. Arias, duets, trios, and quartets told of how the former apprentice had become a master of occult powers and was now living in a state of timelessness, in which he traveled on a golden chariot through the lower, middle, and upper worlds.

The bass provided the solid foundation upon which to build:

> *"Masters were once apprentices.*
> *As apprentices, they learned from other masters,*
> *Spending a long time,*
> *The apprentice uncovers and unblocks*
> *The artisan, the craftsman."*

The response from the baritone blended in perfect counterpoint:

> *"Masters are artisans and craftsmen.*
> *Masters create masterpieces.*
> *My Inner Master is my ally and my teacher."*

As the music soared, Adima was caught up in the experience and transported outward. Watching the spectacle, listening to the timeless dramatic themes, he recognized an aspect of himself within each one.

The tenor's voice sustained each simple phrase:

> *"My Inner Master.*
> *My ageless timeless Self.*
> *My Wise One.*
> *My Elder.*
> *My Circle."*

The soprano's lyrics were poetic, restrained, intimate...

"Mastery—fully in body,
Taking direction from Spirit,
Balanced male and female,
Balanced Master,
The Master knows the quiet place,
The timeless place—
The Heart Center."

Singers rather than actors, their appeal lay in their ability to pronounce the notes and the words accurately, coloring the tone, sustaining each beautiful phrase to the point where the listener could experience the most extreme possible range of emotions.

As the last note sounded, the audience rose to its feet as a single being. Ten thousand throats roared forth their praise. Twenty thousand hands created deafening applause. They would not let the performers off the stage. For endless minutes they continued to express their appreciation, calling the performers back for one curtain call after another. Finally, almost half an hour later, the gorgeous velvet drapes closed for the final time, and the audience began filing out of the amphitheater.

At home later that evening, Adima and Cybele sat out on the veranda under the stars, listening to the waves. The twins had gone to bed, so they were quite alone. No need to speak, for to do so would have broken the enchantment that the opera had produced. They shared the silence comfortably, simply holding hands and enjoying the evening.

This new art form was intriguing, in that it had come so close to imitating real life in such a novel way. It was not purely drama, nor was it only music. It if had been a play, the production would have been complete with just the dialog. If it had been a concerto, the music alone would have sufficed. The opera was, instead, a combination of the two, in which each single element—drama and music—could not stand alone.

Drama is not confined to the plot, Adima thought as he listened to the melodies playing over and over in his head. It is contained in the music as well. Opera without music is incomplete, but half of a dramatic entity. The music is essential for providing that missing "something." And then the realization struck him. He knew what the missing "something" was, although he could not put it into words. It was the same "something" that had made him whole—that spiritual essence which had combined with his physical self to transform him from a boy into a man.

Like the opera, one without the other was not enough. A spirit without a body to inhabit was incorporeal and insubstantial. A man with no connection to Spirit was fragmented and separated. To be whole, the two must be combined. *The opera was about Mastery. So, too, was his whole life!*

"I know now that Mastery is about having the humility and willingness to approach life as a beginner—with *Beginner's Mind*," he said, looking at the Scorpion sparkling high in the western sky. "I know it is all right to make mistakes, as long as I have the right intentions and try my best. It is not about being *perfect*. It is about being *perfectly human*."

They went upstairs to bed. Lying there in the dark, Adima prepared himself for sleep. Tomorrow would be an eventful day, and he was grateful for the evening's respite. "What is the energy needed to bring peace to my heart and soul?" he asked before closing his eyes. He knew the answer would come in the form of a dream.

It did. During the night, he experienced a wonderful vision of a mighty warrior searching the world for a mythical lost kingdom. So real it was, so vivid! Not wishing to forget a single detail, Adima awoke long before dawn, took pen in hand, and wrote in his journal.

*****

From Adima's Journal...
Dawn
Last Day of the Month of the Willow
Year of the Tower

In Search of the Kingdom

Once there was a Warrior who wandered the world alone, without king or kingdom to serve. Brave was this Warrior. Great were his skills. Strong was his willingness to serve, protect, and defend. But he was alone, and great, too, was his loneliness, his longing for the companionship of other warriors, lords, and ladies. And most of all, he longed for the blessing of the king.

"Where are you?" he cried out in the long, cold, lonely nights, wrapped in his blanket before a pitiful fire. "Help me," he cried to no one in particular. "I am afraid." He voiced the words only in the deepest darkness in the barest of whispers.

Far and wide he traveled. He had all sorts of solitary adventures—jousts and contests and tournaments. He heard of wars and rumors of wars. He visited oracles and wizards and teachers. He sought comfort in wayside inns, where he found temporary relief in a warm meal, a tankard of ale, and a woman's arms. But always on the morrow, he would awaken with the same feelings of emptiness inside him...feelings of anxiety, frustration, and deep longing.

Longing for what? He could not explain the feelings, nor could he fight, eat, drink, or love them away. He might cover them up for a while, but only for a while. It was only a mask. Always the feelings and longings came back in the cold gray light of dawn.

So the years went on, and the Warrior experienced many adventures, saw many wonders, and learned many lessons. One day, he came to a fork in the road, where he had to make a decision about which way to proceed. Now he had heard about this fork for quite some time, but he was not quite prepared for its sudden and unexpected appearance right there in the middle of the path. There they were—two roads, one leading left, one right. And he without a map or a clue about which way to go.

So the Warrior got off his horse and sat for a while, lost in thought. Which way should he go? What should he do? He began to observe others along the way. Some took one fork, some the other, apparently with no rhyme or reason. He questioned many about their decision. They told him many things. All had strong and compelling reasons for choosing the path and direction they did. He did not know what to do. How could he make up his mind?

"I can't decide this for myself," he realized after a long time. "I need help. Who can help me?" He looked around in frustration. At that moment, he saw a mysterious couple walking along the road toward him. They were ancient, an old man and an old woman. Hailing them, the Warrior stepped onto the trail. He knew intuitively that they had come with a message for him, but he was quite unprepared for the words they uttered. The crone spoke first.

"Brave Warrior, you seek so many things—comfort and riches and companionship and glory. All these things you seek as you roam this vast world alone. Know you not that you are seeking in vain, because you are seeking the wrong things in the wrong place?

"Let us tell you of a kingdom—a great and glorious kingdom unlike any other. An expansive kingdom, one of great worth. Where the streets are paved with gold. Where there are many warriors and wise men and women. And an omnipotent king, like no other king you have ever served. A king so great, so strong, so kind, so wise, more so than every other king in every other kingdom. Seek first this kingdom, brave Warrior, and all else will be given to you."

"But where is this kingdom!" cried the Warrior. "Tell me that I may go there."

"Within," said the sage with a mysterious wave of his arm. "The kingdom is within."

"A strange answer," replied the Warrior. "Speak not in riddles."

"I speak the truth," said the ancient one. "The kingdom you seek is not where you have been seeking, else you would have found it already and be content now. No, you must go into the deep, dark Forest of Yourself. There you will find the kingdom."

"The Forest of Yourself!" cried the Warrior. "I have never heard of it. Where is it!"

"Yonder lies the entrance." The old woman pointed a bony finger at the center of the Warrior's chest. It seemed to pass completely through his midsection to an undetermined point behind him.

"But it is dark in there," cried the Warrior, "and I do not know the way. Give me a light. Draw me a map."

"The light will be there when you need it," replied the sage. "Sometimes it will appear quite dark. At other times it will be clearer. But the light is always there if you let it shine forth."

Then the crone spoke. "As for a map, there is none, but that does not matter. You do not need a map. For you know the way. You have been gone a long time, but you know the way. Remember!"

"How could I know the way!" asked the Warrior, bewildered. "I have never even heard of this kingdom."

"Ah, but you have," they cried together. "It has been a long time, and you have forgotten much over the years during your long wanderings, but the kingdom is your true home. You were once a great Warrior there, much loved by the king and all. You went forth one day to seek your fortune, young and full of your strength and power. Along the way, you fell under a great enchantment, the enchantment of the world outside the kingdom. You have forgotten much, including who and what you really are and where you come from. But always in the back of your mind, and especially in your heart, you hold the memory of your home and your desire to return there."

"Go there now, gentle Warrior. The enchantment is broken, broken by your own call for help, by your desire for communion—the Eucharist. This world holds no more illusions to ensnare you. You know what you want. You have all you need to get home. The kingdom is not far away, nearer than you think. Yonder lies the way...within."

As they spoke these final words, the Ancients vanished, leaving the Warrior at the edge of a great green wood with a wide path leading within. Many were walking along the path, which went forward straight and true into the heart of the forest.

"Within," remembered the Warrior. "The kingdom is within." Something stirred in him, a memory of things long forgotten, but true nevertheless. "And I know the way—down the old familiar road, the Straight Path, which leads directly to the shining gates. Long have I sought the way—and there it lies, straight and true before me. Long have I asked, and lo, the answer has already been given me."

Where else was he to go! He had seen the world, tasted the sweetness of its riches and pleasures, drunk of the bitterness of its sorrows and disappointments. It held no more appeal. And it had not soothed the deep ache in his heart. In the distance, he could hear music and laughter, the sounds of a great feast. "They are waiting for me, waiting to greet me with open arms," he thought in delight. "I need but stand at the gates and knock, and I will find that they swing open easily...that they were never locked but always open, just waiting for my touch."

So, taking a deep breath and drawing himself to his full height, the Warrior took a step forward. Doubt flickered like lightning for a moment as he stood on the threshold. But only for a moment. A rush of wind blew around him, and he seemed to hear a Voice whisper softly in his ear.

"Seek first the kingdom, and all else will be given unto you."

Repeating this silently to himself, the Warrior stepped across the threshold and onto the path, wondering where his new journey would lead.

*****

"That was so long ago," Adima mused, placing his pen down and shutting his journal. "Now here I am today. I stand ready. I have accomplished my goal, mastered my fear."

That did not mean that he was not afraid, that he did not have doubts, that he did not make mistakes. All of those things still happened. But the drama was gone now, and his behavior was different. No longer was he motivated by fear and doubt. He didn't do things because he was afraid of what might happen otherwise. Fear and doubt still crept in, his emotions still surged, but such things did not drive him as they used to.

And when the old feelings came back, as they sometimes did, he knew what to do. He had a full bag of tools, a full Circle of Allies for dealing with life on life's terms. Now it was not so much a crisis to be dealt with as much as it was old patterns wanting to be cleared. Lying there in the cool darkness before the dawn, Adima felt wonderful in every aspect of his being. Physically, he was in superb health. Mentally, his mind was clear, his thoughts pure. Emotionally, he was calm, with no doubts or fears to disturb his calm Center. Spiritually, he felt a strong, unbreakable connection with the numinous, the Divine.

It was a time of supreme satisfaction, supreme joy, supreme celebration. There were no parties, no gala festivals, no diplomas. Adima celebrated quietly, content with the knowledge that he had endured the long journey. There was no arrogance, no noise, no bragging or boasting. His dominant emotions were humility and compassion, not pride. He did not strut around, saying, "Look at me! Am I not wonderful?"

He knew that he was not going to be honored by all for his great achievement. Rather, he was about to become the servant of all, quietly and without fanfare. There was no denial of what was real, just a refusal to acknowledge illusions in any form, including Belial's. He felt as much compassion for the world as he felt for all aspects of himself—even those once viewed as not nice, wrong, or negative.

The transformation had been quiet, so very, very quiet. Outwardly, there was no change. The change was entirely within. He smiled as he remembered how he had used to fear change. Change had always meant pain, the end of what he knew and loved. Change had meant death and judgment and condemnation, over which he was powerless.

Now, of course, he had come to understand the true nature of change, not as loss, but as absolutely essential to the continuation of life. Changing seasons, changing cells in the body, changing ideas, changing emotions, changing actions, changing conditions...change was necessary for survival. Out with the old, that which no longer served, in with a new and better way.

He smiled to himself, remembering Enoch's words when a fearful, ignorant boy had asked to be rescued from life. "The only way out is through," the old man had said. Now he was out. He had come through the long, dark tunnel and emerged into a bright new world. He repeated his favorite affirmation, one that he had been saying each morning for almost twenty years.

"I am a strong and peaceful warrior and a master of the ways of Love."

Essentially, the journey had been one of finding his way to wholeness, with many and varied lessons in which he had learned to tap the inner resources of the King, Warrior, Lover, and Magician. He had undergone a powerful and irreversible transformation. Asking the right questions, he had found the right answers.

"Who am I? Where am I? Where am I going and why? What is my goal? Does my goal have great worth and value? Am I willing to do whatever it takes to accomplish my goal? Am I committed? What are my tools? Who are my allies? What is my power?"

He remembered all of those snippets of wisdom and advice, hearing Enoch's voice in his head. One by one, the words came back to him out of the dim recesses of his mind. Strong words, true words, words that were now a part of him, part of his very being.

"What is Mastery? Simply the courage and willingness to empty the vessel of Self and approach every day with Beginner's Mind."

Yes, it was a time of joy. He lay back in his bed, hands behind his head, staring at the ceiling. Waves of gratitude filled him. Savoring the moment, he let the feelings of pride and accomplishment fill him. Too often, he had gone through the cycle from fear to doubt to guilt to anger, forgetting to stop and revel in the joy.

Well, he would not forget again. For *Joy* was the natural outcome of all of the other parts of the cycle. It was the part for which he had been striving. Now that it was here, he had to be sure to savor it fully. He relaxed, pausing to experience the joy, knowing that his journey was far from complete. It was not over by any means. This was only a restful pause along the way.

For the universe was in constant motion. Nothing remained static. Too soon, the cycle would swing back upon itself. Then the learning would begin anew. The Fear-Joy Cycle would come full circle, and he would take up the journey once again, but from a loftier place and lighter place. This was the way of the world. This was the way of the journey.

*****

At the beginning of spring, a bright blue-crested bird had built a nest in the dogwood tree outside the bedroom window. Blue Jay, whose very name was a derivative of Gaia, the Great Mother's name. "Take particular notice of the markings on her wings," Adima had told the twins. "Black Earth separated from white Heaven by blue sky—they carry the signs and colors of the connected yin and yang. Blue Jay, like Dolphin, has the ability to link Heaven and Earth. It can move between both worlds and tap the primal energies of each."

Her three eggs had hatched several weeks ago, and the chicks were chirping hungrily when Enoch knocked softly. "Are you awake?" the old man asked, coming in with a steaming cup of tea.

Adima could not help but laugh. "I'm about to embark on what could be the final day of my life, and my last meal is going to be a cup of your witches' brew."

"Never mind," Enoch shot back. "This witches' brew, as you call it, has warmed you and many others on many a night, and it has never done anyone any harm. If you think it's so bad, then you'll just have to start making tea for yourself. That's something you've never done, so far as I can remember. You've complained mightily, but you have never refused the gift or made some for yourself. So how bad can it be?" Theirs was the relaxed, easy camaraderie between two old and dear friends who had no secrets to conceal, who knew all there was to know about each other and loved each other very, very much.

"You know, I'm not really looking forward to addressing the Council," Adima admitted. "There is a certain amount of fear." He did not want to admit to that fear, but the truth was the truth. "At best, I'll make enemies. At worst, I could get killed. Look at the many who have fallen into disfavor. The Sons of Belial have a way of making those who disagree with them and who are in open competition with them disappear."

Enoch nodded his head slowly. "I understand your fear," he said. "This kind of fear is good, and you are using it wisely." Adima looked surprised. He had never heard Enoch describe fear as something good.

"Fear is an ally when it serves to protect, as it is doing for you," the old man continued. "Fear is only negative when it becomes a motivation for human behavior, as is demonstrated by the fear-based motives of the Sons of Belial. Let me tell you a parable."

> The path of those seeking a new land begins with much excitement and enthusiasm. Then later comes a fear that it cannot be found, and most never get past this stage.

"Do you know the moral lesson?" the old man's eyes twinkled.

"The cheap moral is that you should never underestimate the power of fear," Adima laughed.

"Absolutely right," Enoch agreed. "But the more complex moral, worthy of a real Sojourner, is that by not understanding the nature and source of all fear, one will always overestimate its significance." They sat for a while in silence, sipping their tea while the dawn broke in full splendor around them. Mother and father jay were busily engaged in feeding their babies.

"They'll fly this morning," Adima remarked. "They're just getting a last meal, and then they'll be on their way. They're already jostling each other and standing on the edge of the nest. No more room in there," he called softly to the birds. "Time to fly." He remembered when they had been no more than balls of fluff...all beaks and feathers, with but a single motivation—to satiate their enormous hunger. Now, only a few short weeks later, they were going to fly away and live on their own.

"Have you thought about what you are going to say the Council?" Enoch asked after a while.

"I'm going to tell them the truth," Adima said. "They may not like it, but they're going to hear it. The time for pacification is over. It's far too late for that. When we drifted down from the high places and abandoned the wild ways, forsaking hunting and gathering in favor of agriculture and commerce, we began to forget the ancient ways, the ways of the Goddess, the Divine Feminine, the Great Mother. Now the worst among us have established themselves in power, and we've let them."

Enoch nodded his head in agreement. "You know, of course, that your words will never be strong enough to change the minds of the Sons of Belial. They have embraced their path, and they will follow it to its inevitable destination."

"I don't think it's my purpose to change them or anybody else," Adima answered. "It will not even be to them that I shall be speaking. I want to address the others, those who are still somewhat awake, those who do not understand, those who are unaware. Those who have good hearts and might—just might—try to do the right thing, given the right opportunity and proper support."

Enoch agreed. "There's a shift of immense proportions taking place. The new world order that ensues will last for a long time, until the time of the Great Awakening, just before it all breaks apart once and for all."

"How so?" Adima asked. "You and Sophia keep referring to this time of sleep and a time of awakening. What does it mean?"

"It is very simple," Enoch sipped his tea. "The people of Atlantis have shifted into the Spell of Matter, in which the material realms of three-dimensional space, time, and number are the only things of significance. So caught up are they in the excitement of what these materializing forces can do, they cannot acknowledge anything else. In fact, they do not even want to."

"That's the falling asleep." Adima understood his teacher clearly now. In fact, it had almost happened to him, when he had embraced the teachings of the Sensate philosophers at the university. Falling asleep was a metaphor for limiting one's consciousness to a purely external awareness of the way the world worked. It was a set of false beliefs in which external events and stimuli would come to be more "real" than the ever-present Divine direction coming from within oneself. Spiritual experiences and values had no place in the Sons of Belial's worldview. Such things were out of the acceptable range and therefore not worthy of consideration.

"And it is all by choice," Enoch revealed, sensing his thoughts. "It doesn't have to be this way."

"How so?" Adima asked in surprise.

"Free will." The answer was simple and direct. "Falling asleep is a fear-based decision. The First Ones chose to hide after eating the proverbial apple because they were afraid. Belial and his followers are no different. They repeat the same decision daily. It wasn't necessary then; it isn't necessary now; it won't ever be necessary."

A wave of sadness swept over Adima as he considered the Sons of Belial and the choices they were making. Spiritually blind, they perceived a multidimensional universe in only three dimensions. "What are they so afraid of?" Adima thought he knew, but he wanted to confirm his ideas.

"As Sophia and I told you on your wedding day," Enoch replied, "their fear is a form of the Original Fear. The First Ones' fear stemmed from a lack of trust. There was so much to manage on such a vast scale that they were overwhelmed. So, too, are the Sons of Belial."

It was fully daylight now. The birds had been fed, and now they were jostling each other in the nest, fluttering their wings, standing up on the edge, venturing out onto the branches of the tree. Mother and father hovered nearby, knowing the time of departure was near.

No fear in them, Adima thought to himself. They want to fly. They're ready to fly. They can't wait to fly. It would be wise to add Blue Jay to my Circle of Allies, he realized, for its fearlessness will help keep me connected to the deepest mysteries of Heaven and Earth. He returned his attention to Enoch. The old man was still speaking of the First Ones and their descent into fear.

"Doubts appeared. They lost self-confidence. They made so much mental, physical, and emotional noise that they could not hear that still, small Voice of Spirit speaking to them in their hearts. So they became unstable and fell out of balance," Enoch continued as Adima kept one eye on nature's spectacle outside the window. "To compensate, they instituted the false deities and beliefs we know today as fear, reason, social convention, and tradition."

Adima shook his head in disbelief, scarcely able to comprehend the vast ramifications of a single, fear-based decision that had happened so long ago. He tried to contrast human action with the actions of the wild creatures. "Lack of trust," he repeated. "Lack of trust."

How had something so unnatural become so "natural," part of the Atlantean cultural code passed on from generation to generation? Adima pictured the descendants of Atlantis following in the footsteps of their ancestors, floundering helplessly and hopelessly throughout history in a state of spiritual amnesia. What kind of a world would they create?

His thoughts were interrupted by a flurry of activity outside the window. With a cheerful chirp, the first chick had flown the nest. Now it was perched on a higher branch, calling joyfully to its brothers and sisters to follow. They needed no second urging. A tentative spreading of wings, and they were airborne. After that initial leap of faith, the rest was easy. Mother and father cavorted with them, leading the way, showing them how to land and take off, teaching them how to explore the huge new world into which they had just flown.

"Tell me about the Awakening," Adima sighed, sorry to see the birds go, but also knowing that they would spend most of their time in the garden for at least this summer. He would be enjoying his beloved birds for months to come.

Enoch shrugged. "As with all things, there must be balance. After a time of sleep comes a time of awakening, when they shift out of the darkness of sleep in the material realms and return to the light of the Spirit."

"What will that be like?" Adima asked, extremely interested in the prospects of a world in which people trusted in their natural ability to create their own lives, relying on the inherent understanding and Divine guidance within themselves. "I wish I could be there to see it and experience it."

"They will experience a time of crisis, just as we are experiencing one in our own time." Enoch closed his eyes, looking forward to a time thousands of years in the future, after all of the intervening events of history had played themselves out. "Events will occur that will beckon them to awaken, just as you and all of Atlantis are being called now. You chose to answer the Call, and so you are awake. Chances are, most of Atlantis will ignore the Call. What happens in the future remains to be seen. "It will, however, be a time of great opportunity, for they will have had the benefit of thousands of years of history from which to learn. Their chances of success will be much greater than now, if they are willing."

The old man opened his eyes and smiled at Adima. "However, just as at the Well of Kuneware certain questions had to be asked before the spell was broken, so must they find and ask the right questions that will lift the veil that separates Form and Spirit. It is only the thinnest of veils, as it is the simplest of questions.

"As for your being there, who knows? You have fathered children, passing along your genetic structure to the future. So, too, you have achieved much in the way of wisdom and truth, which you will also pass down to posterity. Such things are always remembered and received, for you do not do such work for yourself alone. Each time you close your eyes in meditation, each time you conquer a fear, overcome another obstacle, or release a false belief, you do it for everyone."

One of the chicks had returned to the nest. It stood there for a moment, as if debating whether to stay or continue to explore the new world. Courage won out over fear. Adima looked at Enoch. "How is that possible?"

"I think you know," the old man answered. "All minds are linked, all minds are one, part of the vast, eternal Spirit-Mind. So what happens for the good of one happens for the good of all. For each one who answers the Call and takes action, a thousand are released. So the Plan is accomplished. You have already answered; you are doing your part, walking along the Path, paving the way, passing along the truth to all who follow in your footsteps. And then it will be up to them, just as it is up to you. The choice will be theirs, as it is yours now."

The old man rose, set his teacup on the nightstand, and prepared to leave. "So, will you be there? Of course you will. You cannot help but be there. In fact, you are already there."

Enoch closed the door softly behind himself. Alone again, Adima looked for the baby birds. Outside in the garden, the chicks had found the bird feeder and were busily crunching seeds. They spilled more than they ate, but it was fun to watch them try to land and take off from the various perches. They were so clumsy, so awkward, but they were doing it.

It was a beautiful morning. Adima stood in the window and watched for a long time. "Speak to me, Blue Ones," he called to the birds. "Sing me your song on this fine morning."

Mother Blue Jay graciously accepted the invitation. Alighting on the topmost branch of the flowering dogwood, she opened her throat and burst forth in glorious song. The melody wafted down to him, falling lightly from the treetop to his ears, drifting in and around and through him, while his heart translated her message.

"A time of greater resourcefulness and adaptability is about to unfold, in which you must develop and use your natural talents and abilities. You are faced with a choice.

"Will you develop the innate royalty within you, properly utilizing your talent? Or will you be a dabbler—a pretender to the throne—as Belial is? As always, the choice is up to you."

Adima shivered in the early morning air. It is about mastery and the proper use of power, he realized. Blue Jay is teaching me to gather my considerable abilities together, reminding me not to get scattered, but rather to stay focused and follow through in what I am about to do.

"Her bright blue crest is reminding me to wear the crown of the true master with dedication, responsibility, and committed development in all things in the physical and the spiritual." He looked at the sharp-eyed, sharp-voiced bird still perched in the treetop, her feathers shining brightly.

How she sparkled in the morning sun! The color seemed to pour forth from her, the blue of her coat mixing with the yellow sunshine flowing around her head and neck. He sensed a deep warmth in his throat as the colors moved into him. His throat muscles relaxed and with a rush of energy, Adima felt his throat chakra open. Now he could speak. Now he could address the Council. For now the words would come!

With a last shrill chirp, Blue Jay flew off to attend to her babies. Adima dressed and went down to the morning meal.

*****

It was the ninth hour. In private quarters off the Council chamber, Adima finished dressing. It had been Enoch's idea to wear ceremonial garb, sending a message just as clearly as Belial had sent one on the night that he had received the Spear.

Unlike Belial however, who had worn heavy and ponderous armor replete with warlike images of raptors, Adima's coat was soft and delicate, almost mystical. Emblazoned across his chest, Dove winged its way from the Sun onto an invisible disc held within the arms of the Crescent Moon. It was the *Sign of the Holy Grail*—the alchemical symbol of the Quest for Enlightenment, representing the relationship between Heaven and Earth, Spirit and Matter, Father Love and Mother Truth.

"See in Dove the feelings of your heart," Enoch explained the traditional symbol of the Mother Goddess, the bird that represented the feminine energies of peace, maternity, and prophecy. "Purified in the Fire of the Sun, these heart-feelings rise up and spread through the cold intellectual thinking of your Moon-brain. It is thus that you are freed from the curse which plagues Belial and his followers—a soulless, three-dimensional conception of the universe."

Adima buckled his scabbard around his waist. The old man came forward carrying the Sword. For a moment they just looked at each other, not speaking a word. Then Adima reached out and took the weapon in his hand. Within himself, there was instant transformation. The ever-changing shadows of the past were gone, replaced by a deep sense of consistency and tranquility. As he had come to rely on his knowledge and count on it in all emergencies, so all of his learning, everything he had been taught, he would be called upon to use now. In his heart, Adima knew that he had entered into a *Period of Achievement*, a stage of real peace, regardless of deceiving perceptions, circumstances, or illusions.

Extinguishing the single candle, Enoch plunged the room into darkness. But not for long. Slowly, an ethereal rose light filled the chamber. The glow seemed to be coming from Adima himself. He looked at his reflection in the mirror. It was true! He was glowing.

"What is happening to me?" he gasped. The room was filled with the light that was shining from him.

"Your Third Eye has opened," Enoch congratulated him. "The blood in your heart has initiated an alchemical process in the pineal gland within your brain." The old man pointed to the Sword that Adima held firmly in his hands. "Use your new-found organ of higher awareness now," he urged, "and with your Third Eye, let your soul read its true name inscribed on the Sword."

Adima looked at the Sword lying across his palms. There was the inscription he had seen at the Well of Kuneware—*Through Compassion to Self Knowledge*. One by one, the letters appeared in his mind's eye—*T* for *Truth* - *H* for *Heart* - *R* for *Remembrance*...

Through his activated pineal gland, he understood that each single letter appearing in the shining surface of the blade named some aspect of himself. Together, they spelled out his whole spiritual biography as his soul had evolved from a dullness akin to sleep to this present moment of spiritual awakening. And with further astonishment, he realized that Time had no meaning here. His personal development was timeless, occurring simultaneously in the past, the present, and the future. All lives were one, all time was one, just as all aspects of himself were one.

"And so you partake of the fruit of the Tree of Knowledge," Enoch spoke softly, so as not to impinge on his concentration, "the knowledge of your Eternal Self."

Now Adima understood why the path he had chosen could never be undertaken by his twin brother. Belial had no compassion for the sufferings and tribulations of others. Belial sought the quick and easy way. Belial lived in fear. Belial was asleep. Belial did not know his own soul. And only a soul that had awakened to the love of the Creator could comprehend, without the aid of black magic, its own Individual Spirit.

It was an ultimate moment of Grace. One by one, the letters faded from his vision. Adima remembered the final piece of the legend as it was written in the *Book of Mysteries*:

NO ONE NEEDS TO RUB OUT THE INSCRIPTION,
FOR ONCE HE HAS READ THE NAME,
IT FADES BEFORE HIS EYES.

Enoch came and stood before him, looking deeply into his eyes. "Who are you?" he asked of the man who held the Sword.

"*I am Adima,*" came the immediate and unwavering reply, giving forth his name, speaking it aloud, unhesitatingly, with power. "*I am a man.*"

In that Holy Instant, Time stood still. All physical and natural laws of the space-time continuum were suspended, along with all cares, worries, and anxieties. The Pendulum ceased its never-ending journey to and fro, yin and yang merged back into oneness, the inbreathing and outbreathing of the universe was stilled. Perfect calm and quiet ensued, and eternity flooded the room.

Out in the sunlight in the piazza before the Great Pyramid, the statue of the great Guardian, Quetzalcoatl, stood frozen in stone, forever in its place. The perfect work of art, it represented the ideal man. In the ethereal rose light within the antechamber in which Adima and Enoch stood, a frozen man had sprung to life, not as life imitating art, but rather life itself becoming the ultimate work of art.

Enoch watched, and others watched with him—angels, Elementals, allies, the Great Mother herself. In that eternal moment, standing before the Masterpiece, they held their breath and admired the Ideal.

Behold the man! Behold the embodiment of the Ideal in physical form—the four archetypes of King, Warrior, Lover, and Magician in perfect balance and harmony. Pure, glistening, sparkling, Adima stood tall, larger than life, rising above pettiness, towering above triviality—a man in the fullness of being.

Behold the body! The hardness of marble coupled with the fluidity of living flesh and bone and spirit—lithe, mobile, supple. The beauty of marble—muscles tensed, rippling, flexed. Relaxed and prepared, all senses alert and aware and attuned, holding just the appropriate amount of tension, like a coiled spring...cognizant of all things in the seven directions around him—front, back, left, right, above, below, and within.

Behold the mind! Mind as Cause, body as Effect, the outer reflecting the inner—clear mind, singleness of purpose, attunement to Higher Self. Mind in control of body and emotions, reflecting in form what the mind knows to be true inside itself. In optimal physical, mental, emotional, and spiritual health—fully developed, peak, prime, unravished and unravaged. Absolutely pure!

Behold the self! Intensity of expression—focused and alert, with a singleness of purpose, at one with himself. Not as the world defines a hero, warrior, or king, but as he *is*, in Truth. No doubt in him, for he has the strength that comes from knowing. Accepting his role, playing his part, he serves the whole of Atlantis—his global community. Untried, unproven, yet ready to face an extreme test, an extreme trial and ordeal, he does what he is called upon to do.

Behold the hero! Not a hero *after* the fact; a hero *before* the fact. Rising to the real challenge—to hold this pose, posture, and state of mind-being *before* and *throughout* the supreme ordeal. For anyone can hold it afterward.

Behold the inspiration! How many would he inspire over the centuries of human history and evolution, those who followed in his footsteps, having the gift of seeing with the Third Eye. Looking back into a vision of the Akashic Record, how many would step into this moment of timelessness and behold the man as he stood in timeless transcendence?

Would the Renaissance Bard glimpse the man before penning the perfect description of the character and form of human nature?

WHAT A PIECE OF WORK IS A MAN!
HOW NOBLE IN REASON!
HOW INFINITE IN FACULTY!
IN FORM AND MOVING HOW EXPRESS AND ADMIRABLE!
IN ACTION HOW LIKE AN ANGEL!
IN APPREHENSION HOW LIKE A GOD!
THE BEAUTY OF THE WORLD!

Ultimate achievement, beyond which the Poet cannot go.

Would the Renaissance Sculptor read the Bard's words, or would he travel with the Angelic Spirit backward through the ages to use Adima as a model for his carving of the statue that so captures the essence of being human? Ultimate achievement, beyond which the Artist cannot go.

In the eternal Now of that moment of non-time, Adima had become the Center of the Universe. The totality of Creation's attention was focused on a single human being standing still at a single point in space and time. In the Spirit world, angels and ancestors—every sentient being in the celestial realms—were watching him. In the world of Matter, all eyes were on him—Cybele, Alta, Charis, Enoch, Sophia, Quetzalcoatl, the Elementals, his Circle of Allies, even Belial and the Adepts. In the silence, that still, small Voice whispered to Adima in his heart.

"This moment—this Now—is all there is. It all depends on you. This is the purpose to which the energies of your life and beyond are and have been directed. Yours is the ultimate achievement, beyond which the human family will continue to go."

Then the Voice was gone, leaving behind echoes of a deep and everlasting stillness. The Holy Instant began to fade, along with the rosy glow of the Heart Light, as he returned to ordinary space and time.

"Who are you?" Enoch asked a final time, lighting a candle and looking at his friend.

"I am Adima," the man repeated again, looking at his teacher and friend with love and gratitude.

"You are ready," the old man said simply. "It is time. Centered, you are the calm Center, remaining calm within the Center." Enoch walked away, leaving Adima to stand alone on the threshold.

He placed his hand on the doorknob. Turning it slightly, a sudden thought occurred to him.

"Heaven is here and now. There is no place else to go. I have sought, and I have found. What could be more desirable than this which I have accomplished and attained?"

Opening the door of the Council chamber, Adima stepped within. Thus began *the Week That Would Change the World!*

EFFECT

THE GREAT MOTHER

CHAPTER 39

And the evening and the morning were the first day.

—*Genesis 1:3*

A week. Seven days and seven nights. Seven cycles of light and dark. Seven journeys of the Great Mother around the sun. An instant as Holy Mother Truth measures time. The blink of an eye as Holy Father Love measures time. *Forever* as the Sons of Belial and the Children of the Law of One measured time. Time enough to create a world! Time enough to destroy a world!

*****

When crises reach a certain critical turning point, time seems to speed up. Problems compound in rapid-fire succession, like bullets from an automatic weapon, their rat-tat-tat staccato ringing in the ears, echoing around the world. Such was the case in Atlantis at the time of the Homecoming Festival in the Year of the Tower. Now things started to happen very quickly. Events followed one upon the other in a mad, headlong tumble toward the final day when Atlantis would breathe its last.

Could the catastrophe have been avoided even yet? Who knows? Of course it could have. It was all but a matter of choice. For the sinking began long before the final breakup of the land. The sinking began in the minds and hearts of the Atlantean people, through *Intention.* The ultimate catastrophe was only an Effect, not a Cause.

Adima knew this, and he tried to tell the people of Atlantis. He tried to approach them and initiate change at the level of Cause. But they would not listen. They had closed their minds and their hearts, too afraid to move forward, too afraid to challenge Belial, too afraid to acknowledge the truth, too afraid to get into the Arks, too afraid to live free.

Through it all, I moved in silence—watching, recording each event as it happened. Looking at their faces, looking into the depths of their hearts, I wrote down their names in my Book. I watched them try to justify their decisions. I watched them try to rationalize their actions. I watched them try to bend and shape the truth to a more comfortable version, one that they could live with, one that did not cause so much pain.

I watched the ignorant blissfully go about their daily lives, not knowing that something was terribly wrong. Completely unaware they were, completely out of touch with the magnitude of the forces at work around them. Completely asleep. I watched the frustrated attempts of those who had heard and were willing to try—the men and women from Al Khemia and Turtle Island, who came to the great island to add their voices to Adima's, to stand beside him as allies, to offer the wisdom and resources of the provinces in a last vain attempt to accomplish the reversal.

I watched as words and actions fell on deaf ears, sightless eyes, frozen hearts, and closed minds. I watched it all, and I wept. So needless, so unnecessary. Poor Atlanteans, poor Atlanteans!

*****

Day one of the final week began with Adima's triumphant return to the Council of Elders. Opening the locked doors and shuttered windows, Adima let in the light to shine upon the darkest corners, revealed all of the secrets, and let the truth be known to all Atlantis.

The timing could not have been more perfect. It was the week of Homecoming—the annual reunion of the provinces and a time-honored tradition from the days of Atlas, when each of the ten kings of the provinces gathered together for a gala festival in the home city on the great island. More than a festival, it was a time for the leaders and elders to review the state of the society. First they assessed where Atlantis was in its current stage of development, then set the right goals and direction for the future by asking three questions at the beginning of the conclave:

What social and economic issues need attention? What laws need to be created or modified? What needs of the people must be addressed so that the society can continue to grow, prosper, and run smoothly?

This had been Poseidon's greatest gift, although the form of the Homecoming had changed greatly over the centuries. In the beginning, when Atlantis was young, the earliest rulers, the Orphean Bards, had legislated through music alone. Their Homecomings were joyous celebrations of sound—not just random sounds, but grand tones...harmonies and scales whose intervals were those of pure geometry. In later times, the priests and priestesses carefully upheld and preserved those traditional musical scales, understanding what the Orphean Bards had already known and recorded in the *Book of Life*:

SUCH MUSICAL RESONANCES ARE INCLINED TO INVOKE
CORRESPONDING HARMONIES IN THE HUMAN SOUL.

Thus it came to pass that when the Ancients codified their law, innovations in musical form were expressly forbidden because of their disruptive tendencies. As Quetzalcoatl had observed in the *Book of Life*...

CHANGES IN GOVERNMENT ARE BROUGHT ABOUT BY CHANGES IN MUSIC.

Over the centuries, however, those dreaded changes in government *had* come about one by one, until now, in the era of the Sons of Belial, the Homecoming event had degenerated into a week of debauchery and drunkenness. An excuse for orgiastic revelry, it was a time in which the shadow energies of the God of Pleasure came forth unleashed and unbridled. Feasting, drunkenness, lasciviousness—these were the hallmarks of the week in which the Sons of Belial gathered in the home City of Atlantis, not for the good of Atlantis, but for the satisfaction of the base pleasures of the ego.

Of course, they pretended to hold to the old ways. It was, in fact, a grandiose show, full of wonderful words and bright promises, played out with great pomp and circumstance. Great orators presented flowery speeches, railing against the evils and problems of the day. The leaders took pains to extol their personal virtues, integrity, and powerlessness in the face of insurmountable difficulties beyond their control, problems that the common people could not possibly understand.

"Of course we would love to make Atlantis a paradise again," those in power declared vehemently. "Of course that is everybody's intention. Of course there are differences of philosophy between the Sons of Belial and the Children of the Law of One. Be patient," came the exhortations to the masses. "These things take time. They cost much gold. We have to assess the need, for the good of all."

"If we can improve things, we will. We are your rulers, your Elders. We know best. We have the larger view. You cannot possibly understand what we do, you who are so ignorant of the ways of government, sociology, economics, science, and the workings of the world. That is why we are in charge. Trust us, for we know best. Trust us."

Year after year the speeches were presented for all to hear. Year after year the parties and balls were held in the sumptuous palaces that lined the Avenue of the Gods. Year after year the problems continued to worsen and Atlantis continued to decline. Now another year had passed, and it was time once again to "put on the show," as Enoch and Sophia scathingly referred to the event. All of the arrangements had been carefully made according to Belial's master scheme.

The keynote speaker this year was Draco. Carefully positioned by Belial at the forefront of the proceedings, he would begin with a grand description of how great Atlantis had once been, then go on to denounce Lemuria as the root of all evil and call for war one more time. The rest of the week would be spent disseminating propaganda as to why war was the right way, the only possible course, the only chance to save Atlantis. At week's end, Belial would call for a vote, and the decision would be made. If everything worked according to plan, the skies over the enemy's homeland would be raining fire and death before the end of summer.

That was Belial's intention. That was how he planned the week and anticipated its outcome. But that was not how it was going to be. Not this year. Not any more. For Another had a different intention and a better, bolder Plan—one of great scope, power, purpose, and import. Such a Plan required the willingness of a few people of good heart and open mind. Such a Plan required relative strangers to join in uncommon alliances. Such a Plan required the cooperation of the Great Mother. And such a Plan required the full power and backing of the omnipotent forces of Spirit.

There *would* be excitement and fireworks at the end of the week, to be sure, but not the kind Belial had anticipated when planning the grand finale. These fireworks would be far more awesome, presented by the Great Mother herself.

*****

Morning of the first day of the week dawned clear, bright, and oppressively hot—strangely hot for so early in the summer season. Yet despite the heat, the Council chamber was packed. On the balcony tier that circled the perimeter of the room twenty feet above the main floor, the King held court, flanked by courtiers and attendants. Beside him sat Lilith, escorted by an entourage of lesser priestesses and acolytes. And in the center of them all sat Belial—grand master, orchestrator of the event, host, shadowy manipulator.

On the main floor below them, every seat was occupied. Others lined the walls, jammed themselves into hallways, or jostled for position in the gardens, from where they peered in through the open windows and strained to hear.

Rumors had been rampant for several days. The Children of the Law of One had spread the word far and wide that this was to be a most important gathering. A confrontation was about to take place. They did not know much more than that, except to say that it promised to be extraordinary. "If you care at all, if you want to watch history in the making, be there," they said to all whom they reached. "We need all of our allies to stand together in a show of strength."

And so the allies had come. The Ark Builders had come, as had their friends on the Council. Strangers had come, too, honored guests from fabled and mysterious provinces. Isis, Princess of Al Khemia, sat with her attendants in the front row, her dark oval eyes sweeping the room, trying to read the emotions behind the masks on all those faces. More priestess than princess, she was the personification of Al Khemian art and power. Slender and graceful, her striking features were perfectly sculpted, almost chiseled; her slight frame belied her deep inner strength and wisdom.

Directly behind her were Hia and the warriors from Turtle Island. They were beautiful to behold, almost naked, their straight black hair adorned with bright feathers, their coppery skin painted with daubs of color. A clean-limbed, mighty people, they still held closely to the ancient ways, living in the wild places, hunting and gathering, highly devoted in service to the Great Mother.

As honored guests, the provincials were seated in places of honor before a raised platform that jutted out from the west wall and served as a stage and focal point for the action...at least the pretense was made that they were honored guests. They had been given seats on the floor closest to the Elders. They had been well fed and quartered in the most sumptuous of palaces. They had even attended the grand opening of the opera the night before. Yet, strangely enough, neither the Al Khemians nor the Islanders had been asked to address the Council. "A terrible oversight," Belial had apologized personally. "We will find time for you later in the week. You have my personal assurance."

Of course, time would not be made. Events would be arranged to force the "primitives" home as quickly as possible. Belial had seen to that. Even now, the more violence-prone members of the Sons of Belial were en route to the provinces to do their sinister work. It would only be a matter of days, perhaps hours, when word would arrive of a serious crisis in each of their homelands that would require their immediate return.

A gong sounded, calling the conclave to order. Lilith rose and offered a solemn prayer, invoking the Goddess and asking for the light of her wisdom to illuminate the minds of the Elders for the highest good of all Atlantis and the provinces. Then, with a ceremonial wave of his scepter, the King rose and declared the Council to be officially in session. Finally, Draco stepped up to the podium. He paused to look at Belial, shuffled a few papers, and took a sip of water.

Several of the Children of the Law of One glanced at each other. So the rumors had not been true after all. There were to be no confrontations, no challenges, no opportunities for change. This was to be business as usual. They shook their heads sadly, their disappointment obvious. There was nothing left to do but sit and listen, hoping that the speakers would succumb to the heat and not be long-winded. They settled back in their chairs, fanned themselves, and waited for Draco to begin. It was at that moment that Adima stepped into the chamber. Quietly and without fanfare, unannounced and unattended, he was suddenly just there, surveying the room, feeling the presence of the people, attuning himself to the atmosphere and energy of that moment in space and time.

As it was out of doors, so the heat in the room was oppressive. He heard the noises and felt the presence of many living beings closely crowded into a confined space. He smelled the pleasant aromas of fragrant spice, perfume, and incense mingled with the scent of many bodies. Another odor, too, underneath the more pleasant ones, subtly assailed his nostrils as he sniffed the air. Sour, unpleasant, even distasteful, it was the odor of sweat, the scent of fear produced by the heat of all those masculine bodies in an agitated state.

The moment he appeared, a hush fell over the assemblage. Everyone stopped talking to look at the man in the doorway. There were gasps of amazement from the assemblage. Even his friends among the Children of the Law of One had never seen him like this. Those who knew him and loved him smiled. Here was a champion indeed, they realized. Belial was about to be challenged. Look out, mighty one, they thought smugly, a new Defender has arrived, and he is bigger, stronger, and more powerful. Now you're going to get your just rewards for bullying us all of these years...

The Adepts, too, overcome by powerful emotions, squirmed and fidgeted in their seats. Adima already had a reputation as a sorcerer. Now, dressed as he was, armed with a ceremonial Sword, the alchemical symbols of the Grail and Enlightenment emblazoned across his chest, he was an imposing figure indeed, especially to men who could read and translate the symbols and imagery of ritual magic.

The Sons of Belial were all too aware of Adima's power; however, having chosen a different path and dedicating themselves in service to their Dark Lord, they hated Adima and scorned all of his ideals and accomplishments. But because they knew his strength and acknowledged it, they were worried, Draco especially so. Here was a real challenger, not some pretender easily dealt with and swept aside. Here was someone to take notice of and watch out for. Here was danger. It would not be easy to rid themselves of this danger.

Moving a few paces into the room, onto the center of the stage, Adima's gaze locked with Belial's. An instant of recognition passed between them, and a supernatural force caught them and joined them together. Palpable, highly charged, an electromagnetic current wrapped them in its all-powerful embrace. The same current that each had felt in the toxic womb and again in the alleyway at the university was here now, in this very room. Only this time, Adima understood what it was—a force of attraction and repulsion between the two brothers, the opposites, the anti-twins—a bond that both drew them together and repelled them at the same time. It was the Force of Duality.

He knows! Belial felt it instantly as the fear rose up within him. He knows the secret between us. He knows who I am. And he knows who *he* is! he realized in amazement, recognizing the alchemical insignia on Adima's breast. That was even more frightening. For the first time, Belial noticed the Sword, gleaming in its highly polished scabbard. Where did he get that? he wondered in shock, instinctively reaching for the Spear that never left his side and starting to get out of his seat.

Instantly, Adima inclined his head slightly to one side, almost nodding in his brother's direction. It was a subtle gesture. Except for the two antagonists, no one noticed, but it was enough. Before the giant could get halfway out of his chair, he was held motionless. He would describe it later as feeling like he had been kicked by a horse. All of his energy and power left him in a rush of stale air. Oooomph! He deflated instantly. A wave of power drove into him, assailing him, penetrating deeply into his solar plexus. Driving him into his chair, pressing him backward, he was pinned down and held in place...utterly motionless.

This was a new experience for Belial. The pain was startling. It knifed into him, cutting directly into his solar plexus. He had never been hurt like this before. Even more searing than the physical pain, however, was another pain, the pain of being absolutely helpless in the face of a power far greater than his own. For this wave of incredible energy, this blow to his center of power, had come from the only man he feared in all the world. It had come from Adima, his brother. This was not the tiny, helpless infant in the toxic womb, nor was this the innocent boy of the university days. This was the terrible creature Nebo had warned him to beware. Now he was here, and now he was ready.

Their eyes remained locked on each other. The message had been sent, sent and received. Belial sat motionless, using every last ounce of strength to hold himself steady. He dared not show fear, he knew. But it was too late. From his place on the podium, Draco saw, and he knew, once and for all, that his fearsome, terrible, and loathsome master had a weakness. The Master could be hurt. The Master was vulnerable. In that instant, in his heart, watching the interplay between Adima and Belial, Draco made up his mind. For the good of Atlantis, he would kill the Master.

It had taken less than half a minute. Adima strode directly to the center of the stage and looked out at the sea of faces before him. Not to Belial did he address himself, not to the High Priestess, not to the Elders, not even to the King. He spoke, rather, to the people whom he loved. "Honored brothers and sisters," Adima began in a voice that exuded courage, confidence, and strength, "I request permission to address the Council." It was not a request, it was a demand. Adima knew it; Belial knew it; everyone in the room knew it.

"Granted," Belial spoke evenly, still reeling from the blow. That he even managed to speak that single word told how incredible his great strength truly was.

Draco stared at the man in front of him, scarcely able to believe such boldness. To come here dressed as he was, interrupt the proceedings, and demand to speak was either the act of a king or a fool. Judging by the looks of him, the man with the Sword was anything but a fool. With a glance at Belial, Draco bowed stiffly and took his seat.

"You all know me," Adima began, looking around the room. The element of surprise had begun to wear off, and the men and women were settling into silence. With a cough here, a grunt there, they made ready to listen. It was going to be a serious moment, so it took some time to prepare properly. Adima waited patiently, then he continued.

"You have known me all of my life. I was born in Atlantis, I am *of* Atlantis, I will always be of Atlantis. I have called many of you friend. I have walked side by side with you every day, eaten with you, drunk with you, worked with you, played with you, lived with you, loved with you. Never have I harmed any of you. I call you brothers and sisters because you are, indeed, my brothers and sisters."

He raised his arms in a gesture of supplication, addressing an earnest request to the multitude. "How has it come to this? What has happened to Atlantis? There was so much enthusiasm surrounding the coming to power of the Sons of Belial. We all heard the words, even spoke them ourselves:

"For the good of Atlantis...a brave new world...bigger and bolder and better...make Atlantis great beyond the greatness of the Ancients...the art and cultural center of the universe...a haven for all who want to come here...Protector of the Oppressed...Glory of Nations...Jewel of the Ocean of Atlas...a return to the Garden...Heaven on Earth...

"This endless litany of accolades came from everyone I met, whether they lived here in the capital city or were visiting from the provinces, whether they were Atlanteans or not. It seems that almost everyone had heard of the Sons of Belial, had a favorable opinion of them, and had had a favorable experience of Atlantis under their rule.

"Thus, I must ask myself these questions. What do my brethren know that I do not know? What do they see that I do not see? What do they experience that I do not experience? Why am I not enjoying life in Atlantis right now? Why am I not favorably impressed with life in Atlantis under the leadership of the Sons of Belial? Why don't I perceive these men the way everyone else does, *and the way everyone else says I should perceive them?* Why is my experience less than satisfactory?"

Adima looked around the room. People were listening politely, if not attentively. No matter. He was warming to the task. His thoughts were coming clearly and well. His throat chakra was open, and the words were flowing smoothly on a soft current of sound.

"Am I too picky?" he continued. "Am I an elitist? Am I expecting too much? Have I set my expectations too high?" He paused and let his gaze wander slowly around the room, coming at last to rest on Belial. *"Or am I right and everyone else wrong?"*

The giant made no move, his face a blank, expressionless mask. Whatever he was thinking was known to him alone.

"I have been considering this for a long time now," Adima continued, "mulling over the various questions and letting my thoughts wander in search of the answers. It seems that what is going on here is a conflict between what I am being told by others and what I am actually perceiving with my own senses, mind, and heart. Not a conflict, perhaps, but certainly a discrepancy between what *you* say, what the Sons of Belial say, and my *direct experience* being in the world...seeing the sights, walking the streets, eating the food, mingling with the people, smelling the smells, listening to the sounds, riding the Way, living life day-by-day.

"For what you tell me, and what the Sons of Belial portray in their pictures of life in Atlantis, is this:

'Atlantis is a paradise...the Glory of Nations, Heaven on Earth.'

"Such beautiful words invoke even more beautiful images in my mind's eye," Adima said, shutting his eyes and inhaling deeply. "I close my eyes and conjure in my mind memories of a time when everyone in Atlantis lived together and shared. Ours was a society based on cooperation and love. Happy in the Garden, we lived, labored, and played in perfect peace and harmony. Fear, anger, greed...such emotions were unknown in our happy world.

"In my mind's eye, I envision the Golden Age, when the Truth was self-evident...that all life is sacred, and that freedom is the gift of the Creator to its creations, freedom to live, freedom to grow, freedom to pursue happiness in one's own style. The Golden Age, when we acknowledged the principles of the Law of One, out of which the very fabric of our society has been formed, based on the principles of Unconditional Love and respect for all life, regardless of its myriad forms. The Golden Age, when the Great Pyramid and the Lighthouse first soared to the heavens, when the Straight Paths first crisscrossed the Mother's soft skin. The Golden Age, a time when the Dragon Current flowed smoothly and freely, when there was no sin or sickness or suffering or death."

Adima opened his eyes. "Then I open my eyes to the world of today, the Atlantis of the Sons of Belial. The beautiful images are gone, and I am faced with stark reality. What I *experience*, what I see and smell and taste and feel every day of my life, is a static and stagnant civilization, a dead and dying world. I *experience* an Atlantis in which everything is broken, from the way we look at our world to the way we look at ourselves. What started out as the grand idea and vision of the Ancients has now degenerated into a collapsed, dead, and broken mess.

"I *experience* a political system that perpetuates rule by an elite few and forces the rest of us to choose between conforming out of fear, or banishment and alienation. I *experience* an economic system that has produced two distinct social classes—those who have plenty and those who have nothing.

"I watch as the Sons of Belial take over and artificially manipulate the smoothly-running natural processes. The inevitable result is planetary destruction, manifested, as you all know, by pollution, disease, and the earthquakes and storms that come almost daily now. I *experience* the effects of a worldview that has arisen from a consciousness that disavows the Planet Earth as a living organism. Where I see the Great Mother, others see a lifeless ball of dust, to be exploited and used to their advantage. Such a value system glorifies not life and peace and joy, but murder and violence and war.

"No wonder, then, that the Sons of Belial view their fellow creatures the same way—not as brethren, not as kindred spirits, but as mere objects that exist for the pleasure, amusement, and personal gain of the wealthy and powerful elite. Annoyances that must be tolerated because to do otherwise would force the elite into the fields and the factories and the ships to do the manual labor that is so abhorrent to them, so beneath their social status.

"As I move through our world, I *experience* polluted air, polluted rivers, polluted seas, polluted bodies, polluted minds. Daily I am surrounded by the carnage of a continuous war against all of the Mother's children—from her liquid life to her metal life to her organic life; from rocks, trees, and flowers to fowl, fish, and mammals. A war in which we cut and gouge her soft body for metals and crystals, destroy biological species at an incredible rate, and poison the air we breathe, the water we drink, the food we eat. This has been my *experience* of Atlantis the Paradise, Atlantis the Glory of Nations, Atlantis a Heaven on Earth!"

Adima stopped for a brief moment. There wasn't a sound in the room or in any of the surrounding precincts. All seemed caught up in the strength of his words. Not *my* words, he reminded himself humbly, the words of Truth. I am but the vehicle of its expression.

He looked at the provincials seated directly before him—relative strangers, but men and women of honor, nevertheless. Whatever they were thinking, they were keeping it to themselves for the moment. He had visited their lands, partaking of life in Al Khemia and Turtle Island. Each had its own unique customs, climate, and geography. Yet each knew it was part of the collective, the Whole. Once you experienced life with them, it was something you never forgot.

Time to move on, he realized, continuing with the theme he had begun earlier. He was trying to point out the contradictions—how the word pictures painted by the propagandists conflicted with the reality of everyday, direct experience. "For what you tell me, and what the Sons of Belial portray in their pictures of life in Atlantis is this:

'The Sons of Belial care about us, their way is the better way. How great and good the Sons of Belial are for Atlantis!'

"Once again, such beautiful words invoke even more beautiful images in my mind's eye," Adima repeated himself, again shutting his eyes in reverie. "I close my eyes and conjure in my mind visions of great and wise thinkers with open minds, a real sense of self, and a connection to the numinous. Men like Adam, Raja, Baba, Atlas, Woden, and Amon; Women like Eve, Parvati, Qanyin, Dhyana, Barbaras, and Kali. We called them the Titans, the men and women of old, of renown. They gave us the gifts of agriculture and music and metallurgy and medicine and mathematics. They lived side-by-side with us, walking amongst the people they served, not as aloof and tyrannical rulers demanding honor and tribute, but as trusted servants of all.

"The greatest among us tended to the least among us, evolving the loving social structures that brought safety, happiness, and harmony to all sentient beings. For the greatest among us always remembered to bend head and knee and acknowledge the even greater wisdom of Spirit, guiding by example, reminding us ever and always to do the same."

Wide-eyed once again, he continued. "Then I open my eyes to the world of today, the Atlantis of the Sons of Belial. The beautiful images are gone, and I am faced with stark reality. What I *experience* is indeed a new social structure, but not a better one than that of the Ancients. I *experience* instead a government out of control and running amok, a government whose engines of war and destruction and policies of abuse threaten the very fabric of life and the serene harmony of the Great Mother herself.

"I *experience* rule by deceit, falsehood, and treachery. I sit in council with men who idolize the false deities of greed and force. Never do they admit their mistakes; instead, they build upon their errors, piling transgression upon transgression while you and I are invited to approve of and worship them. I *experience* one abuse after another as I watch the Sons of Belial close their ears to the weeping of the poor, turn their backs on the anguish of the provincials, smile at the death of our children, and shut their eyes to the warnings of our awakened ones.

"Worshipping only Force and Money, they listen only to Force and Money. These are their gods, their vain and arrogant selves the only authority they acknowledge. This has been my *experience* of how the Sons of Belial care about us, of how their way is the better way, of how great and good they are for Atlantis!" Again Adima paused, letting his words take effect. Even the hardest of the hardened, men like Draco, were caught in the throes of extreme emotion.

Belial sensed it, too. He stared long and hard at his second-in-command.

Does he know? Does he sense the treachery? Draco wondered, suddenly very much afraid as he felt those demonic eyes boring into him. He tried to remain calm and hide the deceit in his heart. Catching Belial's eye, he drew his forefinger across his neck in a symbolic gesture of cutting Adima's throat. Belial smiled and nodded his head in approval. Draco relaxed, visibly relieved that his Master still trusted him.

All around the room and out in the courtyard, similar interactions were occurring. A whispered comment here, heads nodding or shaking vehemently, people drawing closer together, people moving further apart. The words were having their intended effect—to divide and separate the Camp of Love from the Camp of Fear. Adima continued.

"For what you tell me, and what the Sons of Belial portray in their pictures of life in Atlantis, is this:

'There is plenty for everybody; we are a great nation with untold wealth and riches that will never run out.'

"Once again, such beautiful words invoke even more beautiful images in my mind's eye," Adima said for the third time, shutting his eyes and looking inward to the world of imagination.

"I close my eyes and conjure in my mind images of abundance—grain piled high, content and healthy people partaking of a cornucopia of wealth, while harmony, tranquility, and peace are the order of the world. I recall the Garden, with its bounty of vegetation—seed-bearing plants of all kinds and trees that bore life-giving fruit.

"I see our children at play, safe and secure as we, their parents, labor in the shade of our own vines and fig trees. I see the animals grazing peacefully by our sides, graced by warm sunshine, watered by gentle rains, cooled by soft breezes. I see us turn our shining faces toward the east each morning as we ask for grace to live correctly this day and toward the west each evening, perfectly content, perfectly at peace as we give thanks for another day well-lived."

A third time, he opened his eyes. "Then I open my eyes to the world of today, the Atlantis of the Sons of Belial. The beautiful images are gone, and I am faced with stark reality. What I *experience* is the nightmare illusion of scarcity, in which we are told a great Lie—that the natural inheritance of the Mother's and Father's abundance are not freely available to all. Rather, they are reserved only for those with enough power, status, and wealth to purchase and possess them. I *experience* hoarders—the wealthy among us who have more than they could ever use—struggling madly to accumulate still greater riches. I *experience* a consciousness which denies that giving and receiving are one and the same, a consciousness which believes another great Lie—that giving something away implies a loss for the giver.

"I have only to walk along the Avenue of the Gods to *experience* hungry and dirty children, people living in rags, families without homes, lying in the gutters outside this very building. I have only to stand before the houses of the nobles and watch them partake of their sumptuous lifestyles while naked people just like them eat garbage twenty feet from their doors. I have only to enter the Temple precincts to see people denied healing of mind and body, children denied education, strangers denied entrance across our borders. And, too, I have only to walk into the wild places to avail myself of the abundance and plenty of Divine providence. My *senses* tell me there is plenty for everybody. My *experience* tells me there is plenty for everybody. Why, then, the artificial scarcity? Why the Lie?

"In my heart, I *experience* the cries of my hungry, angry, lonely, and tired brethren as they awaken to another day of drudgery and weariness, as they shoulder their burdens and struggle to survive, collapsing in an exhausted heap each night only to repeat the cycle on the morrow. In my heart, I feel their absolute misery and hopelessness. This has been my *experience* of how there is plenty for everybody, how Atlantis is a great nation, with untold wealth and riches that will never run out!"

A third time Adima paused. The Atlantean nobles were shifting uncomfortably in their seats. These last remarks had struck home. Most of the people in that room lived on or near the Avenue of the Gods. They passed the poor every day on their way to and from the Council chambers.

Not that they were at fault, or that they should deny themselves and live in abject poverty and misery, for the poor had a Divine order, too. Adima's words were not about blame or shame. His intention was to present the Truth and raise their consciousness, calling the Council of Elders' attention to the fact that such conditions existed right before their eyes. Once the awareness was there, then perhaps the changes would follow. As Enoch had told him, "When you know the Truth and are made aware of it, it changes you, and so you change the outside world through your actions." He drew a deep breath and continued.

"For what you tell me, and what the Sons of Belial portray in their pictures of life in Atlantis, is this—"

'We are a free nation under the Great Creator.'

"Once again, such beautiful words invoke even more beautiful images in my mind's eye. I close my eyes and conjure in my mind images of a Spirit-loving, peace-loving, fun-loving people playing naked in the sunshine, gently evolving on our blue-and-white world, each according to the truth of his and her own inner being. Consciously aware of their true identity and relationship to Spirit, they take direction from Spirit and Love instead of from fear."

> AND IN THAT WORLD TRANSFORMED, A HAPPY SONG OF FREEDOM SOUNDS THROUGHOUT THE WORLD. EVERY NEED IS PROVIDED FOR, JOY HAS COME TO REPLACE SORROW, AND ALL TEARS ARE WIPED AWAY.

Adima continued to quote from the *Book of Life*, verses with which every Atlantean was familiar.

> IN THE SHINING LIGHT OF TRUTH, THERE ARE NO CONTRADICTIONS, NO HIDDEN PLACES, NO ILLUSIONS, NO DISTORTIONS, NO DIFFERENCES, FOR NOTHING IS HELD IN DARKNESS.
> NOW THOUGHTS OF MURDER TURN TO ACTS OF BLESSING. JUDGMENT IS LAID BY, AND THE VOICE OF TRUTH IS HEARD BY ALL.

Opening his eyes, he looked at his audience. "Then I open my eyes to the world of today, the Atlantis of the Sons of Belial. The beautiful images are gone, and I am faced with stark reality. What I *experience* is the glorification of material values and the degradation of Spirit by a greedy, lustful, fearful, angry, misguided few. What I *experience* is never-ending struggle, competition, and war—a continual attack by these powerful few on the meek, on the different, on the young, on the helpless, on strangers, and on each other.

"I see the land closed off, fenced in, and restricted for the exclusive use of the elite. I see people driven like beasts from their homes and their ancestral lands, herded behind artificial borders, prevented from roaming freely across their Mother's breast. I see free-flowing communications and individual channels of free thought blocked and suppressed in favor of a state-mandated system of compulsory education, arts, and sciences. Good ideas, new ideas that fall outside a narrow scope of propriety are branded as heresy, impiety, Lemurianism, and a threat to the well-being of the State.

"The wisdom of the Ancients has been deemed dangerous and evil. It has been discarded and suppressed in favor of the propaganda and error-prone thinking of an elite, misguided few, while all who love freedom and creativity are punished for expressing their truth. I see Atlanteans being told how to think, how to speak, how to behave. I see what used to be a nation of rich and beautiful diversity transformed into an island of mindless drones where variety, individuality, and independence of thought are feared, threatened, punished, and suppressed."

"I hear the knocks on the doors in the middle of the night. I watch my brothers and sisters carried off by the Royal Guards. I feel the spies and informers everywhere behind my back, watching, waiting, ready to pounce on any and all who dare to speak freely or think differently. This has been my *experience* of how we in Atlantis are a free nation under the Great Creator!"

Again Adima paused to look around the room. His words had produced extreme reactions. Some were misty-eyed; some were weeping openly. Others remained stonily silent, gazing off into space or out the windows. Yet it was not his place to judge those reactions as positive or negative. His task was to speak the Truth for all to hear. It was time for the Call to Awaken, time to invite everyone to join him on the heroic journey. As he had been called so long ago, so now it was time for the collective's challenge, the world's Call to Adventure.

"To you, Council of Elders, and to all of Atlantis who are willing to hearken to my words, I invite you to take a fresh new look at our world. Use your senses, your mind-brain, and your heart. Look at what there is to see. *What do your senses tell you?* Look at the streets, the buildings, the traffic; look at the social, political, cultural, and environmental conditions. Smell the smells, sniff the air. Listen to the sounds. Touch things, then look at your hands. Talk to the people and listen to what they have to say. Watch what they do. Observe. Pay attention.

"What does your mind-brain tell you? What does it make of all that sensory input? How do you sort it out? What conclusions do you draw? Finally, *what does your heart tell you?* For even more important than what your head tells you, what your common sense and logic tell you, is what your heart tells you. As it says in the *Book of Life*:"

THE HEART IS THE TRUTHSAYER. IN YOUR HEART, THERE LIES THE TRUTH.

"As I have done, so I urge you to do—look beyond the words to the *experience*, for experience speaks truer than words. The words of the Sons of Belial are lofty and grand; they are eloquent and do contain a hint of the truth. However, look at the *effects* that have resulted from the words—murder, death, destruction, greed, and rape, not just of individuals but of the entire living planet."

"For the truth is this—*a culture based on the knowledge that the Earth is a living organism and a divine manifestation of the intentions of Spirit has degenerated into a society that is eating itself...raping, maiming, and killing the very Mother planet on which it lives!*

"See? There is the discrepancy between what I am hearing and what I am observing through the Path of Direct Experience. The two do not match. And the important part is not the dead words; rather, what is important is the *observation* and *experience* of the observable, sensory world around us."

Adima smiled as he spoke. There was no way to soften the words. The time for gentleness of speech was long past. He could, however, express gentleness of being, in fact, he must do so. What better way to express gentleness than with a loving smile?

"All of us, and I am no exception, have surrounded ourselves with an amazing number of false beliefs about the reality of our world. We have convinced ourselves that these beliefs are true in order to maintain some sense of comfort, for to face the truth would bring us fear and make us feel powerless indeed."

"Perhaps to some, this false worldview is still acceptable. Perhaps to those of us falling asleep, what I have described is acceptable, as long as it does not get any worse, as long as the Sons of Belial just leave you alone and do not hurt you any worse than you are already being hurt. I, however, can no longer accept such a worldview. For me, the Atlantis of the Sons of Belial is an atavism, a throwback to the first Period of Darkness."

Adima was alluding to a time that all Atlanteans had heard of, a time long ago, before Atlantis, before the Ancients, before even the Titans. "Don't you remember the story of the City of Nod? Don't you remember what happened?" Heads began to bob up and down in agreement, the words serving as a reminder of that which the people already knew but had, for the moment, forgotten.

"How could you forget? That is the purpose of our myths and legends—to remind us not to repeat the same mistakes of those first city dwellers who built their city and ate themselves up. The few who survived—our ancestors, the Ancients—said, 'No more. Never again will we repeat those mistakes. Let us take steps to ensure that such errors never happen again.' And so they gave us the *Book of Life*, in which they codified the Law of One and the principles of Truth for all to see, all to share, all to cherish, and all to live by.

"And now in Atlantis, history is repeating itself once again," Adima declared as a few mutterings broke out from the crowd, accompanied by a vigorous shaking of heads and harrumphs of denial. He chose to address the naysayers directly, reading their minds and exposing their dark thoughts to the light, repeating their denials aloud for all to hear. "No, you say, it is not the same thing. The past is myth and legend, not real. This is different." He paused briefly.

"My brethren, I ask you, what is the difference? I don't see any. I see the same mistakes repeating themselves. Yet do we learn the lessons from the past? Not apparently, it would seem, judging by the current state of affairs in which we find ourselves. Before you sink further into the gloomy depths of denial, listen to your own words and the words of the people around you. 'Oh, it can't happen to me.' 'It won't happen in Atlantis.'"

"Listen also to your uncaring, selfish words. 'Let it happen. Who cares? It's not happening now, and I'm getting in on the cornucopia and amassing my wealth while I can. Who cares what happens down the road? I'll have gotten more than my share, and I'll be long gone by the time the roof caves in and the bottom falls out.' In truth, brethren, there are no winners. Whosoever believes the Lie and listens to what the liars say, whosoever invests their wealth and their future, whosoever believes that the Sons of Belial are their last, best hope—these same ones are the losers."

"It is time to speak up and speak out, time to bring the Truth into the center of attention and place it before you. The Truth will no longer be silenced. I add my voice now to that of one of our great poets, who gave us a last warning from his deathbed."

> WE HAVE WARNED THEM FROM TIME TO TIME
> OF THEIR INEQUITIES AND BLINDNESS.
> WE HAVE ADDRESSED EVERY AVAILABLE APPEAL
> TO THEIR WITHERED SENSE OF RIGHTEOUSNESS.
> WE HAVE TRIED TO MAKE THEM LAUGH.
> WE HAVE PROPHESIED IN DETAIL
> THE TERROR THEY ARE PERPETUATING.

"Council of Elders, we cannot keep the Truth secret any longer. The Truth is the Truth. It is real. Atlantis is broken and on the verge of ending, and we are sitting back and allowing it to happen!" One final pause before dropping the bombshell. He lowered his voice, forcing the listen attentively. "And now it is time to reveal another secret to you. We had better take action pretty quickly, because Belial has a secret weapon that is so powerful it can pulverize the planet and turn it to dust."

Adima paused to let the full weight of his words sink in. They hadn't known this, not most of them, anyway. Here was a startling truth, one that directly affected each and every person before him, a truth that would affect themselves, their families, their possessions...all that they held dear. This time, it was personal! As it had always been personal between Adima and Belial, so now it had become personal for the Whole.

"Try to imagine that, if you can. I wonder if you can even conceive of the vaporization of the entire world. I know I cannot. Why then, does such a weapon exist? The answer is simple, although astonishing in its very simplicity. Because one man wants it. On the whim of a single man, on Belial's whim, rests the fate of us all.

"Belial gets angry or ambitious, and who suffers? All of Atlantis—its people, its wildlife, its natural resources—and the Mother herself. He names someone an enemy of the State, that person disappears. He decides he wants Lemuria's gold, our children die. He decides he wants your dwelling place, he takes it. He decides he does not like you, you're gone. Period. The end.

"Why? Why do we allow such a thing? Who gave him the power? Who lets him keep the power? Who lets him dictate the social and political agenda? *We* do, my brethren. We let him because we are afraid that to do otherwise would mean death—or worse. Well guess what, dear ones? It is *already* worse. We are already dead, we just don't know it yet. Belial is about to turn on the device, a machine so powerful that it is going to annihilate everyone and everything, including Belial himself, although he thinks he's got his escape all planned out. He is going to bring the ultimate doomsday weapon forth, unleash its power, and we're all going to go *boom*! And no one is doing anything to stop him, from the scientist who designed and built the infernal machine to his unwitting protégé who is going to turn it on."

Adima looked first at Shakala, then at Kafar. The older man appeared to be in shock. His face had gone a ghastly white, and his lips were trembling. Kafar sat by his side, holding his arm, trying to steady the older man.

"This is in open violation of the Truth and the Law of One, and it is about time it stopped. I, for one, no longer choose to support a government that has declared war on us rather than be of service for the good of the people who elected them. If the rest of Atlantis is not able or willing to see that, I am going to point it out. And I would like the Council of Elders to point it out, too. You might be blind or asleep or in denial now, dear ones, but you don't have to be. Ignorance keeps you chained and locked and limited. Enlightenment is power.

"Don't you see that the Sons of Belial are only interested in keeping the rest of us in squalor, ignorance, and degradation so we cannot move up and alongside or even ahead of them? Their agenda is suppression, not the good of Atlantis. This is about oligarchy— two separate and complete states, one of the 'haves,' the other of the 'have nots,' in which the elite few have no intention of letting the power, status, and wealth get into the hands of the very people they depend on to keep them in their elite status.

"It is time for the challenge, the Call to Adventure. Who is going to help me bring this forth? How do we get the message out to our brothers and sisters around the world? Over the communications channels? In public forums and arenas? Through interpersonal conversations? However we do it, the message must go out to everyone. Our brothers and sisters need to hear from those of us whom they trust, admire, love, and respect, like the priests and priestesses, like the Council members, like the ambassadors from Turtle Island and Al Khemia."

He gazed directly at Belial, who was still motionless in his seat. In his mind, he issued a direct challenge, which he knew his brother could hear. Defend yourself, Brother! The words flew silently through space, crackling in Belial's mind. Defend your position. Say it isn't so. Prove me wrong. Show Atlantis that you are indeed a great and wise ruler, if you dare. But, of course, you know you can't, and can't translates to 'won't.'

Aloud he said, "I would like to hear Belial give us his point of view. I would like to see a leader rise up whose primary interest is in serving his people, regardless of his personal feelings and whether he gets appointed again. A leader like Quetzalcoatl, whose gifts to his people were the gifts of medicine, law, order, and education, not the gifts of the scapegoat politics of blame, fear; and finger pointing, unless that finger is pointed back at the accuser."

It was almost time to conclude, one last point to make. It was Adima's greatest gift as an orator—the ability to not only point out the problem, but also to present the solution, a solution that really worked for the highest good of all. His voice grew softer, his tone more personal. Compassion, genuine warmth, love, and affection—these were his motives. Hope, optimism, and confidence, above all, confidence—these were his messages.

"Brothers and sisters, I urge you to take heed and listen to the Truth, for I speak the Truth today. We can fix this. We have proven that we can do anything we put our minds to doing. Behold the Great Pyramid! Look at the vast network of straight paths and standing stones that bring life-giving energy to all corners of the globe! Remember what we accomplished when we decided to travel to the stars and explore under the sea. We did it. Many times. Because we all wanted to go and we all worked together to get there, we *cooperated!*

"That is the key! What the one cannot possibly do alone, the Whole can achieve with ease. Our combined efforts must be based on cooperation, not competition. Therefore, we know that we can succeed once again. But the first thing we've got to realize is that *we are all in this together*. We are all the same. We all have hopes, fears, dreams, likes, and dislikes. We are all the same. Every last one of us. There are no differences, except those of form, and form matters not in Truth.

"This is the Truth. Regardless of what you think or do or say to deny it, you have heard the Truth spoken here today. The Sons of Belial may convince their scholars, philosophers, and orators to refute my words and critique them and present alternative points of view, trying to prove me wrong. But they will not be able to, not really. They might try to couch their lies within surrounding truths, presenting a confusing admixture of facts and falsities in an attempt to lead you to the wrong conclusions. As demonstrated by the Laws of Number, however, one plus one will always and ever equal two, regardless of how one might rail against that fact. So the Truth remains forever changeless. It is forever True.

"This is the Truth from which we have got to start, High Priestess and King, ministers and honored guests. Do you have the courage? Now that you have been confronted with the Truth, now that the Truth is staring you in the face, what action will you take, each of you, personally? Deny it aloud if you will; that is your prerogative. But the question remains—what are you going to do about it in your hearts, where it really matters?

"For you cannot escape the Truth. Either you accept it, embrace it, and be changed by it, or you *consciously* reject it, and thus consciously continue to *live the Lie*. And this time, you know what you are doing because you are conscious—which makes you culpable and responsible. So what's it to be? Will history say of you, 'These were the great ones, the men and women of old, the men and women of renown.'? Or will they remember this as the time when the Fathers fell asleep? The choice is up to you."

As Adima finished speaking, the force that had been holding Belial motionless ceased. The giant could move again and, as his power returned, so did his voice. He would answer the challenge, all right! Make no mistake about it. He would rise up and bring this upstart crashing down. He would make an example of Adima for all to see.

"Sorcerer!" he roared, jumping to his feet and brandishing the Spear. "Behold the Sorcerer! He couches the Lie within the Truth. Here is the real danger, for he has disobeyed the ancient commandments and dared to impose himself—body, mind, and soul—upon others." Belial grabbed the Captain of the Guard and shoved him roughly forward. "Seize the traitor," he bellowed. "Lay hold of him, disarm him, and put him in chains."

There was pandemonium in the Council chamber. Men and women were on their feet, shouting and yelling as the battle lines were drawn. As the Children of the Law of One tried to move toward the front of the room, their way was blocked by those loyal to the

Sons of Belial. Cries of "traitor" and "sorcerer" filled the air, along with curses, oaths, and epithets.

Dakinis, Captain of the Guard, leaped down from the balcony, attempting first to restore order and then to carry out his Master's command. Armed guards milled through the crowd, pressing the people back into their seats and clearing the aisles and the exits.

Order had been restored for the moment. One by one, councilors, elders, and guests returned to their seats. In the relative quiet that ensued, Isis somehow managed to slip past the guards and make her way to the front of the stage. "Enough," she beseeched Belial and the soldiers. "Hasn't there been enough violence? Haven't you heard a word that has been said here today?" Her impassioned plea, however, had no effect. There would be no controlling these men, no appeals to higher reason and emotion.

"Silence, woman!" Belial roared, his deep bass booming through the room. "You have no say here. And since you have forgotten your place and chosen to interfere, you are no longer welcome in Atlantis." He motioned to a burly guard, who immediately grabbed the Princess and held her in a viselike grip.

Before Adima could react, other guards leaped onto the stage, weapons at the ready. Forming a circle, they surrounded him while the Children of the Law of One looked on helplessly. What might have happened had they seized him is anybody's guess. But they were not to seize him that day. The Other Plan was in effect. Although all seemed to be in chaos, everything was under control. Everything was in perfect order.

Adima smiled, remembering the night he had stood in the stream and faced the five-headed snake. Now I stand in a different stream, he thought, a stream of fear and violence, filled with all sorts of vicious creatures that want to devour me. As he had stood his ground then, and thereby received the gift of Snake, so he stood his ground now. There was no fear; rather, a pleasant heightening of his senses as he felt the serpent within him uncoil itself from around his spine and rear up, poised to strike.

Calmly, from his calm center, Adima drew his Sword and faced his enemies. The weapon crackled with energy, radiating enormous light and power. The circle of guards drew back in fear, taken aback by a force they could not comprehend. This is a battle I will fight, he thought grimly, having chosen to stand his ground and not retreat this day. If I am to die, I will die well, having spoken my truth for all to hear. That much, at least, I have accomplished. As for the rest, so be it.

The room grew deathly still. Most of the Children of the Law of One were unarmed, and even the few who carried ceremonial daggers or swords knew they were no match for the mercenaries of Belial's army. So they stood by their seats and watched the drama unfold, too afraid to interfere.

Alone on the stage, surrounded by enemies who wanted to kill him, it was impossible for Adima to be aware of everything around him. So many milling soldiers pressing him from all sides! "Seize him," Belial screamed again from the relative safety of his imperial seat high above the action. "Arrest them both." Slowly, the circle of armed guards began to close.

Adima's first thought was for Isis's safety. Turning to look for her, he did not see the Captain of the Guard approach him from behind, sword poised to strike. Had it landed, the blow would have been fatal. But before the man could bring the blade crashing down, a newcomer entered the fray.

It was Hia, mighty chief from the great land on the western shores of the Ocean of Atlas. The warrior was disgusted by the spectacle he was witnessing, disgusted by the way they were treating Isis, disgusted by the way they were treating Adima, disgusted by the way they were treating himself.

The provinces of Turtle Island and Al Khemia had long been close allies, and an attack upon one was considered an attack upon the other. Hia knew it, and his warriors knew it. No need to speak to his fellow countrymen; they had lived side by side for so long that they could sense each other's thoughts. They were only waiting for the right moment to strike. That moment had come.

There were no warning shouts, no cries to alert the guards. Only action—pure, simple, direct action. With a bloodcurdling yell that sent a chill of fear through even the most inured, battle-hardened guards, Hia leaped to his feet. In a single fluid motion, he raised his axe-blade and threw it through the air.

Time seemed to slow to a standstill. Everyone watched, including the Captain of the Guard, who had turned at the sound to face this new antagonist. The man stood transfixed as the terrible weapon followed the course upon which it had been set, tumbling over and over, flying straight and true. In that instant, a memory flashed in the doomed man's mind. He remembered the night he had seen Belial transformed into the monstrous Beast. A sickly, rueful smile spread across his face.

"I should have run," he whispered in those last fleeting moments of life. I should have gone far away, where they would never have been able to find me. Now it's too late, too late, too..."

The weapon struck with the force of a lightning bolt. Indeed, it *was* a lightning bolt, Adima realized as he watched in amazement. This strange weapon wielded by the skilled warrior from Turtle Island was another form of Hard Lightning. Clutching his chest, Dakinis's eyes bugged out of his head in a look of disbelief. He swayed unsteadily on his feet for a second or two, then crashed to the floor in a lifeless heap. As one, the other warriors from Turtle Island rose and fanned out around the room. Longbows drawn, arrows fitted, they stood ready.

It was an awesome display of primitive power—half-naked men armed with longbows, traditional weapon of the hunter-gatherer tribes of the old days, standing ready to defend and protect. True warriors, they could fit and release arrow after arrow in a blazing display of speed and accuracy. Flying straight and true, the "death sticks," as they had been named by those who had tasted of their potency, unerringly found their mark in a "rain of death" more potent and of greater duration than the raindrops and hailstones of an Atlantean hurricane.

Belial's guards were outmatched, and they knew it. Reluctantly, they lowered their weapons and backed off—all but one, the huge brute of a man holding Isis. Placing the point of his sword against her throat, he dragged her roughly to the center of the stage. "Drop your weapons or she dies," he ordered, exerting just enough pressure on the point of the blade to draw blood. A tiny crimson trickle flowed down the princess's neck, staining her milky white gown a bright red.

There was no response from the Islanders, no attempts at negotiation, certainly no acquiescence to what they considered a cowardly act. A bowstring twanged, and an arrow flew across the room at inconceivable speed, the whoosh of its passing the only sound.

The guard had no time to react, no possibility of stepping aside or making an outcry. The arrow struck with such stunning force that it lifted the two hundred and fifty-pound man off his feet and drove him backward into the western wall of the room. There he stopped, impaled a foot off the ground, a feathered shaft protruding from the center of his throat. Four more bowstrings twanged, four more arrows whizzed through the air in rapid succession, finding their marks, piercing the dead man's arms and legs, splaying him spread-eagled for all to see.

The silence was deafening. No one moved, no one spoke, not even Belial. Another message had been sent, this time from the warriors of Turtle Island. With a bound, Hia leaped to the stage and stood beside Adima and Isis. Here was an imposing ally indeed, for the reputation of the warriors of Turtle Island was renowned throughout the world. Legends in their own time were these mighty warriors, skilled with bow and knife and tomahawk. In fact, never since the beginning of the world had an invader successfully attacked Turtle Island.

Now Adima and Hia had joined forces. Island man and provincial man stood together—two warriors, two allies, two kindred spirits. "I stand with Truthsayer," Hia cried to the assemblage, as his brothers and sisters swept the room with their eyes, lest any attempt more foolishness. "In my eyes, his words are true. In my eyes, he stands falsely accused."

He turned to Adima, placing his left palm over his own heart and his right palm over Adima's. "Your strength is my strength, as mine is yours. I pledge you my loyalty, and from this day forth, I shall call you Brother. All of Turtle Island stands ready to come to your aid. You need only ask. Should you wish to reside with us, you and your family are welcome. Let us go now, and leave this place of deceit and corruption. This is no place for men and women of honor." The Islanders converged on the stage, forming a phalanx around the trio of allies. Before Belial could even think of a course of action, they were gone.

*****

It had been a marvelous oration, full of fire and energy and power; full of pathos and heart and life; delivered as a King standing in the fullness of his power, speaking his truth, walking his talk. Never had such words been spoken in Atlantis. From the heart of a single man to the hearts of all humankind, the Truth poured forth in a perfect blend of reason and emotion. *And it fell on deaf ears!* The people of Atlantis heard the Truth and chose to not be changed by it. They chose, instead, to consciously live the Lie.

Yet in that instant of choosing, the Other Plan went into effect, the bolder, better Plan, the Plan whose success was ensured. That change would be wrought was inevitable. That humankind would come to acknowledge the Truth was inevitable. That the whole reversal would be accomplished was guaranteed. Only the means to achieving those ends would change.

What could have been accomplished in a single instant would now play itself out over a span of thousands of years. Instead of a graceful laying aside of the old in favor of the new, now the people of Atlantis were going to have to experience the long hard lessons of the future. They were going to have to learn by doing, by walking the Path of Direct Experience, for a very long time to come.

CHAPTER 40

The problem with you
Is the problem with me
The problem thinking we're so different
The problem is how to perceive...
                                        —Anne Waldman, *"Duality (A Song)"*

The Plan was really very simple. To ensure its success, so that humankind could experience and thereby learn, several closely-related processes happened within a very brief span of time.

First, the people of Atlantis separated into two distinctly opposing camps—Camp Love and Camp Fear. Then, a massive migration off the island began. This was followed by a new awareness that was birthed in the Atlantean consciousness, an awareness of a heretofore unimaginable future. And finally, the Great Mother shifted on her axis.

No single process had greater or lesser value or significance. Each was equally important to the success of the Plan. Each happened in accord with the others.

*****

Immediately after Adima and Hia left the Council chamber, Belial gave the order for their arrest. He had no choice. His enemies had openly challenged him. They had defied his authority, questioned his leadership, advocated rebellion, and committed murder. "It is treason!" he raged, his spittle forming frothy droplets at the corners of his mouth as his supporters vehemently declared their assent. His hands shook, his whole body trembled, and he wanted only to lose himself in the murky depths of one of Hanuman's magic potions. Yet he dared not lose control of his faculties now, at this most critical juncture.

Within the Council chamber, chaos reigned supreme. Adima's words had had their desired effect—not to unite, but to separate, although Adima had not known it at the time. That little secret had been the intent of the Other whose Plan it was, whose Plan was now fully under way.

Adima's words had served to transform the room from a place of relative reason and order into a battleground. A major rift had occurred, battle lines were clearly drawn, and borders were sharply delineated. For the first time in almost thirty years, everything was out in the open. There were no more waverers, no more fence-sitters. Those in the chamber had been instantly drawn either to one side or the other.

The two camps were clearly defined. In the Camp of Love were the Children of the Law of One—the few, the gentle, armed with truth and virtue, yet hardly a physical match for their opponents. And what opponents they were, adversaries in the truest sense of the word, enemies who wanted them dead!

In the Camp of Fear were the deluded Sons of Belial, the many, the powerful. Hugely strong as the world measures strength, these were dangerous, violent men caught in the grip of the nightmare illusion of separation, wishing death upon their enemies, who were, in truth, their brethren. And Death would come quickly now, for it had been invited. Oh yes, the grim Spectre was approaching ever so quickly.

The conflict began with a war of words. Shouting, accusing, and cursing, each side tried to cast blame upon the other. "Belial, you brought us to this?" cried the Children of the Law of One. "Death to Belial!"

"Your weakling attitudes of peace and nonviolence are the problem," countered the Sons of Belial. "You must all die."

Almost immediately, the conflict expanded into physical violence—first bruising fisticuffs, then weapons striking, drawing blood. The Children of the Law of One were no match for the heavily armed, battle-hardened veterans of several Lemurian campaigns. In just a few moments, there was great bloodshed.

Mouth open in shock, Lilith put her hands to her face in horror, covering her eyes, trying to shut out the sight of so much flowing blood. The King—desperately afraid, desperately weak—made no effort to intervene. Instead, his ministers and Royal Guards hustled him away through secret passages to the relative safety of the country palace on the other side of the Great Plain, in the foothills of the Mountains of the Moon.

The Children of the Law of One had no choice but to flee, leaving their dead and dying behind, the cries and pleas of the wounded going unheeded as their comrades surged through the exits and poured out into the streets. The chaos spilled over into the city, spawning violence, rioting, and all manner of harm against the human person as the once-united Atlanteans split asunder.

They were not used to this; it was a new experience for them. True, they had waged great war upon their enemies, but never had they raised their hands against their own. Violence and murder were unheard of in Atlantis...until today.

Belial watched in calm satisfaction. Everything seemed to be working out perfectly; there was no need to interfere. Now he put the order forth, the order he had waited thirty years to give, the order that would bring about the end of all who opposed him. "Round up the Children of the Law of One, wherever they are, and bring them to me. If they will not come willingly, bring them by force. They will be given one chance to escape the fate of those of their kind who litter the ground beneath our feet." He nodded, indicating the bloody corpses scattered on the floor below him. "If they renounce their ways and swear allegiance and obedience to me, they will be spared. If they do not, they will be killed instantly."

There was no room for compromise, no wavering. Belial had declared martial law. In fact, he had gone beyond martial law, recognizing no law but his own—a shadowy, deluded version of the Law of One, with himself as the "one" authority who held absolute power of life and death over the masses. And in the absence of a strong King, there was no one to challenge him, no one to stop him. The Children of the Law of One stood alone and defenseless, or so it seemed.

At last the violence was squelched, and an uneasy calm settled over the city. The streets were emptied, and people stayed behind closed doors. A few attempted to go to the Temple to pray and petition the gods, but Belial's guards accosted them and rudely sent them home. Within the Council chambers, calm had also been restored. The wounded had been gathered up, the dead bodies shrouded and carried off, the puddles of gore sopped up. But no amount of scrubbing could remove the dull purple stains that soiled the porous white marble floor. As Belial descended from the balcony and stood at the podium, the ghosts of the dead voiced a silent scream, their lifeblood mute testimony to the carnage that had occurred there that day, when brother had turned against brother in Atlantis for the first time.

A lesser man could not have restored order. A lesser man would not even have dared try. Homecoming would have ended in disaster before it had begun, with the diplomats returning to the provinces and Atlantis continuing in chaos. But Belial was not a lesser man. Using all his skills of statecraft, the master manipulator stood before the assemblage and took control. Urging the Council members to remember their purpose in gathering—Homecoming and all of the responsibilities that such an event entailed—he deftly steered the Council's focus back to his original agenda—the war with Lemuria.

In fact, events could not have worked out better, he thought to himself as he looked out at the crowd. Now he could not only start a war, he could also get rid of his most hated enemies at the same time. All that was required was a simple modification of his original plan. Couching the lie within the truth, he would stand before the Council in all humility, confess to the existence of the device, and even offer to demonstrate it to the Councilors. Then, unbeknownst to his victims, a convenient mishap would occur—a mishap in which vast multitudes of the Children of the Law of One would die. And Belial would blame it all on Lemurian spies.

Outside, the afternoon grew gray and damp, the humidity soared, and the barometric pressure dipped sharply. Billowing thunderheads loomed in the east and in the west. The wind blew in fitful gusts, scattering the dust in miniature cyclones. Lightning flickered behind the dark clouds, and thunder rumbled ominously. A storm was approaching.

Inside the chamber, candles were lit against the oppressive grayness of the skies. The debate raged long and hard, but it was not about the suffering of the people. The Councilors who remained, especially the provincials, wanted to know more about the mysterious device of which Adima had warned them. Such men and women were not used to secrets, at least not secrets that weren't of their own devising. "Tell us about the device," they demanded with one voice, firing question after question at the giant on the stage. "Tell us. Why do you have it? What can it do? What is its purpose? Why weren't we told?"

Belial stood unflinching under the fusillade of questions. When he did speak, he was not the angry tyrant who burst forth in an abusive tirade. Rather, here was the Belial of old, the mesmerizing and captivating speaker whose voice rang with strength and power. Holding his audience spellbound, mustering all of his skills of tact and diplomacy, the cunning Beast within the human shell magically and gently calmed the angry crowd. "My purpose in creating the device is as a weapon to protect Atlantis."

"Why does Atlantis need protecting?"

"Because of Lemuria and who knows what other dangers?"

"If the device is so good, why did Adima come here and rail against it?"

"Because he is a sorcerer whose mind has been taken over by demons. He is afraid; he is deluded; he is confused. So many reasons why...all the wrong ones."

The words were having their desired effect. The questions were fewer and fewer, the combative air gradually softening. "Adima is the real enemy here," Belial reminded them, "Adima and the Lemurians. "I act only in the best interests of Atlantis and the provinces. I chose not to tell you of the device until I was sure it would work. Now I know it will. In fact, I was planning a demonstration for you on the morrow and would have announced it this morning were it nor for the interruption. Now you will see for yourselves that Adima is a liar, and there is nothing to fear."

A soft murmur of approval ran through the crowd. The Councilors looked at each other and nodded in satisfaction, pleased with themselves at having asked the right questions and uncovering the facts.

"The device is the future...your future," the Belial-Beast continued to intertwine the lie within the truth. "This is where your future lies—in technology, in expansion, in world domination. In that sense, Adima was right. We have the science, the technology, the wealth, and the infrastructure to do anything we want to do. In fact, the device is perfectly safe. I will show you. I have scheduled a demonstration for tomorrow evening. Shakala will see to it."

And that was that. The session ended and the Councilors left, mollified for the most part, smugly confident that it was their assertiveness that had forced Belial's hand. Little did they know that they were but following a predetermined course over which they had very little control. The device would be set off as planned. They would come to realize its potential as a powerful weapon. Then things would go wrong, and much suffering and destruction would ensue.

But not because Belial had planned it that way. Not through Belial's intention, or even their own would these events come about, but through the Intention of Another, so that another condition of the Plan could be met—the birthing of a Consciousness of the Future. For the major effect of the detonation of the device would be the birthing of the future, a future that would serve to scare the Atlanteans to death.

*****

The events of the morning of the first day of Homecoming were the topic of conversation on street corners, in parks, and in homes. Word spread quickly to the people of Atlantis—to the farmers and merchants, priests and healers, scientists and teachers, vendors and laborers; and to young married couples just starting families. To elderly couples who had spent many years together and had created good lives for themselves. To single men and single women; and to lonely ones, jolly ones, sick ones. By midday, all of them had heard the news.

Sitting in their homes, playing with their children, they heard the news. Eating lunch and dinner with their loved ones, they heard the news. Strolling through the Garden of the Heart they heard the news. At the beach they heard the news. On the mighty ships at sea they heard the news. In the caravans plying the trade routes, they heard the news. In the fields and forests they heard the news. In the provinces they heard the news. On the hills and plains and mountain tops they heard the news.

Questioning, wondering, taking the message to heart, they pondered its contents, trying to decide what to do. At first there was only the message. Then came tales of violence, chaos, arrests, and death. Rumors spread like wildfire, each succeeding story crazier than the ones that had preceded it. "Belial has been killed. The King has been killed. Adima has been killed.

"The Great Temple is burning to the ground. The Lighthouse has toppled into the sea. Lemuria has declared war and is even now attacking the western borders. Belial's death squads are roaming the streets, killing anyone who ventures out of doors." With the rumors came the doubt and fear. At every turn, the old order was collapsing. Only a day ago, such events would have been inconceivable. Thus, no one was in any way prepared or able to cope.

*****

All over Atlantis, deeply personal scenes of tragedy were unfolding. On a quiet street on the outer ring of the city, an elderly couple sat in a darkened room and held each other's hands. "What should we do?" the old one asked his beloved. "Should we try to leave Atlantis?"

"I don't know," came the anxious reply. "Everything we love is here—our home, our children, all our possessions, all that we've worked for. How can we leave our lives behind? How can we abandon our children?"

"You're right," her husband replied, shaking his head helplessly. "Besides, we're too old to move away, even if only for a short time. Where could we go? The provinces? We'd be strangers there. And even if we were willing to go, how could we afford it? No," the old man sighed resignedly, "we will stay here and trust that things will be all right."

*****

On another street on the far side of the city, closer to the central hub of activity, a group of young men and women stood on the flat roof of a house, peering intently toward the Great Pyramid and the Temple, where huge crowds swarmed through smoke-filled streets.

"There's nothing to fear," a young man spoke confidently, the tremor in his voice belying his mock bravado. "We've heard all this talk before. These people know what they're doing."

"You're right, I suppose," a young woman chimed in doubtfully, "They're not going to hurt us. They need us to run things."

"At least in that respect, this Adima guy is right," said a third, even as a group of armed men took up positions in front of the Temple. "I'm staying put. I've got a position of responsibility, a nice home, a comfortable amount of wealth. I'm not going to throw all of that away on rumor and speculation."

*****

Behind a shuttered storefront on the Avenue of the Gods, a group of merchants huddled to discuss their new strategy for averting potential business collapse. They had planned to sell trinkets, souvenirs, clothing, and the like throughout Homecoming week. At the end of the seven-day period, each had expected to amass a tidy little profit. Now there would be no market for such memorabilia.

"How can we profit from this turn of events?" a merchant asked. He had invested heavily in clothing and manufactured goods and needed a way to recoup some of his losses. "There has to be a way."

"People are going to be afraid," another rubbed his hands greedily. "They'll be unable to think rationally or clearly. We can count on them to make hasty, even rash decisions that quite probably will lead to great profit for those of us who don't panic."

"Of course!" another cried, suddenly realizing the opportunity. "Capitalize on their fears. We can provide special excursions to the provinces. We can offer to purchase their homes at drastically reduced prices. We can sell supplies and survival kits in case war breaks out..."

*****

In the forest that blanketed the foothills of the Mountains of the Moon, the Sun Children gathered on a high promontory. A self-appointed shaman-priest squatted over the entrails of a disemboweled rabbit, his brow furrowed in deep thought. A ragged group of men, women, and children looked on fearfully. "It is a great punishment that has befallen us," the filthy old man cried at last, pointing a bloody finger at each member of the group. "This is the price of your sins. You have failed to pay due homage to the Sun God, and now he has turned his face away from you."

"No," the people wailed. "We are sorry. Say it isn't so. What must we do to atone for our sins?"

Again the faux-shaman turned to the grisly carcass, fingers probing the bloody organs. When he rose to face the people, his face was a ghastly shade of gray. "There is only one recourse," he said grimly, wiping his fingers through matted, greasy hair that hung almost to his waist. "We must appease the wrath of the Sun God. The Sun God calls for a sacrifice. The Sun God calls for blood."

He took a step toward the people, who shrank back in fear. Mothers clutched their children; fathers glanced uneasily at one another. Who is it to be? each wondered. That it would be a child was certain, for the Ogre Tyrant god of this radical, misguided sect was appeased only by the blood of virgin youth.

The fanatical priest walked slowly down the row of sun worshippers, gazing fixedly into the eyes of each man, woman, and child. So firmly did he wield his power over them, so thoroughly dominated were they, that no one dared challenge him. To a person, they stood helplessly by, waiting for the victim to be chosen. Each breathed an audible sigh of relief when the horrible, half-naked caricature of a holy man had passed. But there was one whom he did not pass—a young mother whose firstborn was still sucking at her breast. With a single swift motion, bloody hands snatched the child from its mother's arms and raised it high in the air for all to see.

"Behold the sacrifice!" the blood-crazed tyrant screamed in awful glee, his erection bulging visibly beneath his ragged loincloth as the child screamed in terror and the mother collapsed in an unconscious heap on the rocky ground.

*****

All over Atlantis, the individual dramas repeated themselves with astonishing frequency. In each case, the people were different, the forms of the drama were different, but the behaviors were essentially the same. So many people, so many different forms, yet underneath, all were driven by a common motivation. All of their decisions were based on their attachments to things material—to homes, possessions, relatives, memories of the long-gone past; to power, status, and wealth. The old fears were there, the ones Adima had alluded to. "Better to sit quietly by and wait," they said to themselves.

So they talked themselves out of taking action—the elderly, the young, the middle-aged, the greedy, the misguided, the hopeless. Talked themselves out of taking a stand, out of doing the right thing, out of investigating further. Talked themselves out of listening to the Truth. Talked themselves into living the Lie.

Little did they know that they would not have long to wait. Time had run out. The moment of transition was at hand, a mere matter of days now. All was prepared. By the time they would make their decision to flee, it would be too late. There would be no place left to go.

*****

In the peaceful oasis of Elysia, the Twelve gathered to discuss their next plans. "Everything is just about finished," Nuah said. "The crystals are prepared. The geometric matrices are established and in place, and the destinations chosen. Most of what we are bringing in the way of scientific knowledge, art, music, and literature is gathered and stored. All that is left to do is decide where the twelfth Ark is going to go, gather what you are going to take, and place and activate the crystals."

"I can answer the first part," Isis spoke up, her lovely dark eyes filled with tears for the loss of Atlantis. "I offer you my homeland. All that we have we will share with you. You will be welcome among us. You will be treated with love and respect and provided for all of your days. You need but to accept our invitation."

"We do accept," Adima thanked her gratefully. "Yours is a most generous offer. We shall be honored to dwell in your land. We will never forget Atlantis, indeed, we *must never* forget Atlantis. But we will hold those memories in our hearts while beginning anew in the new world—the land of Al Khemia, where we will place the monuments of stone as reminders to our posterity of our former glory."

"Good, then it is settled," Isis said matter-of-factly. "I will take my leave of you now and return home to prepare for your coming."

"That leaves only the Knowledge Crystals," Nuah said when Adima and Cybele had returned from showing Isis to the door and sending her safely on her way. He glanced at Cybele. "Can you get them, Latoné?"

Nabala started. After more than two years, someone had finally uttered the mystical name in her presence. The secret had been revealed at last. Now she had the name; now she knew the secret. Power and glory and riches would be hers! She could not wait to leave the group once and for all and return to Lilith with the news. The others were still talking, but Nabala was not listening. Her head was filled with images of gold and riches and treasures. She imagined herself as high priestess, floating on the sea on her magnificent barge, men swooning at her feet, attendants catering to her every need.

"Then it's all settled," someone said as she returned her attention to the room. "In three days, everyone will convene in Poseidia and the first of us will go. The few who stay behind will be able to leave at a moment's notice."

"I will stay here with the last of you," Hia said, speaking for the first time.

"This is not your fight," Adima answered.

"It *is* my fight," the Islander replied. "It became my fight the moment Belial attacked my homeland. You think I don't know what he tried to do by sending his henchmen to Turtle Island? They were intercepted the moment they arrived and their lifeless bodies are even now on their way back to Belial with a message from us to stay away. No longer is Turtle Island part of the Atlantis of the Sons of Belial. So you see, my newfound Brother, it is indeed my fight."

Hia walked to the doorway that opened onto the veranda, looking wistfully out to sea, as though he could see his homeland shimmering on the horizon. Alas, he would never see Turtle Island again. "Even with your mighty Sword and Wand and Shield, and your great teachers," he nodded in deference to Enoch and Sophia, "you and Cybele cannot fight Belial and his army alone. You must have allies; you must have warriors at your side. We are those warriors, and we will stand by you to the end. If you fall in battle, so we will fall. If you are successful, so we will be successful. Either way, we now share your fate, whatever that fate may be."

Adima looked at the man beside him. They had known each other only a few hours, yet already he loved him deeply. This man should have been my brother, he thought. It would have been wonderful to have had a brother like Hia while growing up. How they could have played and roamed and learned together! But no, I had Belial instead, he thought grimly. Then he remembered his adopted brothers, whom he loved—the elder gone these many years, the younger sitting quietly out in the garden with Alta and Charis. In that moment, the grimness vanished from his heart, replaced with love and happy memories.

"No matter," Adima realized without regret. "Hia is my brother today, and what we did not do as boys we will do now, as men."

*****

In another part of Atlantis, a dark and mysterious and secret place known only to a select few, Draco plotted the death of Belial. "He must be destroyed," the Adept reasoned aloud, his thoughts coming in little bursts and phrases. "For the good of Atlantis. Not because Adima is right. In fact, I still hate him, and he, too, must be destroyed. But because Belial is crazy and out of control.

"He will destroy us all. He is in the grip of madness and delusions of megalomania. We cannot have him leading Atlantis. He will bring the destruction down on all our heads."

Why now? Draco wondered silently. Why the change of heart? If Belial were to find out, he would kill him for sure. And it would be a terrible death; he could count on it. He shuddered, remembering all of the grisly executions he had witnessed over the years. "Yes, but this time, I can beat him," Draco insisted, remembering what he had seen that morning. "Up until now, I was afraid to try, because I thought him invincible. But Belial has a weakness. He can be hurt. I saw it today with my own eyes. I saw Adima do it to him. If Adima can do it to him, then I can, too."

Long he sat steeling himself, resolving to follow through on the course he had set while the small fire burned itself down to glowing coals. It was almost midnight when he rose to return to his home and his bed. As he left, Draco did not see the eyes—eyes that glowed with the dull red of the smoldering and sulphurous fires of the infernal regions. Peering out of the darkness at the edge of the clearing, the eyes of the Beast were upon him.

Hideous, evil, malicious, and highly intelligent, the Beast skulked into the center of the clearing, pausing to sniff the ground and catch the scent of its prey. After a moment, it straightened up and stood perfectly still, sniffing the air. Was that a smile that creased its hideous countenance? A thick black tongue lolled out of its gaping maw. Viscid, evil-smelling drool dripped onto the dying embers of the fire, making tiny, evil hisses. The Beast threw back its head, cast its baleful eyes to a silvery crescent moon, and gave vent to a fierce, mournful, bloodcurdling howl.

Farther down the mountainside, Draco stopped dead in his tracks. The tiny hairs at the nape of his neck stood on end, and he cast a fearful glance over his shoulder. "Coyote," the Adept tried to reassure himself, but it didn't work. "Or worse!" the recognition sent a thrill of terror through his body. He said nothing more, drawing his cloak more tightly about his person, wanting only to get home to safety behind locked doors.

*****

Throughout that night, the first night of the week, incredible portents appeared in the air and on the land and in the sea. They began at dusk, when a red light appeared in the sky where before there had been only empty space. It was not the light of the War God, nor the light of any of the seven errant Wanderers that prowled the heavens. The astronomers called the light a comet. The astrologers heralded it as a message from the Sun God. The awakened ones recognized it for what it was—a harbinger of doom, carrying calamity, war, fire, and pestilence within its icy tail.

At the same time that the comet was flashing across the sky, other signs and wonders were occurring all over the world in the elements of earth, air, fire, and water. Throughout the night, violent tremors shook the central plains of Turtle Island and the mountains of Mu and Lemuria. All along the Ring of Fire that bordered the Sea of Peace, volcanos spewed fire and brimstone. Torrential rain and gale-force winds battered the barrier islands off Atlantis's eastern coast.

If these natural upheavals were not strange enough, even more mysterious supernatural happenings struck fear into the hearts of the Atlanteans. As he was riding through the forest, the King met with disaster when his horse shied so violently that it threw him to the ground. An excellent horseman, no one could remember him ever falling, being thrown, or having any kind of equestrian mishap. Now Gadir lay in a state of partial consciousness, barely breathing, while the Palace floundered in darkness and despair.

At the Temple of Poseidon, the magic words of the Ancients carved into the granite lintel above the great front doors mysteriously disappeared. One moment the runes were there, etched deeply into the stone; the next moment they were gone, throwing a crowd of pilgrims and attendant priestesses into a state of near hysteria.

When word reached him through frightened messengers, Belial scoffed, refusing to admit that any of these events could have any connection to or effect on his personal affairs.

"These are signs that Adima spoke the truth," said one frightened Adept.

"The end times are at hand," cried another.

"We must all repent and beware," admonished a third.

"Nonsense," the giant replied, laughing at their foolish fears. All was working according to plan, and he would not be swayed by superstition resulting from a few ill-timed coincidences. Little did Belial know the true meaning of such signs. For if he had bothered to take the time to attend to them, to listen to their messages, he would have known what all of the awakened ones knew—ownership of the Spear was about to change hands.

Further and even more significant, an important death was imminent, but on this matter even the omens were vague. Could it be the death of the current holder of the Spear? Was it to be the death of the one who held the Sword? Or would it be the death of the once-great Nation-State itself? It was but the evening of the first day, and the answer would not yet be revealed. Only time would tell!

*****

The parties were quiet that night. Try as they might, the Councilors could not get Adima's words out of their minds. They kept hearing the phrases, kept hearing the exhortation to judge for themselves, to look past the words to the experience. And in their hearts, the place of Truth, they knew that it was all over. But so frightening was that knowledge, so secret, that they could not admit it, even to themselves. They fell asleep trembling, dozing fitfully, waking with a start at the slightest sound...disoriented, not sure of where they were. Falling back to sleep again, the cycle repeated itself as they wrestled with the Truth in their hearts, struggling to deny it, trying make it all go away so they would not have to look at it. And all the while, the Truth remained, unchanged and unmoved by their struggle within themselves.

Sometime toward morning, Belial's sleep was disturbed by a strange rustling sound. He tossed and turned fitfully but did not get up to investigate. Had he done so, he would have been shocked to see an enormous bird standing on his window ledge. Black as pitch, mysterious as the Great Void in which it dwelt, Raven—*Guardian of the Ceremonial Magic*— had arrived with a warning for the Master.

"*Beware, you who have embraced the Dark Path,*" the Messenger of the Ancients croaked as a smoky light filled the bedchamber with its supernatural glow. "*For you have forgotten the magic of life. You wish to move into higher levels of consciousness, but you cannot because you have not yet achieved mastery of your current level. You wish to harm others, and so you have invited harm to be visited upon yourself, that it may teach you what it feels like to be harmed.*"

Silent as the night, the great bird soared back and forth over the sleeping giant, pecking at the door to his consciousness, offering to fly through his dreams, offering him a taste of its most potent medicine. But the door remained closed, the Beast-mind enshrouded in clouds of sooty black smoke produced by an intellect that could not conceive of a magic greater than its own. Thus did Belial reject both the gift and the giftgiver. Thus did he reject the magic of the darkness and a call to awaken. Thus did he choose to remain asleep. Upon rising the next morning, he was amazed to discover a single iridescent blue-black feather on his pillow.

*****

Adima lay quietly in bed, listening to the words of the Great Mother as she spoke to him.

"I am grateful to you, Adima." The Mother was smiling, whispering her thanks on the breeze and in the song of the nightingale. *"The choice has been offered—accept Belial or reject him—and the decision has been made. Many of your brothers and sisters have chosen to accept him, or at least to passively sit by and do nothing. Therefore, the time has come. The course has been set. Now I shall act. Have no fear, my son. There is no danger. All is as it should be. All is in accord with the Plan."*

Adima smiled contentedly. Snuggling closer to the sleeping woman beside him, he drifted into a deep and peaceful slumber.

*****

And the evening and the morning were the first day.

CHAPTER 41

And the evening and the morning were the second day.
—*Genesis 1:8*

Kafar was upset. The young protégé had listened intently to Adima's words, and what he had heard had disturbed him very much. He hadn't slept at all well, tossing and turning as dream memories and images of the events of the previous day filled his subconscious mind. Finally he could stand it no more. It was still dark when he arose, washed, dressed, and prepared a small breakfast of fruit and bread.

Could Adima be right? he wondered as he ate. Aside from the contradiction between the words and the experience, could there be any truth to the fact that there was a device such as had been described? Of course there is! Kafar realized almost instantly. He was not a stupid man, and it was quite easy for him to fit the pieces together. Secret chambers, off-limit laboratories, covert meetings, forbidden experiments, high-level security, Belial's mood swings, hidden agendas...everything fit together into a picture that he did not like the looks of, not at all.

He had been duped, he knew that now, misled into doing research into a forbidden area, told that he was looking for a solution to exploding crystals (which was the truth), but not told why. Now he knew why—to power this mysterious device, a device that would bring death to billions and lay waste the entire planet, if Adima could be believed. He shuddered to think of the shattered and broken world it would leave in its wake.

Then another thought occurred to him, and his mouth slowly widened into a smile. The device could not work if the crystals did not maintain their structural integrity.

Finishing his meal, Kafar activated his musical player and selected soft woodwinds and strings. He always thought better with a little background sound, and music always inspired his best ideas. He sat back, closed his eyes, and tried to relax as the peaceful strains filled the room. Breathing slowly in and out, he tried to clear his mind of the chatter. Underneath all of that noise, he knew, lay his real feelings.

"Ah, there they are," he said aloud to no one in particular as the guilt and anger welled to the surface from deep within him. "So I helped them," he realized ashamedly, speaking to the empty room. "Unwittingly or not, I helped them create their device. They couldn't have done it without me. They tried and tried and tried, but it wasn't working. Then along I come with my brilliant IQ and my high ideals and my confounded eagerness, and what do I do? Make it easy for them!"

Eyes still closed, still concentrating on his breathing, he slammed his fists into his sides in disgust, desperation, and self-loathing. How he hated himself for what he had done! How he wished he had never come to this place. How he despised his own prideful ambitions!

The music filled the room, evoking ever stronger feelings. He sat for over an hour as various melodies ebbed and flowed, carrying him through an entire gamut of emotions. Now the deadly shame and guilt were gone, replaced by a different kind of anger. Neither rage nor self-contempt, this was an ennobling anger, a righteous anger that carried its own inspiration to action.

"I can fix it!" he exclaimed suddenly as the music soared in a lofty crescendo. "I found the solution; I can un-find it. I can fix the crystals so they do explode after all. I can't be responsible for all those deaths. I must correct my mistakes. I've got to change the formula!" He sat quietly for another thirty minutes, eyes still closed, breathing softly, growing more relaxed, more confident. When the music finally stopped, he opened his eyes and rose to his feet, alert, refreshed, and ready for action.

His first task was to make sure. He had to really know. He had to prove to himself that there was, indeed, a device, that it was a weapon of destruction, and that the Sons of Belial had malevolent intentions for its use. He could do that quite easily, of course. As long as they kept records, as long as they stored their information in the data crystals, the information was there for the taking.

He had no doubt that they did. Shakala was schooled in the scientific process, after all. He would have kept meticulous records, documenting all of his ideas and observations from initial design through prototyping, testing, and implementation. No doubt the records went as far back as Shakala, if not farther.

Then there was Belial. The Master probably kept records, too—minutes of meetings, lists of enemies of the State, agendas, communications and correspondences, databases. Everything would be there, available to whomever knew where and how to look.

"That is the key!" Kafar was excited now, pacing back and forth as he thought through the details of his plan. What Belial thought safe from prying eyes was a matter of open record for one who knew the secrets of the crystals. Kafar was one who knew. He knew how to tap into the inner recesses of the crystals, delve into their internal structure, and view all of the information stored there. He had learned as a boy, when he had invented his own device for a science project.

And what a device it was! Not a weapon of destruction, but a new form of communication. He smiled as he recalled himself as a youth, proudly explaining his work to a panel of judges. "I call my invention a neural interface." That raised a few eyebrows. "It allows me to enter the consciousness, if you will, of the crystal itself and view all of the information stored within its crystalline matrices."

Higher again went the eyebrows upon hearing such mature words and ideas from one so young; higher still when the demonstration proved that the words were in fact true. It was such a brilliant concept that it had earned him immediate acceptance into the Science Academy in Al Khemia. Over the years, he had tinkered with his prototype whenever he had the time, but as his interests changed and his worldly ambitions mounted, he had laid it aside in favor of more financially rewarding pursuits. He hadn't even thought about his device in months.

The last time he had seen it was when he had packed to come to the city. He thought it might provide something to do if he got bored or, if nothing else, make a nice conversation piece with his new friends. Little had he known that it would serve a far more significant purpose.

"Aha!" He voiced his muffled cry of triumph from the bottom of a small closet. There it was, in a box buried under a pile of dirty laundry. A simple-enough looking device, it resembled an article of headgear—a helmet and goggles, with wires and electrodes attached to a pair of leather gloves. "You look like a robot," his schoolmates had teased him when they had first seen the outfit. But their jeers had turned to cheers when he won highest honors.

Of course, that demonstration had been presented on a tiny crystal that he had impressed with a small amount of relatively simple data structures. Now he was going to try it on a much more sophisticated and complex crystal being. At the door to his chambers, he paused for a moment. Holding the strange contraption in his hands, he looked at the jumble of wires and electronics. Would it work? Time would tell. Kafar stuffed the device into his pack, wrapped his cloak around his shoulders, and headed out the door.

*****

The light breeze and cool morning fragrances were a welcome tonic as Kafar made the long walk from his living quarters to the Great Pyramid. The eastern sky was just starting to lighten as he approached the main entryway. His admiration for the builders had never left him. Today, however, those feelings of amazement had been replaced with a strong sense of foreboding.

Atlantis was a large, busy city, and even at such an early hour, people were usually up and about, making deliveries, opening shops, exercising, and engaging in all of the normal activities of a large community slowly waking to a new and productive day. This morning, though, the streets were strangely deserted. Doors and windows remained shuttered. Not a person was about, not a sound reached his ears, not a single light gleamed in the houses and shops. Such abnormal quiet was unnerving.

As he walked, he thought long and hard about the best way to approach the problem. In a flash of genius, he hit upon a brilliant and cleverly simple solution. All of the crystals were living in the truest sense of the word. Not carbon, but silicon-based life forms, each pulsed with life. And each was connected to its crystalline counterparts, some by a system of neural networks invisible to the naked eye, others by using rudimentary "senses" of speech and hearing to communicate with similar crystals in close proximity, usually within a few hundred yards of each other.

It would simply be a matter of connecting to a single crystal, speaking to it in a language that it understood, and essentially asking it to show him around, lead him through the otherwise incomprehensible maze of data passageways, and reveal its secrets to him. There were no encryption codes to worry about, no passwords to decipher. He could use the crystal in his own laboratory as a starting point. No one would have any idea that he was there, and after he was gone, there would be no trace. It is a simple, foolproof plan, he thought confidently.

The Pyramid was empty at this time of morning. No one was working yet, although he knew from experience that there were Adepts in the building. Belial had spies everywhere. Kafar had probably been observed already. His behavior was not unusual, though. He liked to work during odd hours, often arriving before dawn and leaving late in the evening. So his arrival this morning would not be noticed, or if it was, it would hardly be looked at askance...or so he thought.

Even now, a guard monitoring the various public and secret entrances to the Pyramid had observed him and was speaking into a communications device. "Yes, Great One," he replied, "it is just as you predicted. He arrived moments ago and went straight to his laboratory. No, Sir," he said after a pause, "he is alone. Shakala is not with him." Another pause. "Yes, Master. He carried his usual duffel, although it bulged more than normal and seemed far heavier than usual." The guard was silent for several moments. "Certainly, Master," he said at last, ending the communication. "As you wish."

*****

In the laboratory, the diamond glowed silently on its pedestal. It was not a particularly large gem, but, like all of the crystals in the Great Pyramid, it was flawless and perfectly shaped. Closing the door, Kafar strategically placed a chair where it would provide a barrier against unwanted guests. If anyone tried to get in, he would hear the noise and be warned.

He wasted no time in setting to work. With a conflicting sense of eagerness and dread, he donned the helmet, placed the goggles over his eyes, and gripped the crystal with his gloved hands. Instantly the outside world vanished, and he found himself in a beautiful, crystal universe. Kafar paused for a moment to look around. He had forgotten how breathtakingly beautiful it was there inside the crystals. He had entered a vastly different world, an alien world comprised of a wonderful latticework of crystalline structures and landscapes.

It was the world of the crystal Supermind, and its singular, omnipresent feature was light—multifaceted, creative, structured light. The whole terrain shimmered with a soft yellow pastel glow, vibrating with a regular rhythm and pulse. There was no motion, not in the ordinary sense of the word. There were no breezes, no moving elemental particles like electrons or protons of which he was aware, just the three-dimensional, living crystalline patterns. "Consciousness in form," Kafar breathed, intrigued by the marvelous shapes, shapes of all kinds and sizes—squares, triangles, tetrahedrons, trapezoids, octagons, pentagons, and countless other polygons—the living geometry within the crystal world.

Pure mineral, pure beauty, pure thought. It was indeed wonderful—a world full of wonder, in which thought had become visible, a form of crystallized consciousness. He relaxed and let his own thoughts float freely. His device would enable him to communicate with the consciousness of the crystals. Whatever he thought would first be translated into an image and then expressed in a universally recognized three-dimensional mathematical pattern or equation. These were "words" that the crystal could understand and to which it would respond.

"It is simply a matter of thinking holistically." Kafar smiled to himself, remembering the first time he had spoken those words, a boy-genius explaining his theory to the distinguished scientists at the Academy. They hadn't quite been able to grasp what was so simple to him.

The Supermind worked just like his own human mind. Like his own mind, the Supermind was a vast repository. Anyone could input raw data and creative ideas. Even emotions and feelings could be stored there, as could memories and every conceivable sensory input. Then, as within his own mind, all of that seemingly random, chaotic, and perhaps meaningless data was all reassembled according to an innate systematic order inherent within the crystal's own intelligence. What had once been meaningless in and of itself was now organized, logical, and structured.

How was this possible? Again, it was simply a matter of holistic thinking. Each facet of the crystal was part of a greater whole, just as each part of his own mind-brain worked together. He could see relationships and classify information. He could see the essential and prioritize. He could evaluate and make judgments. He could use logic, reason, and intellect to make decisions. He could feel emotions. *So could the crystals!*

Now here he was, standing at the threshold, in the awesome presence of the Atlantean Supermind, boldly asking to enter within, to explore its structure and order, to see how it worked, what it looked like, what was important to it, and what secrets it held. So like the individual Atlantean mind was this vast crystal Supermind—solid and practical, tidy and efficient, and above all, ordered and balanced. It was the King Mind!

For this complex crystalline structure was modeled on the minds of the Ancients— Poseidon, Atlas, Athena, Hera, and the rest. Ages and ages ago, they had cultivated, nurtured, and grown this living crystal network as a gift to all the world, from generation to generation, forever. They recorded their experience in the *Book of Life*, that all might read and understand.

> EVER AWARE OF THE UNDERLYING ORDER BEHIND ALL PHENOMENA IN THE
> UNIVERSE, WE HAVE IMPRESSED OUR FUNDAMENTAL KNOWLEDGE WITHIN
> THE STRUCTURE OF THE CRYSTALS AND ALL OF THEIR MULTIPLE FACETS
> AND OFFSHOOTS.

Upon this foundation, the Ancients had built their whole world, the living crystals forming the solid yet ever-expanding base upon which they established Atlantis' own sense of order, harmony, and proportion. As these truths were written in the *Book of Life*, as they exemplified them in their own lives, so they programmed them into the crystals.

Kafar's first thoughts were thoughts of greeting. The Supermind responded immediately. The muted yellow background began to glow and sparkle. Images of dark, cloudy skies swam in his vision, soon giving way to a bright, clear sunshine. "Wake up!" he seemed to hear the words inside his head, although there was no sound. "Open your mind, clear your vision, let your own brilliance shine in harmony with ours." A sparkling lemon-yellow sunburst filled his vision. "Behold the dawning of clarity."

"Good," Kafar thought, appreciating the harmonious colors and images and the warm greeting. He took a deep breath and relaxed a little, growing more confident with the assurance that his device was working as designed. "I'm in, and I'm welcome." He wasted no further time in small talk. "Show me the Device Project." Kafar pictured Belial's device in his mind's eye, thinking about the crystals he had worked on and trying to imagine what such an engine of destruction would look like. At first there was no response.

He added Shakala to his thoughts, then Belial, along with images of exploding crystals and using the device to attack Lemuria. He was trying to form a composite image of the men, their machine, their crystals, and their motives.

What was that? Something was happening in front of him. The shapes and colors were visibly changing. Gone was the geometric landscape. A passageway was opening before him, a triangular-shaped tunnel leading deeper into the depths of the crystal consciousness. He felt his mind being carried along the passageway. "Such a strange sensation," he marveled. Reason told him that his feet were planted firmly on the floor of the lab, yet he could feel himself moving, being whisked through space at incredible speed.

As he traveled, Kafar looked around in wonder. What sights! The walls of the tunnel were a soft pink. Here and there, multifaceted nodules protruded from the walls. Kafar knew that they contained information that had been stored within the crystal. "It feels like I'm in its central nervous system," he realized. It was a perfect simile. At various intersections along the way, branching tunnels led off in different directions. The whole network, glowing with various hues of pink, reminded him of his own neural bundle of nerves, neurons, and spinal cord. The explorer aspect of his nature wished that there was time to investigate all of those byways. What secrets they must contain! But his scientist self knew he had to stay focused on the task at hand.

Holding the images of the device in his mind, he continued moving through the maze. He turned left, then right, trying at first to keep track, but soon giving up. He was hopelessly lost, but that was no matter. He need only think about "home" and he would be returned to his original point of origin...he hoped.

The colors and shapes were changing now, and he realized that he was no longer in communication with the crystal in his lab. He passed from the pink neural system through a whole spectrum of crystal worlds—an amber world, an emerald world, a turquoise world, an agate world, a ruby world...at last entering a carbuncle world. Carbuncle—the Crystal of War and Bloodshed!

Kafar knew that he was in the core of the data center. He recognized these dark crystals, having seen them on occasion in Shakala's secret laboratory. "Wouldn't the old man be amazed," he thought, "if he knew where I was and how I got here!"

The light grew darker and darker as he approached the center of power within that multifaceted crystal Supermind. His forward momentum slowed, and he came to rest in a perfectly round chamber, a perfect living sphere within the pure center of the crystal, in the midst of which floated a flawless tourmaline. There it was, the information he had been seeking.

Kafar stood still and let the images come forth. They floated to him seemingly out of thin air, or whatever it was that passed for atmosphere in such an alien world.

He saw diagrams and prototypes. He saw blueprints and schematics. He saw the device in its fullness, perfect and complete, from every angle. After a while, he sensed that something was missing. There was more to the device than just these simple technical diagrams. But how would he be able to coax the data from its crystal hiding place? It was a most frustrating set of circumstances, until he remembered something his mother had told him when, as a boy, he had stubbornly tried to cling to an idea that just was not working.

"Try looking at it in a different light," she had said, sending him outdoors to play. "As you turn your mind around, whole new viewpoints will open up before you."

It had worked then; why shouldn't it work now? Feeling more comfortable within that alien environment, Kafar began to move about, slowly circling the floating tourmaline, examining at it from all sides. How surprised he was at what he felt! It was a strongly sensual experience. He felt the Supermind reach out and embrace him, an offer of union and communication from energies outside himself. Having a naturally creative and curious mind, he allowed himself the freedom to indulge in the commingling.

His willingness was well rewarded. What at first glance had seemed perfectly smooth, round, and symmetrical was in fact quite abstract, amorphous, and variegated. And as his perspective changed, so did the images that came to him. From this new angle, he saw the device's victims—poor creatures scurrying to and fro as fire and death rained from the sky. Beneath the tourmaline, he beheld the elements in total disruption, causing destruction and devastation on a vast scale. Looking down on the tourmaline from above, Kafar realized that he was looking on a vision of what might happen to Lemuria if such a device were to be unleashed on them.

On he went, continuing his circumnavigation of the chamber. Scenes of exploding crystals burst around him. He saw himself working on those crystals, and Shakala and Belial smiling in satisfaction as he presented his new formula.

Kafar had many questions to ask. "I wish I could talk to the crystals in their own language," he thought in frustration. It was a direct expression of inspiration and friendship, to which the crystal Supermind responded immediately. Instantly, the images faded. Back within the neural web, Kafar felt himself hurtling headlong down a dark, narrow tunnel. The pace was breathtaking, and his head spun dizzily as powerful waves of nausea swept over him. Closing his eyes made him feel better in spite of the lack of light, but he lost all sense of time and direction. On and on he sped, alone in the darkness of the unknown. When the motion finally stopped, he lay still, his whole body tingling and highly sensitized. That was when the voice spoke for the first time.

Where was it coming from? Not from the outer world, of that he was certain. No, the voice was coming from within the Supermind itself. Could the crystal consciousness be speaking to him? Indeed, it would seem so, but how was that possible? "Kafar," the voice called his name. It was not a human voice. It had a definite metallic sound and timbre. It was the voice of a silicon-based life form, he realized in amazement. And it was female!

"I'm here," he answered, not at all sure of what he was doing. Opening his eyes, he gasped in astonishment. He found himself floating in a sapphire sea, while all around him, the liquid crystal glowed a deep, cool blue. It felt like he was inside his own heart, but he knew that couldn't be true.

"Good," the voice replied. It seemed almost at his elbow.

Kafar turned toward the sound. Again came the involuntary gasp of astonishment. Floating in empty space at eye level was the disembodied face of a woman. Her features were bold and somewhat distorted, as though he were looking at a ceremonial mask constructed out of highly polished metal and crystal.

It was a striking, beautiful, enigmatic face, at once cold and warm, hard and soft, impenetrable and open. Dispassionate, detached, non-judgmental, and non-involved— here was a woman in touch with the higher laws and values of the universe, existing in a pure state of awareness. Looking into the cool blue pool of her single sapphire eye, Kafar sensed a depth of wisdom and serenity that he could barely imagine. Intuitively, he knew there was nothing to fear.

"We are glad that you are here and that you have asked to see," the Crystal Priestess reassured him, her lips reshaping themselves into what appeared to be a smile.

"A living kaleidoscope," Kafar breathed, remembering the beautiful, complex, ever-changing patterns he had viewed in his mother's kaleidoscope when he was a boy. The entire multifaceted face absorbed all of the images around it and reflected everything back out at the viewer—light, shadows, geometric shapes, even his own reflection.

"Long have we awaited your coming," the voice continued calmly. "Long have we awaited someone willing and able to speak to us in our own language. You are that someone. While you have been exploring us, we have been exploring you. We have scanned your motives and intentions and know them to be pure. That is why we have chosen you and allowed you to come inside us."

Kafar wanted to remind the creature that he had not asked permission. He had simply donned his own device and plunged within. There was no mystery about. He certainly had not needed to ask the crystal's permission.

"Do not think it was your meager device that allowed this." The alien priestess seemed to read his thoughts. "That was a part of it, but there is so much more. We are attuning our crystalline vibrations to the relatively meager powers of your pituitary gland to show you this glimpse of the Atlantean Supermind and let you read the records. It is our crystal Supermind combined with your Mind's Eye that presents these virtual images which you see displayed before you."

Kafar wanted to ask so many questions, wanted to understand how such technology was possible, but he was barely able to speak. All he could manage was a single hoarse question. "Who are you?"

"I am the Priestess-Guardian of the Supermind," the being replied from her elevated place above the jumble and confusion of mundane life. "I am the *Intuiter of the Truth*, speaking to you in the voice of the crystals themselves, or rather, their combined group consciousness. By your human standards, I am an alien life form. By universal standards, I am one with all life."

The ever-changing crystal face shimmered in the liquid sapphire sea. "We are not ambulatory; we remain forever motionless and at rest. Our purpose, for which we are well suited and with which we are quite content, is to store data and live peacefully with the knowledge that is stored within our all-knowing consciousness. We do this impartially and objectively, seeing with non-judgmental awareness, always obeying the prime directive of our creators:"

Achieve equanimity through dispassionate analysis.

"Ours is a balanced world in which we remain forever free of emotional attachments. We live according to the highest principles and values of the Law of One, but because we are sentient beings, we cannot avoid making value judgments. We want to share those judgments with you now."

"Let us show you the Truth. Let us show you how sick your world really is. Let us show you the dark side of the Atlantean Supermind, the side belonging to the Sons of Belial." The shimmering face moved close, asking a single question. "Are you ready?"

It was no time for fear, yet the fear was definitely there. Anything other than an affirmative response would end the experience forever. Kafar's inner struggle raged for several moments, the two hemispheres of his brain battling for supremacy. Reason argued against creativity; the thirst for knowledge fought with logic. The priestess waited patiently for the synthesis to occur. At last it happened. Kafar's versatile mind achieved the evenness and balance to formulate the only possible answer.

"I am ready."

Hardly had he spoken the words when the priestess' face burst asunder, shattering into countless pieces. From the wreckage, four crystal fragments emerged and floated magically in space before him. The first was jagged, the second dark, the third opaque, the fourth glittered enticingly.

"Welcome to the Shadow Worlds of Confusion, Narrow-Mindedness, Dullness, and Delusion," the disembodied voice echoed hollowly in his head. "Select a starting point."

Never having seen the likes of such crystals before, Kafar could only surmise their purpose and contents. Feeling like his own world was broken, he reached out and tentatively touched the jagged Crystal of Confusion.

Once again, the shapes and colors changed. Once again, he was transported deeper into the labyrinthine structures of the crystal Supermind. Surprisingly enough, the first of the Shadow Crystals was not at all shadowy. At least, not at the outset. Kafar had no idea where he was, probably not even in the Pyramid any more. No matter, he was being shown something important.

There were crystals of all sizes, shapes, colors, and qualities, each representing an idea or an aspect of the rich Atlantean culture. Moving at dizzying speeds, they floated through space, sometimes merging with each other to form new shapes, other times colliding and shattering. Out of this confusing interplay, a vision of Atlantis was opened up to him, and he saw. From the swirling mists of color, patterns and images began to take shape as the crystalline records released themselves from their long-frozen state.

First he saw Atlantis in its former glory. He watched the Ancients as they studied the creative energies of the universe and penetrated the essence of Nature's storehouse. Such vast and diverse knowledge they had—of the vibrations of plants, jewels, and metals; of the highly advanced sciences of agriculture, astronomy, and astrology; of the meaning of numbers, the stars, and the elements; even of the activity and effect of the morning dew. So great they were, those ancient giants who could neutralize the pull of gravity and who understood the mysteries of the origin of humanity and the five races. They had a full understanding of the laws of metaphysics, of spiritual and scientific truths that were essentially the same.

It was all a blur, so quickly the images came, so rich and varied and full. Kafar felt giddy, overstimulated, drunk. He found himself standing in a wild and tangled garden, hopelessly lost and confused. "I'm losing my mind," he cried in anguish, closing his eyes and shaking his head in an attempt to clear away the chaos and confusion. "I've got to get out of here."

With the asking, the colors changed again, growing brighter, more sparkling as he moved on, alighting this time in the glittery, artificial realm of the Crystal of Delusion. Hallucinations assailed him from all sides, his mind attempting to convince himself of the reality of things that were not at all true. A huge crystal whirled around and around, its flecks of iron pyrite catching and reflecting the sunlight.

> ALL THAT SHINES AND SPARKLES IS NOT OF GREAT VALUE.
> ALL THAT GLITTERS IS NOT GOLD.

Kafar remembered the words of his father's favorite quotation from the *Book of Life*, one that he never hesitated to remind his son about, lest the boy be led astray by promises that could not be fulfilled. How he wished now that he had taken his father's lessons to heart.

Suddenly, without warning, an image loomed up at him from nowhere. Two shapes fairly leapt out of the reflections at him—huge shapes...dark, bold pictographs twelve feet high that cast blood-red shadows.

Project Nightside

"What does it mean?" he wondered. He had never heard such an expression. He doubted if even Shakala knew the term.

He would soon learn that "Project Nightside" was more than mere words. It was so pervasive and terrible, so dangerous and malevolent, that it carried a vibration that caused an actual tremor in the crystalline structure. For Project Nightside was the name given to a secret society so hidden, so sinister, so corrupt that their machinations were destined to alter the very course of human evolution for thousands of years to come...indeed, for all time, if the originators of the idea had their way.

Kafar was anxious to learn more, but the crystal seemed to want to unveil its data in its own way. Where once his thoughts had elicited immediate and direct responses, now he was forced to peruse the data according to the dictates of the Supermind.

"Be patient," he sensed the words in his mind. "First you must see your world as it really is."

Kafar relaxed, knowing he had no choice. Image after image followed, each showing an Atlantis that he never knew existed. He saw how the wealth of knowledge possessed by the Children of the Law of One was usurped, abused, and misapplied by the Sons of Belial. All in secret, all hidden away, out of the light of day! Hidden behind smoke and mirrors and all sorts of illusions that had effectively created delusions of grandeur and a false sense of security and well-being among the Atlantean race! Couched in the glitter of false hopes, false beliefs, false promises, and false dreams!

Now Kafar saw the underlying truth. Acknowledging only material existence, the Sons of Belial rejected not only the principles of the Law of One, but also the warnings of those who understood the Law. Bitter tears filled his eyes and trickled down his cheeks as he watched the forces of Nature and the Great Mother being misused and the wise ones tortured and killed. He saw all of the sordid details, the complete picture of Atlantis under the Sons of Belial. He saw, and he was astonished, completely overwhelmed at the scope, depth, and pervasiveness of the corruption that lay spread out before him.

The Fire Crystals, magnificent source of life-giving light, heat, and regenerative forces, had been cruelly transformed into instruments of coercion, torture, and punishment. Deep in the secret dungeons below the Great Pyramid, Belial's victims screamed in agony as the Terrible Crystals did their work. Occasionally out of fear of death, but more often as a result of succumbing to temptation, many of the Children of the Law of One listened to the arguments and yielded, becoming collaborators with the Sons of Belial. Priests, priestesses, scientists, geomancers, alchemists, musicians, merchants, artists, scribes, poets, farmers, philosophers, legislators, elders...the ranks swelled year after year.

As the satisfaction of personal desires became paramount, there came a corresponding increase in the growth of disturbing social, political, economic, and environmental factors. There was no stopping the degeneration. As fundamental spiritual laws and truths were misapplied to the goal of satisfying physical desires, spiritual temples degraded into temples of sin. Human sacrifice and sun worship prevailed, as did adultery and corruption.

There was conflict everywhere—contention over the use of explosives, gases, and weapons for selfish purposes. Bitter, bloody battles were waged to determine who would be the leaders among the ruling class. Even more disgusting were the degradations that ensued as the fawners and sycophants vied with each other for special privileges and recognition. Among the working classes, slavery, poverty, disease, and ignorance flourished. The peasantry were not only abused and oppressed, but heavily taxed as well.

Within government and business, in all dealings with each other and with their allies in the provinces, deceit flourished. The lie became the most common form of speech, and treachery replaced brotherhood. Evil spread throughout the realm. Intrigue and conspiracy were alive and well, from Belial's secret lair to the Council of Elders to the King's court itself.

The mind games and delusions perpetrated by the Sons of Belial had brought about a new nadir in morality and human dignity, spawning false expectations, delusions of grandeur, and messianic thinking. Atlantis had reached the depths of moral and spiritual degradation. Now violence and rebellion spread across the land. Such was real life in Atlantis under the government of the Sons of Belial. Yet still the question remained. "Why?"

Now it was time. He had been shown the *effect*. Now would be revealed the *cause*. The Supermind, anxious to cooperate, relieved to unburden itself of its terrible secret at last, projected the answer in graphic detail. Kafar gasped as he was shown images of Project Nightside.

Not just a term for the political agenda of a tyrant named Belial, its true nature was so much more frightening, so much more insidious. For Project Nightside was, in fact, a secret society—a cult, a coven, a single, elite Dark Brotherhood reserved for a chosen few; a dangerous, misguided, and demented Brotherhood dedicated to embracing the *Nightside of the Law of One*.

Eyes still wet with tears, watching breathlessly within that strange mirage world, Kafar saw the origins of the most insidious conspiracy ever perpetrated against the human race. Formed from an aberration in human consciousness, the group existed for one purpose and one purpose only—world domination.

What could this mean? He would soon find out. Images swirled around him, coalescing into a darkened chamber deep below ground, out of sight of the eyes of men, far from the light of day. In this hidden room, a Circle of robed and hooded figures met. Kafar could not help but notice the similarity between these men and Belial, from their pale white skin and hollow black eyes to their dark robes and heavy cowls.

As candlelight flickered and a smoky blue haze floated over the heads of the men, a sinister figure arose and addressed the Circle. It was the Puppetmaster, that strange and mysterious figure who had loomed up out of the darkness of the Great Plain, handed Belial the Spear, and then vanished back into the darkness from which he had come. Swearing the Circle to an oath of absolute loyalty and absolute secrecy, the Puppetmaster called upon these men to renounce the world and philosophy of the Ancients and embrace a new and better way, the way of the Dark Brotherhood, a way that would bring power, status, and wealth to these men and their sons forever. And its terrible price was the curtailment of human evolution and the domination and manipulation of the human mind, will, and destiny.

The mists swirled around him, static electricity crackled as the crystal consciousness struggled with the enormity of the secret it was unveiling to the man-mind who had entered its consciousness. Kafar felt his arms and legs tingle, and a chill of terror swept over him as he listened to the Puppetmaster utter the secret order, the terrible injunction known only to the most select of Adepts. Not, *"Subdue the Earth,"* as Spirit had commanded the Garden-dwellers. But rather, something far worse:

Subdue one another!

Such was the injunction that drove these men, causing them to invert the world order and create a world in which only the elite few controlled the masses. Such a terrible perversion of the Divine command to the First Ones!

"How?" Kafar was beyond tears. It was as though all the water in his system had dried up in the shock of the revelation. As the question formed in his own human mind, Kafar saw the answer as it was encoded in the crystal Supermind. He saw the Dark Brotherhood not only as it was now, in its formative stages in Atlantis, but also as it would become over the millennia, growing stronger and stronger, its false teachings becoming more and more entrenched in the consciousness of the human race.

Through the control of information, the Dark Brotherhood would keep the truth hidden, reserved only for the "Initiates," those of their own kind, whom they could trust to pass along their doctrines and thus preserve their goals. Hiding knowledge from the masses, robbing them of their inherent right of access to wisdom and the truth, the plan was to keep the people ignorant. For knowledge was power, and truth was enlightenment. Knowledgeable and enlightened people would never accept a world created by the Dark Brotherhood.

Through manipulation and deceit, they would initiate the *Consciousness of Differences*, devising an elaborate hierarchy of class systems and class consciousness, while advocating racial purity and fomenting racial hatred. Ever careful to remain out of view and beyond scrutiny, they would incite competition, strife, and violence, constantly playing one side against the other, silently "assisting" both but actually helping neither, all the while secretly profiting from their vast manipulations.

Through control of financial institutions and natural resources, the Dark Brotherhood would institute a system whereby the basic prerequisites for a peaceful, happy life would be assigned a monetary value. By setting that value above the reach of the masses, suddenly life would become a struggle, a series of forced labors and endless drudgery. And while the masses sank ever deeper into a quagmire of perpetual debt from which they could not possibly hope to escape, the Dark Brotherhood would grow immensely wealthy from interest collected on that debt.

Through the control of health and well-being, the Dark Brotherhood would create many forms of physical, mental, spiritual, and emotional disease. Thus, they would promote suffering, keeping the masses weak and helpless, off balance and without hope. With the loss of hope would come the loss of desire and ambition as the masses focused on their physical infirmities, constant suffering, and constant struggling. The focus would be on the problem rather than on the solution. And most importantly, all attention would be diverted away from the Dark Brotherhood, so it would be free to grow unmolested and unimpeded.

Through the control of philosophy, culture, and society, the Dark Brotherhood would invent and promote organized religions in which spontaneous prayer and symbolic ritual would give way to rigid dogma; any deviation from these " divine laws" was punishable by disgrace and torture in this life, as well as eternal, horrible, and painful punishment after death. Further, they would create elaborate caste systems and theories of reincarnation which taught that the only way to raise one's status was to live a good life and hope to be reborn into a higher plane. In this way, the masses would focus on the struggle of life on the material plane, linking their immortal souls to their physical bodies and accepting suffering as both a part of their fate and the will of a vengeful, omnipotent Creator against whom they could not possibly fight.

At the same time, the Dark Brotherhood would be free to partake of all of the fruits and wonders of the world at their whim, without having to share it with the masses. Free to indulge themselves, free to squander and waste, they would also be free to use and abuse...because it was their destiny and right to do so, a privilege of being the most powerful.

Through the control of politics, the Dark Brotherhood would breed generation after generation of Ogre-Tyrant kings, who would gain and maintain control of the ruling bloodlines down through the ages, fostering deceit and dissension, secretly starting wars and inflicting all kinds of ills. Openly blaming the weak or a particular racial group, these Shadow kings would thereby have scapegoats on whom to blame the ills of the world whenever human consciousness rose up, looked around, and realized something was wrong, that there must be a better way.

"Subdue one another!" Such was the injunction of the inner Beast that drove the Dark Brotherhood. And as it drove them, so also it drove Belial, their first initiate, their first unwitting pawn...drove him as mercilessly as he in turn drove all of Atlantis.

As the crystalline patterns swirled and changed shape, Kafar found himself looking at a point in space and time far in the future. How different the world was, yet how similar. The basic human form had not changed so much, although the human body was far sicklier and more fragile. Technology was as advanced as it had been in Atlantis, and as in Atlantis, the population was spread out across the globe.

Kafar was amazed that so little had changed in so many thousands of years. As in Atlantis, here too were war, dissension, and the constant struggle for survival. Suffering and strife were rampant, pollution and the ravaging of the Great Mother were still the order of the day. As in Atlantis, a great new plague had spread out across the population, claiming life after life, year after year, while the scientists and healers proclaimed their powerlessness and those filled with anger and rage pointed accusatory fingers and blamed each other. As in Atlantis, great masses of people were forced to labor by the sweat of their brow to purchase those things which were required for their survival and physical comfort. As in Atlantis, what once had been free for everyone now had a huge and oftimes unpayable price tag.

As in Atlantis, the leaders and people in power mixed the truth with a vast network of lies designed to keep the people under their control—lies about the Creator, lies about the fundamental laws of creation, lies about the true nature of the cosmos, lies about the body's relation to the soul, lies about every aspect of every thing.

As in Atlantis, the people found themselves smothered under a variety of organized religions. All claimed to have an exclusive hold on the Truth. All claimed to be the best and only way. Many screamed for the death of those who did not embrace their way. Many were led by a tyrannical, Patriarchal, all-powerful, all-knowing deity who dwelt separate and apart from his creation—a creation that, by the way, was inherently imperfect, corrupt, and evil. Subject to a set of inhuman rules and unattainable standards that could not possibly be met and obeyed, the adherents of these religions were preyed upon not only by a tyrannical supreme being but also by a whole slew of predatory spirits—demons, fallen angels, and the Lord of Darkness himself, all bent on a single goal—the annihilation of the human race, body and soul.

As in Atlantis, the Dark Brotherhood remained openly neutral while secretly playing one side against the other, keeping the masses too busy fighting amongst themselves to ever realize that it was not each other who were the problem, but rather a common enemy toward whom they should be directing their combined efforts to overthrow once and for all.

And as in Atlantis, which was ruled by the Sons of Belial, so now, high above the struggle and chaos, fat and comfortable and safe from it all, the elite few continued the work of the Dark Brotherhood, continued to fulfill the prime directive—*Subdue one another!* Aging, greedy, lustful, hating and stifling all that was beautiful, all that might live and grow, these corpulent, pasty-skinned patriarchs continued to control and manipulate...continued to amass more and more wealth, more and more power.

The systems that their ancestors had started so long ago in Atlantis had grown incredibly strong over the years. Philosophical, social, and political systems—all were now imposed across the globe, either by force of direct pressure or through an elaborate and firmly entrenched system of ritual, tradition, law, language, customs, etiquette, education, and division of labor.

Project Nightside! The name had changed, but not the purpose. What Sophia had named Patriarchy in her vision in the Cave had now become a paradigm with such a strong hold as to be practically unassailable. The Brotherhood had done its work well. So entrenched, so powerful it was that no one even thought to ask two basic and fundamental questions.

"Is Patriarchy based on the right premises? Is Patriarchy based on the Truth?"

Throughout recorded history, from Atlantis forward, the doctrines of Patriarchy had remained the one unchallenged belief, accepted without question, thus forming the basis for all the wrong that followed. These doctrines had become so universally accepted that they had come to be perceived as the laws of Nature, and indeed were presented as such.

In this manner did the Dark Brotherhood maintain its success. Taking elaborate steps to remain hidden, their agents worked subtly, covertly, presenting their philosophy and beliefs not as ideas to be questioned, challenged, modified, and adapted for the good of all, but as Universal Law, the Word of the Creator, to be unquestioningly obeyed on pain of physical death and the loss of one's immortal soul! Presented in this way, what choice did the human race have but to obey? For who would dare to challenge God? How futile to rail against that which "Is"! Such "victims" had no choice but to accept their lot, for that was how things worked. Poor deluded humans. They did not even know who they were obeying.

The plan was brilliant, the execution even more so. Thus did the Dark Brotherhood guarantee its survival by ensuring that no one would challenge their fundamental premise—the absolute rule of the Patriarchy.

There was no need to ask if the human race had learned the lessons of history. The question itself was foolish, Kafar realized. There had been no human evolution, no progress, no change of any kind—from Atlantis all the way forward into the future. The world had not changed or grown or evolved because control by the Dark Brotherhood had never been relinquished. The long march into the future had been a sham, an illusion!

"There is no way out!" Kafar cried aloud, overwhelmed by the enormity of the deception. "They cannot even fight against it because they do not know it exists. The power of the Dark Brotherhood has been all-pervasive, influencing the most basic ideas about human nature and one's relationship to the universe. And it has been a complete and total secret!"

The colors and shapes changed again, and he realized he was back in his own time, back in Atlantis. Kafar could not believe what he had been shown. "Where could such a state of consciousness have come from?" he wondered. But there was no time to look for an answer. Answers were not stored in the Supermind, just facts. He would have to find the answers elsewhere.

"It's like a disease," Kafar thought, "a corrupt and deadly disease invading the body of Atlantis." With the realization, the images changed once again as the Supermind accommodated his thoughts. Onward he moved, through a close, twisted tunnel studded with jagged, spiky crystal outcroppings.

"I'm in prison," Kafar thought as he came to rest inside the dark Crystal of Narrow-Mindedness. All around him was darkness, except within a limited field of vision shining out before his eyes. As he turned his head, the beam of light also moved, illuminating mysterious openings and passageways heretofore hidden in the darkness.

Walking through the tunnel was like walking through the inside of a disease-ridden body. The killer virus was everywhere, preying upon every system, organ, and tissue. The body fought and struggled, but there was no way to defend against the Invader as it spread to every organ and tissue. Or so it seemed. The Invader was hungry, voraciously devouring everything in its path, an insatiable Beast feeding upon the body, consuming it. And as the Invader grew stronger and more robust, the body grew weaker and more emaciated, closer and closer to death.

"Behold the source of the Invader," the voice spoke.

"I can't see it," Kafar cried, straining his eyes, moving his head to the left and the right, then up and down as he vainly searched for what he did not know. At first there was only blackness. Then suddenly, he saw it—a shadowy blot of even darker darkness, so subtle as to be almost missed.

A sudden thought occurred to Kafar.

As subtle as the beasts of the field.

Wasn't that a verse from the *Book of Mysteries*? Wasn't that how the Tempter worked? Find a healthy body, enter in so very subtly, hide from view, then spread out and encroach, consume, overwhelm.

"There is the disease," he cried as he looked down on the great Nation-State of Atlantis. "That is the Invader who has crept in and is destroying the body." The body—the human body and the Atlantean body. The metaphor was clear and obvious. How clear it was to Kafar, once he knew where to look. What he had not even noticed before was now so overt, so obvious, he wondered how he could ever have missed it.

The Atlantean body lay spread out before his field of vision. As with the human body, on the surface of Atlantis all appeared well. Nothing was out of the ordinary. Yet within, hidden and subtle, he watched the Shadow spread and spread, entwining itself, weaving its roots deeply into every crack and crevice, its tendrils entangling and suffocating, squeezing and choking the very life from the Nation-State. Kafar heaved a deep sigh. Now that he had seen the Invader, it could not be missed again. He would always know how to recognize it, even if he did not as yet know how to deal with it.

For with his newfound ability to see came the desire to heal. He wanted to blurt out the obvious question. "How do I combat the Invader?" But wasn't there more to this than just combat? Was combat really the answer? he wondered while the Supermind waited patiently. At last the realization came to his weary mind, and he voiced the question in its correct form. "How do I effect a cure?"

Again the images changed shape, and he found himself in motion once more. Into a different crystal now, a crystal so clear, so absolutely quiet, absolutely serene, absolutely pure, that Kafar knew he was inside the living Knowledge Crystals lying in their sacred repository deep under the Temple of Poseidon.

"Are you the Ancients?" he asked, suddenly aware of who had been guiding and orchestrating his entire sojourn. He felt the strength of the life-pulse all around him, filling him completely with an emotion he realized he had never actually experienced until now—absolute, unconditional, fearless Love.

"We are," came the metallic reply. The voice was different now, no longer one voice, but the voice of many, the voice of the Collective. "And we have brought you here to give you answer, for the question you have asked is the right one. There is a sickness in Atlantis, as you have seen, but it is not a sickness of the body, although it appears to you that an Invader has encroached upon that sacred domain. Therefore, the cure cannot be effected within the body. For this is a sickness that began in the Mind—the collective Atlantean Mind—when it welcomed the alien ideas that you have named the Invader. What you see in the Atlantean body is but an effect. Therefore, the cure must be effected at its source— within the Mind."

"How?" Kafar asked reverently. He was well aware of the stories of the Knowledge Crystals. This was not "wu-wu babble," as his mother liked to refer to the preposterous ravings of the fanatics who lately seemed to be shouting from every street corner. Every Atlantean believed in the story of the Knowledge Crystals. He was awestruck in the presence of such powerful Mind.

"By following the Plan," came the equally reverent answer.

"Plan?" Here was a new reference. Could it be that somewhere within the crystal Supermind there was stored data that would provide a solution to the problem of the Dark Brotherhood? A means of fighting them, of defeating them? As if in answer to his thought question, the image of a white bird floated in three-dimensional space before him. Dove opened its mouth to sing, and Kafar understood the song, recognizing the words in his heart.

> When the decision to separate was made,
> In that instant was the Plan established.
> For the Plan, you see, is the perfect answer
> To the imperfect choice.

Kafar was impressed, although he did not understand. The melody was lovely, however, and he listened to the poetry with great pleasure.

> The answer to the problem,
> Given in the instant that the problem occurred,
> At the moment when the First Ones
> Metaphorically ate the apple.
>
> The choice to suppress
> The feminine side of Creation
> And the Female aspect of the Creator,
> Elevating the Masculine
> To an unbalanced state of dominance.

The melody soared to ethereal heights, light and lofty, almost angelic in its harmonies and cadences.

"I think I understand," Kafar breathed as Dove was reabsorbed into the geometric images that filled the chamber. "Tell me more, please."

The music continued to play, and a fluorescent sine wave took shape, oscillating in the space before him. The gentle S-curve undulated like the coils of a perfect geometric snake as a new voice took up the explanation in the simple language of prose. "The Plan's function is not to judge or condemn what just is. The Plan accepts that which is and work from there to restore balance."

"Even evil?" Kafar could not help but interrupt. "The Plan even accepts such evil as the Dark Brotherhood and Belial?"

Patiently, as though explaining to a very young child, the voice continued. "In the nature of things, there is a force called Maia—the pulse, the oscillation of all reality. All Duality results from the Maia. The Maia is the fundamental force behind the manifestation of the Creator in form. Were there no Maia, there would be no form."

Behind and around the sine wave, a shimmering yin-yang symbol pulsed with life. Kafar could almost hear the sound of the pulse, like the beating of an immense cosmic Heart.

"All forms are an oscillation and pulsation of Duality itself. The Duality is built into the nature of all manifestation." The images began to move, rotating and repositioning themselves to represent different viewing angles. "The key is in getting a whole different view of the nature of the Dark Brotherhood and utilizing it all to achieve a harmony of function. That doesn't mean to extinguish it, doesn't mean to kill it off, doesn't mean to deny it, doesn't even mean to define, compartmentalize, and contain it." Here the voice softened. Kafar could almost hear the smile within the words...so simple yet so profound. "It simply means to bring it out of the darkness and into the light. And, as always, that is done according to the fundamental precepts of Universal Law—through application, utilization, and realization."

Again the images faded, along with the music, leaving only the original geometric patterns and the voice of the Supermind teacher. "This is Cosmic Truth. This is how and why the Plan works. It simply restores order and balance and returns creation to the natural way."

"How brilliant!" Kafar marveled at the symbolic way in which the Supermind stored data. Dove, symbol of the Goddess, the feminine energies of peace, maternity, and prophecy, contained the cure for the problem of the Dark Brotherhood. The answer was there for the asking, yet the Sons of Belial and the Dark Brotherhood would never find it, because they could not bring themselves to acknowledge the significance and worth of anything feminine. Thus, the Plan would remain safe and secure and available to all for as long as the crystals remained intact.

Yet still, there were unanswered questions. The voice had used simple language and imagery to explain, but the concept was so difficult that Kafar still did not really understand. "This is too complicated for me," he gave voice to his frustration. "What are application, utilization, and realization?"

"The answer is simple, the cure is simple," came the reply. "*Mind Change!* So simple, yet at the same time so complex. For what begins in the Mind also ends in the Mind. How easy it is to change one's mind, yet how difficult."

Kafar knew this to be true. How often had he tried to change his own mind about something, but for one reason or another he could not. "The difficulty is due mostly to my attachment to things," he suddenly realized, things he liked and did not want to "give up," even though they were not necessarily good for him.

"Shall we show you how simple and difficult this is?" the voice asked. Was it his imagination, or did Kafar sense a hint of playfulness? As if in answer to his thoughts, the voice asked, "Would you like to play a game?"

"Okay," Kafar replied hesitantly. "How do I play?"

"It is an easy game," the voice replied. "All you have to do is use your imagination. Imagine Atlantis as you want it to be. Picture your imaginary world in your mind, and we will show you the effects of your thoughts. You can see your world any way you want, from any point of view—yours, Adima's, Lilith's, Poseidon's, even Belial's. Entertain the thoughts in your mind, then make up your mind that this is how it is, in truth. Believe in your creations. We shall do the rest."

Kafar was intrigued. This was an exciting game, one that he would enjoy playing. Closing his eyes, he gave his fertile imagination free reign. He pictured an Atlantis ruled by a kind and benevolent Belial, a man motivated by love instead of fear. It began as a simple thought, and he tried to make the image stronger and clearer. But he did not have to. Instantly, the images flew past him, showing him Atlantis in the weeks, months, and years ahead.

The centuries flew by, as did the eons, while he beheld the brand new world that his thoughts had created—a beautiful land where his brothers and sisters dwelt in peace and harmony, soaring to unimaginable heights of achievement. Descendant after descendant of Belial, good king after good king sat on the throne, ruling with love, affection, and tenderness.

"All that you have seen are the Effects of a single motivation within a single mind," the voice said as the images faded. "From the seed of your single starting thought sprang an entirely different world from the one you now know." The voice was gentle and encouraging. "Now try another thought."

Again Kafar created a virtual Atlantis in his mind, this time ruled by a maleficent Belial, although one who did not have the present levels of science or technology to cause massive destruction. The images were as horrifying as the first ones were beautiful. Over the centuries, over the eons, Atlantis continued to sink into depravity and degradation, until at last the people had devolved into mindless, filthy savages, not even recognizable as the once noble race from which they had sprung. Kafar shuddered as the images stopped.

"See how simple a mind change is and yet how difficult, and what effects it can have?" the voice asked. "Now do you understand where the cure lies and why?"

"I do," replied Kafar, "but there is one more world I'd like to explore. Can you show me this?" He pictured Atlantis as it was now, with Belial in control and the device working perfectly. Kafar waited for the images to come, but there were none. Only the clear, pure chamber, devoid of geometric shapes or imagery of any kind. "What is the matter?" he cried. "Have I done something wrong? Why won't you show me?"

"You have done nothing wrong," came the soft reply. "We cannot show you because there is nothing to show. The scenario you envision, based on the decisions of the mind that created it, cannot exist. Such a future cannot be. Such decisions of mind lead only to annihilation."

"Annihilation!" Kafar gasped in shock, the realization searing him like a living flame. Absolute nothingness. Absolute and total destruction. He stopped, tearing his hands from the crystal, ripping the apparatus from his head. Drenched in sweat, hands shaking violently, he could not catch his breath. His mouth was bone dry, his tongue thick and foul-tasting. "Annihilation!" And he was the only one who knew.

They had to be warned. They had to be stopped. He had to tell them.

His first emotion was guilt for what he had done and for the part he had played in helping the Sons of Belial accomplish their evil plans. But that passed quickly, replaced with a far more satisfying emotion. Kafar was angry, angry at being lied to, angry at being used, angry at having his world destroyed, angry at having no future, angry at being ripped from existence. So angry, in fact, that he was willing to do whatever it took to stop them. He turned to rush from the room, then halted dead in his tracks. As if he hadn't had enough shocks and surprises for one day, now here was another! His jaw dropped open, and he gaped in dumfounded amazement.

"What do you think you are doing?" Shakala was standing just inside the door to the laboratory. "Sit down. You're not going anywhere."

*****

With the initial shock of discovering his mentor watching him, Kafar tried to remain calm. How much did the old man know? How long had he been standing there? The questions flooded his mind. There was no use in trying to deny what he had been doing. He had gone far past the denial and cover-up stage. In fact, in a way, he was glad that Shakala had found out. It would make explaining that much easier.

As though they were still with him, he heard the crystal voices exhorting him to regain and maintain his composure. Remain calm. Don't give Shakala a chance to point the finger of blame. Don't give him a chance to accuse or threaten. Take charge. Get control and stay in control. You run this show.

It was excellent advice. Kafar took a deep breath and looked the old man squarely in the eye. "We have to talk," he said, instantly taking charge and deflating any anger that Shakala might been holding. "I have made an astonishing discovery, and I don't know what to do. I'm glad you're here. It saves me the trouble of coming to find you."

Kafar took the chair and placed it in front of the older man, motioning him to take a seat. He himself perched on the edge of a lab table. "They are disavowing the Ancient ways, the ways of the Goddess, the Divine Feminine, the Great Mother Earth, the hunter-gatherer culture." The words tumbled over each other in a breathless release of pent-up excitement.

"What do you mean?" Shakala asked as he took his seat. He looked at Kafar strangely. What was this highly agitated young man trying to tell him? What had he been doing with that strange apparatus which had so frightened Belial that the Master had ordered him to seek out the young scientist and stop him at once?

Kafar told him, revealing everything—his conflicted feelings of doubt and guilt after listening to Adima; his misgivings about the device; how he had explored the crystals and uncovered the hideous secrets of Project Nightside. The old alchemist sat motionless while the younger man spoke. For an hour, the young idealist's words penetrated that hardened, cynical heart as no weapon ever could. One after another, the pointed barbs of Truth struck home, each one stinging, each one burning, each one bringing its own peculiar pain.

Where had it all gone wrong? Shakala wondered. How could I have been so blind? How did I allow myself to be so misled? He had not known about Project Nightside. This was something new to him. Another secret revealed, another Shadow exposed. Such a secret, such a dark and hideous secret! Who could have known? Who could have possibly known that such an aberration was taking place? He could not be blamed, could he? It was not his fault. Oh yes it was. Of course it was. There was no doubt. He was as much to blame as anyone else. He had let it happen, even supported it as it had happened. And now it was probably too late.

"This is wrong, it is really and truly wrong," Kafar cried.

Shakala sensed the strength of the young man's passion. It was hard not to be affected by it. He knew it, too—it *was* wrong. What Belial was doing was very, very wrong. Now, listening to Kafar, the alchemist acknowledged this. He had known it when he had listened to Adima's words just a short day ago. He had known it all along but had never admitted it to himself. In the hardness of his heart, he had denied the Truth and buried it where it could never make its presence felt...until today.

With the realization and the acceptance came the softening. Over the past several days, a real bond had developed between the two scientists. "We are not so different after all," Shakala realized. The younger man before him was he, himself, as he might have been had he not become so bitter, so driven, so anxious to prove something to the ghosts of the past.

Long they talked, these two brilliant men. They spoke of shattered hopes and dreams, broken promises, lost opportunities. They spoke of being misled and deluded, of following the wrong path, of taking the wrong turn, of making the wrong decisions. They spoke of their affection for each other despite everything else, and the gifts each had brought to the other. How each had learned from the other, how their lives had been enriched through knowing each other. Shakala paused to look at his timepiece. It was almost midday.

Kafar was speaking. "You've got to stop him. You've got to try and reason with him. You're the only one who can."

Shakala knew it was true. He did not relish the idea, but he knew he had to try.

"I will go with you," Kafar offered. "And if that doesn't work, we'll change the formula. Belial will never know. The device won't work, and we'll run away and be long gone. He'll never find us..."

"No," Shakala interrupted, slowly getting up and making his way to the door. "This is something I must do alone. The Collector has arrived to gather in the dues. It is time to pay for all of my sins over the years."

*****

Alone once again, Kafar felt terrible. Shakala would not allow him to play any further part in stopping Belial. He was to stand helplessly by and not lift a finger while the old man faced the Beast alone. It had all been so overwhelming—Adima's speech, his own encounter with the crystals, talking with Shakala. His head was bursting with pain. His temples throbbed, his neck ached, and he wanted desperately to close his eyes and sleep a deep, dreamless sleep. Still, there was something left undone. He felt it intuitively—some unfinished business with the Supermind. Exhausted, he donned the device once again, gripped the diamond in both gloved hands, and returned to the crystalline world.

"Please help me!" his mind cried out, picturing images of aid and succor. The crystal priestess appeared almost immediately.

"You left us in such a hurry," she spoke kindly. "Are you all right? How do you feel?"

"I feel like something is missing, like I haven't heard everything."

"Indeed you have not," the priestess replied. "Would you like to finish?"

"I would," Kafar answered. "As tired as I am, I truly would like to see this through to completion."

With the answer, the colors changed, growing dark and somber as he moved forward. The sensation was quite familiar now, bringing with it a deep sense of relaxation as he was taken to the last of the four Shadow worlds—the world of the Opaque Crystal of Dullness. He felt thick and heavy, weighed down by a boggy, oppressive gravity. Tired and confused, his innate curiosity and imagination had left him, and he barely noticed the swirling geometric patterns that filled the space within the purple amethyst—the Lodestone.

"This is your place of refuge." The priestess was gone, only the alien sound of her voice echoing in that healing place. "Here you will let your thoughts go, let your body relax, and give your mind a rest."

Kafar wanted to refuse this most generous offer. There was too much to do, too much at stake to rest right now. He struggled to stay awake, struggled to remove his hands from the diamond he was holding. His arms felt like lead; he could not lift them. His eyelids, too, grew heavy, and the world grew darker and darker. The safety of Dullness spread over him, and his conscious mental processes blessedly shut down.

*****

"With all due respect, Master, you cannot do this. It is wrong. There will be too much destruction." Shakala was alone with Belial in his private chambers. A single candle cast a feeble light against the closed and heavily shuttered windows. The heat in that fearsome chamber was almost unbearable—stifling and oppressive. Not a breath of air flowed, not a single cool breeze, no respite from the awful, bone-burning heat.

Doesn't he sweat? Shakala could not understand how Belial managed to stay dry and comfortable in such blast-furnace conditions. Great beads of perspiration stood out on his own forehead, and his skin was clammy and feverish beneath his loose-flowing robe. Despite the heat, he shivered a little, remembering how, as a child, he had once gotten too close to his grandfather's kiln, where they had been firing pottery. The little boy was badly hurt, suffering severe burns on several fingers and the palm of his hand. He carried the scars to this day.

"Now you know the punishment that awaits you in the fires of the Netherworld." His grandfather had showed no sympathy. "So you had better behave well in this life, lest you die a sinner and roast forever on the Blacksmith's forge in the eternal heat of the Mother's bowels."

Little Shakala was so terrified that he had hidden in his room all the rest of the day. Fingers throbbing and burning, his simple child's mind could not conceive of worse pain. Yet his grandfather had said it was so, and thus it must be so. Alone in the dark of night, the child had promised the gods that he would live a good life. So deeply had he been impressed with the physical pain, coupled with images of the huge, deformed Blacksmith impaling him on a spit, roasting him forever over the hot coals, that he never forgot the experience. Burned into his sense memory, the feelings and impressions remained forever a part of his psyche, smoldering, waiting for the right time to resurface.

That time was now. It was like a kiln in that room, and Shakala, a rational, thinking scientist who prided himself on his reason, regressed in an instant to a frightened, burned five-year-old awaiting death and damnation from a mad, devouring monster.

"Why is the device still not ready?" Belial asked angrily, interrupting the old man's reverie. "I will not tolerate your coming here this day, Shakala, to tell me it is not ready."

"The device is ready," the alchemist said defiantly, retaining his poise and nerve in the face of the Master's rage. "That is just the point. It is so ready, so perfect, that it could very well destroy us all."

Belial raised an eyebrow questioningly, but made no reply. Slightly encouraged, Shakala continued despite his fear, despite the heat.

"We don't really know what will happen when we turn it on. It has only been tested in theory. There could be serious side effects that we would be powerless to stop. We could set off a chain reaction within the Earth's crust and in the atmosphere. There would be violent upheavals and terrible storms. We could all be destroyed."

"Nonsense!" Belial was in no mood to be reasoned with. He had heard all of this before. Now was not the time for caution, nor was it the time to get cold feet. He had been drinking a strong potion ever since yesterday afternoon. It was the only way he could control his thoughts and put Adima out of his mind. Now he was so deeply under the influence that his reason had left him, and he was ruled by the Beast. The Beast was in no mood to negotiate. The Beast liked the dark; the Beast liked the heat.

"We will be safe enough within the Great Pyramid," Belial replied. "The Pyramid can withstand any onslaught Nature can throw against it. As for the rest, what does it matter if they all die? Their ignorance and whining grows tiresome. I am ready to destroy all of Atlantis and start again. Do not press me or I will. I just need an excuse. In fact, I don't need one after all!"

The giant's normally white face was a ghastly shade of gray. His deep-set black eyes had sunk even further into their sockets, surrounded now by huge black circles. Livid purple blotches mottled his skin, as though the blood in his veins had congealed into clotted pools.

Shakala knew there was no way to reason with the Master, but he really had nothing left to lose. A deep, gut-wrenching pain seared through his abdomen. The wasting disease was growing within him and making its presence felt, just as the Belial-disease was making its presence felt in Atlantis. For weeks now, the cancer had been steadily worsening. The pains were coming more and more often. He was losing weight, and now he could barely keep food down. Sleep was impossible; nausea and diarrhea kept him up all night. Exhausted, completely spent from the heat and the disease, there was no fight left in him, no fear left in him, no life left in him. His own death was near, he sensed, just as he sensed that the death of Atlantis was near.

Shakala was no longer afraid of Belial. The once dreaded Master merely disgusted him now. He wanted to stop him, but he knew he hadn't the strength. That fight would have to be fought by another. Yet he could make one last attempt to reason with the Beast that had once been Belial, if only to assure himself before he died that he had left nothing undone, that he had made at least this single effort of atonement for his great sins over the years. He tried to moisten his lips, but all of his saliva had evaporated in the heat. Having no other recourse, he wiped the back of his hand over his face, using his own perspiration as a source of moisture for his dry mouth. He would make one more speech after all.

"POWER IS A BLESSED THING," Shakala cried, quoting the *Book of Mysteries* and slamming his palm on a table. "POWER MISUSED IS A HORROR. What good is the expression of power if it does not help improve our people, our world? What good does it do you to have all of Atlantis bow down before you in fear, acknowledging your strength, your abilities, your greatness, if they are so frightened of you that they abhor your very presence?"

As the old man spoke, Belial stood looking into the candle flame, his back to the room, his ghastly features hidden for the moment. Suddenly he turned and faced the old man. "What do *you* know about power?" His features were twisted and contorted in rage. The man was waging a powerful internal struggle against the Beast, who wanted desperately to be loosed.

"Not much, I'll grant you." The pain was coming in great, rolling waves now, and Shakala had to lean against the table for support. The more beastly Belial grew, it seemed, the more his own pain worsened. "But I do know now that the power of Love is greater by far than the power of Fear. I saw that yesterday, when Adima and Hia challenged you and defeated you. Hear this, Belial!" The old man spoke through clenched teeth, his body wracked with anguish. "They have the true power—the Power of Love. And because they have it, they will use it to overcome other expressions of power...your power."

"They would not dare challenge *me*!" It was the Beast who hissed the words. The man was no longer there.

"They have no choice," Shakala was on the verge of collapse, his voice barely a whisper. He wiped his mouth with the back of his hand, the metallic taste of his own blood on his lips. "They are obligated to challenge you, and they will defeat you. Your motives are wrong, but they fight for what they believe in. You have the device, but they have more powerful weapons. They control the vibrations—the vibrations of Love and Truth. You have your shadowy allies, it is true, but they have an even greater Ally. Theirs is the power of the Great Mother herself."

"Fool!" At mention of the Mother's name, the Beast recoiled as though stung. Belial paced restlessly back and forth, hands covering his ears, trying to shut out the terrible words of his most trusted servant.

Shakala continued, undaunted. "The Mother knows you have misused her energies for your evil purposes. She knows you have harnessed increased power sources to use for control. Are you that arrogant that you really believe she will let that happen to herself and her children without mounting a defense?" The old man shook his head, almost laughing aloud at the ridiculousness of Belial's blind, wanton arrogance. "The Mother will strike back. She will defend herself. There will be explosions in certain of the Fire Crystals. A chain reaction will occur, and ultimately, this will become the cataclysm that destroys Atlantis."

Shakala felt his bowels clenching and tightening. It would not be long before his own lifeblood poured forth in an unstoppable flow. On his knees now, barely able to support himself on the table's edge, he pronounced his final sentence. "This is the mistake you made, Belial. This is the reason why you will be defeated. You have forgotten the Source of Creation's most powerful weapon."

Unbelievably, the air in the room had grown even hotter. Gasping for breath, blood pouring from his mouth and nose, the dying man doubled over in agony, collapsing to the floor in a heap. He struggled to remain conscious, whispering a quiet prayer as the giant loomed over him. "Please, gods, do not let me die in an unconscious state. Let me retain my wits and meet my fate fully alert and fully awake."

As though reading his mind, the Belial-Beast loomed over its doomed victim. "You will not die today, old man," the frightful creature roared, flecks of scalding spittle dripping onto the body on the floor. "You will be taken to the Temple and healed. Then you will be arrested and placed in the dungeons, out of the sight of men forever."

Belial opened the door and motioned to two Adepts who were quietly standing guard. "Take him away and see that he has healing and that the bleeding is stopped," he ordered. "Then throw him in the dungeons and guard him well. As soon as he is properly taken care of, prepare the device and summon the Elders and Councilors. The demonstration will go on this evening as planned."

The Adepts obeyed, lifting their burden lightly. Mercifully, the old man had fainted, but Belial could not resist a final taunt of triumph. "And there you will wait alone, in the absolute darkness, for the mercy of death. And just when you think it will not come, it will approach. 'Death, be swift and merciful,' you will cry, but it will not be so. Death will toy with you, taking its time, playing its merciless game, the outcome certain. By the time it wins, you will not even know it. But I will know it, for I will give the ultimate command. 'Take him,' I will cry, pointing to the wasted, dehydrated shell that had once been my master alchemist. And death, whom I control, death, the servant of Belial, will comply."

The door shut, leaving Belial alone. Wave after wave of monstrous heat poured up from the floor and out of the walls and down from the ceiling. Then the Beast sprang forth in all its hideous evil. Strutting and swaggering, it paced to and fro, opening its hideous mouth in frightful roars, reveling in the heat, growing stronger in the heat, thriving in the staggering heat.

With a guttural roar and a shake of its hideous head, the Beast dropped down on all fours and reached for an iron rung set into the floor. Giving a mighty tug, it pulled up a stone slab, revealing a gaping hole. Down into the stygian blackness it jumped, landing on all fours. Red eyes glowing like two fiery coals, it paused for a moment to sniff the stale, foul air. The smell of death and decay was strong. The Beast loved that smell. It was in its native element. Breaking into a loping trot, the creature ran for almost an hour through the blackness, coming at last to the base of an iron ladder set into the limestone. Now the Beast rose up again, pausing to catch its breath, waiting for the transformation to reverse itself, as it knew would happen.

Slowly the bestial features softened, changed shape, and became human once again. Its color and skin tone returning to normal, if indeed that ghostly complexion and those hard, chiseled features could ever be called normal! It took several moments, but at last the metamorphosis was complete. Where the Beast had stood only a moment before, now stood Belial. Climbing the ladder hand over hand, he stepped out onto a small wooden platform. Pressing an invisible release, a portion of the wall swung silently back, and he stepped into Shakala's secret laboratory.

The device gleamed malevolently on its pedestal as Belial stood before it. There would be no demonstration for the ignorant, weakling Councilors who had gathered for the Homecoming. Indeed, he had never intended that they see the device. He would send out word that there were "technical problems" that must be overcome. The gullible idiots would believe him, being satisfied to wait until later in the week.

Thus, unfettered by their ridiculous restrictions, he would be free to pursue his real intentions. The device would be used this night after all, not as a demonstration, but for the destruction of Adima and Lemuria, of course. But first and foremost, the device would be used as a lesson for all who dared oppose him. Although the words would never be voiced, they would be understood. He, Belial, could send messages too.

*****

And so it came to pass that, deep within the hidden recesses of the Great Pyramid on the mighty island of Atlantis, on the second of the seven days of the Week That Would Change the World, Belial turned on the device. Not as a test, not at low power, but at almost full force...almost unlimited power. It took but an instant to make up his mind, throw the switch, and effect the change. Yet it would take thousands of years and tens of thousands of lifetimes before the world would recover. And even then, the world would never be the same, the Great Mother would never be the same, and humankind would never be the same.

The only sound was a low hum as a narrow beam of blue light shot through a crystal rod up into the ceiling, through the stone of the Great Pyramid, and out into the twilight. So seemingly innocuous but so deadly in truth, burning the atmosphere, tearing a long, gaping hole in the tender, fragile skin of the Mother.

It would take a while for the forces to gather. What appeared to be a natural storm would in reality be caused by Belial's manipulation of the elements. Belial controlled those forces now. The elements obeyed him and did his bidding. Although he knew it, he still marveled at the depth of his power, the extent of his control. "I am a god," he roared in triumph. "A god! Bow down before me, all you weak and small ones, and tremble. For the time of your desolation is at hand."

Outside, heavy clouds began to form in the east and the west. Their black underbellies stood out in sharp contrast to the white, billowing tips, which were highlighted with hues of red and pink and rimmed with the brilliant orange light of the setting sun. The wind blew in fitful gusts, lightning flickered within the thunderheads, and thunder rolled in from the sea, echoing all the way to the Mountains of the Moon. Evening was approaching rapidly, bringing with it a mighty storm, as life in Atlantis continued toward its inexorable climax.

The piazza was practically deserted, except for a few pilgrims making camp for the evening in the Garden of the Heart. Looking up, one of them happened to notice a slender blue beam shooting up from the tip of the Great Pyramid into the darkening sky.

"I wonder what that is?" he thought to himself. But before he could explore the matter further, his wife called him to supper. He would forget all about the phenomenon as the evening wore on, and by the morrow, before he could tell anyone what he had seen, he and his family and friends would be dead.

CHAPTER 42

...a world that is as old as the Earth itself—the primeval meeting place of the elements of earth and water, a place of compromise and conflict and eternal change.

—Rachel Carson

As the sun went down on the second day of the week, the Great Mother's children began their migration off the island. Those that crawled and crept and walked on the ground sought the inner places—the caves and tunnels within the body of the Great Mother, where they would be safe. Those that swam and flew were visible for all to see. It was supposed to be that way. It was intentional, part of the Plan.

"Fly, my winged ones," the Great Mother exclaimed. *"Leap out of the sea and flash in the sun, my finned ones. Let the people see your flight, that they may awaken to the Truth, hearken to your message, and follow your example."*

Doing their part to give the warning, helping wake up the people and turn them to the light of Love, great flocks of birds took to the air, and great schools of fish leapt above the waves of the Ocean of Atlas. Everyone saw it, and everyone was amazed.

"What does it mean, Grandmother?" the young ones asked.

"It is a sign," the old ones who remembered their origin cried. "The times are changing. See how the wind blows? See how the birds fly and the fish swim?"

"Just changing migratory patterns," a few alchemists and geomancers tried to rationalize, but they knew it, too. They felt it. Something was in the air—a sense, a feeling. Adima had told them to attend to their experiences. Well, they were experiencing something now—something important, something incredible, something terrifying, something they were powerless to do anything about.

*****

That summer, for the first time in anyone's memory, the Grounded Ones had not returned. On the beach, the twins had waited patiently each night for the sea turtles to come and lay their eggs, but there were none this year.

"I don't understand it," Alta had discussed his frustration with his father several weeks ago, after three nights of unsuccessful watching. "No turtles again. They ought to be here by now."

What he did not know, what he could not possibly have known, was that the turtles were intentionally staying away. Knowing that their eggs would not survive the imminent destruction, the few who did choose to come had a different purpose. Theirs was an act of self-sacrifice, dying in the toxic waters as a message to the two-legged polluters, that they might see the error of their ways and stop the poisoning. Theirs was a message from the Great Mother, with whom they were intimately connected.

With the help of their father and mother, the twins had interpreted the signs. Cracked and broken shells—no groundedness, no place of safety any more. Better run! A warning of the geological shifts occurring deep inside the Earth—another fault slipping and breaking, the subterranean waters moving into place. "All is being prepared," Turtle said to any who cared to listen.

It was a wild night on the beach, early in the season for such forceful weather. A violent storm was brewing, and it had all the earmarks of a major meteorological event. "Be careful," Cybele had warned them before they left, glancing apprehensively at the ominous-looking clouds. "I want you home in two hours. This is going to be a big storm, and the beach is no place to be in such weather."

It never occurred to her that they might be in danger. How could it? No one had ever been in danger walking along the beaches that ringed the great island. Even with the events of the past two days—Adima's address to the Council, his confrontation with Belial, the killing of Dakinis and the guard, and all of the civil unrest—the thought of harm coming to her children from human perpetrators just never entered Cybele's consciousness.

"We promise," the twins had replied with all of the good intentions of youth. Then they were off, out into the moonless night.

Alta and Charis stood on the windswept beach, salt spray stinging their faces, wind blowing straight in from offshore. It was too dark to see the great schools of sea creatures heading north and south, too windy to hear the mighty rush of many wings as enormous flocks of birds followed the swimmers in the water far below.

The tide was running around eight to ten feet. Long combers broke continuously on the sand, their sound filling the air like the mournful songs of the ghosts of shipwrecked sailors. There should have been turtles everywhere. Off in the distance, the beam from the Lighthouse swept the stormy seas, revealing the frothy white surf cascading over the slick black rocks. The deep bass of the foghorn sounded its mournful, melancholy dirge every thirty seconds. There would be no ships this night, but just in case, the Keeper of the Light was awake and alert, warning the huge oceangoing vessels to stay away.

The twins could see him, a strange and solitary figure high up in the light, his dark shadow silhouetted against the glass. "There's something very spooky about that place," Alta insisted. "I still say the Lighthouse is haunted and he's a ghost."

His sister agreed with him. So did all of their friends. Stories abounded about the Keeper of the Light...how he prowled the beach in search of victims to lure into his mysterious lair, where he preformed all sorts of evil rites using innocent children as human sacrifices.

They stayed away, they always had, never venturing close. Actually, they had never seen the old Hermit, but they had a pretty good idea of what he looked like—a huge, misshapen monster, its long fangs dripping blood, its huge, clawlike fingers capable of gripping its victims and tearing their flesh to shreds. It was a delicious kind of spookiness. Alta and Charis were old enough now to realize the foolishness of their childish beliefs and terrors. Yet the old memories and stories still lingered, and the Lighthouse was always there, a constant, mysterious presence.

In the two years since returning from Mount Kylene, the twins had matured greatly, especially emotionally and spiritually. They were developing a strong ecological consciousness, recognizing the interconnectedness of everything while at the same time acknowledging the fragility of living systems...their mutual strength and their mutual vulnerability.

"What's that?" Charis pointed along the beach.

"I don't see anything," Alta said, straining his eyes in the darkness.

"There. There!" Motioning her brother to follow, she started moving slowly in the direction in which she had been pointing.

Alta did not need to be reminded to move slowly and silently. He knew that if frightened, the turtles would return to the sea and lay their eggs in the water. He did not want that to happen. It was much better to stand far enough back from the water line and watch the mothers from a safe distance as they crawled out of the sea and dug their holes.

It was an amazing sight to watch, a marvelous glimpse of continuity—great Loggerheads lifting their enormous bulks out of the water and crawling up onto the sand. Completely out of their element, they moved slowly and ponderously, using their flippers to pull themselves forward. Instinctively knowing what to do, they followed an ancient code established by the Great Mother herself. Reaching a desired spot safely above the high tide point, the turtle mother would begin to dig the hole, using her front flippers as shovels.

Of course, all of this took a lot of time. It takes a three-hundred pound Loggerhead quite a while to get things done on dry land. Patience was the lesson; Turtle was the exemplar. Only when the cavity had reached the proper size would she turn around and begin laying her eggs. One by one they would drop into the soft sand, round and white and somewhat leathery, so as not to break when they tumbled against one another. Once again, the magnificence of the Grand Design was revealed for all to see.

At this point, the twins could approach without disturbing her, assuming they did so quietly. The mother was in a kind of hypnotic trance, and human presence would not stop her from laying all of the eggs. As she laid them, the tears would well up in her eyes, the mother weeping for her children. "When the turtles come to cry..." Adima liked to say.

When it was over, the exhausted mother would bury the eggs and camouflage the nest, moving around the original spot in ever-widening circles, covering all signs of her tracks so as to secure the eggs from predators. Then, ever so slowly, she would drag herself back to the sea. This was the part Alta and Charis liked the best. They would walk beside the great creature, talking soothingly to her, assuring her that they would watch over her nest and help the hatchlings find the sea for the first time, so that they could return to her.

By the time Turtle got to the water line, she was so exhausted that she could barely move. Coated in sand, her great strength almost spent, she lay in a few inches of water and waited, just waited. And then it came. That first wave broke over her, cleansing, restoring, and washing away all traces of the beach, rinsing off both the sand and the salty tears. With the second wave, she was lifted up and carried a few yards out. Back in her native element, now she was home. Now she was safe. Floating freely once again, she lifted her head high above the water, gazing around for one last look at the shore. Then, with a flash of her mighty flippers, she was gone.

And that was it. That was how it happened each night during nesting season, on beach after beach all over the world. Except for now. Except for this year. Where were the turtles? What could be wrong?

"Shhhhh," Charis whispered, approaching the dark object at the water's edge.

"What is it?" Alta cupped his hands and whispered in her ear. Something had definitely washed up on the beach, a dark blob, a huge bulky something. "It's just some driftwood," he was about to say. That's when the mysterious object moved.

A chill of fear ran up each twin's spine. Whatever the object was, it was definitely not driftwood. It was alive, and it was in trouble. A huge wave came rolling in, a mighty wall of water powerful enough to lift the object and carry it several feet farther up onto the sandy beach. Approaching cautiously, the twins could still not make out what it was. A light drizzle began to fall.

"It could be a dolphin or a whale," Alta suggested. A lot of them had been sick lately, and many had come to the coastline around Elysia to beach themselves and die.

"Too small," Charis said, "and too round. I think it's a sick turtle."

Another huge wave came crashing in, moving the unknown creature still farther onto the sand. Now they could see clearly. Indeed it was a turtle, but it was not sick. It was upside down!

Again the chill of fear swept over them, and their skin crawled. The twins instinctively reached out for the security of the other's touch. There on that lonely, storm-swept beach, under cover of dark and scudding storm clouds, in a maelstrom of wind and rain, they beheld an astonishing sight—a shocking vision neither of them had seen before. A vision, perhaps, that not even the eternal Mother had seen before. There on the beach, flat on its rock-hard shell, flippers flailing helplessly in the air, lay an enormous Leatherback turtle. It was just beyond the surf line, too far up on shore for the waves to lift it and right it so it could regain its balance.

"It must weigh a thousand pounds!" Alta exclaimed. He had to shout to make himself heard above the rapidly-intensifying storm.

"What are we going to do?" Charis agonized, staring in disbelief. "She's helpless. She'll smother and drown. We've got to get her back into the water."

"We can't move a thousand pound turtle," Alta reminded her.

"But we've got to!" His sister was crying softly now. "If we don't, she'll die. Look at her. She's afraid. We've got to help her."

It was raining harder now, a biting, driving rain. The wind had intensified, too, gusting to gale force, whipping the waves to a frothy, boiling stew and driving the huge raindrops straight into their eyes. Thoroughly saturated, the twins had to turn their backs to the ocean in order to see. The roar of the storm and the waves filled their ears. Up to his knees in swirling water, Alta approached the helpless creature cautiously. He tried to move her, even a little bit, but there was no budging that massive bulk. The living turtle might as well have been a block of granite.

"Be careful she doesn't hook you with her fins," Charis warned him. She was kneeling by the turtle's head, talking gently to her, trying to soothe and calm the helpless creature. The look in its eyes was one of desperation and hopelessness, like the look in a mother's eyes when she loses a child.

"We've got to help her," Charis pleaded frantically as she waded to her brother's side.

"There's nothing I can do," he shouted over the din. "I can't budge her."

"We've got to," Charis insisted stubbornly, standing waist deep in water. A huge wave crashed over her, knocking her off balance and immersing her in the boiling foam. The girl screamed as the rip tide caught her and carried her out into deeper water. She reached out desperately to grab hold of something, but her hands clawed at empty air.

Struggling to catch her breath, powerless against the enormous force of the current, she felt herself being swept out to sea. In panic, she opened her mouth to call for help, but a crashing wave swept over her, and she swallowed a huge gulp of salt water. Alta reacted instantly, diving after his sister and averting a tragedy in the making. What could have been a disaster was all over in a few seconds. He grabbed her quickly, his strong arms pulling her up and out of the powerful grip of the tide.

"Thanks," she gasped when she could catch her breath. She held tightly to her brother's hand, shuddering to think of being swept out to sea in the storm. Together they hunkered down in the gale, too concerned for the turtle's welfare to abandon it, too tired to make it home if they had tried.

"We're in trouble," Alta said, recalling his mother's warning. "We need help."

"Help, help," they cried in unison, but there was no one there to hear. Even if there were, who could have heard their small voices above the din of the mighty storm?

"Please," Charis cried again, "help us."

And then it happened. A brilliant light—brighter than anything they had ever seen—bore down on them, bathing the whole scene in a circle of white light. Strangely enough, the brightness did not hurt their eyes. It caught them, held them, captivated them. Unable to help themselves, they looked directly into the glare, trying to follow the beam of light back to its source. Eyes wide open, they were mesmerized by swirling patterns of color. Together they watched and shared the same experience.

"Look," Alta pointed. There, in the center of the circle of light, a tiny black dot appeared, holding steady amidst the other colorful dancing and sparkling dots.

So very small at first, shimmering round and black, it began to swirl and grow larger. Taking shape and form, coming forth from within the light, the specter moved directly toward them, as though being born from the very center of the beam itself. Becoming recognizable now, assuming human shape, a mysterious figure arose within the brilliant rays and emerged from them. Charis screamed in shock and fear as the eerie figure materialized before them. The twins held tightly to each other's hands.

"The Keeper of the Light!" she gasped, scarcely believing her eyes. Yet there was the mysterious hermit standing directly before them. Now they knew the source of the beam. They could see it emanating from the Lighthouse far down the beach.

The twins glanced apprehensively at each other. Each was struck by the unearthly quality of the light. "It was definitely not of this world," they would later describe the experience. Alta looked into the mysterious stranger's face. It was a strong, kindly face, neither old nor young, it seemed. There was a look of strength and compassion, wisdom and safety in that face. The twins felt reassured.

"I am Enoch," the old man introduced himself, shouting over the noise. "I am your father's friend. Do not be afraid. You have nothing to fear from me. I am here in answer to your call for help. We must right the turtle so that she does not drown."

"How is that possible?" Alta protested. "She weighs half a ton. I can't even budge her, and she's too far up on the shore to catch a wave."

"You *must* right her," Enoch insisted again, as though he hadn't heard the boy. The power is within you to right her, the same power that is used to raise and cut the stones, the same power that can move mountains. Learn to use it now. Learn to tap into those forces which are part of you." The old man extended his arms, beckoning the twins to join him in the rescue attempt. "Take hold of my hands, both of you."

The twins did as they were told. It was an eerie scene—a surreal circle of bright light amidst the surrounding blackness and the raging storm. The wind blew, the rain pounded, the waves crashed. The turtle just lay there, watching helplessly.

"You are not powerless," Enoch shouted, squeezing their hands tightly in his own. "You are not weak. Yours is the power of the universe. Learn now how powerful the universe is, and how powerful *you* are."

Everything was happening so quickly, the twins did not have time to think about the experience. They were cold, they were desperate, they were anxious to save the turtle. Here was a possible way. Because they were used to the mysterious, the non-ordinary, because this man claimed to be a friend of their father, each made the decision to trust him.

"Focus your attention. Everything is light. See the turtle. See how light she is. She is a creature of light. In the light, she has no weight. Place her in the light and watch her rise."

The twins did as they were told, picturing the Leatherback gently bathed in clear, white light. They did not know what they were doing, let alone whether they were doing it correctly, but something was happening. Illuminated in the beam, the turtle began to glow and sparkle. Suddenly, the huge creature was not lying helplessly on her back. She was floating gently above the sand, slowly rising upward, moving slowly down the sloping sand toward the water's edge.

How is this possible? Alta remembered thinking, but there was no time to even begin to postulate an answer. An enormous wave, at least ten feet high, came rolling and crashing over them, dousing everyone in a deluge of water, spray, and foam. The twins held fast to

Enoch's hands, struggling to retain their balance as the water swirled all around them. After what seemed an eternity, the wave receded, leaving the three bedraggled rescuers standing alone on the sand.

"Where is the turtle?" Charis cried, straining her eyes for some sign of the poor animal. She was firmly convinced that the creature had drowned.

"Behold!" Enoch pointed out into the water. The turtle was floating on the surface, bobbing right side up amidst the waves like a giant cork. Lifting her head high, the grateful messenger cast a single backward glance at the trio on the beach. Then, with a kick of her powerful flippers, she disappeared beneath the waves, seeking refuge far out to sea in the safety of a coral reef.

"We must get inside," Enoch urged them, glancing at the boiling clouds overhead. "The storm is growing worse. Belial has done his work well this night." Without a word, he led them along the beach, their path illuminated by the beam from the Lighthouse holding ever steady before them.

"He's not taking us home," Charis realized as they headed farther north. "He's taking us to the Lighthouse." She was too tired to be afraid, too exhausted and overwhelmed by the experiences of the past hour. All she wanted was to be inside and dry in front of a warm fire. At last, battered and bedraggled, they reached the massive structure. Up close, it was even larger than they had imagined. It soared upward into the night, a white beacon amidst the surrounding darkness.

"Welcome," Enoch said, opening the door and leading them within. "Make yourselves comfortable."

They were in a small anteroom devoid of furniture or the trappings of home. A spiral staircase rose out of the floor, disappearing into the gloom below and rising up toward the light so high above. Instinctively, Alta started to descend, seeking the shelter of the Earth to protect him from the storm.

"Not that way," Enoch smiled, sensing his confusion. "Not down, but up. Tonight, we go up." He pointed to the light above and started to ascend, motioning for the twins to follow.

*****

They climbed for an eternity, up and up, around and around in the darkness of the stairwell. Yet always above them, the light served as a goal, so they would not feel completely lost in the darkness. Finally, they emerged from the stairwell into the upper room.

"What happened out there?" Alta asked when he could catch his breath. He had seen the builders move the great blocks of stone by projecting their thoughts through the crystal-powered devices. A ray would surround the stone, bathing it in light. After that, it was a simple matter to hoist the block and move it into place. But this was different. This mysterious figure, whoever he was, had no machine. He did it through the power of his own mind. It was very strange indeed, but more than strange...exciting. Alta wanted to learn how to accomplish this marvelous feat for himself.

"Simple," Enoch answered. "We helped the animal to alter her molecular structure to match that of the wind. Then it was a simple matter for her to rise up when the gust lifted it. When the wave swept over her, she righted herself, returned to her natural molecular state and swam away, confident that she had delivered her message."

"What message?" Alta was soaked and exhausted, but he wanted to know more about this stranger who had appeared from the middle of a beam of light, levitated a half-ton turtle, then returned it to the sea. "Where did you come from? How did you levitate that turtle? How do you know our names? Who are you?"

"Patience, Alta, patience," Enoch handed each twin a soft cotton robe and a flannel blanket. "I will answer all of your questions. But first, step behind there," he pointed to two beautiful hand-painted screens, "and get out of those wet clothes. I'll make tea."

They needed no second urging, for they were soaked and chilled to the bone. As they changed, they heard the comforting whistle of a kettle as water boiled.

"Drink this," Enoch said, handing two steaming mugs to the twins as they sat in luxurious overstuffed chairs. They were high up in the Lighthouse, wrapped snugly in soft blankets, drying out nicely.

"Ychhh," Alta grimaced as he sipped the scalding liquid. He did not mean to be rude, but the beverage had an awful taste, bitter, almost dry. How can something so wet taste so dry? he thought.

"Alta," his sister admonished. "Don't be rude."

"That's all right, Charis," Enoch smiled. "He's just like your father. I remember the first time I offered him tea. He took a sip and just about spit it back in my face. 'You make a lousy cup of tea,'" he told me then, "and apparently I still do. I guess I've gotten used to my own cooking over the years, so I don't try to improve on my recipes."

"You know our father?" Alta asked in amazement.

"Of course I know your father. I know your mother, too. And I know both of you. I've watched you grow up into a fine young man and woman. I've waited for this day when we would finally meet. I don't go out into the city very often. I much prefer the solitude of the Lighthouse. Here is where I do my work and where I observe what's going on around me. That's how I saw you on the beach tonight. What were you doing out in such weather?"

"Looking for turtles," Charis answered quickly. She was enjoying the company of this pleasant old man. He was really nice...kind, gentle, and easy to talk to. And what an interesting place! She looked around the glass-walled room. It must offer an incredible view when the weather is clear, she thought.

The Lighthouse was obviously Enoch's home. There was a table and a bed and cooking utensils. But what really attracted her attention were the books—huge volumes, ancient tomes and manuscripts. And in the center of the table, on a golden stand, stood a beautiful clear crystal globe.

Outside, the storm raged. Rain pelted the glass, the wind howled with fierce intensity. Inside, though, all was warm and snug and cozy. "You can't even feel the storm," Alta observed. "The wind has no effect on the building, even up this high. This Lighthouse must be very strong."

"Very strong, indeed," Enoch replied. "It was the first structure build by the Ancients when they arrived on the island. They needed it to endure, because it would serve as the Wayshower for the others who would follow them. It had to be strong enough to withstand the ravages of wind, weather, water, and salt, as well as the shaking of the Earth and the ravages of time. "No, it will not be this storm that will cause the crumbling of the Tower. Other towers are falling even now, but this Tower will not fall tonight. Soon, perhaps," he muttered under his breath, "but not tonight."

Charis was reminded of a snatch of one of her mother's poems. How did the verse go?

> When the Tower falls and the world seems small,
> Here I sit with my Shadows one and all.

There was more, of course, but these two lines said it best, summing up not only what was she was feeling in her own young life, but also what everyone around her seemed to be feeling. Expressing in a beautiful couplet the condition of the Atlantean world. Sipping her tea, she looked about her. It does taste awful, she thought, making a sour face. All this talk of crumbling towers reminded her of the immediate situation in which she and her brother now found themselves. They were far from home in the middle of a hurricane with a stranger who had kindly offered them shelter. Their parents would be frantic. She fidgeted restlessly.

"You're thinking that your parents will be worried about you," Enoch said. "You promised to be home in two hours, and now here you are."

"How did you know that?" Charis asked. "Can you read minds?"

"It doesn't take a mind reader to realize that you'd like be home with your parents rather than causing them worry. Let's tell them that you and your brother are safe from the storm and that you will join them as soon as the weather clears."

"How can we do that?" Alta asked, looking around for electronics equipment. "You don't have any communications devices up here."

"I have a mind, don't I?" Enoch's eyes twinkled mysteriously.

Alta did not understand. He was about to speak further, but his sister laid a cautionary hand on his arm, put her finger to her lips, and nodded in Enoch's direction. The old man had grown quite still and was sitting upright in his chair, facing the center of the room and gazing at the beautiful globe.

"Yes, it is time to tell your parents that you are all right." Enoch stood up, walked over to the globe, and placed both palms around the polished crystal, careful not to actually touch the surface. "Come stand beside me," he winked. "I'm going to show you a new way to talk to people who aren't close by."

The twins wrapped their blankets about them and walked to their host's side.

"Form a circle around the table," Enoch directed, taking hold of their hands, more gently this time than earlier that evening. "Now look into the globe and try to see your parents' faces. Concentrate, but do not strain. Just let their images come to you. If you do not see anything, that's okay. The message will still get through."

"Adima," Enoch called softly. After a pause, he called again. "Cybele."

The twins watched, skeptical but willing. After their night on the moaning rock and this latest adventure in the storm, they were pretty much open to whatever came along. This, it seemed, was going to be another one of those times.

"Father!" Charis gasped. There was Adima's face, floating deep within the crystalline structure of the globe.

"Mother, too," Alta whispered, amazed that he was really seeing Cybele's image in the glass.

"Tell them that you are all right," Enoch instructed. "Don't say the words out loud. Just think them to yourselves. Say them in your mind, and try to project your thoughts into the crystal."

The twins did so.

"We're fine." Alta sent his thoughts. "We're in the Lighthouse with your friend, Enoch. He's taking care of us. He makes a lousy cup of tea," the thought just flashed through the boy's mind inadvertently. His father grinned broadly.

"He hears me!" Alta marveled.

"Sorry we got caught in the storm," Charis said the words in her mind. "We were trying to save a helpless turtle and wound up needing to get rescued ourselves." She saw her mother nod her head and smile, as if to say, "As long as you're safe, all is forgiven."

Now it was Enoch's turn. The twins heard the words in their heads just as clearly as though he had spoken them aloud. They heard them and marveled, just as their father had done almost thirty years ago on the Great Plain on the night that Belial had received the Spear and Enoch had come to him for the first time.

"They're fine," Enoch communicated. "A little wet and tired, but I'll keep them here until the storm passes. Then I'll bring them to you. I assume you will be in the usual place?"

Adima nodded. "Don't go telling them any stories about me," his shimmering image laughed within the glass.

"Never mind," came Enoch's laughing reply. "It's time they learned more about their father and mother."

It was all over. The images faded; the communication ended.

"How did you do that?" Alta couldn't wait to ask.

"It isn't such a great miracle," Enoch said deprecatingly. "In fact, it's quite easy if you know how."

"Can you show us how to do it, too?" Charis requested politely.

"You already know how," Enoch smiled at her as he sat back down on the couch. "You just did it. It's perfectly natural. Everyone could do it once, long ago, but most of us have forgotten how." He sighed wistfully.

"You don't really need the crystal; you can do the same thing without it. But I thought the images of your parents would help you concentrate better and hear their voices more clearly. The secret, which is really not a secret, is the knowledge that all minds are connected. We have no idle thoughts, no separate thoughts. We are all part of the same collective Universal Mind. Therefore, it is a simple matter to talk to one another. That part is easy. The hard part is paying enough attention to our thoughts and attending to what we think so that we don't overwhelm the circuits with a lot of noisy chatter. Just keep practicing and the ability will develop naturally, as easily as learning to walk."

The old man arranged several cushions into two piles on the floor. "It is growing late," he said, motioning for them to make themselves comfortable on the makeshift beds, "and I want to tell you a story before you go to sleep."

The twins looked at each other. Weren't they a bit old for bedtime stories?

Enoch seemed to sense their thoughts. "Go over and take a look out the window," he suggested. "What do you see?"

Alta and Charis got up and gazed out at the ever-intensifying storm. They couldn't see much, it was too dark. Being in the Lighthouse was deceptive. So strong it was, so solidly built, so well sealed, that they had little indication of how severe the tempest really was. Had they known what catastrophic destruction was occurring even now, and how much more there was to come, they would have been immensely terrified. Had they been out on the beach, they would not have survived. Mercifully, however, they did not know, nor were they out on the beach. Mercifully, they were in the top of the Lighthouse, safe and warm and dry.

Nestling back into the soft cushions, wrapping their blankets snugly around them, the twins relaxed in cozy comfort. And as they made themselves at home, Enoch also relaxed, sat back, smoked his pipe, and talked.

"You cannot see it, but what is happening is the next step in a Plan that is older than the Great Mother herself," he began, "a Plan inspired, ordained, and put into place even before the very atoms and molecules that comprise the universe were created and shaped." It is of that Plan, and the part you two will play in it, that I speak to you now. I will begin with your father and mother and the land of Atlantis. Then I will take you back to a time before the beginning, to the birth of the first created being."

The candles were growing dim, and they sat in semidarkness as Enoch told them about their parents, told them tales of Atlantis in the old days, told them of the times when their ancestors had visited other worlds and colonized beneath the sea. The old man was full of magical, mystical stories—stories of the wonders of Atlantis and of the spiritual side of Atlantis. Stories of the Earth Spirit, the beneficent Dragon by which the Atlantean civilization was sustained. Stories of the men and women who utilized the sacred principles of spiritual engineering and sacred geometry to built the ridges, earthworks, and lines of stone that linked various parts of their world—men and women who cleared the way for the spiritual irrigation of the countryside, sculpting gigantic patterns in the landscape, titanic images of the heavens patterned on the skin of the Great Mother—the living Earth.

Stories of the creation of Light and all the Souls, from the time when all were one, before the descent into separation and the formulation of the Plan. Alta remembered his father's stories and how he could sit for hours and listen to them, letting himself be caught up in the experience of the words. Enoch's voice grew soft as he came to the heart of the tale.

> Into the sea of peaceful and harmonious vibration came one Amilius, the Light, the first expression of Divine Mind, the first manifestation of the Spirit, the first Son who emanated from the Source as a beautiful thought is created or as an idea is born. This was the first creation.

> Amilius was by necessity endowed with free will and reason, otherwise he would remain *of* the Whole, *at the will of* the Whole. Although a part of the Source and aware of his identity with the Source, he was a separate entity and conscious of his own individuality while still one with the Creator in spirit and in purpose.

> It was Amilius who fostered the coming of other soul-entities into the electro-spiritual world, for all souls were created in the beginning; none were created later. With their free will and reason, they existed in a state of perfection, in full accord with the Divine Will of the Source.

> But not for long did the will of the souls remain the will of the Source. They began to experiment, fascinated with the power of their own creative individuality. Desire and self-aggrandizement gave birth to their destructive natures.

> Amilius realized what was happening. A Plan was conceived whereby a means of escape was devised from the predicament into which the "lost" souls" had fallen. In accordance with the Plan, materiality came into being. For Matter was essential in order to demonstrate physically the *separation of Spirit*, so that the souls might become aware of their fall, although the Earth was not created solely for humankind. The Mother has other children, too.

> The solar systems and the planets and the Earth took form, created by the same thought vibrations and the same Life Essence emanating from the Mind of the Creator—the two eternal partners, Holy Mother Truth and Holy Father Love.

> The poles—the positive and negative, the yin and yang, the opposites around which the Mother revolves—were the keystones. The atom, made up of negative electrons revolving around positive protons, was the building block. Every atom, every cell is a world in itself and motivated by the same life-giving Spirit; they are not the Creator, but the *manifestation* of the Creator.

> The Cosmos—the Order—was built by and upon the principles of harmony, structure, and balance that became known to the Ancients as music, arithmetic, and geometry. By changing the rate of vibration, various movements, patterns, forms, and substances came into being.

Enoch took out a beautifully carved flute and blew several clear tones. "Each design inherently carries within itself its own plan of growth and evolution, which corresponds to the sound of a musical note." He blew a single note—A above middle C, vibrating at

440hz. The sound held long and clear, its tone and vibration sweet, filling each of them with a sense of well-being.

"Notes unite to make chords." He played an A-major triad.

"Chords become phrases." Next came a progression of the I, III, IV, V, I chords. The twins were quite interested. They had never heard music explained like this. Enoch's teaching provided a whole new meaning for them now.

"Phrases turn into melodies." The old man piped a tune based on the underlying structural harmony.

"Melodies intermingle around and between each other to make a symphony." He played the whole piece. The twins were so caught up in the moment that they never thought to question how a whole symphony could come forth from a simple woodwind instrument that was only capable of playing single notes.

"Thus is the universe." Enoch laid the flute on the carpet beside him. "Thus is Atlantis. Thus are you and I and everyone. Each is a unique note, phrase, or melody, and all are part of the Master Symphony."

> Back and forth the Mind of the Great Creator played upon the universe, unlimited within the imagination of an all-creative Spirit. All matter moved and changed, assuming its design according to its own vibration and maintaining its activity by the Law of Attraction and Repulsion, the positive and the negative, the Tension of the Opposites. Everything that came into being was an aspect of Mind, the Spirit of the Creator.

The old man was interrupted by a loud crash. A large limb had been blown into the wall below the light. The glass was thick and strong, however, and held firm.

Charis was frightened. She had almost forgotten the storm. Now she was reminded of the danger. "Why are you telling us this?" she asked politely. "Are you trying to teach us something?"

The old man smiled slowly. "You are wise, Charis, like your father and mother. Indeed, I do have a reason for telling you this. It is to prepare you for the coming destruction so that you will not be afraid, so that you will understand. It is all part of *the Plan*. It is all okay."

"What destruction?" It was Alta's turn to be frightened.

"The end of the Atlantean civilization," Enoch said simply. "But more than an end, it is at the same time a beginning. It is a shifting of the positive and negative poles around which the Great Mother revolves, a rearranging of the atoms and molecules so that we can build anew, and to ensure the success of the Plan."

He paused to let them reflect on the meaning of this. So young they were! They could not grasp the full significance of his words. Having never experienced total devastation, they could not conceive of it. Fortunately, their minds could not paint sufficiently vivid images of the coming onslaught to frighten themselves too much.

"You see, Atlantis as a race and a civilization was built as a part of the Plan," Enoch broke the silence. "So too, the Fall of Atlantis is but part of the Plan. There will be other parts before the Plan is complete. Your parents have a part to play in the Plan, as do I, as do you. What will be your roles? Do you know?"

The twins shook their heads.

"You will be the Seed Carriers. You will lead the ones who will carry all of what is pure and good and right about Atlantis forward into the future, into the next stage of the Plan. You will step out of the destruction and the chaos into the new world, where you will plant the seeds. Then, during your lives, you will take the necessary steps to ensure that the seeds are protected. Some may fall on barren ground and not take root. Others will lie dormant for a long, long time. But some will sprout right away. Those are the ones that you must tend and cultivate, so that they mature and propagate and bear strong, good fruit.

"How?" asked Charis. "How will we do this? We've never even planted a garden."

"I speak metaphorically," Enoch replied. "The seeds you will carry forth are ideas—the germs of thought. Your minds will carry forth the memories and the ideas, which also are contained in the crystals that your mother will turn over to you when the time comes. Fear not. You will be guided, as your father and mother were before you and as your children will be after you. You will not be alone. You will never be alone."

On the old man droned, the fragrant aroma of his pipe commingling with the melodic tones of his voice to soothe his young guests. Such interesting tales, full of magic and whimsy, and not a little bit of dread. Tales of heroes and heroines and grand adventures. The twins listened as long as they could, but they were, after all, still children, and the events of the day finally caught up with them. Alta dropped off to sleep first, followed a few moments later by his sister.

And as the hurricane continued its devastating sweep across the great island, the twins slept soundly and undisturbed. That was good, Enoch thought. They would need all of their strength in the days to come. It would be their last good night's sleep for a long time. He blew out the candles and tucked the blankets in around them, making sure they were warm. Then he stood by the windows and gazed out into the night. The only light was from the great beam in the room above him, revolving, ever revolving, warning all travelers to stay away from Atlantis. Refilling his pipe, Enoch smoked and looked out to sea as the melancholy knell of the foghorn boomed its dire warning to the world.

*****

The hours passed slowly as the Keeper of the Light kept watch over the gigantic storm that was destroying the City of Atlantis. The raging tempest seemed to stand still over the island, battering it with incredible winds, inundating it with torrential rains, pummeling it with devastating lightning. Looking into his crystal ball, he beheld the destruction in vivid detail. There was Elysia. The sandy shores of the once-lovely lagoon were completely under water, as were the gardens, the veranda, and most of the first floor of the dome. Only the very highest part of the house was visible above the raging, boiling ocean. He strained to see Adima and Cybele, but there was no sign of life. Enoch winced as a huge wave swept over the beehive-like structure and the dome collapsed and sank into the turbulent waters. The image faded. It was all gone.

Almost midnight. The children still slept comfortably, wrapped snugly in their warm blankets. What feelings passed through the old man's mind? First and foremost, there was an incredible, overwhelming anger. He was angry at Belial, at his stubborn refusal to move beyond his present level of growth and development. "How I hate him!" Enoch realized aloud, shocked at the strength of his emotions. "Belial the malevolent, Belial the dark one, Belial the accursed spawn of the Tempter!" The old man felt a sharp pain in the center of his chest as the dark thoughts pressed in on him. No matter. He would let these angry thoughts come once and for all. For too long he had been suppressing them, denying his feelings, pretending that he felt nothing, that he understood everything and was in perfect accord with the ways of Spirit.

He knew that the destruction of Atlantis was occurring for many reasons, but none angered him as much as the monster Belial's refusal to continue to seek and expand himself. How could he remain so limited, content with his achievements, locked into a consciousness of fear? How could he be satisfied to simply exercise a dictator's power and control? How could he be so blind and unwilling to move beyond his present station?

Enoch was also angry at his fellow Atlanteans—angry that they were killing the Mother, angry that they were killing themselves. "They are really no different," he muttered, pacing back and forth as the twins slept undisturbed. "So blind, so asleep. Letting this happen instead of standing up and saying 'Enough. It ends now. The insanity stops here. Atlantis is ours. Let us take it back.'" Again he walked over to the gorgeous crystal globe and gazed deeply within its dark interior. The images formed slowly, as though the crystal itself were protecting him from the image that he wanted so desperately to see.

There it was at last, that face shimmering in a ghostly, surreal light...the face of a vicious, monstrous Beast, its long snout drawn back into a ferocious snarl, its feral tongue lolling out of its hideous mouth, its sharp fangs dripping poison. The Beast seemed to sense that it was being watched. Turning its head, it looked straight into Enoch's eyes.

It was an eerie scene. Two mortal enemies—personifications of the opposites, Good and Evil, Wise and Foolish—faced each other across Time and Space, each standing his ground, each facing the other with unwavering gaze, confident of his own strength and power. Not a sound disturbed the air around them, but the space inside their heads was filled with the deafening noise of battle as each sought to unbalance and cripple the other with the force of his mind.

"I see you, old fool!" The Beast struck first, a mighty blow. Enoch recoiled as the force of the words burned themselves into his mind. The voice of the Beast was like the roar of many wild animals. "You thought you could stop me. You thought you could take the little one and teach him the ways of Light and Truth and that would be enough." Laughter, deep and mocking, chilled the old man's soul.

"You are the fool, Beast!" Enoch cried, striking back from within his own mind, his voice deep and clear and strong. The power of the words drove the hideous creature backward, throwing it off balance, forcing it to use all of its strength to remain standing upright. "You have chosen to stand still. You have become warped and distorted, no longer a man, not fully a beast."

In the darkness, the old man placed a trembling hand on the Book of Life, knowing the Beast would see the holy image in its own gazing globe. "Universal Law dictates that you cannot stand still. You are either going in one direction or another. When you attempt to stand still, you are actually going backward. And that direction leads only to expressions of negativity, doubt, ego, and personality-controlling thoughts. In that direction, you will *never* find the enlightenment you crave."

The words struck home. Enoch knew it instantly. The Beast was gone, and Belial stood in its place, wincing as though stung by a serpent. How he craved enlightenment! Could Enoch's words be true? "Of course not," the voices within him countered. "You are already enlightened. You are already there. You dare not show weakness to your enemy. Strike back. Do it now, before he can pounce again and strike you down."

"Silly, foolish, weak old man," Belial roared, drawing himself erect, allowing himself be strengthened and driven by the darkness within. "Learn this lesson well. Learn once and for all that you can never defeat me. I am all powerful. My allies are the forces of Darkness. Project Nightside will succeed, for I command the shadowy host."

Floating in a hazy sea inside the crystal, the image of the Belial-Beast placed a twisted claw on the lever of the device and pulled it downward. Simultaneously, a huge gust of wind shook the Lighthouse. The ancient building groaned and quivered on its foundation but held firm. Enoch looked at the twins, who continued to sleep peacefully. Within the crystal, the Belial-Beast threw back its feral head and laughed long and hard, until finally the image faded into darkness.

The pains in his chest were stronger now. Enoch leaned against the window sill, anger and hatred surging and churning in his breast, increasing the sensation of constriction and pressure. He closed his eyes and breathed deeply, counting slowly, focusing only on his breath. Little by little, he managed to calm himself.

Such strange feelings, he thought. Never had he experienced such physical or emotional discomfort. As the negative emotions had intensified, so also had the physical pain. He shook his head, thinking of all of the negative emotions surging through Atlantis on this terrible night. How much pain they must be bringing! How badly his brethren must be feeling! Enoch's heart went out to the people of Atlantis, and he was filled with compassion for them and their plight. And with the compassion came the grief, grief at so much unnecessary loss. He cried out to the Great Mother in despair.

"What is happening to you, Mother?" he whispered aloud. "What will become of you? What will happen to your children? You but protect yourself, I know. You but rid yourself of this parasite that invades you and threatens your very existence."

Ever so quietly in the darkness before the transition from one day to the next, the Great Mother spoke to the son who loved her so. Explaining her purpose and her ways, helping him to understand, and finally, declaring her love for all of her children.

"It is not Belial against whom I take my stand," the Mother whispered, *"for he himself is not the parasite. I rise up against the Beast-consciousness that drives Belial—the alien thoughts within his mind, the thoughts of separation and power and lust. Fear-based thoughts, shadowy thoughts. Sick, twisted, perverted, thoughts, not worthy of such noble creatures; not worthy of my children.*

"Divisive thoughts that separate the physical from the spiritual, eventually forgetting the spiritual completely. Oppressive thoughts that keep my children locked in fear-based consciousness. Limiting thoughts that keep my children from achieving their full potential, from even realizing that they can do so much more, that they are capable of creative and generative powers beyond their present limited abilities to conceive. These are the thoughts that have created the effects of which I now choose to rid myself.

"Belial!" The Great Mother cried out, writhing in agony as she spoke the name. *"I weep for the loss of my son. I wept when he forgot that he was part of all that was around him, when he no longer acknowledged the oneness of all things, coming instead to rely solely on the physical mind and its carnal interpretations. I wept as he came to accept those beliefs which he knew instinctively were not true. I wept as he rejected his Divine nature and became less and less aware of the Source from which he had sprung. I wept as he put ego of self above everything else."*

The Great Mother grew silent, except for the sounds of wind and rain and the roar of the storm. Enoch marveled at her compassion, at the depth of her unconditional love and forgiveness. No thoughts of malice at those who hurt her so; simply a matter of protection and survival. Her love for her children remained constant and unchanged.

"I wish I could feel as you do, Mother." He spoke softly, but the bitterness and resentment in his voice could not be concealed. For Enoch was, despite his knowledge, enlightenment, and understanding, still a man, with all of the attendant human emotions. He found it so hard to forgive, so hard not to judge the Sons of Belial and their actions, equating the two, making the men as evil as the thoughts and actions that came forth from them.

"Power!" The anger erupted again. "They have no idea what power means, although they use it without even knowing it. For power is not in weapons or armies or wealth or the possession of material goods. True power is in the ability to wield thoughts as things, to have the idea first, and then turn it into a reality."

Careful not to wake the twins, he clambered up to the room above, where the light continued to sweep the sea with its powerful beam. It was more exposed up there, and the noise of the storm was louder. Wind whistled through the cracks in the masonry, and the floor was slick with rainwater.

"Behold the disease, the sickness, the evil that must be dealt with!" The old man was breathing heavily, and he had to shout to hear himself above the din. "Behold the lack of awareness within the human family of the fact that their seemingly idle thoughts are indeed the very things they must learn to control the most...are in truth the most powerful tools in the physical universe. Yet they choose to remain ignorant. They choose to remain irresponsible. They choose to remain in darkness." A sharp spasm seared across his chest, and the old man grimaced in pain.

"Well," he cried hoarsely, placing both hands on a huge lever that protruded from the machinery. "If they choose to *embrace* the darkness, let them *live* in the darkness!" With a mighty heave, he pulled the lever toward him. Metal groaned against metal, and in an instant, the great light was extinguished. For the first time in the history of Atlantis, the seacoast was enshrouded in darkness, with no illumination to guide the way. For the first time since he had entered into his service as Keeper of the Light, Enoch relaxed his vigilance. The old man leaned his back against the rough cement walls, sank to the floor, and burst into tears as he realized that there was no one to watch over Atlantis anymore. "They are so stubborn," he sobbed, "so very, very stubborn."

"And whose fault is that?" the Mother asked patiently, understanding the anger but refusing to give in to it. *"The Invader tells them that this is not so. The Invader tells them that they can do whatever they want. The Invader deceives them with the Great Lie. It is the Invader on whom I must focus my attention. The Invader is attacking my children. This can no longer be. I will not let my children continue to be attacked. I will see to it that the Invader is stopped."*

"And then what?" Enoch asked, the tears still flowing softly. "After the Invader is gone, what will be left? Nothing, only ignorance and wasteland and darkness. Where will the human race go then, after Atlantis is no more?"

Obviously Enoch was afraid, although he concealed it well. It was all right, though. The Mother would help him understand and thereby have no more cause for fear or doubt. She spoke softly and patiently, gently helping him release his own anger and fear, all that was bothering him.

"There has always been direction for those who seek the Light. My children are never alone. I and their Father are always with them. We are always One, although the illusion that we are not is still so very strong. Throughout the coming sleep of world history, many civilizations will rise and fall upon the Slaughterbench of History. Some will achieve great levels of good, others will sink to utter depravity, all in proportion to the exercise of their will toward good. Behold!"

Opening his third eye, Enoch looked into the future, seeing all of the mighty empires of the great nations of the world to come. Sumeria and Egypt, Greece and Rome, the Soviet Union and America. So much bloodshed and violence, oppression and tyranny. So much music and poetry and invention and tenderness. So much *passion*. Now he understood what the Mother meant, and he told her so.

"And underneath it all remains the powerful reality of Spirit—the *Absolute*. Spirit, whose essence is *Freedom*. As the fathers sleep, so Spirit will teach them the meaning of their own freedom, through their own passions and desires, the expressions of their human will."

The Mother smiled at her son. *"Yes,"* she replied. *"That is how the whole reversal will be brought about. In each civilization, in each nation-state, it will be accelerated, retrograded, or remain stationary in proportion to the exercise of the human will toward good. For desire and passion are the keys. They are what motivate my children. In your personal goals you find the satisfaction of your personal desires. And nothing is ever accomplished unless individuals desire it and find their satisfaction in bringing it about. Nothing great in the world has ever been accomplished without passion."*

Again Enoch scanned the future, marveling at the complex web of human desire with which Spirit would work to bring about its goal of freedom for humankind. The pain and pressure in his chest were gone, as were the fear and doubt, for now he knew the purpose behind the destruction of Atlantis. Now he understood completely. Spirit would use human will as a means to bring about its own Divine Will, which was to restore the human race to the consciousness of its unified nature.

One by one, the At-one-ment would happen to each individual, to each soul who chose to sojourn on the Earth. In each one's development, the first to be conquered would be the Self. Thus it had been for himself, so it was for Adima and Cybele and the Children of the Law of One, so also would it be for Belial and the rest, one by one, throughout the millennia. And as each individual mind became harmonized and balanced, so also would the Nation-State itself become harmonized and balanced, and thereby the whole world. As it was written in the *Book of Life*:"

LIKE BEGETS LIKE.

For this was part of Universal Law.

The old man smiled in gratitude and appreciation at the scope of the Plan. Atlantis would indeed be reborn and rise again—not the conflicted Atlantis in which he now lived, but a wholly transformed Atlantis, gleaming brightly in the light of a new dawn of consciousness. What an Atlantis that would be—totally functioning, unified, and harmonized, in which all of the Mother's children remembered and accepted their Divine origin, their inheritance!

So the Great Mother spoke, so she promised to Enoch. She would help her children, she was taking the necessary steps to help them return Home, to the Consciousness of Freedom that was their birthright. She would accomplish her goal with the help of Belial and Adima and Lilith and Cybele; Alexander and Caesar and Elizabeth and Joan; Martin and Teresa and all who would follow them, using each unique individual personality to bring about historical changes so that the Consciousness of Freedom would grow and evolve.

The first step would be a difficult one, of that there was no doubt. Much would change after the destruction of Atlantis. Much of the old would fall away. Throughout the world there would be massive shock, massive resistance, and massive upheaval. But in Truth, nothing would really be destroyed. Old forms would dissolve, patterns would shift and change, but the human Form would endure, the human Soul would endure, and the human Spirit would endure, taking the next steps along the Grail Path on the wonderful journey Home.

*****

And the evening and the morning were the second day.

CHAPTER 43

And the evening and the morning were the third day.

—*Genesis 1:13*

And so the future was born in a hail of wind and water and destruction and darkness. Born with the detonation of the device and the extinguishing of the light. On the second night of Homecoming, Atlantis had gone to bed in a world that had functioned perfectly. A few short hours later, they awoke to a world that was irretrievably broken.

In an instant, life as they knew it had been completely transformed by a monumental physical disaster. It was all gone—harmony, structure, and order; beauty, balance, and precision. All that was good and true and beautiful had been replaced by conflict, wreckage, and discord; ugliness, instability, and chaos.

As an ominous gray dawn broke over the ruined city on the morning of the third day, the people of Atlantis sat up and looked around them, horrified by what they saw and heard and smelled and tasted and felt. In that damp, muggy, stifling moment in time, a new thought suddenly projected itself into the Atlantean Mind. A powerful thought, a frightening thought, a thought that had never been conceived of before. As the killer storm had burst across the unsuspecting landscape—unannounced and uninvited—so now the demon thought burst into the unprepared Atlantean Mind, unwanted and unwelcome.

Suddenly, the future was thrust upon them. Suddenly, the unthinkable was real! Suddenly, the people of Atlantis sat up and took notice. Suddenly, it was personal. What would the future bring now? Indeed, would there even be a future? Suddenly, it was quite easy to imagine a world that no longer existed. People everywhere were quite easily able to think the unthinkable—no more Atlantis!

Like wildfire, such thoughts spread from person to person, following the myriad links among the passageways of the interconnected Atlantean Mind. No one had ever entertained such thoughts before. Now everyone knew that they would never be able to *NOT* think such thoughts again.

Recovery from the effects of the storm would prove to be impossible. Assuaging the fear spawned from the thought would prove equally impossible. As frightening as any thought that had ever intruded into human consciousness, this thought and others like it would continue to plague humanity throughout the ages. Absolutely terrifying, they would haunt the sense memory of the human race for millennia to come. Long after the actual events had been forgotten, the sensory impressions generated during that final week would stay locked in the human subconscious, locked in the genetic code. There they would fester and breed, forming the basis of all future myth and legend, laying the foundation for the primal, fundamental, motivating fear. Reminding the human race of its origins, of the time when they fell from grace in the Garden and were expelled from Paradise.

The real problem, of course, was that events were happening too quickly. Time had run out for Atlantis! There was no time to react, no time to adjust, no time to get used to these powerful and terrifying new ideas and circumstances. Change was occurring in such a fury of activity that there was no time to evolve gently into the necessary behaviors and thought processes necessary to compensate. The only thing there was even a bare minimum of time for was getting out alive—with whatever good they could salvage for the rebuilding.

Absolute and overwhelming, the fear spread to all corners of Atlantis. From young families with infants at the breast to the old and feeble who could not protect themselves or their loved ones, fear and panic gripped the world. Suddenly they knew the awful truth. There was no way out—no escape route, no place to go, no safe haven, no help in coping with and adapting to the changes. Except for the Arks. Rocking gently in their berths in the Bay of Parfa, the Arks remained their last, best chance.

*****

Atlantis awoke that morning to the aftermath of the most furious and intense storm in all of its history. The storm's fury had been palpable, causing destruction on an immense scale—huge, vast, and total. The hurricane chewed up and spat out everything in its path, carving a swath of destruction from the coastline and beaches to the tops of the Mountains of the Moon and beyond. With no warning, no time to prepare, nothing had been secured, boarded up, stowed away, or tied down, and very few had sought strong, safe shelter.

To the west and south, much of the Great Plain lay under several feet of water. Where there was dry land, megaliths and standing stones lay toppled and broken, littering the landscape like so many colossal broken limbs. Gone were the ley lines, unrecognizable the ancient Straight Paths, buried under branches and leaves and debris.

To the east and north, the harbor lay in ruins. Only days before, the magnificent sailing vessels had arrived for Homecoming. Painted like great birds of prey, sails unfurled in a riotous blaze of color, the tall ships had floated majestically along the peaceful canal. Sailing past Elysia, negotiating the bend to the north, they had come gently to rest in their berths. Throngs of people had lined the docks, cheering and waving to the passengers crowding the decks. Cries of "Hail!" and "Welcome" had filled the air. The harbor had been alive with the sounds of joy and laughter as the Atlanteans greeted their foreign cousins.

There would be no cheers today. Cargo and cruise ships alike lay swamped in their berths, floundering at precarious angles. A lucky few merely listed to port or starboard, depending on how much water they had taken on. The majority, however, had sunk, and now only a few black masts jutted above the waves to mark their graves. A thirty-foot storm surge had picked up scores of smaller craft like so many children's toys, carrying them hundreds of yards inland. Pleasure craft, fishing boats, houseboats...there they sat, incongruously perched in treetops, on rooftops, even high and dry on the hilltops.

As the water had encroached upon the land, so also had the land been carried to the sea. Plucked from their age-old soil as easily as a child helps her mother weed a flower garden, old forest giants lay splintered on the shoreline, their roots entangled among the slick black rocks. Massive logs jammed the canals and beaches, while leaves, twigs, and smaller branches floated in the tidal pools, marshes, and estuaries.

Within the city itself, the once alabaster streets were now buried under mountains of debris. Pools of stagnant, dirty water filled every natural and man-made depression. The meticulously carved cobblestones were covered over with several inches of silt, and the gleaming white buildings were splattered with mud from foundation to rooftop.

The largest and strongest structures—the Lighthouse, the Temple, the Palace, and the Great Pyramid—were intact and relatively undamaged. But the mansions along the Avenue of the Gods were no more. Red stones were piled one atop the other. Clay tiles, jagged shards of pottery, and broken glass littered the ruined yards and gardens. Walls and fences had vanished, and the people who dwelt in the mansions were as homeless on this morning as the naked, sickly beggars who had lain unnoticed and unattended in their gutters for so many years. Now they were one—if not in consciousness yet, at least in physical condition.

The Garden of the Heart was no more. Every flower, shrub, and tree had been uprooted and blown away. A score of pilgrims who had made camp in the lovely garden lay sprawled in the mud, their drowned and broken bodies mute testament to the fury of a killer storm that had yielded no mercy on the unprotected who happened to lie in its path.

The odor was amazing, larger than life—a foul brew of vomit, defecation, and rotting flesh and blood mixed with a thousand other unidentified stinks that, when combined, formed a single, all-pervasive stench—the smell of death. Perhaps a third of the population of the city had been lost—some drowned, many crushed under falling debris, others blown away by tornadoes or swept out to sea by the storm surge. Everywhere were the bodies of the dead and the carcasses of drowned animals!

In the streets, where the bodies lay, feeble cries for help came from under the heaps of rubble. Dead parents still held dead children in their arms, helplessly trying to shield them from the storm's fury. Homeless dead lay on doorsteps, their fists bruised and bloody from pounding on doors, crying out for help, begging for shelter, their desperate pleas going unheeded and unanswered. They had died as they lived, in the streets and the gutters, while those behind closed doors died along with them. Thinking they were safe in their houses of stone, those very domiciles of safety had let their wealthy owners down, collapsing upon them, crushing them as the stones tumbled one on top of another, until not a single stone was left standing.

The fires burned, filling the sky with soot and ash from thousands of small and large conflagrations. Barely an hour into the morning, a new danger loom. Thunderous explosions shook the ground as, one by one, the power crystals exploded in a catastrophic chain reaction across the city. Great showers of sparks and burning debris rained down upon the people as they scurried for shelter, only to be injured or killed as they stepped onto live power conduits that slithered across the ground like a thousand hissing serpents.

In the east, the rising sun, source of all energy, lay hidden behind an impenetrable curtain of clouds. There was no power this day, no energy to run the appliances, power the Way, or offer illumination. Communications were out, leaving no way to contact outlying districts or cities on other parts of the island. From Al Khemia and Turtle Island, there were only silence and static where there should have been multiple channels of communication. The Atlanteans were cut off, isolated. They were alone!

Through the devastation and carnage, the survivors struggled to cope and understand. The Atlanteans were not prepared, for it had not entered their consciousness that such a thing could happen. They had no frame of reference for total chaos. Their history, myths, and legends told of horrors and disasters, it is true, but those stories were limited in scope and location, recounting events that happened to somebody else, in another place, at another time. Such disasters, however, did not happen in Atlantis. They might happen in Lemuria and the provinces, but they did not happen here. Until now, until the morning of the third day of the Week That Would Change the World.

And so they were caught by surprise. Yes, there had been storms before, even severe ones. They were the natural consequence of living in a watery world. They knew how to deal with the hurricanes that battered their coasts each summer. They accepted the storms as part of the natural way, living in harmony with them. It had always been thus. Storms had hurt people and taken lives before. Storms had caused damage and destruction before. But never like this. This was different—so very, very different. And they did not know how to deal with these kinds of differences.

They did not know how to deal with injury on a national scale. They did not know how to deal with hunger and thirst on a national scale. They did not know how to deal with homelessness and no shelter on a national scale. They did not know how to deal with death on a national scale. This was their first experience with the ravages of the Destroyer.

Their books, writings, sacred teachings—nothing told them how to deal with anything like this. The most they had were the words of the *Book of Life* about treating each other with love and compassion and kindness, about treating their brethren the same way they would want to be treated themselves.

These Atlanteans, shocked as they were, needed specifics. Lofty words were not going to do it, were not going to be enough. They needed wayshowers to arise and show them how, lead them up and through and out of all of this darkness and death and confusion. So many questions that needed attending. "What do we eat? What do we drink? How do we decontaminate the food and water? Where do we live? Where do we put the bodies? What happens now? What do we do now? Who's responsible?" Questions for which they had no immediate answers, questions that would have to wait until they had taken care of more immediate problems.

As the morning wore on, a few wandering bands of troublemakers roamed the streets, preying on the weak and helpless, looting, robbing, even raping. In other places, a few who had managed to salvage limited supplies of food and water tried to sell such necessities for vast sums of gold. These were the Dark Ones, still motivated by lust and greed even after all that had happened. Still afraid, still craving wealth and personal gain at the expense of their brethren. Still thinking theirs was the right way.

But they were the few, the exceptions rather than the norm. For the most part, the Atlanteans who had survived had been profoundly changed. One and all, the survivors drew together, working side by side to provide aid and succor to the trapped, the injured, the dying, and the dead. Nobles, beggars, and everyone in between—all tried to help each other. Digging through the rubble in search of the living, whose weak and muffled cries they heard. Tearing their clothes to make dirty bandages to staunch the bleeding. Cradling the heads of the dying in their arms. No class consciousness this morning, no status symbols to separate them. This day, all were Atlanteans, all were one, all were victims, all were survivors.

Throughout the city, individual heroes rose up, like the beggar who single-handedly dug a ten-foot tunnel to reach a group of five people buried alive under a dozen tons of concrete and steel. Reaching them at last after hours of backbreaking toil, he had dragged them out one by one, staying with them and tending to their every need, until he finally collapsed from shock, exposure, and dehydration. Likewise, a prostitute whose house was left miraculously untouched turned what was left of her home into a hospital. Covered in blood, she was everywhere at once—washing wounds, bandaging open cuts, sewing gaping holes with thread and needle—an angel of mercy in the eyes of those to whom she ministered.

But the majority of the people could not do much of anything. Helpless, dazed, and hurt, the victims shuffled aimlessly through the rubble and smoke and ruin. Calling out the names of their loved ones, turning over the bodies, they peered intently at the dead faces, not knowing whether to be happy or sad that the victim was not the one for whom they had been searching.

They were hungry, but there was nothing to eat. They were thirsty, too, but the water was contaminated. Drinking it brought violent illness within a few minutes—vomiting, chills, and gut-wrenching spasms leading to fever and perhaps death, although it was too soon to tell.

No one spoke the words aloud; nevertheless, everyone knew the truth. It was all gone—Atlantis was no more! In a collective state of shock, the survivors wandered around their lost world—lost, forlorn, without hope. It was a condition that was to last, give or take a few exceptions here and there, for thousands and thousands of years.

*****

"What time is it?" Charis called sleepily to the old man who stood looking out of the glass windows of the Lighthouse. Enoch had let the twins sleep late. They were going to be in for a tremendous shock when they woke up, so he wanted them to be well rested.

"Mid-morning," Enoch smiled, turning to her.

Alta stirred and sat up, rubbing his eyes sleepily. "I'm hungry," he said, heaving a mighty yawn. "I hope mother has made a big breakfast."

"You won't be having breakfast at home today," Enoch spoke softly, coming to sit on the floor beside them. "In fact, you won't be having breakfast at Elysia any more."

"What do you mean?" Charis was alarmed. What was this strange old man saying?

Enoch held her and soothed her, speaking gently. "Much has happened while you were asleep," he said, holding their hands. "The storm was devastating. The city has been destroyed, as has most of the island, and along with it, your home."

Elysia! They could not believe it. It could not be so. The twins rushed to the windows and looked out. The sight was too much to comprehend, even from that great height. Where once there had been a beautiful, shining city, now there was only mud and rubble and matchwood scattered as far as the eye could see.

"Father and mother?" Alta asked in shock, looking helplessly at Enoch.

"Fear not, Alta and Charis, your parents are unharmed," the old man soothed them. "As soon as you are dressed and have eaten something, I shall take you to them. Remember last night when I told you about the great Plan? Well, this, too, is part of that Plan. Even though it seems like all is lost, such is not the case. All is well. All will be well. Come, get dressed and eat. We must leave with all haste to join your parents. They are waiting for us."

"Where?" Alta asked, but the old man was already half way down the spiral staircase. "There is food on the table," his voice drifted back up to them. "Join me when you are ready."

The twins wasted no time in doing so, putting on their now-dry clothes, gobbling a few mouthfuls of fruit and nuts, and gulping swallows of juice. Bounding down the stairs with a clatter, they dashed out the door into the gloomy morning, with its damp drizzle and horrible stench of destruction and death.

"Where are you going?" Enoch called to them from within the Lighthouse. They stopped in their tracks, looking at each other, suddenly doubtful, suddenly unsure.

"Where are we going?" Alta wondered. "I don't know."

"Neither do I," his sister replied, tears in her eyes as the full realization hit them. They were homeless. They had no place to go. They didn't even know where their parents were. They were alone with a relative stranger, albeit one whom they had come to trust in the past few hours. But they did not know what to do.

"Come back inside," Enoch called again, beckoning from the doorway. His black-robed figure filled the empty space. They shivered as they looked at him. He was suddenly not a little bit scary. He had just told them to hurry up, that they had to leave, that he was going to take them to their parents. Now they were outside, and he was standing in the doorway of the Lighthouse in his flowing black robes, beckoning to them to come back inside. Why? Their parents were not inside. What reason could he possibly have for wanting them back in the Lighthouse, unless it was a sinister one?

Sensing their fears, reading their thoughts, Enoch came to them, smiling his peaceful smile, always ready to teach, always willing to give, always able to turn disaster into an opportunity for learning. "My dear young people," he said, "you are right to question. You are right to have doubts and wonder. Now let me tell you how it is."

Gathering his robe about him, the old man sat on a slippery black rock, his back to the Lighthouse, and looked wistfully at the storm-tossed sea. The twins sat beside him, listening to the booming surf as it sang its plaintive song of lamentation for the death of Atlantis. "Everything that you think about your home being destroyed and the world being topsy-turvy is true. You cannot go back."

The truth was frightening, and tears began to well in their eyes as the twins contemplated the enormity of their plight for the first time. Enoch's voice, however, was strong and confident, his smile kind and reassuring. "You are right as far as you have gone. But you must continue your thinking and carry it to the proper conclusion. You are not lost, you are not without hope, you are not without allies, and most of all, you are not alone. Think!"

It was a command, not a request, and the twins started at the intensity of the old man's voice. Through tear-filled eyes they looked at him in amazement as he fired one question after another at them. "Who is your greatest Ally? Who would never abandon you and leave you helpless? Who will always take care of you and all of her beloved children?"

The twins thought. This was not unlike a lesson their parents would have taught them. It was Charis who realized the answer first. "The Great Mother!" she exclaimed, wiping her eyes. With the realization that there might be a ray of hope after all, she suddenly felt much better. "We can turn to the Mother for help."

"How?" Alta was more practical. "You may be able to communicate with the Mother at will, Enoch, but we certainly can't. How can she help us now? As if to confirm his words, the body of a drowned bird was washed ashore at his feet. A powerful sign, Alta thought. "Look around you," he cried, staring at the lifeless form with tears in his eyes. "The Mother herself is pretty badly banged up. I doubt if she can help us in any way. In fact," he picked up the bird and laid it gently on a flat rock, beyond the reach of the destructive surf, "it is we who should be helping her."

The old man rose and gripped the young man's hands with deep fervor, eyes shining brightly as he gazed intently at his student. "Again, what seems to be in your limited perception is not what is, in Truth," he replied. "The Mother is fine. She is always fine. And she certainly can help you."

He placed a strong arm around Charis as she came up to join them. "There is more to the Mother than that which you see on her skin." Enoch spoke quietly, revealing a powerful truth. "She is a great and vast Mother. Her body is enormous, for it is the entire globe." Arms around each twin, he walked as he spoke, gently guiding them back toward the Lighthouse. "Come with me now and learn more of your Mother. Come with me now within."

The empty doorway gaped before them like the black maw of a lion, open wide to devour its prey. The metaphor was not lost on the twins. Instinctively they shrank back, suddenly not wanting to enter the building that had provided them with sanctuary only moments before.

"You are cautious, and that is good," Enoch approved, his tall, straight form framed in the doorway. "But there is nothing to fear. For the Lighthouse not only extends above the ground, above the Mother's skin; it also extends within, penetrating her body, covering one of the twelve entrances to the Underworld, where there are many places of safety and refuge. As you go within your own minds whenever you need to rest, whenever you have doubts, or just to find peace and quiet and connection with Source, so you can always go within the physical body of the Great Mother for safety and refuge. It is within that we must go now. That is where your safety lies. That is where your parents await us."

Without another word, the old man turned, his black robe billowing in the still-gusting wind, and entered the Lighthouse. For an instant, the twins hesitated, silently wrestling with their doubts as they stood on the threshold of yet another adventure. Then they stepped within, following the dark figure to the spiral staircase, descending ever downward, around and around, until finally they stepped into the vast network of tunnels that honeycombed the crust of the Earth, entering into the body of the Great Mother for the first time.

Lighting a torch, Enoch led the way through rough-hewn passages. On and on they walked, ever downward, ever deeper, through a dark and mysterious world. Dozens of passages branched off in all directions, varying in width from a few inches to several feet. The twins had no idea if they were in the right tunnel or not. How could Enoch know his way? they wondered, but they did not ask aloud. They walked in silence. The old man seemed to want it that way, and the twins complied without question.

After a time, a dull roar began to echo through the tunnel, and the air grew warmer. Something was happening up ahead, and as they approached, the noise increased in volume. Alta recognized the sound at last—the thunderous roar of a waterfall. Enoch held up his hand, signaling caution. Rounding a sharp bend, they halted, stunned by what they were seeing.

The passage opened into a good-sized chamber, one of many through which they had passed. Each was a unique geological masterpiece—sculpted stalagmites and stalactites combined with innumerable crystals and minerals in colors and shapes that delighted the eye. "A giant's playground," Charis had remarked. It was true. The huge caverns were the perfect setting in which fairy-tale creatures might romp and frolic.

This chamber was unique, however. There would be no playing here. Their way was blocked by a powerful torrent of steaming water pouring from the mouth of a huge cataract. Spilling down onto the cavern floor, the dark, hot water swirled and churned, forming a wide, swift-flowing river that disappeared into a gaping black hole in the opposite wall. There was no way to cross the deluge. Enoch watched the torrent for a while, saying nothing as the spray formed tiny droplets on his face. Then he turned and spoke for the first time since they had entered the tunnels.

"The flooding has begun," he remarked cryptically, shouting over the roar of the rushing water. "The Mother is preparing herself, twisting and turning so that the water can move into place. We shall have to take an alternate route."

And so they did, backtracking for several hundred yards, then turning down a side passage. It was narrower and lower for a while, but the way was clear, and they continued on. An hour passed as they descended through the limestone and into the bedrock. At last they emerged into a wide, high tunnel that stretched out of sight in both directions.

"Now the way will be clear," Enoch smiled, extinguishing the torch and plunging them into total blackness. It was incredibly dark, a fluid inkiness that seemed to reach out and smother them. The twins were frightened once again.

"Just be still and let your eyes adjust," the old man's voice reassured them. "As soon as your pupils dilate, you will see clearly enough."

It was just as he had predicted. After a few moments, the darkness gradually diminished, giving way to a soft green light. The very walls and ceiling were glowing. "Meet another of the Mother's creatures," Enoch introduced them. "The living lights that illuminate the way for all who travel the paths of the Underworld."

The Underworld! Indeed, that is where they were. It was an amazing place, an alien world, so different from the world of the surface, the world of the outer. They were in a wonderland of stone. The twins could not begin to grasp the magnificence and diversity around them. *As above, so below.* How true!

Here was life on a monumental scale—liquid mineral life—magnificent, diverse, and incredibly beautiful, filled with delicate formations that had been carved drip-by-drip into shapes undreamed of by human sculptors. All were washed with the natural colors of the Great Mother's palette—red splashes of iron ore streaked with the purples and blues of manganese dioxide on a background of glossy white. It was the Underworld—the world within the Great Mother—a world that had begun before the human race had walked the planet, a work in progress that had been going on for hundreds of millions of years, long before there was an Atlantis, a Mu, or even a Lemuria.

Over rock as soft and smooth as velvet they walked, following pathways of stone that wound along the base of magnificent ornamented cliffs that soared to dizzying heights or skirted the rim of broad canyons that dropped into bottomless depths. They passed through vast chambers filled with surreal sculptures and strange formations...plants made of stone, with spiny branches subdividing and twisting as they grew from walls, floors, ceilings, anywhere and everywhere.

Careful not to touch the fragile formations, the twins enjoyed it all and expressed their appreciation. "I'm going to name this place the Stone Garden," Charis exclaimed in delight. Thus began a playful game in which she and her brother tried to give meaningful names to the various rooms and formations through which they were passing.

"This has to be the Land of Giants," Alta gasped as they passed beneath a row of huge stone monoliths that soared over fifty feet high. Formed where stalagmites rising up from the floor joined with stalactites reaching down from the roof, the vast columns were adorned with intricate layers of delicate dripstone.

"And this is the Queen's Bedroom," Charis named another lovely chamber, lightly running her fingers over flowing draperies of silken stone that gracefully cloaked the walls and ceilings.

They paused for a moment at the edge of a pool so clear and still as to be virtually invisible, eternally serene. "The Lake of the Mother's Tears," Enoch exclaimed, joining in the fun.

On and on they went, walking backward as often as forward, looking up as much as down, turning their heads, craning their necks, using their sense of touch and sight to drink in all of the beauty and newness around them. Here in this hollow, subterranean world, time and space had been altered, and the Mother had wrought her transformative work. The twins had been changed, deeply changed. Gone were the oppressive feelings of darkness and gloom, forgotten for the moment was the destruction. All that mattered was the beauty.

Passing from a particularly large chamber that Alta had appropriately named "the Big Place," the trio entered a wide, flat tunnel. In the distance, two human figures were walking toward them. The twins recognized them at once. "Father and Mother!" they cried, running toward their parents, arms outstretched. The family embraced, hugging each other long and hard, crying softly, loving each other, smelling each other's comfortable smell, feeling each other's strength and familiar sense of comfort. It was good to be together again. It was good to be together again. It was good to be home.

"You see," Enoch came up to join them. "You are not homeless. Your home is wherever you are together. Home is not a physical place. It is a state of mind, a state of being. It is within you, whenever you are with family and community and those you love."

The twins smiled at him gratefully. "Thank you," Alta said, extending one palm forward over Enoch's chest, placing his other palm over his own. "Thank you for everything."

Charis was more demonstrative. "I love you, Enoch," she cried, throwing her arms around the old man's neck and kissing him resoundingly on the cheek.

"And I love you too," Cybele said softly, taking his hand as they walked the last hundred yards to Sophia's Cave in the belly of the Great Mother.

Adima alone remained silent until they reached the entrance to the subterranean chamber. While Cybele and the twins went inside, he lagged behind, alone with his teacher. "Thank you for taking care of my children, dear friend. They are alive and unharmed because of you. Once again, I owe you more than I can ever repay." Adima placed both arms around the old man's neck and drew him close, burying his head in Enoch's shoulders as the tears flowed.

*****

Belial was thrilled. The device had worked perfectly, even better than planned. Actually, he couldn't remember setting it off or how it had gotten to such a high power level. After having drunk deeply of a particularly strong potion, the events of the previous evening were a blur. He vaguely recalled some sort of confrontation with Enoch, but his thoughts were dull and his head ached too much to think about it.

No matter. The device had worked very, very well, and that was all that was important. All that remained for him to do was convince the Council of Elders that the destruction was all Adima's fault—Adima's and Lemuria's. Belial actually believed the lie, so long had he rehearsed it, so many times had he repeated the story over and over to himself. Adima had brought them to this, having stolen the device and the technology and sold it to the Lemurians so that they could unleash it against Atlantis.

The Council would believe him, too. Early last evening, he had cancelled the demonstration, claiming that there were "technical difficulties." The delegates had grumbled and complained. Some were openly angry. They would soon focus their wrath on another, however. When he addressed the delegates today, on this third day of Homecoming, in the aftermath of the storm, it would be easy to convince them that the "technical difficulties" had, in fact, been the theft of the device by Adima and Hia.

Belial smiled as he imagined himself speaking the lie to the delegates. Not wanting to alarm his guests, he had made up the story of technical problems. He would go on to say that a massive manhunt was underway, expressing the hope that the guards would recover the device before any harm had been done. Indeed, they had tried to catch the perpetrators, but they were too slippery. Now look at what they had done! Adima and Hia were obviously traitors. Of course, the Council would have no choice. They would issue orders for their immediate arrest and trial.

Belial gloated with satisfaction. His plan was working. All was progressing as it should. So close to the truth he was, and yet so far away. Of course the Plan was working! Not Belial's plan...the Other's Plan.

*****

Kafar awoke from his long sleep feeling thick and dull. It was dark in his lab, and he had no idea what time it was or how long he had been unconscious. Fumbling around, his fingers searched for a glow bulb, which he tried in vain to light. Strange that it would not operate!

At first he could not grasp the idea that there was no power. Fumbling again, he found a candle, which he lit. In the soft, yellow glow, he looked around. The room was normal, yet it was not. What was wrong?

It suddenly struck him. All of the electrical objects were off. Not a single one was lit. He tried several power switches, but nothing worked. Everything was dead. Strange indeed. Now he began to wonder. What could have happened? He had never heard of the power being off. Power was something that everyone took for granted. Power was always there, just like the sun, which rose every morning and set every night. Power was a fact of life. Until now. What could have gone wrong?

He opened the door and walked out into the passageway. There wasn't a soul around. At first, Kafar thought he must have slept until after dark and that, since it was late at night, everyone was at home or in their private quarters within the Pyramid. He had no idea that he had slept for over twenty hours. Eventually he made his way to the main passageway. Still no signs of life. "This is getting stranger and stranger," he muttered to himself.

He stepped outside, fully expecting it to be dark. He was not prepared for the shock. It was as though he had stepped into a nightmare, a surreal world where everything was upside down, inside out, and broken. Knee deep in a gooey, oozing mud, he gazed upon a wasteland. The magnificent statue of Quetzalcoatl lay broken into fragments, the mighty head severed from the body, the body itself shattered beyond recognition into a thousand pieces.

The once spotless piazza was littered with the carcasses of birds and small animals. A few human bodies lay sprawled at precarious angles, half buried in the mud, those on their backs staring with sightless eyes at a dull, gray sky. The stench was awful. Already the dead had started to bloat and decay in the midday heat. The once-lovely piazza had become a deserted graveyard, except for the crows, vultures, and other scavengers already feasting upon the carrion.

Kafar dropped to his knees and vomited until his stomach was empty. Still he continued to be sick, great dry heaves wracking him apart, as though his body, disgusted by what it was witnessing, was trying to turn itself inside out in revulsion. "No such luck!" he muttered when he could finally stand upright again. Wandering around like one in a daze, he followed the perimeter of the Pyramid, completely unable to believe what he was seeing. The destruction was everywhere.

Could his mind have been damaged by his last encounter with the crystals? He did not think so, but one never knew. He was about to begin a series of mental exercises to test his rationality when he ran into Nargal. The man who had been responsible for bringing him to Atlantis was sitting on top of a pile of rubble, bleeding from a ghastly, jagged wound across his forehead.

"What happened?" Kafar cried, rushing to the scribe's aid.

"Hurricane, hurricane...wind, water, destruction...from the sky, from the sea, from above and below." Finding speech difficult, the wounded man babbled slowly and incoherently, making very little sense. "Everywhere at once. No time to prepare, no time. Couldn't get away. Should have said no. Should have told him to turn it off."

All at once, he stood up and grabbed Kafar's coat, staring with unrecognizing eyes. Highly agitated, he screamed and cried at the same time, his tears flowing in greasy rivulets down his bloody, dirty face. "Should have turned it off!" Nargal cried. "Should have killed him. Should have agreed to help Draco. Should have let Shakala out."

Shakala. Kafar thought of his mentor for the first time. "Where is Shakala?" he asked the dazed man.

Nargal shrugged and shook his head, mumbling under his breath. "In the dungeons, in the dungeons. Bowels collapsed. Belial wants to kill, wants to ki..." Voice choked off in mid sentence, he collapsed back onto the pile of rubble, barely breathing. Kafar placed his outer cloak under the dying man's head and tried to make him comfortable, but there was nothing he could do. With a soft sigh, Nargal shook his head and expired.

It was the first time Kafar had been this close to death, and it frightened him. Gently closing the corpse's eyes, he covered the body with his cloak. Then he offered a silent prayer and went in search of Shakala. What Nargal had said did not make sense. Why would Belial want to imprison Shakala and kill him?

Of course! he realized, as the cobwebs cleared and he remembered more of the previous day. The alchemist must have challenged Belial. He pictured the confrontation in his mind, just as though he had been there to witness it as it happened. Belial had gone into a rage and arrested the old man, and now he was going to kill him. Then, in complete defiance and disregard for life, the Master had dared to turn on the device. And this is what happened.

"My parents, what of my parents?" Kafar called out to the dead man. "Are they alive? Are they hurt, or are they gone too?" He had no idea of the extent of the damage. It might be limited to the city, although he doubted it. More likely it was widespread, encompassing the entire island, perhaps even beyond. Somehow, he was sure it was the latter. "I have to get help," he cried in frustration. "I have to find Shakala, if he's alive. He'll know what to do."

Rounding a corner of the Great Pyramid, Kafar stopped in his tracks. On the east side, the destruction had been the greatest. The stone walls and arches leading to the Temple and gardens were completely demolished, as though a titanic wrecking ball had gone berserk, pulverizing everything it its path. The Temple itself stood relatively unscathed, but it was surrounded and half-buried amid piles of rubble.

He still had not seen another living human being, although there was a lot of noise coming from somewhere ahead of him. Continuing to the north, he rounded the corner and was greeted by a sight that sent him scurrying for cover. From behind a pile of crumbled stone, Kafar looked out on an incredible scene, one that challenged his rationality more than anything he had witnessed so far. There were the soldiers herding his fellow Atlanteans into a fenced-in enclosure, standing guard over them, issuing orders, virtually imprisoning them. And standing tall in the midst of everything was the monster, Belial. The giant turned as Kafar thought his name. "He's seen me," the young scientist realized in panic.

"Seize him," Belial snarled, pointing to where Kafar had vanished around the corner of the Pyramid. Instantly, several guards started in pursuit. Kafar ran for his life. There was no time to think, just time to get away from that horrid place and hide, to get back into the Great Pyramid and lose himself within its huge maze of rooms and corridors. He was young and swift, he had a good head start, and there was so much rubble that the guards could not move quickly. Outdistancing them proved easier than he thought.

Winded, gasping for breath, he reached the entrance to the Pyramid and ducked inside before any of his pursuers were even in sight. Pausing to catch his breath, a sudden realization occurred to him. He was filthy and would leave tracks if he tried to move about in his clothes and sandals. He dashed headlong down the hall, rushed into a dormitory room, stripped off his filthy garments, and donned a plain white laboratory gown. Remaining barefoot, he dashed back down the hall to his own laboratory, where he hastily gathered supplies for the attempted rescue—rope, twine, candles, dagger, water, and other tools. Then he sought out the lower levels.

It seemed to have taken a long, long time, but in actual fact, only a few minutes had passed. There was no pursuit. The guards managed to trace him to the point where he had changed clothes, but there they lost him. It was futile to try and search for anyone in that multilevel warren of twisting, turning passages. Returning to Belial, they reported their failure, assuming it would mean their death. But the Master surprised them.

"No matter," he boomed. "Let him be. Let him find the alchemist if he so chooses. Let them converse. Let them scheme. Let them think they can make a difference. They will both be dead before the sun rises on a new day." And the Beast threw back its head and laughed long and hard.

*****

Down and down Kafar went, ever deeper into the Earth, past his own level, past the level on which he had found the aberrations. He had no idea that there were so many levels to the Great Pyramid. It penetrated as deeply into the ground as it soared above. He wandered about for hours, completely alone. It was only a matter of chance that he found the vaulted passageway leading to the dungeons. Or was it? Could it have been that Another wanted him to find them? That it was part of the Plan that he find Shakala and have one last conversation with the old man?

Kafar stood before a flight of stone steps that led down into a small chamber. A strange combination of letters and numbers was carved into the stone lintel above the doorway.

ALCOR   59-59-50

At the foot of the stairs, in the center of the room, a life-sized statue guarded the entrance to a narrow tunnel. Holding his torch higher, Kafar examined the hideous figure. Its left leg was horribly bent and twisted. "Asmodeus!" He gasped out the name of the lame demon. Almost dropping the torch, he shrank back in terror, so great was the shock of recognition.

Etched into the wall behind the demon was a pattern of stars, forming the figure of the Great Bear that floated majestically in the night sky over Atlantis. Four winged angels pointed to the sixth star in the constellation, the double star known as Alcor. Another inscription formed a half circle over the darkened portal.

BY This sign you will conquer.

Kafar knew where he was now—at the entrance to the spiral labyrinth that was rumored to exist beneath the Great Pyramid. This was the maze of legend, at the center of which lay a great treasure guarded by an equally great demon. Could the maze also contain other secrets? he wondered, such as the bodies of the missing enemies of State who had disappeared over the years? Could part of the maze also be a dungeon?

Kafar seemed to think this was so. He was not interested in any golden treasure, not today. Perhaps the dungeons weren't too deep within the maze. Perhaps, with a bit of luck and ingenuity, he'd be able to explore this fabled place and find the human treasure for which he was seeking—Shakala. Kafar remembered the legend that his mother had told him when he was but a boy.

> Within the innermost cavern lies the great treasure, guarded by a ferocious monster who stands ready to devour any who dare try to uncover the secret of the maze. In order to conquer the monster and attain the treasure, one must be well prepared.

> The Initiate is given the thread by Ariadne, the Spider Goddess. Only in this way can he return after penetrating into the dark underworld and seeking out the monster who lurks there. For to do otherwise means certain death!

Kafar shuddered as he thought of being trapped alone in the depths of the Earth, with no hope of rescue. He could wander around in there for ages and never find the center or the treasure or his way out...not without a map or a guide, and he had neither. What was he to do? "The Thread of Ariadne," he mused, thinking of the legend. "I wonder..."

He had plenty of twine—hundreds of yards of it coiled over his shoulder. It was a simple matter to fasten one end near the entrance and tie the other end around his waist. Thus would he be able to retrace his steps with ease. Confidently, he entered the tunnel. The maze was structured and ordered; he knew that as soon as he stepped within. This was going to be easier than he thought. First came a series of left turns, followed by a straight path, after which came a pattern of alternating rights and lefts. To Kafar's scientific mind, the geometric design was simple and straightforward, and he walked with confidence, his bare feet making no sound on the smooth stone floor.

He came at last to a dark, musty-smelling tunnel hewn out of the solid bedrock. At regular intervals along each side, massive oak doors were set deeply into the living rock on rusty iron hinges. Enormous iron locks and small barred windows set high in each door indicated the nature of the chambers. They were prison cells! Smoky wicks burning in vats of oil lined the walls, providing fitful light and casting grotesque, flickering shadows. Kafar knew instinctively that this was the right place.

"Shakala," he called softly. "Shakala, are you here?" He continued to walk along the corridor, pausing before each cell to call the old man's name. At most of the doors he got a faint response. "Yes, I'm here," or "Who is that?" or simply a cough or a grunt. But the voices were unfamiliar, and when he peered through the tiny windows, the living skeletons looking back at him were unrecognizable, hardly the man for whom he was searching.

The tunnel continued to slope downward in a gentle curve. Having wandered for so long, Kafar had lost all sense of direction. He did not know if he was heading north, south, east, or west. Fortunately, the twine was still firmly attached, so he would be able to retrace his steps and find his way out. He was at the end of the tunnel now. Only one door left, set into the middle of the wall at the back of the cul-de-sac in which the passage ended. The light was dimmer here, but he could see the heavy door directly in front of him.

"Shakala," he called again. "It is I, Kafar. Are you in there?"

"I am." There was the distinct rattle of chains, then the familiar face of the alchemist appeared in the window. The two men let their fingers embrace through the bars. "What has happened?" Shakala wanted to know immediately. Even as deeply buried as he was, he had felt the vibrations during the night. When no one had come with food or water, he had feared the worst. Now Kafar confirmed his suspicions.

"It's like a war zone," the younger man told him, "like walking through the rubble of a Lemurian bombing. I've seen pictures of such things, but never until today have I experienced it. You can't imagine what it's like. It can't be described, it can only be lived. And I'll tell you, I never want to live through it again!" he declared vehemently, although he knew he would eventually have to leave the Pyramid. Now, though, he was filled with guilt and remorse. "I'm so sorry for what I did. I feel responsible..."

"No time for such nonsense," Shakala interrupted him harshly. "There is work to be done, and you have to do it. If you are really sorry and want to help, you will do this. If not, go now and let me die in peace."

Kafar was taken aback by the stinging words of his mentor. "What do you mean?" he cried, only too anxious to help his teacher. "Of course I'm sorry and want to help. Just tell me what to do."

The prisoner's face softened a little behind the bars. He had not intended to hurt the young man's feelings, but the urgency of the situation required extreme measures. Now that he had Kafar's attention, he could relax and explain his plan.

"I'm trapped in here, unless you can find a key and get me out," Shakala sounded resigned to his fate. "And somehow, I don't think you're going to find the key. No matter." He dangled a rolled piece of parchment through the bars. The edges were ragged, and it was tied with a piece of cloth torn from the old man's robe.

"This parchment contains the instructions for stopping Belial from effectively using the device," Shakala explained. "They are the instructions for sabotaging the Fire Crystals. You must take the parchment to Adima and give it to him—only to him, do you understand? He will know what to do." His voice anxious and insistent, his fingers gripping the bars with such intensity that his knuckles turned white, Shakala stared at his would-be rescuer, repeating the question. "Do you understand?"

"I understand." Kafar was miffed. "But why Adima? I'm just as capable of doing this. More so, in fact. The crystals are my life. No one knows them better than I do."

"You cannot gain access to the crystals," Shakala explained impatiently, his face pressed against the bars. "Don't you think I've thought of that? Those crystals are hidden and secured behind magical doors. You would never find them, and even if you did, you could not gain access."

"What makes you think Adima can?" Kafar asked, still not convinced.

"Because he has the power," came the simple answer. "He understands the ways of the Ancients. You may not understand, as I did not for so long. But a man's mind grows very clear when he is facing his own death. And it is all very clear to me now." The flickering light cast dark shadows on the old man's face. Framed as he was in the tiny window, Shakala looked pale and drawn. "Adima is the one," he sighed, as though reluctant to admit the truth even now. "He has always been the one. And he will stop Belial, one way or another. However, he needs allies. We have fought him long enough. Now it is time to help him. Take this, therefore, and go."

The old man thrust the parchment into Kafar's outstretched fingers. "You may find him at Elysia, if it is still standing, which I doubt. In that case, I suggest you try the area in and around the Lighthouse. If he is not there, he will be. Or the Keeper of the Light will be. Finding one is the same as finding the other." The old man's tone grew softer, losing its sense of urgency. There were tears in his eyes as he forced his withered hands through the bars. "Now, before you go, give me your hand one last time."

Shakala reached for his student's fingers, gripping them with deep fervor and intensity. "You have been like a son to me," he said lovingly, "the son I never had. I am so proud of you. I respect you, I admire you, and most of all, I love you. I could not have asked for more from a son of my own. I could not have had a better son."

The prisoner paused, crying softly as the intensity of his emotions overwhelmed his ability to speak. Kafar gently caressed the old man's face, wiping away the warm salt tears, remaining silent until Shakala found his voice again. "I have nothing to give you other than my love and my advice. My love you have always. My only advice is to be very, very careful. Belial knows all. He can read minds. He is a sorcerer. If there is a way to find you, he will try to succeed. Be silent as the wind, cautious as a fox, quiet as a mouse, dark as the night. Do not let the Beast find you. You are my last hope."

Kafar was weeping openly now. "I can't leave you here," he cried, dropping the torch and throwing his weight against the door, trying desperately but futilely to break it down. The massive barrier would not budge. Time and again he launched his body against the unyielding timbers. Time and again they mocked him. At last, exhausted, out of breath, and severely bruised, he gave up.

"I cannot free you." Kafar was sobbing, holding the old man's fingers tightly in his own. How he wanted to break down the door and hold him, carrying him from this frightful grave where he was buried alive. But he was powerless to do so, possessing neither the physical strength nor the spiritual skills. Kafar had lost, and he knew it. He had come to a dead end within the labyrinth beneath the Great Pyramid in the dungeons of Belial. There was nothing left to do but pour forth his anger and grief. How could he say good-bye to someone for the last time, knowing he would never see him again? How could he let go of him whom he loved?

Then came the images of his own parents reaching out to him as they died, calling his name as they breathed their last, and the tears flowed harder. And while Kafar cried, the candles sputtered and demonic shadows danced on the walls. From its place of concealment deep within the labyrinth, the Guardian Demon paced back and forth, its mocking laughter echoing among the stone passageways. It would enjoy devouring this pitiful mortal who did not know the magic words. The treasure was safe, for the moment. Let him take the worthless writing to the upper world. He would never reach his destination. By midnight he would be dead. The creature licked its lips and slunk from the maze by way of a secret exit.

Shakala let the young man cry, and he cried also. At last, there were no more tears for either of them. There was nothing more to be said. "I love you, too, old man," Kafar said softly, squeezing the feeble old fingers tightly one last time. "And I am truly grateful to you for all that you have given me—your wisdom, your advice, your scientific learning, and your love. You are a good and kind man. May you always be blessed." Then, without a backward glance, Kafar turned, picked up the torch, and ran back along the passageway.

"May the Messenger lend you his wings this day," Shakala's voice rang in his ears as he rounded the first turn. Kafar knew that he would never see the old man alive again.

*****

Alone in his cell, Shakala prepared for death. So much to think about, yet his thoughts were surprisingly clear. He knew why. The *Double* had left him—the anti-man, the merciless and inhuman Shadow element in his human soul. The part of himself that had forsaken family and friends, companionship and love, choosing instead to live in opposition to the good, the true, and the beautiful. The part of himself who had formed an unholy alliance with Belial, embraced his lies, and helped in the creation of the device. Dehumanizing his activities, dragging him down into Belial's inhumane world, it had forced him to forsake the dictates of his own conscience.

All his life, Shakala had experienced the constant tension between the longings of his soul and the vicious desires of the Double. That tension was gone now because the Double was gone. That shadow being of fear and darkness had left precisely three days ago, at the exact instant that Adima had looked him in the eye during the address to the Homecoming assemblage.

He had felt it go, had almost heard it go. Why? Because the Double was afraid. Because it was a creature of the shadows, a being of fear and darkness, it dared not face the light. It had seen the light in Adima's eyes that day, and it had recognized it as the Light of Spirit. Not daring to face such light, it had fled. For the past three days, Shakala had been filled with an inner sense of peace and harmony the likes of which he had never felt before. His thoughts had come easily and peacefully. Now Death stood by his side, waiting patiently for him to lay his wasted body aside in favor of existence in the Light of Spirit.

"It will not be long," the old man muttered to the shadows. "Patience, patience, please, while I collect my thoughts and compose myself."

The guards had not thought to search him when they had thrown him into the cell. He still had a small ceremonial dagger strapped to his leg and a crumpled sheet of parchment in one of his pockets. It was that dagger which he had used to pierce his flesh and collect enough blood to use as ink for his letter to Adima. It had taken a long time and a lot of blood, writing with the point in the flickering semidarkness. But he was patient and persevering. Now his responsibilities to the people of Atlantis were ended. The only responsibility that was left was to himself.

The exhausted old man leaned back against the rock. He tried to clear his mind of all worldly thoughts, but it was not so easy. His head was abuzz with all sorts of chatter. First came the regrets, all those phrases beginning with, "I would have..., I should have..., I could have..., I might have..."

"If only I'd done what I really wanted to do," he cried in frustration. "I wasted my opportunities. If only I'd followed my dream and my heart instead of my pride and my greed. I thought a little time was given me as mine alone, a little time called my life. So short a time it has been from birth to death, a narrow current in the ocean of eternity." Pacing back and forth in his cell, Shakala suddenly realized that he was speaking out loud.

Who cares! he thought. It's not like I'm disturbing anybody. It's not like I have any secrets left to keep. That's when he heard the voice for the first time—a soft, sibilant whisper coming from an even deeper blackness at the far end of the cell.

"Shakala," it whispered his name. *"Shakala, why do you hesitate to come to me?"*

"Who's there?" the old man cried, peering intently into the darkness. He could not see anything, but something was definitely there. Of course he knew who it was—the disembodied voice of Death itself, its awesome Presence filling the cell with a deep, overwhelming blackness.

He had felt Death's nearness for many months now, but never had he spoken directly to the shadowy form as it loomed beside him. He had been too afraid, denying the possibility that Death might be there for him. Now, though, his feelings had changed. Both repelled and attracted at the same time, the old man tried to peer into the gloom for a glimpse of the figure behind the voice. All he could see were swirling mists of an even deeper blackness.

Shivering, Shakala was reminded of the grim tales he had heard of the chill of the grave and Death's cold presence. Yet the room was not cold. In fact, this Presence was quite comforting. This shiver, then, was something different—a thrill of extreme excitement and trepidation upon embracing the ultimate unknown, the greatest of the mysteries. His scientific self leaped at the prospect, ready and eager to enter the void. His human heart, however, hesitated.

Was this the right thing to do? How could he be sure? What if this Presence were not kind, sweet Death, but something more sinister, something evil? It was possible, after all, was it not? His grandfather had warned him of the trickster demons who wanted to torment his soul. Could this be one of them? Still, he had nothing to lose and no real choice anyway. Life was as good as over. Without food or water, sick as he was, there were but a few days left, perhaps only a few hours. Deciding to be bold, Shakala addressed the unknown Presence enshrouded in the darkness. "Who are you?" he whispered hoarsely.

"Who do you think I am?"

"Are you Death?"

"I am."

"And you have come for me?"

"I am here to offer you a way out. I have been waiting for you for a long time. It is not quite your time yet, but if you are willing, you may cross over sooner..."

As the voice trailed off, suddenly the fears and doubts abated. The quiet words were soft and soothing and very, very welcome. Shakala was not completely convinced yet, but he would listen to what Death had to say, even engage in a dialogue with the grim specter before him. There was so much he wanted to say, so much to confess, and now, apparently, the opportunity for purging and release was being given to him.

"You have achieved success," the voice of Death continued. *"What more can you ask?"*

The dying man snorted derisively. "Success?" he repeated. "You call what I have achieved success? All my life I have been in conflict, yet I thought I was in control, that I had choices, that I was free, that I could escape the fear and troubles of the world. How wrong I was, how disillusioned and misled!"

"I thought I could choose the roads that would lead out of conflict. I walked them all. The road of the good son, which led to a dying grandfather who cursed and despised me. The road of the frustrated student, which led to rejection by the Academy of Science because I was not quite good enough. The road of occult alchemist, which has led to a cancer-ridden body and imprisonment in the darkest of dungeons, disgraced and forlorn and without hope." Shakala felt his skin crawl as a chill breeze gusted across the cell. Death was speaking once again.

"So many roads, so many seeming different ways. On some you walked with fear and dread, experiencing the full-blown, excruciating pain for all to see. Then you embraced Belial's world, thinking it would offer consolation and escape from the problems of life."

Shakala shivered at the truth of Death's words. How well it knew him! How well it had observed his life.

"You are right," he agreed. "In fact, that road brought a semblance of happiness for a while, until the bleakness entered once again, and I realized that the pain had never really left. Always it was there, gnawing, ever gnawing at my entrails."

To which Death calmly replied, *"So many seeming choices, so many seeming different ends. Yet in truth, all leading back to where you started. All leading hopelessly round in circles. All leading nowhere. All leading but to me."*

Shakala shuddered as another shiver of cold air passed over him. He was suddenly very frightened, not of Death itself, but of retribution beyond the grave, punishment for all of the sins he had committed against himself and humanity. "I am afraid!" he cried, rushing to the door of the cell, rattling the bars, trying desperately to escape, "afraid of punishment for my sins, afraid of the great debt I owe to all of Atlantis."

Again the soft voice whispered from the darkness. *"There is nothing to fear in my embrace,"* Death assured him. *"You were only obeying orders."*

The old man calmed somewhat and laughed disgustedly. "Only obeying orders? Like the guards who blindly obey Belial? Like the Adepts who hearken to his beck and call? Like the courtiers who pander to his every need? Like the High Priestess who shares his bed and offers him her body? Like the people who trust him to do the right thing? Like anybody who needs an excuse, wreaking havoc and destruction because someone in authority ordered me to do so? That is no excuse. It never is!"

For a second time, the cold breeze swept across the cell. *"You had no choice,"* Death replied. *"Otherwise, you would have found me even sooner, before your time on Earth was through."*

"Ah, but I did have a choice," the old man countered tearfully. "I have free will. I could have said no. I am responsible." Sinking to his knees, face in his hands, Shakala sobbed out his guilt and remorse. So much pain, such deep, expressionless grief, yet all he could manage to say was "I'm sorry, I'm sorry, I am so, so sorry!" over and over and over again. At last there were no more tears. The cell grew unutterably quiet.

"So then, do what you must do," Death whispered. *"You have admitted the truth. Now come to me and embrace me. Let go of struggling with the pain of your guilt over the destruction of Atlantis and in having aided and abetted Belial. Take your life and give it to me, and I will give you rest and release from the pain."*

"You are right," Shakala gasped, straightening up and gripping the dagger firmly in his hand. "I must atone. I must pay the price...with my life. I am not fit to live. Besides," he reasoned in his fevered brain, "life is all futile anyway—futile and hopeless and worthless and a lie. It is all for naught. I must die. I have no choice."

"Where is this truth written in the *Book of Life*?" he screamed bitterly, his voice echoing out into the corridor and along the tunnel. But there was no one to hear, no one to answer his desperate question but the other poor wretches like himself, whose reason had left them long ago. Now they were drooling, babbling idiots. Let Shakala scream all he wanted. There was no one there to care, save only Death.

"Show me, you wise and mighty Ancients! Show me where it is written that there is no choice where every end is sure. That all the seeming different roads are just one road, and that one leads but to Death. There is no pathway offered by the world. All lead to nowhere. If only I had known then what I know now. I could have saved myself so much time."

In the ensuing silence, Death smiled its grim, rapacious smile. It had won, as it always did, as it always would. The grave had risen up and embraced the man, pulling him down into its cold and gloomy depths, covering him with dirt and darkness, blocking out the Light, returning him to the dust from which he had been formed.

Shakala sensed the smile and returned it with one of his own. All fear had left him now. His mind was made up, and he was ready. "And so I choose now to step off the path." The old man spoke for the last time. "To step out of the world; to cease my endless, painful searching where there is no gold, no Grail. I choose to stop struggling and striving for that which I know now does not exist; to end the excruciatingly painful process of holding the Double at bay while trying to overcome its merciless influences. If nowhere is my final goal, then I will not prolong the inevitable. I am old and sick and tired. Oblivion will be a comfort after all."

He leaned back against the cold black stone, almost spent. He was through speaking, and a deep weariness swept over him as all his bodily functions began to shut down.

In the darkness, Death waited patiently. There was no rush. The end was assured.

Taking the dagger once again, Shakala had one last act to perform. Feeling for the vessels, he inserted the razor-sharp blade at a point just above the place where the wrist connected to the hand and drew the cold steel backward for three inches up his forearm. Twice he repeated the maneuver on each arm, opening the veins and letting his lifeblood spill out onto the cold, dirty stone floor.

He lay back, gasping for air. Surprisingly, there was no pain, only a delicious wave of release as his senses faded one by one.

As he lay bleeding, a light began to shine, gradually taking shape in the blackness. It was a very bright light, but it did not hurt his eyes. Shakala decided to move toward it, reaching out with both arms. In an instant, he was gone.

CHAPTER 44

*The hills are shadows, and they flow
From form to form, and nothing stands;
They melt like mist, the solid lands,
Like clouds they shape themselves and go.*

—Alfred, Lord Tennyson

Beyond the city walls, the people were virtually on their own, for the soldiers did not venture into the countryside. So much the better, at least for now. Unlike their urban brethren, the rural folk were free to mill about in relative peace, making it easier to adjust to the loss, sift through the wreckage, and decide what to do next.

Adima and Cybele were the first to leave the Cave, stepping out into a world transformed. Now they stood above the broken ruin that had once been Elysia. Alta and Charis were aghast. Enoch had tried to prepare them, but the reality was far worse than anything their innocent minds had imagined. Home—the only home they had ever known—had been obliterated in one single, devastating act of Nature.

Adima scanned the rubble, searching for the nest and bodies of the blue jays, but there was no trace. He could only hope that they were all right, but that was doubtful, for the storm had been too severe. He sighed, realizing that he would never know the true fate of the delicate creatures who had inspired him and graced the gardens with their beauty and songs only a few short days ago. There was nothing to salvage, for there was nothing left. The gardens had been washed into the sea, the trees had been bent and broken, the veranda pulverized. Even the corn, springing up year after year, ever since they had planted it on their wedding day.

A few scattered remnants of flotsam bobbed on the surface of the lagoon, where the erosive force of wind and tides had done their most creative work. A sand bar had formed in the center, and the river had spilled over its banks to follow a new channel. Being one of the strongest of architectural structures, part of the dome itself was still standing, The wind, however, had broken all of the glass, and the storm surge had flooded in and swept everything away.

Holding tightly to each other, the family looked down from above, surveying the ruin. No one spoke, for there was nothing to say. Deeper than words could express were the feelings of loss—loss of home, loss of possessions, loss of roots. They were all gone.

"Yet not all gone," Cybele said, smiling through her tears. "We still have each other. We are together and unhurt. Houses can be rebuilt, gardens replanted, new memories created through new experiences. We will build again."

And build they would, although not for a while yet. First they had other things to do, more important priorities. The rebuilding would come later, not in the form they imagined, not on the scale they imagined, not in the place they imagined, nor by whom they imagined. For the task of rebuilding would fall to the children.

The ocean breeze picked up, and a light drizzle began to fall, yet no one made a move to seek shelter. Although they were together, each felt so alone...alone with a ravaged home and fond memories and shattered hopes and dreams. Down they went, descending into the ruin, picking their way amidst the wreckage. Slowly they drifted through the empty rooms, each lost in a personal reverie, each with personal memories of the joys and sorrows they had shared there for so many years.

Father and King memories stirred in Adima. He remembered how he had felt when the point of his spade had first broken ground. How he had anchored the foundation, placed the beams, and built the dome with his own hands, piece by piece. How proud and satisfied he had been—a young king creating his castle and kingdom, although he hadn't known it at the time.

Mother and Lover memories stirred in Cybele. She and Adima had loved each other there. Their children had been conceived and born there. With Sophia and Adima beside her, she had brought the twins into the world. Face first they had emerged...first Charis, then Alta a few minutes later. How joyful the lovers and parents had been, experiencing the bright promise of the future and long, happy lives together.

Childhood and Innocent memories stirred in Alta and Charis. Playing there, toddling in the gardens, swimming in the lagoon, feeding the squirrels and deer and birds, this was where they had learned to walk and talk, where they had been introduced to Dolphin and Osprey and Turtle. On that rocky point, Charis had fallen and cut herself. She still carried the scar on her leg. Over there, Alta had composed his first poem in honor of a butterfly releasing itself from its cocoon.

One by one, the family offered their thanks in each room. Then they wandered out into what had once been the garden. The late afternoon light cast long shadows as they walked among the tangle of broken plants and trees. The silence was unnerving. The birds, the birds whom they loved and who loved them, were gone.

"What now?" Alta broke the silent reverie, speaking for himself and his sister. In their young minds and hearts they had no idea what to do, so they turned to the only source who might.

"The first thing to do is be grateful that we are alive and unharmed and together," Cybele reminded them all. "In our sorrow over what we have lost, let us not forget to acknowledge that which we have." Taking them by the hand, she closed her eyes and stood silently for a moment, her auburn hair blowing in the strong offshore breeze. The wind sighed loudly as it gusted around them, but for this moment, Cybele's voice was stronger than the wind.

"Thank you, Father and Mother, that we are safe and well and whole," she prayed in a clear, pure voice. *"Thank you that we are together with the ones we love. Thank you for the strength and talents and willingness to endure and carry on and rebuild. We accept the present, and we place the future in your hands."*

She grew silent, letting each one stand with eyes closed, offering their personal prayers, making their personal petitions. Slowly, Adima opened a pouch of tobacco and handed some to each of them. Following his lead, the family scattered the sacred herb to the four winds in an offering of thanksgiving, purification, and release.

Then the tears came, and there was no holding them back. All of the sorrow, grief, and fear just gushed forth. How long they held each other in their ruined garden cannot be said. It was a deep and timeless moment, very different and very personal for each of them. After a while, they slowly walked back up the hill, whispering their farewells in unison. "Thank you, and good-bye."

From the edge of the path that led to the Good Red Road, Adima looked out to sea, lost in thought. The first order of business was seeing to the safety of his family and friends. This meant ensuring that the survivors among the Children of the Law of One and his own wife and children had proper food, clothing, and shelter and were protected from any new dangers that Belial might have in store. There was only one solution, only one possible answer to Alta's question. "We will go to the Arks," he said. "It is time to leave Atlantis."

*****

Kafar waited until it was completely dark before leaving the Great Pyramid for the last time. Shakala's note was safely clutched in his hand. Picking his way through the rubble and filth, he carefully made his way out of the city. It took a long time, because with each little sound, each passing shadow, he hid himself until he was sure there was no danger. At last he left the third ring and crossed the bridge over the outermost canal. Now he could relax a little. There were no more guards, no more danger of being spotted by Belial. He sat for almost fifteen minutes, trying to calm himself and catch his breath. He was trembling, so very, very frightened. After all, everything depended on him.

"Now where do I go?" he asked to no one in particular as he stood at the beginning of the Good Red Road. Shakala had suggested that he try Elysia first, although Adima probably would not be there. If not, the Lighthouse was next. Kafar sighed. It was going to be a long night.

The clouds were beginning to clear, and a half moon offered something in the way of illumination. He knew the way fairly well. Everyone in the city knew of Elysia. He had never visited the place, but he had seen it from afar many times.

The Good Red Road led straight south across the Great Plain for about a mile, where it crossed the River of the Rising Sun. From this point, the way turned inland for a while, passing for five miles through a stretch of old-growth evergreens. Gingerly, Kafar stepped out onto the road. This was quite possibly the most dangerous part of his journey because he was so exposed. He was in full view of anyone who might have been looking.

Turning around, he cast a last look at the ruined city. No longer a gleaming jewel shining in the night on the edge of the sea, it lay now in total darkness, save for the glow of several small fires that still burned. The familiar shapes of the Temple and Pyramid were silhouetted on the horizon, and far off to the east, the huge mass of the Lighthouse loomed dark and apparently deserted against the eastern sky like a giant yet impotent phallus.

Kafar had barely stepped out onto the Great Plain when he smelled an awful stench. It was a sickening, gut-wrenching odor, like that of long-dead flesh rotting on a garbage heap. His first thought was that there were victims of the storm nearby, their bodies already decomposing. But the newly dead would not smell so bad, not this quickly. This was something different. He broke into a trot, trying to put the carrion behind him. After five minutes of steady jogging, however, the smell was stronger than ever. How was that possible? No fixed odor could travel that far, especially without a breeze.

Pausing in the middle of the Plain, he cocked an ear. Was that the sound of footsteps behind him? Looking back over his shoulder, he saw only the empty ground shining in the ghostly light. He took a few more tentative paces, completely exposed now. There was no place to take cover, not even a tree or a low-growing bush. That's when he heard the growl. It was soft at first, coming from behind him, almost at his elbow. He wheeled, startled, as a huge, misshapen figure loomed up behind him. At that instant, the clouds parted and the Plain was bathed in pale moonlight.

What Kafar saw froze the blood in his veins and locked him into immobility. Now he recognized the smell, remembering his first encounter with the noxious odor. It was the aberration from the laboratory, of that he was certain. And such an aberration it was! Almost eight feet tall, naked, and covered with filthy, matted dark hair. It stood on two feet, its huge, misshapen arms dangling almost to its knees, a giant caricature of a man—hairy, horrible, hideous. But it was the face that terrified him the most. Huge yellow fangs protruded from wide thick lips below a broad, flat nose. And in the center of its forehead, gleaming malevolently in the pale moonlight, was a single wicked eye.

Terror swept over Kafar like a heavy black fog. His heart fluttered wildly in his chest, and his skin crawled. "I'm going to die," he realized, and there was nothing he could do about it. Was it his imagination, or was the creature smiling at him? It stood there looking at him, grinning horribly, licking its thick, pulpy lips, staring at him from its single, glittering eye. There was murder in that eye! Roaring mightily, the creature took a single step toward him. It was enough to return him to his senses.

There was no way he could defend himself against such a powerful antagonist, so he took the only possible course of action. He turned and ran for his life, forgetting Shakala, forgetting the note still clutched in his fist, forgetting Adima, forgetting the destruction, forgetting everything but that hideous eye chasing him.

Kafar was fleet-footed, but he was no match for the giant strides of the monster. With each step, he smelled the awful stench of death coming closer. Before he had gone fifty yards, the creature was upon him. A huge, hairy paw landed heavily on his shoulder. Sharp, needlelike talons clawed into his back, and he was lifted off his feet.

"This can't be happening," he gasped as the world turned upside down and he was shaken roughly. The hideous face loomed close, and the fetid breath assailed his nostrils. Kafar's last thoughts were of his parents as the sharp yellow fangs closed over his jugular and he mercifully lost consciousness.

*****

High up in the darkened shell of the Lighthouse, a black-robed figure watched the grisly drama unfold on the Plain far below. A magnificent bird of prey perched on his shoulder. No stranger to death, a mighty predator in its own right, even Osprey flinched as it watched those fearsome talons close.

"Another light snuffed out," Enoch sighed as he watched the murder, powerless to interfere. It was over in a few moments. The aberration dropped Kafar's lifeless body to the ground and loped off down the Good Red Road, eventually disappearing into the forest south of the city. "Did it take the letter?" Enoch looked at the raptor, his lips remaining shut as he sent his thoughts directly to the bird, trusting his ally's sharp eyes more than his own.

Osprey looked at him, as if to say, "No."

"It is time, then," Enoch wasted no further words. "Go to the body, take the note, and deliver it to Adima." With a rustle of feathers, the great bird flew to the window ledge, where it paused for one last moment of communion with its human companion. "Be swift, my friend," Enoch crooned softly, stroking the soft head. "The next step is yours to take, and then your task is through."

Tears glistened in the old man's eyes. "Fly away from Atlantis. Fly to freedom. Join the others of your kind who have already left. You have done well. You have been a trusted and faithful ally. I will miss you. Farewell until we meet again." That was all. There was nothing left to be said.

Releasing itself, the bird took to the air, circling a few times to get its bearings. High above the Lighthouse it hovered, soaring majestically on the wind, its white breast shining in the moonlight. "Kreeagh!" Its shrill valedictory echoed through the night air. Then it dove headlong toward the Plain, flying at incredible speed. Landing beside the body, it searched with its beak among the folds of the dead man's robes. At last, parchment clasped tightly in a single talon, Osprey took to the air once again, this time heading south along the beach in search of Adima.

*****

A few miles to the south, Adima and Hia stood on a low rise above what had once been Elysia. Having returned at Enoch's request, they waited now in the darkness for the message they had been told would come. How unlike these two allies were! Adima was the poet, the thinker, the visionary, the King. Hia, on the other hand, had followed the path of the Warrior, having learned the skills of the Warrior, the ways of wildness. Hia was a doer, never hesitating to enter the fray, taking immediate action whenever action was called for. Unlike the King, the Warrior was not concerned with philosophy or theory. Thus, they balanced each other.

Long ago, in Spirit, before they had ever chosen their present bodies and life situations, these two souls had agreed to enter into the three-dimensional world and do their part to help ensure the success of the Plan. Over the years, they had lost all memory of their pact. Why is not known. Perhaps it was the shock of coming into the physical world, perhaps it was intentional—to motivate them to amass more worldly experiences.

They had been born at almost the same time, but there the similarity ended. For almost fifty years they had lived their separate lives, growing up in different worlds, on different continents. Each had his own unique set of experiences, each developed his own set of skills, hopes, fears, dreams, talents, allies, and life experiences. Then, at the perfect moment in time, they had met at the appointed place to perform the rightful deed, carrying out the aims of Spirit as human consciousness evolved along the Grail Path.

Adima's attention was drawn to a faint rush of wings high above the cliff. Sensing Osprey's presence before actually seeing the bird, he looked up. High above, the raptor circled slowly, a dark speck silhouetted against the pale, billowing clouds. The man thrilled at the sight. Osprey never failed to stir a deep sense of adventure in his breast. Reaching out his arm, Adima stood perfectly still, inviting the raptor to join him on the ground. "Come to me, little brother," came the barely audible whisper.

"Krreeeeeeeeag!" came the acknowledgment as the great bird dropped like a stone to land ever so gently on the outstretched arm.

"What is this?" Adima asked, gently taking the parchment that was still gripped in a razor-sharp talon. Powerful waves of emotion washed over him. Instantly he knew...knew of the death of Shakala and of the death of Kafar. His reaction was the same as Enoch's.

"A good man, just confused," he thought of Shakala. "Another light snuffed out," he repeated Enoch's eulogy of Kafar. "They're going out one by one," he remarked to Hia, "all of the stars in the sky."

The Islander nodded his head, remembering the prophecy in the *Book of Mysteries*.

AND THE BEAST WILL LASH ITS TAIL
AND SWEEP A THIRD OF THE STARS FROM THE SKY.

An ill wind blew in from the east, and the troubled ocean foamed restlessly in the lagoon below the ruined dome. Adima looked at Osprey, still perched silently on his outstretched arm. A moment of silent communion passed between them—two powerful creatures, two warriors—a bird of prey and a man of prey. Two allies, two friends, two kindred spirits. Then Osprey spread its wings and lifted itself gracefully into the air. Adima watched as it soared higher and higher, heading out over the island to the southwest, following the others of its kind to safety in their new world, away from the doomed island forever.

"I shall go and seek out this aberration," Hia declared, slinging his quiver of arrows over his shoulder and picking up his bow.

"Be careful," Adima admonished. "There has been enough bloodshed for one day."

"If more blood is spilled this night, it will not be mine," Hia replied grimly as he disappeared over the ridge.

*****

Through a tangle of ruined forest, under the light of a pale half moon, a solitary figure moved. No sound he made, his passing known only to himself and the kindred Elementals who watched him go by. This was Hia, leader of the red race of Turtle Island—a creature of the land, part of the forest, part of the night. If he chose to let himself be seen, he would be seen. Likewise, if he chose to remain silent and hidden, not even his mother would sense his presence from a few yards distant.

He was, first and foremost, a wild man, deeply at home in the world of Nature, the bosom of the Great Mother. Having first conquered his most formidable opponent—his own ego—having first achieved victory in understanding his own Self, only then had he ventured forth into the world, full of Warrior wisdom.

Having explored and conquered the wilderness within, so he had set out to explore and conquer the wilderness without. He went forth a true Warrior, senses pure, attending to the energy pulsing within himself and in the veins of the Great Mother, cognizant of how all of the elements worked and played together in the Dance of Life. Humble in his strength, alert to all things that were around him, he mixed daring, expertise, and unparalleled cunning. Never had he tasted defeat in battle. He knew who to fight, when to fight, and how to fight. And he would fight very soon, of that he was certain.

Owl hooted from the darkness above him. Hia paused to listen, cocking his head to one side, waiting for the bird of night to speak again. "Whooooooooo?" the familiar questioning call repeated itself.

Looking about in the moonlight, Hia found himself in a stand of aspen trees that had not suffered the effects of the storm. Old-growth monarchs, they had remained relatively intact and undamaged by the fury of the wind. Yet even these giants could not have gone so unscathed, unless they had been protected by some enchantment. Might that be the case? he wondered. It was very possible. Aspen were sacred trees. Perhaps there was a special god or goddess who protected this forest and to whom this grove was sacred.

A third time, Owl called out to him. "Whooooooooo?"

Now he was certain. This was, indeed, an enchanted grove, and Owl was inviting him to pause for a while and receive a message. All senses alert, Hia stood absolutely still and listened to the forest creatures speak to him.

"There is no hurry," Cricket chirped. "The killer is following a leisurely pace, confident that it is alone and unchallenged. You can catch up to the creature any time you want."

"But first, you have something else to do," Squirrel chattered. "Before you can do battle, you must prepare yourself for the challenges that lie ahead."

"When better than nighttime in the forest?" Deer questioned. "Where better than in this sacred grove of aspen?"

Hia smiled in the darkness. Everything around him brought memories of home, the cool aspen forests that carpeted the slopes of the high places he loved so well. The familiar voices of the night—Owl and the others—urged him to take time out and attend to the message and the answer that was even now blowing on the winds of change. Above his head, Swan swam silently through a vast, milky river of stars. A warm breeze caressed his bare skin. Hia knew where he was now...the *Sacred Grove of Hesperia*, where the past was revealed and mysteries unfathomed. Would it be so tonight? he wondered.

"Help me remember," Hia whispered to the trees and the stars and the moon. "Open my mind, that I may know." Standing perfectly still, the Warrior listened as the sacred trees sang to him of the time before his birth. The strains of a lyre wafted on gentle currents of air, playing an old song. He had never heard it before, but he recognized the melody and knew the words instantly. Where had he heard it? He could not remember. Snatches of memory—dim, incomplete, vaguely-recalled fragments of a time long ago, before he was a man, before he was a boy, before he was even born.

Suddenly Hia shifts and moves out of his physical body, entering once again into the Fields of Light from which he has come. Colors swirl around him in varying patterns of brightness and intensity. In another place, beyond the rational, three-dimensional world of space, time, and measurement, Hia looks at himself. Once again he is in his Long Body, his unified Self, at one with all aspects of his nature. All traces of duality have vanished, and he experiences himself as he has once been and, he knows instinctively, as he will be again.

His Father-Self is speaking, asking him to provide a service, to go on a mission to a strange and distant world, where he will perceive himself and others as fragmented and separate. Hia is excited. He will go to this place and experience its strange ways and do his part, but he requests one favor of his father. "...that I retain knowledge of my true nature and be allowed to return home when I have completed my task."

"As you wish," his Father-Self replies, and so Hia departs. With a single movement akin to a fish moving its tail, he starts forward, creating ripples and waves in the light fields as he moves through them. Slowly at first, then with ever greater speed as he adjusts to this new form of locomotion, he moves on his course. Suddenly, the light vanishes, and he is alone in unutterable blackness. "I have entered the Great Void," he realizes, not at all alarmed. "Here I shall be shown my destination. Here I shall find my way."

How long he floats there he cannot tell, for Time does not exist in such realms. After a while, he senses that he is not alone. Another has joined him, another like himself. Great waves of unconditional love roll toward him, and Hia moves unhesitatingly to embrace them. Reaching out with his mind, he calls to the kindred spirit beside him. A flash of recognition lights up the darkness as his fellow sojourner responds with a loving greeting.

Details of a long-gone conversation come to him, and he hears the words as the two beings join in their sacred pact. Long they talk, making plans, filled with Spirit, excited and enthused about what they are going to undertake. When the conversation is complete, Hia feels the other move away, beckoning him to follow. Together they move through the blackness and the silence, to where he does not know. Then he sees the goal shimmering far in the distance—a tiny patch of brilliant white light shining like a diamond in an inky sea.

Minuscule at first, then growing ever larger as they move closer and closer, Hia sees that it is not a single point of light, but billions of individual lights moving together in a great spiral mass within the Space-Time continuum. It is his first glimpse of the Milky Way. In the reflected light from the stars, his kindred spirit smiles at him. Reaching out with their minds, they embrace for the last time.

"You go your way, I'll go mine. Entering in together...together yet separate. Born of two different races, dwelling in two different lands, following two different paths. Gathering different skills, honing different talents, experiencing different things. Growing up apart...separate for many years, until the appointed time. Coming together at the appointed time. Until then, farewell."

And now Hia is alone once again, watching the other descend into the star fields, trailing a glorious stream of light as the spirit moves toward the third planet orbiting a small young star on one of the outward spiraling arms of the galaxy.

"Where my brother goes I must follow," Hia realizes, moving forward himself. He turns around for a last look behind him. Far away, so very far away, across a vast sea of eternal night, lie the familiar light fields of Home. "Farewell, Father," he says, already beginning to feel the first effects of duality and separation. "I shall do my part and then return to you. Keep a place prepared for me."

Then he turns around and moves forward once again. And so it is that Hia has come to Earth, following the Wayshower, his kindred spirit, Adima.

Now the Warrior remembered. The whole story presented itself in a flash of recognition. Two spirit beings, two friends, had joined forces before birth. A pact had been made—an agreement, a promise to come together to perform a great and noble task for the good of the whole. Now it had finally happened. They were reunited at last. Each had developed an archetype within himself—Adima the King, Hia the Warrior. Each was complete within himself. Now, as in the inner, so it was to be in the outer. The Warrior had joined forces with the King, and the Kingdom was a single, unified Whole once again.

As the trees spoke to him, Hia smiled, nodding his head, remembering that which he had once known but had forgotten. Now he was sure. Now it all made sense and had purpose. Now he could assuage the longing in his soul. Now he could do his part. Confidently, the Warrior took up the trail once again.

Outside the magical aspen grove, the once-lovely natural forest that surrounded him was as ravaged as the man-made city. Fallen trees lay everywhere, obliterating trails, making the way practically impassable. A great sorrow lay on his heart as he passed through the destruction all around him. Yet that which made it a struggle to pass also made it easy to track the killer. The huge, hairy body had carved a wide path through the otherwise impenetrable tangle, confident that it was alone and unchallenged, or if not, that it could defeat any adversary.

The spoor was strong and clear. Even an inexperienced tracker would have had no difficulty, and Hia was anything but a novice in the woods. The creature had followed the Good Red Road for a short distance, then had left the trail and taken to the denser undergrowth. All along the way, it had left signs of its passing—broken branches, uprooted bushes, the half-eaten carcass of a deer, a pile of foul-smelling droppings. It seemed to be traveling in a large, rough circle, heading first to the south, then turning to the west, and finally coming back around to the northeast.

Hia paused, all senses alert, nostrils quivering as he smelled his prey. The scent of the creature was strong. Its lair was definitely nearby. There it was, not a hundred yards ahead, a huge, shaggy, evil-smelling brute foraging for grubs in the dirt beneath a large boulder. In a single silent motion, Hia unslung his bow, fitted an arrow, and waited for the creature to move out from the shadow of the rock into just the right position. No longer the Hunter, it was the Predator who watched with the eyes of Death, timing his fearsome strike.

The creature was so close that he could almost taste its foul presence, so strong was its repugnant stench. Then the unexpected happened. A low whistle sounded from beyond the rise. With a growl of recognition, the creature leaped up and disappeared over the other side before the warrior could loose the feathered shaft.

With a snarl of disappointment, he dropped to the ground. Creeping forward, he paused at the top of the hill. Here the forest ended, giving way to the southern edge of the Great Plain. Below him lay a dark, ancient building. It appeared to have been a temple once, although the structure had long since fallen into disrepair. The windows were heavily shuttered, although Hia's sharp eyes detected the faint glow of candles between cracks in the wooden slats.

Men were coming and going, heavily armed men. Several of them had thrown a heavy net over the monster and were struggling to get it into a cage without being severely mauled. At last they managed to secure the creature, forcing it behind the strong iron bars. A frightful din ensued, not the voice of a single brute, but the voice of many of its kind. Hia marveled. Apparently, the cage held other aberrations, and the presence of the newcomer was not at all welcome. A few of the men shrank back in terror, while others poked and prodded with sharp lances, trying to prevent the creatures from tearing each other to pieces. In a few moments order was restored, but not before several men had been scratched and bitten.

"Too many to take on alone, on their turf," Hia realized, quite disappointed. He had wanted so badly to avenge the deaths of the innocents and send another message to the hated Belial. Now he would have to wait. No matter. His time would come again. It always did. Meanwhile, he would watch these strange men who lurked far from the sight of other men and controlled such strange, malformed beasts.

Watch and learn. He would learn their strengths and weaknesses. He would learn all there was to know about them...how they walked and talked, how they used their weapons, how they thought. Finding a safe and comfortable hiding place, he settled into his vigil as the activity in the compound continued and the moon climbed higher and higher into the night sky. For hours he lay thus, moving not a muscle, as still as the boulders and stones. The leaves moved in the breeze, but not Hia.

The compound finally grew quiet and deserted. Creatures and men were asleep at last. Silently, Hia crawled back down just below the rim of the ridge. Opening his pouch, he produced flint and steel, the universal, age-old tools for making fire.

Wet as they were, the small twigs and leaves would not burn without help. A few sprinkles of a dark powder, however, a quick touch of flint to steel, and in moments a tiny blaze was crackling. It would not provide much warmth, but then again, he hadn't made this fire to warm himself. Hia was not cold, he was angry.

Again he reached into his pouch, this time producing twine and rags coated with a dark, tarry substance. Cutting the rags into half a dozen strips, he wrapped each one around the shaft of an arrow, fastening it with twine an inch behind the deadly tip. He worked methodically and meticulously, confident of himself, sure of what he was doing. Placing the arrows in a semicircle around the fire, he rose and looked back out over the rise. Although the moon was far to the west, Belial's Lair stood out clearly. There would be no missing those targets—the wooden porches, wooden doors, wooden windows, wooden corrals.

Taking the first arrow, Hia touched it to the fire. The treated cloth blazed instantly. Fitting the arrow to his bow, he took careful aim and loosed the shaft. It found the target— the front door of the Lair. Like a living creature, liquid fire spread out in all directions, licking hungrily at the bone-dry wood, crawling through the cracks, spreading to the interior of the Lair even as the other arrows found their marks.

Again and again he repeated his actions. Six flaming arrows, six blazing targets—the last the very window behind which the Belial-Beast lay sleeping. The Lair was a roaring inferno in less than thirty seconds. Hia paused only a few moments to watch the flames engulf the building. Before the first warning shout had been issued, he had melted back into the forest. It was like he had never been there.

*****

All kinds of creatures lurked in the bowels of Belial's Lair. Some were strong creatures with sharp fangs, powerful rending teeth, and deadly poisons, lurking in the shadows, ready to pounce. Others were weak creatures, soft and delicate, tiny and slow, skulking, ever alert for the deadly sting. Predator and prey, they dwelt together in a constant struggle for survival, a constant battle between weak and strong.

Were they evil, these predators? Not in the human sense. Theirs were the deeds of instinct, of self-preservation. They were not motivated by fear, but rather by the need to survive at all costs. If that meant the demise of a weaker creature, so be it. It was all part of the Circle of Life, and one's place on the food chain was predetermined. What could be done?

One such predator was the female Black Widow. Her bite was pure poison, meaning instant death for smaller prey and severe, painful illness for human victims. Tiny she was, and quick, so very, very quick. Coal black and perfectly adapted, she would hide in the shadows, scuttling out of the light when danger lurked, waiting deep in her web for the right victim to come along. Deadly, to be sure, but even so she was beautiful. The red hourglass on her abdomen served as a constant reminder to her prey, "Time is running out. I'm waiting for you, waiting to pounce."

Ever spinning, ever weaving her web of fate, Spider was intimately connected to the Great Mother. Shaped like the symbol for infinity itself, she represented the infinite possibilities of creation. For Spider wove not only her own intricate webs, she was also intimately connected with the creative force that weaves the beautiful designs of life.

Late on the afternoon of the third day of the week, this tiny predator had just finished spinning a new web when Belial came around the corner. He would have walked right into it had not the sun been setting. In the orange light, the slender, gossamer strands of the web were just barely visible. And there in the center, the Black Widow waited patiently, a glossy dot of blackness in the surrounding silver and light, watching a fly struggle desperately to free itself.

Seeing the creature had sent Belial into a fury of rage. He cursed and swore and swatting at the web, destroying it and knocking Spider to the floor, where he crushed its delicate body under his boot heel. The wrathful act did nothing to assuage the fear. The object of his fear was gone, but her message lingered. He could not get the thought of the spider and its nest out of his mind, recognizing them for what they were—messengers from the Spirit world. Here was a message he did not care to hear at all. Spider weaves the web of fate, he realized. Could what he had seen be a foreshadowing of his own fate?

All evening, Belial wrestled with the demons and predators in his own mind. Before retiring, he had summoned one of the Adepts to his chamber, a man skilled in interpreting signs and portents. He did not like what the soothsayer told him.

"Master, you are like the bug that is caught and about to be devoured. You have gotten entangled in the web of your own illusions about your power and place in Atlantis. Because you are no longer moving forward, you seek to prevent others from doing so. Because you cannot love, you are resentful of all who are loving. Because you feel weak, you lash out and attack. Because you cannot create, you destroy. Thus, Spider comes to you to eat you up."

Enraged even further by the dire prognostications, Belial ordered the man cast into the dungeons, where he might reconsider his interpretation of the omen. But still the dead spider continued to haunt him. So, as was his wont whenever he could not face his own demonic fears, the Master had ordered a potion mixed and brought to him. Drinking deeply, he had spun down into the blackness, where he found some semblance of relief. Hours later, he lay dreaming.

In a strange nightmare world, Belial saw himself watching a spider spinning a huge web. Whichever way he turned, Spider was there, dangling before him, walking delicately along the slender strands, turning every so often to look at him, its mouth dripping venom.

The scene changed. A bug was caught in the web. "I am the bug," Belial realized in horror, crying out in the dream world. "I'm caught in its web."

He struggled powerlessly as the huge spider approached, mouth agape. Fire flashed from that mouth, deadly bolts of lightning landing all around him, setting everything ablaze. Helplessly entangled in the web at the center of the conflagration, he felt the heat and smelled the smoke. Alone and dying, there was no one there to mourn his passing as Spider bit into his soft flesh.

Belial awoke with a start, sobbing. At first, he did not know where he was or what was happening. From far away, he heard hoarse shouts—the screams of frightened men and beasts. Opening his potion-fogged eyes, he looked around the hot, smoky room. Gasping in terror, he wrapped the blankets tightly around him. The flames were inches from his bed.

*****

Had they been left alone, the people of the City of Atlantis would eventually have helped themselves. They would have catered to their own needs and attended to the needs of each other. They would have been all right. They would have rebuilt.

But they were not left alone. By midday, the soldiers and Palace guards had arrived, and then life in Atlantis had become a living hell, for they offered little in the way of help. Surly and uncooperative, they were as apt to kill the wounded as help them. Those had been Belial's orders. "Whoever are feeble or wounded or sick, they will be a drain on the rest of us, and we need all of our resources now. So kill the wounded, do not help them. And kill anybody who tries to stop you or get in your way."

In the first several hours, the soldiers had managed to construct a makeshift tent city on the west side of the Great Pyramid, where the damage had been the least serious. Food and water were severely rationed, as were blankets and medical supplies. As the day wore on, hundreds of survivors had made their way there, hungry, tired, cold, afraid, and desperate. There they sat under gray and lowering skies in a damp, chilly drizzle, with no food, no water, no possessions, no place to go. At the bottom of the pit of despair, with nothing left, not even hope, they sat in the gloomy silence, too shocked to cry, too numb to react, too hard hit to realize what had happened to them. They just sat or lay on the cold, hard, wet stone and stared off into empty space, each with his and her own private thoughts and questions.

"What happens now? What do we do now?" So the questions began.

"We have to stay put." That was the first option they discussed. "Trust our leaders. Trust Belial. Belial will fix everything. He will take care of us."

Others were of the opposite opinion. "No, we must flee the city," they cried. "Go to the mountains. We'll be safe there. Hide out for a while, live in the caves, forage and gather in the forest, where there are food and water enough. Then we'll see. Then we'll see."

"You are right, we do have to flee," still others cried, "but not just to the mountains. We must flee the island. We must leave Atlantis completely. We can no longer stay here. It is not safe."

"That is insane," the first group cried. "How would you leave? Where would you go?"

"Insane?" came the incredulous replies. "It is insanity to stay anywhere on this island with Belial in power. For Belial is responsible. Belial has brought us to this. Adima was right. He warned us."

"You couldn't be more wrong," came the replies from the opposite camp. "It was Adima who brought this upon us, Adima with his sorcery. He is the one who angered Poseidon and caused him to unleash the full power of his fury upon us. Adima is the one who is responsible and must be punished."

The debate raged back and forth from one side to the other. No quarter was given and no answers offered. On one side, the counterculture rose up against Belial, taking a stand, daring to be different, trusting to the larger process, seeking the higher and greater good. On the other side, the traditionalists blindly followed their government and their faith, supporting Belial regardless of the path down which he might lead them, trusting to their gods to save them despite the evidence of their own senses, accepting their own defeat.

So, in their fear and anger and desperation, the people of Atlantis lashed out—not at their common enemy, but at each other. Lashed out at the ones they loved and needed most, themselves and their brethren. Thus, the camps were divided and separated—the Camp of Love on one side, the Camp of Fear on the other. On each side, they made up their minds based on their experiences of the day. Those who were in the Camp of Love were going to stay loving. Those who were in the Camp of Fear were going to stay afraid. There would be no more changing sides, no more changing minds. The decisions had been made.

That night, under cover of darkness, hundreds of people silently began leaving the tent city. Following the example that the birds and the sea creatures had set the day before, they began the mass exodus from the city and the island. Some took as much as they could carry, others took nothing but their loved ones and the clothes they were wearing, trusting that the Mother would provide food and water and shelter. The soldiers made no effort to stop them. That, too, had been Belial's order.

"Let them go," the Master had declared mercilessly. "The fewer who stay, the fewer we will have to clothe and feed. Let them go to Adima and the Children of the Law of One. Let them set sail in their Arks. The Ocean of Atlas will make short work of them."

Some fled to the mountains, where they hid themselves and their families in the relative calm of the great forests. There they stopped and waited, for what they did not know. Alas, they stopped too soon. They did not flee far enough.

Some fled into the sea, leaving the island in any way they could. Walking or on riding on horseback to the coast, then into the sea on makeshift rafts. Floating and bobbing on the mighty waves as the current swept them away from the shore, away from Atlantis, away from the sight of their brethren forever.

Some, however, chose another option, the option of the Arks, the alternative offered by Adima and Cybele. The people had scoffed when the great ships had been discovered only a few short months before, but then they had forgotten again, having had other things to think about. Now some of them remembered.

"What about the Arks?" they whispered in the darkness as they watched the others leave. "Adima said all were welcome. Why don't we give them a try? It's better than living in caves in the mountains, eating roots and freezing and dying a slow death. It's also safer than taking to the seas, where we will almost surely drown. Adima seems to know something we don't. He seems so sure of himself. What have we to lose? He asks nothing of us; he simply extends his hand in friendship and makes us welcome. I say we go. I say we take a chance. It's our best hope for survival, our best hope for life."

And so they left, walking forth under cover of darkness, heading out across the Great Plain, looking for Adima, seeking out the Children of the Law of One. Making the best decision, setting forth upon a new adventure, they left their dying city behind. Bidding farewell, they left home with tears in their eyes, heading into a future they could not comprehend, into a new world they could not even imagine. Would that future bring life or death? They hoped life. They would not be disappointed.

In just three days, three of the four conditions for the Plan had been met. The people of Atlantis had separated into two distinctly opposing camps—the Camp of Love and the Camp of Fear. The migration off the island was underway. A new awareness had been birthed in the Atlantean consciousness, an awareness in which people were suddenly forced to think the unthinkable and imagine a heretofore unimaginable future. All that was left was for the Great Mother to shift on her axis!

*****

And the evening and the morning were the third day.

CHAPTER 45

And the evening and the morning were the fourth day.

—*Genesis 1:19*

The fire leveled the Lair, killing many guards and horses and even a few of the aberrations, although most of them had managed to avoid serious injury. Belial himself barely escaped unscathed by diving through a burning window frame and rolling over and over on the damp ground to smother the flames that were eating away at his clothes. They tried to save the building by forming a bucket brigade, all but draining a nearby pond, but the flames had too much of a head start. In the initial excitement, there had been no time to salvage anything. Now there were a few moments to think.

"Where is the Spear? The Spear is missing!" Belial cried to Draco. In his panic and haste, the giant had not had time to grab the precious talisman. Hopefully one of the others had been able to do so. But when the Adept shook his head, Belial flew into a rage. "I must have the Spear," he cried to a passing guard, shoving him roughly toward the blazing inferno. "Fetch it for me."

The man cowered in fear, the intense heat scorching his face and searing his eyes. Belial was in no mood to tolerate disobedience.

"You will fetch me the Spear," he ordered, grasping the hapless victim by the scruff of the neck and about the waist and dragging him as close to the flames as he dared. The guard struggled to save himself, but he was held fast in that iron grip. Draco watched in horror as Belial lifted the man as easily as though he were a rag doll. "This is what happens to all who disobey me," the Beast snarled, its roars of rage drowning out the roar of the fire. Holding his victim high above his head, giant muscles surging, Belial tossed the poor creature headlong into the flames. Draco shuddered at the man's screams as the flames engulfed him.

For several moments, Belial stared intensely into the fire, not speaking a word. When he could stand the heat no longer, he turned and walked back to Draco's side.

The act of violence seemed to calm the Beast, as was so often the case. The release brought a sudden sense of clarity and normalcy. There was nothing he could do but watch helplessly as the Lair burned to the ground. The Spear was gone. It was gone forever. Now he would have to rule by force and cunning alone. He hoped he was up to it.

*****

From a high promontory overlooking the Great Plain, Hia watched the purifying flames consume the den of iniquity, his face an emotionless mask. He watched as the guards scurried about like ants, trying to save the building. He watched as Belial rolled in the dust, struggling to put out his burning clothing. He watched as the Adepts burned and died in their desperate and futile attempts to salvage the Spear. As the sun rose, he watched as they finally gave up and began the long walk back to the city and the palace grounds, where they would take up temporary quarters until suitable new ones could be found.

When the Adepts were far enough away and the Lair had been reduced to a smoldering ruin, the warrior came down from the hilltop. Dropping to one knee before the ashes, he gave voice to a prayer of thanksgiving to his ancestors and all of the spirits who had helped him achieve a great victory. Then he rose and began the Rain Dance. For several minutes he danced and sang, performing the ritual, asking his spirit allies to send the sacred waters to douse the flames and cool the ruins, that he might search the embers for the object of his desire.

His prayers did not go unanswered. Hearing his pleas, hearkening to his request, the Great Mother smiled on her son. A single bolt of lightning shot from a towering thunderhead, and the rains came. A torrential downpour it was, quenching the last of the flames, turning the embers first to hissing piles of steam, then cooling even the steam until there was nothing left but blackened ash floating in thick, sooty puddles. As the torrent lightened to a drizzle, Hia entered amidst the rubble, poking and prodding with a heavy stick, looking, ever looking for the prize. He searched neither long nor hard. The shining Spear stood out clearly against the charred wood and blackened stone.

It was untouched. How could it be otherwise? Hia realized, knowing the Spear's origin, that it had been created on the Forge of the Gods and could withstand any human onslaught against it. He paused, saying the prayers for protection, guarding himself from the fearful powers he was about to embrace. Invoking the light, he surrounded himself with the light, attuning himself to the highest and purest vibrations of Truth. When he felt safe and protected, he reached out and grasped the Spear.

The potent energy danced all around him, blue sparks and currents flowing up and down his arms and crackling in the air, but the negative shadow current could not penetrate his defenses. Grasping the talisman tightly, Hia stepped gingerly out of the ruins and ran from that place of evil. Far into the forest he made his way, through the foothills and up into the high places. As he moved tirelessly forward, he reflected on the Spear and his part in taking it from Belial. He did not understand the need for such a weapon. Why was the Spear necessary?

"I wish it could be another way," he said to no one in particular, "a way without so much destruction and bloodshed. I wish they could get the message and remember the truth." But they could not, it seemed. He was not privy to the whole Plan, however, although he wished he were. All he knew was that it fell to him to take the Spear from Belial and give it to others for safekeeping. This was his part, and thus would he fulfill it.

The Islander did not know his final destination, never having been in this forest before. The trees, however, were aware of his passage and his intention. They were only too eager to help. Opening before him, the ancient sentinels showed him the way, clearing a path for him to pass. Hia moved forward easily, grateful to the mighty forest dwellers for their support in ensuring the success of his sacred endeavor. When the sun stood at its zenith, he came out into a high meadow surrounded by even loftier peaks. What a contrast to its former glory!

The land lay bleak and barren, devoid of birds, bees, insects, and wildflowers. No gentle deer or elk grazed on the tender grasses, no sweet birdsong filled the air, no colorful butterflies flitted from flower to flower. The dwellers of the high places had all left. Nevertheless, he knew that he had reached the end of the trail. Pausing for the first time in several hours, he stood still, prayed, and waited.

The sky grew dark. Thick, black clouds roiled overhead, and thunder rumbled ominously. A strong wind whipped down from the higher peaks, chilling his bare wet skin. A soft rustle in the foliage drew his attention. Hia remained motionless. Only his eyes moved, searching for whom he did not know.

Slowly, several pairs of brightly glowing dots of light appeared in the low-growing bushes around him. Gradually faces appeared, then the bodies of the Elementals. He recognized them instantly from the stories his grandfather had told him. Making the sign of peace, he held the Spear out at arm's length.

Very carefully, Orange-Eyes stepped forward, arms outstretched. Without a word, he reached up and took the proffered weapon. The Elementals gathered around their leader and looked at the fabled artifact, marveling at the craftsmanship that had produced it.

"Guard it well," Hia spoke gently. "Belial was the first to possess the gift. He has misused it, and so it has been taken from him."

The wind was beginning to gust harder now, and a few drops of rain splattered down around them. Thunder boomed close by, and the Spear glowed with a strange blue light as the warrior spoke to the Elementals. "Now it remains for you to guard the Spear until the others come along," he instructed. "Perhaps its next owner will use its powers wisely. If so, that is good. If not, the Spear will pass to still other hands until the time finally comes for it to be laid aside in favor of a new and better way. Always, however, it will do what it was created to do—help us along the Grail Path toward the Consciousness of Freedom. And always it will be balanced by its counterpart, the Sword—the Hard Lightning carried by the Twin of whomever possesses the Spear."

That was all. The Elementals listened carefully, nodding their heads, taking every word to heart. With smiles and bows and waves of farewell, the Earth spirits gathered together and surrounded the Spear. Stepping back into the foliage, blending in with their surroundings, they melded back into the natural landscape with which they were one. For a few seconds, their bright eyes glowed in the dim light, then they winked out one by one. And so the Spear vanished from the sight of the human race in Atlantis.

Thunder rumbled, lightning flashed, and once again the rain fell. Alone in the clearing, Hia doffed his pouch, his quiver of arrows, and his bow. Stripping off his clothing, he stood naked as great sheets of water washed over him, allowing himself to be cleansed, allowing the Mother to gently wash the dirt and negativity from her beloved son.

*****

The fourth day in the city began with an intensive manhunt for Adima and Hia. Word went out that anyone providing information leading to their capture would be greatly rewarded. Word also went out that anyone harboring the accused would die along with them.

For the first time since the storm, the soldiers ventured out into the countryside, where there were so many hiding places—basements, barns, forests, caves. Now the people really felt the effects of Belial's wrath. All rights of privacy and citizenship were suspended. Armed men were everywhere, searching houses, appropriating what little food and water there was, taking whatever they wanted to take, doing whatever they wanted to do.

Anyone who got in their way came to regret it. The soldiers had become more dangerous than the evildoers for whom they hunted, all in the name of finding and suppressing enemies of the State. And while all of this was going on, Gadir, King of Atlantis, was planning a little surprise of his own.

*****

The King of Atlantis was a weak man. The one who Adima and the people perceived to be the Ogre Tyrant was in reality the Abdicator. Gadir did not want to be king. Kingship had been thrust upon him through an accident of birth, and he could not care less.

Although he was a direct descendent of all of the Atlantean kings and could trace his lineage directly back to Gadir the First, twin brother of Atlas, the present king was a small, weak man with no stately mien, no kingly presence. Oh, he had tried, to be sure. He had tried to be king, but it just would not come. He enjoyed the luxuries and the trappings of office and the riches and the women, but it stopped there.

Gadir did not want to rule. He did not want to govern. He could not care less about the people and their problems and their laws because he could not care less about himself. So low was his self-esteem that he felt he did not deserve to be king. He had not earned the rights and privileges of that station.

He felt as though there was a great ball and chain attached to his leg, holding him in place and weighing him down, keeping him from doing what he wanted to do, keeping him in chains, keeping him a prisoner, alone and isolated in his magnificent opulence. Oh, how he longed to be free, not just from the burdens of office, but also from the limits of his small and weak self.

He could not stand up to Belial. Try as he might, even with all of the trappings of office and the officials of the Court surrounding him, Gadir was no match for the Chief Elder. It was Belial who ran the show, Belial who made the rules, Belial who controlled Atlantis, Belial who held the key that would unlock the ball and chain from around his leg. But Belial wasn't unlocking it. At least, not yet.

Belial wanted the power, but not even he dared usurp the throne. For then, the military would have no part of him. And he needed their support, because after all of the false persona had been stripped away, was also weak, perhaps weaker than the King himself. He needed a strong Inner Circle to help him maintain power and keep it, since he could not keep it by himself. The difference was that Belial disguised his fear well. And Belial *wanted* to rule. He fancied himself destined to lead Atlantis to even further greatness.

So Belial was patient and cunning. He could wait. And while he waited, he continued to curry favor with the advisers and courtiers and generals. "And I can't stop him," the King muttered to himself in the privacy of his chambers, looking out on his ruined kingdom. "There is nothing I can do. I am powerless. Oh, that I were a different man! Oh, that I were like my ancestors...like Poseidon and Atlas and the rest. Then the people would have a king worthy of them. Then they would have a kingdom of bounty and plenty. Every day would be a festival. Every day would be a day of peace and harmony and joy.

"The people would revel and feast in the streets, and they would have me to thank. They would kneel before me and kiss my royal ring and touch my robes and ask me for my blessings, which I would gladly give.

"If only I could! If only I could. But I cannot, and I cannot stay here. I must be true to my fathers before me. I can no longer dishonor their accomplishments. I can no longer be King. I must abdicate the throne and leave Atlantis forever."

Sadly, Gadir picked up his pen and paper and began to write.

Once there was a King who wanted to throw a great celebration for his subjects. All the kingdom would be invited. There would be feasting and singing and laughing and dancing and all manner of making merry.

There was just one problem. The King was bound and held immobile by a great ball and chain welded to his ankle. Try as he might, he could not free himself from its viselike grip.

Oftimes the King would dream of the great celebration. How he longed for that day! He pictured every detail in his mind—the location in the grand ballroom in the center of the kingdom. The sumptuous feast spread out on great carved oak tables. The servants all polished and dressed, standing ready to attend to each guest's every need.

In his mind, the King heard the sound of the great trumpets as the musicians burst forth with a mighty fanfare calling all the kingdom to come in and be welcome. And come in they did, from all over the kingdom and even beyond—subjects and pilgrims, tall and short, fat and thin, light and dark, young and old, male and female, happy and sad, sick and well, broken and whole.

The King received them all and blessed them all. To those who were hungry, he gave food. To those who were naked, he gave clothing. To those who were homeless, he gave shelter. To those who were sad, he gave consolation. To those who were sick, he gave healing. To those who were ill at ease, he gave comfort. To those with less, he gave more. To those with plenty, he gave still more. And to all he gave joy and blessings. "Thank you for coming," the King exclaimed as he took the hand of each guest. "You are welcome here. Come in and be happy."

And as he watched the room fill with the great multitude, a feeling of fulfillment swept over the King. Great tears welled up in his eyes. A profound and heavy emotion filled his breast. From deep within himself, a huge sound began to build, pushing its way forth from the center of his being up through his throat and out of his mouth. His heart and chest felt as though they would burst.

The bright room suddenly grew dim, the vision faded from his sight, and he found himself lying on his bed in the early hours before the dawn. His eyes were dry—no tears. And where the great moan had been waiting to make its escape, only a soft sigh passed his lips. In the silence and darkness, the King stared at the ceiling, remembering the vision that had seemed so real.

"Not today," he sighed as he slowly rose to a sitting position. The rattle of the great chain echoed throughout the chamber.

"Not today," he sighed again as he draped the heavy links across his shoulders.

"Not today," he sighed a third time as he rose and slowly walked to the door, dragging the huge and ponderous ball behind him. The only sounds were the shuffling of his bare feet, punctuated by the dull rasp of iron against stone.

Gadir spoke the final paragraph aloud as he wrote the words:

"Good-bye, my people. I leave you to your destiny, as I go to face mine. My sins are many, and now I add to them the sin of Abdication. We shall all suffer grievously, but I the most, for I have abandoned you who trusted in me. May the Great Mother and Divine Father and all of you forgive me and have mercy on my tortured and tormented soul."

He penned a sad story, the story of what it might have been like if only he had been able to fulfill his dream, if only he had been a stronger man. He shuddered to think of the turmoil that would arise upon their hearing the news of his leaving. He shuddered even more to think of what life would be like with Belial in power. For he knew that the court would appoint Belial, even if only as a temporary ruler, to give the kingdom order and direction. Of course, Belial would rise to the occasion and accept the crown and the throne. And then would come even darker days!

Gadir thought of his people one last time. He hoped they would understand. He hoped they would forgive him. He hoped that not too many more would suffer and die. The King left the parchment on the golden table beside his bed. He undressed, divesting himself of his royal robes. He shaved off his beard and his hair and put on sackcloth.

Walking over to the massive stone hearth that filled one entire wall of his bedchamber, he stepped within and pressed a certain stone. Silently, a portion of the wall slid back, revealing a dark passageway. It was a secret escape route, having been built by a nameless ancestor against the time of invasion or other national emergency. Gadir would use it now to leave the Kingdom.

Where would he go? He was not sure. Perhaps to one of the provinces, perhaps to Turtle Island. Perhaps he might return to the high places and seek solace in the wilderness.

All he knew was that he had to get away from Atlantis once and for all. The King who was no longer King never looked back, never paused to take a last glance around the only place he had ever called home, the only home he had ever known. He straightaway entered the passage and was instantly engulfed in darkness. The wall slid closed behind him, shutting Gadir off from the sight of men forever.

*****

Draco could wait no longer. With the Spear gone, Belial had become a man obsessed. "How can I recapture what has been lost?" the giant had asked him over and over again, pacing the corridors of the Council chambers. "Is there any way to make one last effort to regain control now that the Spear is gone?"

Fate, not Draco, provided the answer. It had come with the discovery of Gadir's letter to the people of Atlantis. Here was the perfect solution, and if Belial were in any way spiritually inclined, he would have dropped to his knees in gratitude. Now that the King had abdicated, he would have himself crowned King. His position would be guaranteed forever. No one would dare to challenge the King. It was unheard of. The King's word was law. The King was Divine.

Belial's scheme was grand, and he would execute it three days hence. In one glorious public display of pomp and power, he would have himself crowned, execute Adima as villain and traitor, and attack Lemuria and achieve a great victory. Atlantis would love him and flock to him as never before, and he would be in power forever. He would finally have all that he wanted.

"I shall rule!" he had cried upon hearing of the abdication. "I shall make this nation great. I am your King. I am your leader."

"But Belial," Draco had spoken up, "you cannot just assume control. You are not descended from the royal lineage. You are only an Elder. The laws of our ancestors are quite clear. Only one of the royal line can be King in Atlantis. That is the way it has always been, and that is the way it must be now."

"You dare to defy me?" the giant had lashed out in a fury. "You whom I trusted now dare to defy me? Get out of my sight, lest I have you burned to ashes along with all of the others." With a mighty shove, Belial had hurled him bodily from the room, slamming the door with such force that the walls shook. Draco had been lucky to leave with his person intact. Now he would face Belial one more time. One of them would not leave the Council chambers alive.

Making his way through the corridors, Draco was surprisingly calm. At first he had wrestled with his conscience, experiencing doubt as well as fear. Once he had made the decision to act, however, internal calm had been restored. He walked with confidence, resigned to whatever fate had in store. Clutching a sharp-edged sword, Draco entered the hallway that led to Belial's private chambers. At once he was seized by half a dozen powerful men.

"Where do you think you're going?" one growled, roughly searching him.

"To kill the Master," Draco replied calmly, much to the amazement of the guards. They disarmed him easily and bound his arms behind his back. Then they dragged him forward to face Belial for the last time.

The Master was waiting in the magnificent Hall of Justice, standing beneath a vast mural of the Orphean Bards. The monumental fresco spanned an entire city block, larger than life, rising up from the floor and filling the circular walls and domed ceiling overhead. Titanic figures of the Ancients towered over the room, presiding over their people, dispensing justice, ensuring fair and equitable treatment for all Atlanteans, where wisdom and peace were the order of the day.

The irony was not lost on Draco. He could not help but laugh at his predicament. He was about to be declared guilty in a mock trial by a tyrannical despot and summarily executed without benefit of jury trial or counsel or any of his rights under Atlantean law. And it was all going to happen in the middle of the room that for centuries had been the centerpiece of world justice and wisdom, under the watchful eyes of the Ancient judges. How fitting!

Belial turned at the approach of the guards. He spoke not a word as he looked over the prisoner, walking around him like a tiger encircling its prey, about to pounce. A strange conversation ensued, so much the more frightening because of the calm, almost matter-of-fact way in which the two antagonists addressed each other. Draco stubbornly maintained his guilt, while Belial tried desperately to give him an out. An immovable object had met an irresistible force.

"Why do you want to kill me?" Belial spoke first, coming directly to the point. His deep voice sounded inordinately loud under the hollow dome of the hall.

"Because you have brought misfortune to Atlantis." The guards exchanged uneasy glances, knowing Draco's accusation was only too true.

"Have I harmed you in any way?"

"As much as you have harmed everyone in Atlantis."

Belial paused, taken aback by the brutal honesty of the accused. He had known the secret intentions of Draco's heart ever since Adima's address to the Council. He had read the thoughts in his mind as clearly as though Draco had spoken the words aloud. So he had set the trap and waited. Now the victim was caught, and Belial was in a quandary.

He could not rule without Draco at his side to advise him. He could never survive without the Adept's cunning and knowledge. On the other hand, he could not let his most trusted advisor betray him and walk away unpunished. The Master wanted this problem to go away. There was too much other turmoil without having to deal with Draco's defection. If only things could revert to the way they had been, even if just for a little while!

He looked up at the titanic figures of the Ancients looming overhead. In one scene, a judge was portrayed mercifully settling a dispute among neighbors. In another, a family was comforted by the aid of the State. Scene after scene showed compassion and tenderness coupled with the dispensation of justice. Normally, Belial would not have even deigned to glance at the masterpiece. Today, however, he paused for a closer look. Could he perhaps learn a lesson from the Ancients after all?

Of course! The common theme in all of the scenes was fair-mindedness and temperance. That was the solution, he realized, a possible way out of this dilemma in which he was now so entangled. Could he persuade Draco to change his mind? If so, all would be forgiven. The all-wise and all-kind King Belial would make an exception and let the transgression pass.

At least for the time being, he thought slyly, until the present crisis has passed. Time enough to take care of Draco later, to settle the score when things were more relaxed and he was firmly established as King. At that time, Draco would just quietly disappear, having served his purpose and outlived his usefulness. Until then, however, Belial would do whatever it took to keep the Adept on his side, using all his powers of persuasion, offering an honorable way out for both of them.

"Who incited you to this crime?" the Master asked, hoping to find an accomplice upon whom he could heap most of the blame. The accused refused to swallow the bait.

"No one. I armed myself because I am firmly convinced that by killing you, I will render the greatest service to Atlantis and all the world."

Belial was nonplussed. He did not understand the man's reaction. Didn't Draco see that he was being given a chance to save himself? Didn't the fool value his life?

"You are mad, or else ill," Belial suggested, not wanting to threaten, but becoming angry nonetheless. Still, he held to his scheme, offering yet another way out.

"I am neither," Draco said softly.

The conversation was turning darker, scarier. Belial felt the demons coming to life inside him. The demon of Rage welled up first, followed closely on its heels by the demons of Pride and Arrogance. Struggling to keep the voices quiet and at bay, grasping at any hope, no matter how wild, he ordered that his personal physician be summoned. After a close examination, during which not a word was spoken, the healer declared Draco to be in perfect health.

With the diagnosis, Belial became panic-stricken. He paced restlessly back and forth, lost in thought, muttering unintelligibly to himself as his heavy footfalls pounded dully on the polished oak floor. All eyes were on him, expecting the worst, yet no one was prepared for what came next. Doing the unthinkable, shocking the guards, shocking the prisoner, shocking even himself, the Master offered to pardon Draco.

"I do not wish to be pardoned," the accused replied, causing even greater consternation among the small group. "I regret that I did not succeed."

Tears of desperation welled in Belial's eyes. "Tell me," came the last pathetic plea, "if I pardoned you, would you at least be grateful?"

"I would still want to kill you just as much."

Belial reacted as if struck by lightning. In a great cacophony of sound, the voices hummed inside his mind, vibrating over and over until he thought his head would explode. "You can do it on your own. Who needs Draco anyway? Kill him, kill him, kill him..." One after another the voices sang. Belial looked around. Didn't anyone else hear the demons? No, they spoke only to him, only to Belial. What more could he do? Draco openly wanted to kill him and showed no signs of remorse.

"Perhaps he is under a spell," Belial muttered in frustration, looking for any way out of the quandary in which he found himself. "Summon the magician."

A magician was summoned and a ritual performed. As with the healer, however, so the magus declared Draco to be free of spells or enchantments of any kind. Belial sighed a deep and sorrowful sigh. There was nothing more to do. He had tried everything. The voices were insistent, and his head throbbed. He placed his hands over his ears, as much to keep his skull from bursting apart as to drown out the incessant chatter.

He looked around desperately. No choices left, no options except, as always, to succumb to the voices.

"Take him away." The giant barely whispered the order, turning his back on the closest person he had to a friend. With a rattle of chains, Draco passed from his sight.

Alone in the domed hall, Belial stood helplessly under the monumental mural. The voices were quiet at last, but he knew they would return. They always did. He looked up one more time. High above him, the Titans gazed down from their lofty aerie. Although their images remained fixed, making neither movement nor sound, the Ancients spoke to him nevertheless, silently conveying their disapproval with their huge, wise eyes.

*****

Martial law, death, destruction, loss, change—the physical aftereffects of the storm had produced remarkable emotional disorder and uproar. For as long as they could, the people of Atlantis tried desperately to restrain themselves, struggling to remain in control. The breaking news of the abdication of the King and the ascendancy of Belial to the throne, however, was more than anyone could stand. Emotions boiled over in a frenetic release of pent-up energy. Now there was pandemonium indeed. As had happened on the first day of the week, so now, on the fourth day, the rumors flew once again.

"Belial has killed the King."

"He has killed Shakala and Kafar."

"The Sons of Belial are responsible for causing the storm and the destruction, and now they are going to kill all of us."

"Someone tried to assassinate Belial."

And above all, the single most prevalent rumor, the most frightening one of all, loomed like a dark and malevolent cloud over the city. "Belial has lost the Spear. He can't control it any more."

On the verge of hysteria, seeking for some way to express their frustration, fear, and anxiety, the people converged en masse upon the Palace. The future King, however, refused to listen, refused even to grant the leaders an audience. Belial's few remaining loyal minions gathered about him, making access to the Palace virtually impossible.

Reaction to this latest rebuff was far stronger than anyone had anticipated. With no other recourse, amid shouts and oaths and curses, the people took to the streets. By midday, life in Atlantis was completely out of control. In the courtyard of the Temple of Poseidon, the crowd had become a mob, taking on a life of its own, an energy of its own, a consciousness of its own. There was about to be a great conflict. A challenge was about to be issued, and war was about to be declared.

Why? Because there was no Trust on which to rest secure. Because of the Doubt inflicted by a single man upon an entire race. Inflicted by one who had embraced the dishonest act that followed the dishonest thought of taking the crown. Inflicted by one who wished only to deceive, for as it is written in the *Book of Life*...

Iᴛ ɪs onlʏ ᴛʜᴇ wɪsʜ ᴛo dᴇᴄᴇɪvᴇ ᴛʜaᴛ ᴍaᴋᴇs waʀ.

As a result, Trust had fled, Hope had fled, because Honesty had fled. The people were about to be harmed, and new attributes were about to replace peace of mind, love, gentleness, and tolerance. Alien attributes—not natural to Atlantis, not natural to the human race—these were the attributes of confusion, fear, anger, and suspicion.

Why? Because the people had laid a judgment on their brethren, declaring each other guilty of a sin that they did not commit. Lying to themselves, so they lied to each other. All because they had come to accept the first Lie—the one told by Belial—that they were separate, they and those beside them. They were not one and the same. They were different. And there were degrees of difference that made one better or worse than the other.

It was about to be the end of Peace and the denial of Love, to be replaced instead by the insanity and conflict that had come from the inevitable result of self deception. Why? Because the people raised so much noise that they could no longer hear the still, small Voice, could no longer receive the messages of Holy Mother Truth and Holy Father Love—the messages of Source. Nor could the human voices of Reason and Love be acknowledged—the voices of Enoch, Adima, Cybele, Sophia and the rest. The people of Atlantis were about to chose Hell because they could see no way to Heaven.

The air still stank of all manner of noxious vapors and odors. Smoke and soot and toxic fumes from the fires and explosions coated everything with a dull gray ash, the taste of which lingered in mouths and noses and throats. As the mood grew ever more tense, self-appointed leaders among the Children of the Law of One—the most vocal, perhaps the ones with the least left to lose—spoke up, stirring the people to a frenzy, encouraging open revolt and the overthrow of the Atlantean government. Across the way, in the Palace compound, their civilian counterparts among the Sons of Belial followed suit, taking great pains to convince their audience that the white-robed creatures across the courtyard were responsible for all of their problems.

In the streets, crowds massed along the Avenue of the Gods. On one side, chants of "Belial protect us" arose as if from a single throat. On the other side, chants of "Death to Belial" rose in grim rebuttal. For an hour it was thus. Faces contorted with rage, the warring factions of Atlantis hammered away at each other. Idealist versus reactionary, they abused and abased each other so brutally and with such seeming relish that it was hard to believe they were, or ever had been, brethren.

So engrossed were the people in their frenzied desire to murder each other that neither party took notice of the cadres of armed and armored soldiers prowling in the background through the Temple, Palace, and Council precincts, quietly taking up strategic positions, setting booby traps, and laying down barricades to keep the people in their place and control the battle lines. For once again, the two divided camps were at each other's throats, this time attacking the fictitious enemies of themselves instead of the real enemies—Belial and the Adepts. Once again, Atlanteans were about to spill each other's blood and their own for a worthless and misguided cause.

It did not take long to turn bloody. The speakers and instigators had done their work well, and the crowds pressed restlessly forward. Anger and fear surged forth like a great red river of molten lava, bubbling and boiling as it welled upward from within the Fire Mountain, where the Blacksmith labored at his titanic forge. Gone were the soft chants, the peaceful meditations of earlier, gentler times. The Children of the Law of One were about to run amok, and the Sons of Belial were only too willing to join them in the blood frenzy.

For just a fraction of an instant, an ominous silence fell over the two camps. How alike they were! Both sides dirty, bleary-eyed, exhausted, afraid, confused, panic-stricken, hopeless, enraged. No one knew who threw the first stone. Perhaps it came from one of the civilians, perhaps from a soldier. Perhaps it came from a rooftop, perhaps from somewhere else. No matter. The tiny rock landed in the middle of the street with a dull thud, a harmless first strike that would serve as the catalyst for all of the death blows that followed. With a mighty roar, the two groups charged at each other, coming together in a crash and grind of flesh and blood and bone and steel.

There were no barriers, no pretenses, no holding back on either side. Innermost feelings and darkest shadow frustration, fury, and hatred—all were unleashed and exposed. Their naked fury was unparalleled...ripping, tearing, and gouging one another in a mad desire to kill, kill, kill. In front of the Palace, armed soldiers watched in silence. Eyes narrowed, faces grim, they stood ready, spears poised, swords drawn, as the mob swarmed toward them.

The Captain gave a signal, and the soldiers entered the fray like demonic harvesters. Swinging their swords like scythes, they mowed down everyone in their path, cutting a swath through the mob as easily as a farmer mowed ripened hay. It was harvest time for the soldiers of the Sons of Belial, and they were enjoying it, working with lethal ferocity, smiling as they chopped and hacked and prodded and thrust at others like themselves. The sounds of Death were awful—the sickening, wet "thwack" of a sword hacking at flesh and bone, the quiet, moist "swshhh" of a lance passing through soft, internal organs.

"What kind of creatures are you?" a priestess shouted from the Temple veranda. "Have you gone mad?" But of course, no one could hear her, so deep were they in their blood-lust. Her first reaction was to liken them to animals, but then she paused. Animals did not behave so. Humans did. This was purely human behavior.

The woman watched as a soldier chased a young man, a boy really, up the marvelous flight of stone steps that led to the massive portals of the Temple. The boy fell just before reaching the first landing, where he lay gasping for breath. Looming above him, the soldier smiled and raised his sword, bringing the blade crashing into the skull just above the left ear.

The priestess rushed forward from the shadows, trying to offer aid to the already-dead youth. Turning with a snarl, the soldier raised his bloody weapon to strike again, only to stop in the nick of time, remembering that it was death to strike the holy women. He hesitated for a moment, as though thinking it over. Then he lowered his sword and moved on in search of other prey. *Was is my imagination?* she wondered in amazement, or *did I detect a look of disappointment on his blood-smeared face?*

On and on the battle raged, the young as bloodied as the old, the innocent along with the instigators. The scene in front of the Temple and at the Palace was only one of many that were repeated all over the city and out in the country. Hundreds were maimed or killed. Hundreds more were arrested and jailed. Arms and legs broken, faces bloodied, skulls crushed, dragged by their feet or their hair, one by one the survivors were bound and gagged and carted off to the dungeons.

At the Palace, making one last-ditch attempt to regain control, Belial ordered Draco and the leaders of the rioters to be tried in the courtyard. The trials were swift, a mockery of Atlantean law. Belial himself presided over them. In a mere two hours, Draco and the other defendants were declared guilty and sentenced to be hung.

It was a grisly scene—naked bodies, their throats tied with wire, suspended from meathooks, struggling and gasping for breath as they writhed in their death throes. Belial watched with smug satisfaction from the window of the King's private chambers. "It is too bad that Adima and Hia do not swing there along with the rest," he thought aloud. "But they will soon, very, very soon. It is only a matter of time."

By late afternoon, it was all over. The rebellion had been squelched, the instigators and perpetrators had been subdued, punished, and destroyed, and Belial was firmly ensconced in power. As night fell, Atlantis grew quiet again, like a great beast after a terrible fight, licking its wounds, grieving its losses, and wondering what would happen next. Life, though, had been irrevocably changed. There was no commerce or trade in the Marketplace, no worship or healing in the Temple, no marriages or consecrations, no joy or laughter. The people could not accept their lot. They could not forget what they once had, nor could they accept the new conditions.

In a single bloody day, in a single rite of passage, another step had been taken on the long journey toward attainment of the Consciousness of Freedom. Atlanteans no longer believed in their leaders or trusted them to tell the truth. Perhaps it had been foolish to have ever done so. Disgusted by what they had seen, one by one the Homecoming delegates and guests made arrangements to return home. The convention had been ruined. There would be no more reconvening.

Belial swore and raged and threatened, but his authority was limited to only the Atlantean Elders. He could not force the provincial councilors to meet or even stay in Atlantis. He might rule with an iron hand, he might be in complete control in his own city, but as far as the visiting delegates were concerned, Belial was anathema...an outcast, a pariah. By leaving, they made it perfectly clear that they wanted nothing to do with the new king, his problems, or the home island.

The events of the past few days had changed these delegates forever. There would be no going back to the innocence of the time before Homecoming. They would carry these memories with them all of their lives, telling the stories to their children and grandchildren, of how they had been there to witness the destruction of the greatest civilization the world had ever known.

And all the while, time continued its inexorable march onward. Everyone could feel it. It was obvious. Underneath, there was a deeper undercurrent of change—larger than the unrest—seething, simmering quietly, like a great cauldron whose lid is about to blow from the extreme pressure of the steam boiling within. The enormous pressures within the Great Mother were almost ready to explode now, were almost at the bursting point.

*****

At the gathering place, the Arks were fully loaded and ready. It was dark by the time Hia made his way to where the great ships lay waiting. The others were all there. Adima told him about the events of the day. "To be captured means death," he said, referring to the note about how to sabotage the Fire Crystals, "but we have to carry out Shakala's instructions,"

"You'll be killed!" Cybele cried.

"What other choice do we have?" her husband replied. "We must try. There are secret ways in and out of the city. I'll use the tunnels. With any luck, I'll be in and out without them ever being the wiser. Then, as soon as I get back, we can be on our way."

*****

Nabala fidgeted uncomfortably as she waited for Lilith to grant her an audience. The Temple was virtually deserted, and she did not relish the idea of being alone within those desolate rooms and corridors, even though the news she brought was of the utmost importance. Even now, she started at the slightest sound, the vaguest flicker of a shadow. To take her mind off her fears, she concentrated on the words she would use in presenting her story.

There was so much to tell—bold, exciting, important news—and only she knew all of the details. Better to reveal them slowly, she reasoned, one juicy tidbit at a time. Begin with Shakala's note to Adima. Then tell of the plan to sneak into the Great Pyramid through the tunnels and sabotage the Fire Crystals. And finally, when the stage had been set and Lilith was tense with anticipation, she would reveal the most important news of all, that of greatest worth—Cybele's secret name.

"Latoné," Nabala could barely bring herself to whisper the name. What would Lilith's reaction be? She imagined herself being hugged and praised and flattered by the High Priestess. In her mind, Nabala was already counting out the pieces of silver and gold and jewels that would be her reward for such loyalty. She pictured herself in the turquoise robes of the select servants of the high priestess, one of the elite, one who was honored and revered. Wherever she went, people would bow down at her feet and treat her with reverence and respect.

Poor deluded child! She thought she was doing the right thing for Atlantis. She still thought there was room for her in the plans of Belial and Lilith. She still had aspirations of glory and grandeur and rising to a position of power in the sisterhood of priestesses. She felt someone shake her roughly. "I must have fallen asleep," she realized, for it was dark outside and her neck was stiff. A servant escorted her into the High Priestess' chambers.

"What is it you want?" Lilith asked curtly, not bothering to get up from the bed on which she was reclining. Her voice was tired and strained, and she looked pale and haggard. The remains of her supper lay untouched in golden plates and sparkling crystal on a bedside table.

"I have come to give you what you have asked for," Nabala began, wanting to draw out the moment and deliver her startling news slowly.

"Speak not in riddles, girl!" Lilith was in no mood for games. "Say what you have to say. Be plain and simple. There is no time for embellishments." The High Priestess leaned close, her voice soft, her smile surprisingly genuine, almost tender. She placed a warm palm on Nabala's arm. "Else you can keep your mysterious news to yourself. And if you try my patience further, I shall have your serpent's tongue cut out. Then you can carry your infernal tales with you to your grave and tell them to all the demons of the Underworld."

The threat worked. With a gasp of astonishment and fear, Nabala opened her mouth to speak. She told all, not with the flair and drama that she had rehearsed, but in a tumble of words and details that barely made sense. When she spoke the name, she looked at Lilith. The High Priestess reacted as though she had been crowned with a diadem of gold. She placed her palm over her mouth and stifled a gasp. A strange light gleamed in her eyes. At last, she had what she so desperately craved—the name, Cybele's secret name.

Pouring herself a goblet of wine, Lilith sipped slowly, savoring the dark red liquid as it trickled slowly down her throat. As the fruit of the vine was delicious, so also was the feeling of power that swept over her. "Latoné," she repeated, saying the word slowly, letting it roll off her tongue, savoring it as she savored the fine wine, savoring the gifts that came with knowing the name. For with the knowledge came the power. Cybele was hers, all hers. She would have complete control over her enemy—control of her person, her being, her very life.

Then came images of herself at Belial's side, as Queen of Atlantis. That would be her condition for sharing the secret name and the power with him. He would have to marry her and make her his queen. It would be a small enough price to pay, would it not, for something so valuable? Lilith pictured herself telling her Dark Lord the news. She could see herself standing in the royal purple, being crowned in front of all Atlantis. After they rebuilt, of course.

Nabala stood silently by, waiting impatiently. Had the High Priestess forgotten her? Had she forgotten the promises and the rewards? Softly, Nabala cleared her throat. As though called back early from a trance, Lilith turned to look at the acolyte, seeming to notice her for the first time.

"Well," she said imperiously, "are you still here?" "What is it that you want?"

"I await your pleasure, Mistress," Nabala said humbly, bowing low, palm outstretched. It was the most polite way she knew to ask for her reward.

Lilith was incensed. All the color drained from her face, and her lower lip trembled as she strove to control her wrath. "You await my pleasure?" she sneered, mimicking the young woman. "You await my pleasure? I shall give you my pleasure. I shall show you what it is that pleases me, and you will be sorry that you asked!"

Picking up the dinner plates and glasses, she hurled them through the air at the astonished priestess. Nabala dodged, but not in time. A crystal goblet struck her a glancing blow, breaking the skin of her cheek. She shrieked in pain, blood flowing from the deep, jagged wound.

"It pleases me that you leave my sight and never darken my door again," Lilith screamed, out of control as she grasped her victim by the hair and pulled her toward the door. "That is my pleasure!"

She struck first the priestess, then her gong. A servant appeared almost instantly, bowing low. "Remove this wretch from my sight and from the Temple," Lilith commanded disdainfully, wiping the blood from her hands. "See that I am not disturbed again tonight."

*****

"So he will come tomorrow." It was evening, and the soft glow of candlelight filled the room. Belial stood looking out the window of Lilith's private chambers at the ruined Garden of the Heart as he slowly sipped a glass of wine. A beetle crawled awkwardly along the windowsill, trying to hide within a small chink in the plaster. Every time it got close, he would brush it backward with a sweep of his huge hand, knocking it over, laughing evilly as it lay on its back, struggling to right itself.

"My little brother thinks he has a surprise in store for me. But it is I who will surprise him. When he exits the tunnels, I will be there, ready to pounce." He crashed a huge fist down onto the bug, squashing it on the stone, then turned to look at Lilith, lust in his eye—not the lust of a man, but the lust of a beast.

"You have done well, my dear," he purred, setting his glass on the nightstand, licking his thick lips as the sexual frenzy built inside him. "I shall pay your price. You will be Queen of Atlantis and rule by my side. Now come to me."

Feeling both excitement and revulsion at the same time, Lilith hesitated not a moment. Using a golden snuffer, she extinguished the candles one by one, then turned to face her lover. In the darkness, the soft rustle of silk made a sensuous whisper as her gown slipped from her shoulders and fell in folds to the floor. Silhouetted against the lighter background of the night, she glided slowly across the room and gave herself to the Beast.

As their passion welled, the sounds of their coupling mingled with other noises—chthonic grunts, groans, and the guttural growl of an animal. Lilith pretended not to hear. There was another sound, too, the high, almost musical jingle of shattering glass as the crystal decanter broke. Wine spilled onto the golden nightstand, staining the snowy damask tablecloth with the Mother's blood, the blood of death and sacrifice. Drip, drip, drip. One by one the droplets splattered on the stone floor, ticking off an ominous countdown to the final moments of Atlantis, forming a small, dark puddle, a fitting libation to the dead.

*****

And the evening and the morning were the fourth day.

CHAPTER 46

And the evening and the morning were the fifth day.

—Genesis 1:23

They came to Poseidia in droves—mothers and daughters, fathers and sons, families and individuals, alone and in groups, singly and by twos, with everything that they could possibly carry or just the clothes they wore. Young and old, rich and poor, weak and strong, healthy and sick, they flocked out of the city, forming a great processional along the Good Red Road. Across the Great Plain, into the forest, through the hills, and down into the valley through which flowed the River of Many Waters, the people of Atlantis wended their way to the Arks.

Yet for as many as came—and there were hundreds—so many more stayed behind. The few who made the decision to leave comprised only a small percentage of the entire population, several hundred in a land of millions, less than one tenth of one percent. It was not enough. There needed to be at least three percent in order to effect change. And there would not be three percent for a long, long time.

By first light on the fifth day of the week, the great ships were loaded and ready to sail. The Twelve stood by, welcoming the refugees, helping them feel safe and secure in the face of so much overwhelming disruption of their lives. Each Ark carried a specific cargo—a different piece of the puzzle, a different part of Atlantis—in its hold. Each would sail to a specific destination, separating both the people and the knowledge, scattering the seeds all over the world on so many foreign shores. It was best that way, the Voice had told Nuah. Thus they would be safe, thus the knowledge would survive. Where one might not take root and flourish, others would. Then, at the appointed time, they would come together again.

And so, a process begun by their founders had come full circle. As their forebears had done before them, so now the Children of the Law of One undertook the journey once again. What lay on the other side of the threshold? What initiations lay in store for them? What treasure would they find? And most important of all, would they succeed in returning home with it?

*****

As the people flocked out of the city above the ground along the Good Red Road, Adima made his way back into the city below the ground. Through the tunnels he walked, coming out at last below the base of the Great Pyramid very near the entrance to the labyrinth. Following Shakala's map, he made his way to a huge subterranean chamber. The room was dark and heavily vaulted, empty except for the Fire Crystals, which provided the only source of light, glowing red in the darkness.

Huge they were, twelve giants over thirty feet high and fifteen feet in circumference, perfectly smooth, each surrounded by dozens of smaller crystals of various shapes and sizes. From each tapered apex and base, thick metal rods rose upward into the ceiling and down into the ground, forming a complex latticework grid through which energy flowed to power the great island.

The very atmosphere was charged, each crystal pulsing with enormous power, energy on so vast a scale that it could split the planet in two if not properly controlled. Listening to the hum of the crystals, feeling the hair on his body and scalp rise up, charged with static electricity, Adima thought of the lightning and how he had felt when he had been struck. This experience was not unlike that one. So much electricity, so much power all around him!

And it is being abused, he thought. Used for death and destruction rather than for good. How Belial had thwarted the great purposes of the Ancients! Well, Adima would do what he could to rectify that today. The way was clear, too clear. Suddenly he felt uneasy, sensing danger. This was far too easy. Such precious crystals should have been heavily guarded. Why were they out in the open for anyone to access? Too late, he realized it was a trap. The soldiers pounced, holding him firmly. A single gasp escaped his lips as the black-robed figure of Belial stepped forth from the shadows.

"Greetings, little brother," Belial's tone was cool and mocking. His huge body was an indistinguishable dark black blob against a lighter background. His white skin muted the red light, and his face glowed an unearthly pink, emphasizing the deep-set coal-black eyes that gaped like twin portals to the land of the dead. "To what do I owe the pleasure of this visit?" He reached out and took the parchment that Adima still clutched in his hand.

"What is this?" Belial feigned surprise as he held the paper close to one of the crystals, slowly reading the words in the dim red light. "A message from Shakala telling you how to destroy the Fire Crystals? Shakala the traitor? Giving out forbidden information? Teaching you, also a traitor, how to destroy Atlantis?"

Belial crumpled the brittle parchment into a small wrinkled ball, rolling it in one huge fist as he paced round the room. Adima struggled to remain calm, trying not to panic lest he do something stupid that would get him hurt or killed before he had a chance to think. "Well," Belial said, gently placing the parchment atop one of the smallest of the Fire Crystals, "it may surprise you to know that Shakala is already dead, and you are going to be joining him very, very soon."

There was a sharp whiff of ozone as the parchment ignited in a flurry of sparks and burned to a crisp in a matter of seconds. Adima stifled an involuntary shudder. Belial watched, immensely pleased with his tiny but effective pyrotechnic display. He leaned close and smiled a fearsome, wicked smile. "But before you die, little brother, you and I will have one last talk." Belial pressed his face close to Adima's. That smug grin could not mask the distinct odor of rotting flesh. "That is a promise. I shall be back to see you very, very soon. Take him to the labyrinth."

*****

The soldiers bound him to the stone wall, fastening his arms and legs with manacles and chains so that he could barely move. Then they went out, leaving the door ajar and a flickering torch to cast its feeble light on the walls and floor and ceiling of the dungeon. Adima looked around the tiny cell. There were no windows and only a single door. The walls had been carved out of the solid bedrock, telling him that he was deep under the ground.

Reaching out, he felt the cold, hard stone, so solid and unyielding beneath the soft touch of his fingers. Feeling along the floor, his hand encountered something cold and viscid. He drew back with a shudder of revulsion as he realized that he was sitting in a dark pool of congealed blood. It was a great amount of blood, he knew, and relatively fresh. Someone had bled to death in that very spot not too long ago. He shuddered again, trying to shift his position, but he was too tightly bound. There was nothing to do but wait for Belial's return.

The great links pressed deeply into his flesh, first bruising, then cutting. The pain was terrible, but he kept stonily silent, willing himself to accept the physical agony and helplessness, while at the same time letting his mind soar freely. Thus he waited, bound and chained and alone with his thoughts while the torchlight cast demonic shadows and the blood flowed from his arms and legs, commingling with the blood of the alchemist on the unfeeling stone floor.

*****

The door swung wide and Belial entered the cell. He was carrying a miniature Fire Crystal, a smaller version of the giants that powered all of Atlantis from their repository within the center of the Great Pyramid. Adima blinked and roused himself from the doze into which he had fallen. Even the soft red glow of this tiny crystal was enough to hurt his eyes. He had to shut them tightly until they got used to the light again.

Accompanied by a handful of soldiers, Belial placed the crystal on the floor in the center of the cell and stood before his bound and helpless brother. "Give him the potion," he commanded the guard.

"But Master," a terrified underling protested, "it isn't safe. I could be hurt. We could all be hurt."

"He is bound and chained to the wall and cannot move," Belial noted. Almost as an afterthought, he added, "But force him to stand upright, so that he stays alert and listens. I want him to hear all that I have to say to him."

Adima felt himself lifted roughly to his feet as the guard pulled on the chains and readjusted them so that his feet barely touched the floor. A strong hand grabbed him by the hair and pulled his head backward, forcing his mouth open as a thick, bitter concoction was poured down his throat. Gagging and sputtering, head swimming, he felt his legs collapse as the potion carried him up and out into an altered state of consciousness.

"Now leave us," Belial dismissed the guards and stood facing his brother. They were alone for the first time since they had met in the alley almost thirty years earlier.

Physically, Adima was just as helpless now as he had been then. This time, however, he was mentally, emotionally, and spiritually prepared, strong and able to hold his ground. That made all the difference. Belial's magic and tricks would not work this day. The potion might induce strange and frightening visions, but there would be no psychic wounding, no supernatural display of powers to frighten him. Belial knew better than to try.

Nor would he be killed right away, Adima surmised. His mind was surprisingly clear as he felt himself floating in a gentle ocean of swirling colors. Belial wanted to make an example of him, to be sure. But first, his brother seemed to want to talk, to unburden himself, to get everything out in the open between them.

"So you thought you could get away with it," Belial sneered, pointing to the glowing object on the floor. "You thought you could follow Shakala's formula and sabotage the Fire Crystals so that there would be too little power for the device. How foolish, and how stupid." Making a great effort to control his rage, he walked around the crystal, silently contemplating the prisoner who stood shackled before him. At last, the rage won out.

"Do you think I am a fool?" he roared, grabbing Adima by the chest and pulling him close. "Do you think I was not prepared for your plan? That I was not aware of your coming?"

Adima said nothing, letting his brother rant and storm and gloat. He was deeply under the influence of the potion now, and with his eyes closed, he floated in a vast ocean of swirling lights and color. Moving, living geometrical forms swept past him in a continuously changing equation that passed from richness to more intensely colored richness, from grandeur to ever-deepening grandeur.

At last Belial tired himself out. He just stood there, panting, his great chest heaving with the exertion and strain. Adima opened his eyes. The beautiful lights and colors were gone, replaced by the stark reality of the cavern, where long, dark shadows flickered grotesquely on the walls like a pack of demons waiting for the excitement of a macabre drama to begin.

In the silence, the twins faced each other, the soft red glow from the Fire Crystal reflected in their faces. One wrapped in physical chains, yet so free in mind and spirit. The other physically unfettered, able to come and go as he pleased, yet chained beneath a veil of false beliefs and illusions, bound by the power of the drug-beast that had so strong a hold on him. Brother facing brother, Hero-man facing Shadow-man.

Gradually, an object began to materialize in the cell, a huge polished looking glass floating gently in space. Adima gazed within and gasped. Who am I looking at? he wondered, peering intently at the somber figure from eyes that saw only what the potion wanted him to see. He knew, of course, and he shuddered involuntarily. I'm looking into a perverted magic mirror at some dark and sinister aspect of myself had I chosen a different path.

His thinking was surprisingly clear, and a sudden realization of a great truth came to him. *"I am both Belial and myself, as he is both himself and me. There are parts of us in each other."* But if this is so, Adima wondered, then why have I chosen my path? And why has Belial chosen another? What happened to separate us and make Belial follow the dark way? Adima had to know, and the only way to get the answers was to ask.

He straightened himself and stood upright, taking charge despite his chains, despite the effects of the potion. He was not afraid. If he were about to die, so be it. He regretted that he had not been able to do what he had set out to do, but so be it.

Suddenly, a sharp, burning pain exploded in his midsection. "What is that?" he cried in agony, looking out at his reflection in the magic mirror. His body had become transparent, and he scanned it for signs of physical malady as the pain in his solar plexus continued to burn with agonizing intensity. He was amazed at what he saw.

Fire seared his midsection, glowing as red as the Fire Crystal itself—a red hot ball deep in the middle of his third chakra, his center of power. From within the ball, a thin red band of fire snaked out into the cell, threading its way through the Fire Crystal and out the other side, where it penetrated Belial's midsection, which glowed with an even redder, hotter, brighter fire.

With astonishment, Adima realized that he was looking at the source of the pain. It was coming from Belial. Not that Belial was inflicting pain on him. Rather, he was sensing Belial's own internal pain, the physical and emotional pain that his brother carried inside himself every minute of every day.

"Such agony," Adima muttered, stifling a groan. "Belial is a tortured soul, and now he is making me feel the same torture that he feels. He wants me to be as tortured as he is. He wants me to hurt as he hurts. He wants me to know how life is for him. I could probably stop this," he told himself, "but I will not. If I am to understand my brother, I must know all there is to know about him. I must feel what he feels, even if it is great physical and emotional pain."

As he accepted the state of empathy that the drug had induced, his third eye opened to a grim and ghastly vision of the future. Within the magic mirror, all kinds of strange new engines of destruction swam before him. Alien machines of torture and death, he had never seen the like of them before. The human race, however, would come to know them very, very well. For as they stepped onto the Slaughterbench of History, many would be broken and killed on those terrible instruments.

Adima knew their names—the rack, the screw, the press, the guillotine, the gun, the cannon, the atomic bomb, the electric chair, the lethal injection. Some primitive, some quite sophisticated, all shared the common ability to inflict pain, terror, and death. All created from the same dark and perverted desire to inflict the personal pain of the torturers outward onto others in the misguided hope that another's physical agony would somehow ease their own emotional anguish.

Images in the mirror flashed and swirled, beckoning to them, inviting the brothers to step within. They accepted. In a flurry of rushing wind and flashing colors, Adima was transported into the Chief Elder's personal chamber of horrors, where he was thrown roughly onto the rack, bound hand and foot, and stretched out spread-eagled in the form of a human cross, a grotesque caricature of the image etched into the floor of the Temple of Poseidon.

Belial stood by his side, about to turn the huge wheel that, if pulled tightly enough, would ever so slowly stretch the victim's muscles tighter and tighter, straining joints, eventually pulling his arms and legs from their sockets. Although he knew it was a drug-induced illusion, the pain and the terror were quite real. From his supine and helpless position, Adima looked up at his brother looming over him.

Belial stood there looking rather lost and forlorn, not the man of power and might who controlled the Council of Elders, who spoke so eloquently, who could crush an opponent with a single withering glance. This was a different Belial, one whom Adima had never seen. Could this be the real Belial? Taking a deep breath, resigning himself to the experience of the pain, Adima addressed his twin. "What is it with you, brother?" he asked the giant. "What ails you?"

Belial's face grew strained, as though some deep emotion were fighting to express itself and did not quite know how to find the release it craved. Features twisting into a terrible, ghastly grimace of absolute sorrow and despair, he struggled to control himself.

But Adima had asked the single right question, the one that invoked compassion, the one he had learned at the Well of Kuneware. It was a magic question, unlocking the dam behind which all of Belial's emotions had been stuffed, where the Truth lay bound by the confusion in his mind-brain-heart. Like long-blocked waters that had suddenly been unstopped, the words and emotions came pouring out. The release came, and Adima listened in silence as his brother spoke at last.

"I tried, I tried so hard," the giant sobbed, standing with stooped shoulders and clenched fists in the middle of the cell. Suddenly he was not a giant, just a pitiful little boy with huge tears running down his pasty white cheeks. "I sought for merger and union with the Divine. I sought through the potions. I drank them, hoping for a glimpse of the Spirit-world. I sought through wizards and magicians. I listened to them and did their bidding, hoping for love and approval. All I ever wanted was to know my Source—to step into it and be one with it. And I never could!" Belial spat out the words as he paced back and forth like a caged animal.

"Do you know what that feels like, little brother?" the giant asked, tightening the wheel for the first time. "You will know. You will feel the pain now, the excruciating torture of being pulled and stretched in every direction." The wheel clicked, and pain seared through all his joints and limbs. Adima felt as if he were about to break apart. The irony was not lost on him, nor was the scope of his brother's suffering.

He felt his twin's affliction, shared the agony of being stretched and pulled and torn. It was extreme torture, yet he had been undergoing the gruesome physical experience for only a few minutes. Belial had been experiencing it emotionally for a lifetime.

"No matter how hard I tried, I never could find that connection," the tortured soul wailed. "Someone always prevented me from achieving my goal. Someone like you," Belial hissed, anger stepping in to replace grief as he tightened the wheel another notch.

Click. The pressure increased, and Adima felt the rage shoot out at him, its powerful shock waves pulling at him, ripping and tearing and pressing him down onto the table. The pain was excruciating now, but he managed to speak between clenched teeth.

"Why, brother?" he asked, truly wanting to know. "Why is your heart so filled with hatred? Why is there no love in you? Why do you hate me so?"

"Because you were the chosen one," came the simple but confused reply as Belial pulled the rack ever tighter, his voice rising in fervor and intensity. "You were the beloved of the Spirit-world. They favored you, they loved you. So what was left for me? To be second behind you? To stand in your shadow? To watch while glory and riches and honor were yours alone? To lie at your feet and hungrily beg for scraps and leavings from your table of plenty? No, little brother. I could never accept that. I could never be subservient to you. I could never watch you exalted and myself humbled."

Belial groaned, and with the groan, Adima the empath felt all the emotional and physical pain of unrequited love, of seeking and not finding, of wanting to belong and being locked out of the world of togetherness and companionship, confined instead to a dark world where there was only misery and solitude.

"So I sought for material comforts," Belial paused in his confession, his voice soft once again, his face taking on a look of resignation. "If I could not get the love and affection that came with the blessing of Spirit and merger with the Divine, I would get them from the world. Power, status, and wealth would be my gods. I would merge with them and they with me. And they would bring me what I so desperately craved."

He paused, releasing the pressure on the wheel. For a moment, Adima thought he was going to be released as his brother quietly admitted his mistake. "How wrong I was. I know now that power, status, and wealth are not enough. There must be something more. What is it?" Belial shrieked, pacing to and fro in emotional agony, tearing his hair, flailing his arms in frustration. "Where is it? Why is it being kept from me? Why do you have it and I do not?" The look in his eyes as he implored his brother caused Adima more pain than the physical torture of the rack.

"You bastard!" Belial's mood changed again, growing darker and angrier. He turned the wheel a notch tighter. Click. "It was so easy for you. You asked, and Spirit answered." Click. The wheel turned again, and Adima screamed.

"You bent your knee, and the angels caressed you. You lifted up your eyes, and they came down to you." Click. Another turn of the wheel, a few more ounces of excruciating pressure, another scream.

"Why?" It was not a word, it was a cry of absolute frustration and despair, ringing loud and long, echoing through the chamber, out into the corridor, up through the Great Pyramid, and out into the streets, where it floated up to Heaven. "What makes you so special?" Click.

With the final turn of the wheel, Adima felt his body break. He was pulled apart, arms and legs torn from their sockets as the relentless pressure overcame the strength of sinews, muscles, tendons, and bone. He screamed too, giving voice to his agony, mingling his voice with his brother's. Weeping with his brother, for his brother, feeling the pain, the anguish, the frustration, the rage. After a time, he found himself floating once again in the peaceful, warm sea of light and color. The pain had passed for the moment, but he could not see his physical body, just a glowing white form that had a vaguely human shape.

What can I do, how can I help? Adima wondered. Am I even supposed to try? He felt he had to say something, to make some sort of response, not in defense of himself or his choices, but rather just a statement of the truth. If his brother could listen to the truth and be changed by it, so be it. If not, so be that, too. It was, after all, still his brother's choice. From that peaceful place, floating in the ocean of color, Adima attuned himself with Higher Mind, that place he had come to know so well over the years whenever he entered a deep, meditative state. From that place of calm knowing, he called to his dark twin, speaking to him of Love and Truth, trying to comfort and console him, offering a soothing balm to ease his pain and cleanse his wounds.

"Brother, what you think is not the truth. You are as loved as I am, as we all are. There are no degrees of love. No one is first or second. We are all the same. Your being is as legitimate as mine, as loved as mine. Therefore, your worth is equal to mine—no better, no worse. Had you known this and followed your true path, whatever you would have done, whatever offerings you made or gifts you brought would have been pleasing and acceptable in the eyes of Spirit, *had your motives been right.*"

"You hate me and wish me dead because I have a heart open to Spirit and understand that true worship is based on gratitude to the Creator rather than attempted merit by human efforts or works. Your problem, which is really a misapplication of the Truth, is a wrong motive rather than the wrong type of offering." The words flowed gently forth. Adima watched them float out of his mouth, each a tiny point of light gently falling over Belial like soft, golden rain.

The giant stood mesmerized for a moment, caught in the spell of the healing, cleansing shower of Truth. But then a change came over him once again, and he roused himself and brushed the golden words away like so many annoying insects.

"Nonsense!" Belial scoffed as he stormed and raged around the cell. "Just plain nonsense! Keep your pious, self-righteous words and attitudes to yourself. Save them for the Children of the Law of One who hang on your every word like doting simpletons. They are wasted on me. I have no need of them."

His form had begun to change along with his mood. He was suddenly larger, more upright and erect. The Belial-self was slowly being pushed down, and the Beast-self was beginning to come forward, taking shape before Adima's very eyes.

Why? Adima wondered, and then he realized right away. Because his words were true, and some part of his brother knew it. That knowing-self wanted to embrace the Truth, but the Beast-self was stronger and would not let it happen.

Adima realized the difference between the first encounter and this one. A few moments ago, he had been talking to his brother, a vicious brother who hated and despised him and wanted to hurt him, but nevertheless a brother. Now, though, he was in the presence of the Beast, and in order to survive, it could not let the Truth be heard for long. In order to ensure its own continuance, the Beast had to take charge, suppressing the real Belial, hiding him away, stuffing him deep within his pitiful self and keeping him there.

From the ocean of light and color, Adima stared at the creature before him. It looked like his brother, and perhaps his brother was even there somewhere, underneath all of the layers of armor and protection and masks. The personality in control, however, the personality in charge, was that of the Beast. There was no room for remorse, no room for willingness to change, no room for forgiveness, no room for tears or a cathartic experience. This time, the torture was going to be a lot worse.

The magic mirror shimmered and beckoned once again. Together, the antagonists stepped within. Instantly, the comforting ocean dissolved, and Adima found himself back in physical form, chained and bound to a cold slab of stone. A great weight pressed down on him, that of a heavy wooden slab which covered him from head to foot.

"Easy for you to say, you who had it all," the Belial-Beast roared, meticulously placing huge stone weights at specific locations on top of the board. "You condescend to me and look down on me and presume to teach me. How dare you!" He placed a huge stone on the center plank. "Feel this, little brother. Feel the burden of carrying the weight of the world on your shoulders, of being locked into a course of action and a way of life from which there is no way out, no escape."

The stone pressed down mightily. Its weight was immense, and Adima experienced a choking, smothering sensation. It was a physical version, he realized, of an even more stifling emotional experience, one that Belial lived day in and day out, all the days of his life.

"Let me tell you something, great savior of Atlantis," the Belial-Beast added another stone, and another. Adima tried to look around but could not. He was hemmed in on all sides, and the floor and the slab were closing in on him, crushing him under their relentless weight. "You have not seen the last of me. The world has not seen the last of me." Maniacal laughter filled the chamber as the Belial-Beast struggled with a great slab of iron.

"Even if you strike me down, I shall not die. I shall return again and again and again. And each time I do, I shall find the Spear, take it up, and resume where I left off." Iron muscles bulged as he raised the anvil high above his head. Pausing for an instant, he looked down at his helpless victim. "You will never crush me, you will never defeat me," the man-thing roared. "I shall live and rule forever and ever and ever!"

In slow motion his fingers opened, and the force of gravity reached out to pull the great weight to the Earth. It landed on the wooden slab with a sickening crunch. Adima felt the rush of escaping air as his chest and lungs caved in and his internal organs were crushed. Unable to take in air, he struggled to inhale as the breath of life was pushed out of him. There was no room to move, no place to go, no choice but to succumb to the enormous weight, the weight of all the world, as it pressed down on him.

As suddenly as it began, the pressure was gone, his lungs filled with air, and he felt himself floating peacefully in the ocean of color, back in the sea of compassion and understanding. Now he understood, knowing the truth at last, understanding his part and Belial's part too. They were brothers, and they were also opposites, representing the two sides of human nature—ego and alter ego, light and dark, active and passive, positive and negative, waxing and waning—the two hemispheres, the two poles. But they did not have to be at enmity. There was no need for one to serve as sacrifice at the hands of the other, the sacrificer. Just as Adima and Hia had a part to play, just as Cybele and Sophia and Enoch and the twins had their roles, so too did the Belial-Beast.

Because this was so, there was no need to struggle with the Beast or fight against it any more, no need to be guilty about what he, Adima, was about to do or what Belial was about to do or how events would play themselves out in Atlantis. Their paths were set, their courses chosen. There was no right or wrong, it was simply the way it was. And the reasons were far beyond Belial's limited ability to understand.

The effects of the potion had almost worn off. Adima's head was clear and his heart full of compassion and gratitude. With a smile of love, he addressed the Belial-Beast, but it was really his brother to whom he spoke. He hoped that his brother could hear his voice, and so be comforted by the truth and finally freed of his guilt.

"You debase yourself needlessly, big brother," Adima replied calmly and gently, "for your purpose is as great as mine, as anyone's, for that matter. We are one, you and I. Part of the Unity, experiencing the Duality, you walk one path, I walk another. Why you walk yours and I walk mine, I do not know. I do not yet understand the workings of the Plan well enough to presume that I have all the answers. All I know is that it is a wise and good Plan, and that each of us has a part to play, a part we chose."

As he spoke, the Belial-Beast howled and roared, pacing restlessly to and fro, trying to drown out the sounds of Truth. The vibrations of the words, however, were stronger than any discord the Beast could produce.

"The part you have chosen is as great a part as the one I have chosen. For through you, the world will receive the gift of awakening to the Consciousness of Freedom. Through you in your many incarnations, they will learn what freedom truly means. That freedom is not just for the one—Belial, or whatever name you may take in your future incarnations.

Nor is freedom only for the elite and the ruling classes or the Patriarchy alone. But rather, freedom is for all created beings, male and female, old and young, black and red and brown and yellow and white, human and nonhuman. Carbon-based life, silicon based life, star-based life...it matters not. All are created equal, and freedom belongs to us all. The gift of that knowing will come from you, my brother."

What was that? Adima wondered. A faint flicker of recognition, a tiny nod of the head, a sigh of hope? Had he seen a reaction from the real Belial, hidden so deeply under the visage of the Beast? Encouraged, Adima continued to speak.

"What a wonderful honor has been bestowed upon you, my brother. What a wonderful gift you offer to the world. We are forever grateful to you, for without you, we are incomplete. Without your part, the Plan cannot succeed. That is why I shall not judge you, why no one must judge you." Adima waved his arm, and the magic mirror appeared again, floating in space, the Belial-Beast reflected in its shiny surface. A shadowy, ragged symbol appeared on the forehead of the man in the mirror, although it did not appear on the living creature who stood before the glass.

"Behold. You are marked by an invisible sign that shows you are forever under the protection of Spirit," Adima explained. "Justice and judgment upon you belong to the Divine, with whom you seek so desperately to merge. It is the long-suffering mercy of the Divine that awaits you throughout the ages as you seek the light and learn to overcome the dark part of your Self."

This was more than the Belial-Beast could bear. A huge paw reached out and encircled Adima's neck in a death grip, squeezing and choking the life force from him. Out came the Beast, roaring in all of its fury. Belial was gone, replaced by the hideous, growling creature with the long snout, feral tongue, and dripping fangs.

Adima felt the fear well up in him. This was no potion-induced illusion. This was real. He had to defend himself. The flames still burned dully in his solar plexus, still maintaining the connection to the creature who held him through the Fire Crystal. Fighting to stay conscious and in control, he reached out with his mind, reached out to the consciousness within the crystal, aligning his mental patterns and vibrations with those of the Supermind, as Enoch had showed him, sending out a plea for help.

The Supermind responded. As the Beast squeezed, the Fire Crystal glowed redder and redder, the hum grew louder and louder. The Beast was aghast. How was this possible? How could this puny human creature have mastery over a power as great as the Fire Crystals? Squeezing harder, it tried to make him stop, tried to make him dead.

On the verge of blacking out, Adima concentrated more deeply. If he were going to die, better that it be by his own hand than by the hand of the Beast. Better to vaporize the crystal and both die in the resulting explosion than to be choked to death by his Shadow Brother Self. The crystal pulsed with enormous energy, releasing a shower of fiery sparks. The room glowed with a fierce red light as predator and prey struggled in the depths of the labyrinth under the massive bulk of the Great Pyramid.

Which force will win? Adima wondered. Which will be stronger, the Fire Crystal or the Beast? He shut his eyes, waiting for the outcome, forgetting the existence of a Third Force, an all-powerful Force capable of overcoming even the combined energies of the Fire Crystal and the Beast.

Just when the crystal seemed ready to explode and the life force leave his body, Adima felt the pressure relax, and his airway was clear once again. Something had stayed the Beast's hand. The demon had vanished, and Belial had returned, a tired, forlorn, hopeless, weak, and fearful man.

"No, I will not kill you now," he hissed, trying to hide his fear. "That would be too easy. I will wait until my coronation day. As the crown is placed on my head, I will watch as your head is lopped off. It will be my first official act as King—the punishment of the greatest traitor Atlantis has ever known."

With a bound, Belial strode out of the cell and slammed the door shut, plunging the chamber into total darkness and leaving Adima completely alone.

*****

Alone, deep within the Earth, the third torture was visited upon Adima, not a drug-induced hallucination, but a physical experience that was all too real. There was no physical pain, yet his suffering was far greater than the suffering of being stretched and broken on the rack. There were no physical marks upon his person, yet his anguish was far more excruciating than the anguish of being crushed under immeasurable weight. There was no physical harm to his body, yet his misery was far more agonizing than the misery of strangulation at the hands of a murderous monster.

This was torture of a far more virulent and effective kind—the exquisite torture of the mind, in which all of the pain and anguish were created by the victim himself through succumbing to his own worst fears and misperceptions. Not even Belial's demonic rage and imagination could have dreamed up such appalling and inconceivable horrors. No, such torment could only come from the demons within Adima himself, demons of thought whose creation had sprung to life on the day of his own conception.

The sense memory of his hideous existence in the toxic womb and ensuing struggle through the birth canal had smoldered deep in his subconscious for decades, waiting for the right time to emerge. Always, those memories were with him, although he did not understand what they were or what they meant. All he knew was that he had a distinct and overwhelming dread of tight, dark places and being confined therein.

Adima's worst fear had just become a reality. He had been buried alive in a tight black hole, arms pressed closely to his sides, legs immobilized—stuck, helpless, and hopeless. No way out, no chance of rescue. No light to see, no air to breathe. No one to hear his cries for help, no one to come to his aid.

The damp air in the cell grew rank and foul, and he could scarcely draw a breath. The walls seemed to come alive, closing in upon him, the living stone reaching out to crush and smother him in their relentless and unassailable hold. Panic-stricken, struggling desperately to free himself, he cried out in terror, lashing against his bonds, pressing against the unyielding rock, trying desperately to get loose. The more he tried, the more afraid he became, the more he lost control.

Fearing for his sanity and his reason, all that his mind would focus on was the fact that he was trapped. Trapped! The fear screamed through his consciousness. His mind railed at the thought, although his body could not physically move.

Trapped beneath the Earth, within the Earth, surrounded by the Earth—forever trapped, forever helpless. Never to get out, never to see the light of day again. Never to move arms or legs, never to be free again. Never to walk on the bosom of the Great Mother again. Never to hold his wife in his arms again. Never to see his children again. And never to die! Such was the ultimate torture, a powerful aggressor that seared into his being, attacking with vicious ferocity.

He was trapped in that awful hole forever—alive and conscious and absolutely alone. No amount of trying to control his thoughts could ease the terror. No amount of struggle could release him. No amount of screaming could inform his loved ones of his plight. They would always wonder what had happened to him, never knowing his fate. He screamed out in terror, heart pounding in his ribcage. He thought his heart would burst through the walls of his chest. Indeed, he *hoped* it would, but it did not.

He craved death, but it would not come. He tried to die but could not. Adima was in the grip of the Supreme Ordeal. Enoch had told him the experience would come one day, but he had never imagined anything like this. Words could never describe the agitation and turmoil within his tortured mind.

As he struggled, Enoch's voice rose above the chatter and unfolding drama. "Go," the old man ordered. "Enter into the teeth of the Great Mystery and confront it. Confront the Void. Confront your fear. Confront solitude. Confront life in death and death in life. Confront the Beast within yourself. Confront the Creator. Confront Death. Confront the Mystery."

"I don't want to," Adima screamed, pulling at his chains to no avail. His wrists and ankles were slippery with blood, but he could not manage to slip loose. "Help me, get me out of here, let me out. Argghhhhhhhhhhhhhhhhh!"

"Are you a man?" Enoch snapped back at him. "Or has this all been for nothing? How long are you going to run from it?"

Adima didn't even bother to try to look for the figure behind the voice. He knew this was a projection from Enoch's consciousness to his own. The old man could not possibly be in the cell, could not possibly effect a rescue.

"All you have is you—not Cybele, not me, not the twins," Enoch continued, his tone stern and commanding. "Only you. There is no one else, nothing else. Go off and confront you!"

"What if the demons come when I'm all alone?" Adima wailed, barely realizing what he was saying, so exhausted was he from the fear and the struggle."

"Then let them come, once and for all." That was all. Enoch's voice faded, and Adima was alone once again, alone with his greatest fear.

He had no choice, so he went—into the wilderness, into the teeth of his greatest fear, into the solitude, into the mystery. Alone—no Enoch, no wife, no children, no shield, no sword. Alone, with only himself to greet the demons, confront the mystery, and face death. His body went limp as he tried to catch his breath. The cell had been hewn from the solid bedrock, and his back seemed to nestle into a little depression in the living rock.

There he stood, no longer struggling, no longer railing against or resisting that which he was absolutely powerless to move or change. Dread and emptiness were his sole companions now, and he welcomed them, letting these cold, dark emotions embrace him, fill him, and consume him completely. With such complete surrender, his consciousness changed, and his mind grew quiet, expectant, as though a great secret were about to be revealed. A circle of impenetrable blackness appeared before him, so absolutely devoid of color as to be visible, even in the total darkness below ground.

His mind seemed to step outside itself, peering into the impenetrable blackness, watching and waiting for what he did not know. "Come in," the Void seemed to beckon, and Adima knew that he must indeed accept the invitation. With a shiver, he willed his mind to enter a strange shadowland between life and death, where physical laws were suspended and space and time did not exist. Slowly, his consciousness began to be transformed.

First came the tears, then the fears, and finally, alone in the dark, the night terrors. Deprived of the input of his senses, his mind wandered, and the nightmares came. Horrible dreams they were, images of beasts and dragons and monsters, only to be followed by moments of lucidity in which he would mumble and cry out for answers.

"What are you, Death?" he addressed the Great Mystery. "What happens in your black embrace? How will this all end? When will I be free again? I've got to know. Tell me."

To which the Void responded with ineffable silence until at last it spoke. *"Don't know,"* came the chilling reply. *"Don't know. Embrace the Mystery."*

Adima swooned, only to awaken to another period of altered consciousness, stronger this time, deeper. Gone were the nightmares and terrors, to be replaced by a different kind of experience. He was buried alive within the rich, fertile Earth, only his head sticking out above the ground. This is how I came into the world, he realized with a thrill of recognition. Stuck in the birth canal, head free, but the rest of me still buried in my mother's womb.

Far off in the distance, a drum was beating. Adima listened, embracing the sound, taking comfort in its slow, steady cadence. After a while, the drumbeat became the beating of his own heart. At some point during the ordeal, his body ceased to exist. This was a different experience from those when he and Enoch had floated freely through the astral plane, for here he was still chained in the cell.

His body, however, had merged with the body of the Great Mother. He could not tell where his body stopped and where hers began. Adima felt as if he were one with her. The Mother's body was his own. The Mother's heartbeat was his own. The Mother's blood was his own. Surrendering himself to the embrace of the Great Mother, he lay in her warm and loving arms. Individuality lost all meaning as he experienced unity with his physical source.

After a time, he felt himself rising up along a beam of fire. "I'm inside a bolt of lightning," he realized, "traveling up it to its source beyond the ether." Ascending higher and higher, he soon found himself floating in a blissful realm of absolute tranquility. "I remember!" he cried, experiencing a strong sense of peace and well being as he recognized the familiar light fields where he had once made his home. Gorgeous colors swirled around him, caressing him, touching him, welcoming him. It felt so good to be there that he cried soft tears of joy.

He had ascended beyond the Great Mother. She was far away, yet he could look back on her, back on the sun and the moon, back even on the solar system and the Milky Way. From his place in the Light, he realized that the heavenly bodies were not separate entities and objects. Everything was alive! The whole universe was connected to a Universe of Universes, and there was but a single Spirit moving through all of life.

"*Welcome,*" a Voice said. He looked and beheld others like himself. "*Welcome to the Brethren. We have been awaiting your arrival, and we are glad you are here.*"

"Where am I?" Adima asked, sensing total acceptance, hearing the words as thoughts within his own mind.

"*You are in the Light,*" came a reply of perfect patience, perfect gentleness. "*You have ascended into a new level of consciousness. You are at the place for which you have been striving and searching for so long. You are Home.*"

The tears fell harder now, great warm tears of absolute ecstasy. The journey was over at last. He had found the Grail, he had overcome, and now he had made his way back home. Or had he? The Presence so like his own continued to speak.

"*You have a choice, a decision to make,*" his Light Brother explained. "*You are welcome to stay with us, or you can continue to evolve while being of service to your brethren on Earth.*"

Adima thought long and hard. It was so peaceful there. How he wanted to stay! He could learn everything he wanted to learn, explore all that there was to be explored. He was on the threshold of coming to understand the Great Mystery and move beyond the veil that separated Illusion from Truth, the Dream from Reality. How could he pass up such an opportunity?

Then he looked back down at the Earth, the beautiful blue-white world swimming silently in space. Compassion filled him like waters from a warm spring—compassion for the Great Mother and all of her myriad forms of life. What other course could he choose than to return to Earth?

"You have made a wise and loving choice," the Light Being commended him, sensing his decision even as the thought was birthed in Adima's consciousness. Floating gently in the swirling colors, the Presence hovered before him. *"Receive this symbol, a reminder to yourself as well as a sign to all the world of what you have achieved and who and what you are."*

Adima bent his head as the ahnk was placed over his neck, not just an ahnk, but inscribed with the figure of a man. The explanation was forthcoming.

"Like Enoch and Sophia and ourselves and the others before you, now you have reached a state of being that would be thought of as immortal in the world to which you are returning. Because this is so, when you arrive again on Earth, you will be known by a new name—Thoth—and you will assume the mantle of Teacher."

Another of the Light Brethren hovered before him, shimmering in iridescent splendor. Adima sensed curiosity, and opened his thoughts to receive the question.

"How long will you stay?" the Radiant One inquired.

The answer was easy. Everything had become so very easy from this state of heightened awareness and vibration. He remembered everything—his agreement with his Father-Self, his pact with Hia, the whole Plan. It was so loving and so simple, so perfectly loving and simple.

"Until the planet has reached a certain level of consciousness," Adima-Thoth replied. "When humankind reaches that level, they will be able to survive by themselves. Then, when the Light is finally stronger than the Darkness once again, I will return here."

"That may take a long time," the Radiant One replied.

"It would take a long time," Adima-Thoth replied with a wise and knowing smile. "But I will not go back to Earth empty-handed. I will give the world a gift that will help them greatly. This gift will effect marvelous changes in human civilization. For it is a gift that will help to free them from their entanglements in polarity consciousness after the Mother shifts to save herself, a gift that will help them return more quickly to their natural state of Unity Consciousness."

The Light Brethren pressed close, excited by his words, eager to know more about this marvelous and mystical gift. *"What magic will you give?"* the Group Mind asked in unison. *"What could you possibly give that would accomplish in the human condition what you have described?"*

Adima-Thoth smiled his familiar, human smile. "I will give the gift of Writing to the darkened world," he said. "No longer will the art of writing be reserved for the priests and priestesses and cultural elite, thereby forcing the people to rely on the Elders to interpret royal edicts, news from the provinces, and ancient texts like the *Book of Life*. No longer will the texts be structured around limiting and codified pictographs whose meanings are known only to the initiated, thereby forcing individuals to devise crude, personally-defined symbols to record what is in their minds and hearts.

"Now writing will be transformed into something beautiful—a sacred art form available to all races, all cultures, for all time. And serving as Scribe, I will record the history of the world and present it to humankind.

"A great and precious gift," they all replied. *"This will have a far more beneficent impact on civilization than even the invention of the wheel and the rediscovery of nuclear fire. May they be worthy to receive it. Now rest yourself and renew your form identity, that you may return refreshed and strong and ready to teach."*

Adima-Thoth did as he was told, letting the light play about him and caress him, massaging him gently, cleansing wounds, healing psychic traumas and scars, strengthening, refreshing, and invigorating him—body, mind, and soul. Someone began to beat a drum, a soft, steady cadence. It felt so peaceful and serene that Adima closed his eyes. When he opened them at last, his body was bathed in the soft glow of candlelight. He had returned to the cell, and Enoch was holding him, cradling his head in his lap.

Amazing! Somehow, his beloved friend and teacher had sought out and found the dungeon at the center of the labyrinth. Evading the guards, shielding himself from Belial's farseeing eye, Enoch had opened the chains, released the prisoner, and wrapped him in a soft blanket. Now the old man was crooning softly, chanting in harmony to the drum that he beat. "Welcome back," Enoch smiled as he began to rub Adima's arms and legs. It wasn't long before feeling returned and he could sit upright again.

He felt strange, as though he had been newly born after his encounter with the Light Brethren. What had happened out there? "I can't remember." He looked at his friend in puzzlement. He was awake and conscious, he knew, but still he did not feel as though he belonged in his body."

"Easy, easy," the old man soothed. "Your memory will come back to you. You are just experiencing the shock of returning to your body and this realm. In a little while you will remember." He glanced around, senses alert. "Now, though, we must leave this place."

"How?" Adima asked, suddenly remembering where he was. He looked at his wrists and ankles. There was no blood, no bruises, no marks of any kind. How had he been healed? How had Enoch gotten past the guards and through the locked door? How had he freed him from the chains? It was amazing. The only possible explanation was that Enoch had slipped into the labyrinth under a cloak of invisibility and released him. "How did you get in here?" he managed to ask.

The old man smiled, helping him to his feet. "It was quite simple," he said, steadying Adima as the younger man got his bearings. "I just filled my heart with Love."

With a gentle push of his hand, the heavy oak door slid silently open. The two men stepped out into the corridor and walked past the guards as they stood at their posts. Further and further into the maze they walked, knowing the way, descending into the body of the Mother, coming at last to the tunnel that led to Sophia's cave.

*****

The Supreme Ordeal was over. Adima had done well. Physically he had changed, although he did not know it yet. His face shone with a new and intense light. "He has ascended," Cybele exclaimed to Hia when she saw her husband.

Still in a very altered state, he embraced his family. Hia placed a strong arm on his ally but said nothing, fingering the ahnk and contemplating its meaning. Adima lay down and took the proffered food and water, drawing additional strength from the nourishment. Then he and Cybele walked out into the tunnel to be alone for a while.

"I have found the answer to everything," he whispered excitedly as he held her in his arms, "and it is so simple. The answer to it all—the key to understanding the Nature of the Divine, even and including and especially the Great Mystery—is Love, the all-encompassing embrace and totality of Love. Love is the only pathway to walk. Love is the only protection we need. To the extent that we resonate with Love, we are invisible to the forces of chaos. The highest point of safety lies in our own hearts. Love is the Alpha and the Omega, the First and the Last, the Beginning and the End. When it all comes down to it, Love is all there is."

*****

And the evening and the morning were the fifth day.

CHAPTER 47

And the evening and the morning were the sixth day.

—Genesis 1:31

It was the In-Between Time. The Light had not quite been extinguished, and the Darkness had not yet taken hold as I came to sit on the sacred rock at the top of the Mountains of the Moon to watch the sun set on Atlantis for the last time. A single point of light glowed in the western sky, that wanderer known to all as the Evening Star. How silent it all was. No birds made their way to the trees and roosts for the night. No crickets chirped. No bats ventured forth in search of insects. No whales or dolphins sported and cavorted on the waves.

I faced west, into the dying light, looking out upon a silent world, a waiting world, a world tense with anticipation, hearing only the beating of my own heart and the soft inhale and exhale of my own breath. Atlantis was deserted, her myriad life having left her in search of shelter and safety and a new home. The eternal sky though, as always, was ablaze with color, the fiery orange sun setting behind dark, billowing thunderheads, casting great rays out from behind the clouds.

The corona glowed a violent shade of pink, overlaid on a background of deep magenta. "The Aura of the Divine," I breathed, the double halo reminding me of the dual nature of the Divinity and its creation. I recognized a particularly magnificent ray of light shooting up to the heavens and down to the Earth. "The Solar Gate," I cried, awed by the Divine emanations, recognizing the portal that led from this world to the next.

As I gazed to the west, the sun glowed redder and redder as it sank ever closer to the horizon. My heart beat a bit faster in anticipation. Even though I had seen the sun set every day of my life for so many years, tonight's sunset was different. This would be the last sunset over Atlantis. Tomorrow the sun would set on a vastly different world. After tonight, sunset would never be the same.

I focused all of my senses at a single point on the horizon where the last tip of that great flaming ball would disappear. I wanted to see something one more time, to ensure that it was still there, that it had not died, that it had not left with the others. The winds of change roared in my ears, first just a whisper, then building to a mighty roar. The voices of the past echoed in those winds, voices of the Ancients and the ancestors and all who had gone before me, ghosts from the past crying out their compassion for Atlantis, crying out their anguish over what was about to unfold.

The sun was almost gone. I held my breath and drew myself fully erect. The last crescent tip sat for a timeless moment on the horizon before sinking beneath the sea. For an instant it lingered, and I hoped it would last forever, that it would always stay that way and never disappear. Alas, the moment could not last, but the gift was given to me nevertheless. A brilliant green flash burst up out of the water, followed instantly by the sun sinking out of sight of Atlantis forever.

Tears filled my eyes—tears of gratitude. The Dragon still lived! The Life Essence had not died! How quickly the light vanished. How dark it had become, how melancholy. No night sounds to cheer me, no evening lullabies to carry me gently into a peaceful, restful sleep. As the sky continued to darken, I gazed steadily westward into the violet-velvet emptiness as the tears began to flow and the silence floated mightily down on me. Distancing myself from the individual dramas about to unfold, alone I sat, far from the haunts of men, and talked to the Great Mother.

"Tell me, Mother," I cried. "What are you doing? What will become of you? What will become of us?"

The Mother heaved a great sigh, almost a groan. My question had not gone unheard, and she spoke to me on the voice of the wind, giving the answer, explaining herself, justifying her ways, that all who cared to listen might understand.

"*I had hoped they would chose another way,*" the Great Mother began, "*but they have not. Now I must do my part, to protect myself, to protect my children. For the sake of the Elect. For the sake of the Plan. If I do not shift myself, all will be destroyed—all civilization, all culture, all life. This very day, in the Kingdom of Atlantis, at the end times, Belial can destroy it all—and he will!*"

The air grew cold. I shivered as I considered the ramifications of the Mother's words.

"*The Sons of Belial have the technology, they have the weapons, and most importantly, they have the arrogance. It would be a simple matter to blow themselves up. And then it will all be gone, even my body itself, the beautiful planet Earth. Just so much dust and debris drifting in the vacuum of space, waiting for some errant interstellar traveler to wonder about what those particles might once have been and how they came to be pulverized. Watching the molecules of my body speed through the atmosphere of some alien world, blazing with fire as they streak across the night sky. Meteor showers, shooting stars. How beautiful! Make a wish!*"

What an ironic twist, I thought, that the feelings of awe and mystery inspired by a shooting star were actually the death knell of another being. The Mother sensed it, too. The wind gusted fitfully, soughing through the pines in a series of dreadful shrieks.

"*It takes eons to create a world!*" the Mother cried aloud. "*How long does it take to destroy one?*"

Dirt and twigs and leaves swirled around me as the mini-cyclone raged. I had no fear. The Mother was but expressing her frustration and grief, and I was sheltered by a stand of evergreens anchored firmly to the ridge. I waited patiently for the return of her soft voice. Gradually, the wind calmed, and the Mother spoke again, her sweet breath scented with the fragrance of night-blooming jasmine.

"*A Shift will avert the immediacy of the impending disaster. A Shift will bring a dark time, a period of forgetting, a scattering of the people, a breaking of the technology, a loss of power to the weapons. A Shift will make the world a colder place, a darker place, a more hostile place.*

"*After I shift, the focus will be on survival, not on power, status, and wealth. On survival, not on destruction. Humankind will be primitive once again. They will have to relearn and rebuild, piece by piece. They will be cold and hungry and frightened, focusing only on the essentials of food, clothing, and shelter. Huddling in their dank, dark caves around their meager fires with the elements raging without, there will be no time to even think about destroying each other and themselves. No time, and more importantly, no way—because the technology will be gone. With the Shift will come the forgetting, the loss of conscious contact with the Ancient wisdom.*

"*And by the time they do rebuild, thousands of years will have passed. Thousands of years, thousands of experiences from which they will learn—learn and hopefully remember, so they will not repeat their mistakes and recreate the crisis all over again. Because they will rebuild, of that there is no doubt. The knowledge will still be there, waiting for them to remember. Universal Law will still work as it always has—the Law of Love, the Law of Propagation, the Law of Evolution, the Law of Cause and Effect, the Law of Attraction, and the rest, as they are written in the* Book of Life.

"*So I have no choice,*" the Mother sighed. "*I shift to save myself. For without a Mother, the children will also die, and I cannot let that be. As the fearful dream progresses, I might not appear to be a loving Mother, or even to be alive. But I will always be their Mother, whether they remember me or not, whether they understand my ways or not, whether they acknowledge me or not. And I shall always love and nurture my children.*"

The breeze ceased, and I sat in the silence, contemplating the Mother's words and the beauty of the Plan. The Shift would buy the human race time, and it would buy the Mother time. What might seem cold and cruel, even harsh and hostile to the unenlightened eye was, in truth, a great gift—the gift of self-preservation. For nothing would really be lost. The immortal human Soul would rest forever safe and unharmed. The knowledge would always be there—waiting to be rediscovered and applied lovingly in accordance with the highest ideals of creativity and good.

The only thing lost would be time, and time was meaningless as measured by the Mother and the Father. Those who perceive themselves as limited to a little life, measure time in units they can understand—minutes, hours, days, weeks, months, years. The immortal Mother and Father measure time in aeons. In fact, they do not measure time at all. Such a concept is meaningless to them.

So the Shift was to be the safety valve. The Shift was to be the Mother's great gift. She would not abandon her children after all. A light breeze ruffled my hair, and I was instantly alert. The Mother had more to say, and I listened with gratitude and hope.

"Over the centuries, throughout the ages, I shall teach my children, nurture them, help them remember and grow stronger and wiser than ever. And when the time is right and my children are ready," the Great Mother sighed a third time, *"I shall shift once more."*

I saw, and I understood. How wonderful! I marveled at the Mother's great wisdom and her unconditional love and selflessness. Still, I had questions. I wanted to understand how the human mind worked, how it could become so deluded and so egocentric. "How does he get away with it, Mother?" I asked. "How does Belial attract so many followers?"

On the gentle currents of the wind, under a chilly, cloudy sky, surrounded by the aroma of jasmine, the Mother explained. *"You know, of course, that not all of my children have followed Belial,"* she said.

"Even now, many are preparing to leave Atlantis and embrace a new way of being. Their course is set, their intentions right, their success ensured. As for the rest, they follow Belial because it is the easy way, the safe way, the comfortable way."

I blinked in astonishment, startled by the Mother's words. I had not expected such an answer, and I did not understand. She sensed my amazement and confusion.

"Are you surprised to hear this? Do not be. It is easy, safe, and comfortable because they can blame everything on someone else—project it outward on Belial. They do not have to take responsibility. They can place the entire burden on their shadow King.

"Because this thinking is misapplied, they will have to learn another way. They will have to learn that the responsibility is always within themselves. The learning will take a long time. Many thousands of years will pass, many nations will rise and fall, many Belials will come and go, until they finally understand. Until, as Adima-Thoth has said, the Light is once again stronger than the Darkness."

Again the night grew calm, and I reflected on the Mother's words. Patience—the Plan was very patient. So was the Mother. "What will you teach them, Mother?" I asked, eager to understand the new curriculum, which I now realized had been designed to guide the human race up and out of the darkness of ignorance and back into the light of Truth. Of course, as always, the choice would have to be theirs.

"Trust, honesty, tolerance, gentleness, joy, defenseless, generosity, patience, faithfulness, and open-mindedness..." the litany of attributes was long indeed, but were not some missing?

"Good things to teach," I replied. "Good attributes to develop. But what about Love, sinlessness, perfection, knowledge, and eternal Truth? Why do you not teach those attributes to your children?"

The Mother smiled at the lack of understanding in my question. Gently she reminded me of a great truth that I had momentarily forgotten. *"How can I teach what my children what they already have, what is part of their inheritance? When the unhappy dream is over and my children awaken, they will know themselves once again and recognize these attributes about themselves, that they were always there and always will be—part of their birthright as children of the Father and the Mother—the Great Creator and myself.*

"Trust me, my children" the Mother whispered on the fading breeze, speaking not only to me, but to all of Creation. *"All is well. Be not deceived by appearances. Surrender to the process. Do not attempt to control or interfere. Take the leap of faith along with me. Let go and do your part, as your Father and I do ours. All is well, all is well, all is well..."*

The breeze faded, and I knew that the Mother would not speak again that night. As she had no choice, neither did I have a choice. I would have to trust, and with the trust would come, inevitably, *patience*. I would be patient and wait without anxiety, certain of the outcome...if not the time. I would not doubt.

Slowly, I opened the great book, the mighty tome known in Atlantis as the *Book of Life*. Coming to a blank page, I took up my sacred Pen, symbol of learning, and wrote the new words...

IN ALL THINGS, BE PATIENT, TRUST, AND DO NOT DOUBT.
THE TIME WILL BE AS RIGHT AS THE ANSWER.

The Mother had the strength that came from knowing. I, too, now possessed that strength. I no longer believed, now I was certain. And with my *certainty* came, of course, the gift of *Joy* as I turned my back on the dying light and faced east once again.

*****

Far below, the great ships lay packed and ready. Finally, the time of Preparation was over, and the time of the Journey was at hand.

Gathering together in Poseidia, the Children of the Law of One and those who had chosen at the last moment to abandon the ways of the Sons of Belial were about to leave the island. Families, friends, and strangers huddled around the huge bonfires, watching each other make last minute arrangements. Some sat in silent meditation; some wept. Others were sullen and angry; a small few were openly happy, enthused about embarking on a new adventure. Yet always and everywhere were the tears and hugs as friends and loved ones took their leave of each other. "Farewell and good voyage!" Their cries filled the night air.

The Twelve stood before their respective Arks, calling to their passengers, inviting them in, seeing to their comfort, offering reassurance and compassion. One by one, the wayfarers entered into the darkness, not knowing what lay in their future, not knowing that as they embarked on the journey, they would experience privation and suffering as all that they loved was swept away by the mighty arms of the Destroyer. But they had each other—their families, their friends—and they had the course on which they were set. They were committed and willing to do whatever it took to accomplish the goal and ensure success.

The night was dark, the air damp and cold. From the southeast, a strong offshore breeze heralded the approach of another tropical storm. Rain squalls came and went, punctuated by periods of uneasy calm. Every so often, the Earth trembled, a sign that massive forces were at work below ground, out of sight of the people who dwelt above.

Nuah went first, followed by Poet, then Artist and the rest. One by one, the Arks slipped from their berths and floated silently out into the river. In their great wombs, they carried the heart and soul of all that was pure and kind and good of Atlantis—her people, her history, her technology, her laws, and her wisdom.

Despite their heavy cargoes, the arks floated gently in midstream, bobbing like massive corks on the calm surface of the dark waters. Then the current caught them and they were swept downstream to the south, where they passed through the Great Southern Canal and out into the vast expanse of the Ocean of Atlas, en route to the new world.

"It is written that LIFE TAKES REFUGE IN A SINGLE SPACE." Adima stood on the shore and quoted the words he had read so long ago in Enoch's book. Now he understood their meaning—the sacred Arks were the refuge in which the people, consciousness, and treasures of Atlantis would be safe from the terrible catastrophe that was about to occur.

Cybele reached out and took Sophia's hand. They had worked long and hard to plan the exodus and ensure its successful beginning. They had done their part. Now it remained for Spirit and the Goddess to do their parts. The Arks had been placed under the loving care of the Father and the Mother. "Godspeed," the priestess murmured, blessing each vessel as it passed, invoking Divine protection and providence for the travelers.

"What is the matter?" Sophia asked, sensing the younger woman's anxiety. "Do you not believe that they are safe and protected from all harm?"

"I do," Cybele replied, wiping a tear from her eyes.

"Then why do you continue to be anxious and distracted about your loved ones? Are they not children of the Mother and the Father?"

"Of course they are," Cybele replied.

"Could it be that the Mother and Father would somehow refuse to work wonders for them while still performing wonders for you and yours?" Sophia's eyes twinkled merrily as she taught her student.

Cybele thought about it. "You're right," she replied, "but I still wish I could save them from all of this. If there were only a way..." Her voice trailed off as she looked pleadingly at her dear old friend.

"You are not in charge of saving anyone," Sophia replied. "That is Spirit's job, not yours. Nor are you charged with changing things in the world. Spirit will do that, too. Yours, however, is an equally important task—that of loving, forgiving, and interceding in prayer." The old woman wrapped her shawl around her ancient shoulders and settled herself in front of the fire. "Now meditate and pray," she instructed, closing her own eyes. "Ask for the Grace to accomplish this, and let Spirit do the rest. Then be still and trust, knowing that the Mother and the Father will never fail their children."

Cybele followed her teacher's example, sitting still and closing her eyes. She was silent for a long time, accepting Sophia's words, accepting her own part, opening herself to Grace. When she opened her eyes again, the harbor lay empty, the last ship just rounding the bend and disappearing out of sight downstream.

"How long before they find land again?" she wondered. "It is the eve of battle. How will things turn out?" She was merely curious, knowing now that the outcome did not really matter. Good had already transcended Evil; Light had already transcended the Darkness. Even if they were all killed, if their physical bodies died, it would not matter. The greatest struggle had been within their own minds. The Children of the Law of One had already faced and fought their greatest battle, and they had won. They were transformed!

For herself and Adima and the twins, a personal transformation had occurred. Even though they did not know what was going to happen on the morrow, the last scene was already complete, the final act in the drama already written. They had to win because goodness had transcended.

"It is only a matter of how," the priestess mused aloud, sitting in the circle with Adima and the rest. Firelight flickered on her face, playing on her dark skin as her family listened to her wisdom. "It's just a matter of what is the next right step for Atlantis. Everyone is experiencing something incredible right now, something that, according to all of our beliefs and all of the laws of the universe, could not possibly happen. Yet it is happening nevertheless; our senses tell us so. The impossible is happening, and there are three choices that we Atlanteans can make."

She smiled, her face shining with the gift of prophecy as she foretold not only the immediate course of events that would befall Atlantis, but also the events of another time far in the future, just before the Great Awakening, when a similar course of events would occur and humankind would be faced with the same choices once again.

"Not understanding what is happening," Cybele explained, "completely unprepared for the great surges of energy about to be released, many are experiencing intense fear. Many more will choose not to stay on Earth, dying in the natural destruction. For them there will be no next step in this lifetime."

"Some will survive and still be unaware, choosing to embrace the fearful dream of separation. In spite of all that has happened and all that they have witnessed, such as these will still attempt to perpetuate the master-slave relationship within the darkness of ignorance and illusion.

"And some, like our brothers and sisters going into the Arks, will choose to move forward and do something wonderful. This is the interesting part. These are the ones for whom we will be doing our parts, for they will be the launching point for the next step, the next evolutionary leap."

The priestess grew quiet, letting the others contemplate their own feelings. The hour grew late, the firelight grew dim. Alta and Charis fell asleep, and one by one the others did, too. Cybele and Adima, though, stayed awake, holding hands as they sat in the silence and stared into the dying embers.

All told, eleven ships went forth that night; only a single one remained behind. The huge hulk lay dark and ready, empty, waiting to be loaded with its most precious cargo. Waiting to carry the last few humans—Adima, Cybele, Alta, Charis, Hia, and the rest—and the greatest treasures—a copy of the *Book of Life*, the Knowledge Crystals, a Fire Crystal, artwork, the Alchemical Gold, and the Grail Map. If all went well, tomorrow they would go forth, departing from Atlantis forever.

*****

From Cybele's Journal

Did you think you could get away with it, O Atlantis? Did you think you were special, exempt from the Law of Cause and Effect?

Indeed, Atlantis, you are not. Belial has laid a good foundation, and you have followed the example he set.

There is no turning back now. The course is set. Sides have been chosen, positions have been taken, the players are in place. Everything is ready.

It is the beginning of a new time. Time for the Pendulum to swing in a different direction. Time for the human race to embrace a whole new set of experiences along a whole new path of learning. Time to deny Spirit-Source while the Patriarchy takes hold. Time to explore the ways of the ego, the ways of war and hubris and greed and oppression.

Time to suppress the Goddess and the Feminine—the yin—in order to explore the Masculine side of things. Time for the male side of human nature, the yang, to dominate at all costs—no compromise, no quarter given.

Time to lay aside the ancient ways of Spirit to experiment with the ways of the natural world. Time to exploit science and the Great Mother to amass material wealth. Time to focus on the life of the physical body—the time from birth to death—forgetting, ignoring, not even considering the times before and after...the time of the immortal Self. Time to experience the effects of all that has come before—the effects of all the choices you have made.

The effects of the Spear and the Hard Lightning,

The effects of walking the Grail Path,

The effects of seeking Spiritual Bypass,

The effects of abusing the Great Mother,

The effects of abusing yourselves,

The effects of suppressing the Goddess and denying the Feminine,

The effects of falling asleep...

It is harvest time. The seeds were well planted, well nurtured, well watered, well tended. They have taken good root. Time now to reap what has been sown. Time to experience the reality that every action generates an equal and opposite reaction, for every Cause there is an Effect.

*****

From Adima's Journal...

And so the Fathers fell asleep, dropping into the slumber of ignorance and arrogance to dream a strange and fearful dream. So strange and grotesque this dream, so insane, that the natural order was reversed. Illusion became reality, while Truth became the great enemy of humankind.

At first, they tried to change the Truth, to make it be what it was not. When this did not work, they created elaborate defenses against the Truth, setting up great barriers to keep it at bay. Finally, as their slumber deepened and the dream became more real, they disguised themselves from the Truth...ran from it, hid from it, denied its very existence.

Forgetting their connection to the Great Creator, the fearful among the descendants of the Sons of Belial and the Children of the Law of One came to believe that they had created themselves. Alone in all the universe, they saw themselves as alien unto themselves, and all created things as their enemy.

Separate and apart they dwelt, strange and different, attacked and attacking. So they lived their fearful existence, believing fiercely in the dream, clinging tenaciously to it, refusing to even consider that waking might dispel what was, in truth, not really there.

While they dreamed, they forgot the ancient ways. Forgot the Goddess. Forgot the Great Mother. Forgot the Light. Forgot their Source. And in their forgetting, they attacked each other, brother against brother, spilling blood, embracing the darkness. Thus began the Slaughterbench of History.

*****

And the evening and the morning were the sixth day.

CHAPTER 48

Thou shalt shine with horns to determine six days,
and on the seventh with half a crown.

—Sumero-Semitic Proverb

The seventh day dawned hot and red. The sun glowed red, the sky glowed red, the sea glowed red. The great island itself glowed red—the color of the wasteland, the color of calamity, the color of martyrdom. The light of the War God shone down from the eastern sky, the red light of anger, the red light of ferocity. Through the streets of the City of Atlantis, Death, the Red Horseman, rode, leaving in its wake a blood-red swath of guilt, vengeance, and lust.

The air was thick and wet and heavy, pregnant with anticipation. An ominous silence lay over the world, as though the universe itself knew that an event of huge import was about to occur. Everyone and everything seemed to be waiting, waiting, waiting...

In the courtyard before the deserted Palace, a barefoot and bedraggled soothsayer called out a warning. "There is danger, there is danger," the emaciated old crone cried, her thin, reedy voice like the wail of a banshee, foretelling the death of the inhabitants within, and the death of all Atlantis. *"Belial,"* she cried, *"beware the seventh day, the day of darkness and balefulness. Undertake no labor on this day, which dawns in opposition to the sun and thus becomes a day of rest."*

For several minutes she stood before the ruined Palace, muttering strange incantations and inscribing occult symbols in the dust and in the air. Then she moved on, her thin white hair and tattered robe blowing in the wind, her wizened, toothless face creased with a thousand lines, as shrunken, dried, and shriveled as the emotions of the man to whom she cried out her warning.

*****

Belial woke early on the morning of the seventh and last day. The dreams had awakened him—the dreams and the voices, like when he was a child, when the voices spoke to him in the dark, locked closet, where he was most alone.

They had been friendly voices then, but now they were no longer friendly. They were caustic, bitter and so very, very insistent, so overwhelming, so powerful, so terrifying. The voices told him things he did not want to hear. The voices forced him to do things he did not want to do. Nothing could silence them any more, not even the potions. He was completely paranoid.

"He's coming for you, coming for you," the demons jeered in a thousand discordant shrieks. "He is not in the dungeon, he has escaped. He is free. And he's coming for you, with the Dragon and the Hard Lightning and the Islanders and the woman with the Wand and the Shield. They're all coming for you!"

The voices stopped as suddenly as they had started. An eerie silence ensued, more terrifying even than the voices themselves. Terrified, Belial called out to the guards, but there was no one there. How he wished he had the Spear! How he wished Draco were there to advise him and stand by his side! But he had neither. The Spear had vanished, and Draco was dead, his mangled body probably still hanging in the square where Belial had last seen it. Desperately, his fevered mind searched for a way out of the dilemma. Gone were the plans for the coronation and execution. Now he was scrambling just to stay alive. Before he could do anything else, he had to get rid of the approaching Enemy.

Of course! he realized, his tortured brain seizing on a mad scheme. Set a diversion, distract his attention, lure him into a trap, then use the device. The Enemy could never withstand its enormous power. The Enemy would be crushed once and for all in the ensuing explosions. "I'll lure him to the Great Pyramid, then blow it up!" Belial screamed, imagining the force of the blast. "I'll bury him in the rubble under tons and tons of rock. Bury him so deeply that he will never be able to harm me again."

Dressing himself, the Master went out into the city, gathering the soldiers, issuing orders, laying the bait, setting the trap. The Enemy would come...he must. And when the Enemy had been lured to the death-place, Belial would turn on the device, not against Lemuria, but to thwart his brother, Adima, who was coming for him.

*****

Astride a great roan charger, the Belial-Beast rode at the head of a phalanx of what remained of the Adepts, flanked by a cadre of soldiers. Fully transformed, he was a fearful figure indeed, dressed all in red, face hidden beneath a heavy hood, carrying a deadly scythe with which he fully intended to cut off all life in Atlantis.

Under a lowering sky the Adepts rode on their swift passage through the city, horses' hooves thundering on the flagstone, striking terror into the hearts of the stubborn who had yet to leave, who would never leave the city. At the outermost ring, where the Gates of White Pearl opened onto the Good Red Road, they reined in, pausing to regroup and wait for further orders from their demonic Master.

"Remove that symbol of decadence," Belial commanded, pointing to the Atlantean flag flying high above the walls. The Adepts scrambled to obey, pulling down the glorious colors and Great Seal of Truth. "Raise ours." He tossed a dark, shapeless bundle of cloth to a lesser Adept, who caught it, attached it to the ropes, and hoisted it aloft for all to see.

As the perverse symbol rose ever higher, unfurling in the wind, Belial's horse whinnied and reared up, shying fearfully, pawing the air. The man-thing on its back seemed not to notice, however, swaggering in his saddle, a cry of triumph on his feral lips. "Behold our great victory," the Beast shouted, pointing to the ramparts of the once mighty city, where the obscene banner of the Sons of Belial now flew for all to see—a black background surmounted by the alchemical symbol of a white skull filled with rich red blood.

As the transformation of Belial was now complete, so also was the transformation of Atlantis complete. Around this perverted ensign, symbol of the renunciation of life, the dark forces would gather for the final battle. The reversal had been accomplished!

"Sound the call," Belial roared, his chilling laugh booming like thunder under the blood-red sky. On signal, an Adept began to beat a great drum. Its deep, resonant throb reverberated out across the Great Plain, bouncing off the Mountains of the Moon and echoing hollowly back to its point of origin.

Boom! Boom! Boom! Out to the dark places the chilling call went forth, carried on a demonic wind, summoning the ignorant, waking up the powers of Darkness. In the nether places, foul and loathsome creatures stirred to the horrid sound. Rousing from their slumber, they lifted their heads and turned their ears, entranced by the incessant beating of the drum.

From the depths of the Earth they came, crawling out from under rocks, rising from the morass of fetid bogs and festering swamps. Through the veil of morning mist surrounding the forest and the Mountains of the Moon, slowly and lugubriously they made their way across the Great Plain—mutants and mixtures, aberrations and abominations—drawn to the dark banner as moths toward a flame, to stand before their Dark Lord.

Belial looked at the frightful horde, product of years of genetic experimentation and misapplication of the laws of creation, product of an arrogance so great that it believed it could place its will above the Will of the Great Mother. He laughed humorlessly, pleased with himself that he had amassed such a mighty, demonic anti-army to face the meager and pitiful forces of Light. Against these terrifying marauders—manifesting the most fearful magical powers and capable of feats of superhuman strength—Adima and Hia would pit their lesser intelligence and puny warrior skills. There would be no contest. The outcome was assured.

"Kill them all!" Belial issued his orders to the frightful creatures, pointing down along the Good Red Road to the forest from which he knew the Enemy would approach. "But let Adima through. Let my brother come to me."

Boom! Boom! Boom! The drum continued to beat, whipping the soldiers into an ecstasy of blood-lust. It was time to call Adima forth, time to invite him to his own destruction.

"Take up the fire," the Beast cried, producing a large torch from where it hung on his saddle. The soldiers followed his example, restless, anxious to be about their bloody business. All were silent, watching the Master bend the forces of black magic to his will.

The tip of a finger glowed a brilliant red. Fire shot forth, a tiny incendiary flicker that would lead to an eruption more violent and destructive than any the world had ever known. The aberrations shrank back in fear, but the soldiers grinned with excitement.

Belial grinned, too, touching his flaming forefinger to the torch, which instantly blazed into a miniature inferno. Down along the ranks of mounted men he rode, touching his torch to theirs, passing the fire along to the soldiers, who would, in turn, pass it along to the rest of Atlantis. It was a merciless act of self will—the ultimate Belial savagery, which would soon spread in blazing desolation across the rubble of a world. Raising the torch aloft, he looked at the men. Excited by sexual frenzy, they watched their leader for the signal they knew was about to come. For a brief instant Belial paused, then he raised the torch and shouted, "Charge!"

As one, the soldiers moved forward, voicing a mighty, lustful roar, carrying the fire, riding back into the city. Beginning at the outer ring, they moved ever inward toward the center, toward the Great Pyramid. Wielding deadly tridents, they put to the sword any who stood in their path. Carrying the fire, they touched dripping tongues of flame to everything that would burn—houses, barns, markets, carts, animals, people—starting fire after fire, setting the magnificent city ablaze.

It was an event that was potent with evil, scarcely believable—not a sacred, purifying, or transforming fire, but a destructive, evil, demonic fire, bringing death and destruction, charring and mortifying the Earth, turning the heavenly blue and white Atlantis into a black and red hell. And the only thing that would quench the conflagration was water!

*****

In the Great Temple, her trap ready, Lilith waited, knowing that Cybele would come. Outside, the great conflagration raged, while the Belial-Beast laughed and the people ran screaming through the streets. Within, though, she was safe enough. The great stone walls would keep the flames from consuming her. Within, all was prepared. The fire was ready, the sacrificial dagger lay concealed beneath her robe, and her potent magic seethed, eager to burst forth.

The High Priestess smiled triumphantly. She would utter the secret name and render her enemy powerless. The evil priestess would be captured, bound on the altar, and offered as a sacrifice of appeasement to the Flaming God. Lilith herself would plunge the knife into Cybele's heart and light the fire that would consume the body. She had only to be patient. "It will not be long now," she hissed, rubbing her hands in glee.

*****

At the Ark camp, an Islander arrived with dire news. "The city is on fire," he cried, breathless from his long, hard run.

"Then it is time," Adima said, rising to act, a thrill of anticipation coursing through his veins. Cybele stood by his side, joined a moment later by Hia and the rest of the Islanders. They knew the roles they were about to play. They had planned and rehearsed them over and over again. Enoch and Sophia would stay with the twins at the Ark, waiting, while Adima, Cybele, and the warriors went out to confront Belial and Lilith.

Parents and children embraced, exchanging loving hugs, lingering over the moment, letting the memory of each other's touch attach itself to their consciousness. No words passed between them. They had said all there was to say.

The Mystical Pair, too, had been well prepared. They knew about the Plan. Parents and children had talked about it for many hours. All of the questions had been asked, all of the answers had been given. Alta and Charis held hands as they watched their loved ones depart from them. "I know what they're going to do," Alta struggled not to give in to the fear, "but I can't help being afraid."

"I know," his sister took his hand in her own. "But just as they are going out to do their parts, so we must do ours and pray that all will work out according to the Plan."

*****

The horses were saddled and rested. All was in readiness. With a touch of nostalgia, Adima looked into his pouch at all the artifacts he'd collected over the years—a piece of rose quartz; osprey and owl feathers; the black and white stones; the black cross and seven red roses, dried up now after all those years, their petals making a soft bed on which everything else rested. So much time had passed, so much learning, so many experiences. He sighed and slung the pouch over his shoulder.

"You know, of course, that there is to be a total solar eclipse on this day," Enoch said. They were in a sacred grove a few paces beyond the camp. Even at this distance from the city, the acrid smell of smoke was strong, and the red sky was darker now, black and sooty. He and Sophia were helping Adima and Cybele dress and arm themselves with the weapons that had been given them. The Sword and the Wand and the Shield—Hard Lightning and Protection of the Goddess—these were the gifts that the hero and heroine had earned and which they would use as they went forth to do battle with the forces of evil.

Adima looked at his teacher, surprised that the old man had waited until now to reveal such important information. An eclipse. Of course! He wondered if Belial knew, if the giant had taken steps to adjust to this most important celestial occurrence. Adima knew all about eclipses. Like most Atlanteans, he always experienced a certain anxiousness in the face of such a potent natural phenomenon.

Of all the astronomical events that influenced the Earth's magnetic field, the most dramatic was an eclipse of the sun or moon. As any geomancer knew, when this took place, the magnetic activity normally stimulated by the eclipsed body was greatly diminished, and with serious consequences. To put it more simply, when the moon made its way between the Earth and the sun, the Dragon Current was blocked. With the sudden interruption of the even flow of terrestrial magnetism, all Atlantean systems shut down. For the few brief moments of the eclipse, Atlantis was virtually powerless.

In the days before the Ancients, an eclipse had always been an event to be feared, against whose effects certain precautions had to be taken. To primitive people who depended on the Dragon Current for their very existence and who had no concept of past or future, any interruption in the flow of the life force was taken seriously and considered permanent—a punishment from the gods. To appease the "wrathful deities" and insure that the punishment would never happen again, elaborate myths and rituals had been built up, becoming part of the tradition and folklore of the culture over the ages. With the coming of Quetzalcoatl and the sacred science, however, the ancient astronomers had learned the circumstances in which eclipses occurred. With painstaking care and precision, they had built elaborate stone observatories whose sole function was the accurate charting of such phenomena.

Now these celestial events had become both familiar and predictable. Gone were the days of superstitious terror, to be replaced with viable alternatives by those who understood their exact nature and cause. But the prehistoric dread had never faded, and even the enlightened Atlanteans were nervous about eclipses and took extreme care to gain warning of their approach.

How perfect! Adima thought, reaching out to Cybele and Enoch and Sophia. How right that an eclipse should occur now, at this precise moment in time. It could not be a coincidence. It had to be part of the Plan!

The four, joined now by Hia and the Islanders, formed a circle, palms lightly touching in a last moment of joining before the battle. It was time for the blessing, time for the old man and the old woman to empower their students who had achieved mastery. "As we join hands, let us remember that in our unity lies our strength," Sophia prayed. "We are all in this together. Ours is the Power of the Many Acting as One."

"We have spent the night in prayer and meditation," Enoch added. "We know that this is our time, and we have prepared for it well. We are ready."

The energy of Love danced around them, moving from palm to palm around the Circle, lighting their faces, warming their hearts, invigorating and refreshing them, filling each one with great strength and peace. Slowly they withdrew their hands and placed them over their hearts, maintaining the connection to the Whole in their minds.

"The eclipse will begin during the Hour of the Raven," Enoch said. "That is the most effective time to strike. That is when you must move against them—each of you."

Adima and Cybele nodded. "Load the final Ark and prepare to set sail," the priestess said. "If we are successful, you will know it and we shall return. If we are not, seal the doors of the Ark against the deluge and let the waters carry it where they may. Peace be with you. Farewell until we meet again."

Without another word, they mounted the horses and rode off through the forest and out onto the Great Plain of Atlantis toward the city, toward their destiny. Enoch and Sophia watched them go, then they went back to join the twins.

*****

Adima remembered the last time he had ridden across the Great Plain. How different from that long-gone day almost three years ago, when he and his wife had taken the horses and galloped over the land in a wild burst of exuberance on their way to the Dragon Festival. Then, their faces had been filled with joy and laughter. Now, their expressions were grim.

Cresting the last rise, the small group reined in for a moment to give the horses a breather, reconnoiter, and get their final bearings. As always, the view was breathtaking, but not beautiful, as before. Now what took their breath away was the extent of the carnage, the scope of the disaster. The city lay before them, a blackened and smoking ruin. So great was the fire, so hot, that even at this distance they could see the intense waves of heat rising up from the ashes, distorting the atmosphere, also distorting their perspective.

Across that shimmering, wavy horizon, greasy spirals of thick black smoke mounted to the sky, illuminated from within by great red tongues of flame. Belial had meant for the fire to destroy, and destroy it would, burning the city, the gardens, and the treasures. Paradise was, indeed, lost!

From the top of the rise, they watched spellbound as voracious sheets of flame devoured all created things, reducing the city to ashes. Everything was consumed in that insatiable fire—not just buildings and people, but also the truth and knowledge of the Ancients, along with the lies, ignorance, and illusions of the Sons of Belial.

The warriors looked at each other. To their heightened awareness, the dying city seemed to be crying out to the Great Mother, asking for balance. Seeking for the fire's complement—the deluge, the all-purifying water.

The Mother heard, and Nature responded. Massive storm clouds gathered. Huge waves slammed into the rocky coast. A hurricane loomed offshore, a titanic storm, even more powerful then the terrible cataclysm that had pounded them just a few days before.

It was not, however, a time to sit and contemplate. If they had, they might have turned back, their minds recoiling in horror at what was about to happen. No, it was a time for action. A time to move forward. "Hiyahhhhhhh," Adima cried, spurring his mount onward, down into the conflagration. The others followed his example. So did the Great Mother.

*****

As the party rode down the hill onto the Good Red Road, the elements were unleashed. A great wind blew, and the rain came pelting down. Lightning flashed, thunder rumbled, and the ground shook with the first of the earthquakes. Directly in their path, the Great Plain of Atlantis split in two with a mighty convulsion, a deep fissure cutting a jagged gash across the Mother's skin. The noise was spectacular, a mighty rumble from deep within the Earth. From the fiery depths, great jets of hissing steam shot up, frightening both the horses and their riders.

Clouds of steam swirled around them, temporarily obscuring the path ahead. Not completely, though. Within the roiling mist, a grim and hideous apparition took shape— a dark, misshapen mass of living creatures—or were they? The warriors could not be sure.

All they could see were huge, grotesque forms weaving in and out among the shadows. All they could hear were guttural growls, barks, howls, and screams of rage and hate. All they could smell was the stench of corruption and evil. All they could feel was the sense of being stalked as the aberrations circled around and around their prey, blocking the way forward, cutting off the path of retreat. It was hard to believe that anything so hideous could actually exist. Belial's anti-army loomed on the Great Plain like demons from hell, looking like some hideous manifestation of a demented, drug-induced hallucination of the Shadow Mind.

With the enemy now in sight, Hia and the Islanders wasted no time, urging their mounts to battle speed. Fitting the first arrows to their bows, the Islanders stood tall in the stirrups. Their horses never broke their headlong rush. Into the fray they charged, like a pack of ferocious wolves protecting their young.

The battle was fierce, tumultuous, and deadly, drowning out, for a time, even the roar of the earthquake and the conflagration. And the mutants stood no chance at all! The skill and alignment of the warriors far outmatched all of the misguided magic thrown against them. Horses wheeled, arrows flew, tomahawks found their targets, and the air was filled with a great cacophony of sound—the battle cries of the Islanders mixed with the agonized shrieks of the maimed and dying monsters. Entirely cut off from direct connection and perception of Spirit-Source, isolated from their origins, the aberrations were helpless. Confronted with the power of the Light, they became confused, they panicked. Dull, slow, and thick, they could not cope; they could not even compete. It was a slaughter.

Adima tried to draw the Sword, but he never had a chance to use it. This first clash did not last long. It was over almost before it started. Yet the battle would never be forgotten— a strange, surreal encounter pitting human beings against magical and monstrous creatures, pitting Good against Evil, Light against Dark, angelic forces against demonic forces. The battle would be remembered for all time, the legends living in the sense memory of the human race, echoing down through the ages, the myths told and retold around the campfires, of the time when the titans clashed and the Forces of Light overcame the Forces of Darkness.

Hia rode up, his body streaked with dirt and sweat and blood. "Follow me," he cried above the fearsome din. "The way is now clear."

*****

Under a red and lowering sky, they rode through the great gates. "Like in my Grail vision of the War in Heaven," Adima muttered to Cybele as they entered the doomed and dying city. Huge clouds of oily black smoke billowed up around them. The stench of burned flesh assailed their nostrils, while a silent rain of delicate ash fell thick and heavy, choking them, stinging their eyes, clogging their nostrils, filling their lungs, coating everything a uniform gray.

"Tie these over your mouths and noses," Adima suggested, handing rags to each of them. But it did little to help.

"Be careful," Cybele warned, shouting above the roar of the flames and the general noise and confusion. A great flaming beam fell across their path. The horses shied violently. Hia dismounted and tied his rag around the horse's eyes. His warriors followed suit.

Adima dismounted and talked lovingly to the great beasts on which he and his wife rode, speaking in the First Language, soothing the animals, calming them, asking for their help, assuring them that he would let no harm come to any of them. It worked. The animals were calmed, and they continued onward.

Near the end of the Avenue of the Gods, the war party halted, facing a sight that brought a thrill of awe to even their battle-hardened eyes. Again their way was blocked, but not by another of Belial's frightful hordes. This time, their allies had come forth to greet them. In the middle of the street stood an array of dark-robed figures, their faces and features shrouded under heavy cowls. Cybele recognized them immediately. They were the Holy Ones who dwelt deep within the Great Mother, the same Holy Ones who had revealed themselves when she and Adima had taken the twins into the bowels of the Temple on the evening of their birthday initiation. Now they had come to the surface to do their part in the fulfillment of the Plan.

Dismounting and tethering the horses, Cybele approached the strangers. "Greetings, Priestess," one spoke, the voice muffled beneath the heavy folds of the robe. It was impossible to tell if she was being addressed by a man or a woman. "We have been awaiting your arrival and have come to help ensure your success in removing the Knowledge Crystals from Atlantis. Quickly," the mysterious figure turned and beckoned, "there is no time left."

Adima and Cybele looked at each other. This was it, the moment of parting. From here on, they would go their separate ways to wage their separate battles. Would they be successful? Would they meet again? Neither one knew. One last time they embraced, speaking not a word, their love saying it all. Then Cybele was gone. Surrounded by her newfound allies, she disappeared amidst swirling clouds of smoke.

Adima watched her go with tears in his eyes. Then he turned to Hia. "When she returns, take the crystals back to the Ark as quickly as possible. Do not wait for me. The crystals must be protected at all costs."

Hia turned to the warriors, addressing them in the language of the Islanders. They nodded their understanding. Then he mounted his horse and stood looking down at Adima, as if to say, "I'm ready. Let's go."

"No, my brother," Adima shook his head, understanding the intent. "This is something I must do alone. You cannot go with me. I must face the Beast by myself. Stay here and guard the threshold, and when Cybele returns, escort her and the crystals back to the Ark. Do not wait for me. I shall find you in my own way."

Hia made no comment, knowing it would be fruitless to argue the point. With a warm embrace, the two men parted, and Adima rode off in the direction of the Great Pyramid.

*****

In the Temple courtyard, Cybele paused. The monumental Statue of Poseidon lay in ruins, a tangle of bent and twisted steel, the metaphor all too clear. As the Atlantean Founder had tumbled to the ground, so also had the Atlantean civilization fallen from grace. The open doors of the Temple gaped before her like the entrance to a monster's cave, dark and forbidding. For the first time in her life, Cybele was afraid to enter the sacred precincts.

"This magic Shield, gift of the Goddess of Wisdom, will protect you from all physical harm in the presence of evil."

Gaia's words came back to her, reminding her of her strength. She unslung the Shield and slipped it over her left arm. "I am ready," she nodded to the Holy Ones, brandishing the Wand, holding it before her. "Let us go within."

The Grand Hall was dark and deserted, only blackened ashes where once the sacred flames had kept their eternal vigil. The Wand, though, glowed with a brilliant white light, illuminating the way before them. As though she were actually standing there, Eve's words echoed through the cavernous room, reminding Cybele of her great and noble purpose.

"As Adima, your male counterpart, goes forth to wage a mighty battle with Belial, so you must go forth to rescue the sacred Knowledge Crystals from their repository in the Holy of Holies deep inside the Temple of Poseidon. There will be a great confrontation with the Shadow Priestess, but you will prevail if you remain true to your faith."

The High Priestess! Cybele shuddered at the thought of meeting her nemesis face to face in the dark. Using all of her senses of perception and intuition, she scanned for Lilith. The woman's energy was strong—powerful vibrations of jealousy and rage, the resonance of evil. Try as she might, however, Cybele could not locate Lilith's hiding place, although she knew it was nearby. "The High Priestess is lurking in here somewhere," she said to the Holy Ones, "hiding, lying in wait for me. I can feel her."

The Holy Ones made no answer. Taking the lead, the mysterious beings descended immediately to the cavern where the Knowledge Crystals were stored, the soft glow of Cybele's golden Wand illuminating the way.

There they were, behind the magic wall, pulsing softly, lying in absolute serenity—pure, vibrant knowledge. But wait! Only two of the three crystals were in place. Where was the third? "It has been stolen!" Cybele cried. Her first thought was that looters had ransacked the Temple's treasures. Then another possibility occurred to her. "Lilith and Belial must have spirited it away. They have hidden it where no one will find it, and there is no time to effect a search."

Cybele felt a sense of tremendous urgency. Her intuition warned her not to linger. Danger was all around them. As if to confirm the necessity for haste, the ground beneath their feet shook violently. "We shall take what is here and go," she decided. "Better to salvage two of them than to leave with nothing."

Reaching out, she picked up a crystal. It was surprisingly warm and quite heavy, not nearly as fragile or delicate as it appeared. Carefully she wrapped each one in soft cloths and secured them in a leather pouch that one of the Holy Ones held open. Taking the crystals was quite easy. Too easy, she realized, looking about with a shudder of dread as they headed for the relative safety of the outdoors. At the staircase that led both up and down, the group paused. Sensing that it was time for a parting of the ways, Cybele acknowledged the help of her allies.

"My deepest thanks to each of you," she smiled, inclining her head to the one she had come to identify as spokesperson. The Holy One had not spoken since they had exchanged their first words. Now the sacred being placed a gentle hand on Cybele's arm.

"Three of us will go with you so that you are safely reunited with your people. Be very careful. You are not free yet. There is still great danger. It lurks above us. There is still one more challenge to meet before you can get safely out of the Temple." Without another word, the others were gone, making their way back down into the subterranean depths, back to their home, where they belonged. As promised, however, three remained at her side, carrying the crystals, accompanying the priestess as she made her way back above ground. Up they went, reentering the Grand Hall. The Wand glowed brighter now, as if to say, "Beware, beware."

Cybele stopped and looked around the room. It had been subtly changed in the few minutes she had been below ground. The sacred fires had been rekindled and were burning brightly before the altar. For the first time, she noticed that the great doors to the Temple were closed. As far as she knew, they had never been closed in all of the history of Atlantis; the Temple was always open and accessible to everyone.

The foursome had reached the middle of the vast chamber when a disembodied voice rang out of the darkness. "Latoné." The name echoed through the dark and cavernous hall. The Wand pulsed with golden light. The priestess turned, startled. In the dim light, she saw no one. Then, ever so slowly, a swirling, glowing red mist formed at the back of the room in front of the great curtain that separated the Grand Hall from the Holy of Holies.

With a puff of smoke, a whiff of sulphur, and a loud pop, the sinister figure of Lilith appeared amidst crackling red and yellow flames. All in black she was, a dark and deadly menace, her once-lovely face a portrait of hatred, jealousy, and triumph. Cybele held tightly to the Shield, impressed by the black magic behind this most dramatic appearance—fire and smoke appearing out of thin air, melding together to take the form of a human being. So, among her many other talents, the High Priestess of Atlantis—a very powerful and dangerous sorceress—was also a Shapeshifter.

"Latoné," Lilith said again, laughing a deep, sardonic chuckle as she advanced to meet her foe. "Did you think you could fool me? Did you think you could keep your name a secret forever? Did you think you could steal the Knowledge Crystals and betray Atlantis?"

"Latoné." A third time Lilith spoke the name, slowly circling the room, positioning herself between her enemy and the Temple doors.

Cybele moved in concert with the High Priestess, keeping her face always toward her nemesis. The Holy Ones drew back, stepping aside, knowing it was not their place to interfere. This battle was between the two women, the two opposites. Again and again Lilith spoke the name, shooting forth her evil intentions, projecting bolt after bolt of malevolent energy at the woman whom she wanted to destroy. With each utterance, the Shield glowed with a holy light, protecting its charge, absorbing the malevolence and reflecting it back upon the High Priestess.

It was no use. Try as she might, Lilith could not break through the impenetrable barrier of protection that surrounded Cybele. How frustrating! To have waited all these months to learn the secret name and now to be unable to use it to her advantage was more than her Shadow self could bear. All of the darkness welled up from within and came forth, naked and exposed. Her features were no longer beautiful, but dark and distorted into a mask of pure hatred and rage. "I will not be denied," the High Priestess spoke in a barely audible whisper. "I will have my victory, no matter the cost!"

Outside the Temple, in the red light of the noonday sun, the City of Atlantis still burned. Truth and goodness had fled, while death and destruction reigned. Within the Temple, however, none of that mattered. Within, a different battle raged, taking place in the semidarkness, beyond the bounds of ordinary space and time. Within the sanctuary that served as the symbolic home of the Divine on Earth, the Feminine energies—both positive and negative—confronted each other.

Like the mighty walls of the Temple itself, like the towering Lighthouse, Latoné, Queen of Hearts, stood strong and impenetrable, a pillar of strength amid the hallowed but weakened arches of the ruined Temple. An aura of golden light surrounded her, holding her in the safety of its golden womb, protecting the priestess even as she protected the Knowledge Crystals, guarding her even as she guarded the essence of Atlantean life, nurturing her even as she would one day nurture the seeds once again, that they might sprout and grow and bear good fruit forever. In the seven directions the light shone forth—North, South, East, West, Above, Below, and Within. Like a protecting archangel wielding her mighty Word-Sword, Latoné stood strong and unscathed throughout the battle, protected by her Shield.

Across from her, in the center of the room, stood Lilith, Queen of Swords, herself an imposing figure of power. Driven by greed and self-absorption, she had climbed the ladder of success and conquered the world, building her own impregnable fortress, from which there was neither ingress nor egress. No light surrounded her. The eternal flame that burned within her being had long ago been hidden away, blotted out by motives of avarice and ambition. So dim had her own light become that she was surrounded now by darkness, blind to the death and destruction that Belial's insatiable lust for victory and power had produced.

Trapped in the darkness within, now she dared to issue her greatest challenge. As the day had dawned in opposition to the sun, so now Lilith rose in opposition to the Great Mother herself, standing tall and straight, spitting forth the venom of excess that her rapacious shadow femininity had produced as she hungrily aspired to ever more glory.

Latoné was the first to speak, proclaiming a judgment, a condemnation, not on the person, but on the motives, the behavior, the results of her actions. "You have destroyed the Temple, High Priestess, and abandoned the sacred trust that your people have placed in you. Not just the physical Temple is ruined, but also the temple of the human body."

The Queen of Hearts spread her arms to encompass the entire room. "There is no compassion in the Temple any more. There is no healing here, because you have declared it so. There is no faith, and so the Atlantean mind is weak and confused. There is no hope, and so the Atlantean body is sick and dying."

The Queen of Swords laughed her mocking laugh. "What do you know about faith and hope, false priestess?" she accused. "What do you know about spirituality. Spirituality is obsolete, and religion is for weak and simpering fools who lack the courage and fortitude to take what they want."

Lilith withdrew a magnificent dagger from the folds of her gown. The jewel-encrusted hilt scintillated in the light of the fire. "You are right, faith and hope have long since flown away," she fingered the blade delicately, licking her lips in anticipation of its drinking the heart blood of the enemy before her. "Belial rules in their place, and I rule by his side. We answer to no one, neither the gods nor the Goddess, neither the Divine nor the Great Mother. We are our own authority. We make our own laws."

She is insane, Latoné realized, looking at the Dark Queen before her. The transformation was complete. Lilith had abandoned her faith and embraced fear, and her rational mind had turned upside down. The unnatural and the unreal were now both natural and real. Truth had been replaced with falsity, and the fearful Dream had taken hold.

The High Priestess pointed the accusing dagger at her enemy, her voice rising to an imperious shriek. "You are jealous of me. You want to destroy me. But I shall give you one last chance to save yourself."

Again there was a flash of fire and smoke, and Lilith was enveloped in flames. When the smoke cleared, Temptress stood in her place, revealing the breathtakingly lovely figure and dazzling charm that had seduced even the mighty Belial.

"Gaze upon my beauty with envy and adoration," she commanded. "Dazzle me with gifts of flattery." Drawing close, her voice became silky and sensuous. If raw power could not penetrate the Shield, perhaps she could lead Latoné astray by appealing to her femininity. "Come," she whispered in her most seductive voice. "Bow down before me."

But there would be no seduction this day, for the priestess was protected by the Goddess. The Shield crackled with electricity, sending out a powerful charge, hurling the Seductress across the room in a shower of sparks. When she got to her feet again, the Temptress was gone and Lilith had reappeared.

"For this you will die!" she screamed, her face contorted in rage, spittle flecking her thin, cruel lips. Extending her arm, Lilith prepared to cast another spell, when she was suddenly interrupted by a noise from behind the curtain. A third had entered the room—Nabala.

"So it was you after all," Latoné gasped, shocked that she had not recognized the younger woman's complicity until now. The words of the Greeter's warning came back to her.

"Beware those who change shape and form. She is he and he is she."

Of course. In her desire for worldly advancement, Nabala had abandoned her womanhood and embraced the Shadow masculine, hiding behind her acolyte disguise that she might serve as a spy for the High Priestess. "You betrayed me," Cybele continued, "and you betrayed the Feminine and the Mother and the Goddess. How could you? For what purpose? What has your betrayal gotten you?"

Nabala stood with her head bowed. "Nothing, Mistress," she replied in true humility, abashed and chagrined by her behavior. "I am here to offer my life in atonement. I stand by your side."

"Then you will die by her side," Lilith roared, raising the dagger and springing forward like a cat pouncing on its helpless prey. She had taken but three paces when she stopped short, head cocked, listening.

Deep beneath the Temple, a dull rumble began to well up. Soft and low at first, it quickly built in intensity and volume. The marble floor beneath their feet began to vibrate, and in a matter of seconds the whole building was shaking violently. From far above their heads, small pieces of the ceiling fell like miniature stone raindrops, exploding as they shattered on the tile. One after another they fell, hitting the floor with such force that they were either pulverized or driven deeply into the marble. The din was deafening. And all the while, the great sonic vibrations from below continued to increase in power and intensity.

Cybele knew what was happening. She recognized the sound right away. It was the song of the Holy Ones, the polyphonic hymn of praise that they unceasingly sang to the Great Mother. Louder now they chanted, projecting the sacred tones outward, letting the vibrations of each harmonic oscillate, intoning various combinations of harmonies and dissonances, seeking that certain frequency which would match their tones to the exact harmonic resonance of the Temple of Poseidon itself.

Sound—the first Word, the single, holy Word! Latoné remembered the sacred passage from the *Book of Life*.

IN THE BEGINNING WAS THE WORD...

Now the Holy Ones were using the true Word—the First Vibration—to counter and combat the lying words of Belial, Lilith, and the corrupt religion; using the powers inherent in the Word of Truth to defeat the Word of Lies.

Louder and stronger grew the tones, merging into a single, all-encompassing sound, a sound so vast and so marvelous that it was like the first Sound—the Primordial Sound that had birthed the creation of the universe.

Latoné looked around her. There was no need to take any action. She could not have stopped the process even if she had tried. As they listened, the sound moved beyond the range of human hearing and became pure vibration—pure and sweet and oh so powerful. It had become a sound that was felt in every cell of the body. Up through the Earth the Holy Song came, filling the living stone, moving across the floor, spreading from room to room, climbing up the mighty columns, up the walls, higher and higher, wider and wider, until the whole Temple was vibrating in harmony with that Primordial Sound.

Lilith stood rooted to the spot, unable to move as larger pieces of the roof crashed down around her. "Come to me," Latoné cried, reaching out to rescue her enemy. But before Lilith could move, a great slab of stone crashed down between them. The ground shook, and a shower of dust and rubble spread out in all directions.

"Mistress!" Nabala cried as more pieces fell, throwing herself at Latoné, knocking her to the floor and covering her with her own body. Great chunks of debris fell all around them. Dust covered them. Latoné was smothering. A great, dead weight pressed down on top of her, and she struggled to release herself from its life-choking grasp. She felt gentle hands on her, pulling her from the rubble, lifting her up and out of the debris and chaos. The Holy Ones helped her to her feet and took her by the arm.

"Wait," she cried, looking around for Nabala and Lilith. Nabala lay where she had thrown herself to save Latoné. A tiny trickle of blood oozed from her scalp, and she did not move. The priestess knelt by the young woman's side and gently cradled the bloody head in her lap. Nabala's eyes opened, and she looked up with a question.

"Are you all right, Mistress?" she asked with genuine compassion.

"Yes, I am safe," Latoné replied softly. "You saved me."

Nabala shuddered as a spasm of pain wracked her body. She struggled to speak. "Then I have atoned?" It was a question, not a statement. The dying woman's eyes pleaded for an answer, pleaded for forgiveness and release.

"Yes, you have atoned," Latoné smiled at her, stroking the blood-matted hair. "You have done well. Your work here is through. The crystals are safe, I am safe, and you can leave now with no regrets. All of posterity is grateful to you. Farewell and Godspeed."

Nabala smiled a grateful smile. She took a last look around the ruined Temple, then she slowly closed her eyes, let out a soft sigh, and expired. Gently, Latoné laid the wounded head on the stone. Then she rose to look for Lilith. The High Priestess was nowhere to be found.

"Priestess, there is no time," the Holy Ones urged. We must leave here."

Again they took her by the arm, dragging her gently but firmly out of the Temple as the whole domed ceiling collapsed. Down it all came, crushing statues, destroying artwork, pulverizing the thrones where the ancient kings had once held court. Lingering in the doorway, Latoné paused to watch, drawn by a force stronger than curiosity. *Watch and remember*," a Voice instructed her, *"that you may tell them what it was like."*

High overhead, a particularly large, diamond-shaped stone was dislodged from its mortar. It dangled precariously for a few seconds, held in place by a single bead of cement. Then it too broke free, falling straight down, a great projectile whose sharp point was aimed directly at the heart of the human figure etched into the stone floor directly below. The point struck the image dead center, driving through the stone, smashing the magnificent image of the human being in the center of the floor, piercing the symbolic heart.

With the impact, Latoné was driven backward out the door. A sharp, burning pain seared through her breast, the pain of the broken Atlantean Heart. The Spiritual Heart of the Atlantean people was gone, pierced by a giant shard of cold, unfeeling stone. "As the stone man is smashed, so too is the Atlantean human smashed, never to be the same," she thought with remorse and compassion, rubbing her chest as the pain continued to burn within her breast.

Down the steps she dashed with the Holy Ones, stone crashing all around them as the massive columns that supported the stone porch broke into dozens of pieces. Back along the Avenue of the Gods they ran, putting distance between themselves and the Temple, pausing only to catch their breath half a mile away. There they stopped, panting and gasping for air. Still the fires raged, still the ash pelted them, still the ground shook, still the Holy Song was sung.

Then they felt it. The Sound took on a new vibration, soaring to an even higher pitch. Their hands flew to their ears as the sound become painful, but there was no drowning it out. Deep inside the Mother, at the Sound's source, where it was the loudest, the massive pillars that supported the foundation of the Temple began to sway. Back and forth they rocked to the rhythm of the Sound, swaying to and fro like stone dancers come to life, gyrating to some convoluted sacrificial dance. At last the frequency was just right, reaching the perfect pitch. With a mighty groan, the stone pillars buckled, then collapsed under the massive weight.

With nothing to support it any longer, the Temple could no longer stand. Down it came, imploding, collapsing in upon itself. The Pride of the Ancients, the Wonder of the World, the Center of the Universe, the Home of the Divine on Earth—with a deafening roar, it caved in and became a pile of rubble. The Temple of Poseidon was no more. The spiritual center of the great Nation-State of Atlantis was gone, collapsed into a broken and smoldering ruin.

With tears in her eyes, Latoné and her escorts made their way back to the meeting point. Mounting their horses, they turned and rode out of the city for the last time, without so much as a backward glance, the Knowledge Crystals safely wrapped in blankets in the priestess' saddle bags, the Holy Ones holding tightly to the Islanders who carried them on their own horses.

And as they rode across the Great Plain, Latoné wondered. Where was the third Knowledge Crystal? Who had it? And what had happened to Lilith? No one could have survived such destruction. Or could they? She would never know, she realized, glancing at the sky. The sun was at its zenith, and a small, black shadow had appeared across its face. The eclipse was starting.

"I love you, my husband," she whispered, sending the message back across the Great Plain. She only hoped Adima was alive to receive it.

*****

Adima fell to his knees as the ground shook violently beneath his feet. He had been listening to the song of the Holy Ones, attuned with their intent, and he knew at once that they had been successful in fulfilling their part of the Plan. Latoné was safe. She, too, had succeeded, thanks to her noble allies and her own courage and warrior skills.

"Thank you," he breathed as a great wall of sound descended upon him, surrounding him with its fearsome noise. Turning around, he watched as the Temple of Poseidon tumbled to the ground. An enormous mushroom-shaped cloud billowed up into the atmosphere, blotting out the already-darkened sun. As the yellow-brown dust swirled around him, he recalled the ancient prophecy.

LEAVING NOT A SINGLE STONE UPON ANOTHER...

Indeed, the Atlantean connection with the Divine had been broken. At least, their conscious awareness of their connection had been severed, he reminded himself. The true connection to Source could never be sundered, no matter how hard the human race tried to deny that universal Truth. He dusted himself off and headed once again toward the Great Pyramid. Now the shadow of the moon began to cast its dark presence across the face of the sun. There was little time left.

As soon as he and his wife had separated, he had headed for the Council of Elders, but the halls were deserted. In the Palace courtyard, a soldier had pointed him in the right direction. "Where is Belial?" Adima had asked. The dazed man had recognized him immediately, but made no move to arrest him. He only pointed in the direction of the Pyramid.

"Belial is insane!" the soldier had exclaimed, a wild light glinting in his bloodshot eyes. "He went there and took the device and plans to turn it on and destroy you and me and everyone. He's mad," the terrified man cried, grasping Adima's tunic, clinging desperately to the man whom he had only that morning sworn to find and kill. "Stop him, stop him if you can." Without another word, the soldier had run off screaming, trying to put as much distance as possible between himself and the madman he had called Master. At that same moment, the Temple had collapsed.

Now, with a silent prayer for the safety of Cybele, Hia, and the others, Adima headed in the direction to which the Adept had pointed. It appeared he and Belial would have their final confrontation at the Great Pyramid. Once again, how fitting! How marvelous the Plan!

The Great Pyramid, embodiment of the archetypal energies of King, Warrior, Lover, and Magician. Sacred bridal suite for the consummation of the Marriage of Heaven and Earth. Distillery and silo for the Solar Fire. Focal point for all of the power and might of the Dragon Current. A thrill of anticipation coursed through his body. All his life, Adima had been preparing for this single moment in time. He was about to engage in a replay of the greatest of all battles, the War of the Worlds he had witnessed in his vision of the Grail Angel so many years ago.

This time, though, protagonist and antagonist were not the Angelic Hosts of Light against the Fallen Angels of Darkness. Rather, they were flesh and blood and bone—Adima-Thoth the ascended Man facing Belial the degenerate Beast. No matter, however, that they were not spirits. Like their angelic counterparts, Adima and Belial would step out of ordinary time and space into that higher reality. Protagonist and antagonist might be different, but the reason for the conflict, the motive for the battle, was still the same. Light would face Dark, Good would face Evil, not in the astral realms of Heaven and Hell, but in the shadow of the Great Pyramid beneath the darkness of an eclipsed sun.

As he moved through the inferno, the Mother shook herself again, more violently this time. For the second time that week, Adima drew his Sword. The weapon felt comfortable in his hand, giving him a sense of security and connectedness with the spirit of his ancestors. He was not alone after all.

Walking lightly on tiptoe, turning constantly about to face in all directions, he kept careful watch, using the weapon as a sensor to ward off debris and falling stones. As he approached the Pyramid, the light grew dimmer. The sun was about one quarter eclipsed as he stood at the entrance to the piazza. He paused for a moment and looked around, alert for any signs of danger. He was alone except for Belial, who had yet to notice his brother's approach, so engrossed was he in preparing the sinister device for its fiendish purpose.

"It is not my brother whom I attack," Adima reminded himself. "I have come to slay the Beast, to overcome the Dark One and set Belial free." So it would be, with the help of his allies and the protection of Divine providence. He glanced at the darkening sky. It was almost the Hour of the Raven.

Sensing danger, the Belial-Beast turned and saw the Enemy observing him. Adima gasped, so completely had the Beast transumed his brother. Those feral lips twisted into a grim and deadly smile as it cast a furtive glance over one shoulder, toward the dark entrance to the Pyramid. Then, waving a hairy paw, it beckoned the Enemy to approach, to walk into the trap that was about to be sprung.

Adima stood tall, in emulation of the avenging Angel of the Grail. Stepping out in the open, making no effort to hide himself, he started across the piazza. It was a bold walk, a walk of power, a forthright march across the stones. He stopped twenty yards from his foe.

The Beast flew into a fit of rage, furious at Adima's courage, frustrated that it could not frighten him away, screaming vile curses at its archenemy. Then it screamed an order.

From within the Pyramid, where they had been silently lying in wait, a dozen huge, grotesquely shaped creatures emerged. Voicing guttural growls of rage, the cyclopes lumbered forward, moving ominously toward him, their foul smell and loathsome appearance designed to strike terror into their prey.

Adima stood his ground, letting the loathsome creatures surround him. It was easy to read their intent, their simple minds an open book to his intuitive senses. The cyclopes were ferocious predators, to be sure. Timing their attack perfectly, they would surround their prey, gauge the distance for their leap, then voice a bloodcurdling scream and charge.

Adima, however, was prepared. Just as the aberrations were about to spring, he opened his throat, voicing his own mighty roar, aiming the sound directly at his foes. It was the ferocious roar of the warrior who had found his voice—a primal sound, a savage sound, a full, deep-throated challenge that paralyzed the monstrosities with fear. It was the roar of the Wild Man!

The cyclopes paused, terrified and confused. What manner of creature was this, who looked and smelled like a puny man but stood his ground and roared like a wild beast of prey? Before they could reason it further in their dull brains, Adima struck, laying about after the fashion of a mighty beast on a rampage of vengeance. Not demonic, like the Belial-

Beast, Adima's "beast" was a noble, mighty fighter, creature of the jungle, fierce protector of home and family, the warrior in his fullness.

His strokes were bold and powerful, his strength that of a dozen men, blending all of the skills of the warrior with those of the lioness. Masculine and Feminine together—fierce male protector combined with the energies of the female sun—balanced. The first mutant went down without a sound, followed by another and another. The warrior was everyone at once, slaying each cyclops in a masterful display of raw power and swordsmanship. When the last of the creatures was dead, Adima sheathed his Sword and turned to face the real enemy once again.

Despite wanting to flee, the Belial-Beast stood its ground, wrathful and fearful, incensed and not a little panicky. It had thrown its most powerful allies at Adima, and this spawn of jackals had beaten them back without even breaking a sweat. The Beast looked at its vanquished army lying in pools of their own blood. They were all dead.

Screaming obscenities and curses at its hated enemy, now the Beast called on all the demons of the Netherworld to join in its unholy cause. Frothing at the mouth, its tunic flecked with spittle, it presented an icon of bestial humanity and depravity. And it was far from defeated. Extending its powerful arms, it shot great bolts of electricity out of its paws. Like blue fireballs they flew through the air, crackling with energy, packing a potent charge.

Had they struck him, Adima would have been severely wounded, if not killed. But they did not strike, for now Snake uncoiled itself within his breast, its five heads weaving and bobbing in every direction. Protecting his sacred space, the ally swallowed the charges one by one as Adima executed a strategic retreat, making his way not toward the Beast, but toward the Great Pyramid itself.

"Where are you going?" the Belial-Beast roared, thinking it had succeeded in frightening the Enemy away at last. "You cannot escape me. Run if you want, but I shall always find you."

But the man ignored the Beast, continuing to walk away, his back turned to the loathsome creature, walking straight toward the base of the Great Pyramid, to the foot of the golden stairway that divided the east face into equal and opposite halves, just like the equal and opposite halves of his own being. Taking the first step, Adima began the climb. To left and right, the two sides of the Pyramid's face flanked him, reminding him of the Duality that comprised his Wholeness.

On the left, the Feminine, lunar, dark side, representing the Atlantean past and his own past as well. On the right, the Masculine, solar, outward-going principle, representing his own future and the future of the human race. Between the two he walked, following the middle way, holding the Tension of the Opposites, treading the razor's edge.

Up the side of the Great Pyramid he climbed, scaling its face, ascending higher and higher, leaving the Belial-Beast on the ground far below. Time and again the Beast took aim, hurling one powerful charge after another at the puny man-thing on the face of that great mountain of stone. With each blast, great chunks of stone exploded from their age-old settings. Leaving gaping holes in the body of the Pyramid, they skidded and tumbled and fell to the ground. The Earth shook with each tremendous impact, and jagged cracks and fissures spread across the piazza. Hissing jets of steam rose up from below, and the depths glowed a fiery red as molten lava oozed its way to the surface.

Time and again Adima warded off the blows, not even turning to face his attacker, sensing the bolts, knowing when they would come and where they would strike. Then, moving a hairsbreadth to the left or right, he let the energy pass harmlessly, to be absorbed in the rock of that massive monolith. Up and up he climbed, rising farther and farther above the ground and the Beast. And as he climbed, he was transformed, becoming more and more godlike, ascending higher and higher toward the Ideal.

Reaching the middle course, he paused for a moment as thick clouds of grimy yellow smoke drifted around him, temporarily blocking man and beast from each other's sight. The sulphurous smell of fire and brimstone mingled with the sharp odor of ozone from Belial's energy daggers. When at last the smoke cleared, the transformation had become visible. High above, mortal man had become demigod, while far below, man-beast had become demonic. Avenging Angel faced the demonic Shadow Destroyer as it called to Atlantis to descend into the depths and experience its capacity for destruction as well as creation.

Once more the Beast let loose with an onslaught of fiery energy. Each time the charge missed its mark, it screamed and cursed and called for help from its demonic allies. Finally, exhausted from the effort of the attack, realizing that its energy would serve a better purpose elsewhere, the Beast gave up. Turning its attention back to the original plan, it put everything in readiness.

At the same exact instant, Adima took the last step, reaching the summit of the Great Pyramid, stepping out onto the narrow ledge that surrounded the perimeter of the base of the capstone. High overhead, dark storm clouds billowed. The hurricane was moving in from the East, coming closer and closer. So too was the sun almost three-quarters eclipsed. Daylight was fading into darkness. It would not be long now.

For an instant, he swayed dizzily as he imagined himself falling off the edge of the world, no longer in the loving hands of the Divine, cut off from the Mother and all that was good and sacred. Then the strange sensation passed as he let go of his attachment to limitations and took the greatest leap of faith of his life. Letting go, too, of all attachments to outcomes, all egotistical desires for revenge or bold heroics, he turned his will completely over to the care of the Father and the Mother.

"Not my will, but Thine," he whispered, closing his eyes as he spoke the timeless prayer of Surrender. When he opened them again, it was no longer Adima who looked out on the world with a new and clearer vision, but the ascended master, Thoth. Great muscles bulging, skin glistening with sweat, auburn hair blowing in the wind, Thoth straddled the ledge and looked down on Atlantis. Not Atlantis, but Perdition, he realized as smoke swirled all around him.

Even his great gift of language failed him as he surveyed the incredible ruin. Words and intellect could not describe it. It was something that could only be felt with the heart, experienced with the senses. His eyes beheld the Abomination of Desolation. His lips and tongue tasted the bitter gall of poisoned waters. His skin felt the blood of the martyrs in every searing raindrop. His nostrils smelled the foul stench of death, the slaughter of the innocents. His ears heard the weeping and wailing and gnashing of teeth in the darkness.

In his mind, he heard the roar of multitudinous engines of destruction. In his chest, he felt the crushing pain of a heart that had shut itself down and refused to beat again. A single tear dropped from his eye, and a righteous anger filled him as the scar on his face—that old wound given by Belial to terrify him—now burned livid. "Enough!" he cried, his voice lost in the fierce wind. "This stops now. It ends here, once and for all."

Drawing himself erect, focusing on the enemy below, Thoth shouted a single word. "Beast!" he cried out in a voice that was the roar of many waters. Far below, the Beast looked up, startled, driven back by the power of that potent, palpable roar. Seeing its enemy towering high above like an avenging angel coming on the clouds of Heaven, it roared forth a challenge of its own, a fiery, snarling growl of demonic fury.

Thoth thrilled to the fight. At last! The time had come! After so many years, since the time in the womb. The challenge was given and accepted.

"Beast!" he roared again. The sound came forth out of his mouth and took physical form, a swirling spiral of color. Taking the shape of a miniature tornado, a spiral catching on the wind, it grew stronger, descending to where the Beast labored at its demonic work, falling upon it, enveloping it in a wall of furious sound.

Driven back but still unscathed, the Beast worked feverishly now, surrounded by the bodies of the dead monstrosities littering the piazza, surrounded by blood and destruction. At last its work was complete; the device was ready. A sly, satanic grin of triumph spread across that gruesome face. It had won. It had only to turn on the device.

Saliva drooling from its hideous mouth, baleful yellow eyes glinting evilly, the Beast placed a twisted talon on the button and pressed. A blue-white beam of pure light shot straight up into the atmosphere, savagely piercing the heavens with its burning energy.

Thoth heard the universe sigh. "Beast!" he roared a third time. "Not Belial, but Beast, for that is who you are," he cried even as he spoke the name. "It is the Beast who I want. It is the Beast to whom I roar forth my challenge."

Wild, wicked, evil, utterly depraved, the Beast replied according to the manner of its kind, screaming curses, oaths, and obscenities. Once again it extended its arm, shooting powerful bolts of energy out and up at the hated man-thing who dared to challenge it. "Die, die, die!" it screamed with each blast, its yellow eyes focused on the gauges of the device, willing the dial to turn further and further toward maximum power. Fangs dripping poison, it called on the demons for even more assistance.

Mighty as it was, the Great Pyramid could not stand up to such a battering indefinitely. Nor could the Earth. The molten lava, trapped eons ago and now released, bubbled up to the surface in a steaming river of fire. Like a great snake it crept along the ground, slithering and hissing and making its way outward, free at last to go where it pleased. The Beast seemed not to notice, but the man in the sky recognized the signal. The Mother was ready, and she was telling him so.

Slowly, Thoth moved his hand to the bejeweled scabbard hanging from his belt. Casting a sidelong glance at the sky, he waited for the moment to be exactly right. Darker and darker it grew, but a pale sliver of the sun was still visible. The eclipse was almost total. The sky was simultaneously black and red. All Atlantis was aflame before him, and now the very heavens burst into flame above him. Great bolts of lightning shot forth from the clouds, and titanic peals of thunder boomed and crashed all around. Cyclonic gusts of fiery wind—the breath of the Avenging Angel—blew. But Thoth stood firm, hand poised, feet rooted firmly in place at the top of the Great Pyramid.

At full power the device hummed, the blue laser beam shooting up into the heavens, cutting through the ionosphere, boiling the air, vaporizing the very atmosphere of the Great Mother.

Without a word, Thoth drew the mystical Sword for the third and final time, the mythical weapon forged on the Hearth of the Gods, the great Sword that would come to be known by so many names through the ages—Excalibur, Anduril, and the rest. As he unsheathed the mighty weapon, it crackled and glowed with enormous power. It sizzled with energy, pulsed with light.

The Beast cowered in the face of such awesome strength and power. Drawing back in fear, it recoiled as though slapped, its tongue lolling out, growling in rage and fear.

Thoth spoke not a word. Holding the Blade of Light with both hands, he inscribed a sacred geometrical pattern in the air before him—the Sign of the Merkabah, symbol of uniting and unifying Love. Then he raised the Sword aloft, high above his head, pointing the razor-sharp tip to the heavens, pointing to the stars, pointing home...to Spirit.

Crying out in a loud voice, the transformed man, the ascended master—Thoth— invoked One greater than himself—an Avenging Spirit, the Archangel of the Grail. Invoked his greatest Ally, asking the Guardian of Heaven to appear in physical form.

Great bolts of lightning shot out of the heavens, mighty bolts, terrible bolts. No mortal had ever seen anything like them, of such force and magnitude were they. Not since the Beginning had the Mother displayed such enormous strength, such raw power, such potency. Never since the world was new had the skies of the Mother sparkled with such holy Light.

High in the air the angelic spirits danced, cavorting and reveling in the crackling energy all around them. The lightning was everywhere at once, accompanied simultaneously by deafening peals of thunder. The Beast stood transfixed, mesmerized, and totally exposed, standing powerless in the face of the sacred display of the angelic forces and the awesome power of Nature. For the Great Mother had taken the offensive at last, unleashed, unrestrained, in the fullness of her power—the power of the Heavens, the power of the Divine, the power of Truth.

Thoth looked out around him and smiled. *"Thank you,"* he whispered. *"Thank you, Father. Thank you, Mother. Thank you for hearing my prayers and standing by my side. Thank you for not abandoning Atlantis in our hour of need. As Cybele has done her part, as Sophia and Enoch have done theirs, as Hia and the Holy Ones have done theirs, as you have done your part, so now I do mine."*

Ever so slowly, as though time had suddenly stopped, Thoth changed his position the slightest bit. Still holding the Sword aloft in his left hand, he opened his right hand, moving it off the jeweled hilt. With the greatest deliberation and utmost care, he extended his right arm, bringing it down and forward, pointing outward with his index finger. Searching the piazza, he sought out the target and found the Beast.

Under that accusing finger of fate, it stood powerless, watching its destiny approach. What thoughts passed through its malevolent brain will never be known. Thoth opened his mouth. His throat chakra grew warm, and a tone formed within him. Softly at first, then louder and louder, it merged with the lightning and the thunder, a great and mighty sound that rose above the roar of the Storm God.

It was a powerful invocation, a primordial tone in the Language of Light, invoking the Hard Lightning. In the eternal heavens, another ally, Grandmother Moon, positioned herself between the Great Mother and the sun. The eclipse was total; darkness was upon the world.

There was no light at all, and no power. With the interruption of the magnetic field, the deadly device ceased to function. Below, the Beast screamed in rage and fear, to no avail. On high, the sky blackened and the heavens boiled. Above Thoth's head, the clouds seemed to take shape and form. The figure of a mighty Dragon appeared in the swirling mists, its huge head and burning eyes clearly visible in the glow from its flaming nostrils. Looking out and down, the Dragon waited for the Dragonmaster to give the order, waited for the command to rain its fire down upon the Beast.

Within the Great Pyramid, the Fire Crystals sprang to life, and the diamond crystal tip sparkled with light. The very stones glowed crimson as the great transformer called down the celestial Dragon Fire. The skies opened, the Dragon reared up and breathed forth a fearsome blast from its nostrils, and a tremendous bolt of lightning shot down from the heavens. Such a bolt it was! Not since the dawn of creation had there been another of its kind.

Straight and fast the Dragon Fire sped, its aim true, striking the uttermost tip of the great Sword, attuning itself to the steel blade. Filling the metal, tracking down along the shaft, through the hilt, into the Hero's arm, penetrating him, lighting him up, filling him with the Dragon Current, connecting his head and his heart within the tetrahedron of his own being.

There Thoth stood, energy dancing all around him, a channel for the elements. As he had been transformed, so now he offered himself to the purposes of Spirit, allowing the Mother and the Avenging Angel to transform the lightning within his own body. The electricity churned and roiled within him, causing neither pain nor injury, merely making ready, gathering and focusing itself. Then the Dragon Current shot through his right arm and out of his pointing finger in a focused beam of pure white light—the energy of Spirit in Form.

Tracing a brilliant path through the darkness, the holy beam descended from the Heavens to the Sword, from the Sword to the Man, from the Man to the Earth. Streaking toward the Beast, it struck with savage, awesome heat and power, enveloping the Dark Lord in enormous energy. For a split second, as Thoth watched, the Beast withdrew, and he saw the sad and tired face of Belial. His brother smiled gratefully at him, as if to say, "Thank you. I am free at last."

Then the Beast returned, voicing its hate and rage as the angelic light drove it into the stone of the piazza. A great cloud of pulverized stone, smoke, and fire boiled up from below. The cloud itself seemed to take the shape of a Beast, looming over the doomed island, its leering red eyes burning with hatred. Then the Mother exhaled a mighty breath, and a gale-force wind came and dispersed it, blowing it away into the nothingness from which it had come.

The device was gone! As was the Beast!

*****

Silence, utter and absolute silence ensued, accompanied by impenetrable darkness. No sound, no light. The Earth had entered the Great Void. For the briefest of instants, time stood still, and the Cosmic Pendulum paused as it reached the maximum extension of its arc. In that moment of non-time, a great and mighty groan echoed across the heavens, a long, terrible, and mournful cry of ineffable sorrow.

An instant only, as the universe waited with bated breath. Then the moon moved on, and the light of the sun returned. The eclipse was over, and with the returning light, the Pendulum began its slow, inexorable swing back in the opposite direction. Then the Great Mother did her part. With a sigh that resounded throughout the cosmos and reverberated throughout the Universe of Universes, the Great Mother arose, shook herself, and shifted on her axis.

On that very day, the seventh day of the Week That Would Change the World, a singular event occurred, an extraordinary happening of greater power than any the world had ever seen.

> ALL THE FOUNTAINS OF THE GREAT DEEP BURST FORTH, THE FLOODGATES
> OF THE HEAVENS WERE OPENED, AND WATER—BOTH SOURCE AND GRAVE
> OF ALL CREATED THINGS—CAME AND COVERED THE EARTH.

And in those swirling, chaotic, troubled waters, human nature shifted, too—from consciousness to unconsciousness, from awareness to unawareness—and the Fathers fell asleep.

CHAPTER 49

And rival storms abroad are surging
from sea to land, from land to sea,
a chain of deepest action forging
round all, in wrathful energy.
There flames a desolation blazing
before the thunder's crashing way.
Yet, Lord, Thy messengers keep praising
the gentle movement of Thy Day.

—Goethe's *Prologue in Heaven*

Thus, like a giant carcass thrown to the jackals, Atlantis was handed over to the Destroyer. Atlantean pride and hubris were about to be brought low. The most noble and mightiest civilization the world had ever known had degenerated into a house of cards and confusion destined to be destroyed, its ego consigned to the all-consuming fire. Such was the way of Universal Law, I thought, but I had no desire to watch the Destroyer at work. I shut my eyes and turned my head away, for I did not wish to behold the demise of a civilization, even if that civilization had become prideful and arrogant and jaded.

I felt the Spirit-winds shake me, rousing me from my reluctance, and a quiet Voice whispered in my heart. *"Not destruction,"* the Voice explained, *"but rather, Metamorphosis— under the watchful eye of the Destroyer. An invoking of the Law of Purification."*

"Watch and remember," the gentle Voice urged, *"that the Truth might be preserved."*

Then I understood. Atlantis was not being destroyed. Atlantis was being cleansed, purified at all levels of its being from the toxic effects of the ideas of separation and scarcity created by the duality of the opposites. And as with all things, even with the Law of Purification, there must be balance. That balance came in the forms of Fire and Water.

I opened my eyes and watched. For a day and a night, I beheld the breaking up of the land. For a day and a night, I watched a release of energy so great, so powerful, so overwhelming that it plunged everything into reverse. For a day and a night, I watched the careful, discerning dismemberment of the Atlantean heart and mind and body and soul, scattering them to the four winds, where they would lie dormant until the time for them to be reconstituted and reassembled once again. The two Partners immersing the world in their all-encompassing embrace—sweeping away of the old order, making way for the new—in a baptism of fire and water.

Explosive, all-consuming Fire—the alchemical furnace—putting to the flame all that was dark and poison and impure. Searing and scorching the Earth, purging it of all false beliefs, negative thoughts, shadowy motives, and lies. Agitated, ever-flowing Water— liquid light—washing away the ashes, covering up the scarred and blackened Earth. Returning it to the womb, revitalizing and nourishing the Earth in the lifeblood of the Great Mother.

*****

The dismemberment began on the beach. With a mighty onslaught, the hurricane made landfall, its cyclone-force winds blowing a huge storm surge before them, a veritable tidal wave of water. The ocean overflowed its banks, filling every low-lying place, every nook and cranny, every depression in the land.

Far out to sea, those who had left in their makeshift rafts were swamped and capsized in the tempest. The power of the waves broke them like matchwood. Swept overboard, the refugees were sucked up into waterspouts or down into whirlpools, never to be seen again.

At the shoreline, hungry, voracious, the angry waves devoured the land, chewing up and grinding the black volcanic rocks between huge molars of death, regurgitating only the most minuscule of particles. Battered, bashed, and pummeled, the beaches eroded in what seemed like minutes. I gasped as towering black lava cliffs collapsed into the roiling, churning waters.

High on the rocky coast, silhouetted against the sky, the Lighthouse still stood, mute testimony to the skill of the Ancient architects and masons who created it. Bruised and battered, its once gleaming white skin was coated a dull, uniform black.

It would not stand for long! Deep below the sea, seated on a golden throne within his watery Kingdom, I heard Poseidon roar in a mighty voice of thunder, calling forth the Archangel of the Abyss.

"Come forth, Destroyer," the Sea God commanded. *"Rise up from the deep and tear the Tower down, for they have abused the great gift that I have given them."*

"Why do you do this?" the Destroyer asked, gathering itself even as it voiced the question.

"From the highest point of the Tower, they had an unobstructed view," Poseidon explained. *"They could see themselves and all things clearly. But they kept their eyes closed. They refused to look at themselves. They refused to observe, to take notice. They ignored the gift, did not appreciate the gift. Now it will be taken from them."*

The winds howled fiercely, gusting to tornado force. In a mile-wide ring around the island, the Ocean of Atlas began to seethe. The sight struck fear into my heart, and I trembled before the might of the Sea God.

Up from that boiling cauldron of ocean a mighty waterspout rose, a terrible geyser of which even I was afraid when I beheld it. Higher and higher the funnel cloud snaked into the sky, dancing on the boiling water, searching for its prey, eager to do the Sea God's bidding. The Destroyer had come alive, pausing for a moment to find its target and take aim. Then it moved with blinding speed toward the land, straight for the Lighthouse.

That which had withstood the ravages of time and weather was no match for the unrestrained fury of the Destroyer. The Storm God hit with crushing force, surrounding the ancient masterpiece and overwhelming it in enormous volumes of wind and water. There was no resistance, save for a final sigh of surrender as the towering light was battered and pummeled and swept into the sea.

Through the furious sound of the water, I heard the Destroyer cry out. *"Behold your fate, O Atlantis, and weep. As consequence for your misdeeds, you will observe no more from on high. For the Tower has fallen, and the high place has been brought low."*

I sighed a mournful sigh, powerless to interfere. What could I do but observe and record, that I might remember and tell the tale.

I watched as the storm moved further inland, flooding the city with great cataracts of rushing water. The canals became swollen torrents of thick gray mud. Those who had not already left tried to do so now, but it was too late. A group of soldiers dashed headlong from the Avenue of the Gods onto a bridge spanning the outermost canal.

Farther away, the water in the canal had worked itself into a state of mad fury, overflowing its banks, carrying everything along in its wake—boulders, trees, houses, bodies. Now that horrific onslaught was heading right for the soldiers, and there was no place to hide. They gasped in horror as a huge wall of water rushed toward them and the rivers left their beds.

Only a few hours before, these powerful, arrogant men had ridden their chargers at full gallop through groups of innocent people, impaling them on their deadly tridents. The people had screamed in terror and pleaded for mercy, but the soldiers had given no quarter. How different now that they were the intended victims! How different now that the Destroyer was heading for them! Battle-hardened men screamed in terror as the cataract struck, ripping out pilings, breaking the stone, sweeping bridge and men into the flood and out to sea.

I turned my attention to another part of the city. It was already too late for some people. The outermost canals had flooded, and the lowlands outside the city walls were inundated as the water spread out across the Great Plain. Forced from their homes, those loyal to the Sons of Belial who had stayed close to their leaders now floundered chest-high in muddy, swirling water. Higher and higher the thick foam rose. Those who could not swim drowned instantly. Those who could swim treaded water as long as they were able, only prolonging the inevitable.

Inside the third ring, crowds of screaming people surged through the streets, seeking the higher ground on which the Temple, Palace, and Pyramid had been built. Onto the roofs of the mansions along the Avenue of the Gods, atop the rubble of the ruined Temple they climbed and huddled, waiting as the waters swirled around them, rising higher and higher, lapping at the stones below their feet.

On the top floor of the Palace, a group of lesser Adepts huddled together, watching as the water came for them. "Begone! Get away!" they screamed, casting spell after spell, still arrogant enough to think that the elements would obey them. But when the storm-enraged water heeded them not, their arrogance turned to fear, their incantations to cries of atonement, sorrow, and remorse as they pleaded and begged to be delivered from their fate.

From the sea, Poseidon's voice cried out once again, invoking a new ally. In a voice that rode like thunder on the winds, the God of the Sea called upon the God of Fire. Deep below the city, in the scared caverns under the Earth, the Destroyer paused to listen and obey, shifting shape once again, transforming itself into a pillar of fire.

The Fire God had heard, rumbling forth its answer to the call for unity. The Adepts who cowered pitifully on the rooftops heard and screamed curses. I heard and bowed my head in awe and humility before the mighty sound of the Fire God.

"Woe unto you, you vain and prideful people," the voice cried out from deep below the ground, shaking the Earth, causing the entire hilltop to tremble, *"for you have perverted the sacred monument. In your arrogance, you have transformed the Great Pyramid from a repository of science and knowledge into a symbol of ego and vanity. Now you must pay the price for your great sin of pride. Prepare yourselves, for your abomination is at hand."*

I recognized that voice, and my heart skipped a beat. The Blacksmith had come, the Master Artisan with his mighty Hammer, rising up beneath the Great Pyramid and the glowing red crystals housed therein. Now Fire from within the Mother had come to complement the Water from above, the two working in unity, in partnership.

Sweeping into the piazza, water lapped at the base of the Great Pyramid, flowing in through the main entrance, flooding the corridors, pouring down the stairs, seeking the lowest levels. Deep beneath the Pyramid, superheated water lay trapped within the limestone caverns, held at bay by the tons and tons of rock that formed the base. Crying out to be free, the water exerted great pressure, clamoring for the Blacksmith to release it.

Wielding his golden hammer, the Blacksmith complied, striking a titanic, crushing blow. A mighty tremor shook the hilltop, and the base of the Pyramid cracked, splitting the stone and releasing the water trapped beneath it. Up through the ground it surged, great boiling torrents of water, mud, and steam, filling the labyrinth, covering the skeletons and the bodies, rising up from level to level to meet its cooler counterpart flowing down from below.

At the point of confluence, where superheated water met cold, where the Fire Crystals glowed an intense and furious red, the explosions began, releasing tremendous, all-consuming heat, burning and burning and burning, until an enormous opening appeared in the Earth. Such a hole it was! A vast, deep hollow, at the bottom of which the Blacksmith's fires raged. And into that gaping, fiery pit, like a gigantic dead weight, the Great Pyramid of Atlantis sank complete and intact, falling downward, ever downward, until at last it stopped in its final resting place, the Mother's fiery heart.

At his bellows the Blacksmith labored, his titanic, deformed body glistening with sweat as he stoked the fires even hotter, hotter than they had ever been. Strong and perfect as they were, the Fire Crystals could not withstand the assault for long. Deep within their flawless consciousness, chemical and molecular anomalies began to occur, replicating at incredible speed, compromising the atomic structure, disrupting, rerouting, even blocking the natural flow of energy. Enormous pressure built as the crystalline matrices broke apart and atomic meltdown began.

That pressure craved release. That energy needed to go somewhere. As always, it took the path of least resistance...outward. Slowly at first, tiny cracks and fissures appeared in the outer surfaces, then spread with incredible speed until, with a blast as powerful as the mighty Blacksmith himself, the Fire Crystals burst asunder. Far below the ground, I heard the Blacksmith's deep rumble, inciting the lava to rise up and spew forth into the world. Up it surged like a huge wrecking ball, massive amounts of energy blasting out of the ground, vaporizing buildings, pulverizing rock and steel and earth, killing the thousands who huddled there, blowing the entire twenty-five-square-mile top of the city into oblivion.

Thus it came to pass that the City of Atlantis disappeared from the face of the Earth, out of the sight of the human race forever. In an enormous explosion, a toxic fireball billowed up and out, spreading over the city and onto the Great Plain, consuming everything it touched, covering all created things—land, buildings, roads, bodies—with a uniform coating of volcanic debris that clung like a foul and suffocating glue.

The destruction of that which was man-made was complete, wrought by an unassailable triumvirate of gods and goddesses: the Temple—connection to the Divine—by the Goddess of Wisdom; the Lighthouse—high place for observing the Self—by the God of the Sea; the Great Pyramid—site of the Alchemical Wedding—by the God of Fire. The Destroyer paused, satisfied with its work. Then it moved onward again, out onto the Great Plain, where a solitary horse and rider galloped to the south under a shower of mud and water, toward a waiting Ark.

*****

Out of that swirling cloud of smoke and flame, a great white charger galloped, carrying a lone rider on its back. Out of the city they raced, onto the Plain, the fearsome cloud billowing toward them, chasing them. Racing ahead of the cloud of destruction that nipped at their heels, neither man nor horse looked back. As one they galloped across the land, heading south to where a great Ark floated, its open door and anxious inhabitants awaiting their arrival.

All around them, the air vibrated with a great cacophony of sound—explosions, wind, thunder, steam—a vast, discordant tumult. Above them, atmospheric disturbances danced through the sky. Orange and green and white and blue and yellow lightning filled the heavens, each bolt the color of an Elemental's eyes. Below them, a terrible earthquake shook the land, and a huge fissure split open before them.

Hang on! Horse-mind spoke to the rider whom it loved. The man obeyed. Dropping low, he wrapped both arms around the neck of his powerful ally and held as tightly as he could. Horse continued his mighty gallop, never breaking stride, coming nearer and nearer to the fiery abyss. At the last moment, great haunches bulged, and the animal leaped into the air, out across the yawning chasm of death, flying up and out and over, taking the leap of faith, not knowing where the next step lay, or even if there was one.

On the other side, the Mother reached out and caught them gently in her loving arms. As they passed over, a great blast of boiling water burst from the fissure, rising upward, intermingling with the pursuing cloud, the hand of the Mother putting up an impenetrable wall beyond which the Destroyer could not follow.

"Stop!" I heard the Mother command. *"Do not harm my beloved children. Raise not your hand in anger against them, but let them pass unmolested."*

At the sound of the Mother's voice, the Destroyer halted. *"I obey,"* it replied, heeding the command, stopping at the chasm's edge. The Mother's children were safe!

*****

On they flew, man and animal as one, for what seemed like an eternity as the Earth shook and the water rose. At last they topped the final rise, racing downhill to where the Ark lay waiting. Hia and the warriors lined the way, forming a cordon of honor at the end of which Latoné and the twins waited expectantly. The great door in the side was open. Horse rode straight within, where Thoth dismounted. No time for greetings; they had to hurry and seal the doors.

With the Holy Ones, Enoch and Sophia stood just outside the doorway, supervising the final preparations. When everything was in readiness, Thoth extended his hand, beckoning them to enter. The old ones shook their heads. "This is good-bye," Enoch said, smiling that old, comfortable smile. For just a moment, the rain ceased and the Ark and its occupants were bathed in a soft, golden light. The air grew calm, and a gentle quiet descended upon the clearing. Softly, as though from a far distance, came the delightful strains of an angelic choir.

"What do you mean, good-bye?" Thoth exclaimed, glancing about in awe at the sudden change in the weather. "You can't stay here. You'll be killed." He could not believe that after all that had happened, the old people would be so foolish as to remain on the doomed continent. Could they possibly believe that this sudden calm meant the end of the destruction? Surely not.

"No one will be killed," Sophia replied calmly, "but we cannot go with you. That is not our destiny."

"Then where will you go?" It was Latoné's turn to be frightened, questioning her beloved teacher's reason.

"We will go where we belong," the old man said, "where we always go whenever there is danger. We will go within, for therein lies our safety."

"We will go where we always go after our work is done," Sophia added. "We will go Home. As you seek within yourself for Truth, so we follow the same Universal Law, the same path and direction, and go within—back to the Great Mother. "Behold!" the old woman waved her arm, and a hole appeared in the air before the Ark. One minute there was nothing there, the next minute a shining portal shimmered before them, a long tunnel stretching inward into infinity.

"Farewell," the old ones said, following the Holy Ones within before Thoth or Latoné could make a move to stop them. "Be fruitful and multiply. Nurture and cherish each other, and above all, rebuild." As the ancient ones spoke, they seemed to float backward into the tunnel, growing smaller and smaller as they drifted further away, vanishing even as they issued their last directive.

"Atlantis's enormous diversity must not vanish. Your task is to preserve it after the deluge, to protect the knowledge from abuse and misuse until the human race is ready to embrace the energies once again, for good this time. Where we go now you cannot follow now, but you will one day. Remember, the way is within. It is always within. Farewell, until we meet again."

Then they were gone, and the portal closed. The calm ended, and the wind and rain returned. Husband and wife looked at each other in amazement. They hadn't even had a chance to say good-bye. No time to think about that now as they were plunged into the violence of the destruction once again. Without hesitation, Thoth and Hia closed the great doors of the Ark, sealing them against the outside world. Then family and friends sat in the darkness within, their children huddled close. The Islanders squatted nearby, waiting.

Thoth and Latoné lay back and tried to catch their breath, amazed by everything that had happened. But the most amazing event of all had been the vanishing act they had just witnessed. "We didn't even have a chance to embrace them one last time," Latoné said, as she felt the Ark being lifted up and swept away in the force of the current.

"I wouldn't worry about them too much," Thoth smiled sadly. "They know things. They have, in their own words, 'powers we haven't even dreamed of.' They'll survive. Of that I'm sure. As she has done for us, the Mother will open her arms to protect them and take them back to herself and keep them safe until it is time for them to come again."

*****

Simultaneously with the destruction above, the explosive force from the Fire Crystals also surged downward, setting off a chain reaction deep within the Earth's mantle. Awakened from its centuries-long sleep, an ancient Dragon stirred, slowly shaking itself, beginning the breakup of the continent.

The skies opened, and water fell from the heavens. Not a shower of raindrops, but water—a solid wall of water, drenching, pooling, then flooding and rising up. And as the water fell from the heavens, so too it spewed forth from the Earth as the explosions beneath the Great Pyramid spread in a chain reaction across the island, ripping great, jagged holes in the land. From each gaping maw, huge pockets of superheated water, trapped for eons in the Earth, were released by the subterranean earthquakes.

Thousands and thousands of geysers shot up from below. From the very depths of the Mother they spewed forth high into the air, then fell back to Earth in a rain of mud and water pouring down from above in extraordinary abundance. Billions and billions of gallons of water were released minute by minute, flooding everything from the coast to the foothills of the Mountains of the Moon. The Great Plain was inundated, and the city itself had disappeared under a sea of thick, gray mud. There was no place left for the water to go, except to rise higher and higher and higher.

In the outlying districts, the survivors sought the high places, running across the Plain, scrambling for higher ground, climbing into the foothills of the Mountains of the Moon even as the water lapped at their heels. "Go higher," they screamed, "go higher," struggling to reach dry ground, clambering over one another in their frantic attempts to avoid being swept away in the swirling turbulence. A few made it, although most did not, slipping on the wet rocks, breaking bones, falling off cliffs to their death. A few reached the high places, where others who had left the city a few days earlier greeted them. The conversations were accusatory, acrimonious, and contentious.

"We should have gone to the Arks, after all. Why didn't we?"

"You said we didn't need the Arks, damn you! You said we'd be fine."

"You said Adima was the enemy and that Belial would protect us. It's all your fault."

"Don't be crazy. Who needs the Arks? The water will never reach this high. All we have to do is stay here until the storm passes and the waters recede. Then we'll be fine."

So the survivors reasoned, huddled in the caves, soaked and morose, waiting for the end, whenever and whatever that might be, waiting and hoping for something that would not come. "The waters will never rise this high," they convinced themselves, still stubborn, still arrogant, still denying the proof of their senses. "We are safe at last, high atop the Mountains of the Moon."

The Mountains of the Moon, created millions of years ago by the titanic forces of tectonic action—huge slabs of the Earth's crust pushed up from deep below, scraping the very sky. For eons those stone sentinels had stood the test of time and the effects of weather, eroding slowly over the ages, wearing away as the elements of wind and water patiently polished them smooth. Little did the people know that those same long dormant forces which had created such natural wonders were about to spring to life once again. For while they were correct in assuming that the waters would not rise so high, they never imagined that the land itself would sink.

*****

Nighttime. Hanuman the Potion Master and the last of the soldiers, Adepts, and followers of the Sons of Belial cowered in the caves high up on the Mountains of the Moon...feeling what, waiting for what? They did not really know, too numb were they from shock and exposure even to care. Below, where the Great Plain had once been, there was only water—no city, no coastline, no farms, no Lighthouse, no Temple, no Pyramid, no life. Nothing had survived. The animals and Elementals had long since fled. The people had either escaped in the Arks or were now dead.

But still the liquid fire lived, glowing dully beneath the waters far below. Time for it to rise up and put on a show, although there would be no one to see and appreciate the message that was being sent. It would be for me to observe and remember, against the day that I would tell the tale, of the night when the Destroyer came to settle the score, to settle all debts once and for all.

"What is happening?" the Potion Master cried. They were to be his last coherent words. The night had suddenly become as bright as day, although it was long past midnight. The sky was lit up for miles around. For the first time, the Adepts felt the intense heat. The temperature was intolerable, and the air was full of the smell of brimstone. Miles below the ground, a dull roar rumbled, building in volume and intensity. Beneath their feet, the ground began to vibrate as a series of earthquakes rocked the entire length of the mountain chain.

Along the topmost peaks, a patchwork pattern of spider veins appeared, small at first, then widening into hundreds of enormous cracks, cleaving each peak from top to bottom. From those gigantic fissures, great geysers of steam belched forth, accompanied by thick oozings of molten lava, their incandescent glow lighting up the length of each rift with a red-orange ribbon of fire.

I looked out, scarce able to believe my eyes as I saw the Destroyer transform itself once again, this time into the most frightening shape of all. A new kind of Dragon was upon the land, a multiheaded fire-breather, fierce, vicious, and uncompromising. Hissing fiercely, licking the Earth with its many-forked tongue of flaming, molten lava, the Dragon slithered its way down the mountainside, devouring everything in its path.

When the great tongue of flame reached the cave where the Adepts were hiding, the Dragon voiced a roar of triumph. The sound rose up to Heaven, mingling with the screams of the Adepts as they were consumed in the fire. So came the end of the Sons of Belial's reign in Atlantis. As their leader had been consumed by the Dragon's fiery breath, so were his followers melted by its heat, their liquefied bodies swallowed up by scalding tongues of lava, ingested into its mythic belly.

Overjoyed that its hideous task was complete, as if in celebration that the world was finally free of such as these, the Destroyer Dragon danced higher and higher, its many heads weaving themselves into a single, flaming tapestry, forming a veritable carpet of fire across the slopes that only the day before had been graced by green-clad forests. Closer and closer to one another those bobbing heads danced, coming together at last, merging, coalescing into a single wall of leaping, living flame. The rocky slopes bulged as though pregnant, the vast subterranean chambers beneath the mountaintops filled with boiling magma. Rumbling ominously, the heavy, gaseous liquid waited to be born, to burst forth in a mushroom cloud of lava, steam, and ash.

All at once it happened! With a mighty sound that shook Heaven and Earth, the Dragon roared, breathing a giant fountain of red hot lava thousands of feet into the air, ripping apart the Mountains of the Moon. It was a spectacular display of light and sound, so huge and so bright that it was discernible far across the sea. But there was no one to see it, no one to appreciate it except for myself and a small group of seafarers floating in an Ark some fifty miles to the northwest.

I watched as the black of night was replaced by a brilliant glare—not the light of dawn, but a red-orange glow as bright as day for miles in all directions. I listened to the sound of the lava geysers, a deep, throbbing, thunderous roar that never ceased, like the roar of the waters of a great cataract swollen by spring rains. I felt intolerable waves of heat emanate from the lava floes. "How can the Blacksmith stand it?" I wondered, yet I knew, even as I voiced the question. Not only does the Fire God tolerate such temperatures, he thrives in the awesome, all encompassing, all-pervasive heat.

Indeed, the Blacksmith was awake this night, and now he had been joined by another—his lover, the Fire Goddess. Together they danced, gyrating and cavorting with pleasure. With each new undulation the fire spread, traveling along the spine of the Mountains of the Moon, breaking the island's backbone. I smelled the all-pervasive stink of sulphur. The fumes were strong, almost overpowering, an odor so acrid and cloying that I could actually taste it. I sensed the gods and goddess prowling the night, titanic beings wielding a colossal power—the power to build up, and the power to tear down. This night, they would use the power to destroy.

High above the doomed continent, Fire and Water combined and merged into a single, unified force. Immense columns of lava, hot water, and boiling mud were projected thousands of feet into the air, where they congealed into voluminous black clouds. From this poisoned darkness, a mighty rain of volcanic ash pelted the Ocean of Atlas, hissing and steaming, turning the water thick with mud and debris, transforming the once lovely blue-green sea into a fetid, oozing stew of gray-black muck.

As the ash clouds grew larger and larger, the downpour spread for scores of miles in an ever-widening circle from the volcano's center. Far out upon those turbulent waters, solidified lava rained down a shower of fiery stones upon the twelfth Ark, pummeling it even at that distance. The great ship, however, remained seaworthy, riding calmly and securely through the tempest, floating and tossing and pitching in the cauldron while deep within its hold, the refugees rested safe and calm as Nuah's sacred gyroscopes kept the massive vessel perfectly balanced.

All night long the hurricane raged, the volcanoes erupted, the Earth trembled, the geysers gushed, and the rains fell. Morning came, but not the light. A huge blackness blotted out the sun.

I held my breath, knowing what was coming, trying to imagine the force of an explosion so great that it could destroy a continent. And now the final cataclysms began. Far, far below, deep within the crust of the Great Mother, huge tectonic plates slipped apart, creating a great, gaping hole underneath the island. Into the ensuing rift, lava and water flowed, rising, ever rising through every crack and fissure, seeking release. Ever anxious to cooperate, the Mother complied.

As with the Temple, as with the Lighthouse and the Great Pyramid, when the foundation collapsed, there was nothing to support that which was above. So it was with the continent of Atlantis. Great earthquakes ripped through the Earth's crust, not just shaking it, but splitting it apart, tearing jagged rifts for hundreds and hundreds of miles across the continent, which still lay relatively intact a few dozen yards below the shallow sea that now covered the land.

How can I describe it? To this day, although I have relived the experience countless times in my mind, words fail me. Huge volcanic action—not just a single mighty blast, but dozens of them, then hundreds, then thousands, some small, some great—spewed stone and rock and lava, gouging huge holes beneath the island. It happened far more quickly that I had thought possible. With no foundation upon which they might rest, first the mountains collapsed in upon themselves. Then the island itself broke into great pieces. Huge chunks of land floated for a moment like gigantic black icebergs, then disappeared beneath gigantic waves, boiling and bubbling and sinking into the sea.

*****

In a day and a night it was over, but the effects have lingered for millennia. They are with the world even today. For the Shift was an event of greater power than any in the history of the world. It triggering a reversal of the Earth's magnetic field, ushering in a time of massive change, change on a scale that had no precedent.

Not a single part of the planet was unaffected. Tidal waves inundated distant shores, earthquakes shook the provinces, coastal lowlands flooded, continents changed shape and location as the huge tectonic plates rearranged themselves. For months, thick dust clouds in the upper atmosphere kept the light at bay. In the farthest north and south, where the new poles lay, great storms raged. Snow fell, water froze, and giant bergs and floes of ice began to form. The global atmosphere grew drier, too, as the Great Mother closed off to agriculture many of her most fertile plains and river valleys.

The area of greatest suffering and change, however, was the sea. After Atlantis disappeared, the Ocean of Atlas grew inaccessible, so that navigation upon it ceased for scores of years. The calm, pure blue waters had become a roiling, storm-tossed cauldron of sargassum and debris.

"It is on account of the quantity of mud which the engulfed island left in its place," the sailors said as they drank their grog and told tales of the conflagration in faraway ports. But I knew differently. It was on account of the souls of the dead, lest they be disturbed as they lingered beneath the waves. For years the sea grieved along with the spirits of the lost ones, crying out with them in their agitation and anguish as they sought release and rest.

Not until the last one had found the Light did the waters grow calm and clear once again and navigation resume.

And as the Mother physically shifted, so, too, did the consciousness of her children. The world grew colder and darker, not just physically, but emotionally and spiritually as well—a single moment of falling asleep in which a new reality came fully into human consciousness.

It was an extreme lesson, the only way for the Mother and Father to teach. I wondered how many more extremes there would have to be to raise and transform the mind and spirit of the human race enough to embrace the Consciousness of Freedom.

*****

From a window in the Ark, far out on the turbulent waters, they looked back and watched as Atlantis perished. In his journal, Thoth wrote...

> A resinous thickness descended from Heaven, and I saw that the whole of humanity had returned to the mud. Who could look on this and not be changed!

That night, the first night aboard the Ark, he and Latoné shared a strange and powerful dream:

High in a blood-red sky, an all-seeing eye looks down upon a burning world. Up from the ashes, a black Tower reaches to Heaven. No light burns in its topmost window to guide lost travelers to safety. High upon the ramparts, a Warrior stands at the edge and looks out. With a deep sigh, he leaps from the Tower to the rocks below. With the impact, his head breaks off and rolls into the sea, and all the bones in his feet are broken. Moments later, his fractured and broken body is placed in the Alchemical Fire as a sacrifice.

The flames grow hotter and hotter, but the Warrior is not burned. He melts into a puddle and quenches the flames with his own liquid essence. From the ashes a lovely red-winged blackbird rises, heralding spring and the return of fertility to the land. In the morning sun, the Tower shines a gleaming white, and its light shines forth once again.

Within the Arks, as within the grave, the travelers slept fitfully, dreaming their dream of Initiation, in which the Children of the Law of One encountered the Destroyer and confronted their own deaths, their own darkness, their own Great Void. As within, so also without—confusion and chaos, darkness and ignorance were the order of the day. While the land broke up and the pieces of the Atlantean continent separated and scattered, so too the Arks were separated, dragged by the various aimless currents, pushed and pulled in all directions, scattered to all parts of the world. For months, they floated on the storm-tossed seas.

And while they crossed the waters, within their darkened holds another great transformation occurred. The grave was transformed into a womb, and the wayfarers were suddenly no longer corpses but embryos waiting to be born. Love had vanquished the Conqueror Worm, and a new people and a new consciousness were about to be born.

CHAPTER 50

He who knows how to burn by Water and to Wash by Fire, makes Heaven out of Earth and precious Earth out of Heaven.

—carved inscription, Villa Palombara, Rome

At last the waters receded, and dry land appeared once again. One by one, the Great Arks came aground in the new worlds to which the currents of the deluge and the Guiding Hand of the Great Mother had delivered them. The seven days of trial, fasting, and penance were over. The waters of the womb had receded, and the months of darkness, of sitting in the Great Void, were past.

In the womb of the Arks, the old had been let go of, the new had been striven for and attained. In the darkness, the Seed had germinated; new life was about to spring forth. In their love and passion, the Children of the Law of One had created a new child—themselves. Now, changed and transformed, they were ready to emerge from the dark womb and enter the new world that had changed along with them.

A new day had been born into the world, not a day as we measure time, but a day that would stretch into the ages, offering a new Dreamtime for all who cared to embrace the opportunity. It was the morning of the Eighth day, and what a glorious day it was—a day of felicity and perfect rhythm, a day of plenty and renewal, a day of beginning again.

*****

As the eighth day dawned clear and bright, the twelfth Ark touched the shores of what had once been known as Al Khemia, home of Isis, land of the alchemists. Within, all gathered at the door. For the briefest of instants, flickering shadows of fear and doubt lingered on the threshold once again. All of the questions that had dominated their conversations, all of the anxieties that had plagued their dreams during that timeless stay in the darkness of the Void rose to the surface once again. Where were they, really? They knew they had reached the land of Isis, and that they had been invited. What they did not know was what lay in store for them outside the Ark.

What damage, how much destruction had been visited upon this province? How had the people of Al Khemia been affected by the deluge and cataclysm? Was the land even there, and if so, was anyone left alive? How would they be received by their distant brethren? Would they be accepted, loved, provided for? Or would they be outcasts, strangers, forced to eke out a living by the sweat of their brows from a stingy, barren Earth, ever vigilant for predators and marauders?

And what about the Great Mother? Would she still love them, still care for them, nurture them, provide for them? Would the Dragon return to fertilize the land and bring the Life Essence once again? The time of darkness and waiting and wondering was over at last. They were about to know, once and for all. Would they like what they found?

The great door opened, a ramp was extended, and the Initiates stepped boldly forth into the Light once again. In the twinkling of an eye, the fear and doubt were gone, replaced by a new emotion—wonder! Into that perfect morning, Thoth, Latoné, Alta, Charis and all who had entered the Ark with them emerged. For a moment they stood still as their eyes grew accustomed to the light and they surveyed their new home.

To the north and south, a broad, clear river stretched as far as the eye could see. On either side of its banks, fertile belts of pasture and forest wound like green ribbons, testament to the fertile abundance of that emerald valley. There was abundance everywhere—date palms, fig trees, lotus blossoms, a riot of tropical vegetation. A gorgeous city of polished stone rose up amidst the verdure. Houses, palaces, temples—the home city of Al Khemia was lovely indeed, gleaming white in the morning sun. Further inland, a desert of sand stretched from horizon to horizon, the golden dunes undulating like the waves of a vast, dry sea.

So the world had not been destroyed after all. Life still existed; beauty still existed. Their new home was lovely indeed. Now joy and exuberance filled the wayfarers, and they ran out into that magnificent oasis, bending low to kiss the ground, throwing their heads back to smell the fresh air, opening their mouths to taste the sweetness of life once again.

And the Great Mother rejoiced with them. *"Welcome home, my children,"* she seemed to say. *"Finally, after all those endless days and nights of separation, we are reunited once again."* Reunited indeed! Everything was as it had been. The Mother had not abandoned them. She had prepared a great feast in their honor.

The animals had returned. Great flocks of birds soared through the sky, filling the air with their sweet songs. Dolphins cavorted in the waters of the river, splashing and blowing, breathing in and out the rhythms of life, a reminder of the healing power of the breath. Deer and antelope grazed on tender grasses and leaped in exuberance over the savannas, bringing the gift of gentleness as well as a call to action. On the ground, crystal clear dew sparkled like diamonds, a benediction and blessing, offering spiritual refreshment in the light of the dawn. Overhead, the sun sparkled in a cloudless azure sky.

On the shores of the River Nile, at the edge of the Great Desert beneath a gorgeous double rainbow, Latoné gathered everyone together. "Behold the covenant with the Father and the Mother," she exclaimed, pointing to the glorious bow arcing across the heavens. "Behold the Celestial Serpent, the Sky Dragon, who has come to reunite Heaven and Earth once again. On this day, we are reconciled with Holy Father Love and Holy Mother Truth, by whom we are ever protected from the flood of ignorance and unawareness." Bowing her head in prayer, the priestess paused in silent meditation. Then she opened her eyes and addressed the others.

"Lest we forget," she reminded them, "let us bow our heads and bend our knees, humbling ourselves before the Father and Mother, acknowledging their providence. Let us also beseech them to withhold a return of such calamities, praying to them to forever keep the land firm. Finally, let us offer a prayer of thanksgiving to the Angels of Sunlight and Air and Water, reaffirming our kinship with them, asking them to serve us even as we promise to keep our world pure and hold it sacred."

So it was that Latoné instituted the first ritual to commemorate the frightful destruction of the land, setting both a purpose and a standard for all sacred ritual to follow—remembrance of the dark time, humility in the presence of Spirit, thanksgiving for Divine providence, and a promise to remain steadfast and hold to the truth.

From the city, the blast of trumpets filled the air, raising a joyful fanfare as a procession of camels and riders wound its way toward the shore. "Greetings, loved ones," Isis welcomed them from atop her mount. "We have awaited your coming with much hope and joyful anticipation. Come with us now as we celebrate your arrival. All is in readiness. This is a day of feasting and joy."

And so it was. As the procession returned to the city, throngs of beautiful, dark-skinned people lined the streets, strewing flowers and palm fronds along the way, waving, smiling, and shouting greetings. Around a central park and fountain the caravan stopped.

Isis came forward and addressed the Atlanteans. "Brothers and sisters, you are welcome here," she said through joyful tears as she embraced each of them in turn. "Our land is now your land. Our home is now your home."

"Thank you," Latoné bowed gracefully, acknowledging the great gift that had been offered. Around her neck she wore a pearl necklace from which hung a pendant engraved with a cross inscribed in a circle. "We accept your most generous gift, and we are honored to dwell among you." She paused for a moment as Isis nodded her understanding. Then Latoné removed the necklace and spoke again. "We have little left to give, but what we have is yours. Please accept this necklace as a symbol of the new-formed bond between us."

As she fastened the sacred symbol of Atlantis around Isis's neck, a great cheer went up from the people. As one they surged forward, each vying with the others to pay the highest honor and give the warmest welcome to their brethren from across the sea. Huge tables were set and a vast cornucopia of food brought forth. From a raised platform, the musicians began to play. Drummers beat a steady rhythm, and the air was filled with sweet and cheerful strains. Lovers and friends embraced one another, joining hands to form a huge circle around the newcomers, dancing and singing and stomping their feet.

All through the day the celebration continued. There was eating and drinking, dancing and clapping, quiet chatting and ceremonial storytelling, games and contests of skill—a joyful reunion with the Great Mother as her children played and frolicked under her watchful, loving eye.

*****

All over the world, the scene repeated itself. As each Ark opened, as each group of sojourners emerged from the great wombs and stepped out into the new world, they shared the same emotions, the same experiences. There was still much to be done, the rebuilding process had only just begun. All of the raw materials had been provided in this renewed and refreshed world. It would be for the former Atlanteans to determine what they would do with them. It would be for those who had survived the deluge to determine how they would traverse this next part of the Grail Path.

*****

As an enormous flaming orange sun sank in the west, Thoth, Latoné, the twins, and Hia walked along the riverbank, each filled with thoughts of the future. It had been a day they would remember all of their lives for the heartwarming pleasure it had brought them. Still, there were so many questions for which there were, as yet, no answers.

"Will we attempt to recreate the old order, or will we try to create something better," Thoth mused as he held his wife's hand, "shedding those beliefs and values that have kept us confined and limited?"

"Will we discard those dark feelings that have blocked joy?" Latoné asked, squeezing her husband's hand tightly. "Will we divest ourselves of the rage that has hurt us and others?"

Lizard lay warming itself on a rock at the river's edge. Hia stooped to examine the tiny creature, animal of the Dreamtime, dreamer of the future.

"What will we dream in our new Dream?" the warrior wondered aloud, thinking about home and loved ones far away. "Will we dream a future that promotes spiritual growth and ascension? Will we dream about the beauty that comes with courageous and disciplined growth?"

"Will it be a happy dream from which we might awaken?" Alta speculated. He was no longer a boy, but a young man, standing straight and tall, with a wisdom that belied his years. "A dream that, although it has begun in terror, grows ever gentler over the ages?"

"So that we might wake, not screaming, as from a nightmare, but smiling and refreshed, as from a pleasant, happy reverie?" Charis finished, herself a young woman with a deep and reverent spirituality and intuition.

As they finished asking and returned to the park once again, the sun set and the great bonfires were lit. Thoth and Latoné took their places in the circle beside Alta and Charis, across from Isis and Hia. Immediately, several children gathered round. Someone began to play a drum.

"Sing for us, Latoné," the children cried delightedly. "Tell us a story, Thoth."

Alta and Charis smiled at each other. They were home, after all.

Latoné reached out for a lyre, which she held in her lap and strummed softly. Then, in a voice as pure as the finest crystal, she opened her mouth to sing.

> Stay with me Atlantis,
> My love, my life, my dream.
> Fill me with your magic
> And take me where it seems
> That all my fantasies
> Will spark and come to be.
> Stay with me Atlantis,
> My love, my life, my dream.
>
> Keep away the tragedy
> I've had to face before,
> When all was only struggle
> And Spirit closed it's door,
> When nothing but the battle
> Could silence all the screams.
> Come back to me Atlantis,
> My love, my life, my dream.
>
> Crystal clear has come the Dream
> And nevermore the Scream.
> Yes, crystal clear has come the Dream
> And nevermore the Scream.
>
> See my truth, Atlantis;
> The Darkness and the Light.
> Help my soul's eternity
> Exist within the sight
> Of the everlasting Love
> That keeps me free of Fear
> And conquers what would kill the Dove
> That cries a billion tears.
>
> With the vastness of her cleansing
> The Great Mother is my guide
> To resurrect the Goddess' ways,
> Divine Feminine at her side;
> And Logos makes his presence known
> To calm the troubled ways
> Of that which cannot be condoned
> In the Light of coming days.

For crystal clear has come the Dream
And nevermore the Scream;
Yes, crystal clear has come the Dream
And nevermore the Scream.

Be my heart, Adima
And let me be your queen.
Shield us from the frightful Beast
That fights and tries to screen
The Good within the Whole
Of most that live inside this wall
Where all that ever has been
Will once again be called.

Please come to me Atlantis
And open up your door
Where once again I'll be at peace
To love forevermore.
What my soul has cried for
Will no longer be a Dream
And all the service we have done
Will silence all the Screams.

And crystal clear will come the Dream
To silence all the Screams.
Yes, crystal clear will come the Dream
And nevermore the Screams.

She finished, and the people sat spellbound, eyes moist with tears, delighting in the song. Then everyone turned to Thoth. Slowly he looked around the circle, smiling into each one's eyes as he picked up a drum and spoke in a loud, clear voice.

In the beginning, God created the Heavens and the Earth...

*****

Thus it was that in the ensuing darkness, sitting around the campfires, they drummed and sang and told their stories. And so, in the nighttime, the legends were born, legends of our common heritage, our common home.

Over the millennia, countless storytellers would repeat the tales, each adding their own embellishments, their own interpretations, their own cultural nuances. Thus did the original events become obscured, transformed into a vast and diffuse collection of myths and traditions, some sharing common elements, others openly disagreeing. Now, though, you know the Truth—that all such myths share a common source, that they are all but a confused recollection of real events, a universal memory of a great land where early humans dwelt for ages in peace and happiness.

Of the Garden of Eden, the Elysian fields, Olympus, the Hesperides, and the rest of the Paradises; of the War in Heaven, the battle between Light and Dark, Good and Evil; of the Fall from Innocence, the First Disobedience, the eating of the forbidden fruit. Of a terrible convulsion of Nature, in which a whole continent sank beneath the sea, along with most of its inhabitants; of the Great Flood and its survivors—Noah and Gilgamesh and Deucalion and the others who floated to safety in their Arks; of the giants who roamed the Earth, the gods and goddesses, the mighty ones, the Titans, the heroes and heroines of old, those of renown.

Now you know they were not gods and goddesses, not visitors from other worlds, but men and women like ourselves—human beings with all of the basest faults and all of the highest good and everything in between. Walking along the Grail Path with free will—the power to choose. Just like you and me—no difference—spiritual beings having a human experience, learning how to be human, in fulfillment of the Plan.

*****

There were no answers on that first day. Only time would tell, the expanded time of the eighth day—in which to answer the questions that had been asked, not just for themselves, but for all of humanity. A single day, the eighth, in which the Fathers sleep. A single day in which to dream and then wake up. A day of integration, in which the initiates—having successfully passed through the seven trials—are regenerated and resurrected whole, reborn as new Men and Women of Grace.

A single day in which to prepare for another day—the Ninth—the day of completion, fulfillment, and attainment, in which the Tower is rebuilt and Paradise is regained. The ninth day—when the universe rejoices at the reawakening and rebirth, and humankind returns to wholeness. On that glorious morning of the eighth day, the promise held forth in spite of the terror of all that had gone before. It would hold for as long as it took; indeed, it still holds to this very day.

*****

And so the rebuilding process began, bringing with it the first challenge—accepting total responsibility for themselves and their lives, their personal growth and their growth as a community. There was no one to do it for them. Atlantis was gone, and the Children of the Law of One were on their own. That was the hardest truth of all to accept. But they *did* accept it, because the foundation had been well built. It was firm and strong.

They had all the spiritual support they needed to let go of the past and be free to live joyfully in the present moment without worrying about the future. Such was the reward for answering the call, preparing, taking the journey, becoming initiated, and returning home. What a wonderful reward it was!

At first there was a great deal of disappointment with Al Khemia. "It's a hot, burning desert," was the consensus of opinion. "Nothing can grow here. The sand covers everything. What a wasteland!" Gradually, however, they adjusted and adapted, and the desert began to bloom. They were rebuilding, or rather building anew—not the old Atlantis, but something entirely different.

The Children of the Law of One had come full circle—from Innocents who had believed they were safe and taken care of by their trusted leaders, through the Orphan stage of abandonment, then rising up as Warriors, Seekers, Creators, and Rulers, encountering along the way the Destroyer, the Magician, the Caregiver, the Fool, and the Sage. On a great spiritual journey around the Great Wheel of Life, forever Lovers, they arrived at the beginning again, Innocent, yet wiser.

CHAPTER 51

Nothing in this world [is] a gift...whatever there [is] to learn [has] to be learned the hard way.
—Carlos Castenada, *The Teachings of Don Juan*

On another shore, under another sunrise, in a quiet lagoon at the edge of the sea, a dark pile of fresh seaweed washed up on the sand. Tangled within the vines and tendrils was a long, flat piece of wood. As the object lay there, splashed by gentle waves, a shadow crossed overhead. Bare feet kicked at the tangled pile, toes picked at the seaweed, exposing more of the artifact.

The object was not driftwood, for it had a definite shape and structure...that of a wooden chest. Judging by its dull and waterlogged appearance, it had been at sea for a long time. Yet not too long, perhaps only several months, for the wood itself was still somewhat solid. Two hands reached out to open the lid, but it would not budge, fastened as it was by a large rusted lock. No matter. Several crushing blows from a heavy rock fractured the metal and easily split the waterlogged wood. The hands reached out again, and the lid was raised. What treasures were these, nestled safely within the watertight compartment hidden behind the wooden frame?

An enormous leather-bound book, its yellowed pages filled with mysterious runes and symbols. A crystal ball, absolutely flawless, absolutely clear. And the most mysterious object of all, a great talisman of power bearing the markings of a master artisan. Entwined around the wooden shaft just below the shining metal tip was a beautiful golden chain, from which hung a shiny black crystal.

The treasure hunter reached down and placed the amulet around his neck. Then, brushing off the remaining seaweed, he picked up the chest and walked off into the forest that crept almost to the water's edge, leaving only a set of bare footprints in the sand. For a time all was quiet on that peaceful beach. Then, in the distance, from deep within the forest, the savage roar of the crowd bellowed forth, punctuated by a scream of anguish. Ownership of the Spear had been transferred once again!

OMEGA

EPILOG

The Almighty struck the golden disc of the heavens! There was light! There was Song! Light, color, sound, in great whorls of unimaginable energy spread through the Cosmos. Life came into being!

—Elizabeth Van Buren

In the mid-afternoon heat of the desert as the sun glowed in a cloudless sky, a man sat before a tent on the hot, shifting sands, deep in concentration as he wrote on tablets of orichalcum. Having picked up the magical Pen in favor of the mystical Sword, a book was taking shape before him, a great and epic work, the history of the world from the beginning until now, and even into the future. Each day he came and sat, beginning in silent meditation, invoking his all-knowing Muse, his Observer Self who read the Akashic Records with an all-seeing Third Eye. Then the writer stepped up and out into that higher state of mind from which his creativity flowed.

It was a powerful, mystical experience. Time seemed to stand still, he lost all contact with the world around him and all awareness of the writing experience. Then suddenly he found himself back in the ordinary world, and there on the tablets were the words, inscribed in the metal by a magical imaging technique of his own invention. Even though he did it day after day—indeed had done so ever since, as a young man, he had begun telling stories—he was always amazed at what he had penned when he went back and read his work.

It was, too, a sacred and awesome experience, and the only way he could describe it was in the soft, imagery-filled language of poetry, where he stood *"In the Presence of the Magus."*

> Applying my craft,
> Picking up my tools,
> Stepping up and out
> For a while.
> Crossing the threshold,
> Transcending
> Into the presence of the Magus.
> Bringing the raw materials—the dross,
> Mixing in the mercury and silver,
> Applying the wand.
> Making the alchemical change—
> Transforming the dross into gold.
> Receiving the gift,
> Returning to the kingdom
> With the gold.
> Bringing the treasure
> To the King
> For a blessing,
> To share with all the world.

That was how he created the work. In order to ensure its functionality and readability by the world, however, he had had to invent a new way to record information. Not in the crystals, not as pictures, but in a totally new form.

So he created a series of shapes, associating each shape with a particular phoneme of the Atlantean language, so that shapes and sounds thus corresponded to each other. By arranging the shapes in various combinations and pronouncing their sounds together, new sounds were formed. When combined correctly, to those who knew the secret of pronouncing the combinations of shapes, *meaning* occurred.

Suddenly, speech had become visible. He called the individual shapes *Letters*. He called the collection an *Alphabet*. It was his greatest gift to the world, the great aid in developing the sophisticated reasoning and "whole concept" understanding so necessary to achieving the Consciousness of Freedom.

He liked this spot in which he wrote. It reminded him of home. Before him, he could see the fertile plains of Gizeh, which had always stood firm against the floods of the ages. The land was high, higher even than the hill on which Temple of Poseidon had stood in Atlantis. It was no coincidence that the Ark had touched ground near this spot. After the landing, he had studied the terrain along with the geomancers. When they told him that the Gizeh Plateau was virtually the geographic center of the newly-shifted world, he had known, and his heart had leapt in joy.

So the center of the world had not been lost to the human race after all! It had moved after the destruction and the polar shift, but the Garden of the Heart was still there, if one knew where to look. Just as one's individual center was always there; one needed only to look within. "Thank you, Father and Mother," he had cried, "for leading us to this most perfect and sacred site. Thank you for showing us the holy ground on which you have selected to store your treasures."

And so, years ago, the rebuilding had begun there, with the help of the Al Khemian architects, geomancers, astronomers, musicians, masons, stonecutters, and artisans. Behind him, a mighty pyramid was rising up from the desert floor, as yet but partially complete. Beside it, a strange new edifice, half human, half animal, was also taking shape. The Al Khemians called it a Sphinx—a monument in stone symbolizing the relationship of the human race to the animal kingdom.

Off to one side, around a campfire, a tribal people were gathering for the evening. The fires had been lit, and the adults were preparing the evening meal while naked children played happily in the sand. A man emerged from the tent behind him, followed a moment later by another. The three were obviously well acquainted, judging by the easy way in which they addressed each other.

The first to emerge was tall and dark-skinned, with jet-black hair. The seated one was somewhat lighter and shorter, his auburn hair showing the first faint traces of gray. The third, who had appeared last, although much younger than the others, carried within himself the likeness and spirit of the seated man. They were father and son.

"Father, we'd like your help in determining where we place the treasures," Alta requested, drinking deeply from a water gourd. It was easy to get dehydrated in the dry desert air.

"Let us look at the drawings," Thoth said, rising and entering the tent, "and we'll determine the best location." Inside, it was surprisingly cool. The roof was made of a heavy white cloth, the light color reflecting the light and offering shade from the hot desert sun. The walls were drapes of cotton and linen, allowing what breezes there were to drift in and circulate the air.

How different Al Khemia was from the temperate Atlantean climate! So much drier and warmer—hot desert winds instead of cool offshore breezes; spicy fragrances of sandalwood, frankincense, and myrrh instead of sweet-smelling jasmine and citrus. Latoné had never quite adjusted, much preferring her beloved birds and the gentle quiet of the lagoon and gardens. Thoth, though, had come to love the new land, especially the desert heat. It felt good in his bones, warming them deeply.

Hia spread the plans for the Sphinx out on a table, and together they studied them. The base of the mysterious structure had been laid out in channels, forming a grid of passages and chambers.

"There," Thoth pointed to the corner facing the Great Pyramid, "there is the starting point. In that place we will inscribe the story of how all these things were begun and built. But that is not enough. We cannot leave the treasures so exposed. We need a safer place for them, a place where they will not be found until the time is right."

As he spoke, a newcomer entered the tent. "Why not build a separate repository for them," Charis suggested, carrying a tray of figs and dates, which the men accepted gratefully. It was still a while until supper, and they were already hungry.

"That is an intriguing idea," Thoth exclaimed, smiling and kissing his daughter. She looked so much like her mother he sometimes mistook one for another at a distance. "Have you and Latoné been discussing this?"

Charis set the tray down and pored over the plans. "Of course we have," she smiled, tracing her finger over the lines that crisscrossed the page, "and we have discussed it with the Goddess. She has reminded us that the records must remain undiscovered until the patriarchs who will now rule the world overcome their egos and reach true spiritual understanding. So she has instructed us to store the treasures in a special sanctuary all their own"

"An excellent idea," Hia was excited by the plan, and his fertile imagination was already conjuring up ways that they might build such a structure.

"How do we keep this Hall of Records safe and undiscovered?" Thoth interrupted. "There aren't many places to hide on the plateau."

It was Hia's turn to offer a suggestion. This was an idea not unlike those developed in his homeland, where the Islanders buried their treasures deep underground, covering them over with great mounds of stone and earth. "We can enclose the Hall of Records within a pyramid of its own and bury the entire structure deep below the shifting desert sands in a hidden location. Trust me, no will find it until the appointed time."

"Which will probably be many thousands of years in the future," Charis added.

Thoth liked the idea. It was the perfect solution to a problem that had been vexing him. Of course, they would ask the geomancers to mathematically determine the perfect spot between the Sphinx and the Pyramid, but the idea itself was sound.

"Here," he declared, placing a large "X" on the drawings to mark the general location of the secret pyramid. "This is where we will build it. And in the northeast corner, we will place the tablets on which I am writing of the history of the world."

Alta drew their attention to the right forepaw of the Sphinx, tracing an imaginary line through his father's mark to the Great Pyramid. "The desert sands are ever shifting," he reminded them. "One day, the Hall of Records may be so deeply buried that it would take a great effort to find it. Why not make a passage that leads from the Sphinx to the Hall of Records and another from the Hall to the Great Pyramid?" he suggested. "That way, there will always be easy access to the treasures, even if the secret pyramid is lost under the sands."

It was settled. That's what they would do. The Hall of Records would be safely concealed between the Sphinx and the Great Pyramid while remaining connected to both. Satisfied that they had made a good design, the group walked out into the late-afternoon sunshine. The masons were fitting a huge block of stone into place high up on the side of the growing Pyramid.

"I have never quite understood how it works," Alta said, marveling at how easily the huge blocks of stone floated through the air and were fit so precisely into place. From all over the continent the Al Khemians were gathering the finest stones from the quarries. So many different kinds there were—limestone, granite, bluestone, sarsen stone, and so many more.

"It works on the same principle as the physical laws that cause iron to float on water," Thoth explained, "although I don't really understand it either. One of the geomancers tried to explain it to me once, and I listened politely, but the conversation was entirely too technical for me. To sum up what he said, applying those same physical laws, they can essentially neutralize gravity and make the stone float in the air."

They listened as a series of tones floated across the sands. Sound was essential in the manipulation of the stones. "Of course, the process is helped greatly by chanting and singing," Hia explained. "The sacred tones have a special function that the musicians understand. The geomancers and astronomers determine and prepare the site, the architects draw the plans, the masons cut and fit the stone, the musicians sing the sacred songs to move them through the air, and everything fits together perfectly."

They watched as the highly polished white limestone was fitted and cemented in place. When the masons stepped back to admire their work, the joints were imperceptible.

"See, it's all about cooperation and harmony and balance," Thoth exclaimed, perfectly satisfied with the overly simplified explanation. "What could be easier?"

*****

After supper, after the ritual watching of the sunset and bidding the day farewell, Thoth and Latoné sought the pleasure of each other's arms. It was something they always did, a gentle coming together after their individual duties of the day had been completed. "I'm so homesick," he said to his wife as they lay on a soft woolen blanket under a blue-black velvet sky. The ribbon of the Milky Way drifted overhead. In his mind, he heard his old friend's voice speaking to him.

"The Milk of the Virgin," Enoch had called the great band of light. "The spiritual spiral of evolution upon which each soul travels. As you travel round and round that perfect path, seek always the center, for there lies the object of your desire—a marvelous golden disc." The old man had pointed to the exact place in the sky where the center of the galaxy lay, just above the head of the Archer, a tiny cluster of stars collectively known as the Shield of Righteousness. Latoné had carried that Shield in physical form when she had gone to face Lilith. Everyone would carry it in some unique form as they journeyed on their own ongoing quest for Truth.

Thoth snuggled closer to his wife. The stars were so profuse and so close, it seemed he could reach out and touch them. How he longed to do so. For while the homesickness was for Atlantis, it was also for the Light Brethren he had left behind. He missed them very, very much.

"I know," Latoné caressed his head lovingly. Swimming through the river of stars was her own symbol—the Swan, Fire and Water combined, Mother of the Twins.

"We are all grateful to you for the choice you made in returning to this world. And I know how impatient you are. You long to be finished with this task and on to bigger and better things. Such, however, is not the way it is to be, at least, not yet. A time of darkness has come upon the world, but we are using the tools we've salvaged to rebuild the Great Pyramid and the other structures, in which we will store the treasures. In that sense,

Atlantis is not gone. It will never be gone. In that sense, we are always home." She sat up, looking gaily into his eyes and tousling his hair. "And one day, my husband, Atlantis will rise again."

Of course, they both knew what she meant. Atlantis itself would not rise, for there was much that lay buried under the water that should stay under the water. But the consciousness of Love as manifested by and in Children of the Law of One would rise and spread throughout the world.

"Look into the night sky with me," Latoné tilted her head back and gazed out into that milky white river of light. "Let the stars show us what it will be like. Let us look up and out to the future, to a time when the old truths, the ancient ways, long forgotten, begin to resurface as some of our descendants begin to awaken to the Truth of their being."

Thoth smiled and lay back on the blanket, using his arm as a pillow. His wife always knew the prefect thing to say to cheer him. If he could not go home, at least she could remind him to look toward home.

It was enough. Together they looked to the stars, sharing the same vision, becoming one in mind and heart. In the great heavenly mirror, they beheld the future, where a gorgeous blue-and-white world stood, like the Atlantis of old, on the brink of destruction. A world that was the exact mirror image of Atlantis...where the Tension of the Opposites was great, where the Pendulum had swung far to one side, where two opposing paradigms existed side-by-side—the two camps, Love and Fear. A world moving up and out of fear, back toward Love. What was forgotten would then be remembered, the stars told them. The outcome would be a return to the Garden.

"Will they succeed?" Thoth asked the silent heavens, although he knew his questions were not necessary. Success was assured; it was only a question of when, and time, in truth, did not exist. "Will they manage to break the spell and wake up from the dream of separation and scarcity and the sleep of ages?"

"Perhaps," Latoné smiled, "because of where they are on the Grail Path. Because of what they have experienced throughout the Slaughterbench of History."

Thoth wondered. There was a stubborn part to the human ego. Earlier that day, news had arrived of a mighty conqueror whose savage hordes had overrun the lands to the south, raping and pillaging and plundering. He was rumored to be a powerful leader who wielded a beautiful, magical Spear, said to be both source and secret of his strength. "So, Belial has returned, as he said he would," Thoth had mused as the messenger refreshed himself with water and fruit.

"What's that?" the runner had asked, not catching the reference, not understanding the meaning behind the words.

"Nothing," Thoth had replied. "I was just thinking about someone I once knew."

Lying under the stars in the warm desert night, the fragrance of sandalwood wafting on the breeze, he shook his head, thinking of the violence that was being enacted even now out in the world. Somewhere nearby, the survivors of the Sons of Belial had been watching and waiting, preparing for the return of their Dark Lord, now in the form of a new world-historic figure eager to dominate, wreak havoc, and impose his own will upon the world.

Will the Sword have to be used again? he wondered, thinking of the Hard Lightning, which he still kept close by in a place of honor alongside Latoné's Wand and Shield. Would the weapons have to be passed along to new heroes and heroines after all, to balance the effects caused by the new possessor of the Spear? The depths to which Atlantis had sunk apparently would not be enough to sway future generations from their stubborn attempt to cling to the old ways. The Patriarchy's desire to embrace the Dream was strong. Breaking the spell would, indeed, be a difficult task. He hoped it would not be impossible.

"As I learned at the Well of Kuneware," Thoth said, drawing his wife close, "they cannot break the spell until they know the right questions. Perhaps at that time, many will know them and ask. Perhaps then, the spell will be broken, and we all can ascend together."

"What will it be like?" Latoné wondered aloud, trying to imagine a return to the Garden, the ways of Fear replaced by those of Love once and for all. She fell asleep in her lover's arms, the question still on her lips.

*****

Years passed, and years again, and finally the metallurgists swarmed atop the Great Pyramid, molding an alloy of copper, brass, and gold into a shining capstone, in the tip of which they set a tiny, flawless diamond. Beside that perfect mountain of stone, glistening in the midday sun, the Sphinx crouched on the desert sands, gazing fixedly at a point just above the eastern horizon, waiting and watching.

The monuments on the Plain of Gizeh were finished. A long and elaborate ceremony had been planned to mark their dedication. Colorful tents had been erected to house the various artifacts as they were ceremonially presented to the people for one last look before being secreted in the Hall of Records. Within the tents, the Bearers of the Treasures stood by their precious loads, waiting to be summoned forth.

At midday, when the sun reached its zenith, bells pealed and gongs boomed out over the city and Plain, calling the people to come forth. It was the first occasion of what would become a symbol of all faiths and religions, although most would forget its origin and esoteric meaning—a ringing out, a calling to prayer, thanksgiving, and worship, as well as a spiritual call to arms and herald of important events. Such was the first and original intent of the bellringers, and the most sacred.

In the center of the base of the Sphinx, between the forepaws, a dark portal gaped, waiting to receive the priceless treasures that would be stored within. In front of this doorway, the people gathered, and the ritual began. Many of them had not even been born when construction was begun. Now they had come with children of their own. Others had grown quite old, hoping to see the great work completed before their time on Earth was through. Regardless of their ages, however, in each face the excitement and joy were the same. There was magic in the air once again!

"It's just like the Dragon festival," Alta remarked to his sister, feeling all of the old joy and exuberance he had felt as a youth, when he had tried each year to spot the mythic creature as it rose from the sea. "Remember?"

"How could I forget?" Charis replied, a faraway look in her eyes as she recalled the parades and games and revelry. Those were the happy times, the days of innocence before the shadow of the Sons of Belial had fallen across the land. She would always carry the memory of the Dragon Festival with her and share it with her own children, who clung tightly to her hands now, staring wide-eyed as the crowds surged around them.

Thoth and Latoné stepped forward, and the people grew quiet. As the eldest survivors of Atlantis, the Al Khemians had asked them to lead the ceremony. First came the consecration of the Priestly Initiates, men and women who had chosen to dedicate themselves to preserving the holy records and the ancient knowledge. They would keep the information separate and apart, safe from the profane, while ensuring that the knowledge of its existence and purpose was passed down through the ages to their successors. It was a sacred and solemn trust, one that everyone took most seriously.

"Before these hallowed halls, you come today to consecrate yourselves to holy service," Latoné said as she oversaw their vows. Although she had grown older, she still clung steadfastly to her own purpose. It felt wonderful to serve as Priestess once again. "You do this of your own free will, linked to each other by the single unifying thread of ancient knowledge. From this day forth, you are charged with keeping the secrets of the Mysteries of Atlantis pure and safe and passing them along to your successors until the time for secrets is over."

Such a huge task, she thought, to preserve the memory of the archaic world-order throughout history. Would they succeed, or would the lure of power corrupt their selfless act of service even as it had done to the priesthood of Atlantis? Only time would tell.

A deep gong sounded, interrupting her thoughts. Thoth stepped forward to greet the bearers as they came forth, carrying the first of the treasures. Between them, six men and six women carried thirty-two tablets and two columns of orichalcum, which sparkled like fire. On these stelae, the Divine learning—the principles of all knowledge—were engraved in sacred characters.

Thoth placed his hands on the glowing pieces of metal, consecrating them. "In order that Wisdom will not perish, either by fire or water," he declared, "I consign you to your resting place in the Hall of Records. There you will lie buried against the time when the new consciousness will call you forth once again."

A second time the gong sounded as six priestesses brought forth a hand-carved mahogany chest inlaid with diamonds, rubies, emeralds, topaz, beryl, and onyx. Latoné opened the lid to reveal the most precious treasure of all—the two remaining Knowledge Crystals, the living minds of the Ancients, resting gently on a bed of soft red velvet surrounded by pure gold. "Behold the remnants of the Atlantean mind!" Her voice was barely a whisper, filled with emotion. "The sum of all knowledge on Earth."

Closing the lid once again, she thought of all the violence and bloodshed that had surrounded the crystals over the ages. Would they be safe within the Hall of Records, or would someone find them one day, someone who was not yet ready, someone like Belial? As with all things yet to come, only time would tell.

A third time the gong rang out as six priests brought forth a chest of beaten gold. On either side, stylized double-headed axes served as handles. Each blade was formed by a crescent moon placed back to back, the twofold head symbolizing the creative and destructive aspects of the Goddess. The front of the chest contained an engraved image of a cross inside a circle—symbolic map of Atlantis, an island world surrounded by water, in the center of which the four great rivers flowed from a common source. On the lid, in raised golden letters below an ornate "H"—alchemical symbol of Spirit and light of the Sun—a familiar inscription had been etched.

IN YOU REPOSES ALL STRENGTH.

"From the Lighthouse to the Hall of Records," Thoth proclaimed, opening the lid to reveal the precious contents. Lying on a cushion of white satin was an ancient tome, beautifully illuminated and bound in leather. Enoch's treasure, the *Book of Life*.

Tears welled in his eyes as he looked lovingly at the book he had come to know so well, tears for the memory of his beloved mentor and friend. Lying as he had first seen it, the sacred text was open for all to see, that Wisdom might come to all who sought to understand. The inscription read:

PRUDENCE IS THE GUARDIAN OF THINGS.

"When the time comes for the *Book of Life* to be brought forth once again, this is the first inscription they will read," he explained to the people, "a naming of the Goddess— *Prudence*, otherwise known as *Wisdom*. The Two are as One."

His friend's gift had come far from its home in the Lighthouse on the edge of the Ocean of Atlas. Now it would rest awhile in the golden chest alongside the stelae and the thirty-two tablets upon which he, Thoth, had written the history of the beginning, evolution, and conclusion of all things. "Guard the treasures well," Thoth commanded as they were borne into the mouth of the Sphinx, out of the sight of that generation of human beings. "Keep them from falling into profane hands. The uninitiated must not discover them, for on the day that they do, the destruction will surely return."

He glanced up at the sky. It was time to light the cosmic fire on top of the Great Pyramid. A simple thing, really, an invocation of the Dragon. Would the mighty creature come? Thoth wondered. It had been a long time.

The rumble of thunder echoed across the Plain of Gizeh. The Al Khemians glanced uneasily into the air. There was not a cloud in the sky, and it was not the rainy season. What could be the cause of this most unusual phenomenon? Thoth knew, and he smiled. It was his old friend, his old ally, the lightning, carrying with it the Dragon Current. "Welcome, Ally!" Thoth cried to the heavens, spreading his arms wide and raising his voice to invoke the sacred fire.

The answer came immediately—a fiery bolt arced from the sky, seeking out and finding the tiny diamond at the tip of the apex of the Great Pyramid. Striking, fusing with the energies collected within to generate the Life Essence, the lightning penetrated the stone and drove deeply into the ground.

"The Dragon roars with a mighty voice!" Thoth cried as he had done so long ago on the deck at Elysia, when he had embraced his ally for the first time. Turning his face to the crowd, he spoke once more. "The Alchemical Wedding has been consummated. The Great Mother is fertile again."

The blessing had been given. Now it was time to celebrate. As had been done long ago in Atlantis, so now the Al Khemians did again, bursting forth in an exuberant dance of celebration. Cheering, laughing, hugging, and kissing, they celebrated the return of life on the Plain of Gizeh.

Thoth let them enjoy themselves, holding Latoné's hand as he watched the revelry. They had labored long and hard, every one of them, and had achieved much. The cycle had made a full rotation, and joy was upon the land. After a time, the crowd quieted, sensing that there was something more to come. They would not be disappointed. Thoth quieted too, growing pensive, philosophic. "We can be proud of what we have done here today," he said. "We have accomplished a great task. We have given our posterity a noble gift. Let us trust that they will use it wisely. Let us pray that their awakening will be swift and sure."

He felt that old familiar sense of warmth as a rosy glow filled him. The alchemical process had begun, initiated by the blood in his heart, stimulating the pineal gland within his brain as his third eye opened and he beheld the future. "I see an age of great spiritual reawakening and enlightenment coming in the time before us." Thoth's eyes were closed as he described his vision of the human race's advancement along the Grail Path. "An age of new understanding, new life, new science, and new faith."

"Before that age comes about, however, many trials and tribulations will occur as humankind tries a different way, seeking in a different direction. The Patriarchy will rise and the Goddess will be suppressed. But those days, too, will not last. A new time will arise, a time of crisis and opportunity, where opposing and divergent waves merge and crest in a mighty clash between the material-minded and the spiritual-minded."

"Some will fall away, but others will stand their ground. And when those who stand have passed through the seven stages, as we in Atlantis passed through the seven days, they will be ready to find the treasures we have left here today and use them for the benefit of all of the Mother's children. For the important thing is not their discovery, but their correct interpretation. At that time, the Mysteries—which are really not mysteries at all, but rather gifts of the Father and Mother—will be open to and understood by all once again. Until then, the treasures will rest here in safety."

Thoth turned and looked at the Great Pyramid and the Sphinx rising up out of the desert sands. How magnificent they were in their newness. The Storyteller within his breast sprang to life, and he felt a new tale fill his throat. He was an old man, and he had told many stories over his long life. The time for telling them was almost over. But not quite yet. He would tell one more today.

"Behold the symbols," the Bard exclaimed, taking hold of a drum from one of the musicians and sitting down cross-legged on the sand. "The Great Pyramid, symbol of the esoteric content of the Law, containing within its structure a story in stone."

The children rushed forward, led by Charis's twins. Grandfather was going to tell a story, just like he had done at the Dragon Festival, just like he always did. Somehow they knew, as children always do, that this was going to be the best one yet.

"It is the story of our struggle for spiritual wisdom, expressed here, in this monument of stone, whose four balanced sides symbolize the four balanced aspects of ourselves—King-Queen, Warrior, Lover, Magician. Looking out upon the world, the Great Pyramid beckons to the world to look upon it and read the story for itself."

Smiling at the children gathered at his feet, the old man slowly tapped out a rhythm with his hands. The children...the future! As his own Mystical Pair had grown into adults with children of their own, so these youngsters before him would mature, repeating the cycle from generation to generation. The seeds had been well planted. All that remained was to nurture them.

"Can you read the story in the stone?" he asked the little ones, a broad smile creasing his lined face. "It is the story of yourselves as you once were and as you will be again. Listen as I tell it to you now."

The Good King and Queen sit on their thrones and look out over their kingdom. Their minds are peaceful and calm, happy and serene. So is their kingdom. In the kingdom, all is well.

The Warriors watch from the castle walls and guard all the borders. They stand at every crossroad, in the marketplaces and squares, ready to protect and defend, ready to serve. They serve the King and the Queen and the kingdom. They help, and they keep things safe.

The Lovers walk through the kingdom, where all is well. From the King and Queen to the villagers, tradesmen, farmers, merchants, and wanderers, the Lovers do what Lovers always do—hold hands, smile, and chat gaily.

There are fairs and minstrels, contests and games and prizes. There is bustle and activity and singing and dancing and laughter. There are babies being born, picnics, romantic trysts, tender kisses, flirtatious winks, and coy glances. Flowers are blooming, birds are singing and nesting. The sun shines, gentle rains fall, and rainbows arc across the sky. All of the kingdom is in love. When Lovers feel safe, they hold hands. When Lovers hold hands, all's right with the world.

And all the while, the Magi toil in their laboratory and wander the kingdom in a never-ending quest for knowledge...seeking, feeling, looking, touching, tasting, smelling, listening, talking—all senses on the alert. The minds of the Magi are quick and keen. Gathering, always gathering—facts and objects and ideas and perceptions. Keeping them in the vast storehouse of their minds. Sorting through the data, assimilating the knowledge. Analyzing and synthesizing, keeping the good—that which serves—discarding the rest. Weaving spells and chants, incantations and formulas. Experimenting.

In the high places the Master Alchemist dwells, Knower and Keeper of Secrets, wise elder and hermit—he who dwells alone and apart. In the caves the Seer dwells, she who knows so much, she who changes things..who mends what is broken, heals what is sick, transforms what is no longer useful, and transmutes dross into gold.

Apart from the mundane world, the Priest and Priestess dwell in the Temple in the sacred space. They perform the rituals and ceremonies and preside over the various rites of passage—birth, initiation, joining, separating, thanksgiving, petitioning, offering, and dying. They are pure and untainted by worldly things. While others come and go, their place is always within. They provide the link between Heaven and Earth, between Spirit and Matter, between Creator and Humankind.

In the Temple—the huge vessel, container for Spirit—the Priest and Priestess commune with the Great Creator. They lead by example, and they teach the King and Queen how each one can communicate with the Divine in the sacred temple of their own body and mind, their own Self.

The Good King and Queen sit on their thrones and look out over their kingdom. It is peacetime. Crops are growing. Commerce is good. Craftsmen are plying their trades. Artisans are beautifying the kingdom. Farmers are tilling the land and harvesting and reaping the bounty. Musicians and actors and dancers and players are moving in harmony to a great, rhythmic beat. Scholars and scientists are inventing and discovering and learning and teaching.

Children are playing and growing. People are going about the business of their daily lives—working, shopping, cooking, cleaning, mending, laughing, crying, talking, sharing, caring. Couples are courting. Families are growing or shrinking as children come in or leave home to start families of their own. People are making transitions—coming into the kingdom from faraway places beyond the borders, and even beyond the realm. And going out of the kingdom to faraway places beyond the borders, beyond the realm.

The Good King and Queen sit on their thrones and look out over their kingdom. They watch the rhythmic movement and marvel at the flowing, ever-changing shapes and images and patterns. They tap their feet in time to the steady beating of the pulse of life, and they smile. They are content.

The Father is in Heaven. The Mother is in the Earth. Heaven and Earth are connected. Father and Mother are One. All's right with the world!

And that was how it ended. Thoth got up, hugged his wife and children and grandchildren, and then went home. Later that day, after everyone had left, he returned with the masons and sealed up the mouth of the Sphinx, hiding the entrance from the sight of men.

*****

After one hundred and fifty-three years, Hia returned to the Fields of Light from whence he had come. His body was buried in the northeast corner of the Hall of Records, alongside the thirty-two stone tablets that he had helped to write.

The inscription on his sarcophagus reads as follows...

PRINCE OF THE SUN, PRINCE OF LIGHT!

THIS IS THE POTENTIAL OF EVERYONE.

Of Thoth and Latoné, Alta and Charis, Enoch and Sophia, the tale is not yet through. The rest of the story, however, is reserved for another day.

*****

It is the In-Between Time! The old ways have not quite passed, and the new ways have not yet been born, as I came to sit by the banks of the River Nile to watch the sun rise. A single point of light glows on the eastern horizon, beyond the place where the river flows like glass in the summer morn—that most brilliant of lights in the sky, known to all as Sirius, the Dog Star.

Behind me, the eyes of the Sphinx stare at the star in greeting as it rises over the horizon on this, the twenty-third day of July. How red the star glows, lit by the morning sun hovering just below the horizon.

I offer a greeting too, welcoming all who join me in turning their backs on the Darkness, away from the dying light in the West, toward the Rising Light in the East. Sitting at the water's edge, we await the return of the gods—when the Father's Center merges with the Mother's Center, and unity consciousness returns and the human race is reborn.

Out of the Light, that ageless, timeless Voice calls to us.

Where Father and Mother are, there is no fear.
Come into the Temple,
Don the white robes of Innocence,
Step out of fear and chaos into Love.

Align with the energy,
Synchronize with Love,
Soar on the ether up and beyond.
So that the world is transformed!

As the rising light of a new day shines in the East, we move toward it, immersed in love, resonating with love at the core of our beings. Allowing Fearless Love to fill our hearts and minds, nourishing our souls, knowing there is no accommodation for fear in the heart possessed by love.

The Plan is only now coming to fruition. It has taken much longer than seven days, or even eight. It has taken thousands of years. But always with Spirit, as Eternity measures time, it has taken no time at all. For Time exists not where Truth resides. All was accomplished in the twinkling of an eye—instantly, the moment the Plan was put into effect. Success was guaranteed, because of the very Nature of the Planner.

And now the Darkness stands ready to be brought into the Light. No longer hidden. Exposed, visible, to be transformed by the Magician's wand. The opposites brought together at last...integrated, made whole. Yin and yang in balance. Within the Darkness, Light; within the Light, Darkness. So that all can be seen.

On the gentle morning breeze, a far-off sound is borne to my ears, more felt than heard at so great a distance from its source. Is it the wind and the waves, I wonder, or is it coming from somewhere else, from deep within the Earth?

Be still with me a moment and attend! Can you feel it? A soft vibration, a gentle tremor of the Mother's skin beneath your feet. Do you recognize the sound, and, more importantly, can you translate its meaning? It is the sound of the Blacksmith laboring at his forge. Reshaping the Spear, recasting the Sword, molding them anew into a cohesive Whole—the Talisman of Power and the Hard Lightning united...transformed for a great new purpose.

"Who will it be?" the Blacksmith wonders, his voice a deep rumble from far below the ground as he hands his creation to the Winged One to carry to the surface once again, as a gift for humankind. *"Who will carry it gently forward into the future—which is now?"*

A soft, scented breeze caresses my cheek. *"Who stands ready to receive the gift?"* the Mother asks in her softest, most delicate voice. *"Who will take it up?"*

Then silence. An air of hushed anticipation as they wait to see who comes forth.

On the beach, I wait, too. And along with all Creation, I wonder. Who will take up the gift, so near the end of the Grail Path? Who will take it up, so close to the attainment of the Consciousness of Freedom? Who? Is it you—the *Mystical One*—beloved Child of the Creator and the Great Mother?

ACKNOWLEDGMENTS

ABOUT THE STORYTELLER

The story of Atlantis is a Cosmic Chronicle in which past, present, and future are united in a higher dimension of time. It is told from the point of view of an omniscient Storyteller who dwells not in the physical world, but rather in a state of transcendent consciousness, existing out of time and space, taking many forms, living many lives, having many experiences, observing and recording all.

From such an elevated state, Storyteller, through the aid of that transcendent faculty aptly named the Muse, is able to perceive directly the events which took place in Atlantis—a feat achieved with clairvoyant vision. Thus Inspired, and unfettered by the constraints of Time and Space, Storyteller can breach the time sequences of the historical process and travel between both worlds—the world of Atlantis and the world of today; can see into the minds and the hearts of all of the characters and know their deepest thoughts, feelings, and secrets; can truly "tell the tale."

So, too, Storyteller is that Sage-Crone Magus within each of us, that timeless, eternal and all-wise, all-knowing part of ourselves that we have never really lost contact with but to whom we rarely pay attention any more. Storyteller is the one who watches us as we walk along the Path of Direct Experience and calls gently to us to remind us of the Truth. Thus, whenever Storyteller speaks to us, we should hearken to the teachings.

THE WISDOM THROUGH THE AGES THAT HAS CONTRIBUTED TO THIS WORK

This work is a synthesis of many ideas and modalities, the culmination of eleven years of thought, research, prayer, meditation, and listening. It is not mine alone, nor did the vision of *Atlantis* spring full blown from my imagination. Much wisdom besides my own contributed to the telling of the tale. That wisdom must be properly acknowledged.

I have drawn from the works of many authors and lecturers, scholars and thinkers, among them, in alphabetical order:

Frank Alper, Ted Andrews, Kathi Angeli, Alice Bailey, Willis Barnstone, Greg Barrette, Jean Baudrillard, Bear Heart and Molly Larkin, H.P. Blavatsky, Robert Bly, William Bramley, Michelangelo Buonarotti, Julia Cameron, Joseph Campbell, Fritjof Capra, Ken Carey, David Carson, Carlos Castaneda, Edgar Cayce, Hugh Lynn Cayce, Mihaly Csikzenmihalyi, Deepak Chopra, J.C. Cooper, Alma Daniel, Ram Dass, Leonardo Da Vinci, Jennifer DeLoach, Ignatius Donnelley, Mircea Eliade, Clarissa Pinkola Estes, Albert Einstein, Jim Frazier, Robret Gass, Stanislas Grof, Louise Hay, Michael Hernacki, Carl Jung, D.C. Lau, Thelma Z. Lavine, Timothy Leary, Eliphas Levi, Michael Lightweaver, Niccolo Machiavelli, Michael Marshall, Louie McAlpine, Terrence McKenna, Drunvalo Melchizedek, John Michell, Robert Moore, Thomas Moore, Maureen Murdock, Barry and Bess Nobel, Carole Pearson, David F. Peat, David Phillips, Plato, Andrew Ramer, Trevor Ravenscroft, Adrienne Rich, the Romantic Poets of Nineteenth Century England, Jamie Sams, Helen Schucman, Ron Scott, William Shakespeare, Louis Shores and William D. Halsey, Jacquelyn Small, Pitirim Sorokin, Soloviev, Walter Johannes Stein, Rudolph Steiner, Gregory Szanto, Edmond Bordeaux Szekely, Michael Talbot, William Thetford, Lao Tzu, Elizabeth Van Buren, Jan Van Helsing, Christopher Vogler, Wolfram Von Eschenbach, James Wanless, Melissa West, David Whyte, Robert Wilkinson, Tom Williams, Bill Wilson, Amber Wolfe, Marion Woodman, Timothy Wyllie, and the Editors of Time-Life Books.

Even though I have never met most of you, you are my teachers, and I thank you.

*****

Atlantis is, perhaps, the first of a new genre of fiction—not quite science fiction, not pure fantasy-adventure, more than an historical novel. Neither is it pure allegory or parable, nor a simple reworking of ancient myth and legend. Perhaps, in some way, *Atlantis* is a combination all of these genres to achieve something unique—

Taking the great thinking and teachings of the world throughout history and condensing them, collating them, reforming them, and creating a fictional framework around which to present these profound moral Truths.

As Mihaly Csikzenmihalyi, author of *Flow, Creativity, and the Evolving Self*, says, we need to "reinvent the stories that give meaning to our lives." Or, at least, reinvent ways of telling them. To some extent, I think, *Atlantis* is an effort to address that need.

The ageless, timeless words of the masters are perfect as written, their prose and poetry reaching heights of language usage and beauty to which I can only aspire. Rather than struggle in vain to paraphrase their words, or "say it again in worse language," as Robert Frost once remarked when asked to explain one of his poems, I chose, where appropriate, to quote directly from the master works themselves, weaving the quotations directly into the text, presenting them as a natural part of Atlantean lore, wisdom, and culture.

To that end, I have created the *Book of Life* and *Book of Mysteries* as repositories for many of these quotations. Setting the text in a special type font allows it to stand apart as mystical, magical, and deserving of special attention. Other wisdom and research is presented in a combination of journal entries, speeches, songs, poems, dreams, and stories within the story. Each has a unique typeface and type style, depending on the nature of the material being presented.

This being a work of fiction, however, I have no intention of boring the casual reader with a lot of extraneous commentary interspersed throughout the text. The "pleasure of the read" is paramount. Nor might the casual reader be interested in the source material—the Tale itself may suffice. Nevertheless, these wise ones and their works need to be properly acknowledged and accredited. But how? Where the quotes begin chapters, attribution is easy. When they are interspersed throughout the text, however, attribution becomes more difficult.

If this were a research paper or nonfictional work, the presentation would be simple—standard footnotes or endnotes. *Atlantis*, however, is a novel—to be read and enjoyed without interruption to the flow of the unfolding narrative. The best solution, then, is to provide this "acknowledgments" section, separate and apart from the body of the work, which contains titles, authors, and anecdotal information important to properly accrediting those who helped me in the creation of this work. So, in honor of the wise ones who have spoken through me, and for those readers wanting to know the sources that influenced me and whom I have quoted, I offer this section.

- The characters in the story are compilations of parts of my own journey or other events that might or might not have taken place—composites of several archetypal characters from fact and fiction. I have no doubt that some of these events might have happened to people in the course of their lives, and that many of these characters might remind you of yourselves or people you know or are acquainted with. They are, however, fictional, and any similarity to real persons or real events is purely coincidental.

- Grateful acknowledgment is made to the following publishers for permission to quote material from their publications:
  - Thames & Hudson, Ltd. for *New View Over Atlantis*. © 1983 by John Michell.
  - The University of California Press for *The Teachings of Don Juan: A Yaqui Way of Knowledge*. © 1968 Regents of the University of California, © Renewed 1996 Carlos Castenada.
  - The Foundation for Inner Peace for *A Course in Miracles*, © 1975-1985.
  - HarperCollins Publishers for *Vision: A Personal Call to Create a New World*, © 1985 by Kenneth X. Carey.
  - Samuel Weiser, Inc. for The Spear of Destiny, © 1973 by Trevor Ravenscroft.

- For a general description of the Atlantean people and their environs, I turned to those who knew it best—Plato, the first to record the tale and preserve it for us through history; Edgar Cayce, the mystic whose visions offer "astonishing evidence of an Atlantean civilization, its heroes and villains, its challenges and conflicts, its achievements and failings, its rise and fall; and Ignatius Donnelley, the scholar whose seminal research work on Atlantis and the history of culture still stand as the starting point for those interested in exploring the myth in greater detail.

- For the technical facts behind Atlantean spiritual engineering and the sacred sciences of Alchemy, Geomancy, Sacred Geometry, Measure, and Number, I turned to John Michell. He also provides much of the source material for the Atlantean arts, architecture, customs, and culture, and, most importantly, the Dragon.

- The Gaia Hypothesis—the theory that the earth is a living organism—is not a new one. It can be found in several philosophical treatises and the goddess literature of cultures all over the world.

- In intertwining the metaphors of the Holy Grail and the Consciousness of Freedom, I have borrowed from the ideas of author Trevor Ravenscroft and philosopher Georg Wilhelm Friedrich Hegel, whose term "Consciousness of Freedom" represents the great treasure which lies at the end of Ravenscroft's "Grail Path." Ravenscroft also provides the background of the most important symbol of the Spear.

- The philosophy of the Sons of Belial is drawn from a televised lecture by Thelma Z. Lavine, Ph.D., of George Washington University, on the philosophy of Hegel and the Nation-State. Hegel coined two other important terms used in the story—the "Slaughterbench of History," and "world-historic figures."

- Belial's journal entries are lifted from the so-called *Protocols of the Wise Men of Zion*, supposedly centuries-old secret documents translated by Professor S. Nilus in 1901 and again by Victor Marsden in 1921. That such infamous words exist is a fact; that Belial is the original author of such notorious ideas is a fancy of this author's imagination.

- Many of the lessons from *A Course in Miracles* are quoted in the Atlantean *Book of Life*. If ever there were a real "book of life," I've found "The Course," as I like to call it, to be the one.

- The beginning of Ken Carey's most wonderful spiritual book, *Vision*, provides the basis for the creation myth of the Children of the Law of One. Ken's words are as poetic and visionary as anything I've ever read. I'm proud to include them in this work and recommend all of Ken's works to those who seek a new vision of our world.

- The Archetypes of King, Warrior, Lover, Magician, and the rest were first presented by Carl Jung. Today, his theories are being built on by Carole Pearson and Robert Moore, whose writings and lectures I have found to be invaluable in teaching me about the heroic journey and recognizing the archetypes in myself and applying them in my life.

- As J.C. Cooper writes in his introduction to *An Illustrated Encyclopedia of Traditional Symbols*, "Symbolism is an instrument of knowledge and the most ancient and fundamental method of expression, one which reveals aspects of reality which escape other modes of expression." It would be impossible for me to list every individual reference from his book. I turned to him daily for information about colors, numbers, trees, directions, dragons, crosses, thrones, caves, flowers, arks, animals, Chinese and Native American philosophy and symbology, the cosmos, maps, the signs of the zodiac, male-female attributes, fire, water, fertility symbols, gardens, mountains, crystals, pyramids, temples, stones, wands, shields, swords, and just about every noun in the story which might have a symbolic meaning.

- The novel's cover art is an original work entitled, "The Visitors,"© by artist Scott Moore. The cover design was created by digital artist Bob Chernow. Within the text there are three original works by the following artists:

Page 9	"Atlantean Pyramids"	© 1997 by Bob Chernow.
Page 397	"The Seed"	© by Scott Moore.
Page Appendix-1	"Mother and Child"	© 1997 by Cynthia Didio.

Additional illustrations within the text are computer-generated renditions of esoteric symbols using Corel Draw™ clip art.

- Original poetry appears on the following pages:

Pages 568-569	*"Latone' Song: Stay with Me, Atlantis"*	© 1998 by Brett Towery.
Page 316	*"The Divine"*	© 1995 by Cynthia Didio.
Page 459	*"When the Tower Falls"*	© 1995 by Cynthia Didio.

* * * * *

- To my friends in 12-Step programs, out of respect for your anonymity, I won't mention your names. I remain ever grateful for our many conversations about spirituality, miracles, prayers, and a Higher Power working in our lives.
- To my friend and teacher, Kathi Angeli, thanks for taking me within and helping to light up the dark places. Thanks most of all for staying.
- To Tom Bellucci, my paisan—you are an angel in human form who always calls me at the perfect time, always knows the right things to say, and always holds me in your heart, as I always hold you in mine.
- To Bob and Cathy Chernow, dear friends and fellow artists, thanks for listening, thanks for designing, thanks for always being there to lend a hand, thanks for keeping me laughing.
- To my teacher, Jennifer DeLoach, thank you for teaching me the importance of symbols and how to think symbolically.
- To my friend and teacher Jim Frazier, thank you for initiating me into the Warrior, introducing me to the archetypes and Trevor Ravenscroft's work, and ever reminding me to "go for the roar."
- To my agent-partner, Rich Gardner, your friendship and faith in me, coupled with your energy and enthusiasm, are the reasons why this work is published. "Thanks" seems so small a word for all of your labors of love in helping me succed in bringing *The Atlantis Experience* forth. Bless you.
- To my friends Lee Hanks and Michael Marshall—thanks for your love, support, and willingness to help me carry my work forward and put it out into the world.
- To my friend Leigh Hunt, thanks for your enthusiasm, your invaluable editorial comments, and for sharing your knowledge of symbology with me.
- To my friend Dawn Kunofsky, thanks for making me go back and take a long, hard look at so many chapters. Your suggestions for rewrites have made the story that much more heartfelt and compassionate.
- To my friend and teacher Jacquelyn Small, thank you for going out and writing your books and paving the way for the rest of us.
- To my friend Jonathan Wahl, thanks for your invaluable business advice and technical expertise, and just for listening during all of those times of confusion.
- To my friend Lance Warley, thanks for being my "hyperspace advisor" and for being the first one to read the story even as I was writing it. Your enthusiasm and encouragement kept me going even when I got discouraged. Our friendship is one of the great treasures of my life.
- To Robert Wilkinson, my friend and teacher, I am ever grateful for the time we spend together, sitting quietly in your back yard listening to the waterfall, or having a conversation in your "Light House."
- To Mary Anne and David, thanks for believing in me and supporting me in every way. I love you both. And of course, this story is for Uncle Ed, too.
- To my wife and co-creative partner, Cynthia, who has lived the experience right along with me, side-by-side all of these years. What can I say that hasn't already been said? You are the Light of my life, the Love of my life, the Joy of my life, and I am truly grateful and blessed that we are together.

Bibliography

Books

Abrams, M.H., General Editor. *The Norton Anthology of English Literature: Volumes 1 and 2.* New York: W.W. Norton & Company, Inc. 1962, 1968.

Alper, Frank. *Exploring Atlantis: Volumes I, II, and III.* Irvine: Quantum Productions, 1982.

Andrews, Ted. *Animal Speak: The Spiritual and Magical Powers of Creatures Great and Small.* St. Paul: Llewellyn Publications, 1994.

Barnstone, Willis, Editor. *The Other Bible.* San Francisco: Harper & Row, 1984.

Baudrillard, Jean. *America.* London: Verso, 1988.

Bramley, William. *The Gods of Eden.* New York: Avon Books, 1989, 1990.

Cameron, Julia. *The Artist's Way.* New York: G.P. Putnam's Sons, 1992.

Campbell, Joseph with Moyers, Bill. *The Power of Myth.* New York: Doubleday, 1988.

Capra, Fritjof. *The Turning Point.* New York: Bantam, 1983.

Carey, Ken. *Starseed, The Third Millennium: Living in the Posthistoric World.* San Francisco: HarperSanFrancisco, 1991.

Carey, Ken. *The Starseed Transmissions: An Extraterrestrial Report.* Kansas City: UniSun, 1982.

Carey, Ken. *Terra Christa: The Global Spiritual Awakening.* Walpole: Stillpoint Publishing, 1985.

Carey, Ken. *Vision.* New York: The Talman Company, 1985.

Castenada, Carlos. *The Teachings of Don Juan: A Yaqui Way of Knowledge.* New York: Washington Square Press, 1968.

Cayce, Edgar and Cayce, Hugh Lynn, Editor. *Edgar Cayce on Atlantis.* New York: Warner Books, Inc., 1968.

Csikzenmihalyi, Mihaly. *Flow, Creativity, and the Evolving Self.*

Chopra, Deepak. *The Return of Merlin*. New York: Fawcett Columbine, 1995.

Cooper, J.C. *An Illustrated Encyclopedia of Traditional Symbols*. New York: Thames and Hudson, Inc., 1978.

Donnelley, Ignatius. *Atlantis: The Antediluvian World*. New York: Dover Publications, Inc., 1976.

Estes, Clarissa Pinkola. *Women Who Run with the Wolves*. New York: Ballantine Books, 1992.

Hernacki, Michael. *The Ultimate Secret to Getting Absolutely Everything You Want*. New York: Berkley Publishing Group, 1982.

Grof, Stanislav. *The Adventure of Self Discovery*. Albany: State University of New York Press, 1988.

Hay, Louise. *You Can Heal Your Life*. Santa Monica: Hay House, Inc., 1987.

Hicks, Jim, Series Editor. *Mysteries of the Unknown*. Alexandria: Time-Life Books, 1992.

The Holy Bible: The New Catholic Edition. Confraternity-Douay Version. New York: Catholic Book Publishing Company, 1957.

Lau, D.C., Translator. *Lao Tzu: Tao Te Ching*. Harmondsworth: Penguin Books, Ltd., 1963.

Lightweaver, Michael. *A Day of Grace*. Sparta: The Laughing Mirror Press, 1997.

McKenna, Terrence. *The Archaic Revival: Speculations on Psychedelic Mushrooms, the Amazon, Virtual Reality, UFOs, Evolution, Shamanism, the Rebirth of the Goddess, and the End of History*. San Francisco: HarperSanFrancisco, 1991.

Michell, John. *The New View Over Atlantis*. San Francisco: Harper & Row, 1983.

Moore, Robert and Gillette, Douglas. *The King Within: Accessing the King in the Male Psyche*. New York: Avon Books, 1992.

Moore, Thomas. *Care of the Soul: A Guide for Cultivating Depth and Sacredness in Everyday Life*. New York: HarperCollins Publishers, Inc., 1992.

Murdock, Maureen. *The Heroine's Journey: Woman's Quest for Wholeness*. Boston: Shambala Publications, Inc., 1990.

Pearson, Carol. *Awakening the Heroes Within*. San Francisco: HarperCollins, 1991.

Peat, David F. *Synchronicity: The Bridge Between Mind and Matter*. New York: Bantam Books, 1987.

Phillips, David A. *New Dimensions in Health from Soil to Psyche*. North Ryde, NSW, Australia: Angus & Robertson, 1983.

Ravenscroft, Trevor. *The Spear of Destiny: The Occult Power Behind the Spear Which Pierced the Side of Christ*. York Beach: Samuel Weiser, Inc., 1973.

Rich, Adrienne. *Of Woman Born*. New York: Bantam, 1977.

Robinson, Lytle. *Edgar Cayce's Story of the Origin and Destiny of Man*. New York: Berkley Books, 1972.

Sams, Jamie & Carson, David. *Medicine Cards: The Discovery of Power through the Ways of Animals*. Santa Fe: Bear & Company, 1988.

Schucman, Helen and Thetford, William. *A Course in Miracles*. Tibouron: The Foundation for Inner Peace, 1975, 1985.

Shaman's Drum: A Journal of Experiential Shamanism. Number 41, Spring 1996. Bear Heart with Molly Larkin, "In the Footsteps of My Teachers: Lessons with Little Beaver and Old Seer." Pages 19-23.

Shaman's Drum: A Journal of Experiential Shamanism. Number 42, Summer 1996. Louie McAlpine, "Teachings of the Ancestors: The Early Training of an Osage Medicine Man." Pages 55-57.

Shores, Louis, Editor-in-Chief, and Halsey, William D., Editorial Director. *Collier's Encyclopedia*. New York: Macmillan Educational Corporation, P.F. Collier, Inc. 1976.

Small, Jacquelyn. *Awakening in Time: The Journey from Codependence to Co-Creation*. New York: Bantam, 1991.

Small, Jacquelyn. *Transformers: The Artists of Self Creation*. New York: Bantam, 1992.

Sorokin, Pitirim A. *Social and Cultural Dynamics*, 4 vols. New York: American Book Company, 1937, 1941.

Szekely, Edmond Bordeaux. *The Essene Gospel of Peace: Book One*. U.S.A.: International Biogenic Society, 1981.

Talbot, Michael. *The Holographic Universe*. New York: HarperCollins, 1992.

Van Buren, Elizabeth. *Refuge of the Apocalypse: Doorway into Other Dimensions*. Saffron Walden: C.W. Daniel Company, Limited, 1986.

Van Helsing, Jan. *Secret Societies and their Power in the 20th Century*. Gran Canaria: Ewertverlag S.L., 1995.

Vogler, Christopher. *The Writer's Journey: Mythic Structures for Storytellers and Screenwriters*. Studio City: Michael Wiese Productions, 1992.

Wanless, James. *Voyager Guidebook: Tarot Instruction Book and Manual for Voyager Tarot*. Carmel: Merrill-West Publishing, 1986.

Wanless, James. *Voyager Tarot: Way of the Great Oracle*. Carmel: Merrill-West Publishing, 1989.

Wernert, Susan J., Project Editor. *Our National Parks: America's Spectacular Wilderness Heritage*. Pleasantville: The Readers Digest Association, Inc., 1989.

West, Melissa. "The Gifts of the Dark Mother." *BodyMindSpirit*. July/August, 1994.

Wilson, Bill. *Alcoholics Anonymous: The Story of How Many Thousands of Men and Women Have Recovered from Alcoholism*. New York: Alcoholics Anonymous World Services, Inc., 1976.

Wolfe, Amber. *In the Shadow of the Shaman: Connecting with Self, Nature, and Spirit*. St. Paul: Llewellyn Publications, 1993.

Woodman, Marion. *Addiction to Perfection: The Still Unravished Bride*. Toronto: Inner City Books, 1982.

Woodman, Marion. *The Pregnant Virgin: A Process of Psychological Transformation*. Toronto: Inner City Books, 1985.

Woodman, Marion. *The Ravaged Bridegroom: Masculinity in Women*. Toronto: Inner City Books, 1990.

Wylie, Timothy, Daniel, Alma, and Ramer, Andrew. *Ask Your Angels*. New York: Ballantine Books, 1992.

Videos

Geosophy: An Overview of Earth Mysteries. New York: Trigon Communications, Inc.

The Origin of Drunvalo Melchizedek: Flower of Life Workshop. Wimberly: The Light Channel, Inc., 1994.

The Philosophy of Hegel and the Nation-State. Lavine, Thelma Z., Ph.D. George Washington University: Public Television.

World Wide Web Sites

Note: These were active web sites when I was doing my research. I cannot guarantee that they are still active.

About the Character and Nature of Thoth
http://www.cco.net/~trufax/fol/fol9.html

The Alternative HAARP Page
http://www.geocities.com/CapitolHill/1606/akhaarp.html

Breathing and the Breath
http://www.cco.net/~trufax/fol/fol3.html

The Carl Jung Anthology
http://www.enteract.com/~jwalz/Jung

The Declaration of Evolution
http://www.interact.com/~dimitri/dh/DeclarationOfEvolution.html

The Egyptian Sphinx
http://www.cco.net/~trufax/fol/fol7.html

The Hollow Earth Insider
http://www.slip.net/~bch/wwwbwt/thei/thei.html

Hymn to Gaia
http://www.caw.org/poem/hymngaia.html

Leading Edge International Research Group
http://www.cco.net/~trufax/

Leading Edge Research: The Flower of Life Paradigm
http://www.cco.net/~trufax/fol/folmain.html

Terrence McKenna Land
http://www.interact.com/~dimitri/dh/mckenna.htm

The Noah's Ark Home Page and Directory
http://www.intercom.net/user/rgc

The Sirius Mystery and the Dogons
http://www.cco.net/~trufax/fol/fol5.html

Compact Disks

Gass, Robert. *On the Wings of Song: Chants of the World.* Spring Hill Music, PO Box 800, Boulder, Colorado 80306. 1992.

Whyte, David. *Close to Home.* Many Rivers/Ish River Productions, PO Box 868, Langley, Washington 98260. 1989-1992.

Conversations

Kathi Angeli on Mastery, Angels, Spirit Beings, Shamanism, and the Feminine.

Greg Barrette on the Principles and Function of Prayer, Spirituality, and Surrender.

Ram Dass on Acceptance and Dealing with Fear.

Jennifer DeLoach on the Four Attributes of the Heart, the Tong Lin Meditation, Symbolism, Altered States of Consciousness, Sitting in the Circle/Sacred Hoop, Meditating, the Shadow, and Beginner's Mind.

Jim Frazier on Being a Man, the Archetypes, the Shamanic Model of Containment, Initiation, Ritual Eldership, Sacred Space, Wounding, Storytelling, Drumming, the Hero's Journey, Boys Masquerading as Men, and Going for the Roar.

Michael Lightweaver on the nature of Love.

Michael Marshall on the Fear-Joy Cycle and Wellness Consciousness.

Robert Moore on Accessing the Magician Within and the Archetypes of King, Warrior, Lover, and Magician.

Ron Scott on Staking One's Claim and the Week That Changed the World.

Jacquelyn Small on the Tension of the Opposites, Doing One's Being, Wake-up Calls, Mind Change, Spiritual Crisis, Spiritual Emergency, Spiritual Bypass, the Higher Self, the Shadow, the Path of Direct Experience, and the Heart.

Robert Wilkinson on Courage, Conflict, the Function of Doing Battle, When to Fight and When to Flee, Singular Acts of Resistance, Being Bold, Inspiring Others by One's Own Actions, the Play of Invisible Forces, Innocence to Mastery, Shining the Light, Human Nature, Surrender, Attending to the Truth, the Effectual Use of One's Will, Having Fearless Faith in Oneself, and the Adam and Eve Myth.

12-Step Meetings on Acceptance, Surrender, Letting Go, and Higher Power.

Notes from the Text

Prolog

P. 5	The "Dream" and the "Dreamer" are described in *A Course in Miracles: Text*, Chapters 18, 27.
P. 5	Most students of mythology are familiar with the legends of the Titans. For an alternative description of Titans and the inferno, see Van Buren, Chapter 7.
Pp. 6	The term "Talisman of Power" was coined by Trevor Ravenscroft as a synonym for the Spear of Destiny and is described in Chapter 1 of his book.
Pp. 6	The term "Hard Lightening" is a translation of the ancient Celtic word "Caledfwlch," which was the original name of the sword Excalibur. As Deepak Chopra explains on pages 304-305 of his book, "Whoever wields the sword has justice on his side."
P. 6	In conversations with Jacquelyn Small, she taught me about the "Tension of the Opposites." This suggested to me the metaphor of a great pendulum swinging back and forth, which also corresponds to the Buddhist belief that the Universe is maintained by the "inbreathing and outbreathing of God."
P. 7	The term, "Mystical Pair," is used by Clarissa Estes in *Women Who Run with the Wolves*. See notes for Chapter 20, pages 194-195.
P. 7	The Grail Poem is a poetic representation of descriptions and images in Von Eschenbach's *Parsival*, as retold by Ravenscroft, pages 49-50. See also Van Buren, Chapter 1.

Chapter 1

P. 14	The quotation from the *Book of Life* is from *A Course in Miracles: Manual for Teachers*, page 65.

P. 14 The Time of Tribulations was inspired, in part, by descriptions in Time-Life's "Atlantis: The Eternal Quest," *Mysteries of the Unknown: Mystic Places*, page 7.

P. 15 The "Spell of Matter" is attributed to Ken Carey and described in *Starseed, The Third Millennium*, Chapters 2-4.

P. 16 The quotation is from a song entitled, *Turn, Turn, Turn*, by the Byrds, and is based upon *Ecclesiastes* 3:1.

P. 16 The elements of Wind, Water, and Fire are described in Cooper on pages 192, 188-189, and 66-68, respectively.

P. 17 For a complete description of the Atlantean Provinces, politics, sects, and races, see Cayce, Donnelley, and *The Hollow Earth Insider* web site.

The Dragon Festival is a compilation of the myriad fertility and goddess rituals celebrated on the Winter Solstice, as described in the Time-Life Books series, *Mysteries of the Unknown*.

P. 17 The "straight paths," or *leys*, are alignments of prehistoric sites and landmarks, first discovered and named in Britain by Alfred Watkins. They are described in detail in Michell, Chapter 1, "The Old Straight Track."

Pp. 18-19 Ignatius Donnelley's premise is that most of the myths and legends of paradise, the gods, and the goddesses stem from a single source—Atlantis. He states this premise in detail in Part 1, Chapter 1 of his book.

P. 19 In Sanskrit, *Adim* means *first*. Many cultures named their first man a derivative of *Ad*—among them the Persians, the Hindoos, the Hebrews, the Phoenicians. For more on the etymology of Adima's name, see Donnelley, Part 4, Chapter 1.

P. 19 Elizabeth Van Buren tells us that Kybele (Cybele) was the wife of Saturn, known as Father Time. See pages 203-204 of her book for the story of how she became revered as the Grand-Mother.

Chapter 2

P. 23 Charis's descriptions of the hobgoblins is from *The New English Dictionary*, as restated in Michell, page 82.

P. 24 The Dragon Mound was inspired by the megalithic cathedral at Newgrange in Northern Ireland, whose dark tomb chamber is aligned precisely with the sun during the winter solstice, as described in Time-Life's "the Earth's Elusive Spirit" *Mysteries of the Unknown: Earth Energies*, pages 16-19.

P. 25 The Dragon, or "Green Flash," is a common sight at sunrise or sunset at sea level. It was often spoken about by the old conch fishermen of the Caribbean. Anyone can see it if atmospheric conditions are right.

Chapter 3

P. 27 The *Book of Life* quotations and corresponding descriptive text are from Albert Einstein's "Credo"—his beliefs on the topics of science and spirituality— which I found one day while browsing the web. They combine with Jacquelyn Small's explanation in *Transformers*, pages 14-15, of "science and mysticism coming together in synthesis," to form the core philosophy of the Children of the Law of One.

P. 27 The quote, "What is the worth of consciousness..." was found on the Internet. I am grateful to the anonymous author for saying something I could not have said better.

P. 28 Osprey (Hawk) medicine is explained in Sams & Carson, pages 45-47.

Chapter 4

Pp. 31-32 The Atlantean song is compiled from two sources—Ken Carey's *Vision*, Chapter 1; and *"The Other Bible, "* pages 3-9— blended and reworked into a creation myth.

P. 32 For a complete description of Yin and Yang, refer to any book on Chinese philosophy.

P. 32 The three Principles of Wholeness are borrowed from Phillips, page 5.

P. 34 For a good description of the Atlantean crystals, see Alper, Volume I, pages 11-23, 71-74.

P. 34 The pentagram is described in Cooper, page 128.

P. 34 The black crystals are described in Alper, page 71.

Chapter 5

General The design principles followed by Adima and Cybele in finding and setting up their dome are based on ancient Chinese principles of Feng Shui, as described in Michell, pages 62-63, 121.

P. 39 The Dragon Current is described in Michell, pages 60-64.

Pp. 40-41 Atlantean astronomy, geomancy, and mathematics; quotations from the *Book of Life*; and the three principles of Atlantean code of science are compiled from Michell, pages 8, 32-33, 60-64, 121-123, 132.

P. 40 The "vast web of geometrical and astronomical lines" and the building of Atlantis are described in Michell, pages 32-33, 36.

P. 44   The general suppression of knowledge and "elite caste of priestesses" was inspired by Michell, pages 16, 71, 95.

P. 44   The "words of censure" are a quotation from Michell, page 71.

P. 45   The quotation from the ancient prophecy is adapted, in part, from Time-Life's "Atlantis: The Eternal Quest," *Mysteries of the Unknown: Mystic Places*, page 33.

Chapter 6

P. 49   Shakala's journal entry is drawn from several sections of John Michell's book. The "esoteric Atlantean science" is described on page 8; the Alchemist's primary goal on pages 8, 156-157; the "Animated Mercurius" on pages 161-162. The quotation from the *Book of Mysteries* is from pages 189-190.

Chapter 7

P. 55   Horse medicine is explained in Sams & Carson, pages 177-179.

P. 56   I have heard the expression, "As above, so below," countless times, yet I am unable to determine the original source. However, I know that its meaning is true, and that is what is most important.

P. 56   John Michell provides the source material for Atlantean spiritual engineering. Beauty and order in the landscape are described on page 59, the "hidden nature of the countryside" on page 25, the "spiritual principles" of the heavenly bodies on page 47.

P. 56   The quotation from the *Book of Life* is from Michell, page 33. The "flow of the Dragon Current" is on page 29.

Pp. 56-58   The description of the city and surrounding countryside is a composite of descriptions by Donnelley, Cayce, Time-Life, *The Hollow Earth Insider* web site, and my own imagination.

P. 57   The quotation from the *Book of Life* is from Michell, page 33.

Pp. 58-59   The symbol descriptions are gleaned from Michell—colors of the heavenly bodies are on page 62, the Serpent and Winged Circle on page 15, the Blue Dragon and White Tiger on page 60, the children's game on page 63.

Pp. 60-61   John Michell reminds us that "In every continent of the world, the Dragon chiefly represents the principle of fertility." The idea for the Dragon Parade was inspired by page 38; the logan stones are described on page 75.

P. 61   The Dragon Song is composed of Michell's and other references to the Dragon as a symbol of fertility.

P. 61   The "line of songs" is a fertility ritual of the Central Australian aborigines and is described on page 90.

P. 62   Centaur symbology is described in Cooper, page 32.

P. 63   The quotation from the *Book of Life* is from a conversation with my friend and teacher, Jim Frazier, who learned it from Robert Moore. I do not know the original source.

P. 64   The Cosmic Order is described in Michell, page 191.

P. 65   The quotation from the *Book of Life* is from Michell, pages 96-97.

P. 65   The Alchemical Wedding is described in detail in Michell, pages 156-166.

P. 66   The quotation from the *Book of Life* is from Michell, page 16. The quotation from the *Book of Mysteries* and ensuing description of the philosophical schools are from Michell, page 211.

P. 66   Lilith's opening address is drawn from the beliefs of the Australian aborigines, as described in Michell, pages 36-37.

P. 66   The quotation from the *Book of Life* is drawn from *Winbaraku and the Myth of the Jaripiri*, an aboriginal belief explained in Michell, page 90.

Pp. 67-68   Gadir's invocation is drawn from Michell, page 96.

Pp. 70-71   The relationship between the King and the Warrior, and the gifts of the Good King are described in *The Norton Anthology*.

Chapter 8

P. 73   Dolphin medicine is explained in Sams & Carson, pages 197-199.

P. 73   The quotation from the *Book of Mysteries* is from Michell, page 36.

Pp. 76-78   The Dragon Story is a compilation of images from Chinese legends; Native American mythology; references in Van Buren, pages 94-95; and numerous references in Michell—a snippet of a phrase here, an image there—all mixed together in the storyteller's pot and transformed into the Dragon Story.

P. 79   Eagle medicine is explained in Sams & Carson, pages 41-42.

P. 84   Readers of Carlos Castenada will recognize the quotation from the *Book of Life* and related commentary as a paraphrase from *The Teachings of Don Juan*, page 51.

Chapter 9

General   Many of the ideas in this chapter are derived from Capra's discourse on the sociological and metaphysical processes involved with the rise and fall of civilizations—the various social paradigms, culture clash, culture and counterculture, challenge and response, and so forth.

P. 87 The quotation from the *Book of Life* is a paraphrase of Capra, pages 28-29.

Pp. 91-93 The technological data in Shakala's journal are from *The Alternative HAARP Page* on the web.

Chapter 10

General Four separate sources combine to introduce a dominant theme of the story—the journey of self-discovery:

* From conversations with Jim Frazier, and from the works of Eliade and Moore, the Shamanic model of containment based on initiation, ritual eldership, and sacred space;
* From Michael Hernacki, the commitment to a goal of great value and the willingness to do whatever it takes to achieve that goal;
* From the 12-Steps, the philosophy of a Power Greater than Oneself, letting go, and taking things one day at a time;
* From conversations with my friend and teacher, Greg Barrette, the principles of prayer—asking clearly, visualizing the outcome, believing it is already given you, and saying thank you in advance for the right and perfect answer.

Chapter 11

General Many cultures recognize the Divine Feminine, the Great Mother, the Goddess, and Gaia—the living Earth. For a good explanation, see Time-Life's "the Earth's Elusive Spirit" *Mysteries of the Unknown: Earth Energies*, pages 16-38, 120-137.

Pp. 97, 100 The Cave symbology is outlined in Cooper, page 31. The Cave Poem is a poetic expression of that symbology.

Pp. 98-99 Wolf medicine and the connection to Sirius are explained in Sams & Carson, pages 97-98. For more information on the connection to Sirius, see Van Buren, page 100; and *The Sirius Mystery and the Dogons* on the web.

Pp. 98-99 Wolf's walk through the forest is a paraphrase of Michell's "forest ride," pages 52-53.

P. 101 The symbology of the willow tree is from Cooper, page 192.

Pp. 102-105 Sophia's altered state experience is a fictional recreation of experiences described by McKenna and Grof, with additional input from conversations with Jim Frazier, Jennifer DeLoach, and Jacquelyn Small.

P. 103 Higher Self should not be confused with Higher Power, as explained in 12-Step philosophy. In this case, the Other, or Group Mind, as per McKenna and Small, is that part of oneself which reveals Itself during altered states of consciousness.

P. 103 For a thorough description of Patriarchy, see Capra, pages 29-30, 40.

P. 104 The "Dark Mystery of the Feminine Body" is explained in the works of Marion Woodman.

Chapter 12

P. 107 For a detailed description of the Holy Relationship, see *A Course in Miracles: Text*, Chapters 17 and 22.

P. 115 The quotation from the *Book of Life* is compiled from *A Course in Miracles: Workbook for Students*, Lessons 1, 2, 3, 4, and 10.

P. 115 I have never found a better description of what "acceptance" is than on page 449 of the *Big Book of Alcoholics Anonymous*.

Chapter 13

General I am grateful for my many conversations with my teacher, Jennifer DeLoach, in which she not only taught me about the Four Attributes of the Heart, but also helped me to experience them, nurture them, and develop them in myself—sitting in the Circle, my own Sacred Hoop, just as the Atlantean women do in the Cave—while practicing the Buddhist Tong Lin meditation of compassion.

Jennifer, Jim Frazier, and Jacquelyn Small also taught me about the "Shadow," referred me to the works of various Men's Movement authors, and sat for me while I learned to "eat my own shadow," as Robert Bly expresses it.

Lunar and Priestess imagery, description, and conversation during the Cave ceremony, the subsequent moonlight ritual, and Cybele's prayer on pages 188-189 are drawn from Cooper, pages 106-108; Wanless' *Voyager Guidebook*, page 19; and *Voyager Tarot*, pages 60-64.

Pp. 117-118 The prophecy description and Storyteller's subsequent commentary are drawn from Capra, page 29, who, in turn, cites the work of Adrienne Rich, page 40.

P. 118 The words to Suonare's song are from the Sanskrit language: "I purify myself and discover the Oneness that is everything." As Robert Gass reminds us, "Sanskrit is considered a sacred language because its seed syllables were chosen for their transformative effects." You can hear this and other chants sung beautifully on his CD, *On Wings of Song*.

P. 120 — Latoné (or Lat) was the mother of Apollo and Artemis, as explained in Van Buren, pages 109-110.

Pp. 121, 123 — Swan medicine is explained in Sams & Carson, pages 193-195; see also Van Buren, pages 108-112.

Pp. 121, 123 — Moon symbology and the phases of the moon are drawn from Cooper, pages 106-108.

Chapter 14

P. 127 — The first quotation from the *Book of Life* is my own. The subsequent quotations are from a workshop by Jacquelyn Small and Robert Moore.

P. 129 — For a description of the stages of the hero's journey, see Pearson, pages 8-12; Robert Moore's description was explained to me by Jim Frazier. For the stages of the heroine's journey, see Murdock, pages 4-12.

P. 129 — The "Dark night of the soul" is another familiar quotation for which I cannot determine the original source.

P. 130 — The reasons for the destruction of Atlantis are described in Alper, Volume 1, pages 145-146.

Pp. 130-131 — The first quotation from the *Book of Life* is from Alper, Volume 1, pages 145-146. The second quotation is from Clarissa Estes story, "The Mate: Union with the Other," on page 129 of *Women Who Run with the Wolves*.

Chapter 15

General — Part 2 of John Michell's book deals with the importance of measure and number, and his work forms the basis for much of this chapter, from the quotations from the *Book of Life* to the wisdom of the Ancients.

P. 133 — The first quotation from the *Book of Life* and related commentary is from Michell, page 121. The second quotation from the *Book of Life* is from a conversation with Jacquelyn Small.

P. 134 — The quotation from the *Book of Life* is from Michell, page 188.

Pp. 134-135 — To create the Garden of the Heart, I turned to many sources:
- For its design and architecture, and the quotations from the *Book of Life*, Michell, page 64;
- For the evergreen tree, Cooper, pages 176-179;
- For the Four Attributes of the Heart, Jennifer DeLoach;
- For the symbology of the number Four, Jim Frazier and Cooper, pages 115-116;
- For the Archetype of Lover and Eros, Pearson, pages 148-162;
- For additional concepts of Love, *The Carl Jung Anthology* on the web.

Pp. 135-137 — Readers of Ken Carey will recognize this story as the first four pages of Ken Carey's *Vision*. It is the most beautiful Creation story I have ever read.

P. 137 — The quotation from the *Book of Life* is from an unknown source.

Chapter 16

P. 140 — Adima's "tea party" metaphor as an explanation of his way of dealing with fear was inspired by a talk by Ram Dass one warm summer evening in West Palm Beach, Florida.

P. 142 — The images of the Beast lashing its tail are from *Revelation* 12, 1-4.

Chapter 17

P. 151 — Badger medicine is explained in Sams & Carson, pages 153-155.

P. 151 — The quotation from the *Book of Life* is from Clarissa Estes story, "The Mate: Union with the Other," on page 122 of *Women Who Run with the Wolves*.

P. 152 — The first quotation from the *Book of Mysteries* is from Michell, pages 28-29. The second quotation from the *Book of Mysteries* is from Michell, page 122.

Chapter 18

General — Jean Baudrillard's essay, "New York," pages 13-24, provides the inspiration for the tour of the city. For indeed, the City of Atlantis was, like its Twentieth Century counterpart, the center of the world.

For additional descriptions of the City of Atlantis, see Time-Life's "Atlantis: The Eternal Quest," *Mysteries of the Unknown: Mystic Places*, pages 7-36.

P. 155 — Adima's journal entry was inspired by Baudrillard.

P. 158 — Cybele's journal entry was inspired by Baudrillard.

Chapter 19

Pp. 162-164 — The seven wonders of the ancient world and the magic squares are described in Michell, pages 160-162. The symbology of the numbers 3, 4, and 7 are described in Cooper, pages 114-115 and 117-118, respectively.

P. 164 — The inscription over the Temple door is from Van Buren, page 178.

P. 165 — The Great Temple and story of the Atlantean kings sitting in judgement are described in Time-Life's "Atlantis: The Eternal Quest," *Mysteries of the Unknown: Mystic Places*, page 10.

P. 165   Symbology of the oak and the thrones are described in Cooper, pages 121 and 171-172, respectively

P. 166   The healing rooms in the Temple are described in Alper, Vol. I, pages 6-8.

P. 166   Thoughts on sickness and wellness are compiled from *A Course in Miracles* and Louise Hay.

P. 166   The quotations from the *Book of Life* are from Hay, pages 153, 168, 173-174.

Pp. 167-168   The "invisible Temple of Intention" is drawn from the ideas of Michael Hernacki and conversations with Jim Frazier, as are the quotations from the *Book of Life* and the *Book of Mysteries*.

Pp. 168-169   The pattern on the floor—the "message in stone"—is drawn from Michell, Cooper, and Da Vinci.

P. 168   The quotation from the *Book of Life* is from Michell, page 173.

P. 168   The figure on the floor is patterned after Leonardo da Vinci's famous drawing of the Universal Man.

P. 169   The first quotation from the *Book of Life* is from Cooper, pages 45-46, as is the symbology of the cross, the wheel, the directions, the path, and the body. The Sacred Geometry measurements are from Michell, pages 121-213.

P. 169   The second quotation from the *Book of Life* is from Michell, page 188.

P. 170   The Hall of Crystals is drawn from various descriptions in Alper, Vol. I.

P. 174   The quotation from the *Book of Mysteries* is attributed to Machiavelli.

P. 176   The quotation from the *Book of Life* is from Michell, page 171.

Chapter 20

General   The source for much of the descriptive material in this chapter is *Our National Parks*, pages 135, 223-231. Frequent visitors to the parks will recognize Olympic National Park, Havasu Falls, and Acadia National Park as the combined setting for the lowlands, slopes, forests, and high places of Mount Kylene.

P. 179   The quotation from the *Book of Life* is from Michell, pages 52-53.

P. 180   I do not know the actual source of this quotation from the *Book of Life*, but I remember seeing it many years ago in a "destruction of the rainforest" exhibit at the Bronx Zoo in New York City. I have remembered the words ever since, and I thank the unknown author for saying it so well.

P. 181   The "Imagination of Nature" is attributed to Eliphas Levi, as described in Michell, page 94.

P. 181   The quotation from the *Book of Life* is from Michell, pages 94-95.

Pp. 182-188   In writing "The Story of the Four Winds," I drew from many sources:

- For the multiple imagery, colors, and animals associated with each of the four directions, the Chinese interpretations, as described in Cooper, pages 59, 112, 155, and 190;
- For the prehistoric high places and wilderness, Michell, pages 84-86;
- For the "Wake-up Call," "Mind Change," and not fitting in any more, conversations with Jacquelyn Small;
- For the concept of a "broken civilization moving not forward but backward," Terrence McKenna's live talk at the Fez in New York City, as documented in his web site;
- For what is natural and what isn't, and the "way Creation thinks," *A Course in Miracles*: Text, pages 309-311;
- For the progression of human history, Thelma Lavine's lecture.

P. 189   The quotations from the *Book of Life* are from Michell, pages 122-123.

P. 190   The quotation from the *Book of Life* is a compilation of three author's quotes, as cited in *Our National Parks*:

- James Michener—"In violence the island lived, and in violence a great beauty was born." Volcanoes National Park, page 167;
- Thomas Wolfe—"Where miracles not only happen, but where they happen all the time." Yellowstone National Park, page 301;
- Rachel Carson—"A place of compromise, conflict, and eternal change." Acadia National Park, p. 17.

Pp. 191-193   Much of the family's conversation is taken from my undergraduate and graduate notes on the Romantic Poets—Blake, Wordsworth, Byron, Shelley, Keats, and the rest—who, like Mircea Eliade, looked for and found the sacred in the mundane. Indeed, this section is written like a Romantic poem—descriptive and meditative. See also *The Norton Anthology of English Literature, Volume 2*, for more information about the Romantic Poets and their worldview.

- It is especially to Blake's "Mature Myth" that I turn for this section. Blake's mythical premise "is not of a transcendent God, but the 'Universal Human' who is himself God and who incorporates the cosmos as well."
- The "Fall" is not the fall of Humankind away from God, but "a falling apart of primal man," a "fall

into Division." This idea, by the way, is repeated in Ken Carey's works— *The Starseed Transmissions* and *Starseed: The Third Millennium*.

P. 193   The quotation from the *Book of Life* is from Percy Byshe Shelley, as written in *The Norton Anthology*, page 11.

P. 193   "Great spirits now on earth are sojourning" is a quotation from one of poet John Keats' sonnets. The "Spirit of the Age" is the title of a book of essays by William Hazlitt; the term came to be a metaphor for the pervasive intellectual climate of the Romantic period in England. See *The Norton Anthology*, pages 1-22 for more information.

Pp. 194-195   The page 301 quotation from the *Book of Life*, the page 302 quotation and "Mystical Pair," and other references to twinship are from Clarissa Estes story, "The Mate: Union with the Other," on pages 115-129 of *Women Who Run with the Wolves*.

P. 195   I first heard the phrase "Path of Direct Experience" from Jennifer DeLoach and Jacquelyn Small, who have since taught me how to walk that path.

P. 196   Elk medicine is explained in Sams & Carson, pages 49-51.

P. 197   The groaning rock is real—Enchanted Rock State Park in Fredricksburg, Texas. The pink granite heats up all day in the sun, then cools after dark, creaking and groaning as its temperature changes. When I went there, I thought it would be fun to put this in the story in some way.

Chapter 21

General   The Sensate, Ideational, and Idealistic philosophies are from Capra, pages 31-32, who, in turn, cites sociologist Pitirim Sorokin's work, *Social and Cultural Dynamics*.

Ark symbolism can be found in Cooper, pages 14-15.

Pp. 203-209   The Eleven friends treat each other archetypically, as explained by Carol Pearson. Some are Seekers, going out and gathering information; some are Destroyers, helping the rest let go of illusions and false hopes; all are Innocent and Orphan and Caregiver—taking charge of their own lives, symbolically "answering the call" and undertaking what Pearson describes as "the hero's journey."

Pp. 212-213   In Part 1 of his book, John Michell discusses the "hidden nature" of the countryside, and clues in the landscape that lead to spiritual understanding of great truths. So also Elizabeth Van Buren

refers to clues in the paintings and countryside of rural France that point to various spiritual treasures.

Chapter 22

Pp. 217-218   The quotations from the Philosophy of the Sons of Belial are from Lavine's lecture, as are the debates between the Children of the Law of One and the Sons of Belial. Jacquelyn Small describes this conflict as a "paradigm collision"— where opposing ideologies come together in conflict.

P. 217   The quotation "I am the State; the State is I" is an apocryphal remark attributed to King Louis IV of France.

P. 218   The name "Belial" is derived from Beliar, or Satanas, "the angel who keeps Hell," as explained in Van Buren, pages 99-100.

Pp. 218-219   Belial's conception, fetal development, and birth are drawn from Grof, Part 1, "Dimensions in Consciousness." For early childhood and adolescent development, fragmentation, and parental wounding, I drew from conversations with Jim Frazier.

In an Easter Sunday conversation with Jim Frazier, he taught me about the power of archetypal energies; the psychopathology of embracing an archetype without a healthy brain, ego, and central nervous system to function as a protective barrier in containing the energy; and the dangers of being possessed by an archetype. When Jim used Adolf Hitler as a real-life example and referred me to Trevor Ravenscroft's book, *The Spear of Destiny*, the analogy was clear and complete.

P. 220   Belial's descent into the abyss of black magic was inspired, in part, by Ravenscroft, Chapter 5; "the bridge between the two worlds" is from page xiv.

P. 220-221   Belial's dying mother's last warning was inspired by Ravenscroft, page 174.

P. 221   Meeting Nebo and Belial's journal entries are quotations from Ravenscroft, pages xx-xxi.

P. 223   The "other being" speaking through Belial and his vision of his destiny are drawn from Ravenscroft, pages 3-4.

P. 223   The description of Hanuman, the Potion Master, is adapted from Ravenscroft, page 75.

Pp. 224-225   The descriptions of Belial's immature ego and the effects of the potion are compiled from conversations with Jim Frazier, as well as from Ravenscroft, pages xiv, 80-83.

Pp. 225-226   The description of the aftereffects of drinking the potion are from Ravenscroft, pages 128-130.

P. 227   Belial's schizophrenic personality is drawn from Ravenscroft, pages 68-69.

Chapter 23

P. 231   The description of University life in Atlantis was inspired by Michell, pages 121-122.

P. 231   The quotation from Surya's Treatise is from Plato's *Timaeus*, as cited in Michell, page 122.

P. 231   The description of the priests' and priestesses' duties, the importance of Statecraft, and the quotation from the *Book of Life* are from Michell, pages 121-122.

P. 232   The principles of "dynamic equilibrium and fusion" and "like attracts like," which are described in Michell, page 123, provide the basis for Belial's philosophical views.

P.p. 232-233   Belial's skill as a public speaker and his ability to mesmerize a crowd are drawn from Ravenscroft, pages 98, 112, 178-179.

P. 233   The "place of Difficult Passage—the Sword Bridge"—is from Cooper, pages 25-26.

Chapter 24

General   For detailed information about *The Protocols of the Wise Men of Zion*, see Ravenscroft, Chapter 7.

P. 237   Belial's Morning journal entry is a quotation from *The Protocols...*, as cited in Ravenscroft, pages 109-110.

P. 237   The symbology of the hawthorne tree is explained in Cooper, page 80. The Atlantean calendar was inspired, in part, by images from Wanless and Van Buren.

Pp. 237-238   Belial's Midday journal entry is a quotation from *The Protocols...*, as cited in Ravenscroft, page 110.

P. 238   Belial's Evening journal entry is a quotation from *The Protocols...*, as cited in Ravenscroft, page 113.

Chapter 25

P. 240   The Elders' praise of Belial is a quotation from Ravenscroft, page 69.

Pp. 240-241   Belial's secret and public selves are drawn from the philosophy of Hegel, as explained by Thelma Lavine.

Chapter 26

P. 245   The quotation from the *Book of Life* is from Soloviev's *The Anti-Christ*, as cited in Ravenscroft, page 112.

P. 248   Tiwaz's prophecy of doom is from Ravenscroft, page 105.

Chapter 27

P. 252   The term "Spear of Destiny" was coined by Trevor Ravenscroft and is described in Chapter 2 of his book of the same title.

Pp. 252-254   Storyteller's musings on Belial are drawn, in part, from a combination of ideas from Hegel, Ravenscroft, Alper, Cayce, and *A Course in Miracles*.

P. 253   The quotation from the Belial's journal is from Hegel, as explained by Thelma Lavine.

P. 254   The term "Symbiotic Universe" was coined by Michael Talbot in his book of the same title. It provides an excellent explanation of how Life and Mind work in harmony in the Cosmos.

P. 255   Ritual magic is explained more fully in Ravenscroft, Chapter 12; and Time-Life Books.

P. 256   Hanuman's description of himself is from Walter Stein, as retold by Ravenscroft, page 64.

P. 256   The initiatory ranks within the Sons of Belial and their corresponding symbolic armor are described in detail in Ravenscroft, pages 69-70.

P. 256   The description of the Spear box is drawn, in part, from images in Cooper, pages 10 and 84.

P. 256   The description of the Puppetmaster was inspired, in part, by Ravenscroft, page 80.

P. 258   The Puppetmaster's admonition to Belial after he accepts the Spear is from Ravenscroft, page xii.

P. 260   Belial's reaction to "the Presence around the Spear" was inspired, in part, by Ravenscroft, page 64.

P. 261   Storyteller's quotations are from Ravenscroft, page 64.

P. 262   The words of the Counselor were inspired, in part, by Ravenscroft, pages 177-180.

Chapter 28

General   A portion of the first meeting between Adima and Enoch in the Lighthouse was inspired, in part, by the article in the Spring 1996 issue of *Shaman's Drum*.

Pp. 263-264   The public oration by the leaders of the Children of the Law of One is drawn from Capra, page 28.

P. 265   Adima's Grandmother's advice to "feel the fear..." is a common theme in 12-Step meetings.

P. 266   The lintel, monogram, and inscription on the Lighthouse are drawn from Van Buren, pages 105-107.

P. 267   The quotation from the *Book of Life* is from Van Buren, pages 7-8.

P. 270 — I do not know the original source of this quotation from the *Book of Life*, although I have heard it many times over the years.

P. 272 — For more information about the attributes of the Hermit, see Wanless' *Voyager Tarot*, pages 95-98; and *Voyager Guidebook*, pages 22-23.

P. 275 — Hawk's (Osprey's) cry is explained in Sams & Carson, pages 45-47.

P. 275 — Enoch's quote about forgetting one's true identity is explained in detail in *A Course in Miracles: Workbook for Students*, Lesson 136.

P. 276 — Thanks to Jennifer DeLoach, Jim Frazier, and Jacquelyn Small for reminding me that life is a journey, not a destination.

P. 276 — Enoch's story was inspired by an illustration by Gustave Doré depicting the "faintly shadowed track" to the Castle of Astolat in Tennyson's *Elaine*. The drawing serves as the frontispiece for John Michell's book and is described further on page 105.

P. 279 — Enoch's description of Adima's astrological nature is drawn from a conversation with my friend and teacher, Robert Wilkinson.

P. 280 — Owl and Hawk medicine working in combination is explained in Andrews, pages 177.

Pp. 280-281 — Owl medicine is explained in Sams & Carson, pages 121-122; and in Andrews, pages 172-181.

Pp. 280-281 — The scene in which Adima watches the elves dancing in the fairy glade was inspired by a conversation with Robert Wilkinson about acknowledging the play of invisible forces in one's life.

P. 281 — Source material for Owl's dream message is drawn from Andrews, pages 172-181.

Chapter 29

General — Adima's five "Periods of Learning" are described in *A Course in Miracles: Manual for Teachers*, pages 8-10, which outlines the process for the development of Trust.

P. 284 — For a detailed discussion of that which is valuable and that which is not, see *A Course in Miracles: Workbook for Students*, Lessons 128-133.

Pp. 285-287 — Adima's goal—the attainment of higher consciousness—is described in Ravenscroft, page 192.

P. 286 — The concept of "Beginner's Mind" was explained to me by Jennifer DeLoach.

P. 286 — The concept of "Surrender" was explained to me by Greg Barrette and my friends in 12-Step programs.

Pp. 286-287 — The ancient Rosicrucian meditation upon the black cross and seven red roses is explained in Ravenscroft, page 192.

Pp. 288-289 — Adima's meditative experiences and journal entries as a "walker of two worlds" are from Ravenscroft, pages 192-194; and from conversations with Jennifer DeLoach.

P. 289 — The phrase "Knowing of the Imagination" was inspired by the term "Imaginative Cognition," as explained in Ravenscroft, page 193.

P. 290 — "Staking one's claim" and the "Second Force" were explained to me by Ron Scott in his Palm Sunday 1996 sermon at Unity Church in Austin, TX.

P. 290 — I learned about wounded boys masquerading as men from conversations with Jim Frazier.

P. 295 — The quotation from the *Book of Life* is from is from *A Course in Miracles: Workbook for Students*, Lessons 121-122.

P. 295 — "Grandeur" and "grandiosity" are explained in *A Course in Miracles: Text*, pages 165-168.

Pp. 295-296 — Enoch's conversation about Adima's true, kingly nature was inspired by many conversations with Robert Wilkinson.

P. 296 — The two quotations from the *Book of Life* are from Robert Wilkinson.

P. 296 — Enoch's "Prayer of Surrender" was taught to me by Robert Wilkinson.

Chapter 31

P. 301 — "Wake-up calls" were explained to me by Jennifer DeLoach and Jacquelyn Small. For more information, see Jacquelyn Small's books.

Pp. 301-302 — Adima's meditative experience of the War in Heaven is drawn from the real-life experience of Walter Johannes Stein, as retold by Ravenscroft, pages 195-196.

P. 303 — The quotation from the *Book of Life* is from Ravenscroft, page 198.

P. 303 — Reconciling one's will to a Higher Will is described in Ravenscroft, pages 198-199.

P. 304 — The quotation from the *Book of Life* is from *A Course in Miracles: Workbook for Students*, Lesson 16.

P. 304 — The reminder from the Angel is drawn from Ravenscroft, pages 197-198.

Pp. 304-305 — Adima entering into the silence and vision of the Great Void are drawn from Ravenscroft, page 198.

P. 305 — The quotation from the *Book of Life* is from Ravenscroft, page 200.

P. 306 — Enoch's mysterious hint is from Ravenscroft, page 200.

P. 306 — Adima's two goals are described in Ravenscroft, page 198.

P. 307 — The quotation from the *Book of Life* is from Robert Wilkinson.

Pp. 307-308 — The conversation between Adima and Enoch was inspired by a conversation with Robert Wilkinson.

P. 308   The quotation from the *Book of Life* and ensuing remarks about Courage and Fearless Faith in oneself are from Robert Wilkinson.

Pp. 312-314   Enoch's remarks about conflict, doing battle, retreating versus fleeing, singular acts of resistance, and timidity are drawn from a conversation with Robert Wilkinson.

P. 313   The quotations from the *Book of Life* are from *A Course in Miracles: Workbook for Students*, Lessons 2, 9, 15, and 135, respectively.

P. 314   Enoch's description of Adima's "course" is a paraphrase of the Introduction to *A Course in Miracles*.

P. 316   The poem *The Divine* was written by Cynthia Didio (© 1995 by Cynthia Didio).

Pp. 316-319   Adima's encounter with the innocent child in the garden was inspired by a conversation with Robert Wilkinson.

Chapter 32

General   Many of the ideas in this chapter about ritual and marriage were inspired by Joseph Campbell, Chapter 1.

P. 323   The Summer "Alchemical Wedding" is drawn from Michell, Chapter 5.

P. 323   The quotation from the *Book of Life* is from Michell, pages 161-162.

Pp. 323-324   The wedding symbols of bread, corn, water, wine are explained in Cooper, pages 24, 42-43, 188-189, and 192-193, respectively.

P. 324   The quotation from the *Book of Life* is from Campbell, page 6.

Pp. 324-325   Troubled marriages are described in Pearson, pages 148-162.

Pp. 325-326   The reinterpretation of the Adam & Eve myth was explained to me by Robert Wilkinson.

P. 326   The quotation from the *Book of Life* is from Carl Jung's commentary on Love, as cited on the web.

P. 327   The painting of "Dark Warrior and Shadowy Female" was inspired by Carl Jung's commentary on Love, as cited on the web.

P. 327   The "ordeal of marriage" and Yin-Yang metaphor are explained in Campbell, page 7.

P. 328   That "transcendent awareness known as Grace" is from Ravenscroft, page 82.

Pp. 328-329   Turtle medicine is explained in Sams & Carson, pages 77-79; Deer medicine on pages 53-54; Bear medicine on pages 57-59; Lizard medicine on pages 181-183; Buffalo medicine on pages 113-115.

P. 329   The first quotation from the *Book of Life* is from Exodus 20:12, as explained in Ken Carey's *Terra Christa*, page 53.

P. 329   The "still small Voice" is referred to throughout *A Course in Miracles*.

P. 329   The final quotation from the *Book of Life* is from *A Course in Miracles: Workbook for Students*, Lesson 108.

Chapter 33

P. 332   Enoch's teaching about the power of thought and subsequent quotation from the *Book of Life* is from *A Course in Miracles: Workbook for Students*, Lessons 2, 16, and 17.

Pp. 332-337   Enoch's teaching about the Archetypes is compiled from the works of Carol Pearson and Robert Moore, and from conversations with Jim Frazier. The symbology of the lily, the lotus, the mandrake, and the rose are described in Cooper, pages 97-98, 100-102, 104, and 141-142, respectively.

P. 336   The quotation from the *Book of Life* is from Carole Pearson.

Chapter 34

General   The symbology of the dimensions of the earth is from Michell, page 133-136; the scientific facts about the Great Pyramid are from Michell, pages 136-162.

P. 345   The diamond point "cat's whisker" atop the Pyramid is described in Michell, page 152.

P. 345   The first quotation from Quetzalcoatl is from Michell, page 153.

P. 345   The second quotation from Quetzalcoatl is from Plato, as cited in Michell, page 153.

P. 346   The "Parable of the Seeds" is a compilation of ideas in Michell, Chapter 5.

P. 349   The metaphor of the runner in long-distance race was inspired by Wanless' "Man of Worlds—Achiever," as explained in *Voyager Guidebook*, page 47, and *Voyager Tarot*, page 299.

Chapter 35

General   Portions of this chapter were inspired, in part, by the article in the Summer 1996 edition of *Shaman's Drum*.

P. 352   Snake medicine is explained in Sams & Carson, pages 61-62.

P. 354   "Synchronicities" are coincidences that are so unusual and so psychologically meaningful they don't seem to be the result of chance alone. The concept of "synchronicity" was developed by Carl Jung. For more information, see Peat, page 235.

P. 354-355   Enoch's assessment that the Sword has lost its power and subsequent instructions to Adima are drawn from Ravenscroft, page 181.

P. 355 The forest angels are drawn from the Angels of Earth, Air, Sunlight, and Water, as described in *The Essene Gospel of Peace*, pages 14-17.

P. 356 The quotation from the *Book of Life* is from an ancient prayer, as explained by Ken Carey in *Terra Christa*, pages 231-234.

Pp. 357-363 "The Legend of the Word-Sword" and the Well of Kuneware, from the *Book of Mysteries*, were inspired, in part, by Wolfram von Eschenbach's *Parsival*, as retold in Ravenscroft, Chapters 13-14.

P. 357 The four quotations from the Legend are from Ravenscroft, page 181.

Pp. 358 The quotation from the Legend is from Ravenscroft, pages 181-182.

Pp. 359-360 The spell that restores the sword and the two quotations from the Legend are described in Ravenscroft, pages 181-182.

P. 362 The question that breaks the spell is from Ravenscroft, page 182.

P. 363 The quotation from the Legend is from Ravenscroft, page 64.

P. 363 Adima's prayer is from Ravenscroft, page 64.

Chapter 37

P. 373 The term "Cosmic Chronicle" is described in Ravenscroft, page 143.

Pp. 375-376 The metaphor of sleeping men is drawn from a combination of Ravenscroft, pages 136-137; *A Course in Miracles: Text*, Chapters 27-28; and Ken Carey's *The Starseed Transmissions*, Chapter 2, and *Vision*, Chapters 5-6.

Pp. 376-377 The conversation about actions, judgment, combat, and attachments to outcomes was inspired by a conversation with Robert Wilkinson on the subject of Divine Grace and the Light.

P. 377 The quotation from the *Book of Life* is from *A Course in Miracles: Manual for Teachers*, page 10.

P. 377 The "Dream of Sickness" is explained in *A Course in Miracles: Text*, Chapter 10.

Chapter 38

General *Collier's Encyclopedia* provides much of the source material for the technical aspects of opera as an art form.

P. 389 I learned about the Fear-Joy Cycle in a series of conversations with my friend, Michael Marshall.

Pp. 389-390 Blue Jay medicine is explained in Andrews, pages 121-122.

P. 390 I found Enoch's parable and ensuing commentary on the web; the author is unknown.

Pp. 391-392 For more information about the "Spell of Matter" and "the Fall," see Ken Carey's *The Starseed Transmissions* and *Starseed, The Third Millennium*.

P. 393 Blue Jay's song and the ensuing symbolism were inspired by Andrews, pages 121-122.

P. 394 Adima's armor—the Sign of the Holy Grail—is described in Ravenscroft, page 200; Dove medicine is described in Andrews, pages 133-134.

Pp. 394-395 The opening of Adima's third eye was inspired by Ravenscroft, page 200.

Pp. 394-395 The reading the name on the sword is from Ravenscroft, page 201.

P. 395 The quotation from Legend is from Ravenscroft, page 202.

P. 395 For more information about the "Holy Instant," see *A Course in Miracles: Text*, Chapter 15.

Pp. 395-396 The description of Adima in his fullness came to me after a long contemplation of Michelangelo's Statue of David.

P. 396 The quotation is from *Hamlet*, Act II, sc. ii.

P. 396 Enoch's remarks about being centered were inspired by a conversation with Robert Wilkinson.

P. 396 Adima's thoughts about Heaven are from *A Course in Miracles: Manual for Teachers*, page 10.

Chapter 39

P. 402 The description of the Orphean Bards and subsequent quotation from the *Book of Life* are from Michell, page 122; and the second quotation from Quetzalcoatl is from Plato, as cited by Michell, page 122.

Pp. 406-414 Portions of Adima's "experience" of life under the Sons of Belial were inspired, in part, by Timothy Leary's "Declaration of Evolution" and Terrence McKenna's live talk at the Fez in New York City (each of which may be found on the web), as well as from my own experiences.

P. 410 The two quotations from the *Book of Life* are from *A Course in Miracles: Manual for Teachers*, pages 65-66.

P. 411 The quotation from the *Book of Life* is from Jacquelyn Small, who taught me that "the Heart is the Truthsayer."

P. 412 The poet's "last warning" is from Timothy Leary's "Declaration of Evolution," as cited on the web.

Chapter 40

P. 427 Raven medicine is explained in Sams & Carson, pages 101-103

Chapter 41

General The crystals within the Supermind—their properties, attributes, colors, and images—were inspired, in part, by Wanless' *Voyager Guidebook*, pages 33-37; and *Voyager Tarot*, pages 162-164, 174-176,

185-187, 197-199, 209-210, 219-221, 231-233, 242-244, 254-256, 265-267, 282-284, 295-296, 306-308, and 319-321.

P. 432 The quotation from the *Book of Life* is from an unknown source.

P. 435 The "Intuiter of Truth" is from Wanless' *Voyager Tarot*, page 60.

P. 435 The quotation from the creators is from Wanless' *Voyager Tarot*, page 174.

Pp. 437-442 "Project Nightside" and the Atlantean cultural disintegration are explained in detail by Edgar Cayce, pages 60-62; Kafar's vision of the future was compiled from a combination of ideas in Bramley, Capra, McKenna, Leary, Ravenscroft, and Van Helsing.

P. 442 The quotation from the *Book of Mysteries* is from *Genesis* 3:1, as explained by Ken Carey in *Terra Christa*, pages 57-60.

P. 443 Dove's song is a poetic expression of themes from Ken Carey, Fritjof Capra, and *A Course in Miracles*.

Pp. 443-444 The teachings from the voice behind the sine wave were inspired by a conversation with Robert Wilkinson.

P. 444 Dove medicine is described in Andrews, pages 133-134.

P. 449 The quotation from the *Book of Mysteries* is from Alper, Vol. 1, page 148.

Chapter 42

P. 459 The poem *When the Tower Falls* was written by Cynthia Didio (© 1995 by Cynthia Didio).

Pp. 462-463 The complete story of Creation and Amilius can be found in Edgar Cayce, Chapter 2.

P. 467 The "Absolute" is explained more fully in Thelma Lavine's lecture.

Pp. 467-468 Enoch's vision of the future was inspired, in part, by ideas in Thelma Lavine's lecture.

Chapter 43

General The Underworld was created, in part, from descriptions in *Our National Parks*, pages 76-81, 194-199, and 295-299.

P. 480 The reference to ALCOR is described in detail in Van Buren, pages 73-75, and 123-124.

P. 480 The description of the Labyrinth, or Cave of Midrash, and the quotation above its entrance are described in detail in Van Buren, pages 123-124.

P. 480 The story of the "innermost cave" is a quotation from Vogler, page 181.

P. 483 The "Double" is described in Ravenscroft, Chapter 22.

Pp. 483-486 Shakala's final thoughts and conversation with Death are drawn, in part, from *A Course in Miracles: Text*, Chapter 31.

Chapter 44

P. 491 The quotation from the *Book of Life* is from *Revelation* 12:1-4.

P. 492 The Sacred Grove of Hesperia is described in Donnelley, pages 288 and 306.

P. 493 Portions of Hia's experience in the Fields of Light were inspired, in part, by Drunvalo Melchizedek's video.

P. 496 Spider medicine is described in Sams and Carson, pages 209-211.

Chapter 45

Pp. 504-506 Draco's attempt to kill Belial and their ensuing conversation were inspired, in part, by a plot to assassinate Napoleon, as retold by Ravenscroft, page 66.

P. 507 The quotation from the *Book of Life* is from an unknown source.

P. 509 The imagery of bodies on meathooks was drawn from actual accounts of Hitler's People's Court executions, as retold by Ravenscroft, pages 220-221.

Chapter 46

P. 521 Belial's "mark" was inspired, in part, by references to the Mark of Cain in *Genesis* 4:15.

Pp. 522-524 Portions of the scene in which Adima fancies himself buried alive were inspired, in part, by the article in the Summer 1996 issue of *Shaman's Drum*.

P. 525 Source information for Thoth's origin and his gift of writing to the world can be found on the Thoth web page. See also Donnelley, page 278, for a description of the Egyptian god Thoth (*At*-hothes).

Chapter 47

P. 530 The quotation from the *Book of Life* is from *A Course in Miracles: Manual for Teachers*, pages 13-14.

Pp. 531 Cybele's conversation with Sophia was inspired by a prayer that was given to me by my one of my 12-Step friends.

P. 533 Adima's journal entry is compiled, in part, from various themes expressed in *A Course in Miracles*.

Chapter 48

P. 535 The symbology of the seventh day and the soothsayer's prophecy are drawn from Cooper, pages 117-118.

P. 537 Belial's "merciless act of self will" is from Ravenscroft, page 320.

Pp. 538-539 For more information about the Ancient's fear and handling of eclipses, see Michell, pages 86-88.

Pp. 544-545 Portions of the characteristics of Lilith and Cybele in their final battle were inspired by the Tarot and by a life-sized sculpture of a chess set that I saw at an

P. 546   The quotation from the *Book of Life* is from *The Gospel of Saint John*, 1:1.

P. 548   The quotation from the ancient prophecy is from *The Gospel of Saint Matthew*, 24:2.

P. 554   The quotation from Storyteller is drawn, in part, from *Genesis*, 7:11, and is discussed in Donnelley, Part 1, Ch. 2.

Chapter 49

P. 556   The Tower / Lighthouse imagery is from Wanless' *Voyager Tarot*, pages 131-134; and *Voyager Guidebook*, pages 26-27.

Pp. 561-563   The Volcano Destroyer is drawn, in part, from descriptions in *Our National Parks*, pages 167-169 and 186-193.

P. 564   Thoth's journal entry is drawn, in part, from deluge descriptions in Donnelley and Cayce.

P. 564   Thoth's and Latoné's shared dream is a fictionalized compilation of images in Wanless' *Voyager Guidebook*, pages 26-27

Chapter 50

Pp. 569-569   Latoné's song, *Stay with Me, Atlantis*, was written by Brett Randall Towery (© 1998 by Brett Randall Towery).

P. 569   The quotation from Thoth's story is from *Genesis*, 1:1.

Omega

General   Edgar Cayce, pages 89-93, provides the source material for Gizeh, the Great Pyramid, the Sphinx, and the Hall of Records.

P. 578   The symbology of the Milky Way is described in Van Buren, pages 110-111.

P. 578   Scutum, the Shield—the constellation at the center of the Milky Way galaxy—is also called "Omega" and "The Swan." "Escutar" in Portuguese means "to listen," "to hark." See Van Buren, pages 110-111.

P. 580   The "ringing out of the bells" is described in Cooper, page 20.

P. 581   The "chest of beaten gold" is drawn from descriptions in Van Buren, pages 107-109.

P. 581   The first quotation from the *Book of Life* is from Van Buren, page 106; the second quotation is from Van Buren, page 108.

P. 584   The quotation on Hia's tomb is from an unknown source.

P. 585   The relationship between the Sphinx and Sirius is explained in *The Sirius Mystery and the Dogons* web site, as is the significance of July 23, when the eyes of the Sphinx are aligned with the rising sun.

P. 585   Storyteller's final thoughts on Love and Light, including the prayer on page 585, were inspired, in part, by the works of and a conversation with my friend, Michael Lightweaver.

Roger Didio has been a successful educator and business professional for over twenty-five years. His personal commitment to writing stories that benefit humankind enables him to draw on an extensive liberal arts background and education, and also from the well of a rich and varied personal life experience. As an innovator and visionary—equal parts artist and technologist—he has much to contribute during this time of shifting values and cultural evolution. And as a Storyteller, he knows how to speak to others in ways that are meaningful for them.